Illywhacker

Peter Carey is the multi-award winning author of six novels, *Bliss*, *Illywhacker*, *Oscar and Lucinda*, *The Tax Inspector*, *The Unusual Life of Tristan Smith* and *Jack Maggs*. His highly acclaimed short stories are now all in *Collected Stories*. His first children's book is *The Big Bazoohley*.

His books have won every major literary award in Australia. *Oscar and Lucinda* won the Booker Prize in London in 1988.

Born in Bacchus Marsh, Victoria in 1943, Peter Carey now lives in New York with his wife and two sons.

Books by Peter Carey

Short Fiction

Collected Stories
including
The Fat Man in History
War Crimes

Novels

Bliss
Illywhacker
Oscar and Lucinda
The Tax Inspector
The Unusual Life of Tristan Smith
Jack Maggs

Screenplay

Bliss

For Children

The Big Bazoohley

Biographical

A Letter to Our Son

PETER CAREY

Illywhacker

University of Queensland Press

First published 1988 by University of Queensland Press
Box 42, St Lucia, Queensland 4067 Australia
Reprinted 1985 (twice)
Reprinted in paperback 1986 (three times), 1987, 1988, 1989, 1991, 1993, 1999

Printed in Australia by McPherson's Printing Group, Victoria

Cataloguing in Publication Data
National Library of Australia

Carey, Peter, 1943–   .
   Illywhacker

   I. Title.

A823'.3

ISBN 0 7022 2762 5

For my mother and father,
with love and thanks

Australian history is almost always picturesque; indeed, it is so curious and strange, that it is itself the chiefest novelty the country has to offer and so it pushes the other novelties into second and third place. It does not read like history, but like the most beautiful lies; and all of a fresh new sort, no mouldy old stale ones. It is full of surprises and adventures, the incongruities, and contradictions, and incredibilities; but they are all true, they all happened.

Mark Twain, *More Tramps Abroad*, London, 1897

illywhacker A professional trickster, esp. operating at country shows [derived by Baker (1945: 138) from *spieler*]

1941 Kylie Tennant *The Battlers* 183–4: An illywacker is someone who is putting a confidence trick over, selling imitation diamond tie-pins, new-style patent razors or infallible "tonics" . . . "living on the cockies" by such devices, and following the shows because money always flows freest at show time. A man who "wacks the illy" can be almost anything, but two of these particular illywackers were equipped with a dart game.

1943 Baker 40: *Illywhacker* A trickster or spieler.

1975 Hal Porter *The Extra* 15: Social climber, moron, peter-tickler, eeler-spee, illy-wacker.

G. A. Wilkes, *A Dictionary of Australian Colloquialisms*, Sydney, 1978

Book 1

1

My name is Herbert Badgery. I am a hundred and thirty-nine years old and something of a celebrity. They come and look at me and wonder how I do it. There are weeks when I wonder the same, whole stretches of terrible time. It is hard to believe you can feel so bad and still not die.

I am a terrible liar and I have always been a liar. I say that early to set things straight. *Caveat emptor*. My age is the one fact you can rely on, and not because I say so, but because it has been publicly authenticated. Independent experts have poked me and prodded me and scraped around my foul-smelling mouth. They have measured my ankles and looked at my legs. It is a relief to not worry about my legs any more. When they photographed me I did not care that my dick looked as scabby and scaly as a horse's, even though there was a time when I was a vain man and would not have permitted the type of photographs they chose to take. Apart from this (and it is all there, neatly printed on a chart not three feet from where I lie) I have also been written up in the papers. Don't imagine this is any novelty to me – being written up has been one of my weaknesses and I don't mention it now so that I may impress you, but rather to make the point that I am not lying about my age.

But for the rest of it, you may as well know, lying is my main subject, my specialty, my skill. It is a great relief to find a new use for it. It's taken me long enough, God knows, and I have not always been proud of my activities. But now I feel no more ashamed of my lies than my farts (I rip forth a beauty to underline the point). There will be complaints, of course. (There are complaints now, about the fart – my apologies, my fellow sufferers.) But my advice is to not waste your time with your red pen, to try to pull apart the strands of lies and truth, but to relax and enjoy the show.

I think I'm growing tits. They stuck their callipers into me and measured them. That'd be one for the books if I turned into a woman at this stage of life. It's only the curiosity that keeps me alive: to see what my dirty old body will do next.

I'm like some old squid decaying on the beach. They flinch when they look at me and they could not guess that there is anything inside my head but gruel, brain soup sloshing around in a basin. My voice is gone, so they could not know what changes have taken place in me: I may even, at last, have become almost kind.

I read too. I didn't read a book until an age when most men are going blind or dying in their beds. Leah Goldstein, who has a brain as big as a football, deserves the credit. She was the one who got me going and once I was started they couldn't stop me. By the time I was in Rankin Downs gaol I was known as "The Professer" and I was permitted to take my Bachelor of Arts by correspondence.

Back in 1919 the books on Annette Davidson's bookshelves meant nothing to me. But now, if I wanted to, I could invent a library for her. I could fill up her bookcases carelessly, elegantly, easily, stack volumes end to end, fill the deep shelves with two rows of books, leave them with their covers showing on the dining-room table, hurl them out the window and leave them broken-spined and crippled, flapping on the uncut grass.

Books! Books are no problem to me any more, but until I was in my late fifties I could only recognize ten words in print and two of those made up my name. I was ashamed of it. The ingenuity and effort, the deception, the stories, the bullshit, the lies I used, just to persuade people to read me the paper aloud, all this was far harder work than learning to read.

It's a blessing my eyes are as good as they are and with all my other vanity gone this one remains: my eyes. I speak not of their efficiency, but of their colour, which is the same colour, that clear sapphire blue, which illuminated my father's pale-skinned face. These eyes – which I so much admire in myself – I detest in him. I will tell you about him later, perhaps, I make no promises.

My father will wait. I'd rather start with a love story. It's not the only real love story I've got to tell – there'll be plenty of hanky-panky by and by relating to love of one sort or another – but there is little that I look forward to like this one, this flash of lightning, which occurred in November 1919 when I was thirty-three years old and already dragging out too many hairs with my comb each morning.

2

I wished to discuss Phoebe, but there is Annette Davidson to explain first. As usual, she is in the way.

12

They are, the pair of them, in that little rickety weatherboard house in Villamente Street in Geelong. It is a dull overcast day and there are, below the blanket of gloomy grey, lower clouds, small white ones scudding along from the coast at Barwon Heads. A red-nosed boy is driving a herd of pigs past the house towards Latrobe Terrace and the windy railway station. The pigs sum up everything Phoebe hates about Geelong. She would drive them over a cliff if she could, just to have done with it, just as now, as she sits down, she does not do it like a normal person, happy for life to take its easiest course, but impatiently. She drops into the chair. The windows rattle in their frames and Annette Davidson, in the process of fitting a de Reske to her cigarette holder, looks up and frowns. There will be no ignoring her. She insists on an explanation.

In November 1919, Annette Davidson was twenty-one years old. It was three years since she had left teachers' college in Reading, one year since she had fled Paris, and fourteen months since her affair with Jacques Dussoir had ended. Dussoir is meant to be a French impressionist of some note, a friend of Monet's, etc. However the only book in which you will find his name mentioned is the one Annette Davidson wrote when she lived in Sydney: *Paris Soir, Paris Noir* (Angus & Robertson, 1946). Dussoir apart, it is typical that she chose to write about eight months in Paris in 1916 and ignore twenty-eight years in Australia, but we will not go into that now.

She found a job teaching history at the Hermitage Church of England Girls' Grammar School in Geelong and it was there that she met Phoebe who was seventeen.

Annette Davidson was a striking woman. Norman Lindsay used her as a model in *Perseus & the Beauties* which is now in the Art Gallery of Victoria. Lindsay got her to a T, not an easy thing, because although she had a proud, strong face and quite remarkable Amazonian breasts, she also had a masochistic cast to her mouth and her shoulders looked as if they were ready to mould themselves around the trunk of a man (deceptively, as it turned out).

I cannot blame her for disliking Geelong – in the end, I didn't care for it myself. Teaching at the Hermitage she got the worst of it: all those stout-legged daughters of squatters who displayed the dull certainties of their type. But it was in that mullock heap she found a muddied stone more valuable than any of the fool's gold the staff so proudly presented her with.

Phoebe was an awkward misfit. Her fingers were smudged with ink. Her knees were ingrained with dirt, her toes raw with tinea, her fingernails black and broken. She was the daughter of a bullock driver who had made his pile, and a dizzy overly-talkative ex-barmaid who did not know her place, although – Christ knows – she tried hard enough to find it.

Phoebe had a beautiful voice. She sang deliberately off-key. She had a gift for painting but "dashed off" something at the end of a lesson when everyone else was washing their brushes. It was known that she smoked cigarettes. She was one of the group known as the "Dorm 5 Co" who were suspected of active homosexual relations which, if the stories were true, left the school's more normal Sapphic romances looking almost Christian. She was known in the common room as "the little horror".

God knows what the common room said about Annette. She wore black or grey with flashes of brilliant colour: a shoulder panel of red, a pleat that opened obscenely to reveal a heart like a plum. She had a way of walking, a sort of slouch, with long strides, which may have been all very well on the boulevard St Michel but was not the thing at the Hermitage. Miss Kane, the headmistress, had reason to talk to her about this walk. She had noticed several of the older girls were imitating it.

Amongst the imitators of the Davidson walk, Phoebe was by far the most accomplished. She was in love with the new history mistress, even before her ears had been caressed by that round, soft north country accent. Within a month they had formed an alliance. Soon Phoebe (said to be "thick as a brick") was writing poetry, keeping a diary, passing examinations in French and history. She knew the names of the streets of Paris and many of the people who had walked on them. She knew the stations on the metro. She knew what a bidet was. She read Ruskin and learned to scorn Henry Lawson (whom her father loved with a passion) and learned to mock his bush poetry with her mentor's one-sided smile. With Annette's help and petroleum jelly she removed the ingrained dirt from her knees.

She began to imagine a place in the world where she might not only belong but also be admired, a place where there were other problems than the price of wheat or wool, or whether the waterside workers would be engaged in Yarra Street or Corio Quay.

Annette had been the subject of schoolgirls' crushes before, but she had never thought of herself as homosexual until Phoebe, who boarded during the week and went home at weekends, came creamily into her history mistress's bed on the second night of the final term.

No matter what the pleats of her dresses suggested, no matter how recklessly she walked, Annette was both cautious and sensible. She hated her enemies silently and smiled at them politely. She tried to please her employers. She attended chapel and sang the hymns out loud. She argued with Phoebe, reasoned with her sensibly and listened for footsteps in the corridor outside: but none of this was any defence against Phoebe. There was no denying the force not of her arguments which danced from peak to peak as unpredictably and carelessly as lightning but of her almost unbelievably soft lips, her smooth skin, her tender strokes, her shocking tongue and Annette Davidson (not without a tiny Protestant tremble) gave herself to her student's embraces which compared most favourably with those of the impressionist Dussoir.

I like to think it was on this night, with her ugly brown uniform and heavy brogues shucked off on to the floor, that Phoebe revealed herself as a beauty. It had occurred to no one that she might be. And when it happened it caused a terrible confusion. The boys from College and Grammar not only seemed to overcome their distaste for her vulgar background, but gave her presents of school scarves. And when the anxiously awaited invitations to the prestigious end-of-year dances began, at last, to arrive, slipped into the green-felt letter rack, to be collected and displayed like trophies on study walls, the "little horror" had more than her share. But by then Annette (cautious, careful Annette) had taken the house in Villamente Street, West Geelong, and Phoebe gave not a fig for the Manisides or Chirnfolds or the Osters or any of the other social luminaries of the Western District. She attended no dances and created a perfect scandal by tearing up an invitation to the Geelong Grammar School dance, before witnesses. She might as well have spat in the altar wine.

There were elm trees and peppercorn trees in Villamente Street and the people next door kept a cow. It was a quiet, almost rural, lower middle-class street. Phoebe (who had left the school at the end of 1918) had persuaded her parents to pay "Miss Davidson" to give her history lessons there.

Some history.

There they are now. Their conversation is as clear as crystal. I simply have to reach out and take it.

"It cannot be immoral", Phoebe says, "to have a clear idea of how one looks."

"Not as long as it doesn't become a preoccupation."

A match is struck, slicing through the squeal of pigs. Cigarette smoke streams urgently towards the ceiling.

"Oh Dicksy," Phoebe sighs, "if only there was something to make me forget it."

"That", says my *bête noire*, "is exactly what I mean."

Phoebe, gazing out the dusty window at the retreating pigs, knew exactly how beautiful she was. She had a creamy skin, brilliant waving red hair, long legs like a water bird's, a small waist and breasts which were just . . . so.

To look at a photograph you would not understand the extent of her beauty. There is no doubt that her face was not classic. The chin and lips were perfect, as if the imaginary almighty had lavished extravagant amounts of time on them and then, realizing it was getting late, had rushed on to the small nose and forehead, cramming them in where there was hardly room. In photographs the forehead looks a little low, the nose too high in the face, the magnificent chin and lips too dominant. Yet in life this was not the effect at all. Only the loveless camera shows these things in this way, blind to her strength, her spirit, the intensity of those small brown eyes, the porcelain complexion, the hypnotic way she spoke, hardly opening her mouth to allow the passage of words between her small, fine white teeth.

Annette Davidson did not doubt Phoebe's beauty. But she did not like the way Phoebe had begun to speak about it. She thought it was unhealthy, or unlucky. She brooded on the consequences but none of her insights, which were numerous, did anything to free her from her pupil.

"Your beauty", she said, "will be your downfall. You'll end up like Susan Bussell."

Phoebe groaned. "How could I be like Susan Bussell?" She turned from the window. She wore a short black dress with a flash of chartreuse on the shoulder. The light was behind her and Annette could not see the hurt in her eyes. "Susan Bussell is a cow," she said, and turned back to the street.

"A dull, complacent cow," said Annette, "who doesn't bother to think or feel because she knows she will marry a rich farmer and knows exactly what schools she will send her children to."

Phoebe pulled a face at the dusty window.

"She is waiting for life to come and court her, and it will, in

16

exactly the way she thinks it will. She doesn't need to work, or think."

Phoebe flattened her nose against the glass. "A nose like a pig," she thought, "in a street full of pigs."

"You have to *work*," Annette said softly. "And *think*. If you go on like this, you're going to be very unhappy."

Phoebe felt it. She felt the unhappiness push into her, thread itself through her like piano wire, push out through her stomach and bind her wrists. "You're horrid," she said, betrayed. The face behind the rain-flecked dusty window crumpled and her shoulders collapsed.

Annette drew the curtain slowly, discreetly, so as to attract no attention from the curious Mr Wilson who was laying out tomato seedlings not twenty feet away, and then (only then) held the crying girl and buried her face in the blissful softness of her neck.

"Why are you so horrid, Dicksy?"

"Because", Annette hissed, surprised at her own passion, "you are waiting for something to happen to you. You must *do* something."

"I will do something," Phoebe said quietly, running a finger thoughtfully across her lover's lips. "It will just be something unusual. It will not be something I can plan for. It won't be what you expect or what I expect either."

"What will it be?" Annette whispered, but by then she was no longer interested in the answer and she rubbed her nose into the softness of my darling's eye.

"It will be something," Phoebe said. "I guarantee you."

Later, when she was in Sydney being notorious, Phoebe went around telling people that she had "foreknowledge" of the event. She had known she would see my aeroplane suspended in the sky above Vogelnest's paddocks at Balliang East. She convinced many people, and I won't say it can't be true. In any case, it is a pretty story, so I will leave it hovering there, like an aeroplane, alone in the sky, gliding towards her with a dead engine.

3

Phoebe sat on the big kitchen table and kicked her legs and listened to the commotion, the little cries of pleasure, as her mother and Bridget set about packing the hamper. Phoebe frowned and bit her nails. She watched her mother like a parent

17

who knows a child will shortly stumble. In that odd household it was the parents who were the children: Jack and Molly fussing over each other, touching each other, walking around the roses hand in hand, turtle-doving and cooing at fifty years of age while their only child watched them, nervous lest they hurt themselves.

They did not understand Geelong society. They were friendly and neighbourly. They offered hatfuls of hens' eggs across the fence.

Phoebe understood Geelong all too well. She shuddered when she heard that her mother had invited the A. D. Collinses to a picnic at Balliang East. Molly and Mrs Collins were on the committee for the Wyuna Nursing Home, and although they were both on the committee because their husbands were rich, in Molly's case this was the only reason. Molly did not know the other reasons even existed. She thought she could ask Mrs Collins to a picnic.

It was perfectly clear that the A. D. Collinses would not come and then there would be food not eaten and her mother would become brighter and brighter, chattier and chattier, and the moment would come when a particular laugh – Phoebe would recognize it instantly – would shudder and twitch and then fall apart in tears.

Phoebe jumped down off the table and embraced her mother. Molly was white-skinned and ginger-haired, sweet and soft as roly-poly pudding.

"Isn't it lovely?" Molly said. And Bridget stood back so that they might admire the hamper.

"Yes," said Phoebe. "It's lovely."

It was probably just as well the Collinses would not come. The McGraths always picnicked at the most dreadful places. They picnicked without shame; they picnicked thick-skinned and jolly at places Phoebe would not have stopped to spit at.

Phoebe no longer pleaded and no longer sulked. She understood the parameters of the picnics all too well. E.g. they could not go to the beach because of the sand. They must keep away from areas frequented by mosquitoes, trees with limbs that might fall, forests through which bush fires might suddenly sweep, places known to be frequented by bull ants or similar in soil or vegetation to places where bull ants had been observed. Last, and most important of all, there must be plenty of running water, water of impeccable credentials (a river, with the constant risk of dead heifers just a mile upstream, was quite unacceptable).

A good brass tap was, to Molly McGrath, the thing around which a good picnic could confidently be built.

They all knew, or thought they knew, that there was something wrong with Molly's brain. Neither father nor daughter mentioned it, but why else did they pamper her so, bring her bowls of bread and warm milk, and fuss over her like an invalid when she was – anyone could see – strong as an ox. Molly worked at her picnics like she tended her roses or worked on her veggie garden, breathlessly. Phoebe could feel terrors in the air when the cries of delight were loudest. Her mother was a creature building a fragile stick nest on a beach that will shortly be deluged by tide. She made happy optimistic cries but a practised observer would see she did not quite believe them.

However, the first time I saw the ritual of picnic preparation, I saw no terrors. I saw Molly's fine green eyes alight with anticipation, heard her laugh, saw her throw her small plump hands into the air with girlish delight, watched the same ringed hands accompany the hamper, like an escort of anxious doves, to the trunk of the Hispano Suiza.

And what newcomer, seeing the hamper, the car, the excitement of the hostess's eyes, would understand why Phoebe's lips were so pale and eyes so dull?

Jack McGrath was a man who was happiest without a collar. He preferred his trousers a size too large and his boots loosely laced. You might confuse the roll of his walk with that of a sailor's, but you have not made the study of walks I have – this was not a sailor's walk, it was the walk of a man who has covered twenty thousand dusty miles beside his bullock teams. He had drunk champagne from metal pannikins and called it "Gentleman's Grog". He had slept beneath his wagon and on top of it. He had hidden his gold in a hollowed-out yoke and drunk from dams that held more mud than water. He had, before he became a rich man, eaten a picturesque array of animals, reptiles, and birds. But he was not, not in any way, upset by his wife's restrictions in regard to picnics. "It was as if", Phoebe said later, "he was *proud* of the whole nonsense mother went on with, as if it suggested some height of gentility and femininity few women might hope to attain. I don't think he ever saw how bleak the picnic spots were. All he could see was an advertisement for the sensitivity of his wife's beautiful skin. He was very proud of her."

Good dear Jack would never understand why anyone would slight his wife. He could not see that there was any difference between a picnic and having a drink with old A.D. (which he did often enough) in Finch's Railway Hotel. He would never learn the difference between having a drink with a man and sharing a feed with his family. You never met a man who seemed to make so few social distinctions. He would have anyone to his house who would come – bishops and rabbit-ohs, limping ex-service-men and flash characters from the racetrack. They brought him presents or took him down, told lies or their true life stories and he stamped his foot and filled their glasses and took them for joy-rides in the Hispano Suiza. He was one of the worst drivers I ever met. He had no feel for machinery at all. (In all the years I sold cars to cockies I only met three men who were worse, and one of them killed himself on that narrow bridge at Parwan North.)

It's a strange thing that men who could handle animals with great feeling and sensitivity (and Jack was one of them) suddenly turned into clumsy oafs the minute they got behind the wheel.

There he goes – out the driveway, Molly sitting rigidly in the front, Phoebe hiding behind a wide-brimmed black hat in the back. They lurch on to Eastern Avenue. Jack rides the clutch. The engine roars. He grates it into second before he has sufficient revs and then shudders along beside the beach, heading north towards the brass tap at Balliang East.

To the McGraths' neighbours the style of departure proved everything, i.e., that he had no right to own such a car. He had no right to be in Western Avenue at all or, for that matter, to send his daughter to the Hermitage. He had built an ugly yellow-brick garage to house his flashy auto, and offered his filthy hen eggs across the fence, holding them out in a hat whose sweaty felt radiated an offensive intimacy.

But as Jack drove north he gave not a thought to the effect of grating gears on neighbours' ears. He held the wheel so tight his burly arms would later ache. He called this ache "arthritis" but it was caused by hanging on too hard. His wife suffered similar aches and pains which, although occurring in different places, were caused by the same fearfulness. Only when they were past the cable trams, the Sunday jinkers and the T Models did the older McGraths relax a little.

It was a hot day and the wind was dry. Phoebe sat in the back and reduced the landscape to its most pleasing essentials. She half shut her eyes and allowed her eyelashes to strain out that which was not to her taste. She removed those piles of hard volcanic rocks, those monuments to the endless work of young soldier settlers. She eliminated those lonely treeless farmhouses with the sun beating on their shining gal-iron roofs. She abracadabra'ed the sheep with their daggy backsides. She turned those endless miles of sheep and wheat into something the men who farmed it would never recognize. All she retained was the cobalt blue sky above a plain of shimmering gold. You couldn't make a quid in one of Phoebe's landscapes.

She loved the hot dry wind. She liked speed.

"Drive fast," she demanded. "Oh please, Mother, let him."

Did Jack want to drive fast? I doubt it. As for Molly, I know she didn't. But they knew also that this was what a Hispano Suiza was for.

"All right," Molly commanded, "drive fast, as far as the saltpans."

Jack tensed his great thick arms and gripped the wheel until his fingers ached. The Suiza's eight cylinders responded to his large foot without reluctance and did not question (with the slightest hesitation or hiccup) whether he was man enough to manage it.

They made the wind rush faster for her. They made the flat dull land exciting. She drew down her eyelashes and thought of humming-birds' wings. They spoilt her, of course. They flew across the saltpans at fifty miles an hour and didn't even slow down.

4

There had been too many Germans in Jeparit. The minute the war was over Ernie Vogelnest sold up his farm there and moved away. It had been too hard to be with other Germans. It made the Australians afraid and then nasty. In 1917 there had been all the fuss when they found the dug-out on his property. They said German prisoners of war had been hiding there and he had been feeding them. The Jeparit paper as good as called him a liar. Well, maybe he had lied, and maybe he had not lied, but he was determined to live in a place where there were no other Germans and perhaps there was time yet – he would learn to speak so they could not know, to speak like his son.

When the war ended he bought this land at Balliang East. Not the best land in the world, but better than Jeparit. Five hundred acres and, for an old man, he was working hard. There was another German twenty miles away, at Anakie, but he was happy with the land and the number of Germans.

They made fun of him at the shops at Bacchus Marsh when he went in for supplies, but at least no one said they were going to lynch him. When they said, "Ja, ja," he grinned and ducked his head as if to say, "Ja, ja, I know." Sometimes they cheated him, not much, just a little. He smiled. But now they had written things about him on his road, well, not his road, of course not (the road belonged to the Australian government) but the road that ran in front of his house. It was the soldier settlers, he supposed. They had painted an arrow with whitewash and written words, "Kaiser Bill, the silly dill". He did not know what a dill was but it gave him a sick feeling in the stomach just the same. He had the feeling even now as he tried to remove the paint with turps, kneeling on the hot macadam.

He did not hear the Hispano Suiza until it was nearly on top of him. The wind was swinging around to the north-east and all he could hear was that bit of gal iron from the O'Hagens' place: bang, bang, bang. Sometimes at night it kept him awake, but he did not like to ask the O'Hagens to shift it. He was a German and he wanted no trouble.

The horn blared and he jumped. He saw the car as the brakes squealed. He stood back from the road, his heart beating. The car then turned and lurched into the parking place in front of the Balliang East Hall which was opposite his house. He watched it. The people got out of the car and then passed out of sight behind the pine trees.

Ernest Vogelnest went back to his house. He climbed up on his tank stand from where he could see that the people in the big car were pretending to have a picnic.

It did not seem credible.

5

Phoebe could not believe her mother and father were not acting out a charade. They *must* know the A. D. Collinses would not come. They sat in the dead shadow of the pine trees. They had a good view of the rusted water tank lying on its side in O'Hagen's paddock, and a collection of assorted rocks with a sheet of roofing iron lying across it. The north-easter occasionally picked up the sheet of battered iron and then put it down again. They could also see an old rock fence, and, running parallel to it, a new barbed-wire fence. The paddock was half full of thistles, the white flowers from which drifted before the wind and one had lodged in Molly's hair. Her eyes had pouches, and she had a tendency to jowliness but the hair was splendid, young hair, just like her daughter's.

Molly talked on and on. She could not stop but her face was colouring and she started to complain about the heat.

Phoebe sat on the wooden steps of the Balliang East Hall, in front of its single door, beneath the peeling sign that read BALLIANG EAST HALL. 1912. She felt desolate.

"I wonder what has happened," her mother said. "Unless there has been an accident."

Phoebe sighed, just at a moment when the iron was not rattling and when everything, even the ewe caught in O'Hagen's muddy dam a quarter of a mile away, became silent. And Jack, sitting twenty yards from his daughter, heard the sigh.

He was a plain man. He had a large, thick-necked, jut-jawed head. He had big square hands and a big square backside. "What you see", people said of him, "is what you get." But he understood his daughter's sigh exactly. It slipped through his defences like a knife and made him feel small and foolish – Jumped-up Jack.

"Can't you see?" he barked at his wife. "The snobs have cut us."

It was at this moment, as Phoebe turned to avoid a painful scene, that she saw the aeroplane. It appeared, clear as day, between two branches of a pine.

She stood and walked quickly to the road, her pale yellow silk scarf floating behind her. Ernest Vogelnest, still on the tank stand, called his wife to watch.

The aeroplane was completely silent. It hung there, its propeller lifeless. She could see the struts and crosswires between the two wide wings. The pilot was suspended in a cockpit between the wings. The craft was sandwiched in the cobalt sky like a dragonfly in amber. A magpie sang, its notes as clear as glass. The craft came lower, became bigger, and still there was not a sound from it. It seemed to fly towards her. It seemed it must fly straight into her. She did not flinch, and then it paused, hovered, dipped, and just before it came gently to rest against the fence of Vogelnest's front paddock, she heard a voice utter two words.

"You cow," I said.

23

The problem in that area is the rocks. It's not what you'd call Bad Land. There are few trees. You can get down in almost any of these paddocks. But there are rocks, and that was what I was thinking about as I kicked the rudder bar, and shoved the stick over. Frigging rocks!

There was a lot of low-level turbulence over the ploughed land round Bald Hill, and the nor'easterly was starting to gust as I brought the Morris Farman around into it. I was cursing Mr Farman for only putting one magneto on an eight-cylinder engine when he should have used two. I cursed myself for buying the damn thing. I cursed the damn public who would no longer pay the sort of money they had for a joy ride. I used to get five pounds for half an hour above Melbourne, and then it dropped to two quid in Ballarat. And now the best I could get was four and tuppence ha'penny from a lanky cyclist who wanted to look at the gravel pits at Commaida from the air. Four and tuppence bloody ha'penny. It was all I had, that four and two pence ha'penny, including the four threepences with old plum pudding still stuck to them. I flew him for half an hour and he complained about the bumps. Bumps!

I had just enough benzine to make it to Barwon Common in Geelong. God knows what I was going to do. I forget. I would have had a scheme. I always had a scheme. But when the magneto went I was in a mess.

I owed the RAAF five hundred pounds for the plane and parts.

I owed the publican in Darnham over twenty pounds.

I owed Anderson's in Bacchus Marsh another fifty pounds for building materials for the house I was building for me and that girl from the Co-op. It was a nice little house. It was one of the nicest little houses I ever built but she wouldn't even walk in the front door when she saw how I used the wire netting and mud.

"It's mud," she said.

"It'll outlast you," I said.

"It's not your land," she said. "It's Theo Craigie's and you're trespassing."

I was thirty-three years old and nothing was working out. I

built a lovely kitchen table for that girl. She was broad and strong and she had a nice laugh. We were going to have babies but she thought I was a liar and I found the cyclist and got his four and tuppence ha'penny.

I knew the land around Balliang East. I had sold plenty of T Models and Dodges round that area, to the Blowbells, the McDonalds, the Jenszes, the Dugdales. So I knew the rocks.

When I saw the shining new roof of Vogelnest's new house I decided to put it down in his front paddock. I was a bit high for it. I really should have put it down in O'Hagen's. But no matter what the *Ballarat Courier Mail* wrote about me frightening cattle and causing them to break their legs, a cocky liked to have an aeroplane just like anybody else did. A cocky liked to have an aeroplane in his front paddock. It added distinction. I probably had a plan to stay there a while and sell them a car.

I was still thirty feet up and doing thirty knots when I was over his cow bails. I shoved the stick down and landed so hard I half winded myself. There would, just the same, have been no problem, but as I came to the fence the left wing skid hit a pile of small rocks and stopped it dead. I heard the skid tear off. The plane swung and the lower right wing hit the fence. The wing struts crumpled and the fabric ripped.

"You cow," I said. I could have cried.

I sat there for a minute. When I jumped down I nearly landed on a snake. He was a long king brown, sliding through the grass as silky as 50 SAE motor oil as it pours from the can.

The snake was lucky, and I don't mean that in the sense that snakes are said to be symbols of good fortune. I didn't even know what a symbol was. It was lucky because it was worth five bob to Mr Chin – who rightly belongs in a later part of the story – he was a herbalist with a practice in Exhibition Street, Melbourne.

The snake stopped. It felt my admiration. It raised its head to look around and I stood stock still. Just as it lowered its head again, I pounced. I never picked up a snake the correct way. I always did it wrong. But I was fast. I fancied I was as fast as any snake. I grabbed him behind the head and held him tight and before Mr Joe Blake knew what was what, I was carrying him back to the plane where I had some hessian bags I used as cushions for my passengers.

Two different sets of eyes were already looking at me.

Phoebe did not stop to read the "Kaiser Bill" sign, but the heady scent of turpentine rose from the hot bitumen where Ernie Vogelnest had been battling with the insult. She stood in the middle of the Bacchus Marsh–Geelong Road enveloped in a shimmer of turps, her feet bridging "Kaiser" and "Bill" as I jumped from the cockpit.

She could hear me breathing as I concentrated on the snake. She could hear her mother crying.

As I walked back to find a hessian bag with no holes in it, she was climbing the fence.

I heard the twang of wire and turned.

I saw the most beautiful woman I had ever seen in my life. She was sailing through the air about level with the top wire of the fence.

Phoebe landed lightly on the summer-hard ground (only when darkness came did she realize she had twisted her ankle) and smiled.

Herbert Badgery stood there staring at her. I can see him. He is almost as much a stranger to me as he is to her. He is tall, slim-hipped, broad-shouldered. He has bowed legs which he is ashamed of and which she finds attractive. He has an Irish mouth, like a squiggle of a pen, which is sensuous and attractive. He has all his teeth and the skin that will later become as fragile and powdery as an old kerosene-lamp mantle, is brown and smooth. He has taken off his leather helmet and goggles and there are marks around his eyes. The eyes are stunning. They are the clearest, coldest blue.

Later, when she was in a different frame of mind, she said the eyes made her shiver. A lie. She also, later still, told her son that I had used the eyes to hypnotize the snake. If you could see the eyes you might grant it possible.

She was close to the Farman. She could smell the oil and petrol. The smell would always, from that day, be a perfume to her as heady as musk. This weakness would be used against her, later, later.

She did not see the man as good-looking, or handsome, but something better. She saw the strength and smelt the oil. She longed to make him smile. "Like hard woody cases of eucalypts", she wrote, "that burst open to reveal the most delicate flowers."

No one noticed little Ernie Vogelnest who was nervously hovering around the edge of his front paddock.

"What's the snake for?" Phoebe said.

The tin flapped again. The ewe resumed its bleating.

"It's a pet," I said. I did not wish to admit I needed the five bob so badly. In any case, it was no trouble to lie. I always lied about snakes. I always lied about women. It was a habit. I did it, in both cases, charmingly. I was so enthusiastic that I could convince myself in half a sentence.

"Did your plane crash?"

"No," I said. "It didn't. I am surveying." I paused. "For airstrips."

"This will not be suitable then?" She smiled.

"No," I said.

"Is he really your pet?"

"Yes. He escaped when I landed. He bounced out of the cockpit."

"Isn't he dangerous?"

There is no doubting the power of a snake, which is something I've proved time and time again. "Not if you know how to handle him," I said. "A snake can smell your fear. If you feel fear it will attack you. If you show no fear you can be its friend and it will protect you", I said, "from enemies."

Listen to the bullshitter. If snakes could smell fear this one would know that I was soaked with it. I wasn't thinking about what I was saying. The snake and girl both demanded my attention. The nor'easterly blew against her and pressed her extraordinary dress against her legs. It was a "flapper's" dress, made far away from Balliang East. I had never seen such skin, such creamy skin. I spewed out words about snakes, like muslin out of a medium's mouth, but all my thoughts were full of Phoebe's skin. I wondered if she thought I was old.

"You hold that snake", she said, hardly moving her lovely lips, "as if you are frightened it will bite you. I don't think", she smiled, "that it is a pet at all."

In those days I would have done anything to get written up in the papers and anything for the admiration of a woman. If it hadn't have been for those two factors I would probably, by 1919, have been the Summit agent in Ballarat. I would have had a lot more than four and tuppence ha'penny in my pocket.

27

"Not a pet?" I raised my eyebrows.

"Is it?"

Look at the fool! I shudder to think of the risk I'm taking. The king brown snake is cranky and cantankerous. It can kill with a single strike. That dull Mr-Smith-type name is an alibi for a snake almost as deadly as a taipan. But Herbert Badgery will do anything to insist his lie is true – I let the snake run down my arm, across my trousers, to the ground.

And there it should have ended, with the five bob slinking off through the grass. The pet declared free. A good deed done, etc. But Phoebe came forward and picked the damn thing up herself. She held the writhing, deadly twisting rope out to me. My throat was so dry I could not speak. I took it with a shudder and got it into the hessian bag and tied the top with binding twine. I had to shove my hands into my leather jacket when I'd finished. They were trembling.

It was then that Ernest Vogelnest chose to make his entry, scuttling crab-style round the end of the good lower wing. He didn't beat around. He launched into his conversation before I saw him.

"How fast does it fly?" he said.

He made me jump, speaking up like that.

"Sorry," he said. He was a funny-looking little coot. He had thin wiry arms, a red face with a walrus moustache that was far too big for it. He wore his moleskins with foreign-looking leggings. He smiled and ducked his head.

"A very nice aeroplane, sir," said Ernest Vogelnest, nodding his head to the young lady. "Very nice. . ."

"I apologize", I began. . . .

"No, no, no. It is very interesting." He patted the air in front of my chest with the palms of his hands. There was so *little* of him. What there was was held together by dirt and sinew.

"Where will you go now?" He patted the nose cowling like a man admiring a neighbour's horse.

"Nowhere," I smiled. "It's no good. Broken. Kaput."

As it turned out we had quite different ideas about the aeroplane. From the corner of his eye Ernest Vogelnest saw his wife come out of the shed with a shovel. She carried the shovel to the fence and waited. A shovel was not such a wonderful weapon. He should, perhaps, have told her to bring the fork, but it was too late now.

"Kaput," I said.

"Oh no," Ernest Vogelnest said firmly. "Where to next?"

"We stay here," I said.

But Ernest did not want anything as strange as an aeroplane in his front paddock. It would bring crowds of people who would stare at him. He rubbed his papery hands together and saw them, in their teaming thousands, writing things on the road. They would think the plane was his. They would decide he was a spy. God knows what they would do to him.

I misunderstood him. I offered to pay.

"No, no," he rolled his eyes in despair. "No, no money."

"I will pay three shillings."

"I will pay more," Ernest Vogelnest said desperately, smiling and ducking his head. "Much more."

"He doesn't understand," Phoebe said.

Vogelnest ignored her. "I will pay you, sir, one pound, if you push your aero across the road," he smiled slyly, "into O'Hagen's."

We shook on it. I had made a total of one pound and five shillings since arriving in Balliang East. My gross assets were now one pound nine shillings and tuppence ha'penny.

Success always went to my head. I got too excited. I went from despair to optimism in a flash. And my day was only starting, because a dangerous meeting was about to take place.

I.e.: Jack.

There was nothing to protect us from each other. We were elements like phosphorus and air which should always be kept apart. But he was already standing up from his picnic and picking pine needles from his trouser cuffs, but even if Molly had somehow known, had seen the result of that fifty-yard walk across the road, what could she have done?

Jack McGrath was a man with an obsession, about transportation. He could discuss the wheel as a wonder, and he could talk about it for hours in relationship to the bullock team, the horse and jinker, the dray, the cart, the T Model, the Stanley Steamer. He could talk about it in relationship to Australia and its distances. He never got sick of it.

He had money in the bank. He owned a Hispano Suiza, a fleet of taxis, a racehorse, but none of those things made him happy. What he liked to do was talk. And when the house was empty of guests he'd put on his hat and walk three miles down to Corio Quay where he could still find, in 1919, bullock wagons unloading wool. He could yarn with the bullockies for hours. They talked record hauls. They boasted. Jack told them how he'd got the boiler into Point's Point in 1910. He advised them to move into trucks. He spoke enthusiastically about the future of the automobile but he looked with envy on their teams: Redman, Tiger, Lofty, Yallarman, he knew the beasts almost as well as he knew the men. He shouted them "Gentleman's grog" and, in his cups, made plans to go back on the track. When Lauchie Barr's team brought thirty-two tons of bagged wheat in from Colac and broke the Australian record, Jack brought him to dinner and presented him with a handsome cup with a silver cricketer standing on its lid.

He was exactly the sort of man I had wished to land on: enthusiastic, willing, and impressed with the idea of an aeroplane. But when I saw him stride across the road in his expensive suit I didn't realize what was coming. I saw a rich man. I was never good with rich men. They made my hackles rise.

This false impression didn't last a minute. Jack whipped off his jacket and ripped off his tie. He lost his collar studs in the grass. He collected his cufflinks and rolled up his sleeves while his wife, a pretty ginger cat in fluffy white, watched from the safety of the road.

To get the craft into O'Hagen's it was necessary to remove a few fence posts. Jack picked up a crowbar and set to it like a fellow who is starved of work. He raised the crowbar and sank it into the red earth. "That's the go," he said. "*That's* the go." He did not mean to overpower Ernest Vogelnest or snatch tools from his hand. He was being polite, useful, and although he was bursting with curiosity about the plane, he did not say a word that could be considered nosey. He gave himself wholly to the task at hand, to remove those four posts, replace them, get the plane through O'Hagen's broken fence, and hide it behind the hall.

The posts were out in a moment. Jack stacked them neatly and then I explained to them where they could push or lift and where they couldn't. You have to be careful with a plane like a Farman – you lift under a strut, never between. When I was sure they understood the requirements, I ordered a start, but although the farmer was quick to get his back under a strut, Jack McGrath would not have a bar of it.

It was all very well, he said, to rush into digging out a fence or putting one back in, but only a fool rushed into pushing anything, whether it was a dray or an auto or an aeroplane, without first looking over the ground and assessing the problems. He knew this from all his years with bullock teams. The secret of his success had not just been, as everyone thought, that he knew his beasts, each individual, like you might know a man or woman, each one with their strengths, their weaknesses, their little quirks. His success had been sealed on all the nights he had gone to sleep thinking out a problem. The way he got that boiler into Point's Point is the most famous example, but he would approach a difficult log in the same way. His success had been in thinking it out, and often when he met someone on the track, bogged to the axles under ten tons of wool, or in trouble on a pinch, he would see that they were only in strife because they had not stopped long enough to think. So at Balliang East he walked with me over to O'Hagen's, and unearthed a nasty hollow and a tangle of barbed wire which had been hidden in the dry summer grass.

When we had cleared the wire away, we came back across the road to the craft and, seeing the daughter occupied the front cockpit, I enquired whether the mother might not like a ride in the back.

Jack was surprised to see her accept – she was always so nervous – but he didn't reckon on my eyes. I took her hand and helped her up. She giggled like a young girl and her daughter was nice enough to say nothing of the third passenger: the king brown snake beneath her mother's seat.

When the Farman was safely behind the hall, I tied it to the fence on one side and lashed it to some heavy rocks on the other. The women stayed seated in the cockpit. Vogelnest edged towards the road, but seemed reluctant to make the journey alone. Jack wanted to talk about knots. When he began, tucking in his shirt over his strong man's belly, I thought he was criticizing the knots I had tied. I missed the point – Jack liked the "idea" of a knot.

"It is a great thing, the knot," he said. "A great thing."

Vogelnest seemed to understand more than I did. He squatted on the ground and surveyed O'Hagen's paddocks with a critical eye. As Jack continued the light grew mellow and the colour started to come back into the landscape.

"What sort of fellow," he said, "would invent the Donaldson lash?"

"A fellow called Donaldson," I suggested.

"An astonishing man," said Jack, mentally picturing the unsung Donaldson in some draughty shed alone with his ropes. "What a grasp he had of the principles. And what a memory. Two over, then back, down, hitch, double hitch and through. It's a knot you need to practise for a week before you get the hang of it."

I never heard of the Donaldson lash before or since, or half the other knots I heard celebrated that afternoon while the sky lost its intense cobalt and went powdery and soft, and the grasses that had looked so bleached and lifeless now turned dun and gold, pale green and russet.

Jack wondered out loud about the saddler's bow and argued the comparative merits of the reef and the double latch. Phoebe stayed in the front cockpit with her hands folded in her lap. The late sun set her hair afire. Vogelnest saw me looking at her and smiled and ducked his head.

"Ah," said Jack who seemed, at last to have exhausted his subject, "I do like a good knot."

Everybody started to move like they do in a church when the bridal party has gone out to sign the registry. Phoebe yawned and stretched. Vogelnest stood and brushed his knees. Molly declared herself frightened of snakes and would not walk back through the long grass. Jack picked her up like a bride and carried her across the paddock and when they arrived, laughing, on the roadway, he refused to put her down.

Molly squealed like a young girl and Mrs Vogelnest, still standing guard at the fence with the long-handled shovel, allowed a small smile to break up the unhappy lines Jeparit had engraved on her tiny clenched-up face.

8

Ernest Vogelnest sat in his kitchen. His wife was in bed, asleep. He was finishing the last of the schnapps. He had been keeping the schnapps for five years and tonight had been the right time to drink it.

He could hear the music, the piano accordion and the young girl's voice. It drifted across the desolate paddocks from O'Hagen's where the aviator and the picnickers had gone to explain the aeroplane. It was a party. He guessed, quite correctly, that there was dancing. He raised his glass towards the house where Herbert Badgery and Mrs O'Hagen were doing an Irish jig.

Ernest Vogelnest had spent his pound well. He was not merely happy, he was overwhelmed by the niceness of people, the blissful absence of the aeroplane. It had been a quid well spent.

When he saw the lights of the Hispano Suiza come bumping down the long dirt road from O'Hagen's he extinguished his hurricane lamp and watched the car pass by his darkened window. He thought he saw the aviator in the driver's seat, his face reflected in the glow of the instruments, and he raised his glass to him, wishing him well.

9

I always had an aversion to hotel rooms, guest houses, boarding houses or anywhere else where a man was forced into giving up money for a place to stay. I always built a place of my own when I could. I built from mud and wire netting (which is better than it sounds and more comfortable than the girl from Bacchus Marsh had realized). I was also a dab hand at a slab hut, a skill that has now died out, but which made a very satisfactory house, one that'd last a hundred years. I made houses from the wooden crates they shipped the T Models in. I made houses from galvanized iron (from rainwater tanks on one occasion). I even spent one summer in the Mallee living in a hole in the ground. It was cool and comfortable in that hot climate and I would have got married but a poddy calf fell in on top of us one night and broke the woman's arm. You can call that bad luck, but it was my stupidity. I should have fenced it.

You could say I was obsessed with houses, but I was not abnormal. My only abnormality was that I did not have one. I had been forced to leave my houses behind me, evicted from them, disappointed in them, fleeing them because of various events. I left them to rot and rust and be shat on by cattle on the land of the so-called legal owners who were called squatters because they'd done exactly what I'd done.

While a house was always my aim, it wasn't always possible in the short term. I was an expert, however, at getting "put up". I was not just an expert. I was an ace. I never had to be formally invited and I always left them before my welcome was worn out. Don't think I cheated the legal owners, because I never did. I delivered value in whatever way it was required.

I applied this principle to the McGraths.

I was an Aviator. That was my value to them. I set to work to reinforce this value. I propped it up and embellished it a little. God damn, I danced around it like a bloody bower-bird putting on a display. I added silver to it. I put small blue stones around it.

33

By the time I swung the headlights of the Hispano Suiza on to the McGrath house in Western Avenue, Jack McGrath could *see* the factory I said – it was a pleasant whim – I was going to establish, a factory that was going to build Australian-designed aircraft. It was splendid. Everyone in the car could see it, shimmering in the moonlight.

You call it a lie. I call it a gift.

When I saw the size of the house, I was pleased I had taken so much trouble with my story. It was the equal of the lace-decorated Victorian mansion I saw in the headlights. It was capped with a splendid tower and the tower was capped with a crown of wrought-iron lace. For a building with a tower I could not have taken too much trouble.

In an instant, it seemed, they had the mansion blazing with electric light. It poured forth in luxury from every window, washed across the flower beds and flooded the lawn. Even the yellow-brick garage had its own set of lights and as I garaged the Hispano Suiza I could hear the voices of the two women as they called to the maid who fluttered like a moth inside the kitchen windows and threw fleeting shadows out across the lawn.

I liked the electricity. I liked the sheer quantity of it. It was right that a house like this, grander than any I had ever stayed in, should be so enthusiastically illuminated.

The cicadas, as if they were wired on the same circuit, suddenly filled the garden with a loud burst of celebration. If fireworks had now illuminated the summer sky they would not have been out of keeping with my emotions. I had never seen anything like it. I had never seen anything approaching it. There was a ballroom, a music room, a library, a tower. Don't worry that there was no dancing in the ballroom, no music in the music room, and not a single book in the library. To dwell on those empty shelves would be to miss the point. There were stained-glass windows made by M. Ives of Melbourne. There were carpets, wall to wall, made in Lancashire from Western District wool. There were ice chests, music machines, and electric wiring everywhere.

Jack had introduced the electricity himself. He hadn't messed around. He ran the wires like streamers across the ceiling, tacked them on to wooden architraves, hung them from a picture rail and looped them around the curtain rods. The neighbours in Western Avenue might not have cared for this frank approach, but I liked it. It made me comfortable. It was a house where you could put your feet up and drink French champagne or Ballarat bitter according to your mood.

The other remarkable thing about the house was chairs. There were so many of them waiting to be sat on that you could see, immediately, that the McGraths were hospitable people and they'd never pass up a chance to buy an extra chair if it took their fancy. Their taste was catholic, although that is a term they would not have used themselves. Was there Chippendale? Perhaps. And Louis-Quatorze? Probably, but the Herbert Badgery who looked on that array did not even know such names. They were all chairs to him, some old, some new, some tatty, some gilt, some comfortable, some overstuffed, some bursting with horsehair which would prickle the back of your legs and make you itch. I got the feeling that my hosts expected, at any moment, a hundred people with weary legs to walk in off the street.

I could hear the women making supper. Jack showed me to a room. He opened up the big French doors on to the veranda and the room filled with the smell of flowers, salt from the bay, the humming generators of cicada engines. The cupboard was full of clothes that Molly had collected to sell for the Wyuna Nursing Home appeal.

"Help yourself," said Jack. "There's some first-rate stuff in here, I warrant you."

I got myself a new wardrobe that night, selecting carefully, thinking of the winter ahead.

"Snaffle every staver," I told myself as I admired myself in my new suit. I thought I was a real smart bastard.

10

They tell me now that there was no wireless in Geelong in 1919, but I tell you there was. It had a big round dial depicting not only the stations but the world itself. We sat around it on our chairs. Phoebe drank a cordial and clinked her ice inside the glass. Molly had tea. Jack and I drank Scotch. Alcohol was always dangerous for me when I was excited: I sipped. Not Jack. He confessed he had been a teetotaller to the age of forty and he appreciated his drink the way he appreciated knots. He wiped his mouth with the back of his broad hairy hand and marvelled at its effect on his constitution.

"By Jove," he said, "that was good."

There was wireless, all right, and they read the news on it. Jack, like my father before me and my son after me, was a bit on the deaf side and he leaned attentively towards the set. The rest of us stared at the amber glow behind the map of the world: there was news that night of the Australia–England air race. Ulm, so the plummy-voiced announcer said, had crashed in Crete.

My God, it was the year to be an aviator. We could do no wrong. When the press wrote up a pilot he wasn't just a pilot; he was an "eagle soaring above our skies" and no matter how often some ex-RFC type crashed while publicizing War Bonds, the public never seemed to get tired of it. The Australia–England air race fed them on tales of heroism and danger.

As it happened, I had known Charles Ulm. Possibly I had known Charles Ulm. To tell you the truth I can't remember whether I really did know him or if I claimed it so often I came to believe it myself. Photographs of Ulm never looked like the man I described but people always blamed the photographer for that, not me. In any case, when the news was over I told them all about Ulm, what he was like as a man, what he looked like and so on. In short, I delivered value.

I gorged myself on cold roast lamb and beans and beetroot. I hadn't had a feed in two days.

11

Phoebe watched the man who kept a snake for a pet, who shared, it seemed, a bedroom with the creature. She thought he devoured the table with a most peculiar passion, a passion as cool and blue as his eyes, as controlled and modulated as her own careful speech. She watched her mother as she fluttered – a humming-bird – in the cage of the aviator's oil-stained hand.

"That is so, Mr Badgery?" said Molly who had gone all plummy-voiced. "Is it not?"

Molly was so shell-shocked by social life in Geelong that she had lost all confidence in her normal manner. She now crooked her finger in a monstrous way when drinking tea. People thought her affected.

Phoebe would one day grow into the most formidable snob yet she did not judge or reject her mother for her anxious affectations – her mother was vulgar, but she loved her. Phoebe put the whole responsibility upon Geelong. It is in matters to do with Geelong that she was a snob and she would, given half a chance, have made invidious comparisons with Paris. She did not get a quarter of a chance. The talk was all aviation. They quoted the farmer from Myah-Myah who built an aeroplane in 1910 based solely on a newspaper photograph of the Wright Brothers' plane. They talked of Smithy and Ulm and were momentarily silent for the first Kingsford Smith, Ross. And Phoebe missed the point: the talk was really a celebration of towns as plain (and plainer than) Geelong. They were eyries, the birthplaces of the great. Australians, it seemed that night in Western Avenue, were born to rule the skies.

We drank a toast: "To our eagles." The owner of the antiquated Morris Farman on whose side was strapped a bicycle for seeking help, did not even have the grace to blush.

Phoebe, however, invented me according to her needs. She imagined she saw Jewish blood, or Semitic blood anyway. She thought of Arabs in ships with odd-shaped sails, traders from Sumer, Phoenicians selling their rare purple dyes swept here in the eddies of time to a dull bay and an electrically-illuminated supper in Geelong.

But she saw also, in an ebb in the conversation, that I suddenly looked so sad, so lost, that my mouth lost its shape. In my eyes she saw the shape of brilliant dreams, and also (like a private drawer stupidly left open) the stubbornness, the wilfulness in my lips, a cruelty, a fear of my own weakness. Her perceptions were a dangerous mixture of deadly accuracy and pure romance.

I did not speak to Phoebe during that meal during which she silently, picking at lamb gristle, nibbling at lip-staining beetroot, made a number of decisions that were to affect her for the rest of her life. The first of these was that she would learn to fly and the second was that I should teach her.

That night she would glide into sleep on the double wings of a Morris Farman. I stayed up talking to Jack for another four hours but when I lay, at last, on the cool sheets of my bed, I spat carefully on my forefinger and rubbed, ever so lightly, the head of my penis which was filled to bursting with dreams of creamy skin.

12

I had some funny dreams about Jack McGrath in later life, but there is no benefit to be obtained from discussing them here, even if I do compare that first night to the first night with a new lover.

There was passion, sympathy, excitement. We were tireless. We were so *pleased*. We talked of aeroplanes and motor cars, bullock teams and the bush. We recited Lawson and Banjo Paterson. We were still beneath the naked light globes in the ballroom when the milk cart went clopping down Western Avenue. We heard the clink of the ladle in the bucket, the sweet sound of pouring milk, the seagulls restless on the Quay a mile away.

Jack must have been dressed in the suit he had worn in honour of A. D. Collins, but I choose to remember him differently, with stubble on his folded face, the patch of dark hair on his ruddy cheek, his collarless shirt unironed, his old vest, his patched trousers, his unlaced boots placed beneath his chair (where they would be lost on the morrow), his toes curling and uncurling inside his carefully darned navy blue socks.

He told me the story of his life, and I'll tell you too, later.

I also told him the story of my life, or rather the parts of it I had never told a man before. It has to be told again now, and I find it harder than I did when I looked at Jack's soft eyes in his crumpled sympathetic face.

This story concerns my father who I always imagined to be an Englishman, who made such a thing, as long as I knew him, of his Englishness, who never missed a chance to say, "I am an Englishman" or, "as an Englishman" that I was surprised to find out he was born in York Street, Warrnambool, the son of a shopkeeper. Yet for all that, I must carry his lie for him. For he made himself into an Englishman and my first memory of him is being chastised for the way I spoke.

"Cahstle," he roared at me, "not kehstle." He did not like my accent. He did not, I think, like much about me. My brothers were older and they got on with him better. They were useful to him in his business and I was too young to do any more than feed the animals and jump down to apply the brake on hills.

His business was to represent the English firm of Newby whose prime product was the Newby Patented 18 lb. Cannon, and with this machine in tow we covered the rutted, rattling, dusty pot-holed roads of coastal Victoria, six big Walers in front, the cannon at the rear, and that unsprung cart they called a "limber" in the middle.

Always we were in a hurry. There was never a time when we might stop at a pretty spot, or a morning when we could lie late in bed. Always there was some group of squatters who had got themselves together or – and this must be what really happened –who my father thought could be persuaded to get together to buy a cannon to protect themselves from Russians or Chinese or shearers.

He was a man who saw threat everywhere – thin but very strong, pale-skinned, blue-eyed, black-bearded and as cold to his children as he was charming to his customers. I have seen him at table with fat mayors and muscle-gutted squatters, laughing, telling jokes, playing them as sweetly as if they were his own violin, warming them up, getting their pores wide open before he hit them with the icy blast of fear that was his specialty.

It was from my father that I learned about the Chinese and he painted pictures of such depravity that when I met my first Chinaman I expected him to kill me.

God knows what I learned from my mother. I did not have her for long. I cannot tell you what she looked like, although, of course, I thought her pretty. I can remember sitting beside her on the limber – she is nothing more than a shape, but warm and soft, quite different to my two brothers and father who rode postilion on those huge Walers – they were as hard as the iron leg guards they wore on their right legs.

My father dispensed with my mother when I was still very young and I always assumed that he sent her away, but it is more likely that she died. Only two things are certain. The first is that he would not discuss it. The second is that I blamed him. I was left alone on the bench seat with only the rounds of ammunition to keep me company. The limber was unsprung and iron-wheeled. They steered a course over logs and pot-holes just to jar me. And although I saw a lot of country it was not much of a childhood, moving as we did through threatening visions of Russians, Lascars, Jews, Asiatics, Niggers and other threats to our safety.

My father was always very mean with his ammunition, and it was because of this that we finally parted. There was never a group of men, or an individual man, who did not like to see the cannon fired and there was nothing guaranteed to get him into a fury more than firing off a salvo for someone who did not buy a machine. He never showed his anger to the men who caused it ("A sale", he said, "is never lost, only temporarily postponed") but only to his family and we soon learned what to expect.

My brothers seemed to accept their beatings but then they spent their day on horseback and shared their task, their understanding of life, with my father, while I sat alone on the limber with my thoughts which were only interrupted by my father hollering "brake". There was such weight in that cannon that the brake must be applied at the top of hills, and I was meant to know without being told, to jump down off the moving limber and turn the big wheel at the back of the cannon; this applied wooden blocks directly to the cannon wheels and, making a God Almighty scream, prevented disaster on steep hills.

My father did not normally beat me badly, but there was an incident during the shearers' strike that resulted in a bloody beating. It was his fault, not mine. He got carried away with some wool cockies in Terang, and although I was only ten years old at the time, I could see that he wouldn't get the sale. These were fellows who wanted some fireworks, but my father missed the signs. He drew them pictures of mad-eyed shearers coming down to rape their wives and burn down their sheds. He let off ten shells and demolished a stand of iron-barks, leaving nothing but bleeding sap and torn splinters as soft as flesh. When it was over I could see the look on the men's faces – you see the same look outside brothels as they put on their hats and hurry away – a flaccid, shamed, satiated look.

These squatters told my father: "We'll think about it."

Well, he was nice as pie to them, but I felt the skin around my little testicles go hard and leathery and I sweated around my bum-hole and I will not describe for you the beating he gave me on account of this, but rather paint you the picture of my revenge, for it is this that I count as the day of my birth, just as it is from 1919, from the day I landed at Balliang East, that I count the days of my adult life.

My revenge did not take place immediately, but I did have an idea. I imagined, as I sat alone on the limber with my bruises, that I lacked the courage to carry it out. But the idea would not go away. It grew inside me. At night it comforted me. Soaked to the skin on the road to Melbourne – we were covering about twenty miles a day – the idea made me smile, but I remained dutiful, applying the brake and letting it off as required.

In Melbourne he had some work for a Grand Tattoo. He was paid for releasing showy blasts above the river Yarra; I don't know the occasion.

But on the 15th June 1895 – when the squatters had defeated the shearers without the use of cannon – we came down the Punt Road hill towards the Yarra as part of a procession. My father had a uniform on, and my two brothers were also dressed up with leggings and hats like officers. My father had promised me a uniform too, but at the last moment he decided it wasn't worth the money.

I did not honestly think I had the courage, but courage is a funny thing.

"Brake!" called my father. "Brake!"

Well, I jumped out. He turned and saw me. Have you ever seen the Punt Road hill where it comes down past Domain Street towards the Yarra? By God, it's steep. Well, I put the brake on at the top. The blocks of wood screamed against the steel, but as we came down the hill, I did it. It was such a well-oiled wheel. It moved so swiftly, so easily. Even a boy of ten could make it come whizzing back.

I had not planned to destroy whatever home I had and it only occurred to me in that moment, that moment when I had released the brake, when the screaming wheel suddenly went free and silent, that instant before the other screaming began, it only occurred to me then as my father's eyes, panicked by the sudden silence, found mine, it only occurred to me then, as I said, that I now had no home. Yet the only thing I regretted afterwards was the damage to the horses. They were gentle creatures. I meant them no harm.

"Poor little fellow," said drunk and sentimental Jack, releasing a tear or two which he smeared across his furry cheek. "Poor little chap."

Thus encouraged I could not stop. I spewed out the rest of my story, which is not as harsh as it might sound today. In the Great Depression of the 1890s there were plenty of street urchins and plenty who did it harder than I did, plenty more who worked in factories where the air was so foul it would make your stomach turn just to stand in the doorway.

I do not believe in luck. It was not luck that I was adopted by a Chinaman. I was adopted by a Chinaman because I chose to be. I did it, you might say, to spite my father. I did it because I liked his gravelly voice, because I saw him pat a little Chinese boy on the head, and pet him, and give him something to eat. (This was Goon Tse Ying and there is a whole story concerning him that I will come to later.)

Now if Jack McGrath had been a shrewd man he would have seen the pattern of my life already, i.e., there I was at ten years old telling lies, saying my father was dead, getting myself put up, and giving value to the Chinese by working in the market. But Jack did

41

not see it. He was full of pity for the little boy who had to be adopted by filthy old John Chinaman and this common prejudice kept him from thinking about anything else. He stood up and stamped his stockinged feet on the ballroom floor. He dug his big hand deep in his pocket.

"Here's a pound," he said.

13

I went to bed at four o'clock in the morning, but I couldn't sleep. I tossed and turned, not in misery, but with the sort of uncontrolled excitement of a man who knows he is, at last, where he should be.

I was up at six and strolling in the garden. I wasn't tired at all. I breathed deep and smelled the salt and seaweed from Corio Bay. I had that loose-muscled feeling of a man on holiday. I strolled across to the beach with my hands deep in my pockets. The peculiar shell-grit sand of Western Beach crunched beneath my brand-new patent leather shoes. The *Casino*, a steamer carrying wool from the Western District, rode at anchor in the bay. The *Blackheath* with ninety thousand bags of wheat was berthed at the Yarra Street pier. The big wool stores rose high above the bandstands, bathing boxes and steep manicured lawns.

Geelong, that clear fresh morning, struck me as a town of wealth and sophistication, a lush green oasis, a natural compensation for the endless plain of wool and wheat behind it. It would be a city of parks, gardens, grand public buildings and elegant private ones.

I did not intend to laze around, bludging on my new friends. I had work to do, making certain unstable parts of my story become strong and clear.

There was, for instance, the snake, about which I had made certain claims. I did not intend to shirk my obligation to care for the snake, although if I could have seen what this would lead to (all this industry on behalf of a casual lie) I would have shipped it off to Mr Chin on the first train.

I strolled along the beach in the direction of that wide-verandaed weatherboard building which in those days housed the Corio Bay Sailing Club. In front of the Sailing Club there was an old man shovelling shell-grit into a hessian bag. I did not need to be told why he was doing it: the shell-grit from Corio Bay was, and still is, particularly beneficial to hens – it gives an eggshell substance.

I wasn't normally one for idle chat, but I liked all the world on that morning, and I stopped for a yarn.

"Grit for the chooks?" I said.

"That's right."

"Laying well, are they?"

"Not bad."

The old man did not seem inclined to talk, but I wasn't offended. It was peaceful standing there with my hands in my pockets watching him work.

"Would you happen to know", I asked after a while, "a good spot for frogs?" The frogs, of course, were for the snake.

He was a little man, dried up like a walnut. His freckled skin hung on his arms, like the skin on a roast chicken wing.

"Yes," he said, "I know a good place for frogs."

"Where's that?"

He was an old man used to being granted his due of respect and patience. He drove his spade into the sand with a grunt.

"France," he said.

I could imagine the old bugger sitting at the head of a table and calling his fifty-year-old son "the boy". He was far too content with himself for my liking.

"You should be on the wireless," I said, "telling jokes like that."

"You reckon, do you?" he said, and he made a slow study of me. He did not rush over any of the details. He observed, as I had not, that the trousers of the new suit were an inch too short and the jacket was a fraction too tight. "That's what you reckon, do you?"

"Yes, I reckon," I said. "I reckon you're a bit of a wit."

He wasn't frightened. He knew he was too old to be hit. "What do you want the frogs for?"

"I'll pay sixpence a frog. I'll be wanting two frogs every day." This scheme was not what I'd intended, but now I wanted to force him to do something for me.

"You don't say," he said without a sign of interest. He went back to his spade and shell-grit.

"That's a shilling a day, seven shillings a week. It's good money."

"Who'd pay money for a frog?" His eyes were half clouded with cataracts but his scorn glowed through them.

"Do you want the seven bloody shillings or not?" I said.

"No," the old man said with great satisfaction. "I don't." He picked up the sack of shell-grit and hoisted it on to his shoulder. I watched him trudge down the beach – a sack-carrying burglar who had stolen my sense of well-being.

I was always up and down in my moods and now I looked around the bay with a jaundiced eye. I saw a broken lemonade bottle in the sand. I began to suspect that Geelong might have the capacity to let me down, to be one more malicious, small-minded provincial city with no vision, no drive, no desire to do anything but send young men off to fight for the British and buy T Model Fords. However, the rest of that December Monday restored my faith in the city which, although it was not quite as grand as my vision of the morning, was still more than receptive to Herbert Badgery, Aviator.

I have had a long and wearing relationship with Henry Ford and it was only weakness that brought me back to him. The first thing I did in Geelong was introduce myself to McGregor, the Ford agent. I showed him my newspaper clippings and he was happy enough to engage me as a commission agent at five pounds a car. So when I arrived at the *Geelong Advertiser* I was able to park outside their window in a brand-new T model. I put my book of newspaper clippings under my arm and went to see the editor.

The suit I was wearing had previously belonged to Mr Harold Oster, and the Osters being the Osters I made no secret of the fact. So although Harold Oster's arse was built too close to the footpath and although his arms were an inch too short, I made no secret of the fact. I even ventured, as few in Geelong would have done, a few jokes at Mr Oster's expense. My familiarity with the Osters served as a better introduction to Geelong than any suit I could have had tailor-made in Little Collins Street.

My clothes, I told the editor, were at present in transit to Ballarat where I had been on my way to investigate the establishment of a new aircraft factory. Now, forced to spend the time in Geelong while the craft underwent repairs, I was keen to conduct discussions with local business men. I had already, I was pleased to inform the editor, found a degree of intelligence and enthusiasm in regard to the idea which was quite extraordinary. I would not let myself be drawn on the possibility of switching the site from Ballarat to Geelong but the editor found himself bold enough to run the following headline which my host, bright red with pleasure, read to me at breakfast: "AVIATOR'S MISHAP MAY BRING NEW INDUSTRY TO GEELONG."

Jack McGrath was not only flattered to find himself described as intelligent but also gratified to learn that his new friend had flown the first air mail in South Australia. He read also that I had served in the Air Corps, was a "noted zoologist" and a "motoring enthusiast whose Hispano Suiza is currently on loan to a distinguished Ballarat family".

Photographs, supplied by yours truly, were also used by the *Advertiser* (this, mind you, at a time when photographs in the newspaper were a rarity). The most notable of these showed the Morris Farman "in three positions of flight in a storm above Digger's Rest Racecourse". Quite a lot of this information was correct.

A week later I was able to mail a postal order for twenty pounds to the publican in Darnham.

14

It was nine o'clock at night but the temperature was still above 90 degrees. There was no air in the room. There was not enough air anywhere. From the bathroom window in Villamente Street you could see the red glow in the sky: fires covered the Brisbane ranges at Anakie and Steiglitz.

The front room crawled with insects with long brown abdomens. They fell into the jug of sweet lemon squash and died there. Phoebe had placed a thin book of Swinburne's poetry on top of the jug, but the insects still managed to enter through the pouring lip.

Annette was limp and soaked with perspiration. Her grey dress was too heavy for the climate. It clung to the back of her knees and got stuck beneath her arms. Phoebe, on the other hand, did not seem at all affected. This irritated Annette. Phoebe was so wrapped up in her own feelings that she was insensitive to everything else, even the stinking heat. Phoebe also wore grey: a soft silky grey with a slightly paler grey scarf.

"For God's sake," Annette said, brushing insects away from Swinburne, "aren't you hot?"

"A little," Phoebe said, "but not much."

"It doesn't make sense." Annette knew how pasty she looked.

Her hair was plastered against her forehead, a pimple was emerging from her chin, her top lip shone. "I don't think he's a herpetologist at all. A man of science, surely, does not keep his charges in a jute bag in his bedroom."

"Annette," Phoebe said, "where else would he keep it? We really have no proper facilities for boarding snakes."

"And yet," Annette said, "there you are with *two* of them."

(She is already defeated, before it has begun, while Phoebe is no more than a creamy shape in my dirty dreams.)

"You should be going back to school," Annette said.

Phoebe smiled. "Where I'm safe from nasty men?"

They sat side by side on the cane couch. Annette put her hand on Phoebe's but it was a sticky contact and not pleasant. She removed it.

"You could go to university."

"Ugh," Phoebe said. "How bourgeois."

She learned this sort of talk from Annette and it drove Annette crazy to have it thrown back at her.

"Last year you didn't know what bourgeois meant."

"But I know now," Phoebe said happily and Annette had to fight an impulse to disarrange that cool copper hair which her lover had piled high on her head, perhaps for the heat, perhaps to show her long lovely milky neck to Herbert Badgery.

"Do you really want to have babies and spend your life picking up after a man?" said Annette, who later omitted certain things from her description of Bohemian life in Paris.

"Who said anything about babies?" Phoebe said. "Or picking up. I only said I liked him. I said he was 'interesting'."

"I know what you find 'interesting', you little brat."

Annette had never met me, but she had already heard too much about this man whose only human imperfection was bow-legs. And even this was meant to be "interesting", as if they were shaped like this to accommodate what Phoebe liked to call a "door knocker" of extraordinary dimension.

She had heard (twice) already how Herbert Badgery had brought the Farman back from Balliang East to the airstrip at Belmont Common, how he had circled over Belmont and then flown up river to the woollen mills where he banked the machine before flying it beneath the bridge. What she didn't know is that I had done it for a bet. I got good odds because everyone remembered how Johnny O'Day had killed himself doing the same thing three months before.

It had all been in the *Advertiser*. Annette had read it the day before. But now Phoebe was telling the story a third time. She wasn't doing it for Annette's sake. She was yelling into an empty well, only wanting to hear her happiness amplified.

"You are going to make yourself very, very unhappy," Annette said.

But it was she who burst into tears, not Phoebe.

Phoebe tried to comfort her but she jerked away. She picked up the Swinburne and threw it at the wall.

"It's ridiculous," she screamed. "It's stupid. You haven't even *spoken* to him."

15

I did not like the Geelong snake, nor did I trust it. But I was stuck with it, this cranky creature in the hessian sack beneath my bed. I had considered "losing" it, but I'd already had some nasty experiences "losing" snakes. A lost snake can unhinge the most stable household and produce conditions that are most unfavourable for a man who wants to be put up. That aside, the McGraths were almost as proud of my relationship with the snake as they were of my connection with aviation. Jack brought an odd collection of characters home from the racetrack to view my performance with the snake. Sharp-looking punters and toffee-nosed horse owners all collected in Western Avenue and were as different from each other as the chairs they sat on. I was called upon to demonstrate my "pet". The manager of the National Bank, whose cast-off Pelaco shirt I wore, was nearly bitten on his beckoning index finger and was foolish enough to giggle about it.

You can do nothing to protect yourself from a brown snake except keep well away from it. You cannot milk its poison for (in summer especially) it'll have another batch ready in seconds. There would be no peace with the snake, no treaty. It would not become tame or even accept its captivity. All day long it pushed its head against the sack, as persistent as a blowfly against glass. It was a cunning thing and not capable of being bought off.

By the Wednesday morning I had found no one to supply me with either mice or frogs and I set off early to walk along the Melbourne Road where, one of the punters had told me, there was a soak with plenty of frogs in it. I left the Ford at home and walked. I always liked to walk. I strolled like a Gentleman.

I had observed, very early in life, that the way a man or woman walked gave a much better indication of their place in society than their accent. Although I was now very careful not to say "ain't" and "I never done it" and other habits of speech I had picked up working for Wongs at the Eastern Market, I was happy enough to use the natural nasal Australian accent which had so enraged that imaginary Englishman who sired me. I despised those people who pommified their speech but I was, always, very particular about my walk.

A man who lives by physical labour will move in a different way. A man who lumps wheat will move differently from a man who shears sheep – he will carry his muscled arms like loaves of bread; he will lock the muscles at the base of his spine and lean forward to take some imaginary weight. I had thousands of classifications of walks and I adopted the "Gentleman's Stroll" because I fancied it would make people trust me without ever knowing why.

It wasn't a very scenic route to the soak, but that didn't worry me. I followed the main Melbourne Road beside the railway line. There were few houses out there in those days, just a few weatherboard workmen's cottages dotted here and there along the road. A wagon or two, piled high with ingeniously balanced goods for country towns, passed me and I gave them a nod. I didn't pay much attention to the look of things, the colour of the horses, their breath in the early air, the quality of the light, and so on. But I did enjoy my movements. The walk not only convinced others, it convinced me and, strolling in the manner of a Gentleman, I became one.

The soak lay in the shadow of a towering redbrick flour mill. I got down in the gully out of sight of the road, but the blank windows of the flour mill continued to stare down at me. I didn't like it, but I had no choice: I took off my suit coat, my trousers, my socks. I stood in my underwear in sight of the flour mill and felt self-conscious about my bowed legs. I walked through the black squelching mud, to the far side of the swamp. The calls of frogs drew me on like sirens, although I had no hessian bag.

It is my belief that there are few things in this world more useful than a hessian bag, and no matter what part of my story I wish to reflect on I find that a hessian bag, or the lack of one, assumes some importance. They soften the edge of a hard bench, can be split open to line a wall, can provide a blanket for a cold night, a safe container for a snake, a rabbit, or a duck. They are useful when beheading hens or to place under car tyres in sandy soil. You can stuff them full of kapok to make a decent cushion and there is nothing better to carry frogs in.

Which is why it is surprising that in all the McGraths' possessions I could not find a single hessian bag. I had been forced to come in search of frogs with two small white paper bags which smelt as if they had held confectionery and, indeed, when the snake eventually devoured the first frog he would find it lightly dusted with icing sugar like a special treat from the ABC Tea Rooms.

With paper bag in hand, I felt foolish. I imagined lines of women in white aprons behind the windows of the flour mill. They were laughing at my legs.

I was confident enough of my shoulders and my arms. I was proud of my height and even arrogant about my general carriage. Even my calves, in isolation, met with my approval. But my bowed legs mortified me and I turned sideways to the staring windows, presenting myself at my least ludicrous angle.

That was the problem with a Gentleman's Stroll. It produced expectations that could not be met. It was not the right walk for a man who must, when it is over, take off his clothes and walk in black mud.

When the editor of the *Geelong Advertiser* had used the word "herpetologist" to describe me, I had readily agreed. Later, in answer to a question from my host, I persuaded him to look it up in the dictionary. At the time it had seemed an interesting thing to be, but now, in the middle of the soak, it did not seem so fine.

I found my first frog where the small stream disappeared into the soak. It sat there, brown, shiny and horny-skinned. Its eyes bulged up at me and I grabbed it with a shudder.

It was then I heard the cough.

The first thing I thought of was my legs. I turned, still holding the frog in both hands, and saw a swagman, although that is not much of a description of the fellow. He was a swagman who had let himself go, a swagman who had long ago given up trying to wash his shirt once a week in summer, a swagman whose natural affection for pieces of string and odd discarded rags had entered a virulent phase where it overwhelmed any of the conventional restraints placed on fashion and became a style of its own.

His face, where you could see it through his rampant beard, was weathered and beaten by the combined forces of sun, rain and alcohol. His teeth were rotting. His bulbous nose made its own confession. His hair was grey and matted and one eye, half closed by a blow or a bee sting, gave him an untrustworthy appearance.

He was squatting on the ground like a blackfellow, quiet and still and cunning. I thought the swagman was looking at my legs.

"Good tucker?" the swagman asked.

I tried to hold the Gentleman's stance while I held the frog and walked in a modest fashion through the mud.

"You scared me, man," I said.

"You scared me," the swagman said. "Walkin nekkid like that." He watched me place the frog in the small white bag and then place the bag in the inside pocket of my folded suit coat. "Is it good tucker?"

I was always fighting people I didn't need to fight. I feel like I've been awake all my life with a gun across my knees, waiting.

"Yes," I told the swagman, "very good tucker."

"That a fect?"

"Like chicken," I told him. "You can't tell the difference. That is what they serve the kings and queens of France. It's only the ignorance of the average Australian toff that stops them doing the same thing."

"That a fect?"

"Yes," I said, tucking my singlet into my underpants, "it's a fact."

The swaggie shifted on his heels. His attitude was uncertain. "I thought they killed the kings and queens of France," he said. "I seem to recall that they were killed. They had their heads chopped off, so I was told. They don't have kings and queens in France any more."

This was all news to me. If I had not been a pig-headed fool I might have learned something, but I was more worried about two contradictory things – my dignity and the other frog. I went back into the soak while the swagman took the opportunity to have a closer look at my suit.

"I used to have a suit like that," he said, "but it was took from me up in Albury."

"That a fact?" I mocked.

"Well," the swaggie shrugged away his suit, "you know those Albury types."

I got my second frog and walked carefully back to solid ground. The swaggie watched me put it in its bag.

"We ate roof rats in Albury but we never tried the frogs, never even thought of them. I'm much obliged to you for the information, I must say, much obliged."

I perched on the edge of the stream and washed my feet and then my hands. I managed to dress standing on a grass tussock.

I was given to doing things suddenly. I had strong emotions like unexpected guests and the urge to laugh or fight often overwhelmed me without warning. Similarly I was often beset with the desire to be good and generous, and I have no idea where this part of me comes from. Certainly not from my father who was never held back by his scruples. He was a fine man for talk of Empire and loyalty but it wasn't the Empire or loyalty that made him successful: he was a liar and a bullshitter and hungry for a quid.

If my father had seen me hand the pound note to the swagman he would have laughed out loud.

"Here," I said, "get yourself some flour and tea. Don't eat frogs. Christians don't eat frogs."

We were both, the swaggie and I, puzzled at this development. He held Jack's pound between the thumb and forefinger of both battered hands and turned it over and over.

"If you don't eat frogs," he said at last, "why the dickens do you catch them?"

"My damn snake, man," I said. I was furious about the fate of my pound note. "I've got to feed my snake."

"Of course you have," the swagman said sympathetically, "of course you have."

"I'm deadly serious, man."

"Of course you are."

His mistake was to wink.

The pound note disappeared from the swagman's hand before the wink was over, but even when I held it, tightly crumpled, in my pocket, I did not feel any release from my confusion, I felt worse. I felt guilty, and this did not seem just.

"Charity is good for no one," I said. "Would you like to *earn* a pound?"

Later, when I recalled how I had made the deal with the swagman, I always felt ashamed, not of the deal itself which was certainly fair. (The swagman honoured it too, delivering two frogs each morning for the snake's breakfast.) I felt ashamed of reneging on the grander gesture which was more in keeping with how I would like to be.

I felt the swagman had looked at me and seen something less attractive in me than my bowed legs.

16

The whole household was in love with me, and although I knew it I doubt if I knew how much. Bridget blushed every time she put a plate in front of me, and Molly banned her from serving in the dining room, whereupon Bridget burst into tears and had to be comforted. I bought her an ice-cream from the ABC and she left the empty cone on her dressing-room table for weeks. However, she was not readmitted to the dining room. That was Molly's territory; she cooed and fluttered, big-breasted and blowzy, over dishes of vegetables, and Phoebe saw how she took such care with the arrangement of vegetables on my plate and also (a telling point this, for a woman raised in a poor family) that she gave me bigger portions, so *discreetly* bigger, so *marginally* bigger that they were, in Phoebe's words "like brief eye contacts made between secret lovers, like the shadow of a moth passing across a night-time window".

This was not only lost on me, it was lost on Jack as well. He did not notice that Molly folded my three pairs of socks, how she darned them when they holed, how carefully she placed my two clean shirts in my drawer, how she dabbed and brushed at my single suit coat.

Phoebe noticed. Sometimes her mother's behaviour embarrassed her but she also shared her mother's silent hurt when the subtleties of the vegetable servings were lost on me. I devoured them with the same indiscriminate passion I turned on all of life, whether it was the manager of the National Bank or a roast potato.

As for Jack and me, we got on like blazing houses. It would not have mattered a damn if I had had no snake or stories about aeroplane factories, in fact it would have been a damn sight better, but it is too late to alter the past and regret is a fool's emotion. And while we built a thousand aeroplanes and charmed a lot of snakes, there was plenty else to keep us interested. We had as many theories as peas on our plates and talked with our mouths full and spilled our drinks with sweeping gestures.

"You were like a pair of love-sick jackasses," Phoebe said

later, "and you talked a lot of rot, but I loved you and I didn't mind."

"Isn't it true," Jack said, "that if Leichhardt had an aero, we'd have had none of the tragedy, none of the loss, poor chap."

I pointed to the problems of landing, of clearing a strip, supplying fuel and so on.

"Ah yes," said Jack, stamping his stockinged feet and wiping his chin, "but what about the parachute? Now there's an idea."

"Bourke was a poor policeman," I said, "I doubt he could have managed it."

"We're not talking of Bourke, man, it's Leichhardt. And in any case you've told me yourself, there's nothing to it."

"A bit more than nothing," I said, "but less than a lot."

"All right, granted," said Jack, wiping up his gravy with grey Geelong bread, "a bit more than nothing."

"And he was a big man too, and possibly slow-witted."

"Leichhardt?"

"No, Bourke."

"I never read anything that suggested it."

"Perhaps you didn't," I said, being pleased to hear his ignorance was as great as mine. "But not all of it is published. He had kangaroos in his top paddock."

"An expression," Jack said, pushing back his chair and holding Molly's hand, "I never understood."

"It is clear enough," I said. "Anyone with any presence of mind does not permit a kangaroo, or a wallaby for that matter, into his top paddock."

Jack stroked his wife's hand. He was always at it. Sometimes at dinner I would look and see father and daughter both stroking the mother's hands, one on the left, one on the right.

"I have seen it," Jack said, "on the best properties."

"In exceptional circumstances."

"Granted, yes. A tree across a fence in a storm."

"Well," I said, "you understand well enough."

"I don't like expressions", Jack said, suddenly becoming serious, "that are like officious coppers, with no sympathy in them. The sort of expression like a beak throwing the book at you without allowing for all the circumstances. An expression like that is not fair or sensible. What would you say, for instance, to the term galah being used in the way it is?"

"The galah is a pest," I said. "No one would doubt it."

"But not stupid."

"No," I said, "I grant you, the galah is not a stupid bird."

"I don't think," Jack said, "that we have taken the same trouble with our expressions that the English have."

And off we would go again, not just on one night, but every night, with company or without it. We talked right through breakfast and then went for a stroll along the beach together and we never stopped talking.

Phoebe watched me. In truth we both spent a lot of time watching each other. We fooled each other so much we believed we were mutually invisible.

I had to be away from Western Avenue at times. I was selling T Models again although I was ashamed to admit it. I told them it was for business, related to the aircraft factory.

When I was not there, Jack was listless. He sat in front of the wireless and changed stations and banged his hearing aid with the heel of his hand. He was like a bored child on Sunday afternoon. He did not go down to the taxi company he owned. He did not visit the stud to see his horses, or the track to lose money. The bludgers at the Corio Quay Hotel (who knew him as "Here's-ten-bob" McGrath) did not see him. He had long "naps" and waited for my return. And then, in the summer evening, Phoebe would see us on the beach again. Her father was built like a bullock driver, was the son of a bullock driver, and there was still, as he walked along the beach with his friend, plenty of bullock driver left in his walk and she could see in those broad shoulders, those heavy arms, that thick neck, a man made to endure the dusty day and the solitary night, a man whose natural style would be reserved, who would be shy with men and women alike, but yet here he was – Phoebe saw it – building an aeroplane factory with a stranger. But yet it was not so simple, this factory. We did not approach it so directly. We approached it like Phoebe and I approached each other, shyly, at a tangent, looking the other way, pretending to be interested in other things while all the time we could see that big slab-sided shed of corrugated iron with "Barwon Aeros" written in big black letters on the side.

"The wheel", Jack said, "seems an easy thing when you have it, but if you don't have it then how would you ever know you needed it? Flying is an easier thing to imagine. You can see a magpie doing it. But tell me, Badgery, where is an animal, or bird, with *wheels*?"

"There is a snake", I said, "that makes itself into a wheel and chases you."

"Is that a fact now? In what country is that?"

"In this country. A friend of mine was chased by one up at Jindabyne."

"There is no doubt", Jack said, "that if an animal would do it in any country, this is the country for it. It is the country for the aeroplane as well. But if you take up the question of your Jindabyne snake, there was no white man here to see it when it was wanted."

"They say it was a Chinaman invented the wheel," I said. I said it out of loyalty to Goon Tse Ying, but this is not the place to discuss Jack's attitude towards the coloured races.

"Is that so?"

"It is."

"And not a white man?"

"A Chinaman."

Jack shook his head. He found it hard to credit it. "Do you know his name?" he said.

"I don't," I said. "It was too long ago."

"I doubt a blackfellow could have managed it just the same. He'd be watching the snakes wheeling past and never give them a thought except eating them for his dinner. It was a wasted opportunity," he said. "If we'd had the wheel here we would be well ahead of Europe."

"If the blackfellow had the wheel," I said, "he'd have run rings around us."

"But you forget," Jack said, "that by the time we arrived we had the wheel ourselves, and gunpowder too."

"It was a Chinaman invented gunpowder," I said.

It was too much for Jack. He could not abide Chinamen, no matter what I told him. He sucked in his cheeks and blew them out. He kicked a jellyfish back into the water.

"Twist and giggle," he said, "turn and spin / Squirm and spit and grin / Just like a bally Chinaman / When someone pulls his string."

"There is no kinder soul on earth than the Chinaman," I said.

He narrowed his eyes a fraction and stared at me hard. By God he would have been a hard man in a fight, but he would never allow himself to get into one – he would always find a comfortable way to take in the most uncomfortable things.

"The poor little chap," he said. "Poor little fellow." I was Romulus and Remus to Jack, a poor little chap suckled on the tits of wolves.

Phoebe felt she had become invisible. She accompanied Jack and me to Belmont Common for flying lessons but no one spoke to her. She sat in the back seat and listened.

It never entered my head that she might want to fly. She expressed no interest. She said nothing. Sometimes I saw her listening with a little smile on her face. She made me flustered. I lost my train of thought.

She knew her father would never master the aeroplane, no matter how many lessons I gave him. He had even less feeling for it than he had for the Hispano Suiza. But she watched the circus silently, biding her time. Her father could never bring the stick down enough to land it. It was horrible to watch. The Farman floated in unsteadily, Jack in the front, Herbert in the back.

She could see me leaning forward and thumping her father in the middle of the back with my fist. She could hear me shouting, "Push it down, down, down." But nothing would persuade Jack to push the stick down towards the looming earth.

She visited Annette but they both made each other irritated. They bickered and fought. Her mother, once so concerned about the quantity of balls Phoebe attended, the parties she was invited to, and the friends she had, no longer seemed to worry. She made up her Christmas parcels for the orphanages, put money in envelopes for the men at the Ainsley Home, and fussed about with Herbert's socks.

For Phoebe the days over Christmas passed in a strange daze. Sometimes she felt so tense that she wanted to scratch her face until it bled but sometimes the feeling turned a degree or two and then what had been pain became pleasure. And in between those two extremes she spent whole days in a distracted state, a sort of mental itch that did not let her pay attention to anything or anyone.

She went to a few parties around Christmas (I watched her go, hopeless with lust and jealousy). She had her feet stood on by the sons of Western District graziers, two of whom proposed to her.

She hid amongst the throngs of bathers on Eastern Beach and burnt her creamy skin, perhaps deliberately. No one reprimanded her. She shed her ruined skin with fascination and did not answer desperate letters from poor Annette who spent her Christmas in a rejected lover's hell.

Phoebe did not speak to the person whose image remained continually in her mind's eye. She would not even ask him to pass the bread. She ignored him at bedtime and would not even say good night. She was reprimanded for her rudeness. She shed her skin in a bedroom curtained from the February heat, and waited.

18

It is time to deal with the neighbours and I am like Goon Tse Ying, capable of becoming invisible, sliding under doors, lifting rugs from floors on windless nights. I get a dirty pleasure sifting through their private cupboards amongst the dust and fluff and paper-dry conversations. I push my invisible nose deep into the sheets of beds and breathe in the odours of their unheard farts.

There were so many ways the McGraths had upset the upper crust in Western Avenue. The offences were as numberless as flies and even Mrs Kentwell had given up on counting them.

For a start: the yellowbrick garage Jack had built in the middle of the lawn. He had built it himself, but not too well. It was as blunt and as useful as a cow bail and two deep wheel ruts ran towards it, not neatly, for there were places where the Hispano Suiza had been bogged and other marks made by horses called to pull it out.

There was also what was known locally as "The Wall". The function of this redbrick wall which ran from the garage to almost the middle point of the house (it arrived opposite the big windows of the music room) was to protect Molly's flower beds from the winds that howled off Corio Bay. This function was not obvious to the Kentwells, the Jones-Burtons and the Devonishes who met to discuss each new offence, and if they had known it would have made no difference. They had no sympathy with Jack's bush-carpenter's approach to aesthetics.

The McGrath mansion had been built in 1863 and was originally called "Wirralee". This name had been incorporated in a leadlight window above the front door. They had seen Jack McGrath remove this window one afternoon in 1917. Mrs Kentwell saw it first.

"He has the ladder out," she told Alice Jones-Burton.

The two women put their hats on and plunged their hatpins home. They strolled along the promenade like policemen on the beat and on October 25th, 1917, shortly before noon, they witnessed the man with the binding-twine belt remove the

"Wirralee" and replace it with a plain piece of glass on which a single cloverleaf had been sandblasted.

To understand the effect this had on the two ladies you have to remember that there was a big fuss going on about military conscription for the Great War, that the Catholics were against conscription, and what's more they were winning. On November 1st, 1917, the last attempt to introduce conscription would fail. In this heated climate a cloverleaf might easily be seen to be a shamrock, and the two ladies declared the McGraths not only traitorous, not only tasteless, but also Catholic.

If Jack had known all this he would have been terribly upset. He didn't like Catholics much more than he liked Chinese, although in the case of Catholics he would always say it was not the Catholic people he objected to but the religion and the priests particularly who "swig down all the altar wine themselves, and not a drop for the rest of them". He never knew that Molly was a Catholic, was still a Catholic, and had risked her soul by marrying him in a Protestant church in Point's Point.

Jack put the cloverleaf above his door because he was bored and because he was lucky.

There were no end of offences. The presence of Herbert Badgery Esquire was an offence. My Gentleman's Stroll did not impress Mrs Kentwell at all. She peered at me from behind fence or curtain and judged me a sharp character and a ruffian.

Western Avenue, she said, was on its way to being a slum, and when she saw the swagman arrive early one morning she knew her fears were well founded. She found it impossible to convey to her allies the true nature of this character. For when she referred to him as a swagman and they nodded their heads she knew she had not painted a proper picture of this grotesque.

"But, my dear," Mrs Devonish said, "they *all* use string." And then she prattled on about the useful nature of string and how her father, the late Reverend Devonish (who was remembered by Mrs Kentwell for being too High Church) had always kept brown paper bags of string in various parts of the house, none of which information was sensible or useful to Mrs Kentwell and anyway did not fit too well with her memory of the late High Church man who had caused more than one upset due to his fondness for silk and satin. String, Mrs Kentwell thought, was not High Church at all.

So she dispensed with the string. She snapped it up, so to

speak, with the cutting edges of her squeaky dentures and took the dryness away with a cup of sugarless tea.

"This *gentleman*," she said, "is introducing cane toads to the area."

Laura Devonish blinked. "Do you think, dear, we could have more hot water."

"Hot water," Mrs Kentwell said, "is what we have, Laura. We are in it."

But the cleverness of this was lost on Laura Devonish who insisted the silver hot water pot was quite empty and the tea now far too strong. There was no choice but to provide the water. It took for ever, or long enough for Laura to eat the two last slices of butter cake.

"This swagman", Mrs Kentwell said, when the tea was to Laura's satisfaction, "is bringing in cane toads."

"Why?"

"How would I know?" snapped Mrs Kentwell. "How would I know why they do anything? But the fact remains, cane toads! In sacks. The poor maid was screaming. There were toads all over the kitchen."

"You saw?"

"Heard, quite distinctly. 'Frogs,' she screamed. I heard her perfectly."

"Not toads?"

"Toads, frogs. It is not the point. Laura, you must listen and stop eating. Eating will not fix the problem. The swagman was given money at the back door."

19

I too was sorry about the first delivery of frogs. The swagman had been too enthusiastic. He had not contented himself with two or three frogs but had kept on collecting until his sack was half full. When he arrived at Western Avenue he entered the kitchen without introducing himself to Bridget who was nervous. Then he began to show her frogs and was misunderstood. Then when yours truly at last arrived, bare-torsoed with my trousers half done up, the swagman, overcome with excitement, emptied the whole lot on to the floor. It took me some time to sort out the mess, educate the swagman, mollify Bridget and retrieve most of the frogs. For days afterwards my hostess's scream would alert me to the presence of a hitherto hidden frog in some corner of the mansion.

I had been expelled from houses for smaller upsets, and I waited for a little note slid under my bedroom door, the quiet chat after dinner, an eruption of anger on the lawn. My hosts surprised me. They laughed. They repeated the story and derived pleasure from telling it. When I accompanied Jack on his daily round of what he was pleased to call "interests" the story had often preceded me and I was forced to take another step closer to becoming a herpetologist by discoursing on the dietary habits of the brown snake.

I had never been in a situation before where my lies looked so likely to become true. I did not achieve this alone. So many people contributed creamy coats of credibility to my untruth that the nasty speck of grit was fast becoming a beautiful thing, a lustrous pearl it was impossible not to covet.

The aircraft factory began to achieve a life of its own. Letters were despatched to various suppliers in Melbourne and Sydney and Jack, who loved the telephone with a passion, was chasing timber suppliers in Queensland and waking up squatters in the middle of the night to talk about investing in a wonderful new enterprise.

I can still hear his giant deaf "Hellos" echoing through the house.

We had meetings with solicitors to draw up the company for "Barwon Aeros". We looked at a piece of land at Belmont which Jack already owned. I engaged a draughtsman in Geelong to draw up my plans which incorporated an Avro engine, although we later planned a totally Australian motor. I engaged the services of a stenographer and began to dictate my series on aviation for the *Geelong Advertiser*. I began to think of marrying Phoebe. I gave back Jack the money he had lent me. And even while all this was happening I still continued selling T Models.

I sold T Models with such ease that the local agent could not understand why a man who could acquit himself like this on the ground could contemplate risking his life and his capital by taking to the air. He made this opinion known to me on one stinking February afternoon while the blustering northerly brought red dust down into Ryrie Street and rattled a loose sheet of corrugated iron on the top of the dark hot garage. I flicked flies away from my mouth and, without really trying to, made the agent uneasy. What the agent could not have guessed, what prompted the slight madness in my cold-eyed stare, the ambiguous movement of my lips, was that I loathed Fords on principle, that I was eaten up with selling them, that I did it from laziness because the Ford had the name, because it was American and people were more easily persuaded to buy a foreign product than a local one.

There was another factor in all this, and one I would not have admitted to myself in 1919, and it was that the Tin Lizzie was a better car for the money. It wasn't much to look at but it was deceptively strong and very reliable. This, however, did not suit my idea of how things should be. And if there was a suggestion of arrogance in my lips as I talked to the Ford agent it was prompted by my thought that if there had been an agent for an Australian-made car (like the Summit) in Geelong I would have taken great pleasure in out-selling the Ford agent. It would not have been easy, but I could have done it. I would have applied myself to it, not done it like I now sold Fords which was in a sloppy, showy sort of style, like an expert tennis player disdainfully defeating novices, only deriving pleasure from a loose-limbed flashness and not from any great demands on his skill or any pride in the final victory.

"Any mug can sell a T Model," I told the agent, and was not liked any better for the comment which was not only untrue but also unflattering to the man himself who watched me drive away with feelings, I warrant you, identical to the ones I had every time I put the snake back in his hessian bag.

20

I did not, if I am honest, intend to sell the O'Hagens a Ford. Had I really meant to make a sale I would not have called so early in the day when a salesman is a nuisance to a farmer, but at the end of the day when he is coming in from the paddocks. I would have helped him unharness his horses and then joined the family for dinner. At the end of the meal I could have helped the farmer clear the table, and if he assisted with the washing up (and many did) then I'd have done my share.

As I motored along the Bacchus Marsh Road it was about ten in the morning and the hot blustering wind suddenly fell away and I could feel, before I saw it, the storm building up in the south. I swore softly. The farmers did not want rain yet – they were busy ploughing in the stubble of the last harvest. I did not want rain either. I wanted the O'Hagens to stay outside so I could have a chat with Mrs O'Hagen. It was because of Mrs O'Hagen, I admit it now, that I was arriving early on this day. I had seen a light in her young eyes that I recognized.

I shifted the position of my balls in my underpants, adjusted a penis I imagined had a life of its own, and drove north towards the O'Hagens with my erect member pointing optimistically upwards.

21

I could hear the ring of axes. The air was still and heavy and smelt of dust and treacle. I guessed, correctly, that Stu O'Hagen and his sons were clearing new land in the scrub to the north.

I knocked on the wooden frame of the flapping fly-wire door at the back of the house while a yellow dog flung itself against its chain in fury.

"Anyone home?"

But even before I entered I knew that Mrs O'Hagen was not inside and had not been inside for many days. It was a man's kitchen. Flies crawled across the unwashed dishes. An open can of bully beef occupied pride of place amongst the crumbs on the oil-cloth table. It stank of depression, like unwashed sheets on unmade beds.

Mrs O'Hagen, stone sober, had danced like a woman drunk on city dreams. I did not doubt that she had left and I knew I would never savour her as I had imagined in all the miles that led here: my mouth at her breast, buried between her sturdy legs, my nostrils filled with warm wet perfumes.

I would have to sell a Ford after all.

I took off my coat and undid my tie. I hung the coat on the back of a chair and placed studs and cufflinks and collar in the inside pocket.

I did not hurry across the stubble-slippery paddocks. I strolled with my hands in my pockets and when the axes became silent I knew the O'Hagens were watching me.

I would have walked properly, but I had come in city shoes, and it is almost impossible to walk across slippery stubble in smooth-soled shoes without moving like a draper's assistant. To walk correctly in a paddock you need boots, and heavy boots at that.

The O'Hagens, having paused to examine me, went back to work. As I listened to the axes I had a sympathy for them and what drove them on. I had hacked at life like the O'Hagens hacked at the bush, ring-barking, chopping, blistering my hands to bring it to heel, always imagining a perfect green kikuyu pasture where life would be benevolent and gentle. But where the bush had been bracken and thistles always appeared and then these had to be conquered as well.

I walked sideways down an eroded gully and when I reached the other side I could make out the three O'Hagens on the slope ahead. Two saplings dropped and three rosellas danced a pretty path across the thunder-ink sky. Black cockatoos screeched and scratched at the bark of a big old manna gum as if they couldn't wait to see it done for.

When I climbed the last fence I could see their faces. I remembered, with a shock, how ugly they were. They had heads like toby jugs. They had large square heads with ruddy complexions. Their hair was fair and thin. There was a meanness in their faces that conveyed an unaccountable sense of superiority. They were not easy to like.

The father had ears that stuck out from the side of his head and the youngest boy, who was as tall as me and only fifteen, had inherited his father's ears. They were ugly, of course, but they were quite at home with those square red heads, high, bent noses, and small pale blue eyes. They were faces squeezed from the one lump of clay.

But the eldest son, who was eighteen, had different ears. He had his mother's tiny delicate ears. They sat, flat and lonely, on the side of his great head like beautiful objects stolen by an ignoramus. Although you wouldn't have looked twice at him in the street in Geelong, out here, beside his brother and father, his head was as embarrassing to look at as a withered hand or an ex-soldier with his chin shot off. If the O'Hagens had been butterflies this one would be valuable – a rare exception to countless generations of O'Hagens with big ears.

He was known as Goog, which, until we started to forget our language, was the common name for a hen's egg. I always supposed he was called Goog because the tiny flattened ears did nothing to interrupt the goog-like sweep from crown to jaw.

The O'Hagens (Stu, Goog and Goose) did not stop working as I approached them. They swung their axes and chopped the small trees and scrub off level with the ground. They ring-barked the large trees and those of in-between size were chopped at waist height, after which they belted the bark from them with the back of their axes and piled this bark around the splintered stumps. When the burning season arrived the bark would help burn them to the ground.

They did not acknowledge me. I was a pest, arriving at the wrong time. I squatted with my back to a tree and waited. It was Goose who broke. He came to sharpen his axe with a file. He squatted near me, studying the axe with great care before he pulled the file from a hessian bag (a use for hessian bags I neglected to mention earlier).

"Come to sell us a Tin Lizzie, have you?"

"Come to show it," I said.

A blackwood wattle dropped behind me.

"Should watch where you sit," the old man said, and came over to sharpen an axe that needed no attention at all.

Goog belaboured the stump of a tree with the back of his axe, but when he had finished, and the stump stood wet and naked, he put his axe down and joined the others.

He nodded in the direction of the Ford. "How much do they ask for one of them?" Goog asked.

"He hasn't got two bob to his name," Goose said, handing the file across to his father.

"I never said I did. I was just inquiring."

No one said anything for a while. They watched the old man sharpening his axe.

"What happened to your wonderful flying machine?" old Stu said at last. He was not such a bad fellow, but he couldn't help himself; that whingeing sarcasm came out of his mouth without him even thinking about it.

"It's in Geelong," I said.

"Found someone, did you?"

"I don't follow you?"

"Found someone to buy it?"

"I wasn't trying to sell it."

"Oh yes," Stu said, and the three O'Hagens smirked together like three distorting mirrors all reflecting the one misunderstanding.

"Why did you bring it here," Goog said, "if you wasn't trying to sell it to us?"

Their misunderstanding was so ridiculous, I didn't even try to defend myself.

"We heard you were having a try at motor cars now," Goose said.

"And who told you that now?"

"Patrick Hare told us," said Stu, standing up and putting his hands on his hips. He crooked one knee and put his square head on one side. "He told us how you tried to sell him a Ford. Patrick says the Dodge is a superior machine. That's his opinion."

There was a saying in those days: "If you can't afford a Dodge, dodge a Ford." It was a salesman's lot to listen to all this rubbish. "That's Patrick Hare's opinion," I said.

They stood around me in a semicircle, Goose mimicking his father's stance exactly. They all shared the same smile.

"So tell me," I said, not bothering to stand up, "would you want his opinion on how to plough a paddock?"

"Ah," Stu said, "that's a different matter, a different matter entirely."

I didn't smile, but it was an effort. I'd heard a lot about Stu O'Hagen on the Bacchus Marsh Road. It was said (although I found it hard to credit) that Stu came from behind a shop counter in Melbourne twenty years before. They said he wouldn't take advice from the first day he got there, that he went his own stubborn way and made his own stubborn mistakes. They said he would have spent his life inventing the wheel if one hadn't run over him one winter's morning in Ryrie Street and thus brought itself to his attention.

"Ploughing", he said, "is a different matter to motor cars, an entirely different matter."

I did not turn and look at the eroded hillside behind Stu's house which was easy to see from where we stood. I said not a word about the virtues of contour ploughing. It was not a subject on which Stu had shown himself to be able to benefit from advice.

"So you come to give us a hand, did you?" Stu said. He was being sly, but you couldn't call it nasty.

"Don't mind," I said.

"Use an axe?"

"After a fashion."

"Well," the old man said, handing me his axe, "plenty to use it on."

I was pleased to be using an axe.

22

You can build a good hut with only an axe and not much else, so I had plenty of experience under my belt. My hands were a bit soft, but clearing scrub is a piece of cake in comparison with making a good slab hut and my eye was good and my rhythm perfect.

If the O'Hagens were surprised to find a salesman using an axe so well, they didn't say it. But when lunchtime came they shared a tin of bully beef with me and gave me a mug of sweet stewed tea.

There was bad weather in the south, so after lunch I walked back across the slippery paddocks and put up the side curtains on the car. When I came back Goog said, "You could have saved yourself the walk – that rain won't come here." He sat on a fallen trunk and assessed the weather with an expert eye.

"That a fact?" I said.

"It's called the Werribee Rain Shadow," Goog said, "so I'm told. It accounts for the lack of rain here."

Stu was driving his "Kelly" axe into the shuddering trunk of a blackwood wattle twenty yards away but his ears were as sensitive as their size suggested.

"Who told you that bullshit?" he shouted.

Goog looked uneasy. He shaved some blond hairs from his arm with the axe. "In at the Marsh," he said at last, "at school."

The blackwood teetered on its wound and Goog looked at his father apprehensively.

"What would they know?" Stu said, stepping back from the tree to admire its fall. "Werribee Rain Shadow." He looked scornfully at the sky. "What sort of bloody shadow is that?"

The southerly caught the tree and tipped it. It fell with a crash, pinning a large brush-tailed possum to the ground.

They stopped work to examine the possum whose shoulder had been speared by a small broken branch. Stu tapped it with the flat of the axe. The possum quivered and a trickle of blood ran from its mouth.

"Rain Shadow," Stu said, "Christ Almighty!"

I am making Stu O'Hagen sound like a pig-ignorant bastard, and it is not fair to the man. If I look back on my life I can hear myself saying similar things every day. We all did it, and it has been our loss.

The Werribee Rain Shadow kept Stu amused for the last hour of the afternoon. He kept up a steady niggling stream of witticisms and the boy with the stolen ears worked silently with the colour slowly rising from beneath his frayed collar. It was not the son he was attacking. It was his wife's ears, I swear it, that drove him crazy.

When Goose decided to join in the baiting, Goog stood slowly and walked to where his brother was working. He waited for his brother to finish the sapling he was felling and then dropped the young boy with one round-house punch. Goog fell on top of him, pummelling him around the head. Stu walked over, watched them for a moment, and then kicked them until they stopped.

"All right," he yelled, "you can get off of him. Goose, you can do the chooks and pigs and when you're finished you can do the milking. Goog, you can prepare the meal."

Goog kicked a blunt boot sulkily into the broken soil. "How do you mean, prepare it?"

"God help me," his father yelled. "When they were telling you about shadows of rain, didn't they tell you what 'prepare' means? Prepare it. Prepare it."

"It means get ready," Goog said quietly, his face burning red. "I know that."

"Well, for Christ's sake, do it."

The two boys walked off, Goog in the rear, still red-faced, muttering threats at his brother who looked back continually over his shoulder. Stu and I watched them go down the eroded gully and climb the fence on the other side.

"They're good boys," Stu said.

Goose, seeing Goog was gaining on him, began to run towards the sheds and Goog, having half-heartedly thrown a rock in his direction, trudged unhappily towards the house with long ungainly stride, all boots and wobbly ankles.

"Wife's staying at her sister's," Stu said, looking at me carefully for any sign I might not believe him. His pale eyes looked frightened.

I tried to think of something comforting to say, but it evaded me.

"No dancing tonight," Stu said. His mouth quivered. He turned abruptly and began packing the thermos and files into a hessian bag. He picked up the axes, looked at the sky, and then put them down again. Then he fussed around covering them with bark.

"Might as well leave them," he said, but his accusing eyes were not concerned with either rain or axes.

"How about a run in the car," I said, "before tea?"

"Directly," he said, fussing about with the bark.

I was always offended by what I understood to be the Irish sense of the word "directly" which did not mean, as it appeared to, something that would be done in a direct manner, immediately, without delay, but rather the opposite – it would be done indirectly, after taking time, having a smoke, wandering about, having a piss down the back and then approaching the object under discussion along a meandering sort of a path. It meant maybe. Or later.

But the meanders on this afternoon were shorter than I had feared and after Stu had satisfied himself that Goose was attending to the animals and after he had glanced with satisfaction at the eroded hillside in the south and the box-thorns in the east, we began to walk towards the T Model while the yellow dog threw itself hysterically against its chain.

As we passed the crooked front fence of the little cottage, Goog came out, holding a leg of mutton like a club.

"Dad."

Stu sighed. "Have you prepared that yet?"

"I dunno," said Goog.

In four angry strides Stu was through the front gate and on to the veranda. He snatched the leg of lamb from his cringing son. He swung it in the air and belted it so hard against the veranda post that the whole house shook and a wooden bench, heavily loaded with lifeless flower pots, collapsed and spilt dry red earth and dead vegetation at his feet.

He swung the mutton again, and again. The veranda post quivered and then fell. It landed on the ground at my feet with a single rusty six-inch nail pointing at the sky.

"There," Stu said, handing the leg of mutton back to his son, "it's prepared."

A hundred evicted maggots writhed amongst the dry red earth on the veranda floor. Stu stomped on them with his boot and made a half-hearted attempt to kick them off the veranda.

"Now," he said, "cut up the spuds."

I was never a fussy eater, but I did not care for maggots. I took a few steps towards the car and spat. It felt like I had a maggot stuck in my throat.

"You're staying for a feed," Stu said as we resumed our walk towards the car. "I've got a few bottles in the house."

"Kind of you," I said.

The storm was coming down like a boarding-house shower: water all round the hills on the edges and dry in the middle. I was inclined to grant Goog some credit for his Rain Shadow, and saw that I would be able to do my demonstration in the dry.

"Now," I said, "you'll be wanting a drive. Have you ever driven an auto before?" The biggest job was always to persuade a farmer that he actually needed a car, but once that was done he would normally buy the car he drove first. (I wasn't too worried about his remarks about the Dodge which cost two hundred pounds more than the T Model.) So I did not do what the Yanks at Ford said you should do which was to go round the car, starting with the radiator, and point out the features in a methodical way. My first objective was to get the customer behind the wheel.

Stu, however, did not appear to be listening. He was looking back over his shoulder where he found, as he'd suspected, that his son's attention was taken up with the car and not the spuds. Goog stood on the veranda with the leg of mutton still grasped in his bony hand.

"Go on," the father bellowed, "get on with it before I come and give you a clout across the ear-hole."

Goog disappeared into the house.

"Have you driven an auto before?" I asked.

"They're good boys," Stu said, "but they never batched before."

"Have you ever driven an auto before?"

"Not a lot in it, is there?" he said, not wanting to look at me.

"You'd need a few lessons."

"Lessons. Everybody wants me to have bloody lessons," Stu said and I did not ask him whether it was dancing lessons that he had on his mind. "Patrick Hare tells me there's nothing to it. I'm not a boy. I'll get the hang of it without any lessons. You charge for them, do you?"

"Only three pounds."

Stu nodded bitterly. "That's right," he said.

We were now circling the car, but not in the manner recommended by Ford.

"That's three quid I wouldn't consider," he said, scratching his balls, "if I was going to consider making a purchase at all", he paused, "of a Ford."

"It's a useful machine," I said, "and very reliable."

Now we were back at the radiator and Stu was nodding his head towards the car. It took me a moment to realize that my customer wanted to see the contents of the engine compartment.

"Show us its innards," he said.

"I think you'd be making a mistake," I said, "to skimp on the lessons." But I did what he asked me and opened it up.

He looked over the engine like a man checking something as familiar as the contents of his own suitcase: toothbrush, trousers, two shirts, etc. It was O'Hagen's weakness that he could not stand to make a fool of himself so he tried to give the impression that he knew what was what with a motor and was suspicious that some vital part might be missing.

When he let me know he was satisfied I closed the compartment.

"All right," he said. He took in his belt a notch and jutted his chin. "Start her up."

The sun emerged from a keyhole in the clouds and bathed the weathered whiskered face. Goog and Goose came out on to the veranda where they stood, silently, side by side, staring at the gleaming car whose radiator was suddenly full of golden light.

By 1919 the Ford had a starter motor. No crank was needed. I simply turned it on and the engine caught first time.

"Hop in," I said.

O'Hagen shook his head and plunged his hands deep into his pockets.

"No," he said, "I want to watch it go."

I did as I was commanded. I drove around the house, passed in front of the imprisoned dog, and heard, above the noise of the engine, the clumping boots of Goose and Goog as they ran from one side of the house to the other.

I was a ballerina on a show pony. It seemed a damn fool way to make a living.

23

Goog was wide awake. He lay amongst his bundle of grey blankets and listened to the noise of drinking. The drinking was a new thing. He didn't know what to do about it. Goose was no help. Goose was asleep and nothing would wake him. Goose had slept all last night while their father chopped up dinner plates outside the window. It was Goog who had put their weeping father to bed. It was Goog who lay sleepless while his father vomited in the kitchen sink.

He could hear the voices clearly and if he sat up he could see, through a chink in the shrunken wallboards, his father pouring sweet wine from a demijohn into Herbert Badgery's glass.

"To life," Stu O'Hagen said.

"To life," said Herbert Badgery.

"I'm not a drinking man," Stu said, "but by God it warms you."

There was a pause. Stu traced unstable patterns in the spilt wine on the oilcloth.

"I never liked the idea of lessons," he said. "I never took a lesson in anything."

"You've done well."

Stu tilted back in his chair and surveyed the room. He picked up the kerosene light and held it above his head.

"I built it myself. I was working for a real estate agent, selling blocks of land in Melbourne. I was doing well. They wanted to promote me. But I had it in my head I wanted to make something myself. You could say I had tickets on myself, but I wanted to *make* something, not just sell things. So I bought this land and I didn't know a sheep's head from its arse."

"You've got a lot to be proud of."

We drank. I made appreciative smacking noises with my lips which were sweet and sticky with the wine.

"Lessons were something I had no time for. No one gave me a lesson. But look at it."

"It's a fine house."

"It's a shamozzle," Stu said firmly.

"Come on, man. . . ."

"It'll fall over."

"No."

"You haven't been here in a southerly. You wouldn't know. You haven't lain here like I have listening to the damn thing moving in the wind." He stood up and carried the lantern across to the outside wall. The studs showed on the inside, the outside was clad with rough-nailed weatherboards. He held the lantern high in one hand and banged the wall hard with the fist of the other. The wall bowed and shuddered and a plate fell from the dresser on the other side of the room. Stu kicked at the broken pieces.

"I never learned to dance," he said as he sat down. "I never got the hang of it."

71

I was embarrassed. I had a bad conscience about my motives for visiting O'Hagen's. I leaned to pick up the shards of plate.

"Leave them," Stu said. "I've been wrong. I've been very wrong."

I didn't know where to look. "You've got two fine boys", I said, "and a good wife."

"That's true," he said, "about the boys at least." His eyes were brimful of moisture. "I'll buy the car," he said, "and I'll pay the three quid for the lessons."

I had the papers in my pocket and I could have signed him up there and then. I sat there, worrying at them, folding them back and forth.

"No," I said, "I couldn't."

"Yes, I've been a fool. I've been a fool in most things. The bloody German is a better farmer than I am. The little coot looks like he'll blow over in the wind, but he's made something of that place. He's *made* something. He's a lovely little farmer."

"He is."

"I'll buy this Ford," Stu said, "and I'll take lessons."

"I couldn't," I said. "I couldn't let you."

O'Hagen blinked.

"Well, what", he said, pulling the demijohn back to his side of the table, "did you come here for?"

"To show you the Ford, that's true."

"You came here to come dancing," O'Hagen said. "You came here to prance around my kitchen."

"No, I assure you."

"Well, what for?"

I could not sell a Ford to a weeping man. He made me feel grubby. I too was smitten with the desire to do something decent.

"I told you," he said, "I'll take the lessons. I'll take them." Tears were now streaming down his cheeks. "I'll pay the three quid. I don't care who laughs at me."

"No one will laugh at you. That's not the point. The point is the Ford is the wrong car."

He wiped his eyes with his grubby sleeve. "So Patrick Hare was right then? The Dodge is a better car."

"Not the Dodge. The Summit. It's the Summit you should have."

"What in the name of God is a Summit?" Stu shouted.

"A car," I shouted back. "A vehicle, made in Australia. An Australian car."

72

"An Australian car," O'Hagen said. "What a presumption."

"A what?"

"A presumption. Are you sitting there and telling me we can make a better car than the Yanks? God Jesus Christ in Heaven help me. Mary Mother of God," he whispered and seemed to find her in the gloom above the roof joists. "You're a salesman, Mr Badgery," he said. "The country is full of bloody salesmen. You don't have to know anything to be a salesman. All you need to do is talk. That's why everyone does it. But if you want to really do something you need some bloody brains, some nous. Now tell me, tell me truly, is this Australian car of yours a better car than the Ford?"

"It's not the point about better," I said, "it's a question of where the money goes. You'd be better off with a worse car if the money stayed here."

"You're cock-eyed, man. You're a bloody hypocrite. You go around making a quid from selling the bloody things, and now you tell me I shouldn't buy one. You're making no sense," Stu sighed. "Sell me the bloody Ford before I lose my temper."

"I will not," I said. "If you give me leave I'll travel up to Melbourne and pick up a Summit and bring it down here. It's a beautiful vehicle."

"Is the Summit", Stu said slowly, "as good as a Ford?"

"The difference is not worth a pig's fart."

"A subject", my host said, "of which you would be ignorant."

I was never good with drink. I got myself too excited and I did not express myself as well as I might.

"Do you want Henry Ford", I roared, "to tell you when to get out of bed in the morning."

"Sell me the Ford," Stu roared. "Give me lessons."

"I won't."

"Sell it to me, man, or by God I'll learn you."

"Learn you! Learn you! You talk as ignorant as you think."

"Ignorant," said O'Hagen quietly, "but not so ignorant I don't know why you came here." He stood and walked unsteadily to the wood stove. I paid him no attention.

The poker crashed down on the table. It missed my hand by less than an inch.

"You silly bastard," I hollered, leaping up, and falling backwards over my chair.

And then everything was confusing. I wrestled the poker away and O'Hagen was on the floor but sómeone was still pummelling me.

I found Goog, in a nightshirt, punching me around the head. And then Goog was lying on the floor in the corner near the stove. A small trickle of blood came from his nose. He was whimpering.

I was sick at heart as I stumbled from the house. In my mind's eye I could see, not Goog, but a brush-tailed possum laid waste in the fallen branches of a tree.

24

I woke just before dawn. The Ford was in the middle of the saltpans and my mouth tasted disgusting. I had run off the road on the north side of the crossing and the meandering wheel marks on the saltflats had left no corresponding impression on my memory.

Rain was falling in a fine drizzle. My right shoulder was wet. The line of dwarf yellow cypress pines along Blobell's Hill was smudged by dull grey cloud and nothing else in the landscape was distinct except the particularly clear sound of a crow above the saltpans flying north towards O'Hagen's. It sounded like barbed wire.

My whole body was stiff and sore but my hands, still clamped around the wheel, were stiffer and sorer than any other part of me. The skin on my palms was torn and blistered from the axe work and had dried hard. My knuckles were bruised and broken. I felt everything that was wrong with my character in those two painful hands – the palms and knuckles always in opposition to each other.

My mouth was parched dry. My head ached. I regretted hitting the small-eared boy. I regretted wishing to put my head between Mrs O'Hagen's legs. I regretted that my actions confused people. I regretted being a big mouth, a bullshitter and a bully.

I was thirty-three years old. I turned the rear-vision mirror so that I could see my face. It teetered on the point of being old. One morning, I knew, I would look into a mirror and see rotting teeth and clouded eyes, battles not won, lies not believed.

It was then I decided to marry Phoebe.

It came to me quite simply, on the saltpans south of Balliang East. I would marry Phoebe, build the aeroplanes at Barwon Aeros, be a friend to Jack, a son to Molly.

When I stepped from the Ford I found the distance between the running board and the ground unexpectedly short. I stumbled and, stepping back, found the T Model up to its axles in the salt-crusted mud.

A crooked smile crossed my face.

"Serve you right," I said.

The Ford had been a tumour in my life. I had fought battles with it in the way another man might fight battles with alcohol or tobacco. I had walked away from it and returned to it. I had rejected it only to embrace it passionately. I admired its construction, its appearance, the skill that had produced it so economically. And these were also the things I loathed.

So on this Tuesday morning at six thirty a.m., when I walked away from a T Model in the saltpans, I felt an enormous relief, a lightness. I was finished with Fords and the dizziness, the dryness in my throat, the pain in my hands, did not stop me appreciating the beauty of this landscape with the black motor car stranded and dying like a whale.

I walked ten miles back to Geelong. I could see myself. I saw how I walked. There, on the road: a man entering the first decent chapter of his life.

25

While we waited for the pudding, Jack discoursed on flying.

"I don't want to hear it," Molly said, holding her small hands across her ears. "It makes me giddy, upon my word it does. It makes me giddy and faint."

Jack prized a hand from the side of his wife's head and placed it on his napkined lap.

"I'll fall," she said, not daring to look down at the floor.

It was not easy to understand Molly's antics, because they were only partly a joke. She performed these girly-girly acts continually.

"You won't fall, my petal," Jack said, "and if you did fall, I'd catch you. And if I didn't you wouldn't get hurt – no more", he smiled, "than a bruise on your backside, a big blue one."

"Shush," said Molly, colouring.

They both coloured, husband and wife. It was a dirty sight, because anyone could see that Jack's blush was not caused by embarrassment but by excitement.

"Like a map of Tasmania," he said.

"I'm going to lie down," she said, but must have remembered the pudding, for she sat down almost as soon as she had stood up. There was something very odd about her eyes which were flirtatious but also fearful. Of course this was a game (Jack loved it) but sometimes you could feel real terror in it. She clung to Jack as a giddy person clings to a tree on a steep mountain when everything underfoot is dry and slippery with dead gum leaves and shiny grasses. She held his hand, patted his knee, tugged his sleeve, tucked in his shirt tail, filled his glass, took lint from his shoulder.

Only puddings seemed to soothe her. She cooked them in plenty: steamed puddings with jam sauces, queen puddings with wild wavy egg-white toppings, roly-poly puddings, plum puddings out of season, apple charlottes and rhubarb pies. She had small ankles, shapely legs, delicate bones, but her body was a tribute to puddings and the bread and hot milk Phoebe made for her when she had queer feelings.

There was something definitely wrong with Molly's brain, but whatever it was she so churned up with imitations of helplessness, knowingness, self-mockery and God knows what else that it would have been easy to forget it entirely if Phoebe (silent Phoebe) had not watched over her with such a protective air.

I did not mind these frailties. I loved my new family. I was an old dog lying before an open fire, warming myself before them. I liked to see them show affection to each other.

I had shone my shoes before this dinner. I swung my legs beneath the table. I whistled. I brimmed with marriage. It radiated from my skin in heady waves like sweet-smelling gasoline, and I whistled, not even aware that I was doing it, or that my companions at the dinner table (even Phoebe) were starting to smile because of it.

Bridget, restored to the dining room, hovered with a large steamed pudding – a treacly lava of jam sauce engulfed the yellow mountain in a slow sweet flood. She tried not to giggle at the whistling guest who now gave her a broad, lewd wink. She coloured to the roots of her dark Irish hair, placed the pudding heavily in front of Jack, and fled to the kitchen for the custard.

A veil of marriage fell across the table. I watched my future father-in-law dole out the pudding in heavy country slices and could easily have got up and hugged him. My mother-in-law was busy with the custard. My bride sat pale and beautiful with her head bowed.

76

"I've been thinking", I said at last, "of marriage." My head was so full of it, it did not occur to me that they might find this news surprising.

But I was too enthusiastic to notice any puzzlement. I was carried away, and relying, as I always relied, on the heat of my enthusiasm to ignite my listeners. By these means, by the sheer force of my will, I had seduced women and talked my audiences into the air above astonished cities.

The silence did not trouble me. I did not think to liken Phoebe's pale silence to that of a prisoner staring at a judge with a black cap. I did not notice Bridget run from the room, or Molly pull in her lips on disapproving drawstrings. Jack ate in a dedicated manner, with his head down, and all that any of this meant to me was that I had not properly communicated my feelings to them.

I allowed the hot jam sauce to cool while I devoted myself to my new enthusiasm. I praised the joys of children, and contrasted married life with that of the lonely bachelor. I praised women. I placed candles in their hands and gave them credit for great wisdom. I celebrated motherhood. I pushed against the silence like an old stubborn bull who will lean hard against a fence until it falls.

"Who", asked Jack, without very much enthusiasm, "is the lucky girl?"

"Ah," I said, "that would be giving the game away."

"Is it", asked bleak Molly, "anyone we know?"

I hesitated. The heat was leaving me and my sense of the world around me was becoming clearer. I saw I was in danger of committing a serious blunder.

"No," I laughed, "no one you know." And then, in a stroke that saved me, "No one I know either."

They all laughed (everyone, that is, except Phoebe who carefully divided her slice of pudding into nine pieces and separated them, one from the other).

"What a man you are, Mr Badgery," said Molly pouring on more custard.

"I see nothing so peculiar," I said, happy to pretend that I was offended.

"Nothing peculiar", Jack said, "in marrying without a bride? It's not a thing I'd be game to have a go at myself."

"Walking up the aisle", Molly said, "all by yourself."

"Here comes the bride," sang Jack, "fair, fat and wide."

"Here comes the groom," recited Molly, "all by himself in the room."

"There," she laughed, "I'm a poet and I don't know it."

Phoebe sipped water and watched us all. I dared not catch her eye.

26

I can remember few days when Corio Bay looked really beautiful – even when the summer sun shone upon it, when one would expect to recall diamonds of light dancing on an azure field, the water appeared bleak and flat, like a paddock too long over-grazed. This, of course, is why the city fathers turned their back upon it and placed vast eyeless wool stores on its shores.

Of my evening walks with Jack McGrath, I remember no pretty colours in either sky or water but rather, on the evening now in question, only the coarse sand on its shores which were littered with the bodies of stranded jellyfish.

"You had me worried." Jack hitched up his baggy trousers and buttoned up all four buttons of his waistcoat and all three of his suit jacket. "My word you did."

"How's that, Jack?"

Soiled clouds hung over the bay and the wind came from the south where there was no land at all, just a white-tipped ocean that reached all the way to Antarctica.

"There are two things I've never gone for. Chaps that cheat at cards and grown-up men marrying young girls."

The wind blew through my jacket. My nipples were hard and uncomfortable. They scratched themselves against my cotton shirt. "I don't get your meaning," I said, but I got his damn meaning well enough.

"Molly thought you wanted to marry Phoebe," Jack laughed. "She thought you were going to ask for her hand."

I laughed too. It was a virtuoso performance, an isolated, technically perfect, joyless loop in the cold blue evening air. "And what", I said, when the laugh was done, "did she think of that?"

"It's a thing that always makes me feel ill. I can't abide it. Old men and young girls. It makes my flesh creep."

"Surely," I said miserably, "there must be occasions. . . ."

But there was a stern and unrelenting streak in gentle Jack and his big blunt face looked taut and the laugh lines refused to fall into their natural furrows.

"No, no," he said. "No occasion. No occasion at all."

We walked on in silence.

It was the trouble with the world that it would never permit me to be what I was. Everyone loved me when I appeared in a cloak, and swirled and laughed and told them lies. They applauded. They wanted my friendship. But when I took off my cloak they did not like me. They clucked their tongues and turned away. My friend Jack was my friend in all things but was repulsed by what I really was. I admired and loved him, even though he could not abide the Chinese; but he could only like the bullshit version of me. He would have condemned me for what happened at O'Hagen's, for my lust, my greed, my temper, my impatience. He would not have seen the abandonment of the Ford with any sympathy.

Yet this did not put me off. Quite the opposite. All it did was make me want to tell him *more*, to grab him by the scruff of the neck and force him to look at me as I was, to make him accept me. I wanted to prop his eyelids open with matches and say, I am what I am for good reasons and a man with half a soul would understand and even sympathize.

I had vertigo. I wanted to fling myself off the edge of my confession and somehow, with the force of my passion, with the power and courage of my leap, command respect, understanding, sympathy.

Roughly equivalent, of course, to punching him in the face.

Before I could stop myself I told him that I had lied about the aircraft factory, that I had no experience in the business at all.

"You're a queer fellow, Badgery," he said, when I had finished. "Do I get you right when you say you have no interest in a factory?"

"Of course I have an interest?" I said. "I could think of nothing better."

We walked on into the gloom.

"You have an interest?" he said at last.

"Of course I do."

"And so do I."

He stopped, and stood stamping his big boots into the sand.

"So where is the problem?" he said.

"I wasn't going to Ballarat at all. I was broke when I met you."

"That's Ballarat's loss," he said.

He turned back towards the house.

"The point is not whether you're an engineer or whether you're broke. The point is that you've got a grand idea. And you've also got enthusiasm, which is the only quality that makes a business go. We can buy engineers, Badgery, but we can't buy enthusiasm. You say you're a liar, but I've seen nothing dishonest in you. You paid me back my thirty pounds. You don't go ogling my daughter. I'd be happy to have you for a partner."

I couldn't understand why, but he made me feel unclean. He gave me no comfort.

"I've got a few acquaintances," Jack said, "wealthy men down at Colac who are interested in this venture. To hell with Ballarat," he laughed as the street lights came on in a long electric line above our heads. "We'll do it. By Jove, see if they can stop us."

Hooper the grocer, cantering his team home along Western Avenue, saw two men standing with their hands in their pockets by the side of the road. He tipped his hat to Jack McGrath who stared right through him as if he and his wagon were glass things in a dream.

27

Jack was arranging his expedition to Colac and he could not leave the telephone alone. His deafness made him bellow. When he was engaged in telephoning the whole house stood still and waited for him to finish. It was a big house, but even in the music room you could not escape his optimism. He did not give a damn for the expense. He talked on and on.

In the midst of all this, the roof above Phoebe's bed had begun to leak. Jack was too excited to give much of his mind over to such a mundane thing.

"It's a tile come off," Jack said, still puffing from the exertion of his phone call and putting four spoons of sugar in his tea, "that's all."

Phoebe said nothing.

"Mr Johnstone used to do the tiles," Molly said. "But he's dead, at Gallipoli, and he borrowed your bicycle," she told her daughter, "so he could go up to Ryrie Street to enlist. Do you remember, Jack? Do you remember Bob Johnstone coming here to borrow Phoebe's bike? I said to him, you'll look funny, a big man like you on a girl's bicycle, but he didn't seem to worry."

"It's hard to get a man to do one tile," Jack said. "I'll get up in the weekend, when I come back from Colac."

"I'll do it," I said. "Let me."

"We couldn't," Molly said, "could we, Jack?"

"No," Jack said, "we couldn't." His mind, however, was on other things.

I smiled. They all (except Phoebe) smiled in return.

"I am not frightened of heights," I said (I looped the loop in the skies of their imagination). "Just tell me where the ladder is."

It was late March and the morning had a fresh edge to its sunlight. When I folded my napkin and placed it on the table it looked, with its eggshell white and blue shadows, like a detail from a painting by the impressionist Dussoir.

28

Phoebe lay on her bed. It was five minutes past nine on the monstrous black clock her father had given her for her fifteenth birthday. She could hear me on the roof above her bed. She stood. Her feet were bare. Her mother did not like her to have bare feet, but her mother had taken Bridget to the market in Moorabool Street and as Phoebe stepped out on to the veranda she looked forward to the cool feeling the wet dewy grass would give her unnaturally hot feet.

At the back of the house there was an old fig tree, an easy-climbing tree whose branches now shaded the roof of the back veranda. When she was younger she had played in it. Now she could walk up the branch without so much as stopping. She ran lightly across the veranda roof and crawled, loose as a cat (arched back, purring) to the next ridge.

I was somewhere in the next valley, fiddling inexpertly with wire and pliers. In a moment I would look up and see, perched on the ridge above me, a beautiful young woman with hair the colour of copper, her bare legs dangling towards me, her face a shaded secret, dark against the pale blue morning sky.

I sucked in my breath. I stood there, staring.

I stopped breathing. I put down the pliers. They made a small noise (clink) against the tiles.

Did I speak? Later I tried to remember. Probably I said "come" in my mind, silently, and motioned with my hand. She came down the ridge, that steep face of red tiles, standing up, her lovely

81

feet sure-footed. Only the blind eyes of the empty tower looked down on us.

I will go to my grave remembering the high flush in her face as she came to me, the cool of her arm (hot and cold) and, oh my God, such a kiss. I would have been content, would have ventured no further than the kiss (it was a meal, a feast in itself) but Phoebe had not come climbing trees and roofs merely to taste my mouth and stare at my glittering eyes, and when I felt those fingers like birds' wings fluttering at the buttons of my fly I closed my eyes and moaned. The pliers skipped across the tiles and clattered down into the box gutter in the valley.

Her eyes were a match for mine. They did not falter or flutter, but gazed straight back. She undressed me and I did not fight or attempt to assert the masculine prerogative. She undressed me to my farmer's body: tanned arms, tanned neck, and the blue-white skin traced by veins and, most curious of all, a hard but soft-skinned penis with its toadstool head and its great blue vein stretching along its length. She had talked with Annette about men's organs and how they would look, but nothing had prepared her for the softness, the baby skin stretched so tight.

When she touched me with her finger, I moaned ("So sweetly," she wrote, "the sound enough to make me cry."). She bent and touched me with her lips, just brushed me, silk on silk.

Somewhere, in another world, a door slammed.

I straightened her and removed her dress, a dress left over from a younger summer with daisies repeated on a blue field. I lay the dress against the slope of the roof and she lay there quickly before the dress slid down the slope. The tiles were rough on her back, hurt but did not hurt. She had a mole on her shoulder. She thought my penis was silky and strong. I knelt before her. She took it in her hand and introduced it, ever so gently, into her.

When she hurt, her mouth opened and her green eyes went wide. My left knee was on a roll of copper wire, my right on tiles. I trembled. My eyes never left her. She thought I was a Phoenician with a bow to my bottom lip. She sent the pain away, dismissed it, pulled me to her and felt like she had felt on the day she discovered surf, fear and pleasure, pulled this way, tumbled that without being able to control or understand it; but there was also a place in the water where you melted into it and she found the place and gave herself over to it until the swoon, the swoon she had felt in Annette's arms started to approach like a cloud of distant bees.

"Mr Badgery!" Down below us, unseen, Molly McGrath, in apron, her arms full of snapdragons.

"Yes," I called. "Yes."

"Would you like a cup of tea when you've finished?"

Phoebe giggled. I placed my hand across her mouth, but gently.

"Thank you, Mrs McGrath."

We smiled at each other and she nibbled the fingers of my censoring hand, but her mother's voice had changed me and I moved swiftly, thrust guiltily, made love to her like a thief with the eyes of the tower glaring down on me.

I reared back suddenly.

Phoebe watched the semen spurt in the sunlight. I held her hand. She looked at the cloudy sperm, red tiles. As she scrambled for her clothes, she did not have time to think about how she felt.

"You go first," she told me. "Go and have tea with her." The first words she'd spoken to me in eight weeks.

"What about the ladder?"

"I don't need a ladder."

Phoebe McGrath kissed Herbert Badgery. She kissed him on the nose. She kissed him on his Phoenician's mouth.

And then I was gone, scurrying off like a burglar, leaving behind my pliers and my wet cloud of semen. Phoebe tried to think what she felt but could not touch what it was. The semen on the roof looked like mucus from your nose, yet it was full of life. It was dying in the sun where no one could see it.

She put her finger in it and wrote "Phoebe loves Herbert" on a tile.

She held her finger to her nose. It smelt like flour and water.

29

I cannot say that Jack's feelings did not enter my head, but rather that I trussed and tethered them and threw them into some back room in my mind where I would not hear them struggling. Now, as I drag these old items out, I am surprised at the number I chose to forget (a wife and child in Dubbo come to mind) and how effectively I did it.

I felt strong and confident and wonderful to be alive. I poured tea for Molly in the front parlour and accepted one of Bridget's heavy lamingtons as my right. I devoured it with pleasure, and took a second one when it was offered. In the afternoon I would go to the Barwon Common and service the Morris Farman. I looked forward to it. I had brand new plugs to fit, a new oil seal, and twenty feet of piano wire for new rigging. I would clean the magneto again, time it, and have the Renault engine looking clean and splendid for the backers to whom I would demonstrate the wonders of flight.

I stretched and yawned. There was a soft noise above the ceiling, a pattering.

My hostess stared at the ceiling, a deep frown creasing her forehead, a lamington held between thumb and forefinger. I returned her anxious smile.

"A possum," I said.

"Surely not."

"Almost certainly," I said, and languidly constructed a tale about how, during my attempts to fix the tile I had been confronted with "a big brown fellow" who had "a brush-tail as thick as your arm".

"No," said Molly, putting down her lamington and holding her hands tightly together.

"And cocky as all get out," I said. "Sat there like Jacky and wouldn't budge."

"You don't say."

"In clear daylight." I saw the possum with complete clarity as it came to take its position, the position Phoebe had occupied in the dazzling moment when she appeared on the top of the ridge.

"And wouldn't go away?" Molly shivered.

"No harm," I said, but I was surprised to see goose-flesh on my hostess's arms.

"I live in terror," she said, leaning forward and shifting in her chair a little so that her dimpled knee almost touched me. There was hardly room for a piece of French toast to slide through the space between our knees. She meant nothing untoward. She was merely moving closer to seek the protection of a man, an instinctive move she was not even aware of having made.

"In terror?" I asked as she put her hand on my arm.

"In terror. Do you know," and she widened her eyes accordingly, "a very good friend of mine, a dear lady, very sweet, was in a house, her house, when a possum", she held her white throat with a hand where Jack's gifts glittered expensively, "came down the chimney and quite destroyed . . ." she waved her hand around the room, "everything."

"Surely not." I discreetly separated my penis from the spot where it had glued to my woollen underpants.

Molly blinked and drank her tea.

Phoebe appeared silently in the doorway.

"I was telling your mother, Miss McGrath," I said, "that I have seen possums on the roof."

"Oh," Phoebe said disdainfully, *"really?"*

"You be polite to Mr Badgery when he speaks to you, my girl."

"Frankly," Phoebe said, her cheeks flushed, coming to address her mother with dangerous green eyes. "Frankly, I think he's lying."

I took refuge in a lamington.

"What was it like?" she asked.

I swallowed the cake. My throat was dry. I needed tea to wash it down. "A big old fellow," I said, "a brush-tail."

"That seems an unlikely story, Mr Badgery," she said coolly. I held my half-eaten lamington between gluey fingers and hoped she would sit down before her mother saw the patch of blood on the back of her dress.

"No," I said. "I assure you. Your mother has heard it, just a minute ago."

"That was me," Phoebe said wickedly. "I ran all over the roof."

"Phoebe," Molly said. "Don't tell fibs."

"I must say, Mr Badgery," Phoebe smiled at me, "all that exercise has given me an appetite."

She sat down, at last.

My muscles slowly untensed and let me enjoy the splendid vision of my beloved who happily ate her lamington in the deep shadow of the parlour while the windows were filled with blue sky and the air with the white cries of seagulls.

30

In his cups Jack McGrath confessed to me that he had no affection for the Western District of Victoria. It filled him with melancholy: those great plains of wheat and sheep, those bland landscapes perfectly matched to the forlorn cries of crows. He did not care for the towns: Colac, Terang, flat sprawling places where Arctic winds cut you to the bone in winter. The cockies, he claimed, got a look in their eyes that came from staring at such uneventful horizons; but perhaps the look was in his eyes, not theirs.

As Jack McGrath motored out of Geelong in his Hispano Suiza there were many who saw him who judged, correctly, that he was a rich man in a Collins Street suit. They could not have guessed at the store of memories he carried with him like Leichhardt in the wilderness with his vital provisions: ice crystals in the high country, smoke, sawdust, the flavour of yarns with old men with age-blotched faces, a snake of apple peel dropped into sunlight. No one watching the bullock driver's body, the city man's suit, the grand automobile, would possibly guess that he had, somehow, missed the track, taken the wrong turning and ended up in Geelong by mistake, guided by a luck that was really, if he could have admitted it, no luck at all.

The things that really pleased Jack McGrath were all in the high country of the Great Divide, two hundred miles away from wool-bound Geelong. He could still read off their names, like a Catholic does his beads: Howqua, Jamieson, Woods Point, Mount Specu-lation, Mount Buggery, Mount Despair, The Razorback, The Governors, Mount Matlock. And whenever, in the middle of his bright electric nights, he wanted a peaceful place to rest his mind he shut his eyes and found a place on the ridge between Mount Buller and Mount Stirling, on the way down to the King Valley; there was a place there called Grassy Knoll and he could still, day-dreaming, sit there and feel the cold air in his lungs and let his mind float across the deep valleys to where the Razorback Ridge showed its clear sharp edge against the pale blue evening sky.

He had never meant to become rich. He had never planned anything. He had trusted his life and let it carry him along never expecting it to mislead him. He could not acknowledge that it had. And although depression often enfolded him as he sat alone in an armchair he could not, would not, admit that he was unhappy. He built brick walls. He placed sheets of glass above the door. He laced his home with electricity and thumped across its polished floors in heavy boots.

His father had been a bullock driver; Jack McGrath did the same. He had a talent for it, a sympathy with the beasts that got them moving when other drivers whipped and swore and tangled themselves in hot confusion. By the time he was sixteen he was entrusted with old Dinny O'Hara's best teams and he worked the long rutted miles between Melbourne and Mansfield, a broad young man with a full beard who soon became famous for two unlikely qualities: he used none of the profanities for which bullock drivers were renowned, and he was a teetotaller.

It was March and the shearers were on strike and if everyone in Melbourne and the bush knew about it, if they imagined gangs of shearers were burning down wool sheds and setting fire to the squatters' paddocks, it was news to Jack McGrath who travelled innocently beside his team in his faded red shirt, his moleskins, bowyangs, and heavy boots. He did not read the newspapers. He did not sit drinking around the campfire, telling yarns or singing songs.

When he found out he did not even know what a strike was and it was Dinny O'Hara who had to explain it to him. O'Hara was a huge man, withered with age, whose enormous cauliflower ears dominated his blotchy face.

"The shearers is on strike," he spat.

"What's a strike, Mr O'Hara?"

"A strike is when the buggers won't work," he spat again. "So we got no wool to carry. The Fergusons got no wool. The Rosses got no wool. The McCorkells got no wool. It's all on the sheep, not in the bale, and there'll be bloody war before there is."

They sat on the back veranda. Jack McGrath stared at Dinny O'Hara. He had never heard of such a thing. "A war."

"A war, a bloody war, that's what they want", O'Hara said, "and that's what they'll get. Boozers and bushrangers", he said, "galloping around with their guns and their speeches. So I'm giving you the sack."

Jack didn't say anything. He remembered breaking a gum twig in half and then in half again. He threw the pieces of broken twig on the ground. He could not understand the justice of it. He was so used to being liked by men. His eyes were suddenly, surprisingly, wet with tears and he turned his head into the shade of the veranda on the pretext of finding something amiss with his kangaroo-hide belt.

"I hear tell," O'Hara said, "there's a fella in Point's Point with a team doing work with the timber. His driver got kilt, run over by his own wheel, the silly bugger."

They didn't shake hands. Young Jack McGrath rolled his swag and started walking the sixty miles to Point's Point. He walked through the bush all night and all the next day. He sang hymns as he walked, not because he was deeply religious, but because they were the only songs he knew. He walked for twenty-four hours and stopped, dead beat, three miles short of Point's Point. He unrolled his swag and slept beneath the bridge at Gaffney's Creek.

The next day he found there was no job and no one had been run over by a wheel. He walked up to the gold mine to try and get work but there wasn't any. The manager of the mine was an Englishman known locally as Twopence Thompson, a name that related to his cunning in money matters.

Twopence Thompson's problem was a thirty-six-ton steam boiler that a previous contractor had abandoned sixteen miles away on the mountain road to Point's Point. He offered Jack McGrath two hundred pounds to bring it into the mine and whether from desperation or a rare fit of generosity, advanced half of the money to enable Jack to buy a team.

The opinion of the town was that they were both fools, Jack for accepting the job and Twopence Thompson for parting with his cash.

Jack McGrath chose his team, paying forty pounds each for good polers and ten pounds each for the rest of the team. He made the yokes from Queensland brush box and spent two weeks rigging together a new harness. Then he walked sixteen miles to the abandoned boiler and studied it. Where the other contractor had tried to pull the thirty-six tons uphill, Jack worked out a series of pullies so his team could move downhill. He anchored the pullies to giant bluegums and began the job. It took him three months. Sometimes he was bogged for a week. At other times he moved it a hundred yards. But move it he did, and Twopence Thompson parted with his other hundred pounds.

His luck had started. He had a good team and he was well respected. He worked in the timber and had he wished he could have drunk himself to death on French champagne as plenty of bullockies had done before him.

He banked his money. There was nothing he wanted to spend it on.

When, in 1910, he bought the charabanc he was thought insane and then shrewd. In his opinion, he'd been neither. He'd been lucky. The gold mine was working hard by then and there was plenty of money in the little town. He took his share of it: running sober miners down to Warburton and bringing drunken ones back.

Ten years later, on the road to Colac, he could still smile about those days. By God it had been fun. He'd driven that Ford, the first of its kind in Victoria, around those winding mountain tracks, stopping every mile or so for men to empty their bladders or settle disputes which were often funnier than the arguments that had begun them. And coming back after a big storm! That was the go. The road blocked by fallen trees. How he had loved shifting them.

They called him "Jack the Gelly" in Point's Point.

He blasted those trees with gelignite and never, as long as he did it, did he ever learn to carry enough fuse so as they approached home the fuses would be shorter and shorter and once, just by the Sixteen Mile Creek, he had been blown nose first into the mud and had a dagger of splintered wood driven into his broad backside by the force of the blast. When the dust settled, his drunken passengers clapped and cheered.

He could still wax poetic about the smell of cordite which had become, in memory, the perfume of the eighteen-ounce gold nugget – shaped like a swallow – he had accidentally blasted from that roadway. He could still feel the soft clay mud as he rubbed the swallow in his hands. He could still smell the sweet sappy wounded wood of the great gums, see his breath suspended in the air above the road in 1910 while his passengers, suddenly sober, gathered in the headlights of the charabanc. They stood in the spluttering light of the acetylene arcs, as silent as men in church, and handed the nugget one to the other.

The Point's Point Historical Society has a cast that was taken of the nugget at the time. It is named, in that dusty little-visited room, "The Swallow". The real name for the nugget was not "The Swallow" at all. It was "Gelly's Luck".

It was also Gelly's luck that he had the honour to drive Molly Rourke from Warburton to Point's Point for the first time: a more proper barmaid than any he had ever seen, a more beautiful woman than he could have imagined.

There are people alive in Point's Point today who have never heard of Molly Rourke but they can tell you the story of how old Sam McCorkell spent a pound one night just on swearing, and how he paid up, meek as a lamb, before going home to strangle his wife and children. The swearing box in the story is Molly's. It changed the Grand Hotel and those who didn't like the restrictions would walk across to the Sandy River Hotel. More often the traffic was the other way and Dusty Miller, the publican of the Sandy River, became disheartened and sat in the parlour drinking Queensland rum. Molly sent men across to cheer him up. A small group, known collectively as Dusty's Bridesmaids, sat with him on his veranda above the river and drank tainted beer from unwashed pipes.

Molly Rourke hated the bush. As everyone said, she was a city girl (she came from Ballarat) and they liked her for it, even while they teased her because of it. She was a point of distinction about the town, like Bert McCulloch's German clock and Mrs Walter Abrahams's fine bone china set. She was something that set them apart from other dusty streets in the middle of the Australian bush.

Jack McGrath drank his lemon squash and fell in love with her, although it took him an awful long time to do anything about it.

On one Saturday afternoon in May he was observed to drink a total of sixteen lemon squashes. The Cavanagh brothers kept a book on it and Bert McCulloch won ten quid.

When, at last, he courted her, it was as delicately as he might (had he been permitted) have picked up Mrs Walter Abrahams's bone china between his big calloused fingers. Dusty's Bridesmaids would smile to see them together, the big clumsy man bending over her so attentively, so delicately, as they took their Sunday stroll down the two miles of macadam to the Boggy Creek ford and back again.

He was told often enough how lucky he was to have found Molly. He never doubted it. He expected they would marry and have children and live out their lives in Point's Point and be buried on the hillside amongst the bracken above the river. It was the place where, the man in the Hispano Suiza at last admitted, he really belonged.

His soul was a jellyfish stranded on the shell-grit shore of Corio Bay. All he wanted to do was feel something as good as the air on the Warburton Road in 1910.

31

Molly McGrath sat in the parlour with the curtains drawn and would not say why. She had Bridget bring her fingers of toast and weak black tea. There were noises. She did not like them.

On the previous night Phoebe had made jokes about possums and Molly had left the table hurriedly, leaving us to finish our jelly unchaperoned.

"She knows," I said.

Phoebe shook her head. "More tea, Mr Badgery?"

If I had been less besotted, I would have taken more care of Molly, would have trod more cautiously, but we left her to suffer her terrors alone on her bed and were pleased to be left so dangerously together. We knew nothing about the electric belt, and even if we had known there is every chance we would have continued to torture her.

At breakfast next morning Phoebe announced her intention of visiting the library in town. I knew exactly what she meant. Ten minutes after her departure I decided, out loud, on a stroll. I wore a three-piece suit and a watch with a gold chain. I walked up the fig tree and crossed the steep tiled roof with my shoes in my hand.

Phoebe waited for me, artfully naked, reclining in a valley on a travelling rug under a powder-blue sky.

She was like no woman I have ever known. Please note: I said woman, not girl. This was not a case, as Jack would have imagined, of a grown-up man, already fearful of death and decay, falling for the smooth untroubled skin of a young girl. (Later I will sing you some songs to ageing flesh, a woman's body with scars, stretch marks, distended nipples, breasts no longer firm, a slow sweet song by a river, not a bay.)

She climbed naked to the roof ridge and wanted to be taken from behind while she watched the farmers and their wives promenade along Western Avenue. She licked my nipples as if I were a woman and laughed when they stood erect. She told me I had a Phoenician's mouth and stared so hard into my eyes that I shut them to protect the poor bleak rooms of my life from such intensive scrutiny.

Phoebe looked into those blue clear eyes and thought I was the Devil. There was nothing soft about me, she thought, no soft place, just this cold blue charm. She wrote all this in her book. Sometimes she showed it to me, holding her hands to hide what was before and later.

"He is an electric light," she wrote. She was well pleased with this description, suggesting as it did both electrocution and illumination.

Baked by hot tiles, goose-pimpled by breezes from Corio Bay, she shucked off Geelong and left it lying in the box gutter of the roof like a dull tweed suit. She held a testicle in her mouth and listened to me moan. She shocked me with the attentions of her tongue.

"I like him", she wrote in the book, "because he is probably a liar."

And when I protested, she said: "You have invented yourself, Mr Badgery, and that is why I like you. You are what they call a confidence man. You can be anything you want."

Of course I loved her for more than breasts and tongue. I had never stood so naked and felt so whole. She spoke like a ventriloquist speaks, hardly moving her splendid lips. It was a constant wonder that words emerged at all and that, when they did, they were so velvet soft, the tips of fingers encircling my ears. It was she who was the magician, and I the apprentice.

"We will invent ourselves," she said.

Geelong did not exist for us. We were oblivious to discomfort in our inconvenient nest. We lay, sat, squatted together in the valley of the roof while Molly lay, half crazy, on her bed below and Jack was entertained by his backers in gardens of Western District sheep.

"Will you teach me to fly?"

"My word, yes."

"Could we fly to Europe?"

"Yes."

"Have you ever made love to a man?"

"Good grief, no."

"I have made love to a woman," she said.

I was shocked, jealous, lustful and my voice was hoarse, half strangled with it all. "What woman?"

"You must teach her to fly too."

It is no wonder I did not take to Annette. I was jealous of her before I met her.

The hair around my penis was already damp and matted but when Phoebe extended her white hand the organ seemed to reach out towards the hand.

"Just like a flower", she wrote complacently in her notebook, "towards the sun."

32

Molly had not seen Phoebe climb on to the roof or me follow her. Yet she had a strong sense that something was wrong. This sense overpowered her and gave her what she called "her symptoms": a feeling of vertigo, like the panic she felt on high bridges, ledges, winding mountain roads. And once this feeling had appeared, like an old crow from a childhood nightmare, it stayed there and brought its own fear with it and she bitterly regretted the day she had so rashly thrown away the electric belt.

The electric belt had been purchased in 1890 from the Electro-Medical and Surgical Institute, a three-storey building in Sturt Street, Ballarat. Molly had been fourteen. She sat in the office of Dr Grigson with her two young brothers and her aunt, Mrs Ester. Mrs Ester's real name was Mrs Ester McGuinness but she was known as Mrs Ester to everyone in Ballarat and she was the licensee of the Crystal Palace Hotel.

Mrs Ester was in her late thirties. She had a slim figure, thrown slightly out of kilter by the unusual length of her body in relationship to her legs. She had a high head, a longish chin and quite extraordinary cherubic lips of which (together with her small, arched feet) she was secretly proud. Her eyes had a tendency to bulge and Dr Grigson, on first sighting her, had privately diagnosed a tendency towards an overactive thyroid gland.

Mrs Ester did not much like children but she had a strong sense of responsibility and these three children beside her were her brother's and it was her duty to safeguard them properly. The minute she knew of Molly's mother's madness she knew what had to be done and she used her newly installed telephone to call Grigson for an appointment, although she could, almost as easily, have walked across the street.

There were plenty of people in Ballarat who made fun of Grigson, men Mrs Ester thought should have known better. But Grigson occasionally took a small brandy in her establishment and she had felt honoured to listen to his talk of Pasteur and Lister and the Power of Electricity, the latter being a proven method for dealing not only with such things as constipation but also general debilitation and hereditary madness.

She was impressed by Dr Grigson's offices. They were a hymn to modernism and enlightenment. Models of the human body displayed the electric invigorators. Smartly dressed secretaries used telephones, Remington typewriters, and what she later discovered to be Graphaphone dictating machines. Mrs Ester, having seen the doctor (small, neat, precise, with a slightly Prussian appearance) driving his Daimler Benz down Lydiard Street, had expected modernism, but she had not been prepared for the scale of it.

Molly McGrath was Molly Rourke and she was fourteen. She sat wedged in between Mrs Ester and her brother Walter and saw none of what was around her. One of the secretaries offered her a sweet in a coloured wrapper. Molly shook her head and triggered off an echo of shaken heads in the two small boys. She had long copper hair that fell across her shoulders. Her young body reflected her diet of bread and potatoes. Her dimpled knees were properly hidden beneath her threadbare dress.

Walter had pooed his pants again. She had her nostrils full of the smell as she gazed down at the patterned carpet (roses and delphiniums entwined) and was unusually quiet: she thought everyone was looking at her because she was mad.

It was not like Molly to be so quiet. Her mother had called her "my song bird", not because she sang, but because she laughed. She was cheerful, inquisitive, energetic. She did not have to be told to get up in the mornings. She dressed her brothers, lit the fires, and often as not cooked breakfast. She did not complain, as Walter did, about her chilblains or pick at her warts. She could multiply 765 by 823 in her head, or any other number you liked to give her. No one had ever thought she was mad.

It had not even occurred to her that her mother was mad. Mrs Rourke was pale and wiry with dark sunken eyes and if she spent a lot of time being angry she also laughed, and Molly loved those rare sweet moments between storms when her mother was suddenly pink and warm and the troubles of the world were a long way away and then she would sing the soft Irish songs she had learned from her own mother who had carried them to Australia on a perilous voyage and arrived to find half Victoria afire and their ship had its sails set alight by the flying ashes from the bushfires.

It was Molly who had discovered her mother, early in the morning while her father was still at the bakery. She had hanged herself in the wash-house. There was one black shoe on her foot, not properly laced, and the other dropped on the broken stool she had climbed on. The smell of her opened bowels and the bulging, black eyes fused, in that dreadful moment, into one single thing, not a shape, not a colour, not a picture, but a feeling that burned itself into her. It was, at once, as hard as steel and as ghostly as a smell and it was this feeling that enveloped her still in Geelong nearly thirty years later while Phoebe and I were possums on the roof.

When Molly discovered her mother she did not scream. She dressed her brothers and took them next door to Mrs Henderson. She then walked two miles to the bakery where her father worked. She was made to wait for half an hour before she was permitted to see her father and then she watched while the big flour-dusted man roared and wept and rolled in the icy street while the cold winds blew through her thin dress. She listened to the loud cracks as he hit his head and thought that he must die too. She did not cry.

Mrs Ester was called in. She took the necessary steps. A funeral was organized and there was a wake at the Crystal Palace Hotel, in the private rooms, where Mrs Ester surprised everybody by singing "The Shan Van Vogt" and everybody became very Irish and very stirred and chose to remember that the dead woman's father had had his leg broken by policemen at the Eureka Stockade. They embraced Molly and made her eat slices of bread and butter.

After the wake Mrs Ester took the business of madness in hand. She had a small talk with Molly in the Ladies' Parlour of the Crystal Palace Hotel.

"I'm telling you cause you're the eldest – it wasn't just your mother."

Molly played with her dress which had been dyed black for mourning. The dye was not holding. It left black marks on her fingers. She knew that this conversation was not easy for Mrs Ester who had closed the hatch to the bar and shut the door to the passage. It was dark in the parlour and it smelt of floor polish and Brasso and stale stout and smoke.

Mrs Ester was not at ease with children. "Do you see what I'm getting at?"

"No, Mrs Ester."

"What I am saying is that it wasn't just your mother. Do you see what I'm getting at?"

But Molly did not.

Mrs Ester sighed. She fiddled with the big ring of keys she always wore hanging from her waist. "Your Granny Keogh was the same."

Same as what? Molly looked miserably at the painting of the green-eyed cat that hung crookedly beneath the shelf of china ornaments that were intended to make the parlour cosy.

"Do you see my point? For heaven's sake, girl, she drowned herself in Lake Wendouree."

This news was horrible but made no sense. It got mixed up with the smell of whisky on her aunt's breath, the darkness of the room, the green eyes of the cat and the reverence with which Patchy the barman, having blundered into the room, retreated from it, his larrikin's head oddly bowed.

95

Mrs Ester was at her best dealing with the brewery or asking a drinker to leave without offence. She was, by habit, a blunt woman, and this beating around the bush did not suit her at all. She did not intend to be unkind. She was now merely intent on not prolonging the agony.

"I am not having you hanging yourself," she said, "here or elsewhere, now or later."

And having, at last, delivered herself of her burden, she sat with her hands folded on her lap and her head on one side.

"Oh," Molly said, "I promise you. I promise, Mrs Ester, I never would."

"It is not a thing you can promise, poor child," said Mrs Ester, suddenly hugging her fiercely, and crushing the child's nose into a brooch. "It will come up on you. One minute you will be singing and happy and the next. . . . I will take you to Grigson," she said.

Molly had wailed. She had howled, sentenced in the Ladies' Parlour, and felt the black dye of her dress insinuate itself into the pores of her skin.

Dr Grigson, as it turned out, was strange, but not unpleasant. The nicest thing about him was his hands which were soft and dry like talcum powder. When he touched her face or held her hand it had a lovely ministering quality which the girl found comforting. Everything about Dr Grigson was very neat and very clean. Molly had never smelt such a clean smell, on a man or a woman. He had small, stiff movements and when he turned his head he turned his shoulders as well, as if his head and body were all of a piece and had no independence at all.

"I see no reason", he said, "why you should end the same way as your mother and grandmother. Modern Science", said the promoter of Lister and Pasteur, "can do much for your condition."

"She doesn't understand," said Mrs Ester, who was accompanying each of the children on their interviews.

"Do you understand?" Dr Grigson asked her.

She nodded her head.

"Tell me, my child."

She did not want to say it. She did not have to repeat, with words, the fallen chair, the shoe still on the foot, the smell.

"I will go mad," she said in a very small voice, "and get up on a chair, and jump off."

"You will do no such thing," said Dr Grigson, "if I can help it."

She was relieved when he took her hand back. He asked her

many questions. Did she see things falling? Did she hear voices? Was she prone to laughter in an excessive degree? ("Yes," said Mrs Ester.) Did she touch herself between the legs? Did she wake with palpitations?

He was like a nice nun, not the sort that hit your knuckles with a ruler and talked of sin and hellfire, but the other sort. He had gentle Jesus eyes.

"Amazing," Dr Grigson said turning in his chair to look through the window at the big white statue in the middle of Sturt Street. "The child", he swung back to face Mrs Ester, "*must* have an electric invigorator. With it she will have a long and happy life."

Molly multiplied 899 by 32 in her head. A small, light, happy calculation. It meant nothing. She multiplied in relief. A flood of numerals marched across her mind and swept away her misery. 7,676 by 296, she thought, marching down the stairs behind her brothers. The answer seemed almost as long as life itself.

The day that Molly strapped on the apparatus around her waist, hid the battery in the folds of her dress, and stood before the doctor smiling, was the happiest day she could remember of her childhood, better, by far, than her first communion or the birthday picnic out at Creswick. She walked the wintry streets of Ballarat as one invincible. She went into St Mary's on the hill and prayed for an hour to the Blessed Virgin. She did some multiplications for God as well, presenting him, finally, with 5,895,323.

33

Ballarat stretched low and wide, from Battery Hill to the edges of the west. It was made from wood. Weatherboards and wide verandas lined wide streets that baked into claypans in summer, churned into mud in winter. They had planted oaks and bluegums in Sturt Street. They stocked Lake Wendouree with fish. They began to talk of Ballarat with civic pride, but it was Mrs Ester who showed real confidence in the future. She built the Crystal Palace Hotel from brick.

It stood high and solid, three storeys facing a Sturt Street that looked faint-hearted and pessimistic in comparison, as if the gold that had made the city rich might suddenly go away.

Mrs Ester did not worry about gold. The quartz crushers were already more important. The foundries were there. H. V. McKay was manufacturing harvesters which were sold all round the country. She had no need of the custom of miners who drank themselves into oblivion down in the shanties of the east and frittered away their fortunes on chilblained prostitutes. It is true she had a public bar that spilled its dubious contents on to Sturt Street on summer evenings: and there were miners amongst the shearers, fettlers, foundry men, farm labourers, clerks and tricksters and passing thieves, but she had not built her business on anything so flimsy.

The Duke of Kent stayed at the Crystal Palace Hotel in 1873 – that was the sort of hotel it was.

Molly had visited the Crystal Palace Hotel before her mother's death made it her permanent residence. They had come once for Christmas dinner and once for a funeral, but they had come with tingling skin scrubbed hard by a mother who felt out of place amongst such finery. They had come with new shoelaces, their eyes downcast, told not to stare at the lady with the cherub's lips and bulging eyes.

But now she could enter the Crystal Palace Hotel through the grand front entrance. She did not quite skip up the steps. She certainly did not laugh or giggle. But she could, whilst walking briskly, carrying the morning's newspapers, smiling sweetly at the guests, feel that she was a part of the complicated mechanism of this important place.

Her father had taken a room in a boarding house close to the bakery. Sean had been sent up to Creswick to the Rourkes' and Walter went to Ballarat South with the Kellys who wrote complaints about his bed-wetting. He had also been sent home from school with his underpants wrapped up in newspaper after soiling his pants in arithmetic class. And Molly had begun work as a housemaid for Mrs Ester. She was paid no money, but she was fed, given shelter, and she had her electric invigorator.

She worked hard and lost her fat. She rose at five and lit the fires. She toiled along the carpeted passages upstairs and the highly polished wooden ones downstairs. She could clean a room and leave it so that one would imagine it never slept in. She could clean a mirror so a guest might feel that no face had ever been reflected in it before. She collected squeezed lemons from the kitchen every Tuesday and went from brass doorknob to brass doorknob, rubbing them hard until the lemons fell to pieces in her hands and the brass gave up its grime to the sour sticky juice. She liked the hotel. She liked the quiet clink and rustle of breakfast in the dining room, the rumble of kegs being rolled down to the cellar, the smell of brewery horses, the songs in the saloon bar late at night, and the sound of Mrs Ester's high-heeled shoes and rattling key as she passed in the corridor on her way to bed.

She ate her meals with Mrs Ester in the dining room where there was always food in plenty – meat every day, even Fridays – and almost nobody, it seemed, could eat what they were given and the black-uniformed waitresses were always carrying back plates that had not been scraped clean. The hens in the hotel yard ate better food than Molly had been used to.

She had her friends: an old yardman who told her stories and showed her his odd socks sticking up above his boots and Patchy the barman who gave her pennies when he was drunk, and even Mrs Ester, on three occasions, read her stories from a book about India which, although she did not quite understand them, were appreciated all the same. However, it was not until Jennifer Grillet arrived that she had someone of her own age to talk to. Jennifer was a distant relation of Mrs Ester's. She had red hair that sat on either side of her head like a spaniel's ears and she was very thin. Jennifer arrived with a proper suitcase just after Molly's sixteenth birthday and when the door was shut in their small room above the stables, Molly began to talk.

"My," said Jennifer Grillet, "you are a chatterbox," but she listened just the same and showed Molly the birthmark on her shoulder.

Their friendship was not to last long. Before a month was out Jennifer had begged Mrs Ester for a room of her own because Molly kept her awake all night talking, but by then the real damage had been done and Molly had told her everything, how Walter pooed his pants, her father banged his head, her mother hanged herself. She had made no secret of her electric belt. She explained its purpose. She let Jennifer try it on and thought she was secretly envious, not only of the exotic apparatus but of Molly's figure which had become, by that sixteenth birthday, decidedly womanly.

"A real hourglass," she told herself proudly, standing before the mirror in petticoats and electric belt.

There were others who thought so too, and Mrs Ester was not slow in realizing the girl's potential behind the bar.

The bar Mrs Ester had in mind was not the public bar where Patchy ruled, sometimes ruthlessly. The bar she had in mind was called the "Commercial Room". It was not downstairs, it was upstairs. There were no tiled walls in the Commercial Room. You

99

did not clean it as Patchy cleaned the public bar, with a hose and water. It had a woollen carpet on the floor and several leather chairs and low tables.

The Commercial Room was a meeting place for mutton-chopped merchants and frock-coated doctors, chalky-skinned solicitors and the moustached graduates of the School of Mines. Visiting gentlemen and their crinolined ladies could sit in comfort, drink champagne if they wished, and only occasionally be reminded of the realities of Ballarat when a fight erupted on the footpath below or fire swept through the wooden cottages on Battery Hill, and even these events could be comfortably observed from a balcony above the street.

It was quite clearly understood by everyone concerned, in particular by Molly and Mrs Ester, that this bar would, sooner or later, furnish an excellent husband. Certainly they did not hope for a dentist or a barrister, but a successful farmer or a stock and station agent would not be out of the question, provided Molly abandoned her habit of running along corridors and, when walking, shortened her stride, and swung her arms a little less enthusiastically. In conversation she should think more carefully about what she intended to say and when she said it, say it slowly, not breathlessly.

With these instructions firmly in her mind Molly stood stiffly behind the bar while Mrs Ester conducted her final examination.

"Two Scotch whiskies, one pink gin, one rum and cloves," said Mrs Ester.

"Four and sixpence," said Molly.

"One ladies' beer, two pints Ballarat Bitter, one *crème de menthe*."

"Six and sixpence ha'penny," said Molly.

"Do you have a decent burgundy, dear lady?" said deep-voiced Mrs Ester.

"Yes, sir, Chambertin and Côte du Rhone."

"And what is the price?"

"The Côte du Rhone is ten shillings and the Chambertin twelve and sixpence ha'penny."

"Very good."

"What is three hundred and five multiplied by eight-six, Mrs Ester?"

"Heaven knows," said Mrs Ester.

"Twenty thousand, six hundred and fifty-three," said Molly.

"Oh Mrs Ester, I'm so excited."

When Mrs Ester had removed the pencil from behind her ear and checked this calculation she took Molly to her office where she examined her in arithmetic. She discovered that the girl could add up columns of figures in her head. She did not even move her lips.

"Now, my girl," Mrs Ester said, "you listen to me. You will not throw yourself at the first man who comes along."

"No, Mrs Ester."

"You are a decided commercial asset, you mark my words."

"Yes, Mrs Ester."

"You are only sixteen. There is no need to rush off and marry in a hurry."

"No, Mrs Ester."

"Would you like to learn about the business, how to pay the staff and the brewery and add up figures? I will pay you a pound a week."

"Thank you, Mrs Ester."

"You will not spend the pound, Molly. (Do *not* fidget.) You will put it in the bank every week as long as you work for me, and when you get married you will not tell your husband about it, is that clear?"

"Yes, Mrs Ester."

"Do you swear?"

"I cross my heart, Mrs Ester."

"How much is a glass of best stout?"

"Three pence."

"You are a good girl, Molly," said Mrs Ester taking the girl's two hands in hers in a rare, grabbing, embarrassed gesture of affection. "You will be a credit to the Crystal Palace Hotel."

And, had it not been for Henry Lightfoot, she would have been right.

34

Walter and Sean had not been given electric belts, and they were not happy. It was only Molly who was happy and she knew she had no right to it. No one could say that she was not a good daughter or a loving sister. Indeed she was, when she could be, a perfect Little Mother. When the remains of the family assembled on Sundays she brought a needle and thread for Walter's trousers, a newly knitted balaclava for Sean, wool and darning needles for her father's socks.

Walter was dark and silent and hit at the trunks of trees with stick or boot and Sean clung to her side while she darned their sleeping father's socks. Beside the weed-choked waters of Lake Wendouree their mother's death lay over them. Sean tugged insistently at her skirt. The men in their rowing sculls could not move freely through the water.

She hid the pleasures of the Commercial Room from her family. She did not tell them about Henry Lightfoot. She did not confess her hopes for the Hospital Auxiliary Ball. She fled these Sunday afternoons earlier than she should have, and was punished by guilty dreams because of it.

Henry Lightfoot had a property at Bunningyong and did not come to Ballarat as often as he would have liked, but when he did come he always wore nice suits, and although he was a big man his body did not fight against the constrictions of his suit and his neck did not bulge against his Oxford collar.

"Do you like to dance, Miss Rourke?" he had asked her. He had a warm sweet smell, like straw.

"Oh, yes, Mr Lightfoot," she said.

He had fair hair and dark black eyebrows. Apart from a slightly beakish nose he was decidedly handsome. He was going to ask her to the ball but she saw him frown, lose courage, and order a pint of bitter instead. She liked him better for his loss of courage.

Tonight, she knew, he would come again, because there had been sales in Ballarat and Henry Lightfoot had sold fifty fattened beasts for a record price. The little Scot from Elders Smith had already given her the details of the sale. He said it was a great day for Henry Lightfoot.

Her heart was beating too fast. It fought to free itself from the magnetic restrictions of her belt. It wanted to go wild, on its own loud boastful erratic dance.

Henry Lightfoot entered the Commercial Room. He was aptly named. He walked on the balls of his feet, and she saw that he was already a little drunk. It was not like him to be drunk, but she was pleased he was drunk. She hoped he was drunk enough to ask her to the ball.

He smiled at her; he did not come to the bar immediately but joined the ruddy pipe-smoking Scot from Elders and the round-shouldered man from the *Courier Mail*. His mind did not appear to be on the conversation he was having. He rocked back and forwards on his shining black shoes which showed only the faintest smear of sale-yard mud.

When he came, at last, to the bar, he was carrying his companions' empty glasses. He was smiling, but she was too excited to look closely at his smile.

She blushed.

Had she not been so intent on trying to stop the blush she might have looked more closely at his face and she might have detected a malice in the smile which the men who had dealings with Henry Lightfoot knew to be part of his character. He was both handsome and charming, but he was also a bully with a keen nose for weakness.

He stood at the bar, jingling the loose change in his pocket, swaying gently. His smile was moist, his handsome mouth a little slack.

Molly's red hair was piled handsomely high, and although it accentuated a tendency towards jowliness, it also showed the soft white skin of her neck. There was nothing to hide her blush.

"You've been keeping a secret from me, Miss Rourke," said Henry Lightfoot.

"No," she said, "I promise you," but blushed even deeper, because she had confessed her hopes about the ball to Jenny Grillet.

"It's not a secret," Henry Lightfoot said. "It is too wonderful", he teased, "to be a secret. It is too extraordinary. No, no, dear Molly Rourke, 'tis no secret any more."

He had never called her Molly before. The blush spread down her neck until it seemed it would take possession of her shoulders.

"Everybody," he said, "all Ballarat knows."

"Oh," she dared look up. She held him with her bright green eyes. "And do they now, Mr Lightfoot?"

"Indeed, Miss Rourke. Indeed they do."

"And what secret is this?"

"They say", he whispered, "you wear a belt to stop you going mad."

She did not leave the bar. She stayed working. She gave correct change. She counted the money in the till at closing time. She helped Patchy wash the glasses in the public bar.

35

I had this in common with Molly: we had both pretended our fathers dead, although for different reasons. And while Jack had heard of Mrs Ester, he knew nothing of her father or Walter or Sean. He knew nothing of the electric belt, Dr Grigson, or that Molly had risked her mortal soul by marrying him in a Protestant church.

And although there were many times when she came, teetering, giddy, her hand in his, to the very brink of confessing her faith, she could not. He made it impossible. He had no time for Catholics. This is not to say that he would not, journeying down to Colac to visit his backers, make a detour to Koroit, that Catholic town, drink in the pub and be a good fellow amidst Murphys and Keoghs and Hanrahans, but that he carried a schoolboy's prejudices with him and was always only a hairbreadth away from those sing-song insults that Protestant children call out to the Catholics on the other side of dusty streets: "Catholic dogs sitting on logs, eating maggots out of frogs." He was for Australia and the Empire, had voted Yes to conscription and regarded Archbishop Mannix as nothing less than a traitor.

And in Cocky Abbot, that dimple-chinned, ruddy-faced giant, he found a kindred spirit. They could relax together, in their certainties. They were both big strong men in their fifties, men who had begun life poor and ended up rich. They trusted each other's money. They trusted each other's size and their hands, when shaking, fitted together like two halves of the one puzzle. They were, as the farmer put it, practical.

They sat together on the veranda of the Abbots' homestead late in the afternoon and rolled up their sleeves in defiance of the chill in the evening air. Had you seen them, sitting on their rattan chairs, you would have shared their conceit, that they were two of a kind, and you would be wrong. For the farmer was a harder, tougher man, ruthless in a bargain and with a head for figures not suggested by his slow countryman's drawl.

"This aviator bloke," Cocky Abbot asked, kicking off his boots in a manner Jack approved of, "is he practical?"

The autumn rain had turned the landscape green but at six in the evening it was laid over with a rich golden mist; the farmer's sheep looked like splendid creatures, not the daggy-bummed animals Jack McGrath loathed.

"Is he practical?" mused Jack. "I'd say so, yes, my word I would."

"I'd say there was a definite quid to be made in this business."

"That's his point."

"But my question to you, Jacko, is this: why would we need to go to the expense of building a factory? Now look at your costs. Three hundred pounds for the land. Say another three hundred pounds to put up some sort of shed. Then you've got your labour. You need specialists, I take it, skilled men, mechanics, fitters and turners and so on. Before you've got a penny coming in you're probably up for, call it two thousand pounds."

"This is right, Harold."

"And who's to say you have the best aeroplane? We won't know until it's built and flown."

"That's true," said Jack, but looked miserable, passing his hand over his folded face. "But everything's a risk. Life is a risk."

"Life is a risk, you're right, man. But we've both got where we are by not taking more than we need. Now what does your aviator say to importing a craft?"

"I never asked him, but his point is that we have an Australian plane."

"For Heaven's sake, we're all in the Empire together. I meant a British plane. One we know will fly. Do you follow me? It's a question of risk versus return, and there's no doubt the poms are more experienced than we are. My suggestion to you is: why wouldn't we set up an agency for the best craft available?"

"Talk to Badgery. Talk to him. Listen to him."

"I'll listen to him," said Cocky Abbot. "I'd like to meet him anyway. I believe I knew his father. There was a Badgery here in '96. Tried to sell us a cannon."

"That's the man all right, that's him."

"An interesting man," said Cocky Abbot. "I often think we made a great mistake not listening to him."

36

The electric belt that had saved Molly now damned her. It forced her to flee Ballarat with cheeks still burning and eyes downcast before her fellow coach passengers.

Molly had laboured late into the panicked night, filling five pages with her careful copperplate, but she could not bring herself to be precise about her shame which was, to spell it out, that all of Ballarat was peeking, smirking, at what lay underneath her skirts. Her father went over and over his daughter's letter, searching with his blunt broken fingernail for a place where he might get a purchase. The pages, however, would give up no secrets and remained as mysterious and inviolate as marble eggs.

Melbourne frightened Molly. It was too noisy, too grand. She sought a country position. Had she waited – she had money enough – she might have found a position in a good Catholic hotel. But she could not wait. She must have it settled. In all of the state of Victoria, it seemed, there was only one position, that of barmaid at the Grand Hotel in Point's Point. Sensing, correctly, that her faith would go against her, she told the employment agency that she was not a Catholic.

It was only after she arrived in Point's Point that she understood what a dreadful thing she had done, only after she met the fiercely Protestant Mrs Pearson did she realize that she would never, as long as she stayed in the town, be able to attend Mass and that, even worse, she would be expected to attend services with the Presbyterians.

She resolved, on that first day, that she would tell the Pearsons the truth when they realized how invaluable she was. And certainly, with Mr Pearson half crippled with a stroke and Mrs Pearson too scatterbrained to keep the business together, there was far more to do than simple barmaiding, although it was this skill that gained her the love of the town or, at least, the Protestant half of it. She was, as Mrs Ester had clearly seen, a commercial asset. She ran the dining room, kept the accounts, cleaned six bedrooms, served behind the bar. She was not yet eighteen years old.

If she softened her natural vowels a fraction in keeping with her role as a Protestant lady, she did not put on dog or act in a snobbish manner. If she laughed too much or talked too much or swung her arms or ran when she should have walked, it only seemed to make her more attractive. Her cheeks burned. Her eyes, even in that dismal Presbyterian service, were feverish with secrets she could not share.

The town approved of her courtship with Jack McGrath who may not have been the town's only teetotaller but was certainly the richest and the best-liked one. As everyone said, he had not a nasty bone in his body. Molly yearned to lay all her twisted secrets on him. Yet when, behind the small wooden pavilion on the river flat, a building known locally as the "Football Stadium", Jack McGrath attempted a bit more with his hands than she had expected, there was a great deal more than maidenly modesty to make her leap back from her beloved, her face colouring, her voice shaking.

Molly did not intend that the belt should ruin her chances of marriage. It would have to be done away with; yet it could not be done without. She still, in spite of the belt's magnetic forces, had palpitations of the heart. She did not associate these upsets with the moments when her mind strayed into that minefield, her betrayal of the one true church. Rather, it seemed to her, it was a question of heights. Sometimes, on a high stool in the hotel larder, reaching for a ham or a string of onions, she was overcome with something that was not quite vertigo. It was as if two seconds had been snipped from her life, and the remainder, the past and the future, roughly pinned together. She felt a tiny explosion, a little jump, followed by a wild galloping of the heart. She did not dare think of what would become of her without the belt and yet, if she was to marry this big gentle man, she knew it would have to go. Who, after all, wants to marry a mad woman?

So, on a Tuesday morning in November, just one day before her wedding in a Protestant church, Molly Rourke went out walking in the hour before the sun had entered the valley and when the dew lay thick on the grass and fell from trees on to the tin roof of the Grand Hotel. She walked along one side of the single street. She walked past the last of the new macadam where Reilly's cow stared mournfully at the bracken and blackberries in its neglected paddock and then, just past Crooked Creek, took an old footpath said to have been a Chinese millrace in the 1850s. The path, so she had been told, followed the river to the big swimming hole and the falls beyond.

She had never been along the path before and she did not like it now. She did not like the blackberries that grew along it, the prickly acacias that bent, heavy with dew, across it. She did not like the small dry scurrying sounds amongst the untidy wet floor of the bush. She picked up her skirts and held them tightly to her. She stopped, continually, trying to hear the sounds her beating heart were overpowering.

Black cockatoos filled the air above her and their harsh screeching seemed only to echo the hostile nature of the bush. If she had seen the brilliant scarlet on their tails she would not have thought it beautiful, but rather a confirmation of danger, like the red spot on a black spider.

The path rose higher above the river, along across a rock face. At one place there had been a fall. There was a small gap in the track, easily cleared by children, but when Molly Rourke jumped it was as if the fires of Hell, not a tangle of blackberries, lay below her skirts.

She did not like being so high above the river, but she hurried on (not swinging her arms) until she found herself above the swimming hole; the falls spilled off one end like water from an overfull bowl. People had told her stories of things being swept off the falls and how they were never seen again. It was dangerous, they said. Once a child had been swept away and not recovered.

The water moved blackly over grey rocks. She did not wish to descend, as the children did easily, the rock steps that led to the water's edge.

She stood on the path above, twisting her hands, and young Dave McCorkell, squatting a little further up the hill with two dew-wet rabbits in his hand, thought she looked like a princess in a fairy story. Her long grey dress had a sheen like the underside of gumleaves but it did not camouflage her form or even, with the skirt clutched to her, hide her tiny feet.

He thought he heard her praying, but whatever the words she spoke he never heard them, or if he did hear them they were driven from his mind by the force of his feelings as he watched her hitch, first her skirt, then her petticoats, and remove, in a flurry so confusing he could not be sure of what he had seen, a garment of some type.

It was a belt with some weight attached to it which, as he watched, she swung round and round. She was going to throw it out across the top of the falls, but she was not expert and the thing, whatever it was, flew out and caught itself on the lower branches of a flowering ti-tree which grew out, at an acute angle, from the bank on which she stood.

He heard her cry "Oh no", a lonely desperate cry. He put down the rabbits thinking he would help her. But then he knew that he should not have been watching her reveal herself so completely to him, and he picked the rabbits up again.

David McCorkell was eight years old when all this took place. When he was a soldier in Cairo in 1917 he was known as the "Rabbit", but it was not because he had once held two of them in his hands and watched a lady perform a strange ritual; it was because he had a small twitching nose and a timid manner.

He squatted on his haunches and watched fearfully, his small grey eyes riveted on Molly Rourke.

He felt sorry for the lady trying to climb the tree. He felt sorry when he heard her make small whimpering noises, was glad when she, at last, caught the belt in her hand, and felt for her when she slipped sideways and muddied her dress on the path.

When she swung the belt again he crossed his fingers for her and screwed up his face in sympathy when it caught, in mid-air, on a branch of a big old she-oak that hung above the falls.

The pair of them, Dave and Molly in their separate positions, watched Dr Grigson's electric belt suspended twenty feet above the Sandy River. Molly, recognizing the calamity she had brought upon herself, convinced that the belt hung there as shameful advertisement for her madness which all the world could read, resolved that day that she and her husband would leave Point's Point before the swimming season started.

When she walked back along the track she did not have time for giddiness. She was in a panic that left no room for jolts and explosions. She entered the town wet, torn and muddy, cutting across the back of O'Briens Paddocks where the tall bracken soaked her dress, slipped up beside the blacksmith's shed, and left a large lump of mud on the back veranda (which she would later blame Archie Hearn for and abuse him with unusual heat). She made such a fuss about the little lump of mud and her outburst was so unlike her that Archie concluded, quite rightly, that Miss Rourke had the marriage jitters.

At about the time Molly arrived, torn and panting, in her room, young Dave McCorkell was suspended twenty feet above the Sandy River retrieving Dr Grigson's Electric Invigorator.

He carried his treasure back to where his rabbits lay in a patch of new sunshine. He could not imagine what this treasure was for, but thinking about the cloudy, unnameable, unknowable possibilities made his penis become stiff. He scratched his bare legs and resolved to keep it a secret.

Yet a week after Molly Rourke's Protestant wedding to Jack McGrath everyone in Point's Point knew the whole story about Molly Rourke: that she had worn, for all her time amongst them, an electrically operated chastity belt.

But by then Molly and Jack were on their way to Geelong, Jack marvelling at the way he had managed to make the decision so quickly whilst Molly sat rigid in the train seat: her future madness hung before her, dangling by a rope in her mind's eye.

37

Molly stayed in bed while the voices assailed her.

She had always liked flowers. There had been no flowers in her youth, just a backyard with puddles of stale water unnoticed by sunshine. She tried to think of flowers now, to enjoy what little the view from her bedroom afforded in March. She loved the tender, brilliant complications of flowers, like the folds of ball dresses. She cared more for her flowers than the Hispano Suiza or the house or the society of important people who always left her feeling as if she had been unworthy of their company. But flowers had always made her feel better and she looked at them and drew from them that nectar that Annette Davidson might hope to draw from art.

She had planned her garden in Geelong so that there was always something to see from her bedroom window.

But today was not a good day. The canna lilies, rich red and pretty pink, occupied the midground of her view, and the creamy chrysanthemums the foreground. Yet there was no joy to be had here, and it was not because there was a fine drizzle of rain falling, or because the winds of early winter had begun to whip across Corio Bay making the water an unpleasant green-grey.

Petals loosened themselves and fell and whilst, on a happier day, this early destruction of a flower would have caused her anxiety, today there were other things preying on her mind.

There were voices in the house, and no one else in it.

She had farewelled her daughter to the library. She had seen Herbert Badgery walk away down the esplanade. It was Bridget's day off. She was all by herself and she had, twice, put on her dressing gown and walked through every room of the house and around the wide veranda. There was no one in the house but there were voices. It was not the wireless, which she had disconnected from the wall, nor His Master's Voice.

She retired to bed with voices in her ears. She was having tiny explosions in her head. She detected malice in the voices. Her bed was too far off the floor and made her giddy. She lay in the bed, pale and sweating, while her green eyes viewed the garden from a bed of puffy flesh.

It was then, as one particularly vicious gust of wind shook the branches of the leafless peach tree and bent the fleshy green stalks of the canna lilies until their faces were pressed into the ground, that the naked figure of her daughter sailed slowly through the air above her eyes. She did not seem to merely fall, but to move with dream-like slowness, transcribing an arc while the coppery triangle of her pubic hair, until now protected from her mother's gaze, was exposed quite clearly to its anxious audience.

The figure landed with a thud on the grass beyond the canna lilies.

It said: "Hoof."

Molly McGrath was beset with hot prickling skin and a thundering heart which she tried to still with the pressure of her hand. She saw her daughter stand, and saw her arm hang like a broken wing.

Molly McGrath whimpered and curled her fifty-year old body into a shaking ball beneath the sheets.

When Jack McGrath arrived home, triumphant from his negotiations in Colac, he had great difficulty in persuading his wife to leave her bed. The slightly fixed smile she brought to the table made him feel very uneasy indeed.

38

I find myself, with Phoebe in mid-air, wondering about Mrs Kentwell's nipples, and whether they were ever sucked by man or child, and by God one is tempted to imagine her little black-suited cricket of a brother with his soft child's lips sucking at them, snorting and moaning, and Mrs Kentwell's teeth in a glass on the dresser, but I can't stretch to it, and will content myself with more or less established facts.

Jonathon Oakes, Mrs Kentwell's brother, stole letters.

He was twice arrested, but never charged. He followed the

postman like a nervous dog, always at a distance, hiding in the gateways, behind hedges, dipping into unknown letterboxes in hope of news. He also had two post office boxes of his own, to which certain private correspondences were addressed.

It is easy enough to understand why he got himself into this state, because Mrs Kentwell ruled the house in Western Avenue with an ivory-handled paper knife on which was engraved the image of an elephant-headed god from India.

On the day in question, Jonathon Oakes was doing his rounds and Mrs Kentwell was taking tea alone in the drawing room. She poured with a steady hand and placed the cup and saucer to her left. She then slit open each of the morning's letters with her paper knife. She removed the stamps and placed them in a neat pile and then removed the contents of each envelope. Those from her friends in England she placed on the top, those from Assam (there were two) were placed underneath. The two local letters were for her brother but she would, as usual, read them before he did (which would not be until she had dealt with matters in Assam and England). He was far too timid a fellow to protest at this high-handedness, but not such a dull one that he would not take his own compensation.

As Alice Kentwell concentrated on parish problems in a village in Kent, her brother was puffing up the hill from his morning's work, anxious to get home before he was soaked by rain. Phoebe, meanwhile, was flying from the roof.

Mrs Kentwell looked up just in time to witness Phoebe's fall. She stood, immediately, substituted paper knife for umbrella and strode out on to the veranda in the style of a woman about to lay low a marauding snake. She tapped the metal point of the umbrella up and down on the wooden floor. She hissed. The naked figure of Phoebe McGrath ran with its rag of a broken arm, while the umbrella played an angry tattoo.

Mrs Kentwell was not astonished. She was beyond astonishment. Western Avenue, she decided, must stand up and fight if it was to remain anything at all.

She stood on the veranda, a tall straight figure in severe black which had begun as mourning for a dead husband and now seemed to represent a different mourning altogether. Mrs Kentwell mourned the lost standards of English civilization which wilted and died in this society of Irish peasants and jumped-up cockneys.

She was still on the veranda, a black sentry with a black

umbrella, when yours truly, Herbert Badgery, the ruffian aviator, walked across the roof of the McGrath house and climbed down a fig tree, arranged clothes, and strode out of sight around the north side of the house which had once been known as "Wirralee".

She tapped the umbrella once, a full stop to everything, and returned to her letters whose fine calligraphy danced before her eyes, unravelling before the pull of her anger.

39

When Phoebe fell from the slippery roof she knew, before she hit the ground, that her life was ruined. As the real world rushed up to meet her, she knew she was not brave enough to be what she would like to be. In mid-air, naked, she wished for death, her chest crushed, her heart pierced, her legs snapped like quail bones. Her feelings were not those of a radical, Bohemian, free-lover, but a seventeen-year-old girl in Geelong who faces social ruin.

When her arm cracked she knew it broken. She leapt to her feet. The light was shining into her mother's window the wrong way, and she could not see Molly, only the reflection of her own nakedness. She was winded.

She heard Mrs Kentwell's umbrella tattoo. They locked eyes a second: the naked girl and the black soldier with the umbrella rifle. She moaned as she ran across the veranda in full sight of two Dodges which were racing fast along Western Avenue. One blew its horn.

Damn them, damn them, damn them all.

Yet before she had closed her bedroom door behind her, a change had come over my beloved who was no longer wishing for death but already making plans for her survival.

It is no struggle to imagine the desperate alibis that came to her – half-formed jelly-like things with no proper legs or faces, desperate creatures that fell to powder when inspected, invisible cloaks with holes in them. They swarmed through the sea of pain as she awaited her mother's inevitable arrival. The arm was useless. She dressed none the less. She bit into her lip to stop the hurt. She had mud on her bottom. She managed to get herself inside a dress, and in all this desperation she was careful to choose a yellow dress that was very similar to the one she had abandoned on the roof.

Inept stories came to her, e.g. she had gone on to the roof to fix a tile; she had taken off her dress to avoid ruining it in the rain; worn no underwear for similar reason.

No, damn it.

When the knock on the door came she was still not ready.

"Come in," she said brightly.

She prepared her face for her mother, opened the door with her good arm, and found not Molly, but me, my face livid with fear, my hands trembling.

"Go away," she hissed, "for God's sake."

I was so pleased to see her in one piece, alive, felt such relief that I was faint and wanted to sit down. I opened my mouth and croaked relief.

"Your buttons are undone. Go away." She pushed at me. She was more than my equal. She was definitely my superior, for she had, at last, a plan, flimsy, fragile, but one she would make work by the sheer force of her green-eyed will. "I am not in the house," she whispered. "Take them to sit in the parlour at lunchtime and *watch* the esplanade."

"Are you all right?"

"Yes, yes, but did you hear me? Then please, I beg you, do what I say."

She closed the door and locked it. I did up my buttons as Jack skidded the Hispano Suiza to a halt and left a new set of skid marks on the bright green lawn.

40

The morning's drizzle had turned into heavy rain and the wagon driver with his high load of turnips huddled inside the black oilskin while his fox terrier ran along beneath.

The rain bit into her, sweeping across a bay so hateful that anyone could see the town was right to turn its back on it.

"So much the better," she thought, "so much the better for me to run in this, and slip." But when she came around the corner of Martha Street where she had waited for her wet-glassed wrist-watch to bring its hands to one o'clock, the pain was so intense that she almost fainted. She was soaked through and shivering. She stopped and huddled against one of the esplanade's few trees.

At the other end of the avenue a small grey figure with an umbrella battled into the wind.

It was one minute past one. She prayed her audience were assembled in the parlour, that some talk about aeroplanes would not distract them from her fall.

Jonathon Oakes, the Kentwells' brother, beat into the wind with his illicit letters bulging fat inside the pocket of his waistcoat. He did not lift his umbrella. He was nearly home. He would run the bath and read his letters in delicious privacy.

Phoebe seized this chance that fate had thrown up. She waited for the umbrella to come a little closer to her parents' house before she began to run.

Every step jolted her. She ran with a pitiful "oh, oh, oh" which she said to herself for comfort, a soft cotton-wool bandage of sound around the pain.

Jonathon Oakes had little warning (just an "oh, oh, oh") before Phoebe McGrath collided with him and screamed with pain.

For a second he believed he had speared the girl with his umbrella.

41

Molly McGrath remained in the parlour while the men carried in her wounded daughter. People afterwards remarked to themselves on the curious stillness of the mother who would normally have darted about the room in hysterical activity, billing, cooing, ooohing, and making far too much noise and flutter for most people's taste.

She remained seated by the electric fire with the flex wound round her ankle (a tangle so odd that no one dared point it out to her) and smiled a fixed smile at Mr Oakes who had a small brandy to settle himself down.

She smiled the same smile at the doctor who arrived at short notice with his luncheon gravy still wet on his tie.

She smiled the same fixed smile at the pale, brave-chinned daughter who, lying in state on rugs and pillows in the parlour, shuddered a little before such icy radiance, imagining that her mother had seen through her deception.

She need not have worried. It was the sort of smile you save for the Devil, an attempt at sarcasm in the face of provocative coincidence.

115

42

It was not even Easter and winter had come to Ryrie Street. The owners of T Models put up their side curtains. The vendors in Anderson's Fruit and Produce Markets held cauliflowers in large red hands and the bottle-oh with the cleft tongue rode his wagon wrapped tight in an old grey blanket and had his bottle-oh cries blown westwards before the icy gusts of wind. The big houses on the coast at Ocean Grove and Barwon Heads had been closed down. The jazz bands had returned to Melbourne and the summer's flappers were safely subdued (on weekdays at least) inside the heavy uniforms of The Hermitage, Morongo, Merton Hall and MLC.

I dressed in my suit and walked along Ryrie Street like a gentleman, picking out the puddles with the point of my Shaftesbury Patented Umbrella. A connoisseur of walks might have detected that although my walk was indeed the walk of a gentleman, it also exhibited subtle but obvious signs of depression. What had changed in the walk was not easy to detect, may have been nothing more than a slight scrape of the sole on every third stride, a refusal to pick up the feet properly, a tendency to stumble on uneven paving.

I was in love, and although I had used the term a hundred times before (would have said that I was in love with Mrs O'Hagen had you asked) had, in short, misunderstood, misused, and abused the term, confused it with lust or friendship or the simple pleasures of a warm breast, or a wild whooping fuck on a river bank, I had not known what I was talking about.

For two weeks I had groaned in my sleep and tossed and turned. I was denied the roof. I was denied the merest civility as my plaster-armed beloved affected normality.

Did she blame me for her fall? Did she hate me for jeopardizing her life? I did not know, could get no answer, merely watch her as she took up occupations she had previously rejected. She had taken to socializing with the sons of squatters once again. She had gone, with high hemlines, to "At Homes" and balls, and left me jealous, half mad, to cluck with her parents who were concerned she might be mixing with a fast crowd. I shared their concern. I made it worse. I rubbed at it until it was red and blistered. I wished them to order her to cease, not just the squatters but also the history lessons. I knew what those history lessons were about. But Jack was indulgent, and Molly distracted, and I could get no commitment from them to do anything.

I tried to corner Phoebe in hall or music room, but I could get no reassurance. She hissed caution and passion all at once and did nothing to calm my fears. I attempted dangerous embraces in the bathroom and was savagely repelled. I tried to catch her eyes between spoons of porridge but she refused the very possibility and smiled dutifully at her father and asked serious questions about capital, loans, the structure of companies and the future of an aircraft factory in Geelong.

Her dedication to this deception was remarkable, and was so thoroughly undertaken that, hisses notwithstanding, I felt no hope.

I lost my appetite and could not summon up sufficient interest in the aircraft factory I had so carelessly set in motion. I was forced to imitate my former self, counterfeit an enthusiasm to match that of my host who, in anticipation of our backer's visit, wanted me to tramp around the bush looking at timbers. He had the hang of this aspect very well. We would want mountain ash or white ash for spars; blue fig for struts; cudgerie for the fuselage. He was becoming quite knowledgeable on the subject and telephoned a man at the Forest Commission who promised to conduct tests on our timbers to see they met British Aeronautical Standards. He wanted to dot the "i"s and cross the "t"s but he did not tell me it was because Cocky Abbot had his doubts. He did not wish to offend me.

"What is it, Badgery?" he would ask. "Cat got your tongue?"

"I'm down," I admitted, "there is no denying it."

"You'll see," Jack cried, clapping his hands against his knees, not worrying that his spilt Scotch was lifting polish from the table, not noticing that his wife was sitting alone in the parlour with electric flex wound absently around her wrists, encircled by electricity travelling to and fro from the crackling wireless. "My word, you'll see."

I wished to Christ he would leave me alone, because I had other things on my mind which had no room for Great Plans, or Vision, which in the end have never been worth a tinker's fart in comparison with a woman.

I was busy trying to establish what the papers call A Love Nest.

117

Indeed, the only thing that kept me from shuffling my feet like a tramp as I walked down Ryrie Street was that I had arranged a room above a Chinese laundry. The room had a bed and a wash-basin and was three shillings a week with laundry thrown in. The Chinaman knew what I was up to, and I would say he did not approve, but he let me have the room none the less, and it gave me the strength to get on with other matters. I bought a new jute sack for the snake. I stopped at Griffith's for the *Geelong Advertiser* which contained my third article on the future of the aeroplane in the Western District of Victoria. Although my story contained such attractive fancies as the transport of wool by air, it was remarkable for its dullness, a lack of enthusiasm that set it apart from its two predecessors which had, if I say so myself, shone forth with a luminosity of style that even the editor's meddling could not diminish.

I passed the post office as Mr Jonathon Oakes scurried down the front steps, tucking a large white envelope into his waistcoat pocket. I crossed the street, stepping carefully across a pile of steaming horse dung which lay between the two shining tramtracks.

The draughtsman's office was in an alleyway off Ryrie Street. As I mounted the steel fire-escape I was already at war with the man. I entered the office without knocking, slapping the newspaper briskly against my leg.

It was a poky office divided by a large counter. The draughtsman, with unfounded optimism in regard to his future prospects, had left far more room for his customers than for himself. He huddled at his desk. He was like a thin spider with his web on a dusty window. He squinted at his plans through small steel spectacles.

"Shop."

"I saw you, Mr Badgery," the draughtsman said, spacing his words to coincide with four thin-ruled lines of graphite.

There is an arrogance that seems to come naturally to a certain type of Englishman and this one had it. There was nothing in his gloomy little office above the alley that justified it. There was nothing in his bearing, his physique or his dress that could explain it. He picked up a roll of plans from the desk and brought them to the counter. The undersides of his pale wrists were dirty and his cuffs were frayed.

My eyes narrowed. My squiggly mouth straightened itself into an ungenerous line which left no trace of the lower lip that so entranced Phoebe and along which she had loved to run the tip of her red-cuticled finger.

"There is just one particular", he said (I stared at the pale scalp that shone through his thin black hair), "in which I have not been able to oblige."

"Oh, yes."

"In the matter of the copyright which is already registered and held, you see," the pointing finger had three long black hairs on its bony knuckle, "by a Mr Bradfield of Sydney."

"Do you recall my instructions?"

"Oh, exactly, Mr Badgery."

The draughtsman removed his spectacles and cleaned them with his handkerchief. The watery eyes, thus revealed, showed no respect for his customer.

"My instructions were that you should put my name on the plan in respect," I said, "in respect of the substantial changes I have made to the aileron designs."

Of course I had stolen the damn plans. Never mind that my method of getting them had been clever or that Bradfield himself was never able to get a backer to make his six-seater B3, and that I was, in this way, actually doing the man a favour by attempting to make the craft he had laboured so long on.

Bradfield would have sympathized with me. He would not have grudged me his drawings, his technical data or the stress diagrams and calculations which he had, with typical thoroughness, had checked and passed by Captain Frank Barnwell, the man who designed the Bristol Fighter.

There was only one reason Bradfield could not make his B3 – British interests didn't want him to.

Now another member of the master race was trying to do the same to me. I held my temper nicely: "You don't understand, it would appear, that these drawings you have executed are the foundation stone on which the Australian aircraft industry shall be built."

The draughtsman allowed himself a thin smile at the very thought of such a thing. "Legally, Mr Badgery, a very shaky foundation."

It was very quiet in the office. A horse and dray rattled down the laneway, its driver singing "Annie Laurie".

"Have you ever been to Grafton?" I asked, leaning across the counter as one might lean across a bar.

"No," the draughtsman said, and blinked.

"As you enter Grafton from the south," I said pleasantly, "there is a rather large house on the left-hand side, a big stone place with leadlight windows, three houses before the post office. There is a gentleman who resides there, a Mr Regan, the Town Clerk of Grafton. Perhaps you know him."

"No."

"A pity, because you would know that Mr Regan has only four fingers on his left hand."

The draughtsman tried to look me in the eye, but could not hold it. He blew his nose to hide his confusion. "Why do you tell me this?" he said.

"Because it was I who tore one off," I smiled. "Just like a chicken wing."

"You are threatening me?"

"The same in his case," I said. "Now would you please place my name as the designer of the craft." And I spelt my name out for him slowly.

This Regan story was, at least for the moment, a lie. Unnecessary, of course, but I enjoyed it. I liked the detail of it, the quick fabrication of the large stone house and the nine-fingered inhabitant within, forever sitting at a table which, although I did not trouble the Englishman with the details, was set for dinner. I silently encircled the house with elms and dotted daffodils across its brilliant lawns while the draughtsman hesitated before his vision of the stricken Regan whose four-fingered hand was torn and bloody.

"I will need this amendment by next Tuesday afternoon," I said, putting on my hat. "You will oblige me by delivering them to Mr McGrath's house in Western Avenue."

It was because of this visit to the draughtsman that many people in Geelong said that I was a Chicago-style mobster. It was merely one of the conflicting stories I would leave behind me when I finally departed.

43

Molly unplugged herself, released her anxious coils of wire, and recaptured the kitchen from Bridget who was bidden to make stuffing for the goose. Bridget watched her mistress sew up the goose with too much thread and drop knives and forks in her hurry to have it done with.

Jack arranged chairs in the music room which were destined to be unused (the meeting with the squatters would never move beyond the dining room). He ran new wires to the front porch and hooked them up to a globe of extraordinary dimensions which would give the backers a floodlit entrance and bathe the inside of Jonathon Oakes's bedroom whether he liked it or not.

The snake, confused by winter heating, shed its skin out of season and began to search for frogs which were not forthcoming. It moved at summer speed, its tongue flicking, and bit its discarded skin in irritation.

"It knows something is up," Jack insisted. "Animals can feel these things and if you put it down to heating you are missing half the point."

He was inclined to philosophize on this but I had too much on my mind to take pleasure from conversations about snakes or knots or wheels. I had to take the Morris Farman down to Colac to pick up a squatter for the meeting, an easy enough assignment, but I also had business with Phoebe in Geelong. Time was running short, and I left Jack at the dining-room table, rolling a rubber band off the plans which he had already made worn and grubby in his enthusiasm.

44

I flicked open my fob watch. It was already two o'clock. I should have been at Barwon Common.

I stood on one side of Little Maude Street, Phoebe on the other. She was in front of the milliner's, her plastered arm in a cerise silk scarf which did not make her the least less attractive, not to me, not, I assumed, to the lanky boy who had come, the night before, to drive her to a gathering in an American Stutz. She wore the latest straight-line dress, a dazzling yellow, against which her breasts pushed most attractively and below which her wonderful calves (calves she had wrapped around me, calves I had licked and stroked) were there for total strangers to have dirty dreams about. I ached to hold her, but was totally forbidden.

When Stu O'Hagen drove between us in a brand new T Model with his straw-hatted wife sitting proudly beside him I did not even see him. When Jonathon Oakes (whose pockets included a stolen letter his own sister had written to Jack McGrath Esquire) tipped his hat to me I was unaware of him. Only later, in the air above Warn Ponds, would I recognize these incidents as things from a dream, forgotten on waking, can be remembered later in the day.

Phoebe would not speak to me in public, but she had agreed to inspect the room. Her terms had been clear, hissed quickly. She would inspect it on her own, without me. She knew things that I did not. She had already intercepted one letter from Mrs Kentwell, a terrifying thing with an ultimatum like a scorpion's tail. As for telling me why she was dancing with boys she had once rejected, she assumed that I would know exactly why she did it.

Yet there I was, across the street in front of the ironmonger's, like some moon-eyed boy, and there was Jonathon Oakes, the wrinkled spy, picking his fussy way along the footpath, his little head turning this way and that, observing everything.

The pig-tailed Chinaman was watching too. He stood in the doorway of his laundry and Phoebe was her father's daughter because she saw, not a man, but a cartoon from the *Bulletin*: John Chinaman outside his den.

I could stand it no more. I began to walk across the street towards her. The sweating Clydesdales of the brewer dray missed me by inches and the cockney driver's abuse fell upon love-deaf ears.

Phoebe, having stopped to see me safe, turned angrily upon her heel and carried her broken arm sedately into Maude Street. I reached the milliner's and stopped. Phoebe pretended to be interested in something in a baker's window on the corner – let's call it a dead fly, beside a tray of vanilla slices. I turned and saw that the Chinaman had come to stand in the middle of Little Maude Street to watch our love dance. I walked back towards the grinning sticky-beak who took a few steps backwards before fleeing for the steamy safety of his laundry. When I turned to look for Phoebe, she was no longer looking at flies or vanilla slices and Maude Street was empty except for a tram and a young man in a natty suit swinging on the crank handle of his Chevrolet. The Chevrolet was straddled squarely across the tramlines and the Newtown tram was bearing down on it, its bell clanging loudly.

I felt empty and angry all at once. I walked down Yarra Street to Little Mallop Street and then turned into Moorabool Street with the intention of going to the airfield. It was market day and the streets were filled with the low-crowned, broad-brimmed hats of farmers. They poured in and out of the ABC Grill Rooms and Cake

Shop where I, on a happier day, had bought Bridget her ice-cream cone. On an inspiration I pushed my way in and found my frightened lover sitting at a booth all alone with a dish of vanilla ice-cream whose melted mounds she prodded with a silver spoon held awkwardly in her left hand.

It was now twenty minutes past two. The welcoming committee at Colac were already donning their hats and fussing with their bows. I sat down opposite her. She would not look at me. She mashed her ice-cream with her spoon.

"You didn't even look at it," I said. "I paid three shillings and you didn't even look."

"The Chinaman was watching," she whispered, keeping her eyes on the puddling mess of ice-cream.

"Chinamen don't talk to anyone," I said, "except other Chinamen." I did not even have the fare for a tram to the Barwon Bridge. I would have to walk all the way.

"Please," I said. "For God's sake, have mercy."

"He *saw*," she said.

"Oh merciful Mother of God," I stood up. It was two twenty-three, "save me from the brave talk of little girls."

"You don't understand Geelong," she pleaded and I had to steel myself to stay angry in the face of those liquid green eyes. "It's not like Melbourne."

"I understand enough," I said, looking casually into the next booth and finding the most inquisitive eyes of Mrs Kentwell peering up from a pearly cup of milkless tea.

"Mrs Kentwell," I said, holding out the hat I was clasping to my chest.

She cut me dead.

As I strode from the ABC I realized that my flying suit was not at the hangar at Barwon Common but at Western Avenue. Stratocumulus clouds streaked feathers of ice crystals in the high blue sky.

I strode up the hill in Moorabool Street with a vigour that demanded attention which is how I got myself written up in the Reverend Mawson's sermon.

The reverend gentleman was gazing out of his leadlight window at All Saints Vicarage, his pen handle resting on his pendulous lower lip, when he saw a man of such vigour and optimism that he set to work immediately to embalm the image in his sermon. The congregation of All Saints next Sunday would all see and admire me in their mind's eye, a modern muscular

Christian striding up the hill, his soul bursting with good Anglican intentions.

I brushed through the Reverend Mawson's demands as lightly as through a spider web. I strode past the Geelong West Fire Station, tipping my forty-shilling hat to the men outside. I passed Kardinya Park where the tramline ended and where I had spent a dismal afternoon with the older McGraths, watching monkeys and worrying about Phoebe who had gone away with some people in a Dodge with a badly timed magneto. I pounded across the bridge on the Barwon River where a strong southerly cooled my sweating face too rapidly.

At Barwon Common I enlisted the help of a nearby cabinet maker to swing the prop. He swung it twice to draw fuel into the engine.

I switched on. "Contact."

The man (burly-armed, slow-witted) was lucky not to break his arm. I turned around in my seat to see the prop miss his arm by less than an inch.

I taxied down the bumpy common without the benefit of gloves, goggles, flying suit, or even a cap.

I took off into the wind, banked, and followed the road up the Belmont Hill which lead out to the main Colac Road. It was now ten past three in the afternoon.

Flying is normally an interesting enough occupation to soothe the most troubled man, and I am not just speaking of the much-praised beauty of earth and sky, the people like ants, etc., etc. There is a lot of work involved in flying a craft like a Morris Farman, and it is good for a temper, much like chopping wood can be. But on this afternoon my eyes were watering in the wind and my hands were so cold that when I tried to open my fob watch I couldn't manage it. I did not like the Morris Farman. It seemed a slow, heavy, irritating plane and not worthy of me. This was not snobbishness. It was a fact: the Morris Farman was built as a trainer, and I was a long way from being a student. Ross Smith (who continued to get a three-inch par in the *Geelong Advertiser* every day) would not have been seen dead in it and Bradfield's B3 was ten years ahead in every aspect.

I set my face into a concrete grin and cursed the head wind. All the way I battled to hold the craft in the turbulent sky. I slipped and skidded and, in the face of angry gusts, sometimes moved backwards rather than forwards.

I found the racecourse in Colac without much difficulty and I was momentarily soothed by the sight of a small crowd. It was only natural that I flew low over the ground (as the Shire Clerk's horses bolted in terror and carried his screaming wife and blissfully sleeping baby out towards Cemetery Hill) and did a little fancy flying in a belligerent sort of spirit, pushing the craft a little beyond its safe limits. The spruce-wood frame groaned and the rigging wires sang in the wind. If there was anyone below who was knowledgeable enough to sneer at the plane they would know, at least, that its pilot deserved something better.

I brought the craft in for a perfect landing and taxied to the waiting crowd of townspeople whose numbers had been somewhat depleted by the departure of a search party for the Shire Clerk's wife (the Shire Clerk himself had remained behind, explaining to anyone who would listen that duty compelled him).

Thus a certain confusion greeted me as I jumped from the plane: there were heads turned towards Cemetery Hill, loud shouts, odd cooees, the plucking fingers of the Shire Clerk and the potato farmer's hands of Cocky Abbot (hands which belied his status) which grasped mine to give me a hearty shake. The Shire Clerk made one or two attempts at an official welcome but eventually gave up and, feigning indifference, began to tweak at the rigging wires like a man called to tune an indifferent piano.

Although he was well past fifty, Cocky Abbot was a man of immense strength, famous for his ability to wrestle a steer and throw a bag of wheat. He had a huge head, a high forehead, a long nose, and a big round chin with an extraordinary dimple that I could not take my eyes from.

I hardly heard a word he said. There was too much noise, much grabbing, small boys likely to damage the craft. All I could think of was the dimple, and what a heavy man he was.

A second dimpled chin presented itself. I did not need to be told (although I was – we shook) that this was Cocky Abbot's son. This was a different animal entirely. I did not like this son. He wore an AIF badge and an Old Geelong Grammarian's tie. At the time I did not know what the tie represented, but the camel-hair coat, the military moustache, the way in which cane and gloves were held, all indicated that I was in the presence of an Imaginary Englishman.

125

The son handed me a small suitcase with the distant eyes of a man dealing with a chauffeur. I placed it in the passenger's compartment. I pulled a boy from the wing. A man with a bucket in his hand gave me a letter he wanted posted in Geelong. In other circumstances I would have blossomed in the face of these attentions and turned my eyes to meet those of the Colac beauties who hid their meanings beneath the shade of their hats. But I was late, my passenger was far too heavy, and I was cold and lovesick.

I was disappointed in Jack too. How could he make an Australian plane with Imaginary Englishmen? You would think Cocky Abbot a reasonable fellow until you met the son, and then you saw what was wrong with him. It was what happened in this country. The minute they began to make a quid they started to turn into Englishmen. Cocky Abbot was probably descended from some old cockney lag, who had arrived here talking flash language, a pickpocket, a bread-stealer, and now, a hundred years later his descendants were dressing like his gaolers and torturers, disowning the language, softening their vowels, greasing their way into the plummy speech of the men who had ordered their ancestors lashed until the flesh had been dragged in bleeding strips from their naked backs.

The old man was as rough as bags but he was proud because he had sired an Englishman.

I lost the pair of them in the crowd and then turned to find them both sitting, side by side, in the plane. They were busily arranging rugs around themselves.

"What's this?" I demanded of the old man. "I was only picking up one passenger."

"I'm bringing the boy," Cocky Abbot said, producing a silver brandy flask and taking a swig. He wiped his mouth and passed the flask to his son.

"It's too much weight," I said. The crowd pressed around, eager to hear.

"If you can't carry two men," Cocky Abbot said, "it beats me how you'll ever carry a bale of wool."

When I had envisaged an Australian-made aeroplane it was as a weapon against people like this and I felt an almost overpowering urge to walk away and leave them for the crowd to laugh at. I was so overcome by irritation that I did not know what I was likely to do next. I took the small brass rigging tightener from my pocket and walked around the craft. I tightened several struts which had been stretched by the aerobatics. It was only my desire for Phoebe that brought me back to the cockpit. I seated myself and fussed with the hessian bags to make myself more comfortable.

"I'll need one of you blokes", I called back over my shoulder, "to swing the prop."

"Donaldson will do it," said the Imaginary Englishman, smiling pleasantly at the crowd.

The representative from the *Colac Times* demanded my attention while Cocky Abbot called out: "Where's Donaldson?"

The Shire Clerk, scanning the dusty road behind the grandstand for sign of his wife and child, was summonsed to the craft where, to general hilarity, he grasped the propeller in this fingernail-bitten hands.

I was too preoccupied with poor Donaldson to give the *Colac Times* a decent interview. Donaldson was a small man, all bum and pigeon toes, whose beard could not hope to hide the insecurity of his mouth which quailed before authority and cheeky children. He held the propeller and blushed the colour of a nerine plum. He knew that something bad would happen to him.

The crowd gave him no mercy. "Come on, Donno," they yelled. "Show us your stuff."

"Push your pen."

"Swing it."

He pulled on the propeller twice. Nothing happened. The crowd hooted. They were as ignorant as any crowd: I was simply drawing fuel into the engine and the switch was on "off".

I turned to "switch on".

"Contact!" I yelled.

The Shire Clerk did not understand the terminology. He stared at me, bright red with mortification.

"Again," I yelled, "now!"

Donaldson's scream of pain must have been drowned by the engine, and it was only later, clipping my pars from the *Colac Times*, that I learned of the unfortunate Clerk's broken arm. I dictated a long letter to him, apologizing for the injury and discoursing at length on the ignorance of the townspeople. I hope it gave the man some comfort.

"Mr Badgery", the *Colac Times* of 25th April 1920 reported, "was anxious to return to the air, explaining the uncertainty of winds and the necessity of landing in Geelong before dark."

For once, I had understated the case.

Due to the weight of the two Cocky Abbots the Morris Farman barely cleared the cypress trees at the end of the racecourse. A second line of eucalypts brushed their sparse umbrellas against the undercarriage.

After twenty miles of labouring hard I could not get the craft above five hundred feet. No tail wind in the world would get us to Barwon Common before nightfall.

I watched the wintry sun as it settled behind a low ribbon of cloud and wondered whether it might not be better to land on a road or in a paddock and ferry the passengers to Geelong by some other method. It was only vanity that kept me going.

I glanced back at them and was pleased to see that they were frightened. They sat in their rugs, staring ahead, not daring to look over the side.

Jack, I reflected, kicking angrily at the rudder bar, had understood nothing. He had gone on in his blundering, amiable way, liking everyone without discrimination, anyone, that is, who was not a Chinaman or a Jew. Jack, who had read aloud the poetry of Henry Lawson, had understood nothing about it. He had let me down.

I flew low across the melancholy landscape of long shadows, stewing in the juices of betrayal.

45

Of course the night landing was my fault and no one else's. If I hadn't hung around Geelong mooning over Phoebe I would have been back in plenty of time.

But when I followed the electric lights down Belmont Hill and found no flares at the Common, all my anger was directed at Jack. There was no moon and the Barwon River was a slick of black beneath the lights of the bridge. I couldn't even find the hangar on the Common.

I banked and brought the craft on a northerly course, flying low over Geelong itself. The squatters, emboldened by brandy, thankful to be alive, were all agog at this display of lights and life. The blustering wind (which had made them huddle into rugs and clutch at the bench seat) no longer troubled them. They leaned out, tapped me on the back, and shouted. They had no idea what I had in store for them.

I took the Morris Farman out over the bay, above the ships at

Corio Quay, turned, and began my descent. Western Avenue, bright as day, loomed large before the squatters' eyes. I dropped the craft (none too gently) across the power lines where Western Avenue turns before the park, and skimmed in under the next lot at the Gleason Street corner. I passed beside a Dodge Series 6 whose pale-faced driver swung his wheel, caught in a culvert, bounced out and veered across the road behind the aircraft where Mrs Kentwell saw it lock wheels with a horse and jinker. The jinker's wheel shattered and the Dodge came to a halt at the top of the steep grassy bank above Corio Bay.

I taxied to the McGraths' front door. When the engine was turned off the sound of the terrified horse dragging the crippled jinker made a perfect accompaniment to the old squatter's face.

I was all politeness. I helped the gentlemen from the aeroplane.

46

Madame Ovlisky, Clairvoyant of Little Mallop Street, Geelong, sat before her smudged charts and confidently predicted a resurgence of influenza. There would be deaths in North Geelong, she said, and the dance halls would be empty. She could not see the canaries her customer had lost, although she was provided with the address (Melbourne Road, North Geelong) from which they had been stolen. She saw murder, she said, that very night, and if her customer was uninterested by this news, Madame Ovlisky did not notice it. As she spoke lightning flickered above the distant You Yangs and she was not dissatisfied.

Certainly there was an irritability, a temper, in the air, and Madame Ovlisky was not the only one who felt herself tugged by the sour wind that swept Geelong. It was a mournful, depressing wind, coming from across two hundred miles of denuded landscape to Corio Bay where the shells of cuttlefish lay abandoned in the sandy dark and where Sergeant Hieronymus House stood guard around the flimsy aeroplane that threatened to tip sideways before the stronger gusts. Hieronymus, known as Harry to all except the Clerk of Records, did not need to explain his temper by anything as questionable as the wind. He had been called to duty from the arms of a ready wife, a wife not always ready, not always happy, dragged back from bliss by a boy with a message from the station who had knocked loudly, persistently, at the moment when he had taken the superior position and she had closed, at last, her staring eyes. He had left her bad-tempered and blotchy to sit and watch the fire in a smoky parlour.

And for what? To guard the property of a man who had caused a nuisance in a public place, been responsible for the death of a horse, and damage to a brand new auto. Sergeant House would have locked the bastard up in the cells at Johnston Street without a shit bucket. But the grovelling, forelock-tugging arse-licking police commissioner was closing the street and posting a guard.

Behind the lighted windows of Number 87 Western Avenue there were rich squatters. Their laughter made him feel sour and he did not wish to speak to anyone.

He did not like any of the people who lived in these grand houses in Western Avenue. He would have arrested them all, not the poor bloody swagman with the bag full of frogs they had sent him out to arrest last week. He had been doing nothing but sitting on the edge of a quiet footpath. He had two pounds five shillings and sixpence in his pocket and he said he was off to be a cook in Commaida. But the magistrate gave him three months because "three months might do you some good".

Sergeant House watched Mrs Kentwell walk down the lighted steps of her house and come towards him. He turned his back. He did not wish to speak to her. She had a bad case of "officer's back", i.e., an appearance of a broomstick inserted in the anus with the aim of providing greater rectitude.

"I wish to lodge an official complaint," the woman said. Her hair was done in a braid and she held a shawl tight across her shoulders. Her false teeth were slightly loose, a condition the Sergeant sympathized with, and his countenance softened before the whistling sibilants. He sucked in his ruddy cheeks and settled his own uncomfortable dentures into place.

"Yes, madam," he said.

"This is not an isolated incident. The girl, the flapper, ran down my brother in a similar manner a fortnight ago."

"In an aeroplane?" His hostility evaporated in the face of this unreported crime.

"Not in an aeroplane. Of course not. She ran him down."

"In a jinker?" the Sergeant suggested. He took out his notebook and flicked briskly through the pages of careful copperplate.

130

"Not in a jinker, or cart, not a dray or an auto. Ran him down here," she tapped her umbrella emphatically on the footpath, "on the street, pretending to break her arm."

"And why should she wish to do such a thing?"

"Because she had fallen off the roof in a naked state", whistled Mrs Kentwell, "and broke her arm then."

"So now she ran down your brother, to break it a second time."

"No, no, no. In order to *pretend* to break it."

If he had not observed, through the slightly open curtain, a pretty young flapper with her arm in a sling, he would have thought the woman ready for the asylum. His pencil hovered over his notebook uncertainly.

"I will, of course, wish to speak to your superiors. Perhaps you could have a man call on me."

I am a man, thought Sergeant House, and the police force is not a draper's shop engaged in home deliveries. False teeth or no, he was on the brink of pointing this out when Mrs Kentwell tapped her umbrella for attention.

"My father was a Colonel McInlay," she told the sergeant who had successfully conspired to shoot a major in Ypres. "We have lived in this house for one hundred years, before, *well* before this bullock driver and his flappers came and did this."

And to add weight to her claim and to underline the detestable nature of the aeroplane which rocked fraily before her, she gave it a good poke with her umbrella.

The umbrella speared the fuselage and stuck there.

Mrs Kentwell stared at it with astonishment. Her teeth clacked inside her mouth.

"My brother is very ill," she said defiantly. She withdrew her weapon, leaving a perfect round hole in the fuselage. She looked up at Sergeant House who thought she was going to smile. But she turned on her heel and retreated to the house.

The sergeant regarded the hole in the fuselage, his pencil hovering over the notebook. Then he closed the book and put it away.

47

The other potential investor was Ian Oswald-Smith. He was tall, well built, olive-skinned and his red-lipped long-lashed face was saved from prettiness by the blue cast of his beard. He was also a squatter and an Imaginary Englishman, but he was a different animal to the Cocky Abbots – irony was his great amusement and if it was not detected, so much the better.

He had never seen, in all his travels, such enthusiastic use of electricity. He had already quietly amused himself by drawing Molly on this very subject. He had prevailed upon her to speak of the virtues of all the electrical devices, beginning with the four-globe radiator of which she said: "To ignore the radiator, Mr Oswald-Smith, is to refuse to take advantage of the investment one has already made by installing electricity in the first place." It seemed she was going to say more but was prevented by shortness of breath. She took her daughter's hand, then sipped a glass of water.

The hostess, the aviator, the flapper, the bullocky and the two Cocky Abbots attacked their big unappetizing plates of goose and roast vegetables while he teased his hostess about the bills such a contrivance might accumulate. His teasing was as gentle as a caress and in spite of her simplicity, or because of it, he liked her. They managed to discuss the lighting, His Master's Voice, the wireless, and the kettle on the ornate stand that she used to make tea at the table. And all the while his dark attractive eyes roamed the walls and floors where the hostess's enthusiasm for the electric connection had crossed and recrossed the brown Victorian wallpaper, draped the high picture rails and fallen from the ceiling like crêpe-paper decorations for a progressive Christmas.

For a man with such potential for sarcasm, with such skill at asserting the superiority of his class, he spared his hosts and himself any scorn, drank the strong tea he was offered and did not mind that he was given four spoons of sugar without his tastes being inquired after. The McGraths seemed to him perfectly simple and honest people and he was memorizing them and memorizing the room so that in future he could entertain his friends with stories about their characters.

Whatever winds blew from the western coast affected his equanimity not at all. He studied their daughter, the flapper with the broken wing, and let his dark eyes and long lashes caress her in a discreet enough way. The whole room, their whole coming together, was a symbol of the modern age and when he noticed that the street lights were throwing the shadow of the aircraft on to the curtain, he drew this small wonder to the company's attention and was surprised to find it was the host, the exbullocky, who appreciated the poetry of it the most, not, he supposed, that one would have expected much from such dour Presbyterians as the Cocky Abbots who sat on their seats with the same dry, sly looks they would have brought to the sale-yards. The only thing he had in common with these two was that they were wealthy farmers from the same area. He did not give a lot of weight to the younger Cocky Abbot's moustache or his old school tie. Whatever education he had enjoyed he had remained a barbarian and not even the cloaked vowels could hide it. The Cocky Abbots would not have the poetry to drape their homestead in electricity, if the electricity had been available to them. Any man who'd worked at "Bulgaroo" would tell you stories about the owner's meanness. It was legend in the Western District. It was said that they wrote their correspond-ence on the back of used envelopes and that they would not so much as spare a candle, let alone a bar of soap, for the men. He was surprised to see them here to discuss anything as fanciful as an aeroplane but, watching the way the elder Cocky Abbot listened to Jack McGrath, he saw that he was accorded respect and the respect, he guessed, was based on the fact that Jack had made a lot of money. The old Cocky thought Jack McGrath was shrewd.

48

Jack McGrath scraped the last of the bread-and-butter pudding from his plate and gulped his scalding tea down his throat. He was in no mood for small talk, but a meal was a meal and hospitality must be offered. He thumped his big foot beneath the table and folded his crumpled napkin several times. He did not notice my mood. He was too concerned to get the subject started, to flick off the rubber band, and bring the talk around to factories and their construction. He was ready to explain how he would buy himself a team and bring the timbers out of the bush, who would mill it, who would season it. He wished to be practical. But Oswald-Smith wanted to discuss rabbits, so rabbits it would have to be, and all Jack could do was thump his foot and scald himself with steam from the electric kettle, the flex of which his anxious wife had wound around her wrist.

While Phoebe squeezed her mother's perspiring hand, Oswald-Smith chose to argue in favour of the rabbit. He was one of those men who like a talk so much he will take a contrary position just to get things started.

Jack, whose teams had ripped many an acre of land riddled with rabbit burrows, burying them, cutting them, suffocating them, was shocked to hear a successful farmer speak of rabbits in such terms.

I knew what Oswald-Smith was doing. He was getting me to talk and he laid his argument before me like a fisherman will drop a mud eye, ever so gently, and let it float downstream where a brown trout, old enough and smart enough to refuse such blatant tricks, takes the damn thing anyway.

"I'd have to say, Mr Smith," I said, uncoiling my long bowed legs and stretching back in my chair, "that you are talking rot."

Jack tried to flatten his creased napkin with the edge of his fist, back and forth like a widowed ironing woman.

"The rabbit has no place in this country," I said. "The things that will ruin this country are things like the rabbit."

The things that I had in mind were the Oswald-Smiths and the Cocky Abbots.

"Yes," said Oswald-Smith pleasantly. "Please go on."

"That's it. Nothing else to say. The rabbit is a mongrel of a thing."

I had said nothing new but they were all, except Jack who continued to iron his napkin, ridiculously pleased with me for having said it. It wasn't so much that the subject was rabbits, but that I was addressing myself to it in a definite manner. I could see that the Cocky Abbots were pleased that I was speaking their thoughts.

Right in the middle of my irritation and confusion with everything I smelt a whiff of that interest that comes in every sale, like a wooden case cracking open to spill out honey: a heady, intoxicating aroma.

I tried to use this moment to cross the bridge from rabbits to aeroplanes, but the gap was wide and I misjudged the distance. "We're going to have our own animals," I said. I found myself in mid-air, not knowing exactly what I meant.

There was a silence as everybody tried to imagine what it was that I was trying to say.

"How do you mean?" asked Cocky Abbot Junior helpfully.

"Breed them," I said recklessly.

"How?" asked Oswald-Smith.

"How do you think?" I said so lewdly that Phoebe and Molly,

for different reasons, grew bright red, and only Oswald-Smith, a man who enjoyed the picturesque, permitted himself a quick smile before his sense of diplomacy encouraged him to change the subject.

"I think", he said, "it's time we moved on to business."

"My word," cried Jack, and pushed back his chair loudly.

There was much fussing around as the women tried to clear the table and Molly became entangled in her wire and knocked over the stand of the electric kettle. She was close to tears as Phoebe untangled her but she wished us all luck before she left the room.

"Wireless," she whispered to her daughter. "I'll sit by the wireless."

Bridget removed the tablecloth and Jack stamped around distributing writing pads to his visitors. He was so agitated that even Cocky Abbot Senior realized that the aeroplane factory was more than a casual venture for him.

There seemed to be nothing to prevent a successful meeting. There appeared to be a positive excess of goodwill on the part of the investors. When Cocky Abbot Senior resumed his seat at the table he sat opposite Jack McGrath and winked at him like a conspirator.

I spread out the plans on the table. Bradfield's B3 was a beautiful craft and I had no trouble speaking enthusiastically about its function. I could feel some resistance from the older Cocky Abbot. I pushed against it with my enthusiasm. I discussed the purchase of steel from BHP and the method of bringing in timber from the bush. The young Cocky Abbot caught my eye and nodded. Oswald-Smith made notes on his writing pad. But the older farmer folded his arms against his chest and looked at me impassively.

The wind howled around the house and pushed its fingers under doors, through cracks in the floor, lifted rugs in the long passage so they rode the timber in ghostly waves. The women felt the wind and did not like it, but all I felt was this stubborn wall from Cocky Abbot Senior. I talked and talked, but I could not talk him down. I knew, before I sat down, that I had not made the sale.

"I knew your father," said Cocky Abbot Senior, unfolding his arms at last. "He was a practical man, so I suppose you are too. Now what I want to know, Badgery – and I mentioned this to Jack down at 'Bulgaroo' – why wouldn't we set ourselves up as agents

135

and import the best the world has to offer? I don't doubt you when you say there's a future in the aircraft, but why should we risk all this capital to manufacture something when we can import the best the British Empire can produce?"

"What did Jack say?"

"He said you were a practical fellow."

I looked at Jack. He grinned at me fondly. I sucked in my breath and studied the wallpaper behind his shoulder. I tried to remind myself that the whole thing was only a lie except it was not a lie any more. It was an inch from being the shining thing I had described so lyrically.

"Mr Abbot," I said, "I've sold two hundred T Model Fords and it has made me a lot of dough, but it never made me happy."

The table was quiet. They heard the tremor in my voice and they knew how I felt, but they had no idea why I felt it or what I was saying.

"Happy!" snorted Cocky Abbot Junior.

"Does it make you happy", I asked him, "to be a child all your life? That's what an agent is, a child serving a parent. If you want to serve the interests of the English, you go and be an agent for their aircraft, and you'll stay a damn child all your life."

The younger Cocky Abbot sought his AIF badge on his lapel and, having found it, squinted at it down his long nose. Everybody waited for him. "And yet", he said, "you served the Empire."

"I never served," I said. "I had no intention of dying like a silly goat for the British."

Jack, who had loved every war service story I told him, recognized the voice of truth. His great face folded in misery.

"You're lucky you don't live in Colac," said young Cocky Abbot.

"Lucky indeed. I saw it from the air. It looks like a cow of a place."

"We tar and feather micks for saying things like that. Our mates died for England."

"My point," I shouted. "My point exactly."

"We tarred and feathered a bloke two weeks ago, a Sinn Feiner from Warrnambool. It was written up in all the papers. He wrote a poem you might approve of, in 1915."

"You are fools," I said, and said it so quietly, with such passion, that Cocky Abbot Junior, whose large red fist had been placed very prominently on his expensively trousered knee, dismantled it quietly, and put the pieces in his pocket.

For a trembling instant I had them all.

136

I had a full five seconds in which to say something, anything, to begin a sentence that might, with its passion and precision, convert them to my view.

I did not even get my lips to open.

"I am here to make a quid," said Cocky Abbot Senior, ignoring me and addressing unhappy Jack. "I would not have come for anything else. I would not have risked my life in that machine for amusement or politics. It was only to make a quid."

"But you *can* make a quid, Mr Abbot," I said. "There is a good quid to be made by *us* selling aircraft to Australians. That is the point. *This* is the country for the aeroplane, Mr Abbot, not Europe."

"I must say", Oswald-Smith said sternly, "that I had no intention of investing my money in a political party."

"This is not a political party." My voice rose in frustration. "I could not give a fig for politics." And as far as I understood politics, I was right. It was an understanding I shared with the shivering sergeant in the street outside, a man who had killed an officer and would not join a union.

"It sounds like politics to me," said Oswald-Smith. "Why do you have this chip on your shoulder about the English? Dear God, you are English. You talk English. You look English. You have an English name."

"Not a chip on my shoulder," I said, relieved that Oswald-Smith would at least look at me. "Common sense. Anyone can see that the English are as big a pest as the rabbit. No offence, but they're identical. They come here, eat everything, burrow under, tunnel out – look at Ballarat or Bendigo – and when the country is rooted . . ." I faltered, "it'll be rooted."

"Watch your language," said Cocky Abbot Junior, retrieving his fist.

But Oswald-Smith was a more complete Imaginary Englishman than Cocky Abbot Junior and felt relaxed enough to be amused by this analogy. In fact he was now amused by the whole turn of events and was pleased, more than ever, that he had come. "It makes no sense to the rabbit, surely," he said, "for when the country is," he paused and smiled, "*rooted*, there will be nothing left for it."

"Then they'll get on boats and go home and leave their tunnels and heaps behind."

"Rabbits? On boats?" Oswald-Smith smiled at the fancy.

"Oh, for God's sake, man, this isn't an argument about rabbits. It's about aeroplanes."

"If you two would shut up for a moment," said the older Cocky Abbot, as much irritated with Oswald-Smith as he was with me, "I'd like to say something. The first is I couldn't care if you was a German from Jeparit and I don't mind what you vote about. You can stand on your soap box till the cows come home. The second is I don't think you know a thing about rabbits. And the third thing is I'd like to listen to Jack McGrath, our host, who has had to put up with all this bulldust about rabbits. I'd like to hear Jack tell us how all this is going to make us a quid. And fourth, son," he told me, "I'd like you to shut up and listen."

I pointed a straight finger at him. "I'll be right back," I said.

I strode from the room.

"Come on, Jack," Cocky Abbot said. "What's it to be?"

But Jack felt ill and his deep depression, normally kept at bay by the company of other men, pushed its way into the room and claimed him in public.

"Come on, Jack," said old Cocky Abbot kindly, "let's have a look at what you want."

But Jack could be persuaded to say nothing, and Oswald-Smith, who had been entranced by the scene he had chanced upon, now wondered where Molly had hung his overcoat.

49

Whilst dining on goose Phoebe had seen Mrs Kentwell attack the Morris Farman with her umbrella. It had done no more damage than a knife in water. The craft was a figment, a moth attracted by the electric light of the house. It was Mrs Kentwell's natural enemy and the old hag had recognized it, gone to battle, and discredited herself.

Mrs Kentwell, Phoebe thought, would have no allies in this house. She had attacked the dream and proclaimed herself mad.

Phoebe retired to a chair in the music room and wrote, triumphantly, in her erratic left hand: "Nor shall the bosom proud, / Be hid with shame."

Tomorrow, please God, Herbert Badgery would permit her to fly with him to Barwon Common. She had chosen a scarf. ("Vermilion wraps the cobalt sky.")

And then, if he still wanted to, she would go with him to the

Chinaman and Geelong could say what it wanted to. ("In rooms above Celestial's eyes / My angel's face, my demon's prize.")

She was recording these intentions in her notebook when I burst from the meeting in the dining room and strode down the passage.

She assumed I was going to get the snake, that a performance had been called for.

She tucked her notebook inside her sling and was waiting in the passage as I rushed back carrying the snake. When she saw me she knew that something was wrong, and the snake looked like some writhing demon exorcized from my guts, the source of the twisting emotions hinted at in my angry face.

"I love you," I said, so loudly that she thought her mother, hunched over the wireless in the next room, must surely hear.

She fled to her bedroom and closed the door. When her mother did not appear she took out her notebook and began to write again, attempting to cage the snake with rhymes.

50

"This", I said, as I walked back into the dining room, "is a true Australian."

Oswald-Smith stood up, and then sat down again. Jack stayed at the table shaking his head.

"Ha," I said. "Ha." I threw the snake at young Cocky Abbot who leapt into the air and knocked over the chair he had been sitting on. He scrambled backwards and stood on a wingback chair.

The snake landed where his lap had been. It looked angry and nasty. I cared for nothing. I was beyond it. I picked up the snake without looking at it. I held it behind its neck and at the tail.

"You cannot make this a good little bunny," I told the silent men in the room, "no matter what you say to it, no matter what you feed it. You cannot buy it or tame it or make it nice."

I swung the snake by the tail towards Cocky Abbot Junior and the snake, beside itself with rage, struck out and got a fang into the farmer's scarf and when it was pulled away the scarf came with it, poison soaking into the warp and weft of top quality merino wool.

"Bow," I said to young Cocky Abbot.

Jack moaned. Oswald-Smith pushed his chair back a fraction, closer to the window.

"Bow", I bellowed, "to a true Australian snake."

Young Cocky Abbot tried to look threatening but lacked the conviction. He went down on his knife-point creases and did not have to be told to put his head on the ground.

"Now," I said, "you understand something."

My voice softened a little, and the farmer, having looked upwards carefully, retreated slowly into the wingback chair.

I then addressed the gathering with a friendliness that doubtless struck them as strange. "This snake", I explained, "has been in gaol. It is a mean bastard of an animal and it cannot be bought."

"What are you trying to say?" Young Cocky Abbot tried, without much luck, to combine sarcasm and servility in one intonation.

"I'm trying to say I'm an Australian," I said, "and we should have an Australian aeroplane."

Cocky Abbot Senior now shook his head. He stood. He knew when a man had lost his strength. It had all gone from me now. I stood there in the middle of the room, as if I'd pissed my pants and was ashamed of it.

"I came here to talk to Jack about making a quid," Cocky Abbot Senior said. "I didn't come here to listen to some ratbag and I didn't come here to see a circus with snakes. I would have put my money into this scheme of yours but you've done me a favour by showing me what a ratbag you are so early so I'm saved the horrible discovery later on when you've got your oily mits on the dough I worked so hard to make. I'm inclined to punch you in the nose, snake or no snake, but I think I'd rather ask Mr Oswald-Smith if he'd give us a lift in his auto to the Criterion Hotel."

He went to Jack McGrath and shook his hand. "I'll see you again, Jack," he said, "but my advice to you is to get this bugger out of your house before he does some real damage."

I stood alone with the snake. No one looked at me. They shook Jack's hand as they departed.

51

"Ah," I said, after five minutes of silence during which Jack had poured himself two large tumblers of Scotch. "I'm sorry."

Jack could only shake his head. There was no malice in him, no anger. He had big eyes like a Labrador. "Why? What came over you?"

I was a sleep-walker trying to explain my presence, barefoot, on a midnight street.

"You should have lit the flares down at Barwon Common," I said. "You shouldn't have sent me down to Colac and not have anywhere for me to land."

"You never told me, Badgery. I'm not a mind-reader."

"Anyone knows a plane can't land after dark."

"Well, I didn't know," he bellowed, and the whole household heard his voice and they felt frightened. "I didn't know," he yelled. Sergeant House heard him. Mrs Kentwell and Jonathon Oakes, playing cribbage in their parlour, heard him.

"Ah," I said, wondering if I might have a whisky and then deciding against it. I looked at Cocky Abbot Junior's fallen chair and Oswald-Smith's teacup. "Agents! I've had enough of being an agent."

"We're a young country. We've got to crawl before we can walk."

"If you start out crawling, you end up crawling."

Jack looked at me resentfully and poured more Scotch into his glass. "You were wrong about the snake," he said.

I shrugged. I was not worrying about right or wrong any more. I was only worrying that I had been a fool.

"You don't know anything about animals," my host said. "There isn't a creature alive who won't respond to kindness. You're not a kind man, Badgery, and it hurts me to say it."

Judged, I put my head in my hands.

"If there is one thing I know about," Jack went on, "it's animals. I had a tame kangaroo in Point's Point. I raised it on a bottle when its mother was killed. It used to follow me. You ask the wife, she'll tell you. It followed me everywhere and then some larrikins from Mansfield shot it, with a rifle."

"I dare say," I said, "but that is what they call an analogy."

"I don't know anything about analogies," Jack said impatiently, "but by Jove I know about animals."

"It's not the point."

"It is the point. It's the whole point. If kindness is not the point, what point is there?"

I put out my hand and touched Jack's clenched fist, I was as close to tears as I had ever come. I said a few words to comfort him but I doubt he heard me. He sat with his heavy smudged tumbler before him and looked at this stranger he had invited into his house and wondered how any man alive could not believe in kindness.

"It's a great disappointment," he said.

I always believed he was referring to the aeroplane.

52

There were too many things that Geelong could not explain or understand. Why would a healthy, happy man like Jack McGrath go sneaking into another man's bedroom and remove a hessian bag containing a snake? Why, at two o'clock in the morning, would he open this bag in the kitchen? And why, when he was bitten, would he walk out on to the front lawn to die in public (in his pyjamas) rather than raise his family and ask for help?

It was I who found poor Jack, poor grey-faced dead Jack. I could not bear his staring eyes. I can bear few memories of that dreadful day. I look at them still through half-closed lids against a too bright light. Molly in nightgown howling like a dog inside the music room. Mrs Kentwell standing at the fence ducking the clod of earth Phoebe hurled at her. Sergeant House with notebook suggesting I was not telling everything.

Gawpers, comforters, people with gifts of fruit turned away by Bridget, who would resign next day when the snake was still not found.

I joined the police search for the snake. I supervised the loading of the Morris Farman on to a flat-top wagon and rode with it to Barwon Common on which windswept expanse I tried to weep but all that came from me was a small ugly sound like a man might make when choking.

53

No point to dwell on this episode, to detail the various threats I received from men who thought themselves friends of Jack McGrath, amongst them the elder Cocky Abbot and the once friendly manager of the National Bank, or the strict instructions given mother and daughter to remove me from the house.

They stuck by me, my only allies. And even Molly, unravelled by grief, dizzy, vomiting, summoned up enough love to tell me it was not my fault.

When I did not leave the house as Geelong thought fit, the

142

crowds of mourners who had followed Jack McGrath's coffin saw fit to ostracize the wife and daughter for their indiscretion.

Geelong lined up with Mrs Kentwell and cut them dead. All the fine fellows who had taken quids and ten-bob notes from Generous Jack, who had accepted hospitality, and laughed and drank and danced and scuffed up the floors of Western Avenue, now abandoned his family to solitary grief.

Phoebe slept with her mother. I made them bowls of bread and hot milk. I cannot remember how long this little hell went on for, only that Molly finally expressed a desire to go to Ballarat and Phoebe was sent to withdraw one thousand pounds from the bank. She also, for reasons I never understood, invited Annette Davidson to accompany us.

54

Ballarat, the Golden City, was in decline. The streets were peopled by dour cloth-capped men in braces. Shops were boarded up and there was a mean dispirited air about the place which was made no happier by the big white statue of Hargreaves and his Welcome Stranger nugget, the flower bed in Sturt Street or the feathery cirrus clouds that streaked pink across the pale evening sky.

Annette Davidson was sorry she had come. She, at least, had rallied to her friend and now she wondered why her friend had wanted her. Annette, when neglected, had a tendency to cynicism. She had cancelled two days of classes for which she would lose two days' pay and Phoebe, sitting between Annette and the widow, would not even take her hand. Why ask her then? She answered herself bitterly: to witness the theatre of her grief, to be spellbound, taunted, maddened, by the pale skin and red lips behind the veil.

It had been a terrible journey, conducted in a silence broken only by the small whimpering noises Molly made as she wound and rewound the cord from a bulky electric radiator around her wrists. No one had explained the function of the radiator to Annette and it was too grotesque to inquire after. Molly, however, had been more explicit about a large piece of cardboard cut in the shape of a toilet seat which she would not travel without. It had "UP" written on one side and "DOWN" on the other and, fearful that she might be compelled to carry the ludicrous object into a country hotel, Annette kept quiet about her most pressing and painful problem.

She wanted a pee.

She had assumed we would go straight to a hotel, but no one in the car seemed in any hurry at all. First, it seemed, they would have to find a Dr Grigson. Much as Annette felt pity for Molly she could not see why the visit could not be postponed until the morning.

Annette, who could wax lyrical about the working people of Paris, did not bring this view to those of Ballarat. Small boys with no shoes ran beside the car and their faces frightened her. She thought the Hispano Suiza an insult to their condition. Groups of men on street corners stopped their conversation and stared at us in silence. She saw a drunk vomit into a gutter and another pee against the green-tiled walls of Craig's Hotel.

Molly clutched at her wires. She could not remember the names of streets. She was as confused and shocked as a householder returning to a bombed-out city and her directions to me lacked confidence.

"Down here," she said. "Up here."

Phoebe stroked her mother's arms and dabbed at the beads of perspiration that appeared on her upper lip. She tried to loosen the wires which were cutting off circulation. She despatched me to ask directions. But no one knew of any Dr Grigson. They shook their heads before I had finished my question. They turned their backs. They walked away.

We circled the streets. The Crystal Palace Hotel had vanished. Nothing was the same. People came from their houses to watch the Hispano Suiza go by. They shouted and grinned and sometimes jeered. Annette found none of this reassuring. As a sympathetic student of the Bolsheviks she considered the working class of Ballarat with some trepidation.

"All gone," Molly said, "all gone."

But Dr Grigson's building in Lydiard Street was precisely where it had always been. It was one of those buildings that disappear from the eyes of a city's inhabitants. It no longer had any part in their lives and they did not trouble to spell out the bleached and peeling letters on the rotting fascia of the veranda. We passed it four times before Molly located it in the wrecked map of her memory and experienced, in that drop from memory to reality, the chronological equivalent of an exceedingly large air pocket.

144

"Oh dear," she said as she confronted this desolation. "Oh dearie, dearie me."

Annette was ready to pee on the footpath.

"The good Dr Grigson", she said dryly, "appears to be no more."

"Herbert will knock," Phoebe said and Annette sighed in irritation and held her hands between her knees. Oh God, she prayed, find me somewhere to pee.

I did as I was bidden and gained Annette's best cynical smile for my attempts at kindness.

The windows facing the street were painted cream like a dentist's surgery. I knocked on them. I hammered on the door from which the ancient paint, unused to such agitation, fell in a flurry of green flakes and adhered stubbornly to the sleeves of my dark suit. I stooped to look through the generous keyhole and when I shouted I could hear my voice echo through the empty passage.

I had no idea why Molly wished to see Dr Grigson. It would be another year or two before I became privy to such delicate secrets. For the moment, all I knew was that it was a pressing matter. I did not need to be instructed to go round to the back of the building. I signalled this intention to my passengers.

I scaled the high wooden gate in Dr Grigson's back fence, although the padlock was so rusted I might have snapped it with my bare hands. A pale light glowed in the upstairs window. I picked up a piece of coal and threw it at the window. I fancied I heard a cough. I threw another, larger lump and knew, before it hit the glass, that the throw had been too hard. I sucked in my breath as the window broke.

"Beg your pardon," I yelled.

"Go away," a voice came quavering back.

"Dr Grigson?"

"I have the telephone," Dr Grigson said fearfully. "I shall call the police."

"Mrs McGrath wishes to see you, Dr Grigson. She motored all the way from Geelong to see you."

"Go away."

"Out the front," I pleaded. "Look out the front. In the Hispano Suiza."

"Hispano Suiza?" asked Dr Grigson (whose Daimler Benz sat quietly rusting in the shed beside which I stood). "Did you say Hispano Suiza?" A shard of glass fell to the courtyard and shattered at my feet.

"I did, sir."

The figure disappeared from the window and I went to stand at the back door. I heard footsteps descending the stairs at quite astonishing speed. Minutes later I heard high heels and the voice of my beloved echoing through the house.

I waited. No one came for me. Only after Annette Davidson, unprotected by cardboard, had released a loud cascade of urine into what had once been Ballarat's only upstairs water closet, was I able to make my presence known.

55

Dr Grigson was two days past his seventy-fifth birthday which he had celebrated alone. His hair was almost gone and his neck and spine had stiffened to such an extent that, in order to alter his point of view, it was necessary that he change the position of his tiny feet, which he did with small shuffling movements.

He had been washing his dishes and his rolled sleeves revealed skin of an almost unbearable limpidity, like a fish who has lived at such a remove from the sun that its internal organs are displayed beneath its transparent skin, a spectacle to make the sensitive squirm and turn away at such a display of the squishy vulnerability of life.

It was Annette (her bladder bursting) who had kept him from the motor car. She had taken him by his narrow shoulders and turned him in his tracks.

"I am sorry to be so blunt, Dr Grigson," she said, "but I need your toilet as a matter of some urgency."

Dr Grigson found himself incapable of arguing with such firm resolve and, under the impression that his visitors had driven in an Hispano Suiza simply to make use of his water closet, led them to it without complaint.

"There is no hurry," he told Annette as she closed the door, "we will look at the car in a moment."

By the time Annette had relieved herself and admitted me through the back door, Molly had made the nature of her business clear and was already locked away with Dr Grigson in the consulting room.

Very little had changed in the waiting room in thirty years. The roses and delphiniums still entwined on the carpet which, if threadbare in places, and faded everywhere, was spotlessly clean. The telephones and Remington typewriters and

Graphaphone dictating machines lay ready for the use of secretaries who were now grandmothers, their generous bosoms soft pillows for the bumping heads of their daughters' children.

Phoebe was giggling.

"My God," she whispered as Annette and I came up the stairs, "what an extraordinary place. It's a museum."

"What sort of doctor is he?"

Phoebe shrugged. We stood in the middle of the room. The ancient chairs had the appearance of valuable exhibits easily damaged by the simple demands of everyday life. We hesitated to sit on them.

The consulting room door opened. We had a brief view of the widow in her underwear. She scuttled behind the door as Dr Grigson emerged and shuffled mechanically, jointlessly, amiably across the roses and delphiniums.

He began to fuss at a large wooden filing cabinet whose small drawers were packed with musty filing cards. Long-bottled odours flooded gratefully into the room.

"Ah," he said to me, "the driver!" He nodded to me as a kindred spirit. "Rourke," he called out to Molly who was now safely tucked away behind the door. "There were Rourkes at Creswick. Were you a Creswick Rourke?"

"Ballarat East," said Molly in a wobbly falsetto that betrayed her state of undress. "Mrs Ester's niece."

"Ah, Mrs Ester, yes. Yes, yes." He took out a grey card. "Please help yourself to sweetmeats." He offered the bowl of confections to me. I obliged by offering it to the two ladies while Dr Grigson shuffled back into his consultation.

The sweets had faded wrappers whose substance had long ago melted with what they were intended to contain. We chewed and made faces. I was spitting mine into my handkerchief when I was nearly discovered by the doctor as he scurried out again, turning head and body this way and that, but whether from curiosity or fear of attack was not exactly clear. He flung open a high glass-fronted cupboard and began sorting through cardboard boxes. The odours of perished rubber and elastic joined the must from the index cards in our wrinkled noses.

"I had the first automobile in Ballarat," he said over his shoulder, "a Daimler Benz. They thought I was crazy. When I recommended sewerage at a town meeting Harry Wall said he would throw me into it."

He held up an astonishing elastic and metal contraption for the benefit of his audience.

"There," he said, "she's lucky. Or should I say, fortunate." The distinction was obviously important in Dr Grigson's mind and he did not lower the contraption until I had smiled and nodded my head in agreement. Grigson, satisfied, returned to Molly who burst into tears the minute the door was closed.

"He's a quack," Annette said. "It's obvious. We should take her out of here."

I was inclined to agree with her but one glance at Phoebe showed that she would have none of it. Annette quickly took the place beside her and left me to find less attractive accommodation.

56

Grigson placed Molly's hand on the velvet cushion and stroked it with his parchment-dry hands.

"There," he said, "does that feel better?"

"Yes, doctor," she smiled through her tears. "Oh yes, thank you."

"We are only electricity," the doctor said, and she did not doubt him. She gave herself to the belt and to the soothing strokes of the old hands which became inseparable in her mind. She closed her eyes. She multiplied some numbers, slowly at first.

"Of course," Grigson said, "it offends people to acknowledge it. It offends their primitive idea of themselves. It offends their religious principles. But if there is a god, perhaps", he smiled, "he is an electric charge. And why not? The Ark of the Covenant was an electric generator, although I have been physically threatened for saying such a thing."

Molly silently worshipped the electric god and begged its forgiveness.

"You are fortunate to find me still here," he said, not for a moment stopping the stroking. "I have been considering moving to Dubbo."

Molly shuddered at the thought.

"The town has gone backwards. I blame it on the gold," he said. "A marvellous conductor. The best conductor of electricity known to man and they waste it on decoration. This was a city of great potential, built on gold, and the fools squandered it. There has been no progress, nothing. They would rather go to spiritualists, herbalists. There is no belief in science," said Dr Grigson who had, just the same, borrowed the idea of the velvet cushion from a Chinese herbalist of my acquaintance.

"Rhinoceros horn, monkey foetus, snake livers," he sighed. "It is quite extraordinary. Which is why", he said, "it is an especial pleasure to help someone in an Hispano Suiza."

Molly was weak with relief and gratitude. She smiled at him dreamily. She would have offered him the car as payment.

"Would you like . . ."

". . . a drive?" Grigson smiled. "Would you offer?"

"Of course," Molly said, arranging her stole. She could have sung. "It would give me pleasure."

"I can ask no other fee", the doctor said, "than to drive around the streets of Ballarat in an Hispano Suiza."

57

"No," Annette said as we trooped down the stairs. "Please, Mr Badgery," she whispered in my ear. "Stop him. He'll kill us."

I had no intention of stopping it. I opened the car doors politely and sat beside the tiny doctor in the front seat while I explained the machine's controls.

I have had worse drives, although possibly not quicker ones, for Dr Grigson took to the Hispano Suiza like a demon. He displayed a sensitivity towards the controls that was surprising in such a stiff-necked man and although his frail legs were barely strong enough for the clutch he certainly had no trouble with the accelerator.

He drove recklessly up Lydiard Street and screeched around into Sturt Street where people, queuing for the cinema, turned to stare.

"Barbarians," said Grigson, puffing as he swung the wheel into Battery Hill Road, running down a fox terrier that was too slow to appreciate the danger.

Annette shut her eyes, but Phoebe, unaware of the dead dog behind her, only giggled.

They travelled up the highway and killed nothing more except a Rhode Island Red cockerel outside the Buninyong Post Office.

He drove back into town at a more leisurely pace. "That will teach them," he said, and I was never sure whether it was the display of the automobile, the demonstration of skill or the execution of two animals that was intended to have such an instructive effect on the people of Ballarat who remained stubbornly indoors, leaving Dr Grigson and his passengers to pursue their pagan rites in solitude.

58

Molly disowned the electric radiator. She was irritated, she said, by the amount of space the silly thing took up. She kicked at it with her tiny patent shoes. On the way from Grigson's to Craig's Hotel she made me stop and put it in the boot. There was not sufficient room and I was reduced to tying it on to the spare wheel with its cord – it bumped and rattled over the neglected streets, breaking all four elements and leaving sharp fragments of ceramic to find their way into the hooves of the dunnyman's horses.

Molly held her daughter's hand and kissed her. She fussed over the pale hand where it emerged from the fraying cast. She spat on her handkerchief and cleaned the skin beneath the ledge of plaster. She retied the sling. She pinned up loose wisps of hair that had straggled down from underneath her hat.

The hotel kitchen was closed when we arrived and it was Molly who persuaded them to open it again. When we sat at table in the big high-ceilinged dining room (famous for its pendulum clock and its original oil painting of Alfred Deakin) she ate heartily, demolishing two helpings of very grey roast lamb and only announcing herself stonkered after scraping clean the large monogrammed plate of steamed pudding.

Annette, as usual, was disgusted by the Australian habit of consuming large quantities of lamb, great slabs of dead dark meat smothered in near-black gravy. She scorned her knife and picked moodily at her shepherd's pie with fork alone and wondered what drug the quack doctor had prescribed for the widow's grief. If it had been the gonads of monkeys she would hardly have been surprised. The widow was all fluffed up like a hotel cat. Her plump cheeks were smooth as a china doll's and her fine nose, which had seemed so pinched, now flared its nostrils as if greedy for air and life. She held her knife and fork with a graceless enthusiasm more suitable for cricket bats.

Under the influence of a number of shandies, Molly began to reminisce about her life.

Annette had no curiosity about the subject. The blend of sentimentality and *naïveté* that Molly brought to her tales of the late Mrs Ester offended her, but not nearly so much as the happy smile on Phoebe's face as she decorated her mother's colonial ramblings with "Dear Mummy"'s.

Annette, the faint-hearted, had no confidence in anyone. A few "Dear Mummy"'s and she imagined Phoebe's character changed immediately. She saw her back-sliding into sentimentality and provinciality. Sloth and mediocrity, she thought, would come to claim her.

Annette, as usual, leaped to embrace the thing she feared the most.

She sipped what Craig's Hotel was pleased to call sherry and, although she nodded her head politely, her eyes sparkled with indignation.

Phoebe, she saw, was touching my leg beneath the table and the activity was being noted with disapproval by a silent group of Creswick matrons (who sat stiffly at the next white-clothed table) and with lewd amusement by the young boys who waited on us.

It was typical of her luck in life, or so she thought. She had invented Phoebe (another misconception) only to have her treasure plundered by the barbarian opportunist who sat opposite nodding his head, bringing nasal charm to bear on the widow whom Annette judged to be helpless in the face of such dishonest flattery.

Annette, Annette, for Christ's sake. You do me a disservice, an injustice. My heart, at that table, was as light as Molly's. I felt myself, not incorrectly, a kind man. The terrible whimpering journey up through the Brisbane Ranges from Geelong would have been worth it if it had lasted four days not four hours. It had been worth climbing gates, breaking windows and running over both dog and cockerel. I would have run my wheels over cats and goldfish to achieve this end: that Molly, after all, would not go mad with grief. I wished only, as Phoebe's leg pressed gently against mine, that Jack could be alive to witness, if not his daughter's leg, at least the kindness I had shown his widow. I was not a bad man after all. I was capable of kindness, and the kindness, or at least the anticipation of more kindness, built up in me until my ears were humming with the delicious pressure of it. I vowed, there and then in Craig's Hotel, to do everything in my power to make these two women happy. I would nurture them, protect them, be son to one, husband to the other. If it occurred to

151

me that I had stolen a family from Jack, I must have wrapped the ugly thought in blankets, trussed it up with twine, dispensed it quickly down a laundry chute, slammed the lid behind it.

The cook had, at last, gone home. The young boys stood in the corner and watched the agitation beneath the tablecloth. They were in no hurry to knock off and did not mind that Molly wanted to tell her daughter the story of her journey to Point's Point. They admired Annette's breasts as she leaned back, bored and miserable, in her chair. When she brought an ebony cigarette holder to her wide red lips, they could only think that she must surely be an actress. Thus distracted, they missed the real event at the centre table which was Molly, who had glimpsed a future, like a rosella, hardly seen, swooping through the high umbrellas of the bush.

59

I stayed in my room alone that night, which is just as well, for if I had followed my natural inclinations I would have found my adversary in Phoebe's room engaged in a passionate debate of which I was the subject.

"He is a confidence man," Annette said. "It is there for anyone to see. Even the waiters knew it. They gave the bill to your mother. Doesn't that tell you? They thought he was a gigolo."

Phoebe had taken off her hat and veil and kicked off her shoes. She sat cross-legged on the bed, a little drunk, not caring if she crushed the black linen suit she had, all day, been most particular about. A red toenail peeped through a hole in her stockinged foot and reminded Annette, painfully, of the girl with ingrained dirt on her knees and ink smudges on her fingers.

"What's a gigolo?"

"You know very well what a gigolo is," Annette smiled. "You want me to say something common."

"Perhaps I do," said Phoebe through barely parted lips, "perhaps I don't." Annette felt a short sharp rip of jealousy because she judged, quite correctly, that the excitement in Phoebe's eyes, the high colour in her cheeks, had been triggered by the pressure of a man's bowed leg.

"A gigolo", Annette said, "is a man paid by a woman for certain services."

"A waiter?" Phoebe suggested.

"No, you stupid child." Her pupils dilated and her eyes did not leave Phoebe's

"A man paid to slide his rod," Phoebe whispered, closing her eyes and rocking slyly on her haunches.

Annette moved slowly and sat beside her pupil who smelt of dust and lavender. She kept her hands in her lap and did not risk rejection.

"Oh God," she said. "I'm so miserable."

"Poor Dicksy."

And she was in her arms and Annette was kissing her. "Tell me," she whispered in Phoebe's ear, "tell me what he does to you."

Phoebe told her. She whispered in her ear while Annette moaned and twisted in the opposing tides that would pull at her all her life: pain and pleasure, jealousy and lust, the potential suppliers of which contradictory needs she would recognize in buses and restaurants, on footpaths and in ballrooms, men and women whose sensual lips were never quite in harmony with the unswerving ambition of their brilliant eyes.

60

On Wednesday Molly McGrath ate a breakfast of steak, chops, bacon, fried bread and eggs. Somewhere between the first mouthful and the last she decided that she could not live in Geelong any more. Once she had decided she was eager to be out of it quickly, so quickly that she would, to everyone's surprise, agree to fly in the Morris Farman to Melbourne, leaving behind wardrobes of clothes for the Brotherhood of Saint Laurence and an eccentrically renovated property for Mr O'Brien of Mallop Street to dispose of by auction.

This decided on, although not yet spoken of, she rose from table, went upstairs, packed her case, and, when the urge took her, bustled noisily down the passage to the toilet.

She sat in the huge white-tiled room whose high window contained a perfect square of sky. She grunted happily, pursed her lips, and expelled a turd of such dimension that it would not be flushed down no matter how she tried.

The widow shrugged and turned her back upon it.

Annette, who followed her in, found the thing like a giant *bêche-de-mer* inside the bowl. It lay there, dull and malevolent, a

153

parasite expelled, abandoned on the porcelain shores of Craig's Hotel.

61

I am pleased I have lived long enough to finally meet a psychiatrist, although I cannot believe this one is typical. Jack Slane the lunatic psychiatrist and Maroochydore taxi driver has come out of retirement to take an interest in my case, and when I listen to him I fancy I know why he took to driving taxis.

I told him something (but by no means all) about the snakes. By God, you should have heard him. Snakes and aeroplanes, he says, are not snakes and aeroplanes at all, but symbols. Well, it's entertaining anyway and I would not have missed it for worlds.

When he discovered my tits he nearly wet himself. I expressed a little milk for him and he put it in a bottle to take away.

I told him the tits were just a lie, but he doesn't seem to understand. He has the milk and he is happy and he understands nothing about truth and lies. If my voice was better I would explain it to him. If I had more time I would write a letter for him, but I cannot spend my life amusing him. There are other customers to take care of and I must push on to the years 1920 and 1923 and get them done with. I wish I had been able to control them as well as I can now, for half the time I blundered ignorant and blinkered in the dark, not knowing what was up and what was down, blind as a bat, clumsy as a coot, but now I sit behind my instruments like Christ Almighty summoning up a stolen letter from Jonathon Oakes's drawer to get the next leg started.

62

Oriental Hotel, Collins Street, Melbourne
December, 1920

Dear Dicksy,

You were wrong to write me off and cruel to ignore my letters which I hope you have had at least the decency to open. I know what you think about me and hardly a day goes by when your unsympathetic judgement does not cause me pain and I am determined upon convincing you that you are wrong, terribly wrong. You think I have wasted it all, thrown it all away, but I am far too aware of my life, all life – what a treasure it is – to squander it.

You see today I have flown an aeroplane. My eyes are sore and red from dust because I did not like the goggles H. wanted me to wear and so I insisted on going without them. No, it was not a solo flight, but Dicksy, Dicksy, it was a flight. We took off from Port Melbourne where H. has some land and then went right over Port Phillip Bay. I fancied I could see Geelong but am told this was impossible. In any case, I *thought* about Geelong, and you there in that terrible school and while the air was so fresh and clean I imagined you (not in a scornful way, I promise you) having to endure all the smells I remember and I fantasized a dictionary of smells which I have rendered, not as a proper dictionary, but as a poem which I will enclose if I can have time to make a fair copy before H. leaves.

You would not recognize Mummy. She has been buying (under my guidance) new clothes and she looks quite the grande dame. She has taken a fancy to the theatre and as Herbert also cares for it (I suspect actresses in his past) we take a box at the Athenaeum, the Lyceum or the Royal and make quite a night of it with dinner afterwards.

You did not say a thing about our plans to marry. Please do not be hurt. You must not be hurt. I will not allow it. I am selfish enough to demand not only your approval (for whose else can I ask?) but also your pleasure in it.

We have plans for entering the next big air race as husband and wife. Doubtless you will read about us in the papers but I would much rather, dear Dicksy, that you took the train up one weekend. I have spoken to Mummy and if you are wretchedly poor at the moment she will happily (yes, happily) pay for your hotel room here at the Oriental where we are quite the "Honoured Guests" and are known to all staff who we are privileged to call by first names although they (do not bite your red revolutionary lips with rage) are not permitted the return of this familiarity.

H. will take no money from us. It is a sore point and we have given up offering to help him while he establishes himself again. The loss of the aircraft factory was a cruel blow to him and now he must start to build up again. He is selling cars for Barret's, the Ford agents, working very hard indeed poor dear. He is also building a house although where or what it is he will not tell us. It is to be my wedding present from him.

Dear Dicksy, he is so kind. He looks after Mummy so nicely and does not complain when she wants to be driven here or there or become impatient when she wants to crawl along at five miles an hour, so slowly that men in horse-drawn wagons want to overtake and shout abuse at us. He *does* clench his fists around the steering wheel and look like he could bite a rat, but he is quite lamb-like and does nothing nasty.

I have a lovely room overlooking Collins Street and I see all manner of celebrity walking below. Alfred Deakin, a fat old man, was at dinner last night (not at our table) and Herbert was kind enough to get his autograph for Mummy which was so nice of him, because he is not a groveller and the incident must have caused him pain.

I am writing ceaselessly. I am due for flying lessons on every Wednesday morning. I go to the theatre and the galleries. I remember the things that you taught me, Dicksy. I think of you as a true friend. If you will not answer my letters properly at least send me a postcard, unsigned if you wish, to let me know that you are, at least, opening the envelopes.

With much love and affection, your friend,

Phoebe

63

Melbourne, in case you did not know, has its charms: botanical gardens, splendid churches, a high-domed public library where an old man can read the newspapers and stay cool on a hot day, etc. But there is no use denying that it is a flat place, divided up into a grid of streets by a draughtsman with a ruler and set square. The names of streets are just as orderly. King precedes William, neatly, exactly parallel. Queen lies straight in bed beside Elizabeth and meets Bourke (the explorer) and Latrobe (the governor) briefly on corners whose angles measure precisely 90 degrees.

Melbourne has a railway station famous for showing fifteen clocks on its front door, like a Victorian matron with a passion for punctuality, all bustle, crinolines and dirty underwear. It has Collins Street which is famous, in Melbourne at least, for resembling Paris, by which it is meant that the street has trees and exclusive shops where women in black with violently red lips and too much powder on their ageing cheeks are able to intimidate women like Molly McGrath by calling them "modom".

Oh, it's a good enough town, but it can take a while to realize it.

There is a passion in Melbourne you might not easily notice on a casual visit and I must not make it sound a dull thing, or sneer at it, for it is a passion I share – Melbourne has a passion for owning land and building houses. There is nothing the people of Melbourne care for as much as their red-tiled roofs, their lemon tree in the back garden, their hens, their Sunday dinners. You will not learn much about the city strolling around the deserted streets on a Sunday, no more than you will learn about an ants' nest by walking over it. Thus, when I seek something peaceful to think of, some quiet corner to escape into, I do not think of sandy beaches or rivers or green paddocks, I imagine myself in a suburban street in Melbourne on a chilly autumn afternoon, the postman blowing his whistle, a dog crossing the road to pee on those three-feet-wide strips of grass beside the road that are known as "nature strips".

The people of Melbourne understand the value of a piece of land. They do not leave it around for thistles to grow on, or cars to be dumped on. And this makes it a very difficult place for a man with no money to take possession of his necessary acre.

When Molly, Phoebe and I took up residence in the Oriental Hotel in Collins Street, Melbourne, there was pressure applied to me to accept money from the McGrath Estate in order to purchase land. I will not say I was not tempted, but I am proud to say I did not succumb. I found my land, and took it, although its legal owners (the Church of England) were not aware of it at the time.

What the Church of England wanted with those poor mudflats on the Maribyrnong River I will never know, but anyone could see that it was no site for a cathedral and was of no use for anything but what I intended. It was a place where you could set up a windsock, land a craft, build a house and not expect to be troubled unless you asked for electricity to be connected.

The Maribyrnong is, in places, a pretty river, but as it snakes down through Flemington and pushes out through the flats to the bay it is neglected and dirty, enriched by the effluent from the Footscray abattoirs.

I took possession of my land by circling above it.

"There's my land," I shouted. Not once. Three times.

Phoebe had no goggles. Her eyes so streamed with wind-drawn tears that she could see nothing but the misty confluence of grass and water: brown and green like a runny watercolour.

Later, over cucumber sandwiches at the Oriental, she described my land quite lyrically.

Now if I had never seen Jack's house in Western Avenue, never known a tower, a music room, a library, I may well have built my usual type of structure, something like the place I made for the girl in Bacchus Marsh, or the slab hut I built for the barmaid up at Blackwood. I could not have dug a hole, of course, because the land was not suitable. But I may have set up a series of rainwater tanks, connected them with short passages, and covered the whole with earth for insulation. It would have lasted a year or two. However, you cannot ask women who have lived in a house with a tower to feel comfortable inside a burrow and I was not such a fool as to try to persuade them. On the other hand, I had no money. I could not even pay my keep at the Oriental Hotel and it offended me.

You see, my dear Annette, it was not the way you thought it was – I was not about to milk them dry, buy French champagne, visit actresses, contract syphilis and pass it on, talk sharp, dress slick, steal the Hispano Suiza or use the widow's fortune to buy an Avro 504 and leave them at home to knit while I flew across the world and got myself written up in papers from Rangoon to Edinburgh.

It was Molly and Phoebe who spent the money. By God, they loved it. There were boxes in the theatre, dinners in the hotel, new hats and dresses and picnics in the Dandenongs. I kept a notebook and recorded what they spent on me, and I got a job.

I have put off discussing the job. It was not what I wanted. But tell me what else I was to do? I hated that clever Yankee bastard, but there was no easier motor car to sell. Yes, yes, I took my book of cuttings round to Colonel Tarrant who had the Ford agency in Exhibition Street and he hired me on the spot. I worked right off the floor, which I had never done before, and I cannot say I enjoyed the city style of selling cars. It did not suit me. I would rather have been standing in paddocks ring-barking with the O'Hagens, in some room lit by hurricane lamps while the daughter of the house played the piano accordion. I would have happily suffered indigestion from bad food, done my card tricks, told some yarns, and taken my time to make a sale.

All of this, I tell you now. But for twelve months I did this work and did not let any of my feelings make themselves known to me. I could not. My great talent in life was my enthusiasm and I drew on it relentlessly, careless of how I spent it. I poured it over my new life with the same reckless style with which Molly poured *crème de menthe* over her treacle pudding, not giving a damn for the pounds it added or the pounds it cost. I was protector and provider, or intended to be, and the role, of course, took its toll on me. A portrait taken at the time shows the increasing depth of the wrinkles around my eyes which the retoucher's well-meaning brush made more, not less, noticeable. My black hair was already showing flecks of grey and receding in such a way as to make a long promontory of what had once been admired as a "widow's peak".

I worked early and late, I did deals in pubs and wine bars. I scrounged complimentary theatre tickets for the women. I took them to the aquarium and the art gallery. And, I can confess it now, I stole a church hall from the Methodists at Brighton and had it transported out to the Maribyrnong River where I had the foundation stumps already in their place and waiting.

The Methodists' hall was not a palace, and, being Methodists, they had balked at the luxury of a tower. But it did have a kitchen and the hall itself had a platform. I worked on that hall like a bower-bird, running in and out with nails in my mouth, hammer in my hand. I used the spare wing sections that had come with the Morris Farman to divide up the hall into three rooms. They worked very well. True, they did not go right up to the ceiling, but those wings were the best walls I ever put inside a house. They were made, as you'd realize, from timber struts stretched tight with fabric and they let the light through very prettily. There was not a dark corner, even in the centre room. On sunny afternoons they were like a magic lantern show with the green and amber windows of the hall projected prettily against the canvas.

I found some very good quality carpet at the Port Melbourne tip and bought a brand-new dining-room table from the Myer Emporium. I borrowed a rainwater tank from a building site at Essendon and connected it to the guttering of the roof.

I had no time for the outside world. No one told me that de Garis had made his flight from Brisbane to Melbourne, and if I'd known I don't think I'd have cared. Melbourne was in an uproar about the treatment the St Patrick's Day procession had meted out to the Union Jack, I had no time to make my views known. I taught my customers to drive their cars with a patience that was new to me. If they were upset about the Union Jack I did not contradict them.

I lived for my family, and for Phoebe in particular, who waited in her room for my gentle knock.

Melbourne was a city of dreams and my darling was drunk on them. She made, with her own hands, a bright yellow flying suit and made love to me in it, allowing me entry through the opening she had so skilfully designed. The Morris Farman quivered on its guy ropes beneath the moon, before the wind at Maribyrnong.

In the next room Molly rang for room service and regaled old Klaus with tales of Point's Point while he allowed himself a glass or two of the *crème de menthe* that the widow, magnificent in crêpe de Chine, was pleased to offer him.

64

Annette said she would attend no wedding in a church and it was for her sake that the wedding was held in the register office in William Street, a dusty dismal place which we pretended not to notice. Annette did not arrive, so there was no bridesmaid. Dr Grigson, invited to give away the bride, had missed his train and arrived, puffing and blowing out his sallow cheeks, at the wedding breakfast with a patented electric device for toasting bread which he, confused about whose wedding it was, presented to Molly with a pretty speech.

We had a small private room on the first floor of the Oriental. The windows looked out, through the leaves of a plane tree, on to the dappled footpaths of Collins Street along which the Saturday trams full of football crowds rattled, ringing bells.

When Dr Grigson, formally attired in tails, pronounced the gathering splendid, he was, as was his habit, choosing his words carefully – he did not overstate the case.

Molly wore an emerald green tunic and a dress of gold tusser. She crowned her splendour with a wide-brimmed hat from which ostrich feathers cascaded in spectacular abundance.

Phoebe appeared for the breakfast in a navy and red faille dress with a matching poncho that was short and tailored and did nothing to hide the hugging dress which, as I remarked appreciatively, used no more fabric than was absolutely necessary. She wore a fur hat, a little like a fez, which had the disadvantage of hiding her copper hair but which capped her head tightly and presented her handsome face so pleasingly.

"I could fancy", Grigson said, "that I was sitting, this very moment, in Paris."

I was so happy I could not find it in my heart to ask the old gentleman what was wrong with sitting in Melbourne.

We toasted everyone. We toasted Jack, solemn in black suit and bulging collar, whose photograph Molly had arranged to hang beside the King's. We toasted Annette. We toasted Geelong.

Molly added a little *crème de menthe* to her champagne.

"To a new life", she declared, "for all of us."

Only Dr Grigson, suddenly reminded of the realities of Ballarat, saw reason to doubt it.

65

It can be argued, of course, that I should have consulted my fiancé about the house she was to share with me, to ask her advice, opinion, needs, to see the bedroom pointed in a direction that was pleasing and the layout of the kitchen was a practical one. Shopping at the Port Melbourne tip, she should, you say, have been by my side, and may well have selected a different piece of carpet, a different Coolgardie safe, a better chair, and so on.

I dare say you're right, but the house was my present to her and as it represented no more than the core of the mansion I intended to finally construct, could be altered, pulled apart, demolished and rebuilt, I saw no harm in it. Saw no harm in it! I saw great benefit. It was my gift, my surprise, my work, my love, my tribute to her.

She loved it. As we bounced along the pot-holed track through yellow summer grass she exclaimed with joy. There was confetti spangled on her fur hat. The blustering northerly wind blew dust into her eyes.

She jumped from the car before I stopped. She ran through the house in echoing high heels. She kissed and hugged me. She called me husband.

I never guessed how differently she saw the place. That while her delight summoned up future towers and libraries in my mind, winding paths, flower borders, shrubbery, ancient elms, ponds and statues, children running with hoops and spinning-tops, my confetti-spangled wife saw nothing more than a camp.

It was this she thought so wonderful, and when she wrote her letters to Annette she would talk about it like a gypsy, a place to sing and dance and make love in, but nothing permanent. Phoebe loved it because it wasn't bourgeois. She loved it because it seemed to reject rose bushes and afternoon tea. She enjoyed (my perverse beloved) the rank foul smell that came drifting from the abattoirs, that gave an odd dimension to sunsets and storms in the sky above, and an unexpected perfume to the long-legged ibises.

Our wedding day was a dangerous day for flying. The howling northerly stole great fistfuls of red dust from the over-settled Mallee country, and carried it three hundred miles to throw it spitefully into our faces. But Phoebe, if she felt the spite, ignored it. She wished to consummate our partnership by flying. When she shed her splendid clothes it was not to lie between the stolen sheets, but to dress again in her flying suit and strap on her goggles.

I could not deny her, yet as I swung the prop, I was taken suddenly by the fear that was soon to become the dominant emotion of my life, that an accident would take my treasure from me. I saw her, as I grasped the prop and she, inside her cockpit, flicked the little bakelite switch to the "on" position; I saw her broken, bleeding. She held her thumb up, such a fragile thing, the bone a mere three-eighths of an inch, the skin as snug and fragile as the dope-tight fabric on an aircraft wing. The engine sputtered, then took, and I ran through the swirl of dust, carrying my butcher-shop nightmares, pulling my goggles over my eyes.

We were blown into the air before we had speed, kangaroo-hopped twice, swayed and tilted dangerously before we got the height to clear the dull red brick of the abattoirs. We bounced in the turbulent sky above the Maribyrnong, our noses full of the stink of rendering sheep boiling into tallow just below.

That twenty-minute flight was as frightening as any I ever made, and although I let my bride take the dual controls momentarily, I was forever overriding her, and I took a course out and along Port Phillip Bay, following the hot white beaches in case it was necessary to put down.

When I judged (incorrectly) that she had had enough, I brought the craft back to the river to land it. The ground ran east–west and made no allowance for the blustering northerly. I made no less than five attempts and aborted them as the gusts threatened to smash us sideways to the ground. When, on the sixth attempt, I landed it gracelessly, I whispered a small prayer to the god I did not believe existed and made a number of extravagant promises as payment for our safe delivery.

The exhilaration Phoebe showered on me was sufficient to make me forget the promises, one of which was related to obtaining a divorce from Marjorie Thatcher Badgery, a matter I had neglected to attend to so far and one that I would continue to neglect until it was brought to my attention in a manner I was to find uncomfortable.

We will come, in more detail, later, to the aphrodisiac effect of flying on Phoebe Badgery. Let me merely say that when we returned to the house Phoebe gave not a damn that the floor was adrift with Mallee dust and when she made love to her new husband she accompanied herself with a torrent of words, a hot obscenity that shocked me even while it brought a seemingly endless flow of semen pumping from my balls. It was an auspicious beginning for Charles Badgery who was conceived on that afternoon from the joining of his dry-mouthed father and ecstatic mother in a house whose dry Coolgardie safe contained nothing more than a loaf of stale bread and a tin billy of melted butter.

66

In 1917 I moored a Blériot monoplane in a paddock in Darley and had it eaten up by cattle. The Blériot engine uses castor oil and, messy machine that it is, the castor oil splatters back over the plane, covers the fabric of the wings and makes an appealing snack for cattle. Give them a night and their rough tongues will rip and tear the fabric until the craft looks like a well-picked chicken carcass.

If I had known how important the Morris Farman was to Phoebe I would have coated it in castor oil and introduced a herd of heifers, a nest of white ants, moths, grubs, vultures and men from sideshows whose specialty is eating pieces of machinery.

When you hear what follows you will wonder at my blindness. How can the fellow not know? His wife is besotted with aviation. She spends her days with navigation and maintenance. He assists her in every way he can. And yet he says he never realized the thing was serious.

I will not deny that I knew the thing amused her, but I fancied that, with children, when they came, she would put her fancies away just as I had mine. I had not abandoned my dream lightly, like a man who throws away a half-smoked cigarette outside the theatre. I dropped it with regret and sadness, but I had a family to support and I thanked God I was so lucky.

It was hard work and the hours were long. We didn't have the easy life car salesmen seem to have these days. There were no neon tubes, comfortable chairs, little glass-partitioned offices. We worked, for the most part, from big dark garages with oil stains on the floor and the parts of troubled engines beneath our feet. We did business in the street when it was fine, or in pubs and cafés when it was cold. We drank more than we should, to pressure-cook friendliness. We spent frosty nights waiting outside doctors' surgeries so that the Herr Doktor could, when his last patient had gone, enjoy a demonstration.

In the meantime, Phoebe pursued the mysteries of aviation.

I soon realized that she had no aptitude for things mechanical, had no real interest in the way things worked. She had what I can only call a poetic understanding of machinery, a belief in magic, that did not apply merely to machines but to all the natural world. Thus she planted flowers out of season, ignoring both the instructions in Yates's *Garden Guide* and the ones on the seed packets themselves, as if these rules might apply to everyone else, but not to her, as if it needed only her goodwill, her enthusiasm, her dedication, for all the laws of botany to be reversed and frost-tender species would bloom outside her bedroom window. She was as impatient of the confines of reality in her way as I was in mine. She adopted mechanics' overalls as if, dressed as a mechanic, she would become one.

I bought her a copy of Sidwell's *Basic Aviation* which stresses the importance of a potential pilot understanding the mechanics of a craft, being able to repair, maintain, etc. Thank God for Sidwell. (There are lots of pictures.) I kept her busy with such basic points as making loops in piano wire for rigging. I showed her how to use the round-nose pliers and make the little loops. This looks simple enough when you see it done, but it takes a while to get the knack of it. I was critical of her loops. Perhaps I was too critical. In any case she dealt with this better than she did the principles of the internal combustion engine. She was careless and impatient with the gaps in sparkplugs, insisting that they did not matter, but I kept her at it, and I would find her at home at night with a dismantled magneto on the dining-room table, short of patience, a screw lost, arguing that the thing was incorrectly made, Sidwell wrong, the whole thing impossible.

The more I understood her way of approaching these problems, the more fearful I became of her taking to the air. Well, I was wrong of course, and I've had enough accusations on this subject not to need yours added to it.

If I have made these early months of our marriage sound irritable, I have not explained myself properly. I have merely let my dusty irritations blossom out like one of those Japanese paper flowers you drop in water.

They were heady, wonderful days. The nights were clear, the mornings frosty. We rose early and before I stood in Exhibition Street in my suit ready to sing the praises of King Henry Ford I would have hammered and sawn and worked to build the room for Molly who was soon to join us, planted a tree, explained a mechanical point, made love (sometimes twice), eaten no breakfast, and come to watch the cold-footed ibis (at my love's request) fossicking on the flats.

I returned home at night with a billy of bortsch from Billinsky's in Little Collins Street. I would be tired, worn out and wrung dry by the slyness of doctors, the meanness of solicitors or drapers or widows, sometimes bringing Molly with me, sometimes not. When we were alone we spent the evening poring over maps at the table. I let myself be carried away with flights of fancy across Sumatra and Burma.

Life was so full it is little wonder that I failed to notice several important things that were happening.

The first: Molly was not bored or lonely as I feared, but was busy shopping for a business to buy.

The second: that Phoebe was pregnant.

The third: she was not happy about it.

The fourth: ah, the fourth was Horace the epileptic poet, who I would have killed at the time if I had known the things that stirred his brave and fearful heart, but who I embraced, first in wilful ignorance, and then, now, as I tell you these things I cannot possibly know, in the full passion of a liar's affection for the creatures of his mirrored mind.

67

Horace Dunlop was what is known as a Rawleigh's man – it was his job to travel door to door selling the jars and bottles of milky medication which bear the slogan "For Man or Beast". Yet to call him a Rawleigh's man is to do a disservice to everyone, to the real

Rawleigh's men who went about their jobs in a methodical way and fed their families through their labours, and to Horace himself who was nearly a lawyer and almost a poet.

It has always puzzled me, puzzles me still, how he could have lost his way so completely that he ended up at that isolated spot on the Maribyrnong River. I am tempted to explain it all by means of an epileptic fit: the poet left unconscious, slumped on the seat of his cart while Toddy, his gelding, wandered feeding all the way to Phoebe's door. Yet this will not do. I have seen Horace have one of his fits and it is not the sort of thing that leaves a man on the seat he started out on. It is a wild, banging, eye-rolling, tongue-swallowing, terrible thing and had the fit struck him whilst sitting in his cart he would have catapulted himself to earth to continue his arm-flinging amongst the roadside thistles.

So let us not concern ourselves with how the fellow got there. It is of no importance.

There he is, clear as day, sitting at the kitchen table, speaking to Phoebe who is watching the poet spread lard on one more slice of bread and marvelling that any man can eat so much.

Horace Dunlop was a broad heavy man in his early twenties. He had unusually short legs, a barrel chest, an exceedingly large, closely cropped head. The features of his face were all too small for the large canvas they were painted on and perhaps they appeared more intense because of it: the small intelligent eyes, the mouth with the cupid's bow that would never quite be swallowed up by the corpulence that would later overtake him – even when he was at his most grotesque the eyes would command interest and the lips demand affection.

Horace had no love of lard. He explained this all to Phoebe while he licked it from his short thick fingers. He ate lard to ease the pain in his tongue which had been pierced (well-meaningly) with a hatpin during one of his fits of *petit mal* epilepsy.

He had written a poem to celebrate the event: "The poet, tongue-pierced, / Trussed, gagged, / By butcher's wife in Williamstown."

I would never have viewed the funny-looking fellow as a competitor for my wife's affections, and in this I was both right and wrong. I doubt they ever shared much more than a peck on the cheek, and yet, I fear, there are poet's caresses that are more intimate for not being visible.

While I went to Billinsky's to buy my tin billy full of bortsch, I saw no more than one more steamed-up little café full of drunks in overcoats. I did not recognize the prostitutes and did not know it was a place for poets and artists to boast to each other and recite their works out loud.

I brought back soup from Billinsky's. I won't say it was not appreciated, but what Horace brought from there was treasured more. He spent his evenings drinking tea with jam in it and trying to overhear more prestigious conversations at other tables. He also knew Dawson's wine bar in Carlton where short-story writers and housebreakers rubbed drunken shoulders. He knew little rooms in Collins Street where painters lived in bare rooms divided by Japanese screens, rooming houses in East Melbourne whose moth-eaten felt letter racks held letters that might one day be published in books, whose polished brown linoleum floors led to tiny apartments where people waited until being called to fame in London or New York.

In short, he filled my darling's head with nonsense. He recited his poems and listened to her while Molly tilled the clay-heavy garden beds close by and kept a suspicious eye turned on the events inside the kitchen.

It was to Horace that Phoebe revealed her pregnancy, not me. It was with him that she discussed the complicated state of her emotions produced by the little gilled creature who stirred within her: blood, birth, life, death, fear, and the final decision that she could not, no matter what guilt it caused her, have this child.

The papers that year were full of abortionists being arrested and patients charged. She had already visited Dr Percy McKay who had since been arrested and put in Pentridge Gaol, but not before he had informed her that her body played tricks on her. She was not one month pregnant as she imagined, but nearly three. Dr McKay's last day of freedom was partly occupied with lecturing Phoebe Badgery on the dangers of a late abortion and her perfect situation (in terms of health and financial security) to have the child. He had put no weight on aviation or poetry. He had judged her doubly fortunate to have such hobbies.

From Phoebe's point of view the situation had now become quite desperate. She was anxious, angry, guilty; and frightened of what she read in the papers. Yet, at the same time, she could watch her own drama with an appreciative eye: here she was, twenty years old, married, in Melbourne, a poet in the kitchen, an aeroplane out the window, conspiring to procure a dangerous abortion without her husband's knowledge. All these things, the authentic and the false, the theatrical and the real, were all a part of her nature and I do not mean to belittle her by pointing them out.

"What", she asked Horace Dunlop, "are we to do?"

Phoebe could co-opt people like this – she included them in her life generously, without reserve, and included theirs in hers as readily.

"What are we to do?" she asked, and the poet was flattered and frightened as a clerk given a too rapid promotion. He had no idea what to do. He was an unprepared explorer about to embark in a leaking dug-out on a dangerous journey up a fetid river.

"I will make inquiries," he said, standing. "This evening."

"No, no, you mustn't go, not yet."

Molly coughed, loudly, outside the window.

"But I must, dear lady," Horace said, mournfully arranging his cravat, "must bid adieu."

Phoebe was at the shelf I was pleased to call the mantelpiece. She dug into a large biscuit canister.

"No," Horace said, holding up his hand. "I will not permit you to buy more."

"If I must buy a bottle to maintain your presence, then that is what I'll do," Phoebe smiled. "A bottle, sir, of your excellent product. If it would make my condition disappear I would pay you a thousand pounds."

"If I could make your condition disappear I would consider myself amply rewarded with nothing more", Horace said, "than to be permitted a kiss." And he blushed bright red.

"Mr Dunlop!" Phoebe said, but she was not displeased. "You are absolutely the most immoral man I have ever met."

"A poet", said Horace, "has his own order of morality."

"My husband would kill you just the same," Phoebe smiled. "Here is the florin for your balsam but perhaps you had better give me the bottle another time; I already have four of them."

The poet hesitated. He would rather have denied himself the florin, but he was too impoverished to allow himself the luxury. He took the money and dropped it into his jacket pocket where there was nothing for it to jingle against.

"There will be no doctor in Melbourne who will touch you," he said. He was probably right. The press was in a hysteria about abortion and did not hesitate to report what grisly details came its way. "But I will arrange something."

He would have done anything for this throaty-voiced woman who spoke without moving her lips, and yet the very thing he was to arrange made him clench his thighs together in sympathetic agony and his fearful imagination was peopled with bloody instruments and tearing life.

"It is monstrously unfair," he said, "the whole thing. I would not be a woman for a million pounds."

"Dear Horace," Phoebe said, "you are a good friend."

"Ay," the poet said sadly.

"You can help, can't you?"

"Yes, yes. I will. I will. I will do something. I will make inquiries." He pushed away the bread and lard with a quick shudder of revulsion. He stood up, brushing the crumbs from his vest and tucking in the tail of his shirt. "I will make inquiries and be back by dinnertime."

"My husband will be here."

"Then you will introduce me to him, dear lady," said Horace, allowing himself the liberty of kissing her hand. "I cannot spend my time sneaking in and out of your house like a criminal. Does he not care for poets?"

"Very much," she smiled. "So much that he has impregnated one."

"I will be careful," Horace said, smiling so primly that the small mouth became even smaller and Phoebe, considering the twitching nose, was reminded of a guinea pig called Muffin she had once had as a pet. "Will be *most* careful, that he attempt no such thing with me."

And so saying, he bowed theatrically.

Molly saw the poet depart. She nodded to him as he ran towards his horse and cart. She dug her spade deep into the ground, frowned, and, as Horace began his dash towards the city, went into the house to interrogate her daughter about these visits from the Rawleigh's man.

68

Horace's carthorse was a dun-coloured, sway-backed, lop-eared gelding with furry fetlocks and soup-plate hooves. Nothing in its experience of Horace had prepared it for such a desperate journey. The gelding had been inclined to dawdle and the poet had not been keen to change its mind. It had wandered on a loose

169

rein, eaten flowers when it cared to, and stumbled along the cobbled streets of North Melbourne, Flemington, Moonee Ponds and Essendon, with a low lolling head. The only thing that seemed to have the capacity to excite the animal was a motor cycle, to which category of machinery it had a strong aversion. Horace, on hearing the approach of a motor cycle, would dismount and stand by the horse's head, soothing it, reciting incantations until such time as the offensive machine had passed.

But on this Tuesday afternoon the poet ran to the jinker as fast as his short chubby legs could carry him. His small brown eyes bulged. His button nose shone. He did not take his seat with his usual fussing of cushions and rugs. He did not first introduce himself to the horse's attention and mutter soothing words to it, as if apologizing for the necessary subjugation of one being to another. He stood in the jinker and gave the horse a great thwack on the backside with the end of the reins.

"Geddup, Toddy."

And Toddy did geddup. He started in shock, with such a jerk that Horace fell backwards into his seat with a crash that the horse felt through its bit. There had never been such excitement in the Rawleigh's jinker. The bottles rattled in the wooden panniers. Toddy picked up his great soup-plated hooves and set off in a brisk canter along the pot-holed track beside the Haymarket saleyards. He did not loll his head or try to scoop up dung between his leathery lips. He held his head high. He felt the urgency of the errand and must have hoped, in his slow cunning brain, that it was something that would lead him to flower beds.

Horace flung himself at his errand with a passion, not (as Phoebe thought, watching him depart so dangerously) because he wished the pregnancy terminated this very instant, but because he was a coward in the face of the law. He dashed at the matter recklessly so he would have it done before his cowardice claimed him.

Horace Dunlop loathed the law and feared it, not in any normal degree, but in his bowels. His father was a lawyer in Bacchus Marsh, and much respected in that pretty town. His brother was an articled clerk. He himself had done three years of law at Melbourne University until he could stand it no more and he had flung himself into failure just as he had, now, flung himself into the jinker – eager to get it done with before the thought of his father's wrath dissuaded him.

He did not like the faces of lawyers. He liked even less the faces of judges with whom he had, since childhood, been called upon to dine. He did not like their cruel contented faces, the waxy finish to their folds of skin, the arrogant noses, the hooded eyes.

His terror of the law did not incline him to rebel, but to sneak away and lie very still and quiet, to sit inoffensively in some dusty corner where he vented all his fear and spleen in poems littered with the "cruel cold instruments of reason".

Yet here was Horace Dunlop careering towards the procurement of an abortion. He tried not to think what he was doing. He was not travelling to Carlton to see his friend Bernstein. He was not intent on a conspiracy. He was off to the city to buy a new hat. With only a florin? Well, a beer then. That was all. There is no law against the purchase of a beer, not, at least, before the legal closing time of six o'clock. But, ha, we have a witness who says you do not drink. In secret, yes, in public, no.

Involved in cross-examination, he gave no thought to automobiles through whose midst he cantered. In Flemington Road they passed a motor cycle before either horse or driver could realize what they'd done.

Insisting on his fabricated story, he ignored Grattan Street which led to Bernstein, and went pell-mell towards the city. At the Latrobe Street corner he reined in a little but people stopped to laugh at the soup-plated sway-back cutting such a dash. A street urchin threw an apple core which struck the driver on the back of his closely shorn head. "Fatty fool face," the boy yelled, "fatty big bum," somehow seeing what no one else would see for five years more.

Horace lost his forty-shilling Akubra hat and did not stop for it and the Elizabeth Street cable tram sliced it in half before he had gone another block. He swung left into Collins Street then left again into Swanston, leaving his imaginary beer behind and heading back up to Carlton without legal explanation.

Toddy, unused to such exercise, glistened with sweat and frothed around the bit, but he did not seem inclined to halt for cars or lorries and when they finally arrived at Harold Dawson's wine bar in Carlton he was slow to respond to either the shouts of the driver or the pressure in his mouth and would have, if he had his way, gone all the way to Preston before he'd had enough. Horace circled him around the block and finally pulled him up outside Dawson's, hoo-ing, ha-ing and whoa-ing, his face red with excitement and embarrassment.

171

Toddy got no soft words, no apple, no sugar, no flowers. He looked around, blew out his black lips, showed his yellow teeth, and emptied the steaming contents of his bladder into Lygon Street.

Bernstein was exactly where Horace had expected him to be, drinking plonk from a beer glass in one of the dark booths of Dawson's smoky sawdust-floored establishment. Horace did not need to be told that Bernstein's drinking companion was an actress, but he was too preoccupied to blush or become tongue-tied in her presence. He merely nodded, and reached to remove the hat he had already sacrificed to the cable car.

"Bernstein," he said, "a word in private."

He made a sweeping gesture with his hand towards the street, knocked over Bernstein's glass and made the actress leap to escape its treacly flood.

"To the street," he said, leaving the actress to hover an inch above her seat in the corner of the booth while the wine dripped sweetly to the floor.

Bernstein was a large broad man who was only twenty-one but already balding. He was an atheist, a rationalist, a medical student of no great distinction, an SP punter, a singer of bawdy songs, an acknowledged expert in matters erotic. He was perpetually, attractively, blue-jowelled and sleepy-lidded.

"Bernstein," Horace said when they were standing amidst fruiterers' packing cases in the street, "you must help me."

When Bernstein understood the problem he was amused. He tried to drag the poet back into the wine bar to celebrate his lost virginity.

"No, no," said Horace, glancing nervously up and down the street, "not lost. The lady is a friend. Please, Bernstein, if our friendship is worth anything write me a prescription for the medicine you mentioned."

"It may not work," said Bernstein, meaning that any prescription written by him on plain paper would not be a prescription at all. "Wait, have a drink, and we'll go and see someone later."

"Now, now, I beg you. If it doesn't work, we'll try something else," (imagining his friend was merely worried by the efficacy of the medicine).

Bernstein shrugged his broad shoulders and took out a notepad from the pocket of his jacket. He wrote for a moment and then tore out the sheet.

So: Horace, ten minutes later, smelling as strongly of sweat as his tethered horse, fairly galloping into Mallop's Pharmacy in Swanston Street with Bernstein's piece of paper clutched in his broad-palmed hand. "Give it to the tall man," Bernstein had said. "Wait till he is free. He's an understanding sort of fellah."

Tall man? What tall man? There was no tall man here. There was not a fellow higher than five foot three. He had a boozer's face and mutton-chop whiskers. There was a tall woman, though, not tall for a man, but tall for a woman. She stood beside the man. She towered over him. Horace behaved no different from his horse – he had his momentum up and could not stop. He propelled himself towards the counter, panting, and thrust his prescription into the hands of the tall woman who read it, frowned, and retreated behind a tall glass-fronted cupboard. After a moment she called the mutton-chop man to join her.

Horace stood wet and panting. He had run a good race. He pulled out a scarlet handkerchief from his pocket, wiped his brow, and blew his little nose with relief.

He blew his nose so enthusiastically, so loudly, that the gurgling visceral noise cloaked the return of the mutton-chop man who called twice to his customer before he was heard.

"Do you know what this is for?" asked the pharmacist. He had a peculiar expression on his face, almost a smile.

"Oh yes," said Horace, plunging his snotty red handkerchief into his pocket where it tangled with loose lozenges, string and crumpled poetry.

"You scoundrel," shouted the chemist. "I shall have you put in gaol."

Horace's eyes bugged. His hand was trapped in his pocket, anaesthetized by lozenges and trussed with string. He tried to move but could not. His face screwed up with such astonishment that it resembled the handkerchief: red, crinkled, confused with unrelated things.

"The doctor . . ." he tried, but hat pins pierced his tongue.

"The doctor too," the mutton-chops said, reaching for his telephone.

But Horace was already in retreat and before Toddy knew where he was he was cantering back up to Carlton with his nosebag still on and the reins belabouring his backside while the rhythm of his hooves drummed into Horace's panic: to aid, abet, to aid, abet.

The actress, when she saw him stumble through Dawson's door, carefully placed the wine glasses on the far edge of the table, against the dark panelled wall.

"I'm done for," said the poet, dropping heavily and smellily beside her. "They're after me."

They heard his story and persuaded him to take some wine. He was a teetotaller but gulped it down. Like lard, he thought, giving solace to the injured tongue.

"You're in love, my friend," Bernstein said, lowering his voice to a level which he understood to be a whisper.

"No, no," Horace said hopelessly, "she is a wonderful person."

"Are you really a virgin?" asked the actress who was very young to speak in such a manner. She wore a green headband and smoked her cigarette from a tortoiseshell holder.

"I am, madam," said Horace. "Now, also, I am a criminal. They have my description. They even know the colour of my handkerchief," and he stared into the gloom of the wine bar as if its booths might be filled with policemen.

"You are in love," said Bernstein. "Why else would you do it?"

"She is a poet," said Horace.

"You *are* in love," said the actress, "and I think you're sweet."

"I am not in love," Horace cried shrilly, pulling handkerchief and poems tumbling from his pocket. "I am in trouble," he said, wiping his face and dropping the handkerchief carefully to the floor. He slumped back into the hard wooden bench and, while his companions conferred in a whisper, sipped Bernstein's port while he tried to kick his handkerchief into the next booth.

"Give me a pound," said the actress.

He placed his florin on the table.

No one asked him how he had intended paying for the medicine at Mallop's Pharmacy. Bernstein opened his wallet, took out a pound, and handed it to the actress who squeezed out past Horace. He was so depressed as to be insensible to both his friend's generosity and the passage of the silk-clad buttocks which pressed briefly against him.

"We must buy the newspapers," he said to Bernstein who poured his friend more wine and was polite enough not to laugh at his misery.

The actress was gone an hour and Bernstein would not let his friend depart until she returned. He went out to buy the *Herald* and let Horace pore through it looking for his name.

"Probably in the *Sun* tomorrow," he said, carefully folding the wine-stained broadsheet and ironing in knife-sharp creases with the flat of his hands.

The actress (a Miss Shelly Claudine who was shortly to appear in the front chorus at the Tivoli) returned at last, slightly grim of face, but with a newspaper-wrapped bottle in her handbag. This she thrust at Horace.

"Tell her," she whispered hoarsely, "that she must drink it in the morning when her husband has gone. It will hurt her, but she must not panic." And then she kissed Horace on his astonished wine-wet mouth.

Horace became emotional. He took the actress's hand and shook his head. Tears welled in his eyes but words would not come.

"Go," she said, "for God's sake."

"How can I thank you?"

"Write a poem for me," the actress said, and kissed him again, this time on the forehead (he had never been kissed so many times in a day).

"To hell with the law," Horace told Bernstein, "the law is a monkey on a stick."

"An ass," said Bernstein.

"A billy goat's bum," said Horace, the bottle tucked safely in his pocket, his handkerchief abandoned on the floor. He bowed formally to his benefactors and withdrew.

He threaded his cautious circuitous way to the Maribyrnong River, heading north as if he intended to visit Brunswick, then south as if the zoo had suddenly claimed his interest. He trotted out towards Haymarket along quiet streets and, when he considered himself safe, finally allowed Toddy to wander with his lolling head and stumbling hooves along the last two miles to Ballarat Road. They stopped for snapdragons and roses, delphiniums and geraniums. They stopped so Toddy could shit, or merely lift his tail and consider shitting. The horse, perhaps aware that the excitements of the day were not yet over, prudently threw a shoe four hundred yards from home.

69

The horse had its head at a pile of dung, purchased by Molly, intended for the garden. I saw it in my headlights and read the Rawleigh's sign on the panniers of the cart. My scalp prickled and my hands clenched. I knew that something was wrong. I am not inventing this, not confusing the before and after. I knew something was up before I heard my wife's voice, refracted, splintered, like the glass across a fallen watercolour.

I ran towards the house. I found the kitchen empty. The bedroom was full of light and threw too many shadowed forms against the canvas walls. I ran up the two steps that had once led to the small stage of the hall and found the scene that follows: my wife lying on our bed, spewing green bile into a basin held by a stranger, my mother-in-law sitting on the end of the bed stroking her daughter's feet.

Phoebe wore a woollen nightgown. She twisted, stretched, jack-knifed, clasped her stomach and repeated the fractured moan that had chilled me at the front door. Her hair was wet and plastered on her forehead. My pocket bulged with commissioned photographs of "my house", "my home", "my family".

"What in the name of God is happening?"

Molly would not look at me. The man with the basin could not hold my eyes.

"Phoebe," I said.

"Poisoned," she said, and tried to laugh.

My first and strongest inclination in the face of these conspirators was to hit someone, to bend a nose, crack a tooth, bang a head against a floor.

"What poison?" I shouted and even Molly would not look up. She stared at her daughter's cold white feet. "What poison?" I asked the fat head. I gripped the iron bed with hands on which I had written the price of a limited slip differential.

Phoebe opened her mouth to answer, then changed her mind, moaned, and leant towards the stranger's basin into which she discharged a long stream of green liquid.

"I am your husband," I said, rocking the bed.

The man I later knew as Horace Dunlop opened his child's mouth and then closed it.

Phoebe pulled herself half up and leant on her elbow. "I am pregnant", she said, "and I have taken poison."

I pushed my way round to the head of the bed, my eyes half closed, my brows hooded. I would have unchaired the poet and trampled on him if he had not been wise enough to vacate his position swiftly.

I held the basin.

"No baby," Phoebe said wearily.

176

I shook my head.

"No baby," she said and tried to smile. "No nothing. No Phoebe either. Poor Herbert."

"Get a doctor," I said to the poet who was hovering at the doorway, "whoever you are."

"No doctor," Phoebe said, and took my hand.

"They'll charge her," the poet said. "She won't die. Don't call a doctor."

"Who is this man?" I demanded. "Why is he here? Did he give you this poison?"

"No, no," Phoebe said. "Only the Rawleigh's man."

"She won't die," Horace said, taking a tentative step back into the room. "She is losing the foetus."

"How dare you," I roared, standing up and spilling bile down my trouser leg. "How dare you call my child a foetus."

"It is the name. . . ."

"It is not the name of my child you scoundrel and she will lose no child while I am here."

"It is the scientific name of the unborn child."

"And unborn it will stay, until its time. You mark my words Mr Man-or-Beast, she will lose no child. She will lose nothing."

"Poor Herbert," Phoebe moaned.

"It is a criminal offence," Horace said, plucking miserably at his cravat.

"There has been no poison here," I said. "There is nothing in the house. My wife is ill. She will not lose *anything*." And if you had been there, had you seen me, you would not have doubted that I would keep the foetus clinging to the placenta by the sheer force of my will.

"You get a doctor," I told the Rawleigh's man. "Now, get your horse out of the dungheap and go."

"It is lame," said Horace. "It threw a shoe."

"Then drive my car, man. This is 1921. Only a fool rides a horse."

"I can't drive," he stammered. He had the look you see in public bars when a man knows he is about to get a beating.

"I'll drive," Molly said.

"You can't drive," I said, "you don't know how."

"I can", she said simply, standing and patting her daughter on the knee, "and I will. Come, Horace," she said, "you come with me."

And she took Horace by the sleeve and led him from the room.

70

It was still twelve years before Molly McGrath would come to public notice by refusing to sell her three electrical utilities, those of Ballarat, Geelong and Bendigo, to the newly formed State Electricity Commission. In 1921, however, we had no inkling of Molly's abilities. I did not doubt her passions. One had only to see her gazing at the electrically illuminated cross she had donated to the Catholic Church at Moonee Ponds – her eyes shone with that ecstatic light one sees portrayed in pictures of all the female saints – to see that she had as much enthusiasm for the electricity as she had for God himself.

But we thought her silly. She encouraged us to think her silly. She was the half-mad wife of Jack McGrath, and had I known she was spending her days with real-estate agents examining the books of businesses for sale, I would have done everything I could to protect her. As for driving a car, I would have judged her totally incapable. However I was not there to stop her.

She had looked at the Hispano Suiza for a long time before she finally approached it.

"It's my car," she said at last, and having gone for a pee and put some lipstick on, she rushed up to the vehicle and climbed in behind the wheel. She taught herself (noisily) the principles of clutch and gears; Phoebe came running from the distant Morris Farman to discover the driver of the car that circled round and round the bumpy tussocked ground was none other than her mother.

When Phoebe recovered from her disapproval, she begged to be taught as well.

Somehow they never got around to telling me, but the two women spent less time in the house than I had imagined. They were forever touring here and there – fast, unlicensed, but only sometimes reckless. It was this that gave Molly the idea about the taxi business, but that comes later on.

My mother-in-law did not drive well on the night of Phoebe's poisoning. She stalled three times and lurched across a garden bed. She left huge wheel ruts in excess of anything her late husband could have managed. She could not understand why Phoebe would wish to kill her child. This writhing daughter was a stranger to her. She prayed to the Blessed Virgin who claimed more of her attention than the car she carelessly controlled. She prayed her daughter would not die. She prayed the child would survive.

"I cannot understand her," she said to Horace as they crashed across on to the track to Newmarket. "Why would she ever contemplate such a thing?"

Guilty Horace did not answer. He sank miserably into the big leather seats of the Hispano Suiza, too unhappy to be afraid of the consequences of such erratic driving.

"She loves him," Molly told the poet. "She is infatuated with him. She worships him. Why would she do such a thing? What did she imagine would come of *all that business*?"

The poet did not ask what *all that business* might be, although he guessed that aeroplane wings would do little to muffle the creaks of the marital bed.

"She is a poet," he said (as they rattled over cobblestones towards Footscray in search of a doctor's light), but it seemed a poor defence in the face of the evil bile the victim spilled forth from her once pretty mouth.

"I don't understand. He is so good to her. Poor Herbert," she said. "Poor man. She's broken his heart."

She would never understand, although perhaps she should have. If they had taken three hours to find Dr Henderson's light the conversation would have continued its circular course, like an early-morning dream where the same problem spins on the edge of an off-centre black disc.

71

I sat by the head of the bed and wiped her brow with a water-wet handkerchief. I wiped it to soothe, to erase, wiped slowly, sadly, as I willed my child to remain exactly where he was.

My wife wept and explained, argued, told the truth, lied and apologized while the spasms wracked her and I held her head above the basin.

"The doctor will come," I said, "the doctor will come. He's coming now." I manufactured that damn doctor in my mind. I built his car and gave him road. I turned on his headlights and drew him towards me. Sweat ran from my forehead and caught in the creases of my eyes and coursed down my cheeks in imitation of the tears I could never easily shed.

There were sounds locked tightly in my throat, sounds barely human, steel springs of misery which once released would have filled the room, speared the walls, and lacerated the smooth white skin of my bride and wife. I screwed them down with a lock nut and pierced the shaft with a cotter pin. I wiped.

"Why?" I whispered. "Why?"

Phoebe was stunned by the question.

"Why?"

"No good," she said. "Can't have children."

I soaked the handkerchief and wrung it out. I sponged her arms. "Doctor's coming," I said.

"Can't do it," she said and gripped my hand as another spasm wrenched her womb.

"Can't do what, my darling?"

"Can't fly. Can't do it. Can't poetry."

"We will," I said.

"Did you want a baby?" she asked, very clearly. She raised herself up and stared at me in surprise. I straightened the sheet. I tucked it in.

"Yes," I said, and began to wash the perspiration from her clumsy hands, wiping each finger, one at a time.

"Why?"

I could not look at her. She forced my chin up with her hand so she could see my face.

"I love you," I said. I dragged the words up from the dangerous part of my throat, dragged it out and slammed the door shut behind it.

"Don't cry," she said.

"I'm not crying."

She sat up and held me. I put my arms around her and embraced her so hard she gasped for air. And I would give anything, now, to repeat that clean moment in the middle of such muddy pain.

Phoebe was astonished. She had not understood me. She had never thought me fatherly. She had not imagined me with children. They seemed trivial, beneath me.

"How could we fly? How could I write?"

"You will," I said. "You will do both. You will have the child. I promise you."

Now Phoebe, even in her remorse and pain, was not without calculation.

"Do you really promise?" she said.

"Yes."

"Promise you won't stop me, ever."

180

"Have the child", I begged, "and, God help me, the aeroplane is yours."

"Will you write it down," she said, before the next spasm struck her and the bile she brought up changed from green to yellow.

"Yes," I said. "I'll write it down."

She knew me better than I knew myself and I do not blame her for it.

"Better not die then," she said, and smiled.

In any case, neither of us counted on Charles who was stubbornly clinging on, holding out against the raging seas that threatened to sweep him from his foetus world. He would not let go. Years later his wife would use the story against him and say it was this that had made him stubborn, that he would not go when he was not wanted, etc. However I fancy that Charles was always like it, from his very beginning, when he was a slippery pink thing without a proper face. So while we all made decisions, thinking it up to God, or the doctor, my willpower or Phoebe's connivance, it was none of our doing at all, and it was Charles who fought and won the battle against the cloudy liquid the actress bought in Carlton.

72

Dr Henderson was a small broad man with a shiny ruddy face and thin ginger hair. He answered the door with a vase of lilacs in his hand.

Horace did not notice the vase. He noticed the doctor's tie. It was an Old Scotch Collegians tie and he was so desperate that he, quite literally, grasped it in his desperate hands and hailed his fellow Old Scotch Collegian as a long-lost friend.

"What year?" asked the poet, softening his vowels in accordance with the social requirements of such a tie.

It did not occur to the doctor that the dishevelled tramp on his doorstep might be claiming membership of a particular élite, but rather that he had lost his mind, knew not where he was or what year he was in.

"1921," he answered, looking down his nose to where the warty hand grasped his old school tie.

The poet thought this a great joke. Far too great a joke. He released the tie and slapped his thighs. "Ha, ha," he said, "damn good. 1921."

The doctor smoothed his tie with one hand, holding his vase of flowers at some distance where it would be safe from the enthusiasms of the stranger. "July 1921," he said. "And half-past eight at night."

"I was there in 1915," Horace said.

"You're a returned soldier," the doctor said, imagining a different "there".

"No. An Old Scotch Collegian."

"I see," said Dr Henderson, looking at him with suspicion. "And what can I do for you?"

Horace was so pleased to claim some fellowship with the doctor that all his fears immediately evaporated and he felt ridiculously safe. He told the whole sad story to the doctor who never, all the while, ceased to hold his vase of flowers at arm's length. The effect of the story was slightly spoiled by the laughter he used to punctuate his sentences. This was unfortunate, for it gave the impression that he thought the whole thing was some prank or rag whereas the laughter was produced by relief that he had not, after all, fallen into the power of a hostile stranger.

The doctor did not believe a word he said. He could smell alcohol on his breath and he judged him drunk. Therefore he began to shut the door, stepping back quickly, withdrawing the vase as a tortoise will bring its head back into its shell.

Horace placed his muddy shoe inside the door and would not let it shut.

The doctor stamped on Horace's toe. But Horace seemed insensible to pain. He left it there. The doctor stamped again. But the only effect the stamping seemed to have was to stop Horace's nervous laughter. Horace thought the doctor totally insane.

He left his foot there to be stamped on while he made a speech. It was a bit flowery, a tendency that he had in any case, but which he was inclined to exaggerate whenever he wished to establish himself as a person of substance.

"Sir," he said, "you are behaving foolishly. My name is Horace Dunlop. My father," he lied, "is Sir Edward Dunlop. I am a lawyer. And should you decide not to honour your Hippocratic oath and come to the assistance of this poor woman, I will sue you. I will sue you for neglect, for malpractice and if the poor woman dies I will see you charged for murder. I will sue you for such a sum that you will lose this house, if you own it. You will lose your automobile (and I'm sure you have a good one). The Australian Medical Association will debar you. It causes me great pain, sir, to make such threats against an Old Scotch Collegian who I would have imagined to be both charitable and a Christian, but by God, I will have you sued for every penny you have and every penny you can borrow and you will spend the rest of your life working to repay the loans you will have to undertake to cover the debt you are on the brink of incurring."

Half-way through this extraordinary speech the doctor ceased stamping on Horace's foot and so, given confidence by this reprieve, he finished his speech fortissimo, giving it all the splendour proper to the nineteenth-century novels that had inspired it and Molly, sitting in the car outside, was able to hear the true story of her daughter's poisoning.

The door opened. The doctor stood there with the vase still stretched before him. It was a Dalton vase in the art nouveau style. He smashed it at the poet's feet and made him jump.

"All right," said Dr Ernest Henderson, "I will deal with you."

Horace waited among the shards of pottery and broken lilacs, pondering his own position *vis-à-vis* the law.

73

Dr Ernest Montgomery Charles Maguire Henderson had a hell of a temper. It always surprised those who witnessed it, for ninety-nine per cent of the time he was a taciturn bachelor not given to loud noises. And then: whizz, bang, a plate or a horse's shoe or an Oxford dictionary was sailing through the air, on its way to a windowpane or towards a painting or a wall, and the chunky little man (as hard as an armchair stuffed with too much horsehair) would seem, momentarily, to compress, to compact his muscled frame, and just when you expected the poltergeist that had propelled the object through the air to take possession of him and expand with a malevolent rush, he would go quite limp, bite his small moustache thoughtfully, and go back to the ordinary business of life.

Discovering shards of pottery or dictionaries with broken spines he would be inclined to regard them with surprise, and move them around a little with the toe of his shoe as if they were birds run down by speeding automobiles.

Yet the thing that had made him lose his temper was exactly the same thing that made him, on this April night, leave his empty echoing house happily, with relief, and follow the

Hispano Suiza eagerly: he was in love with a lady already spoken for.

The lights of the doctor's Packard, which blazed into the back windows of the Hispano Suiza, seemed to Horace to be charged with the malevolence of an inquisitor.

"I'm in for it now," he told Molly who had been silent since her tyre-squealing departure from the doctor's house. "He'll have me charged."

Molly sucked in her breath and expelled it. She accelerated grimly. She had heard every word of Horace's speech as it swooped from high falsetto to surprising baritone.

"Love her," she snorted, attacking the gearbox with anger. "Love her. Some way to show your filthy love."

"She begged me," Horace said, aghast to find one more enemy. "She wept. Dear lady, please. . . ."

"Don't 'dear lady' me," said Molly grimly. "If she dies I'll charge you too. I have one hundred thousand pounds", she said, "and I'll spend every penny of it on lawyers if I have to."

"Oh God," moaned Horace. "Oh God, dear God."

"You pray to God. Pray to God she doesn't die."

"The love is platonic."

Molly shuddered at such a dirty-sounding word. She fled from its filth at seventy miles an hour down Ballarat Road with the doctor's Packard roaring at her tail.

"She asked me to do it," Horace cried as they bounced on to the track to the house. As Molly ploughed into her rose bed with the handbrake full on, Horace was catapulted upwards from his seat and slammed his shorn head against the roof.

She turned off the engine. "Pray," she said, "if you know what's good for you."

Ernest Henderson, arriving a minute later, caught the sight of a woman in a huge black taffeta dress splendidly decorated with rose appliqués. Seen in the headlights of his car, she appeared large and blowzy and theatrical. She strode towards the house with the poet stumbling miserably behind.

No one stayed to escort the doctor inside. He entered the kitchen to find the large black taffeta dress at prayer with her knees on extravagant linoleum and her head on the kitchen table. The poet was leaning against a window and staring out into the night.

The doctor coughed.

Horace turned to face his executioner.

"She's praying."

"Yes."

"If you don't charge me, she will."

The doctor winked. "Let's see the patient, mmmm?"

Horace took him to the bedroom where they found Phoebe in her husband's arms. The doctor asked for more light. Horace brought back a second lamp and when he returned he found the doctor standing and silently contemplating the embracing couple. Horace held up the lamp and sadly regarded this evidence of his complete betrayal.

74

When the doctor had contented himself that the patient's stomach was quite empty, he administered a draught of Galls solution to stop the spasms and gave her a strong sedative.

In the kitchen he found atheistic Horace kneeling at the kitchen table beside the mother whose bosom, whether from religious passion or anger, was heaving in a manner that was impossible to ignore.

I leaned against the kitchen sink too weary and worried to counterfeit devotion.

It was Horace (looking up from pragmatic prayers) who asked the question about the patient.

The doctor was pleased to announce that both mother and child would survive the ordeal. He helped Molly up from the floor.

"Just the same," he said to me, "you should be indebted to your lawyer mate. You'd never have got me here if not for him."

Molly gave the poet and the doctor a look of utter disgust.

"If not for *him*?" she said, sitting with a grunt.

Horace stared at Molly with his mouth open, but when she did not continue, he shut it again.

"What lawyer?" I said. Relief had made my face go as soft and foolish as a flummery.

"He's just a Rawleigh's man," said Molly.

"Is he now?" said the doctor, chewing his moustache and raising his eyebrows at the poet in question.

"For Man or Beast," said Molly. "Door to door. Horse and cart."

"Then he makes a prettier threat than any barrister I ever heard. You should have heard him," he told me. "He would have had me drawn and quartered, locked in gaol and left to rot. He had

185

judges and juries and clerks of court ready to grab me and tie me up. So if he is a Rawleigh's man, I'll wager a quid he will end up a rich one, and he deserves it too."

Thus Ernest Henderson brought all his power to save the skin of a man in love.

"You should thank this man," he told me, "and the dear lady who drove so well. It was a performance few men would be capable of."

Molly and I exchanged glances. Somewhere in the air, half-way between us, incredulity met a star-bright beam of triumph.

"She can't drive," I said. "I know it."

"She can," the doctor said. "Like a dream."

Molly blushed deep red with pleasure.

"Granted," the doctor said, "it is a fine motor car, but she raced it like a gentleman."

But Molly could not be appeased quite so easily. She folded her arms across her bosom, as if to ward off further flattery, and demanded to be told the cause of her daughter's problem. The doctor said that he had no doubt it was caused by a gastric attack similar to many he had seen that day, that it was, if anything, milder than normal; there was no risk to the child.

It was I who raised the question of poison. I raised it meekly, pointed to it, as though it were a household mouse I wished a stronger soul to kill.

Ernest Henderson, if you want my opinion, was not normally an inventive or practised liar. But that night the muse was with him and he constructed such a dazzling thread of pure invention and looped it back and forth so many times that I could not work out where anything started or stopped; he buttoned it neatly with Latin words (like bright-coloured pills with shiny coatings) and, although Molly did not trouble herself to believe a word he said, Horace and I, for different reasons, looked at the fabric he wove with appreciation and relief.

Well, tell me then, what was my choice? To believe my wife deceitful? A liar? A cheat? A collaborator with other cheats? Of course not. I took the lies and held them gratefully. I wrapped them round me and felt the soft comfort a child feels inside a woollen rug. And this, of course, is what anyone means when they say a lie is creditable; they do not mean that it is a perfect piece of engineering, but that it is comfortable. It is why we believed the British when they told us we were British too, and why we believed the Americans when they said they would

186

protect us. In all these cases, of course, there is a part of us that knows the thing is not true, and we hold it closer to ourselves because of it, refusing to hold it out at arm's length or examine it against the light.

So I embraced Horace as a friend. I promised the child would bear his name (a promise I later made to several others and all of which I honoured).

We opened beer. I strutted around the kitchen. I found glasses to drink from and a few stale Thin Captain biscuits to eat. I fancy I was like a cocky rooster, with chest and bum thrust out before and after. I erased all memory of bile and tears.

"To wife and child." I raised my glass of warm frothing beer. "To aviation, to Australia."

"To wife and child," they drank.

Ah, they all must have thought I was a mug in their different ways, but their wisdom did not stop them from dying in the end, and my foolishness has not killed me yet.

We had several bottles of that soapy-tasting beer. I became garrulous and told stories about flying. Molly recited Lawson at my request. Horace, unused to alcohol, declaimed two sonnets which confused us mightily.

When the doctor judged his work quite done, he rose to go. I took him by his arm and walked him to the door. There was another matter I wished to discuss with him in private.

I left Horace alone with Molly. The poet was nervous and recited Lawson (whom he loathed) with the same enthusiasm with which he had earlier knelt to pray.

Molly watched him as one might watch a spider that may or may not be venomous.

75

I would not let the doctor go, and yet I could not bring myself to examine the tender matter which so much occupied my mind. The poor fellow found himself stumbling at my side through the tussocked darkness, wandering into flower beds and stepping into horse shit while I thanked him for his trouble and followed a line of conversation that echoed our odd perambulations through the mist-streaked dark.

Ernest Henderson must have thought I had something contagious to admit: syphilis or TB or both.

But it was legs that were on my mind, and nothing else. What I wanted to know was how it was that one characteristic was passed on to a child and how one was not. I gave not a a damn for the shape of a head, or the colour of an eye, or even (as yet unaware of the stubbornness of my unborn son) such things as character and temperament. I wanted to be set at ease about the question of legs, and wondered out loud whether bowed legs (I could never bring myself to say "bandy") were the result, as I had heard, of a poor diet or whether they were inherited from father or mother and, if it was inheritance, then whether the male or female would be the most important in the choice of legs, and if this was something that could be guarded against. I did not put it quite so neatly for, although my thoughts were clear enough, shyness hindered their expression. I had words to say about the Chinese, observing that bow-legs were a common condition, particularly amongst the old. I had seen it in members of Goon Tse Ying's family, seen it before I realized I shared the same condition. Yet I was not quick to come to the point and I confused the matter by discussing the anti-Chinese riots at Lambing Flat where Goon Tse Ying's father and uncle were killed and where he learned to stand in such a manner as to be invisible.

"Should, for instance," I asked the doctor as we turned back for the fifth time towards the dank direction of the Maribyrnong, "I feed her up on vegetables?"

Now Dr Henderson, you will say, had had no time to notice my legs, and I must have been puzzling the fellow to distraction, wasting his time, wearing him out when he should have been home in his bed. But if that is the case, he did not show it. He answered me as best he could, saying that the shape of legs could indeed be determined by a bad diet but he had also observed them to be as hereditary as Habsburg ears and as to whether the male or the female would triumph in the selection of legs for the child, it was a toss-up.

I received this comfortless news in silence. The doctor peered at the luminous face of his watch.

"So it's vegetables," I said, "or nothing."

"There is no harm in vegetables."

I saw him to his car, shook his hand, and waited for him to turn it. As he reversed he caught me in the full glare of his lights. I had no idea whether he was looking forwards or back, but I turned my left foot sideways and stood with my hand on my hip, in such a manner that my deformity, looked at from the doctor's point of view, to all intents and purposes, disappeared.

76

I have made no great study of epilepsy, so I have no accurate idea as to why Horace chose the moment of the doctor's departure to have a fit. It may have been the strain of reciting Lawson's poetry, the excitements of the day, the introduction of alcohol to his overwrought system, or just plain relief that no one was going to put him on a charge. Whatever caused it, the moment the headlights of the doctor's car washed across his bulging eyes all his systems went suddenly haywire. He was a ball of elastic unravelling. He was a full balloon suddenly unstopped. He tossed and crashed on to the floor, thrashing his arms and banging his big head. His eyes rolled dreadfully. He made shocking noises, gurgling up from the back of his throat.

Molly screamed. He heard her. He heard every sound. Every word. He heard my footsteps as I ran inside, and every syllable that followed.

"He's choking."

"It's a fit."

"Pull out his tongue."

A pause.

"Quick, Mother," helpless Horace heard me say, "get a hatpin."

77

It is unendurable, Phoebe wrote to Annette, and she has become quite mad. She is no longer dotty, which she always was, but mad. You would find it hard to imagine, if you can only think of her as the dear happy soul she was in Western Avenue. She has small unblinking eyes like a currawong, turning its head on one side and staring malevolently, as if she thinks I'll pull the needle from the wool and drive it between my legs into the baby's heart. I cannot talk to her. I have tried. Of course we both know what the matter is: she thinks poor Horace is my lover, God help me. Even Horace has the grace to laugh about it.

Annette, I am big and heavy like a fat bloated slug and I am so bored. The aeroplane sits where I can see it from the window. It is the only thing that keeps me sane.

189

No, I am *not* disenchanted with H. He works hard and loves me, but I am bored. You would not recognize me. I sit for hours staring out the window. I cannot even clean the house or cook. Only Horace amuses me, and how can we discuss poetry or life or *anything* while *she* sits there with her hands folded on her lap as if we will, at any moment, leap on to the table and start performing adulterous acts.

I was so *ignorant*. I did not even think to do anything to stop getting in this condition. I assumed it was something *he* would do. What a child I was. Now I feel fifty years old and sad and wizened and I look at my mother and listen to her talk about buying a *taxi* business and you would not believe how sad it makes me. I enclose my latest poems. *Please* criticize them. Tear them to shreds. Tell me. I have only Horace to show them to and he is so sweet. If I listened to him I would start to imagine myself a genius. ARE THEY ANY GOOD? Am I deluding myself? Should I stop all this useless dreaming and be content with what I have? For he does love me, Annette, and I know I can make him so happy yet I did not, even for a moment, guess that what he wanted was so *ordinary*: a fat wife with a dozen children and cabbage and stew every night.

I do not go into town. I do not go to the theatre. I sit on the back step shelling peas and trying to love the child kicking at me. I know you are busy but I beg you to visit. Please write as soon as you get this letter. There is nothing else in my life that brings the prospect of so much pleasure.

With much love,

Phoebe

78

It was not the ghost that made me fearful. I was already fearful before it came. It was the counterweight to my contentment and the greater my contentment grew the greater was my fear of losing it. The eucalypts I had planted now thrust out tender pink shoots that glowed in the spring sunshine like blood-filled skin. My wife's belly pushed against her dress. Her breasts swelled. Everywhere life seemed tender and exposed and I did not need a whistling ghost to make me consider the risks of both life and death.

I could not bear to hear my wife discuss aviation. This subject, which had, so short a time before, contained the juices of happiness itself, was poison in the air we breathed. My mind was filled with visions of ruptured organs and broken struts and I wished to encourage her in gentler safer pursuits. This was one of the reasons I invited Horace to stay. I built a room for him. And while Molly clucked her tongue in censure I cut new timber with my saw and inhaled the sweet sour smell of blackbutt. This was a real room, fifteen feet by fifteen feet, with shelves for books and a proper desk for poetry.

Horace was cosy and comfortable and domestic. He was as fearful as a guinea pig and his nervousness soothed me and made me feel safer. It was comforting to have him in the house, like a pet who can be relied upon to give affection. Also: he could read. I had it in mind that I would learn the knack from him so that when my ink-stained wife offered me her poetry I might have some idea what it was, that I would no longer stare dumbly at the dancing hieroglyphics, my skin prickling with suspicion while I counterfeited understanding and enthusiasm. In the meantime I could have him read the work aloud, pretending that I liked his feathery voice.

Horace was a nice man, but far too gentle. He was no match for Phoebe's will, and when she wished the subject to be aviation he could not and would not swerve her from it. When Phoebe demanded to have her knowledge of Sidwell tested it was Horace who held the tattered volume in his warty hand while I, watching from my place at the head of the uncleared table, did not know whether to be jealous that my position was usurped, pleased that my illiteracy had not yet been uncovered or delighted that I had, at last, a home, a family, a domestic hearth.

"Should the engine stop suddenly?"

"The cause will be failure of the ignition or fuel supply," said my wife, her brow untroubled by the thought of such a calamity.

"To cure it?" Horace turned the page with the same leisurely sweep of hand he brought to his prized edition of Rossetti.

"To cure it, test the magneto and switch off the petrol supply."

"If the engine is misfiring?"

"Ah," said Molly, replacing her fluffy pink knitting in its paper bag and standing. "You should be reading recipe books, my girl."

"If the engine is misfiring on one cylinder," Phoebe smiled at her mother, "it is a faulty plug."

"Or ironing your husband's shirts," said Molly, putting the big kettle back on the stove.

"Herbert doesn't mind. If the misfiring is accompanied by loud banging or rattling it is probably a broken valve. Anyway, Horace irons the shirts."

"If irregular or infrequent firing occurs?" asked Horace, colouring at this public mention of his housekeeping. He looked up at Molly then looked away quickly when she caught his eye.

"You spoil her," she said to me. "I'll never know why you signed that silly paper. It's the most disgusting thing I've ever seen."

The paper she spoke of was a legal document that I had signed to honour my promise to her about the aeroplane.

"It will be because the rocker arm on the magneto contact-breaker sticks occasionally," said Phoebe smiling at me. "It's only sensible," she said to Molly. "He's a liar."

"Phoebe!"

"I love him, Mother."

"Oh dearie me," said Molly, clattering with teacups at the sink. "Perhaps I'm just old-fashioned."

"No doubt about it, Mother. Or", she told Horace, "because there is oil or dirt on the distributor or the platinum points require timing."

The document in question is probably worth including here. I only signed it to demonstrate my kindness to the ghost.

THIS INDENTURE made the twentieth day of September 1921 BETWEEN HERBERT PETER BADGERY of Dudley's Flat West Melbourne in the State of Victoria (hereinafter called the Grantor) of the one part AND PHOEBE MATILDA BADGERY his wife of the other part.

WHEREAS the Donee is possessed of a desire to pilot an aircraft AND WHEREAS in the course of their marriage the Donee has become and is currently with child to the Grantor AND WHEREAS the aforesaid pregnancy has greatly frustrated the Donee in her aforesaid desire to pursue her career as an aviator AND WHEREAS the Grantor is the owner of an aircraft, to wit one Morris Farman Shorthorn (hereinafter called the Aeroplane).

NOW THIS INDENTURE WITNESSETH that the Grantor in consideration of his natural love and affection for the Donee and other good and sufficient consideration HEREBY COVENANTS (subject to the final proviso set out below) that he will not again during the currency of this Indenture impregnate the Donee or make any advances such as may induce the Donee to desire union with the Grantor during such times as she is susceptible to becoming pregnant or otherwise have a second child AND THE GRANTOR FURTHER COVENANTS that he will provide the Donee with all the means and support and will use his best endeavours to teach the Donee to fly and navigate the Aeroplane and that he not withhold either monies or information needed for the maintenance of the Aeroplane in an airworthy condition AND THE GRANTOR FURTHER COVENANTS that from such time as she is delivered of child he will do nothing to discourage the Donee from flying the Aeroplane at any time irrespective of the clemency of the weather or the time of day or night AND THE GRANTOR FURTHER COVENANTS that he will provide the Donee at all times with sufficient funds to purchase her requirements of fuel, oil, mechanical assistance and ground support staff PROVIDED HOWEVER that the Donee will not fly more than eighty (80) miles from her matrimonial home except with the prior written approval of the Grantor which approval shall not be unreasonably withheld AND THE GRANTOR FURTHER COVENANTS and the parties hereby agree that in the event that the Donee does once again fall pregnant to the Grantor this Indenture shall operate as an assignment of the Aeroplane to the Donee free and clear of all encumbrances and in such event the Grantor shall provide the Donee with sufficient funds to maintain herself and the Aeroplane in an airworthy condition and with sufficient funds to fuel and fly the Aeroplane without any limitation whatsoever in terms of distance or time and irrespective of whether the Donee continues to live as the wife of the Grantor or in the matrimonial home AND THE GRANTOR FURTHER COVENANTS that in the event that the Aeroplane is destroyed or otherwise becomes unairworthy and beyond repair he will replace it with another aeroplane of the same make and model or failing that with an aeroplane of equivalent performance and capacity PROVIDED HOWEVER that nothing in this Indenture shall detract from the liberty of the Grantor at all times to sustain the marriage by vera copula consisting of erectio and intromissio without ejaculatio.

IN WITNESS WHEREOF the Parties have hereunto affixed their hands and seals on the day and date first herein before written.

79

A man who wishes his tale believed does himself no service by speaking of the supernatural; I would rather have slipped in some neatly tailored lie to fill the gap, but the gap is so odd, so uniquely shaped, that the only thing that will fill it is the event that made it.

I told no one about the ghost. From March to July in 1921 I saw it often. It sat at the kitchen table. It wandered across the flats. Sometimes it was there every night. Sometimes I would think it gone for good. For two, three, four nights I would be left alone. And then I would wake up and hear it, sitting at the kitchen table, whistling out of tune. The hairs on my neck would raise themselves on end, and those on my arms, and those on my legs that had not been worn away by my straight-legged trousers. I soaked the sheet with perspiration.

The hens were my witness to the ghost. They set up the sort of fuss and panic you hear when a snake enters the chook-house late at night. One of them, a big old Rhode Island Red rooster, died of fright. Molly's verdict was that it had fallen prey to damp and I did not disagree with her. The dead rooster, however, smelt of snake.

The ghost was not a single solid shape, but rather a confluence of lights nestling in a lighter glow, like one of those puzzles for children with dots numbered from one to ninety-five. It sat at the kitchen table with the snake. The snake slithered like a necklace around the ghost, entered into it and streamed out of it. You could see the snake's innards pulsing: liquids, solids, legs of frogs and other swarming substances with tails like tadpoles.

The ghost was Jack. Its gait, as it drifted past my bedroom window, was unmistakable. I saw it move out across the grass flats and on to the mud. It hovered round the Morris Farman.

Now you can say I manufactured this ghost myself, and that it was nothing more than my guilty conscience scorched on to the night. I will have to grant it is possible, providing you also give me credit for killing the rooster and making it smell of snake. You are free to argue it, but it makes and made no difference, not to the story, not to my prickling skin, or to my bowels which loosened and gave me a liquid shit to spray and splatter around the dunnycan at odd and unpredictable hours of the night and day.

These nocturnal visits drove me to excesses of kindness, of which the agreement I signed with Phoebe is only one. I cared for the wife and daughter of the ghost with even greater zeal, dazzling them with my attentions, bringing them gifts of ornaments from Cole's Arcade and peculiar cheeses from the Eastern Markets. I offered liquors to Molly and an array of fountain pens to Phoebe so that she might be a poet in any colour she chose. I bought her red ink and indigo, brown and cobalt blue. I built accommodation, as I've said, for Horace and begged him consider himself a member of my family. Yet none of this seemed to have any effect on the ghost who came and went as he saw fit, whistling, stamping his foot, and displaying the snake in styles that varied from the accusatory to the downright lewd.

I fancied I saw it on the night that Charles was born into the hands of the young midwife. It did a jig, a little dance, hop-ho, a shearer's prance, around the house and out across the mud of Dudley's Flat.

I waited for its return, and while young Charles bellowed with rage at those who had tried to kill him and left the household sleepless and his mother's nipples so sore she could not bear my jealous tongue to touch them, Jack did not return.

Now you may argue that the ghost had simply wished to see the continuation of its line, and now reassured had simply gone away. But a ghost does not bring a snake to flaunt and slither round its neck, to swallow down its ghostly throat and produce from between its legs, if all it wishes is to hear the cries of its assassin's child. He does not go hop-ho to celebrate his daughter's union to an unkind man. He has, therefore, other purposes and less innocent things to celebrate.

When I saw the dance I went quite cold. For I knew that I had been defeated in a battle I did not know the rules of, and my tormentor had slipped inside my defence and thrust his weapon home without his victim being aware of the nature of the wound.

Molly always believed the child was Horace's. And Horace's behaviour simply confirmed it. The truth, however, was that Horace had found, at last, his true vocation which was neither poetry nor law nor Rawleigh's Balsam, but the care of house and baby which even Molly had to admit that he did with greater skill than any of the women could have managed. The house was clean and dusted, the meals were large and simple, the child both neat and happy. Horace cooed over it. He dusted its bottom with baby powder and cleaned its napkins and only when the small puckered lips sucked at his chest could he be judged lacking as both father and mother to it. He loved to watch it stretch and curl its feet, felt relief in its burps, and sheer wonder at its small unformed intelligence.

Molly saw that I, on the other hand, was very careful with the child. I treated it with reserve and caution. I was stiff and awkward. When I held him Charles writhed against me and screamed until Horace took him back again.

All this proved Molly's theories about the child's paternity. No such thought had entered my head. I had other reasons for treating Charles so carefully. I narrowed my eyes and watched him. I spied on him as he lay in his bassinet. And as Charles grew and came slowly into focus I saw exactly what had happened: Charles was Jack with bandy legs put on.

No wonder the jig, the hop, the dance.

I did not waste time thinking about the mechanics of this conception, whether Jack's ghost had mounted Phoebe in the night, driven home his pulsing lights deep into her womb and made her cry out, or whether he sent the snake slithering electrically into the bedroom with its belly full of coded liquids, there to insinuate itself between her legs whilst she slept beside her unsuspecting husband.

Phoebe displayed little of the maternal instinct towards her son and for this I silently thanked her. We did not discuss the Little Jack who toddled silently into places it was forbidden, but I always believed we both understood that something sinister had happened.

A lesser man might have been defeated by such a setback. Yet when I recall 1921 and '22 I recall only my feverish optimism. I built for the future, with the passion of a man who plans to start a dynasty. The house grew. It shot out long branches, covered walkways, new rooms. I built a room for Annette who had failed, as yet, to visit. I was oblivious to the world outside, and most of the world inside too.

E.g.: Dear Dicksy, you are, once again, proven right and there does not appear to be any likelihood of a more modern aeroplane. I am sure there is enough money. I am absolutely convinced. But the whole subject seems to enrage them and they will not even discuss it. He, who introduced himself into my life with all his dreams and ambitions, seems to have become an old man suddenly, weary of trying anything and content to sit in his slippers drinking tea. He is jealous of me. He led me on with all this talk of famous air races, and now he has abandoned them completely and he seems set for the life of a shopkeeper.

The poor little boy will, I suppose, suffer because of us, but at least H. has learned his lesson and seen that he is not capable of normal paternal feelings. We are, neither of us, normal people. I *do* love my son, but much as I imagine fathers love their children, not in the hot entanglement of child and mother, all muddy with tears and pee. Thank God for Horace who is wonderful with him, and leaves me free to master this very antiquated aeroplane which, at least, is not forbidden me and in which I shall, any week, come to visit you. Dicksy, I cannot wait. I am a cat in heat. I lift my tail. I arch my back. I rub against your calves. And for all this, I blame the sky which is so *empty*. You are wrong (or, should I say, Freud is wrong – you are merely wrong to quote him). It may be correct in dreams (his, yours, not mine – I only dream of engines and magnetos with faults I cannot fix) but in real life the feelings are produced by emptiness. I know I would have the same urges in the desert, or in any place where I was me, alone, with no one else to observe or censure me. I have felt the strongest desire in railway carriages when I am alone in a compartment by myself and I know I can do anything, anything at all, without anyone to interrupt. All of which is to say that they are welcome to get cross or unhappy because they have given up their dreams, but I will not.

80

Now you have those letters in your hand it is easy enough for you to take Phoebe's side and look at me as a fool, or something worse. It is your privilege and if I did not wish you to have it, I would have kept the letters hidden. Yet I did not come into possession of them until 1930, when I had the indignity of buying them from a wizened man in the saloon bar of the Railway Hotel in Kyneton. He sat at the little round table, eating a musk stick, drinking stout, and dealing out his wares with yellowed finger. He offered me an envelope marked "personal effects" which contained postcards depicting Cossacks raping village women, then a comic strip of a baby with a ten-inch cock fucking a big-titted woman with a mole on her shoulder. Then

197

my wife's letters to Annette. Jonathon Oakes, for that is who it was, did not recognize me and I did not ask him how his fortunes had fallen so low. I paid him five shillings for his stolen letters.

So this knowledge about my wife not only cost me pain, but also money. But it is yours. Take it. It goes together with the rest.

Yet I must tell you that Phoebe had not been able, or had no wish to, express herself so clearly to me. She did not deny me caresses. She did not fail to greet me with a kiss, to inquire about my work, to fetch my slippers – the slippers she appears to have hated were a gift to me from her. We played with Charles together. We pretended to love him together. My darling expected me, somehow, to be a mind-reader.

Doubtless I expected the same of her. I imagined my passion for building was shared by everyone. I did not doubt that it was understood: that my ruling love was for human warmth, for people gathered in rooms, talking, laughing, sharing stews and puddings and talk. Aeroplanes and cars seemed, in comparison, cold and soulless things, of no consequence in comparison to the family we were building. For the first time in my life I felt I had a place on earth.

But I did not explain myself. I felt it obvious. I thought my building was a language anyone could understand. Did they imagine I added rooms for no reason, that it was merely a hobby, a silly obsession? I built a room for a next child. I began tentatively. It rose as a question. I hung pink wallpaper. Phoebe admired it. I paced around her with a bucket of paste in my hand. It was a courtship dance. I have seen birds do the same in Mallee country. They build a mound. They show it. No words are spoken, but it is clearly understood.

So when Phoebe smiled and kissed me, her lips and eyes erased certain matters in the document I had so rashly signed. Still I did not contradict the cautious calendar my wife drew up. Neither did I ignore the details of the agreement in regard to ejaculatio, not, that is, until one Sunday afternoon when my wife, inflamed with passion after two hours of dangerous flying, clenched my buttocks tight and dug her nails in hard and then – and only then –I ripped forth a joyful sob of semen, a throb, a dob, a teeming swarming flood of life.

It was only then I realized that she could no more read my building than I could read her poetry.

81

The real bitterness did not start there, with Phoebe splashing water up her cunt, but on a July morning in 1923 while Charles slopped his spoon around a plate of soggy Weeties and Horace stood cooking bacon on the stove.

Phoebe left the room to vomit. When she returned she walked up to me and spat her morning sickness in my face.

"You bastard," she said.

I wiped the foul-smelling spittle from my face, dabbed at the small splash on my waistcoat, rolled my napkin and placed it carefully in its ring. I blinked. I walked outside. Not even Molly said a word.

Phoebe followed me. "I want to talk to you," she said.

I stopped. Everyone in that little kitchen must have heard – my voice as dead as stone, Phoebe's quivering and only just controlled.

"I will have this child," she said. "All right?"

"All right."

"That will make you happy?"

I did not answer. How could I answer about "happy" when I saw the liquid hatred in her eyes.

"Then you have my word. You don't need to guard me. I will fly for the first six months, but not the last three. I will spend the last three months writing poetry and then I will give you the child."

And from that point, with my feet frozen in the frost-thick grass outside the kitchen window, I became a different man.

I did everything in my power to regain my wife's affections. The more I tried, the more pitiful she found me. She was one of those people who admire strength and despise weakness. The more I kotowed to her the more she scorned me. She ridiculed me openly.

And yet she did not remove the possibility of hope.

82

One September afternoon, two king parrots settled on the gables of the house while Horace sat in the sunshine peeling potatoes and I cut out fabric for a wing section Phoebe had ripped on a fence post down at Werribee. It was Phoebe, looking critically over my shoulder, who saw the parrots.

"Shush," she said, although nobody was talking.

The king parrot is a magnificent bird, and the clear blue of a Melbourne spring day sets them off perfectly. Their heads and chest are red, their wings and backs green, their long tails green. They stood on the roof and preened each other, and I, estranged from my wife, was overcome with loneliness.

They did not stay long. They landed, preened, looked around, and flew away.

I expressed my disappointment.

"Why would they stay?" said Phoebe, walking to the house. "There are no decent trees. There is nothing for them here. If you had chosen some land with decent trees there would be parrots all year round."

"Not all year," said Horace quietly. He was the only person permitted to contradict my wife. "They follow the blossoms."

"Different parrots," she said, "at different times."

"That is true," said Horace. "But in any case, we have splendid water birds which have their own charm."

"It is parrots that I love," said Phoebe. "It is parrots that I miss."

I held up the fabric to the light. Charles bellowed somewhere in the house. It was, I think, the day he ate Horace's tobacco, and it was also the day I resolved to buy Phoebe parrots.

83

I bought the king parrot from an old bushie in a pub in Exhibition Street. I placed it on the kitchen table on a Friday night.

The gift acted like honey on Phoebe's bitter tongue. Her eyes shone. "Oh," she said, "how beautiful. How splendid. Herbert, you must build it a cage."

"It has a cage," said Molly, "a very expensive one too."

"No, no. It deserves a big cage. A room."

Was I suspicious? Did I perhaps detect the faintest whiff of irony? Was there any there to smell? I still think this first enthusiasm of Phoebe's was genuine, and it was only later, when she saw me working on that cage, that she allowed her bitterness to warp her original spontaneous feeling, to convert it into something artful, ironic and sarcastic.

I did not understand poetry in those days. I imagined it

200

involved rhymes, and if not rhymes at least words. But now I know a poem can take any form, can be a sleight of hand, a magician's trick, be built from string and paper, fish or animals, bricks and wire.

I never knew I was a hired hand in the construction of my wife's one true poem. I knew only, in the midst of its construction, that Horace would puzzle me with his sympathetic eyes which would not hold mine when I confronted him. I observed how he left the room when cages were discussed, how he picked up Charles and plopped him on his pudgy hip and took him outside to play.

Sonia, growing up inside my wife's womb, became accustomed to the noise of hammering and sawing – the king parrot was merely the first bird I housed beneath my spreading roof. My family soon included lorikeets and parakeets, western rosellas, gold-winged friar birds and a cat bird from Queensland.

The cat bird had a forlorn cry, like a whimpering child or the animal it is named for. The cockatoos screeched. The parrots hawked. The house pushed out and grew – rows of cages radiated like the spokes of a wheel.

84

Here: the photograph of the taxi drivers' picnic on September 23rd, 1923. I am trapped in the heart of Phoebe's poem, teetering at the apex of my empire. The photograph shows Molly, Annette, Phoebe, Horace, Charles, baby Sonia, me, and the taxi drivers and their wives and children. It does not show the house, only a little of the lattice I erected to shade the cages from the westerly sun.

The grass was fresh mown, already fermenting, and I was a sexton happily asleep in a fresh-dug grave, my hands muddy, the smile of a fool upon my face.

My house was full. All rooms were occupied. Annette's towel lay drying in the sun on her window ledge. Her bed was made. Sonia's nursery awaited her, but now she lay in her pram in the sunshine, kicking her long straight legs, curling her toes, and gurgling happily while all around her the taxi drivers and their wives and children admired her: just like her mother, but with her father's eyes.

Horace played the waiter. He carried wobbling jellies and drunken trifles, dispensed bread and butter and hundreds and thousands to the children.

The drivers were an independent lot, sharp, shrewd, cloth-capped and street-wise, but you could see they liked Molly who moved amongst them in a vast white dress, her copper hair cascading from beneath a straw hat, dispensing cordial. She was a lady. They called her "Ma'am". When the photographer arrived they lined up their taxis: "Boomerang", the signs said, "fast as an arrow, Australian to the marrow."

I stood between Phoebe and Annette. Annette, I can see, had put her arm through mine. She was nice to me that day, and I to her. I asked her to describe the streets of Paris, and she did, and I enjoyed hearing about it.

Phoebe seemed as happy as I ever knew her to be. When I see her in that photograph, see that proud chin, that soft smile, I can imagine, if I half close my eyes, the way she moved her lips when speaking, the throaty lazy voice. Her eyes, though, are shaded by her hat, and it is just as well they are shaded, those eyes that made the poem.

And it was through her poem I walked, I took the children on tours of my splendid cages. The birds were clean and healthy. They preened themselves in honour of spring. The parrots hung upside down on their perches. The friar birds drove their beaks into the sweet white flesh of Bacchus Marsh apples.

The trees, now three years old, stood as tall as young men, taller than Charles who tottered along in his ghost's gait, following Horace and holding on to his chubby legs.

That night, in the heart of my empire, my wife and I made love in the style that permitted no conception and that, in any case, was the one she now preferred. It no longer hurt her and left her free to increase the tempo of her own pleasure with her hand, but that night she wept when I entered her and her tears wet my nose where it pressed against her neck.

"Poor Herbert," she said.

I did not understand her.

"You'll be all right," she said. She choked. She shook.

"I am," I said. "I am, I am."

But whatever I said to her only made her weep more and I now know what I did not know then, she was suffering from the melancholy that all poets feel at the completion of their work.

"You'll survive," she said.

I did not doubt her. The bedsprings creaked beneath the strokes of my greasy confidence, and if there was shit to smell, I missed it totally.

85

Colonel Barret had long ago abandoned the manufacture of his Barret car in order to be an agent for King Henry Ford. And now, in 1923, he assembled us amongst the spare-part bins on the first floor and made a speech to us, the details of which I forget, but the gist of which I still retain.

"It would appear", he told us, "that Mr Ford is strapped for cash, and now wishes me to pay cash in advance for every car I order. In short, he wishes me to finance his venture and I find I am unable to raise the money he requires. I have informed the Ford company of my position and they have cabled me to say that I may no longer be an agent for the company's vehicles. I have therefore decided to close down the business and retire to Rosebud. I am sorry to have let you down."

It was quiet and still inside that dusty space. Outside we could hear the Chinese children bouncing a ball against the wall. Barret hated that noise but today he sent no one to chase them off.

"I will pay you all your week's wages and a small bonus," he said. "It's the best I can do."

Then he shook hands with all of us. I did not, like the other fellows did, go to the pub and get drunk. I handed in the key of my demonstration model, shook Colonel Barret by the hand, wished him well in his retirement, and caught the tram out to Haymarket. As far as I am concerned that day was the first of the Great Depression.

I was walking down the little lane beside the stockyards when I ran into Horace who was walking the other way, banging a heavy suitcase against his chubby thigh. He was embarrassed to see me.

I told him I had been dismissed and asked him where he was off to.

"I'm sorry," he said, "you have been very kind to me."

I understood that he was leaving. I assumed it was because of Annette whom I imagined he did not like.

"Sonia will miss you."

"Yes."

"And Charles."

"Yes. I'll miss him."

"Where are you off to?" I pushed my hand into my pocket, in search of jiggling keys which were not there.

Horace shifted uncomfortably and kicked at a stone.

"Sydney," he said.

"I hear it's a beautiful city."

I should have known that something odd was happening. He wanted to make a speech, but he could not get the words together.

"I want to thank you," he said, "and to say I never bore you any ill will or did anything I was ashamed of either."

"Thank you, Horace, but if you're leaving because of Annette, she'll be gone soon."

"Oh no," he said, "not Annette. Just time to be pushing on."

We shook hands. He picked up his suitcase. He opened his little red mouth, closed it, hesitated, and then went out of my life, trudging up the pot-holed track towards the Haymarket terminus.

I was still three hundred yards from the house. Phoebe and Annette were at the Morris Farman. The motor was turning, running rough with too much choke. The craft was straining at the chocks.

As I watched, Annette threw a bag into the passenger compartment and pulled out the chocks. Charles came trundling towards her like a little wombat, dense, solid, screaming. My wife opened the throttle. She took a course downwind, away from her bellowing son who tripped and fell. She was lucky the wind was only blowing a knot or two – ten yards from the boundary fence she got the craft into the air.

She left me with two children and a savage poem.

86

I learned a lot about poets and poetry that day and it is my contention that poets are weak shy people who will not look you in the eye. They are like Horace, scribbling spidery things in dark corners, frightened of their fathers, the law, and everything else. They are women who expect their husbands to be mind-readers. They are resentful and cruel. They spend sunny days planning dark revenges where they will punish those who wish them well.

They sit like spiders in the centre of their pretty webs. They are harsh judges with wigs and buckled shoes. They place black caps upon their heads but let others attend the executions for them.

The poem that taught me so much is not the set of rhyming words I found clasped to the king parrots' cage, skewered with a pin from Sonia's dirty napkin. This was just the mud-map, just enough to make sure I did not miss the turning to the Scenic View. While Charles tugged at my trouser legs and bellowed I stared at this crumpled paper as if I could take in its meaning by the sheer force of my will. It would not reveal itself. It contained nothing I recognized, neither the word Badgery or Ford, and it was two hours before Molly arrived to read it to me.

No, this was not the poem. She had no talent for poetry, never did.

Witness:

King Parrot
Then beauty were declared a crime
King Parrot locked with key
Barred and caged on wasted land
Oh angry jewel. Desolate. Ennui.

Do not rush to your bookshop for more of the same. There is none. Phoebe's great poem was not built from words, but from corrugated iron and chicken wire. She did not even build it herself but had me, her labourer, saw and hammer and make it for her. She had me rhyme a cage with a room, a bird with a person, feathers with skin, my home with a gaol, myself with a warder, herself with the splendid guileless creatures who had preened themselves so lovingly on the roof on one sad, lost, blue-skied day.

And it does not matter that she sold the Morris Farman for one hundred pounds and used the money to buy a dress for the Arts Ball in Sydney in 1924. Nor is it of any importance that she spent the rest of her life putting all her wiles and energies into being kept, cared for, loved or that the love she gave in return was of such a brittle quality that Annette Davidson would finally take her own life rather than endure its cutting edges.

It is of no importance that she would reveal herself to be self-indulgent, selfish, admiring herself like a budgie in a cage.

She was a liar, but who cares? The poem was made, set hard, could never be dismantled or unravelled, although on that dreadful night in September 1923 I did not understand, and battled against its timbers with an axe, howling more loudly than my terrified son. I did not guess how long I was destined to live with it.

Book 2

1

In a moment I must tell you how, competing with my son for the affection of a woman, I misused the valuable art I had learned from Goon Tse Ying and brought misfortune on my daughter. I would rather not repeat it. It is bad enough to have done it and I would as soon tear it up, wipe my arse with it, hide it under my lumpy mattress or feed it to my neighbour, the three-legged goanna with bad breath.

Yet, I see, I can postpone it a moment. For first I must tell you how I learned the art itself. I refer to the ability to become invisible, and you may wonder, if I really did possess such an unlikely power, why I should not have already used it to my own advantage.

To explain this I must go back to the days when my father's horses had to be shot at the bottom of the Punt Road Hill and I, a self-appointed orphan, was living, thin, half wild, cunning as a shit-house rat amidst the crates and spoiled vegetables at the back of the Eastern Market. I cannot have lived there for more than a week, but it seems like months that I lay amidst that stinking refuse, making tunnels and nests for myself at night, lying sleepless listening to the rats, shivering amidst the smell of bad cabbage in the early morning, peering through gaps at the family of Chinese whose stall was next to my midden heap. They knew I was there. They left me a bowl of milk on the first day but I would not touch it. I was my father's son. My head was full of stories about John Chinaman: opium, slavery, how they ate the hands of Christian babies.

In the end, hunger might have broken the impasse, but certainly the Wongs, whose stall it was, would never have. They were nervous, polite and law-abiding. Their cousin Goon, however, was a different man and it was he who strode right in, knocking crates aside with his gold-capped stick, who grabbed me by the scruff of my dirty neck and lifted me, screaming and kicking, into the air: pale, skinny, hatchet-faced with hunger. I bit his hand and made it bleed. He laughed out loud, this giant in a butterfly collar and gold-rimmed glasses. I wet myself in terror.

I sometimes wonder if Goon would have taken me in if I had displayed less terror, if his compulsion to prove his benign intentions was not what any human will feel when confronted with a petrified wild animal one wishes to help – the mistaken terror is an insult to our good motives, a goad to greater efforts. But Goon, in any case, was a man driven by a desire to prove himself civilized to the English he despised. He adopted their dress when it suited him and spoke their language without a trace of accent. He was a giant of a man, not in the sense that he might tower over you, my long-limbed reader. Oh, he was large for a Chinese, but that is not the point – he towered over every man I ever met in the size of his spirit, his indignation, his energy, his laugh, and his ability to drink a tumbler of rough brandy in a single gulp.

He was not one of the Chinese who wrote to the legislature: "Dear kind sirs, we the Chinese miners do beg you to treat us fairly as we most respectfully beg you to do. We work hard and mean no harm . . ." or words to that effect.

For these Chinese, Goon had nothing but scorn.

"Roll up," he would taunt them, "roll up."

When he became an old man with a successful business in Grafton, these facts about his younger days would cause him embarrassment and he would deny it all. He joined Chinese–Australian associations and had grandchildren with names like Heather and Walter. He ate chops and sausages, roast beef on Sundays, and the only invisibility he would acknowledge was that which comes from dressing like everyone else.

The Goon of old age is not worth a pinch of shit. It is the forty-year-old Goon we want and to reach him I must walk down Little Bourke Street, Melbourne, as it was in 1896, past drays piled high with wicker baskets, shivering men with long coats and pigtails, past Mr Choo, the fortune-teller with the clever canary, to the worn wooden stoop that led to Wong's cafe. There was no sign at Wong's to proclaim its business, no window to display its wares. There was simply the stoop where old Mrs Wong sat in all weathers, breathing heavily and plucking ducks, the feathers of which drifted down Little Bourke Street and caught themselves in the nostrils of indignant mares, fresh from Port Melbourne with another load of travel-stained Chinese. Over the stoop was a small carved timber arch, its wood grey and cracked. Behind the arch was a trellised veranda, and behind this wooden skirt Wong, his family, and his customers hid their business from the English.

As you came in the door there was a small office on the right where the younger Mr Wong sat at his books, crowded in upon by bundles of goods, some in crates, some wrapped in raffia. There was the smell of dried fish, but also of steel, of grease. Long-handled shovels leaned against jute sacks of mushrooms criss-crossed with sunlight from the latticed window. You would think there was no order here until you looked at Wong's book and saw the neat rows of Chinese characters and Arabic figures and watched his bony fingers as they worked the abacus.

Further along there was the kitchen where Hing butchered and giggled and beyond that the dining room.

And there is Goon at the little table by the courtyard door. "Roll up," he calls, and everyone, all the Wongs, all the lonely single men, all nod and smile at Goon Tse Ying who was a rich man even then and respected because of it.

He had a great moon face with a high forehead and thin black hair that lifted in the slightest breeze. He had big shoulders, strong calves (which he displayed when called upon to sit) and, in Wong's at least, amongst his own kind, a voice like a gravel-crusher. Although he was in his late thirties when he adopted me it is misleading to mention it because he could look much younger and – when dressed in that formidable English suit – much older.

"I will teach you everything," Goon told me. "I will teach you how to skin a crow by blowing air into it with a piece of bamboo. I will teach you how to fight with your feet, my little Englishman," he hissed.

I sat in Wong's and was terrified. My head was full of my father's visions, his cannon balls, his patented breach locks, his naked coastline. His blue prophet's eyes looked at the ducks' feet Goon gave me to eat and saw, instead, the hands of babies.

I was not alone in my nervousness. The other Chinese did not want me there either. They did not approve of Goon Tse Ying adopting Englishmen. They were frightened of the consequences but Goon was a rich man and a natural force whose very laugh could move the brass chimes above the family table.

"I will teach you how to use garlic and ginger to remove pains from the head. I will teach you to read and write. I will teach you everything. Five languages," Goon Tse Ying said, "because I was once an orphan too. Do you understand?"

"Yes," I said.

211

I had never sat at a table without a cloth. I had never heard mah-jong tiles clatter. I had never seen children treated kindly, touched, petted and embraced so readily. The Wong children were all younger than I was. They came and stared at me with huge brown eyes. When the sight of me made them cry they were not slapped. And – ducks' feet and dried fish included – it was this that was the most exotic thing in Wong's café.

"You will come to the herbalist's with me and I will make you a scholar of herbs. I will teach you to shoe a horse. I will teach you to make money. You will polish your boots like I show you. Why am I doing this for you, little Englishman?"

"Because you were an orphan, sir."

"Roll up," roared Goon Tse Ying. "Roll up, roll up. Look at them," he indicated the men playing mah-jong in the corner. "They are in gaol. They have locked themselves up in Wong's. They have made themselves prisoners. They give Wong all their money and Wong feeds them and buys what they need at the shops. They cannot speak English. They do not know what 'roll up' means. I say it and they smile. They nod at me. They think I am moon-touched, but they know I am rich. They respect me and think I am dangerous. I buy them presents because they are lonely and unhappy. Next week I will give poor Hing fifty pounds so he can have a bride come out from China. He does not know. You watch."

"Hing," he shouted in English. "Next month I give you fifty pounds."

Hing, sitting on a chair by the kitchen servery, looked up from his newspaper, took the sodden cigarette from his mouth and gave a stained smile.

"See," Goon Tse Ying said. "He does not know what I am saying. He does not know the meaning of 'fifty pounds' or 'roll up' either. Tell me, my pet Englishman, what is the meaning of 'roll up'?"

I didn't know.

"Pour me brandy, little Englishman, and eat your soup. It will warm your heart and make you forget this terrible country. Why am I kind to you?"

"Because you were an orphan, sir."

"No," Goon said quietly. His voice became soft, amber, vaporous as the brandy on his foreign breath. "It is to show I am not a barbarian like them."

In my confusion I thought he was referring to the Chinese.

"You will sleep here," Goon Tse Ying told me. "I have arranged with Wong. You will share a room with old Hing and his nephew. Hing will cook your meals. In the morning I will come and get you and we will sit at the herbalist's. He does not speak English but he is a good herbalist. I am helping him out for a while, to translate for him. He is a silly man to have bought the business with no English and I don't know what will happen to him when I leave."

My bedroom was on the other side of the muddy courtyard, a long lean-to made from corrugated iron with an earth floor. I could not shut my eyes. Hing coughed all night. His nephew snored. I cried in the dark, assailed by garlic and the sweet smell of Hing's evening pipe.

When, at last, I did sleep, I dreamed the Chinese came and ate my hands.

2

The herbalist was Mr Chin, the uncle of the Mr Chin to whom I would later sell my snakes. He was very handsome with his blue waving hair and his gold tooth but when he saw me his forehead scarred itself with a frown as messy as a bulldog's. Goon Tse Ying listened to what Mr Chin had to say and then he explained to me that I would not be permitted to sit in the consulting room. This was because all of Mr Chin's patients were English gentlemen and ladies and they would be embarrassed, Goon told me sternly, to repeat their complaints in front of a boy.

So I never learned the art of herbalism, nor, for that matter, did I master any of the five languages Goon had promised, although I did learn to count from one to ten in Hokein.

Goon was neither embarrassed nor apologetic about this set-back. He announced that I was to return to the Eastern Markets and learn about vegetables. He himself had been a hawker in the Palmer River rush in Northern Queensland.

It is the nature of childhood to continually encounter things one does not understand, to be thrown here, to be put there, to offend without meaning to, to be praised without understanding why, and I do not remember being unduly unhappy to be sent to the Eastern Markets.

I remember the cold, the paraffin lamps in the early mornings, the chatter of Wong Li Ho, the spitting of Nick Wong. I remember the red-faced Scot with big ears who roared the virtues of his cabbages from dawn till afternoon, the gaunt women with red fingers protruding from their dirty mittens. I remember knocking my chilblains against boxes of cauliflowers. I remember bags of potatoes I could not lift. But most of all I remember that no one hit me and that when noon arrived I was permitted to depart and then I would walk up through the busy streets to Nicholson Street in Carlton and wait for Goon Tse Ying. When the last consultation was finished he would take me by the hand and escort me back to the café within whose walls, it seemed, there was contained everything in the world I would need to know.

In the muddy courtyard, amidst indignant hens, he not only taught me how to fight with my feet but also how to skin a crow by putting a nick in its neck, inserting a bamboo rod between skin and flesh, and blowing. Both of these skills were useful to me in later life. He took me to the kitchen and showed me how to make soup from the crow. He sat me on his knee while Hing butchered a pig and showed me how every part of it could be used for food.

He took me to the front office to instruct me in abacus, but, finding Wong busy with it, demonstrated the pressure points of the body instead, showing me how these could be used to immobilize an opponent. While Wong entered the single men's wages into his ledger, Goon Tse Ying taught me to stand in such a way that I would appear bigger than I was, or, conversely, how to appear smaller. Wong did not complain once. There was such clutter in this dark front room, such a tangle of rope and canvas, incense for jossing, shoes for horses, even a monkey foetus in a bottle of green liquid whose purpose I never discovered, such a disorder of goods, such a tangle of raffia, that the presence of a noisy rich man and a quiet sharp-faced boy did nothing extra to distract him from the wonderful order of his ledgers.

In the dark passage, looked upon by the alien visage of the King of England, Goon taught me the different accents of this King's language and how to use each one. He also instructed me in the importance of clean shoes and how a pair of very shiny shoes can give the appearance of great wealth even if the rest of one's clothes are nothing but rags.

And in the steamy dining room, with rain combing the brick-damp air outside, he taught me history and geography.

"Roll up," he called to the other Chinese. "Look at them, they grin, they do not know. If they were at Lambing Flat they would be dead men. They would hear the English calling to each other: roll up, roll up, and they would go on with their work. What is Lambing Flat, little Englishman?"

"I don't know."

"Of course you don't know. Lambing Flat is near Young in New South Wales. It was a big rush. I was there. We were all there. Roll up, roll up, that is what the English miners called to each other. May you never hear it. May you die never having heard the English come in their horses and carts. They carried the English flag, an ugly thing. They had a band. They had pipes and drums and they came in their thousands. They did not like the Chinese, little Englishman, because we were clever. They sold us their old mines. They thought they would cheat us, but we made money. They drew a line across the diggings and said we must not cross it. Still we made money. We worked hard, even us children. My father was sick. He had ulcers on his feet, and still he worked. My mother worked too, alongside the men. Her feet had been bound. They were tiny pretty things, but she carried rocks in baskets and helped make the big water race. But the Englishmen thought it was all their country and all their gold and they played their band and came out to get us. They drove the Chinese down the river bank. They had axe handles and picks. They ran over my uncle Han in a cart and broke his leg and they broke my father's head open with a water pipe. You will meet people who say that none of this happened. They will say they gave John Chinaman a fright, but they are liars. Roll up, roll up," he bellowed, "roll up. Kill John Chinaman," he roared at the Wongs, the Wongs' giggling children, the dark-eyed single men with no backsides in their English trousers. "My father's brains," he whispered while the thin hair lifted in the draught from the courtyard, "like in the pig Hing cut up. Pour me brandy. What would you do?"

"I would run," I said.

"My uncle Han ran. They had horses and carts. They ran their wheel across him."

"I would hide."

"They would burn down your tent."

"I would fight them."

"There were too many. What would you do?"

I was caught in the terror of Lambing Flat which I imagined to be a great wilderness of rocks as sharp as needles. I had no trouble imagining the terror, the bands of men with my father's merciless eyes.

It was quiet for a moment in Wong's. Hing's mah-jong tiles stood in an unbroken wall.

"Do you know what to do?" he whispered.

"No."

"You disappear," Goon Tse Ying hissed, his great hand totally enclosing his glass. "Completely."

In the courtyard, old Mrs Wong wrung the neck of a Rhode Island Red and in the dining room Hing spat and broke open the wall of mah-jong tiles. I could not take my eyes from the glass that peeked through the fingers of Goon's hand. I did not doubt he could disappear.

"I will teach you too, little Englishman. It will do two things of great merit. The first of these things is to make you safe, and I do this for goodness, because I care for you, because you have no father to help you. But I do it also to show you the terror of we Chinese at Lambing Flat. Because it is only possible to disappear by feeling the terror. So I tell you now that I am giving you this gift as revenge. Are you old enough to understand what I am saying to you?"

"I am ten."

"Why am I telling you?"

"So I can feel the terror." I shivered.

"It is a magician's gift," Goon Tse Ying said. "It is both good and evil. It is because I love and hate you. Will you accept it?"

"I am only ten," I pleaded.

"It is old enough," Goon Tse Ying announced. "We will start tomorrow."

3

Goon Tse Ying was as hard to grasp as a raging sea with waves driving one way and tides pulling the other. He could be loud, play the fool like old Mr Chan at his ugly daughter's pre-wedding feast, going from table to table with his brandy bottle and loudly, raucously even, assuming the role that was expected of him, so that an Englishman, not understanding, would wish to know the name of the old man who was disgracing himself in so un-Chinese a manner. Likewise, if Goon's gravelling laugh and thumping brandy glass on Wong's scrubbed table made him appear impatient or foolish, or even mad, there was also a very cautious and serious part to his character that did not reveal itself while he was playing the rich benefactor. He had many responsibilities which he honoured ungrudgingly. These responsibilities meant that he could not always keep the promises he made to me.

His enthusiasm would have me learn all languages, understand the subtleties of astrology, sex one-day-old chicks and use an abacus. He made me many promises about things which he seemed to forget about entirely. As for the business of disappearing, it could not, he told me, be begun on the next day at all. I had not inquired. But when he brought up the subject it was as a reprimand.

"Not today, little Englishman, and not tomorrow. If you rush at a thing like this you will get nowhere. There are preparations to undertake. Nick Wong must have someone to replace the little work you do for him. There is equipment I need. I must find someone else to translate for Mr Chin whose English is worse than it was a week ago. I also have a marriage to arrange for myself. There are three things," he said, no longer an Englishman, "which are unfilial. And to have no posterity is the greatest of them. What does unfilial mean?"

I did not know.

"Learn," he said, his mouth full of noodles. "What hope is there for you if you know less than a Chinaman? Next week", he said, ladling soup into his bowl, "I will teach you to disappear."

But it was not next week, it was two days later, and Goon Tse Ying shook me awake in my bed at three in the morning. "Come," he hissed, "be quiet. Do not wake old Hing."

He took me to the kitchen where he already had the big wood oven crackling. He fed me a bowl of pork porridge with an egg in it. I broke the yolk and stirred it into the porridge, and, looking up, found him staring at me intently. The flames from the open door of the firebox made his face appear slightly sinister. It accentuated all the foreign features his perfect English and his tailored suits cloaked so densely. "You are learning already," he said, still staring at me. "For now you feel warm and content. You enjoy your porridge. But by tonight you will know terror. You will know the cold of the terror and the warm of the porridge. Now shine your boots and we will go."

He had a good horse and a smart sulky waiting outside. Drugged by the warm porridge in my stomach and the horse sweat and leather in my nostrils, rugged in a thick blanket, I went to sleep. When I awoke I found the dawn already gone and the sulky bouncing along a narrow gravel road through one of those flat featureless landscapes where it is the lot of sheep and their gaolers to spend their lives. Here and there were failed dams and along the fence lines, new plantations of cypress pines which might one day break the wind which now flattened the dun-coloured grasses. It was crow country.

We came to a small depression in the road where a slow creek dribbled its way over rusty rocks. A few eucalypts, spared the new settler's axe, clung to the top of the eroded banks.

Goon reined in the sweating mare and surveyed this scene with satisfaction. "This is a good place to learn," he announced. "There are rocks, a river, ugly trees. It is a terrible place." He rubbed his hands together. "Go and play while I get ready."

I put aside my rug and reluctantly abandoned the comforting smells of the expensive sulky which had evoked memories of days when I had a father beside me and a cannon behind me.

"Play by the creek," Goon instructed.

I was not ready for the lesson. I tugged up my socks to cover my knees and shivered. I walked slowly down to the creek. I was cold. My chilblains itched. I did not like the sound of the crows. I lifted up the rocks and looked for beetles or mud-eyes to torment.

Goon Tse Ying had many voices, but I did not recognize the curdled cry that shortly reached my ears.

Goon Tse Ying, dressed in his formal three-piece suit, his watch chain flashing in the winter sun, came bounding towards me waving an axe handle.

"Roll up," he screamed, "roll up."

The terrible Chinaman leapt from crumbling bank to gnarled root, from root to scoured clay. His face was hideous. The axe handle belted me across the shoulders and sent me sprawling.

I lay across the rocks blubbering, as broken as the beetles I had sought to injure.

"Now, you see," said Goon, standing over me. "It is not so easy. Get up. I did not hit you so hard."

I got up, bawling loudly. "I want my daddy."

"You have no daddy, little Englishman. You have only me. Now pay attention and I will show you how to stand so that you will disappear."

It was a terrible day. I learned to stand in the way he showed me, quite the opposite to what you'd expect for, rather than make me less conspicuous, it seemed to make me more so. I teetered on one leg, with one foot raised and resting on my knee. I stretched one hand in the air as if waving for attention. It did

218

not work. He hit me time and time again. I wept. I begged. I tried to run away, but he caught me effortlessly.

"I will run you down," he bellowed as he chased. "You will go beneath my wheel."

But that night, as I nursed my wounds, he was kind to me. He stroked my head and told me stories about China to which he must return before his death. "To have amassed great wealth," he said, "and not return home is comparable to walking in magnificent clothes at night." He rubbed a cold camphor ointment on my bruises. He wrapped me in a blanket and made a soup heavy with duck. He fed me milk and brandy and put me to bed in the tent.

But on the next morning his great face had transformed. The skin was tight and waxy and the bones beneath it seemed as hard and cold as marble. The camp fire was cold and he showed no inclination to light it. He had rubbed grease in his hair.

"I have no time to play games," he told me, kicking at the dead ashes as if to deny the warmth of the night before. "I am buying a business in Grafton from a man I do not trust. You are slow and stupid. You are too English. You do not believe harm will come to you. Well, I give you my word that if you do not disappear this morning, first time, I will kill you. I do not have time to play games. I am thirty-seven years old and soon I must get married."

If you had seen him you would not have doubted him. He did not look at me. He took out his gold watch and spat on it. He rubbed its glass with a white handkerchief. Then he held it to his small flat ear and listened to it. It was obvious my death had no interest to him.

"Go and play by the creek," he said.

I did not beseech him. I did not cry. I walked down to the creek.

He did not come immediately. He squatted on his haunches and sang "Waltzing Matilda" in a wavering falsetto. I loathe the song to this day.

I did not look at him. When he had finished the song I heard him clear his throat and spit.

"No Chinese," he yelled.

I stood as I was taught. I held my shaking arm high. I teetered on my foot. Urine ran down my leg. I heard the swish of the axe handle. I began to quiver. My whole body began to hum like a tuning fork. My bones vibrated. I was a steel bridge marched on by an army. I was a glass held before a famous soprano.

I disappeared and the world disappeared from me. I did not escape from fear, but went to the place where fear lives. I existed like waves from a tuning fork in chloroformed air. I could not see Goon Tse Ying. I was nowhere.

I cannot tell how long I was like this, but finally the world came back to me and Goon Tse Ying was squatting a little way away from me grinning.

"Now," he said, "we will have a feast and I will teach you to eat chicken's innards."

4

I know for a fact that there are easier methods of disappearing than facing a Chinaman with an axe handle. It is no more difficult to learn than driving a car and does not require real danger for its accomplishment. The terror can be summoned up in the mind, and one does not need to adopt the peculiar stance of Goon Tse Ying: all that is needed is to tense the muscles in a certain way so that they begin to quiver. His odd method of standing helped produce this state but I was a resourceful young chap and soon found I could do it even while lying down in my bed.

Yet only twice did I disappear as a trick and the two incidents are separated by thirty years.

If you know what winter's mornings are like in Melbourne, if you have seen the blue fingers of the Chinese protruding from their grey mittens as they handle the cauliflowers and kale in the Eastern Market, if you have seen their breath suspended before kerosene lights, you might understand why an eleven-year-old might choose to disappear in order to lie in bed of a winter's morning.

I had not calculated the upset I would cause: the prodding hands, the chattering voice of old Hing, the running feet of his timid nephew, the shriek of old Mrs Wong whose heart was bad. I lay, invisible, in the heart of a storm.

When I finally regained my normal consciousness Goon Tse Ying was sitting on old Hing's bed reading the racing form.

"Mr Chin is with Mrs Wong," he said. "She is very sick. She is an old woman and has no use for demons. Look at my eyes and listen to me. I am going to Grafton soon and will not be here to teach you any more. I have already taught you too much. If you make yourself

220

feel the terror when there is no terror to feel, you are making a dragon. If you meet a real dragon, that is the way of things. But if you make dragons in your head you are not strong enough and you will have great misfortune. Do you understand me?"

"I am sorry, Mr Goon."

"You made a terror and now Mrs Wong has been taken by it and you are lucky that Mr Chin is here to care for her. The Wongs will not have you any more and I have spent the morning persuading my nephew to take you. I have had to pay him money and he is only taking you because his greed is greater than his fear, but it is only just greater", he held his thumb and forefinger apart, "that much, and if you make dragons in his house he will send you away and no one will talk to you or help you any more. Further, you will now work all day. When you have finished at the market you will go to the market garden and you will do whatever it is they ask you to do. Do you understand me?"

"Yes," I said.

"Well, shine your shoes," Goon Tse Ying said to me, "and when you walk into my nephew's house make yourself into a small man."

Mrs Wong, so I heard, recovered from the terror I had given her, but I never set foot in Wong's café again and when I had reason to pass by the worn wooden door stoop in Little Bourke Street I made myself small and walked quickly, with short steps and bowed head.

I made use of all the things I learned from Goon Tse Ying – how to appear bigger or smaller, how to skin a crow , butcher a pig, wear expensive shoes when my suit was inferior, how to change my accent, how to modulate my walk, but I always kept my word to him about making dragons until I was stupid enough to compete with my son for the affection of a woman.

5

There is nothing as good as bananas on the breath when it comes to making a horse feel it is akin to you. And it has always been my contention that it was for reasons very similar to this that Charles mistook Leah Goldstein for his mother.

When, on that chilblained afternoon in 1931, he grabbed her around the legs, he imagined his seven years of wandering were at an end, that the declared goal of our travels had been achieved, that we would return to the splendid home he could not remember and abandon the converted 1924 Dodge tourer in which we slept each night, curled up together amidst the heavy fug, the warm odours of humanity, which so comforted his battered father.

You would have met Leah, you might have embraced her and not noticed the smell of snake, buried your nose in the nape of her long graceful neck and smelt nothing but Velvet soap. But Charles – although he had never met a snake – recognized the odour of his flesh and blood and all his belligerence and suspicion melted away like the frost in a north–south valley when it finally gets the sun at noon.

We were camped on Crab Apple Creek, just outside of Bendigo, still six hundred miles from Phoebe Badgery. If I am inclined to refer to frost when referring to Charles's emotions, it is because it was a frosty place. When the frost melted it soaked into the mud. Even the magpies were muddy in that place. They scrounged around the camp, snapping irritably at the currawongs, and held out their filthy wings to the feeble sun, making themselves an easy target for Charles's shanghai.

On the day in question I was panning for gold while I tried to keep an eye on Charles who was reading a (probably stolen) comic on the running board of the Dodge while Sonia was floating sticks down the creek (a rain-muddied torrent that hid the pretty slate you can see in summer). I was getting a little colour, just a few specks, and my time would have been more profitably spent trapping rabbits. However I had a few bob in my pocket and we were on our way up to Darkville where one of Barret's clerks now had a still for making tea-tree oil. He had promised me a month's work cutting the tea tree and I had sent a wire saying we were on our way.

There was a depression on. Everyone knows that now. But I swear to you that I did not. I had lived seven years in an odd cocoon, criss-crossing Victoria, writing bad cheques when I could get hold of a book, running raffles in pubs, buying stolen petrol, ransacking local tips for useful building materials. I had long since stopped trying to impress motor-car dealers and agents. I had a salesman's vanity and could not bear rejection. I could not tolerate talking to men who would not even open my book of yellowed write-ups. Those Ford and Dodge agents in Ballarat, Ararat, Shepparton, Kaniva, Warragul and Colac finished off the work that Phoebe's poem had begun and I entered my own private depression and kept away from anything that might damage my pride any more.

I, Herbert Badgery, aviator, nationalist, now wore Molly's belt and chose not to see that the roads were full of ghosts, men with their coats too short, their frayed trousers too long, clanking their billycans like doleful bells.

I gave up having the newspapers read aloud to me on the day Goble and McIntyre made their flight around Australia in a seaplane. I concentrated instead on the things I could hope to achieve: keeping my children clean and neat, turning the collars of my frayed shirts, polishing my boots and hoping that the brave new signs I painted on the door of the Dodge would convince people who saw me that I was a success and not a failure. The people I imagined were those who peer from a farmhouse window as a glistening custom-made utility goes by, a butcher in Benalla unlocking his shop at seven a.m., a cow-cocky driving his herd of jerseys from one side of the Warragul road to the other, a whiskered garage owner pumping four gallons up into the glass reservoir of a petrol bowser before taking my bad cheque. As for women, the only ones I spoke to were barmaids whose permission I sought before raffling sausages.

I panned for gold whenever I had a spare moment but I no longer hoped for anything remarkable. It was miserable work in winter and on the day Sonia found the emu my bare feet were blue with cold and my bandy legs were as white as an Englishman's below my billowing woollen underpants.

She had crept upstream while I was busy panning. I looked up and found her missing. I bellowed her name above the roaring yellow water that tugged malevolently at my feet. I threw the unwashed gravel back and scrambled up the slippery clay bank just as she came running through the bush with her finger held (sshh) to her lips. My heart was beating so loudly I could hardly hear what she said. I crushed her to me but she wormed out of my arms impatiently.

"Papa, it's an emu." Her appearance, her manner, were a continual joy and a pain to me for she was like her mother in so many ways, in her murmuring throaty speech, in the extraordinary green of her eyes. Yet she was without the imbalances in either her character or her face: Phoebe's low forehead and long chin had rearranged themselves into a more harmonious relationship.

"With feathers, papa." She pulled the sleeves of her woollen cardigan over her hands and flapped them with impatience and excitement. "An emu."

I expected a goldfinch or a chook, but I pulled on my trousers and my boots while she danced impatiently around me, stretching her cardigan out of shape.

"Hurry. Hurry."

I followed her, my laces dangling, mimicking her exaggerated stealth.

Charles came bellowing behind, enraged that he was being abandoned. He did not understand me: I would never have left him behind in any circumstances. I explained this to him. I, after all, knew better than anyone the horrors of being alone at ten years of age. Had I not lived amongst the garbage in the Eastern Markets, living on old cabbage leaves, too frightened to taste the saucer of warm milk the Wongs left for me each night? Charles knew this story. I wished him to know I would never abandon him. I explained it endlessly, but he could not be comforted. He worried that I would forget to pick him up after school. If I was five minutes late I would find him blubbering or running in panic down the street. If I got up in the night he wanted to know what I was doing and on more than one occasion I have had a nocturnal shit interrupted by my son blundering through the dark in search of me. He was my policeman. He would stand beside me shivering while I wiped my arse and only then would he return to bed.

Sonia took her brother's warty hand to lead him to the emu. She never flinched from the feel of those warts, but ministered to them constantly, gathering milk thistles and carefully squeezing their juices on to the ugly lumps that were always marked with ink from one unhappy well or another.

Sonia's hand did not comfort Charles. Now he was with us he became surly. He dragged his boots along in the gravelly mud and scratched the leather I had worked so hard to shine for him.

"Where are we going?" (It was his continual cry, here, and on the road where he kicked against the confines of the Dodge.) "Where are we *going*?"

"There is an emu," Sonia said, "with feathers."

"There ain't emus."

"I *think* it's an emu." Sonia was always ready to defer to her brother but just the same she parted the blackberry briars stealthily.

There are no crab apples on Crab Apple Creek. There is a tangle of blackberries and a number of giant river blackwoods. We came under the blackwood canopy to a clear bit of land by the bridge on the Castlemaine Road and there, amongst the ash of swaggies' fires and the dried pats of cattle dung, was an emu.

It was the cleanest thing in that muddy place. Its feathers shone. Its long neck glistened. It also had the most remarkable pair of legs I was ever blessed to cast my eyes on. They were long and shapely and tightly clad in fishnet stockings.

Sonia squeezed my hand and rubbed herself against me with delight. Charles gawped and went bright red. The emu jerked its head towards us and then away. Sonia hugged herself with pleasure. The emu started to shake. It started slowly, a mild vibration that built and built until it was quivering all over. It stamped its feet, one, two, three. It waggled its backside. It bumped and ground. It went into the most astonishing sexual display I have ever witnessed in my life. There was no mistaking its intention and I was embarrassed in front of the children. It set up a display with its backside, getting lower and lower to the ground, then sprang like a dervish and scissored its legs. It hopped on its haunches. It squatted. It showed itself like I have seen red-arsed bool-bools do in spring.

"Egg," shrieked Sonia, tugging painfully on my wedding ring. "Egg, egg, egg."

"Shut up," said Charles.

The egg was black and shining, about eight inches across, an emu egg of course. The emu pecked it. And out of the egg came a little emu, bright blue, rocking back and forth on a metal spring.

"No, Charlie," Sonia cried.

But it was too late. Charles was running, his head down, his little arms outstretched, his warty hands open, towards the emu. He got a hold of a net-stockinged leg and would not let go.

The emu now unravelled itself. The front of the chest detached itself and revealed itself to be a woman's head with a feathered hat. The emu's head and neck dropped so we could see they were not neck and head at all, but an arm with a glove made in the shape of an emu's head. Another naked arm emerged from somewhere and stroked my son's bristly head.

"Did you get it?" the emu asked.

I stood as gawp-mouthed as my son had.

"Did you get the photographs," the emu said, "or didn't you?"

"Mummy," Charles said.

"Are you a journalist," the emu said, "or aren't you?"

"No," I said, "my name is Herbert Badgery."

"Mummy," said Charles.

"I have waited here all morning," the emu said. "I have waited here for the dills to arrive. God damn them. What do you need to get written up in their silly rag?" She stamped her foot. "I gave them a map. I told them I would be here and I walked here, two miles. They wanted me to do it in town but they don't understand publicity. I need all this," she gestured at the blackwoods, blackberries, the cow dung, the dead winter grass, "for atmosphere. It's not so much trouble for them to come. They have motor cars. Look at my shoes. Look at them. How in the hell do I get a break? Mervyn Sullivan has stolen my act. The police won't make him take down my picture. What do they expect me to do: starve? Bendigo is a lousy town. I should have gone up to Ararat. Where is the boy's mother?"

She squatted down beside Charles and wiped his nose with a little square of newspaper she had tucked away in her feathers. "You should look after children," she said sternly. "They are the hope of the future. Just because you are unemployed it doesn't mean your children should have no hope."

"My shoes hurt," Charles said.

"I am employed," I said.

"Bully for you," she said. "Buy your boy boots then."

I am giving a bad impression of Leah, but she has only herself to blame, for she was not at her best beneath the Castlemaine Road that day, nor I guess would she have been at her best when she asked the police to force Mervyn Sullivan to remove her picture from his sideshow. She was not one of life's diplomats at the best of times, but she could never control herself in the presence of a policeman.

She had an austere face, and you would hardly call it pretty. It was a flinty sort of face, with a small mouth, grey eyes and a little parrot's beak of a nose which I later came to admire although at the time I was not well disposed towards parrots or anything that reminded me of them. She had short dark wavy hair, olive skin, a slight smudge on her upper lip, and a long graceful neck. Her ears stuck out. The emu dance, which she had learned direct from its inventor, certainly made the most of her best features.

226

If I had known she was carrying snakes, I doubt whether I would have let her come to our camp. However, once Charles had decided she was his mother he had no intention of being parted from her again. He picked up her two suitcases and no one could persuade him to let anyone else share the load. He struggled along on his two sturdy bandy legs, jutting his jaw, more like a midget than a child.

Sonia led the way through the blackberries, holding aside brambles for her brother. Leah followed her luggage. I followed her.

She did not walk like a dancer at all. You would not think it the same person. She held her head high on her long neck and locked off her upper body into a rigid unit while her long legs perambulated independently beneath her.

"My name is Leah," Leah said. "And I am a married woman."

6

Bedevilled by vanity, troubled by falling hair, I had my skull shaved quite bald in 1926, a fashion I maintained for twenty-one years. And although I was much given to romancing about the sexual attractiveness of a man's bald head there had been no practical proof of the theory. Nor, with the advent of Leah Goldstein, is there going to be any change. So there is no use – as you watch me roll up a log to the camp fire for her, as my children squeeze on either side of her like bookends – no use at all in you skipping pages, racing ahead, hoping for a bit of hanky-panky. Leah was not only a married woman, but one with a firm sense of right and wrong and, having modestly discarded her feathers, she armoured herself against misunderstanding with a severe black dress, long woollen socks, and a blue-dyed greatcoat of the type dispensed to the unemployed.

The three of them sat in the firelight watching me prepare a meal, a dish known as Bungaree Trout which is made by slicing large potatoes, dipping them in batter, and frying them. If you eat it in daylight your eyes will tell you that you are eating fish, but if you eat it in the dark there is no fooling yourself: you're a poor man eating spuds.

We, the Badgery family, were in the habit of keeping ourselves to ourselves, and I cooked the potatoes in a mingy sort of spirit. If the dancer had once expressed a desire to leave I would not have argued with her. But she stayed and when it was teatime I had no choice but to feed her.

I piled the trout high on a tin plate and invited her to tuck in. The loud noises coming from her stomach had given me fair warning of her appetite.

"So tell me," Leah said, when she was half way through her third trout, "what sort of business are you in?"

"Mining," I said.

You see what has happened: how the lies that once smoked like dreams have diminished to such an extent that by 1931 they are ignoble snivelling things, excuses more than lies, the sort of lies my son told when he was caught stealing at State School Number 1204. They sent him home with notes about it. They strapped his hands; they caned his backside; they hit his warty knuckles with wooden rulers. This did no good at all. He rubbed peppercorns on his palms to stop the pain. He rubbed gum resin on his knuckles to ward off the sting. He put handkerchiefs in his pants to cushion the blows. In Castlemaine he stole an American dollar from the parson's son and claimed he had found it in the gutter. In the gutter! I understood his interest in money, but it was subsistence lying and it has no lasting value no matter how you look at it. And I, with this cock-and-bull story about mining, was no better. I lied to this strange woman (this trout-wolfer) because I was unemployed and could not bring myself to admit it. I did it to ward off the look I had seen in those Ford agents, whose sugary glaze of compassion did nothing to prevent – in fact intensified – my sense of failure.

Likewise, when I was forced to line up with the unemployed at Bungaree at spud-digging time, in Mildura when the grapes were on, at Kaniva and Shepparton for the soft-fruit season, I held myself aloof from my fellows. I, having shone my boots and ironed my shirt, was not one of them. When some stirrers up at Bungaree tried to organize a strike against the spud farmers who were paying only sixpence a bag, I was called a scab. There were plenty of us, don't worry, and it was us scabs who brought in the spuds for those celebrated spud cockies at Bungaree.

"What sort of mining?" my guest inquired politely, while my son, unseen by anyone, jiggled a little piece of wire inside the lock of her battered brown suitcase. (If you look at him now, pressing his body against the dancer while he undertakes his inquiry, you will be certain he will grow up to be a thief. He has all the qualities, the most important of which is sheer persistence.)

"Gold-mining," I said.

The dancer snorted. An extraordinary sound. The shape of her body, the elegance of her legs, the broomstick spine, the tidy contours of her flinty face, gave no indication that such an untidy explosion could emerge from her. Sonia was entranced. She liked odd things and I could see the noise attracted her. She came and sat beside me and squeezed my hand secretly. A joy to Sonia was nothing if it could not be communicated.

"It is gold", the dancer said sternly, reaching for a fourth Bungaree trout, frowning, and then deciding against it, "that is the curse of this country." She wiped her mouth with a little square of torn newspaper, a gesture that smacked of both fastidiousness and complacency. "It is what is wrong with it, has always been wrong with it, and once you look at what gold has done, you can go back and look at the attitude towards land ownership and find it is exactly the same."

I had no idea what she was talking about, but I was offended just the same. I took the last slice of trout, broke it in half and gave it to my children.

"It is gold", Leah said, "that has led ordinary working men and women into terrible delusion; it has made them think that they can be the exception to ordinary working men and women all through history; it has made them think that all they need is luck. They have been blinded by gold. They have imagined that all they need to do is drive their pick into the right spot in the ground and they will be another Hannan – they'll be bosses themselves. It has corrupted them. It has been the same with land. Men who spent their lives suffering from the ruling classes went out and stole land from its real owners. Hey, presto, I'm a boss. There has been no history here," she said. "The country has woken like a baby and had to discover everything for itself and only now are people learning what the ruling class has done to us, that we have been lied to and deceived about some Working Man's Paradise and we need more than luck to have freedom. So if you are still, in 1931, looking for gold to solve your problems, I must say you are barking up the wrong tree."

"I did not ask you to share my tucker," I said, "to hear you insult me in front of my children."

"It's not personal," she said. It may have been a trick of the light but I imagined I saw her eyes flood with tears. "Why do people always take it personally? I try to have an intelligent conversation, but there is no tradition of intellectual discussion here. When a subject is discussed the women simper and say they have no ideas and the men want to settle it with a fight. I am not attacking you personally, Mr Badgery." Her voice was half strangled. "I am attempting to analyse the history of this country and point out why the working classes have always acted as if they're going to be bosses tomorrow. I'm trying to point out why we're in this mess. But if you want to take it personally, that's your right. You can give me my marching orders now, and I'll go."

She took another square of newspaper from her pocket and blew her nose. It would have taken a hard heart to evict her. She rubbed the corner of her eye with the sleeve of her coat and stared into the fire.

"You must understand", she said after I had begged her to stay, "the difference between a criticism and an insult. Do you do well from your alluvial mining?"

Honesty, like temper, has a habit of coming on me without fair warning. Before I knew what I was doing I'd tossed her my specimen bottle and she'd caught it with a snap. A few gold specks glinted in the firelight.

She threw back her head and laughed and her laugh was as remarkable as her snort: a tangle like blackberries, sweet, prickly, untidy, uncivilized, and it is an indication of the difficulty I have with her, for her character will never stay still and be one thing, refuses to be held down on my dissecting board, pulls out a pinned-down leg and shakes it in the air.

Sonia loved the laugh. She nudged me conspiratorially, silently asking me to appreciate this marvel, this genie released from an austere and flint-grey vessel.

While the laugh raged around him, Charles's persistent wire at last hit the secret of his mother's lock and, from the battered three-strap suitcase, came the unfiltered odour of his flesh and blood.

The blue-bellied black snake that came first to his hand was only an average specimen, no more than three foot long and sleepy and stiff with the cold. Yet this is not to take credit away from my son who handled this, his first snake, with an instinctive sympathy.

Sonia gurgled, but whether from amazement or fear I could not tell.

"Shiva," the dancer said softly. "Don't let the others out."

"I shut it," Charles said, stroking a finger along the snake's spine.

"I had it locked."

Charles bestowed a magnificent smile upon his new friend and I cannot remember him smiling at all until that night. Perhaps it was the first time in his difficult life that he dared expect happiness, and when I recall him by the fire it is not, any longer, as a child, but as the big-jawed, heavy-necked, sloping-shouldered, wide-hipped, fifteen-stone business man whose rare smile could so charm those who saw it. It was a smile to treasure, a smile people would try to induce, the more wonderful for being so rare. I have felt a similar emotion when splitting open a dull piece of rock to discover a fist of opal hiding inside: that such splendour could exist captive in such ugly clay.

"There is a rule of the road," Leah told my son gently, "that you do not go messing with another fellow's swag."

"It's a suitcase," Sonia contradicted, leaping to her habitual defence of her brother.

The snake moved through my son's hand, ran along Leah's arm, and stopped. They both stroked it. The creature did not seem inclined to move any more.

"It is an unusual person," Leah said to me, "who will be at home with a venomous snake."

Let me tell you, I was no longer one of them. You can mistreat a horse and be forgiven it. You can kick a dog and it will come back and lick your hand. But a snake is another matter, and once you have wronged it, it will carry the memory of you with it, like a bolted convict with lash marks on its back, criss-crossed, burned in like a loaf of fancy bread. And there is no doubt that the greatest mistake I ever made in my life was to keep that Geelong snake a prisoner in a hessian bag, to starve it, to use it for tricks. Had I not been so foolish my whole life would have taken a different course: Jack would not have died, I would not have been permitted to marry Phoebe, and I would not have been troubled by the sight of my son besotted with a snake-dancer.

I was forty-five years old when I met Leah and a man, at forty-five, is meant to be mature. Certainly he should not be dependent on the good opinion and respect of total strangers who blunder into his camp.

"Most men", Leah said to me, "will run a mile from a snake," and I felt myself compared to my son and found lacking and I was led by my emotions rather than my common sense which told me to let my son have his moment of glory and not to worry that this blue-coated lecturer thought me a coward. My emotions, however, ruled. I could not stand it, this invasion of the one place on earth – my camp – where I might be confident of some respect.

Leah was engaged in conversation with Charles. I poked the fire irritably. "I was doing a show once in Wollongong", she was saying, "with one of Jack Leach's pythons, a dance show. I was a support act to Danny O'Hara's boxers and the snake got around my neck. It was choking me. I was going blue, and not one of those men would come near me. They wouldn't touch the snake."

"I would have," Charles said.

"I know you would have," Leah smiled. "That's what I'm saying."

"What happened?" Sonia asked and I imagined she moved a fraction away from me.

"I bit its tail," the dancer said, "and it let go enough for me to get it off."

"I've often considered show business," I said.

"Oh yes," said Leah, but she was more interested in Charles.

"Yes," I said. God damn it. I did not even want the woman to stay. I would rather she left. I did not like her tone. I did not even care for her looks and I certainly had no thoughts of anything as dangerous as a fuck. I am Herbert Badgery, I thought, a man who nearly had an aircraft factory, a pioneer aviator anyway, a salesman of more than usual skill, and here I am being patronized by a girl who is self-important because she can touch a snake. I, who have travelled the country with a cannon behind me, have built mansions, resumed land, skinned a crow with nothing but air from my lungs, and disappeared from human sight before witnesses.

"Yes," I said, "the entertaining arts have always attracted me."

"It's a hard life," Leah said, "and full of trickery and deception, people like Mervyn Sullivan who will steal your act and leave your picture up when you no longer work for them."

"Magic was my field," I said. For the admiration of a woman I did not know, I spent this little piece of gold which was not intended as currency at all. It was all I had in my empty pockets.

"Disappearing acts," I said, the master of self-delusion, imagining I could simply say it and not have to go through with a performance.

"Very common," she said, "but hardly enough to run a whole show on. You'd be surprised at the number of people I meet who think that they could make a living because they can throw a few balls into the air. One trick is not enough. One dance is not enough. I do the Emu Dance, the Fan Dance, the Snake Dance, the Dance of the Seven Veils. It is the snake that gets them in, but it is not enough by itself. Anyone who has read Cole's *Funny Picture Book* knows how to do a disappearing act. Nothing personal," she said quickly, seeing me rising from my log. "I am merely pointing out the difference between a professional and an amateur."

I stood before them. I can still see their eyes in the firelight, the Dodge, in the distance, half hidden by mist, the frying pan sitting amongst the cracked river rocks of the fireplace, the sheen on the snake's black back as it pressed itself against the warmth of a child's and a woman's body.

I made the dragon.

I put my foot on my knee. I held my arm in the air. I teetered on my toes. I summoned up the terrible flag of the English, the pipes and drums of the band, their blue shirts and white moleskins, the brains of Goon's father like the brains of the pig. The river banks flowed with the Chinese, a yellow river of fear over boulders as smooth and unyielding as dragons' eggs. The cart ran down Han and the bone splintered his leg: it thrust outwards like a dagger, drove through his smooth hairless thigh and he looked at it with astonishment: this enemy he had harboured innocently within him. My father galloped his team, his eyes bright, clear blue, dragging his cannon, cracking his whip.

I wanted to call out but I could not. The dragon came and it was bigger than the dragon I knew before, for a child does not know enough to make a powerful dragon. A child makes a childish dragon from children's fears, a cub with soft paws and breath that smells of warm milk.

Thirty-four years of locked-up terror came spurting at me and I knew I would drown in it. I tried to talk, but the dragon had me and dragged me away into the spaces between the mist of Crab Apple Creek while my audience, I must suppose, innocently applauded such a clever trick.

7

I am forced to tell you more about the history of this woman who finally trapped me into appearing beside her on a dusty stage in Bendigo, and if I begin by showing you her funny-looking family as they take their constitutional it is not so I can blame her parents for her character, but that I may point out the odd silence of the group as they walk. There are five of them, all with sloping shoulders and tall overcoats, but it is not the height I am concerned with, nor the graceful angle of descent from neck to arm, but the lack of chatter. It is my contention that the behaviour of these five people (and to a lesser degree, their appearance) is not the result of genes, but of a house, an odd redbrick place in Malvern Road, Malvern, a drumming, echoing construction which has finally triumphed over them, made them as sparing with their talk as Mallee farmers are with drinking-water: they are at their most comfortable (I must except the mother from the generalization) sitting in armchairs, wordless, bookless, their hands clasped in patient laps. Even released from the house (I except the mother, again) they will only talk for a purpose and never for amusement or diversion. I do not mean to suggest that they are lonely and unhappy because of it. Let me hypothesize the opposite: as they move along the battle-grey St Kilda seafront one can sense a rare harmony between them, although it may be a trick of the light, or a product of their uncanny physical similarities. But there are no tricks of light in the brightly illuminated lounge room in Malvern Road and when they sit with their hands in their laps after dinner – there is no wireless, naturally – one can look at them as, say, a field of poppies which, moving slightly on a windless day, give the distinct impression that some silent conversation is going on. And this impression is confirmed when one of them smiles, another chuckles, and a third stares hard at the ceiling as if trying to catch the gist of it. This, I must warn you, is merely an "impression", a fancy. There is no ESP taking place. The Goldsteins (*père et filles*) are merely engaging in their own quite separate thoughts in the way that has given them reputations for eccentricity in the world outside, and made poor Edith Goldstein have small fits of madness as rare as sunspots when – all this poppy-waving getting too damn much – she leaps to her feet, smashes plates, talks gibberish and (while the poppies stay ramrod stiff) sweeps up the broken pieces and sits down again with a sigh.

Edith Goldstein knew it was the house. The silence had not been natural to Sid who had arrived in Melbourne as a poor refugee from Tsarist Russia. He stepped off the ship with a swagger in his walk, a glide to his step not out of keeping with a man who will shortly make his first hundred pounds in a dancing

234

school in Exhibition Street. When he and Eddie Wysbraum shared both a room and a suit, he was not known to be a silent man. He had opinions which he voiced about manufacturing (he was for it) and religion (against).

Neither was the silence natural to Edith, a fine-boned redhead from Scotland who had made sandwiches in the railway rest rooms during the day and, having added dancing to her list of ambitions, had met Sid and fallen in love, not silently, but in a happy noisy godless confluence of Scots and Yiddish.

It was the house, I swear it, pushed them into its mould, made them meet its requirements. It stretched their necks by forcing them to peer over its high windowsills and Edith Goldstein who was five foot eight when she married Sid was five foot nine and a half by the time Leah got on the train with Sid and Wysbraum to go up to Sydney University.

It was a dark, dull, dank redbrick house that would amplify both success and failure. It made the pages of the Melbourne *Sun* sound like sheets of falling metal. It made the failure of Sid's Electrical Suction Sweeper a deafening event, and while this merely sent Sid back into retailing it produced a profound effect on Leah who came to develop many theories about the "Product" (as it was known) while she sat silently in her chair. Inside that echoing house Leah saw that the Product was a thing that had appetites of its own that must be served. Her father was kind, benevolent, but the Product was the real ruler. It was like a queen bee which must be carefully bred, served by workers huddling around it. The Product demanded a market, economies of scale, it cried for these and, should its needs not be met, it would weaken and die as would the workers who had sustained it.

She did not share her theories with her family and was thus astonished, later, to find that they had not reached the same conclusions; she was incensed that the failure of the Product had so little impression on her sisters; she thought them dull because of it.

Yet the crash of the Product only lasted for a month or two and Sid Goldstein had gone on to other successes. He was now rich, he could afford to move into a nicer house. Toorak was not beyond his reach. He could have paid cash for a house you could sing in, a house where you could tell stories and be extravagant with words, a house that did not insist you remove your noisy shoes at the door. Now Sid, as we will see in a moment, was a rational man, but he was not inclined to push his luck in the

235

matter of wealth; he stayed where he was and kept the suit he had shared with Eddie Wysbraum hanging in its cupboard in the hallway where there was plenty of light for its proper examination.

Sid Goldstein had no time for the god of the Jews, the very mention of which was enough to make his soft dark eyes suddenly harden in temper. Yet I fancy had he only known that the Ark of the Covenant was a powerful electric generator he might have adopted a different attitude entirely, for he was a great respecter of ingenuity. Be that as it may, the god of the Jews was a nonsense to him. A bigot, a pig, the sort of bully one might have found in the service of the Tsar. So although he had been born a Jew and had thought of himself as a Jew he brought up his daughters in total ignorance of what a Jew was. Leah learned she was a Jew at the Methodist Ladies' College. Her mother made some attempt to explain it all to her, but knowing little could not help much. As for her father, he said it was "superstition". He was a modern man, a rational, sensible liberal, but when he visited the suit he had shared with Wysbraum, when he stroked the poor shiny material, when he felt with his long fingers for the tear his friend had made on the second day – a misunderstanding about the workings of cable trams – or when he sought out the place where he had tucked and tacked up the trouser legs for his short-limbed friend, he was not, as he smoothed and touched, a modern man at all.

That Sid, the son of a Minsk tailor, owned fifteen stores, all of which featured high mirror-encased pillars, was one of the miracles of this suit.

But the other miracle was considered (silently, separately) a greater one. And this, of course, was what it had done for Poor Wysbraum.

He had always, Leah remembered, been known as "Poor Wysbraum". "Poor Wysbraum," her mother might say after he had departed, or just before he arrived and the family sat anticipating the amplified sounds of their visitor's high cracked voice. She did not elaborate on what she meant by "Poor". The house did not permit elaboration, and besides anyone could see that Wysbraum was Poor Wysbraum because he was short and dark and ugly, with huge bruised beetroot-red lips far too heavy for his little doe-eyed face, his ears stolen from a bigger man's head, his huge veined hands emerging from his frayed cuffs. He was Poor Wysbraum because he had, it was silently considered, used the suit to take the braver course, the better, more noble course, and had suffered for his goodness.

For Wysbraum had taken fifteen years of his life to become, at last, a doctor. He had given up everything, all hope of companionship, marriage, children, a house, just so he could be a doctor, and, when the time came, at last, on his fortieth birthday, he could afford no more than a new practice in Brunswick where the people were even poorer than he was and could not pay their bills.

When Leah was older she came to resent this description of him as "Poor Wysbraum", found something offensive in it, but when she was a young girl at home she understood the term better, and heard the soft strum of approval, envy even, in the word as well as pity for his loneliness. Later, when she came to analyse things, she did not understand so well and she forgot that it was not just she but all her family who loved Poor Wysbraum who was like food too rich for their ascetic taste, or a scene that was too colourful for eyes attuned to the bleached colours of St Kilda in summer. Wysbraum brimmed with an excess of emotions, angers, fears. He boiled over with stories, his big mouth full of food, while the Goldsteins, quite replete and accepting their headaches without complaint, sat with their hands on their laps and only Sid, their representative, would say: "And then Wysbraum, what happened then?"

You did not need to accompany them on their visit to the suit in the cupboard to know what sort of bond there was between these two men. You could listen to each of them, at table, extol the virtues of the other, and it was Wysbraum, because he spoke more, because he was not restrained by the house, who shouted his praise the loudest.

"An honest man", Wysbraum said, "will always do well. And it is this", he told Sid, "that is behind your success."

"Ah, but it is self-interest."

"Self-interest, yes, of course," Wysbraum would say, eating five pieces of fried fish or ten pieces of bread, not at once, of course, but the Goldstein girls were all counting. "And also self-interest to have your staff paid more than the union demands, and to know their names, but also honest. I drink to your success. It gives me pleasure, Goldstein. If you had been a bad man and done well, then I would be jealous." Lettuce hung from his mouth. "More. I would be angry. But you have behaved honourably."

237

"A kind man", Poor Wysbraum said, "has more importance in the eye of God than a man with a holy book."

"It is only his way of explaining," Sid said. "Isn't that true, Wysbraum? When you mention God it is your way of explaining your idea. He is not religious," he told his daughters. "Which God?" he demanded of his friend.

"Who knows?" said Wysbraum. "Not me. But He would not be much of a God if He did not say the kind man was the better man." Beetroot from the salad widened his lips and smudged his mouth amiably across his face.

"This is not Jaweh."

"Sit still, Goldstein, be calm."

"Because the fellow is a bully."

"Is a bully, was a bully," said Wysbraum. "I agree. I like you better than Him because you are kinder. Ah," he said, considering the table full of uncertain faces, "never tell jokes at the Goldsteins. The Goldsteins are kind, but they are no good with jokes."

When Wysbraum spoke in favour of kindness no one could doubt his sincerity. So who could have predicted his reaction when Sid Goldstein took it into his head to give away the suit he had shared with Wysbraum?

It was not, as Wysbraum assumed, a premeditated act. One minute Sid was walking on stockinged feet to answer the door and three minutes later he was waving to a stranger who, having come to the door selling shoelaces, was now walking away with the celebrated suit.

Sid Goldstein was not sorry to see the suit go. He did not grieve for it. He meant what he said when he spoke to the young man, whose pale blue eyes slid off the dark ones of the donor, embarrassed at the weight of emotion they contained.

"Here," the tall Jew said, "this is a lucky suit. It was lucky for me. I shared it with my friend and we both got what we wanted. May you", he held out the offering, "have what you want also."

He did not tell the young man that he had slipped a ten-shilling note into the pocket of the suit. He did not tell his family that the suit had gone. Neither did he communicate this to Wysbraum until he was, once again, seated at family lunch, devouring roast potatoes which were cooked in excessive numbers in deference to his appetite.

He waited for Wysbraum to begin his final appreciative scrape of the plate, watched the bread being torn, the plate wiped clean, and the gravy-smeared bread despatched into his friend's gaping mouth.

"Wysbraum," he said, when his friend had folded his napkin and threaded it untidily through the silver napkin ring. "Wysbraum. . . ."

Wysbraum smiled at his friend and patted his stomach.

"Wysbraum," Sid Goldstein said with much emotion, "the suit is gone."

Wysbraum blinked. He pulled the napkin out of its ring and opened it slowly, peering at it as if it contained a tiny pearl he was anxious not to drop. "Gone?" he said, and blinked again.

"I gave it," Sid said.

"Gave it?" Wysbraum said incredulously, holding up the napkin to show there was no pearl. "You gave it. To whom did you give it?"

"To whom. A stranger," he smiled. "A nobody. A young man with no money and no suit. I said to him, this is a lucky suit. It was lucky for Wysbraum and I, and now it can be lucky for you."

Wysbraum did not move, but his big hands held each end of the napkin like a paper bon-bon he might tear apart with a bang.

"You had no right," he said quietly, placing the napkin gently on the table.

"Ha ha," said Sid. "Dear Wysbraum."

"Not joking," Wysbraum said softly. "You had no right." His tiny dark-suited body bent over the large white plate and he placed two tight fists on either side of the plate, in the places where the knife and fork should rightly sit.

"I told him our story," Sid said softly. "Maybe, who knows, he will be lucky too, and then," he spread his pale hands, "when he passes on the suit he will pass on *his* story as well."

But Poor Wysbraum, the Goldstein girls saw, was not interested in this fancy. They watched in silence as he squinted his eyes as if to keep out an unpleasant light. Wysbraum's hands uncurled and fluttered anxiously. They took the bread-and-butter plate and stacked it on the dinner plate. They snatched the dessert spoon and placed it on top. Poor Wysbraum shook his head. He rose. He carried his plates and cutlery out into the kitchen. The Goldsteins regarded each other in silent misery, like animals who are unable to express pain. They could hear him clattering out there, but no one moved. The house took the noise of his washing up and blew it up to fifty times its size. The Goldsteins listened to the noise and their frowns deepened and their pale hands began to press hard down into their laps.

Poor Wysbraum emerged at last, holding a tea-towel in his wet hairy hands.

"You," he said to his friend with a great shaking voice. "You have all of *this*." His great lips trembled to hold the weight of his smile as he indicated (waving his tea-towel like a flag) the house, the wife, the three girls. "Past, present, future." The lips quivered but he did not drop the smile. "You have a history. You deserve it, my friend. Well done."

There was a silence while they waited, all of them, for the house to stop thundering.

Wysbraum did not see the girls. He did not see Edith. He saw only Sid Goldstein. It was in his direction he, at last, threw the tea-towel.

"You have given away my history," Poor Wysbraum shouted before he fled the house trampling on the eardrums of his hosts with his shocking oversize black boots.

The Goldstein women considered the desolate eyes of Goldstein *père* with emotions that Leah at least, when she was older, was to recognize as grief of the order one feels in the face of death.

8

That Sid Goldstein then remade the missing suit himself by hand, that he rubbed miserably at the fabric with pumice-stone, rubbed for hours on end to make it shine, that he laid the nap with lard and onion dissolved in gasoline, that he lovingly counterfeited the tear Wysbraum had made falling off the cable car twenty years before, that he shortened and lengthened the trousers almost as many times as he had in the days when he shared the original, that he occupied himself night after night was all known to his family who quietly observed his thin frame bending over the fabric, saw every silent stitch without feeling it necessary to make any comment on the melancholy hobby.

The girls were all at the Methodist Ladies' College that year, and they sat at the dining table with their homework. They knew, surely, that their schoolmates' fathers did not counterfeit suits. Would Leah have invited home her schoolfriends to witness this? She claims the question is a nonsense: she had no friends.

Once, on a sultry Sunday night, with a dusty northerly rattling the windows in their frames, Sid Goldstein quietly asked his wife's opinion of the smell of the suit, but she did not move from her chair. She smiled and shrugged which clearly meant that her opinion was worth nothing, that she had not shared the cheap meals Wysbraum had spilled on the suit, nor had she sniffed at it in its old age as it hung in the hallway cupboard.

Sid, seeing the smile and shrug, sighed and picked up the pumice-stone again.

Another family might, later if not sooner, have chosen to take away the pain from all of this by wrapping it in the bandages of a joke, and, by repeating the correct rituals, have changed it into something smooth and untroubled.

But they made no jokes. Nor did they ever remark that it was at this time that sixteen-year-old Leah announced her intention to be a doctor. There seems no doubt that this serious young lady's decision had something to do with kindness but it is not an easy matter to decide exactly what or how.

Leah assumed her father understood her, that she was paying Wysbraum a great compliment, that she had chosen the course of her life in order that he might have, in future, a history. And when, on the night her father asked her to accompany him (for the first time ever) when he delivered the suit to Wysbraum's surgery, she saw this as proof that he understood.

Yet it seems likely that Sid took her along for moral support, to stop Wysbraum shouting at him and saying ugly words which sometimes, in spite of his awkward good manners, slipped out of his mouth and lay, as scandalous as bird shit, on Goldstein's clean white tablecloth.

It is also possible that, without understanding her kind motives, he wished to discourage her and that he took her to Wysbraum's surgery to show her that being a doctor is not necessarily all roses, and that not all doctors have flowers in their waiting rooms, or even magazines, or even, in Wysbraum's case, chairs.

Wysbraum's practice was in Smith Street, Brunswick, and I am not making a mistake and saying Brunswick instead of Collingwood. Smith Street, Collingwood, is a big wide street. It goes somewhere; it comes from somewhere; it has definition, purpose. But Smith Street in Brunswick is nothing but a smudge, a cul-de-sac, and it was here that Wysbraum's surgery was, in a space he seemed to have (with a foreigner's impatience) elbowed between two terrace houses. It was eight feet wide, one storey high, two rooms deep and smelt of damp. The brass plaque had already been stolen and the small red lantern that he had paid three pounds for had been broken by children with shanghais. It was not an inspiring place.

Sid Goldstein and Leah Goldstein waited in the surgery with the suit. They waited beside the woman with goitre and the man with the slipped disc who interrupted the story of his injury with visits to the doorway, from which vantage he propelled small globs of spittle into the rank summer night.

Leah and her father examined each other's dark eyes.

When Wysbraum at last received them, he was embarrassed. He looked as if he wished to climb into one of the cardboard boxes that littered his office floor. He offered Leah his own chair. He accepted the suit without seeming to notice what it was. He hung it behind the door. He gave Sid the patient's seat. His face wobbled. His lips were like red jelly in a field of iron filings. He straightened a leaking pen in a sea of raging papers. He looked at Sid Goldstein and then away. Someone walked into the waiting room and began to walk up and down sighing (or perhaps it was an asthmatic wheeze).

"Wysbraum," Sid Goldstein said, "we have brought the suit."

"Suit?" Wysbraum was a mess of misery, half rage and half apology. "Suit?"

"Not exactly the suit." Sid stood. He held his hands up. He spread them out. "A copy," he smiled, willing Wysbraum's far larger mouth to do what his smaller one could do with so much less effort.

"Ho," Wysbraum said, slapping his hands together like a hearty man (Wysbraum's idea of a hearty man) while all the time his eyes brimmed with old hurt and new embarrassment. "Ho," he said again. "The suit."

He clumped to the door and lifted down the suit. It was hung on its original coat-hanger, the same one, exactly, with its chipped coat of green paint and its small bag of lavender.

He examined it slowly, carefully, looking over it in every detail.

He was so overcome he could not look at Sid, or even talk to him. He spoke instead to Leah.

"A copy," he said in a choked voice. "A perfect copy."

"She is going to be a doctor," Sid said behind him, smiling at Leah, nodding encouragement.

"Are you?" Wysbraum said, his eyes brimming. "Is this true?"

"Yes," said Leah, pleased but also alarmed.

"Oh Leah," Wysbraum said and embraced her. She felt his tears in her hair and smelt his lard and onions. Her nose was pressed into his stale shirt. It was a long long time before Leah even guessed that

242

the body Wysbraum had held had not been hers, and that his tears had nothing to do with either her ambitions or her kindness.

It was because of this misunderstanding that she wrote, in that letter to her father that caused her so much difficulty, "Please apologize to Poor Wysbraum – I know I have let him down and although I feel I have disappointed you I feel that I have betrayed him."

Sid Goldstein did not know what his daughter was talking about.

9

If Melbourne University would not accept his daughter, then that was bad luck for Melbourne. Sid Goldstein put on his twelve-ounce grey-wool suit and gold-rimmed spectacles and enlisted Poor Wysbraum. The pair of them went on the train to Sydney and made a nuisance of themselves from Rose Bay to Macquarie Street.

They had no shame. There was no one they would not enlist in their cause, no old friend, no new acquaintance, no total stranger who might appear to have some influence in the matter. Poor Wysbraum did not hesitate, at dinner at the Finks', to produce Leah's report cards. They were circulated around the table while their object sat squirming in her uncomfortable chair trying to eat soup with a spoon too big for her mouth while reeling from the waste of all the words that gushed, without modesty or restraint, from the ten mouths gathered, surely, for eating and not talking.

Sid Goldstein and Poor Wysbraum pushed and shoved and elbowed on her behalf until, in the end, they made a gap in Sydney University just big enough to accommodate her.

The acceptance came on a steamy overcast February day exactly three hours before Sid Goldstein must return to Melbourne. Sid did not like to rush, and was already flustered at the thought of what he must do in three hours. Walking across the quadrangle he started pushing wads of banknotes at Leah and giving her instructions on her future conduct. Wysbraum was twenty yards ahead, showing no respect for the neatly trimmed grass, clomping on echoing boots down the flagstoned quadrangle, his trousers too short, his white handkerchief sticking out of his pocket, sweat streaming from his pale forehead. Sid, following after, punctuated his normal amble with an impatient skip.

243

They followed Wysbraum out of the university and across Parramatta Road. They followed him up steps cut into a steep rockface, then on to another street lined with old terrace houses.

"Wysbraum," Sid shouted, "Wysbraum, what are we doing?"

"Digs," said Wysbraum, opening the gate at the bottom of a steep flight of stone steps.

"Digs?" shouted Sid Goldstein. "Wysbraum, we must pack. We must catch our train."

"Yes, yes," said Wysbraum. "Wait, wait," and ran up the steps to the house which displayed a "Room to Let" sign in its front window.

Leah waited with her father amidst the smell of leaking gas and dying nasturtiums while Wysbraum conducted his mysterious business at the top of the crumbling concrete steps.

He was back in five minutes.

"It is taken," he said.

"What is taken, Wysbraum?"

"The room for your daughter, to sleep in, to live."

"Oh no," said Sid Goldstein, loosening his tie. "Oh no, I forgot."

"Don't worry." Wysbraum's ugly face dripped with sweat. "I have discovered she has a front parlour, upstairs. She is a widow. Her husband was Commissioner of Police in Cairo. A big man. She has a nasty case of psoriasis. I have written her a prescription. Her name is Heller", Wysbraum said breathlessly, "and she has three boarders. I have persuaded her she can have four if she permits us to purchase a bed. She wishes only to be sure", Wysbraum giggled, "that we are not Catholics. I have assured her. She asks two pounds for full board. What do you say?"

Sid Goldstein looked at his daughter in alarm.

Leah smiled.

"All right," said Wysbraum, "you will go with Leah and inspect the house. I will buy the bed."

"Maybe", Sid said, "there is a better place."

"Better, no," Wysbraum said. "There is no better place, and besides the train leaves in three hours."

Sid looked at the house. He wondered if this was how Wysbraum had chosen his surgery. He did not approve of buying the first thing. He looked at the rusted guttering, the thistles amongst the nasturtiums, the desolation of Parramatta Road with its lorries, carts, horses.

"I will buy the bed," said Wysbraum trotting sweatily down the steps.

"How much is the bed?" asked Sid helplessly.

"Cheap," Wysbraum said. "I will buy her a double bed and she can sleep in it forever."

Sid frowned. Leah blushed. "Poor Wysbraum," her father said, but more from habit than conviction. They walked upstairs to meet Mrs Heller and assure her they were not Catholic.

10

It was cold at Crab Apple Creek and Leah Goldstein tugged at her long black woollen socks, pulled so hard that the perfect round white hole that had occupied a spot at the very centre of her left shin now suddenly became long and thin, almost invisible, as it darted up towards her lovely knee. She wrapped her blue-dyed greatcoat tight around herself. She found a half-burnt stick on the ground and threw it back into the flames of the fire. She shivered.

"Well," she said.

Charles moved closer to her and she felt his warty hand come creeping towards her, like a lost crab wandering in the dark. The hand was so hungry and cold she held it in both of hers. Its back was hard and rough, its underbelly soft.

"Where's your father hiding?" She rubbed the rough-textured skin, trying to warm it. "If he thinks he's entertaining us, he's upter."

She looked across at the little girl who sat exactly where she had been before the con-man had done his trick. All Leah could see of her emotions was the camp fire reflected in her eyes.

"Timing, Mr Badgery," the dancer said sarcastically to the night. But she spoilt the effect by the way she jerked her head to look, bird-fast and nervous, over her shoulder.

"He disappeared," Sonia said and Leah did not know her well enough to realize that the tone was not quite normal.

"An illywhacker," Leah Goldstein said loudly like someone fearful of burglars who descends the stairs, flashlight in hand, in the middle of the night.

"What's an illywhacker?" said Charles.

"Spieler," explained Leah, who was not used to children. "Eelerspee. It's like pig Latin. Spieler is ieler-spe and then iely-whacker. Illywhacker. See?"

"I think so," Charles said.

"A spieler," Leah gently loosened the painful crab hold of the boy's hand. "Your nails are sharp. A trickster. A quandong. A ripperty man. A con-man."

Sonia pulled her cardigan down over her knees and stared into the fire where solid matter was reappearing in thin blue cloaks of turbulent gas.

"When will he come back?" asked the dancer.

In later life Charles would recall only the brilliance of his father's magic, but now, hearing the nervousness in the adult's voice, he was suddenly very frightened. He began to cry. Sonia immediately moved to comfort her brother.

So they sat, the three of them, side by side on one log, huddled against each other, waiting for Herbert Badgery to reappear. And you, dear reader, will do me the kind favour of emulating my patient daughter and neither make sarcastic comments like the ill-informed Goldstein (who thinks me engaged in some simple trick) nor snivel like my fearful son who is so easily convinced that I am gone for good. Thus you will not waste time staring out into the night but will, alone with Sonia, appreciate the thin green tower of flame which rises from the wattle log to meet – like a comet on a chance collision – the blue penumbra of the yellow flower made by the dancer's broken stick.

11

When Edith Goldstein questioned her husband about their eldest daughter's accommodation in Sydney he realized he did not even know the name of the street it stood in. It was this, not weariness, that gave him flu symptoms. It was panic that his carelessness would be uncovered. His normally sallow face coloured and he opened the taxi window to get air. Edith watched her husband with alarm as he began to talk. She held his hand and, without making any comment about what she was doing, felt his pulse.

The room, Sid told her breathlessly, had a good bed. It was a double bed. He considered this quite appropriate. She could keep this bed forever. It was good enough to marry with, of first quality, made in America. The room had an excellent view ("You see the university, right out the window"). He could also describe (he could not stop himself) the tapestries on the wall and he saw (now he thought about it) that these depicted not only camels, men in red fezzes, pyramids and dancing girls but also, in the bottom right-hand corner, a small shrub that looked very like an Australian Bottlebrush. The landlady was a widow. Her husband had been a Commissioner of Police in Cairo. This is where the tapestries in their daughter's bedroom had come from.

"Stop, stop," cried Edith Goldstein. "I will write to her. She will tell me. Poke out your tongue."

But to write she would need the address. She did not have an address. He could not put out his tongue. "*I* will write," he said, so firmly that his wife – although surprised – did not question him.

"I will write," he repeated, saying nothing about the concrete steps, the odd smells, the nasturtiums, although these were things that troubled him deeply. "I have written", he declared, "already. On the train. The porter is posting it for me."

Thus was invented that rickety thing, the Missing Letter. Edith was too worried about her husband's health to query him as to why he would give a letter to a porter, and so the Missing Letter was allowed to survive. It is mentioned often in the early correspondence between father and daughter, e.g. "Have you yet received the Missing Letter?"

Had it not been for this imaginary letter there might have been no correspondence between father and daughter at all. "I must first tell you", Sid would write in his second letter to his daughter, "what was in the letter that the porter did not post." The letters, at first, are shy and stilted on both sides, and Leah's are ponderous and dull. There is no indication of the dialogue that would later develop. This was not due, on Leah's side at least, to a lack of amusing incidents or new sights to describe but rather to the fact that she was just learning to talk.

Leah, at this time, was unaware of the virtues of discussion and had long been in the habit of making her mind up on important matters without any help from anyone. She would come to a conclusion slowly, tortuously, and she would go over and over it (her hands clasped in her lap, staring at the ceiling) until it was smooth and flawless. In this manner she arrived at ideas that were often original, but not easily accepted by others.

She did not, however, consider herself clever. If she was to succeed at the university she would have to work five times as hard as anyone else. She brushed aside any suggestion of joining debating societies or amateur theatricals and when there were pig worms to be dissected she managed to slip an extra one into her handbag so that she could bring the little pink parasite home to her room and there perform the dissection a second time. The pig worm, being only five inches long, was easily smuggled into the house and escaped Mrs Heller's attention. However, when she carried home a dogfish, the odours of formaldehyde and fish gave her away, and Mrs Heller, her red scaly skin hidden beneath Wysbraum's black tar treatment, came to complain about the smell.

Leah politely declined to place the "thing" in the large brown paper bag her landlady held out into the room. Whereupon Mrs Heller – as white-eyed and black-faced as Al Jolson – announced she would send up Mr Kaletsky.

Leah knew nothing of this Mr Kaletsky. She had promised her mother, in answer to a specific question, that there were no men in the house. She had not noticed the small room, tucked away beside the laundry in the concreted backyard, where Izzie Kaletsky slept. He did not pay full board and so did not come to table.

Leah, waiting for the mysterious Mr Kaletsky, sat in front of her dissection board where the dogfish's nervous system was being untidily exposed. She took out her notebook and began to sketch the pale ganglia, using her eraser too much so that pieces of indiarubber and paper found their way into the dissection.

This is how Izzie found her when she bade him "enter", a very prim and serious young lady, dressed in black, sketching a dead fish. To Izzie, this was an appealing sight. He did not, however, as Leah mischievously claimed on other occasions, introduce himself by saying: "My name is Kaletsky and my brother is a revolutionary in Moscow."

Leah had expected an old man with a belly. This did not look like a "Mr" anyone. He was tiny. He had dark ringlets of hair, small hands, and a wide mouth that hovered in the tantalizing androgynous no man's land between pretty and handsome. His good looks were spoiled only by his skin, and yet even that was interesting, being coarsely textured, a little like a lemon.

Izzie's pointed feet would not stay still. He grinned, mocking either her or himself – it wasn't clear. He had thin wrists like a girl.

"Miss Goldstein."

She was not above a little theatre – she leaned back and sharpened her pencil, squinting all the time at her smudgy drawing. Her cheeks were burning, but who was to know that this was not her normal colour?

"I am Kaletsky."

"Come in," she said. "Complain."

He moved into the room a little but left the door, as was proper, wide open. Leah could hear the voices of the student teachers in the stairwell.

"You are famous," he said. "First they talk about nothing else but how little you talk. Then it is all about how much you work. Now you have given them a smell. They love you."

Leah heard a clatter on the stairs, fast whispers, and then heavy brogues marching across the linoleum in the front hall.

Izzie grinned. "See what excitements you produce. They never talked to each other before you came. Mrs Heller only wanted to remember her husband the Police Commissioner and tell everyone how nice it is to have servants – 'When I had servants my skin was beautiful.' And the students were dull and made toast because they had nothing to say."

He talked on and on. Leah had never heard, she thought, somebody use so many words in all her life, not even Wysbraum, nor seen anyone who made such a confusing, contradictory impression of confidence and shyness. For while his words were so confident (so interesting, so light, with a rhythm like soft erratic rain) his body looked as if it feared rejection – the small feet moved to and fro, the hands clasped each other and the dark eyes could not hold hers for more than an instant. The effect was puzzling but, on the whole, pleasing.

He came to look over her shoulder at the dogfish.

"We are having a meeting about Germany" he said, "tonight. Would you like to come?"

Leah imagined castles on the Rhine.

12

Rosa Kaletsky opened her eyes and surveyed her backyard. It was an untidy place, graceless, with concrete paths. A rusting caravan occupied the centre of the lawn. A clothes-line ran across one corner, above some roses which the sheets now tangled with. Forty-four-gallon drums containing scrap metal stood on either side of the high gate in the paling fence, and Leah Goldstein, when she entered this world fifteen minutes later, would be shocked at its untidiness, the weeds amongst the cabbage bed, the rusting tricycle tangled amongst the passion-fruit. But Rosa, sitting on the cracked concrete step, smelt the salt from Bondi Beach, the lovely perfume of her drying sheets, and when she opened her eyes she saw green oranges and the splendid glow of copper appearing in the verdigrised cauldron her husband was now polishing with Brasso.

Izzie was bringing a girl to meet them and Rosa was at once curious, impatient and also irritable that she would have to surface from her pleasant reverie in the sun. She was a well-preserved woman in her early fifties, large-boned and well proportioned. And although her frock was an old one and her hair was tangled and needed a brush, she could still be said to be a beauty.

"I'm going to give Bo a bath," she said, but did not move. She was looking at the sky between the leaves of the orange tree and imagined she could see the light of the shining copper bathing the green fruit.

"I should get changed," she said a moment later. "And so should you," she told her husband. "Those shorts." But she smiled. "If you must wear shorts you should get your legs brown."

Lenny Kaletsky didn't answer her. He was immersed in the great copper cauldron which stood on a heavy cast-iron base. What sort of scrap-metal dealer, she thought, brings home a bit of junk to polish because it is beautiful? "Mark must have laughed at you," she said.

Lenny looked up and grinned. He had a mass of grey hair and owl-like eyebrows the colour of nicotine. His face was crumpled, like a paper bag. He was broad-shouldered and chested, but his legs were thin, like a cocky little sparrow, Rosa thought. He was shorter than Rosa by a good two inches and looked older. In their early days together, when they were both show people, travelling the tent shows in the country towns, when she had been Rosalind and he Leonard, he had never shown this interest in beautiful things. She had had to teach him how to dress.

Rosa yawned. "I must get changed." Then (was it so late?) she heard the squeak of the front gate. She suddenly felt irritated and not interested in having to talk to anyone and so watched the girl – the first girl this son had brought home – silently, a little critically. She admired the austerity of her beauty, the simple grey silk dress which, she thought, would scandalize her son if he knew how much such simplicity cost. She offered her cheek to Izzie and told him he was too pale. Did he bring this girl home, she wondered, because she was a Jew? They gathered around the cauldron while Bo jumped up on Izzie and then sniffed the girl's shoes.

Izzie was teasing his father.

"Melt it?" said Lenny, smiling at the girl. "Melt a thing like this? An heirloom?" He said nothing of the other thirty cauldrons they would have already melted. Before the day was over he would be showing off, eating fire or bending an iron bar.

"It is disgusting," Rosa said. She was doubly irritable because she did not want to be. "If you say it is beautiful you're not thinking. You would not say it is beautiful if you had to work over it every day."

The girl's grey eyes looked at her with alarm, and then away.

"Ah," Izzie nudged his father, "the Marxist critique."

"A Marxist, perhaps," said Rosa, standing, trying to smile. "A communist, no. Don't you make fun of me." She ruffled her son's head. "You wishy-washy. Look at your clothes. Do you think they make you more appealing? Come and sit with me, Leah. In the sunshine. Leah dresses nicely," she told the men who were standing, as usual, in the shade. "Sit here, the concrete is clean. Have you noticed", she asked the girl, "that the left are always drab? When I was in the Party they thought I was frivolous. They did not trust me because of my dresses."

"Don't listen to her, Leah," Lenny called. "This is her hobby-horse."

"They dressed like they had no hope. It is capitalism, I told them, that is bleak, not socialism. When there is a revolution the people should wear wonderful clothes, streamers, flags, balloons. It should be full of joy and love, not look like a funeral. Do you like picnics?"

Leah Goldstein smiled. "Yes, I do, very much."

"Would you like to come for a picnic with me, one day when you are free?"

"Yes."

"Good," said Rosa smiling, "now I am cheered up," and she laughed. "I apologize for my mood."

The two women sat on the concrete step smiling at each other.

251

13

Leah Goldstein would leave the Kaletskys that night with a splitting headache. She had laughed too much, heard too much, eaten too much peculiar food. There had been discord, vulgarity, and such shifts in mood, from sombre to carefree and back again, that she became lost and dizzy. She had drunk a glass of sweet wine on the grass beneath the orange tree, patted the dog, and heard Rosa's life story, how her young mother had run away from her father and walked all the miles from Poland to Vienna, how they had arrived to find her mother's uncle all packed to go to Australia and how they had gone too. Her uncle, a cultured man, had disliked Australia and within a year he was packing all his books again and dragging his family across the seas, this time to Palestine. Rosa's mother had wanted to go, but the uncle would not pay – she had taken a goyim for a lover and was out of favour. Later the goyim left but she had found another, a man who ate fire for a living. The story went on and on, while the men, sitting in the shade with a bottle of beer, called out their teasing comments.

Rosa had left the Communist Party when they turned on Trotsky and talking about this she began, quite inexplicably, to cry and Leah, bewildered, quite out of her depth, could do nothing to comfort her but pat – she felt so inadequate – the back of her hostess's honey-coloured hand while the dog leapt up and licked her face.

Then Lenny announced he would bend a bar of steel between his teeth and Rosa stopped crying and began teasing him, saying he was an old man trying to impress a young girl and Leah blushed and became uncomfortable. She looked at Izzie who was sitting on the laundry steps, and he smiled at her, and raised his eyebrow in the direction of his cock-sparrow father who was, at that moment, fossicking in one of the rusty forty-four-gallon drums, looking for a piece of suitable iron.

"Too thin," said Izzie when his father held up a piece of bolt-studded metal. "Thicker, thicker."

Lenny frowned, hesitated, and went back to the bin. Finally he found a piece of steel rod that Izzie applauded. The dog raced round and round the yard barking and Rosa was again tranquil as she lifted her handsome face to the sun.

"Do you like to dance?" she asked Leah, but Lenny was now standing before them. He insisted Leah pick up the bar, even though it was oily.

He placed the bar between his stained teeth, shut his eyes, positioned his pale legs like a weight-lifter and began to pull down on it with both hands.

The bar began to bend, but then Lenny pulled a face. He took the bar out of his mouth and spat into his hand. He looked at what was in his hand and looked up and grinned. He had broken two teeth.

"You silly man," said Rosa Kaletsky. "Oh, you silly man." But she did not seem upset about her husband's teeth and indeed neither did Lenny, who having rinsed his mouth out with beer, went back to sit by his son.

Rosa began to quiz her about her family and pretended to be shocked that they observed none of the Jewish customs, not even Passover. She had never heard of matzo, never tasted the bitter herb, never waited, impatiently, for the moment when she could eat the charoset.

"Ha," Rosa called out to her son. "So you were bringing home a nice Jewish girl to meet your mother."

Izzie looked uncomfortable but smiled.

"A Presbyterian, a shiksah. Oh dear," she laughed and Leah's face hurt from trying to smile against the current of her embarrassment.

"Shut up, Rosa," Izzie said, suddenly serious.

"Don't you 'shut up' to me, mister," Rosa snapped, fiercely. "You wash out your mouth."

There was silence amongst the combative, confusing Kaletskys for a moment and then Lenny began to explain to Leah that he was not a real Jew either, that his mother had been a shiksah, a dancer in Ballarat who stole Lola Montez's Spider Dance.

"Her name was MacDonald. You never met a woman so kosher. We had two sets of everything, two sinks, two sets of bowls for cooking. By the time she was sixty she looked like a Jew," he giggled. "Her nose grew. She was very pious. When my father died we had to sit on the floor for *months*. Poor dear Sheila, oh dear."

"A nasty old woman," said Rosa.

"Not very nice," Lenny admitted, feeling inside his mouth with his finger. "I broke a gold one too."

"Whereze cats?" Rosa said suddenly. "Where are they?" The dog jumped out of her lap, its ears cocked, and began to race around the yard. "We will give him a b–a–t–h," she announced. "Come, Leah."

"It is too late for a bath. It is too cold," Lenny said, standing and carrying two empty beer bottles to the rubbish bin.

But they washed the dog anyway and when it was done all ran around, giggling, trying to keep clear of the showers of water the shaking dog sent in all directions. The dog scratched a bare spot in the lawn and rolled itself in the dirt and Leah watched it sadly, thinking herself a dog who has lost its doggy smell. She envied the Kaletskys their jokes and their tempers, their matzos, their gold mouths, their bookish uncles, their shiksah dancers. In comparison her own life felt white and odourless. She felt herself dull, a person without a history, or even a character. She wished she could roll in the dirt like the dog, roll and roll, and rub her chin along the sandy soil and get her doggy smell back.

When, walking to the tram, Izzie held her hand, she did not, as she had imagined in the morning – anticipating this very event – take it back, but found herself, instead, holding it tightly. They both misunderstood her emotions, and the misunderstanding would continue, would grow greater rather than diminish as that year of 1930 continued and finally reached its zenith in 1931 when she would marry Izzie Kaletsky when it was really Rosa that she loved.

14

The letters were an agony to her. Sometimes she would sit an hour between sentences. She could not say that she had danced the foxtrot with a young man who did not reach her shoulder, nor that the young man was a socialist, nor that she had, on one sweet balmy evening, walked past crumbling houses whose tiny gardens were heavy with frangipani, to hear this young man speak in an awful hall which echoed with the heavy boots of working men. Her father had no time for socialists, but how could he have not been moved to see Izzie do battle with his shyness? When he had opened his mouth she had heard, quite clearly, the sound of a throat so dry with fear that its membranes might adhere and strangle him. He wrung his dainty hands and shut his eyes. The audience went, suddenly, very quiet. She did not know that this was the way it was, would always be with Izzie, that he would, in these moments of mute terror, move huge gatherings of people to wish him well, to will him success, to sit with their own throats dry, their own hands clenched, wishing him eloquence. And then his foot, like a band leader, hit three times, haltingly, and then (as if he felt the audience sigh and lean towards him) he began to speak, lightly, intensely, personally. When the meeting was over, she stayed in her seat, limp, quite drained. She saw large working men with arms as thick as Izzie's skinny legs come up and shake his hand.

Nor could she say that the young man made her feel stupid, that almost everything, every day, made her curse the inadequacy of her previous life, the lack of talk, lack of ideas, lack of laughter. There had been few books in Malvern Road, and these were novels, hidden away in the musty big bedroom her mother and father shared, a room she rarely entered and then only secretly, perhaps intent on unearthing the mysteries of marital sex. (She discovered nothing more than a little blue-labelled bottle of vaseline with dust clinging to its greasy lid and two romances by Walter Scott, always the same two, inside which – had she been more curious about books – she would have discovered a rubber contraceptive sheath in a little paper envelope.)

She had walked through the Domain, her high-arched feet blistered from new shoes, and seen men camping in huts made from corrugated cardboard boxes and a little sparrow-limbed girl in George Street dressed in a pitiful fairy costume, begging with a tin in one hand and a silver wand in the other. These things moved her far too much to write about in letters. But this was not the end of the secrets: she had begun to help Izzie in his Labour Party work. She cleaned halls after meetings and ruined her grey silk dress with ink from the Roneo machine. Not only could she not mention this to her father but Izzie had warned her not to tell Rosa who, he said, would scorn her for reformism.

For a person who prided herself on her honesty these burdens were hard to bear.

15

She did not know that she had fallen in love with Rosa, only that her heart lightened when she was called downstairs to the telephone.

"You must not come if I am interfering with your studies," Rosa would say.

"No, no. I am just finishing."

She would run upstairs again, run downstairs to iron a blouse, upstairs to clean her shoes and when the taxi tooted outside she would leave her normally neat room in a mess of books and stockings, discarded slips and rejected skirts, and arrive at the taxi out of breath. At this moment, laughing, collapsing into the seat next to Rosa, she would not think of the guilt and anger she would feel when the picnic was over, when she would walk heavily to her room and look with disgust at the evidence of her indolence.

They picnicked everywhere, in Centennial Park, Cooper Park, but most often near the harbour. They took ferries to Manly, to Taronga Park, to Mosman and Cremorne. They sat, always, at the bow, in front of the ferry captain, and held their hats with one hand while their faces pressed against the soft-gloved salt air. Then, when the engine bells rang, they would clatter down the stairs with basket and rug to see the harbour framed like a painting in the wide wooden doorway.

Then they would walk along paths above tangles of morning glory and wild lantana and spread their rug and take off their hats and let the warm March sun bathe their uplifted faces. When she was with Rosa she felt as if the world was about to burst open, like a delicious tropical fruit, and spill its seeds into her cupped hands.

It was her youth that Rosa liked, her youth that she celebrated, and yet it seemed to Leah that it was Rosa who was young, whose pleasure in the world made Leah feel old and wooden. Rosa was filled with passions and enthusiasms, sudden squalls of anger and equally sudden exclamations of childlike (Leah thought) delight. It was Rosa, for instance, who would stop to point out streaky cirrus clouds that Leah had not even noticed: "Feathers of ice," she had said as they spread the rug on white-flowered clover. "Oh Leah, I love this city. It is so beautiful. Whenever I am unhappy I come to the harbour. It is always splendid, but it is so much nicer when I can share it with someone who does not know it."

Rosa did not show Leah the battle with unhappiness that made these trips so necessary to her, her empty days, all those days, those years of days since she had stopped being Rosalind the dancer. She lived with an almost crippling sense of wasted time and sometimes it seemed that she only lived to read the letters from the son she really loved, the son she had so carelessly thrown into the arms of the revolution.

But Leah saw none of this. She loved the way Rosa sat on the rug, the looseness of her limbs, the way she had of holding her hands together, the right hand circling the left thumb. She liked the fine wrinkles around her blue eyes, the wideness of her mouth, the wind-tangled curly honey hair.

They ate prawns from newspaper and drank wine: Leah, one glass; Rosa, the rest of the bottle.

And it was under the influence of this single glass that Leah, on their third picnic, began to unburden herself of secrets.

"No," Rosa said, when Leah had made her first confession. "You are not dull or stupid. You are young. Of course you know nothing. You are a baby. Don't smile. You have strong feelings and don't know how to argue in their defence. You will spend the rest of your life finding justifications for your strong feelings. I watched you, the day you came to my house – the way you sat, so meekly. Your hands were – so – in your lap, your head bowed, very meek. And inside, I knew, you were boiling with all sorts of things you would like to say. You were not meek at all. So, tell me, what is it you really want to do with your life?"

Leah's hands were sticky with prawns, her head light with wine. She tore a piece of bread from the loaf and threw it to the jostling crowd of orange-legged seagulls.

"I would like," she said, watching the seagulls fight but not seeing them, "to do one really fine thing."

"I knew you were a dangerous girl," said Rosa, laughing. And then, seeing how shy and embarrassed the girl was, added, more tenderly: "What thing?"

"I don't know," the girl said.

"Only one?"

"It would be enough, wouldn't it?"

"I don't know." Rosa poured herself more wine and lay on her back. She held the glass in one hand and shaded her eyes with the other. "When I was young, I was just like you. Very moral. Very serious. But my character was flawed. The real reason I left the Party was nothing to do with what they did to Trotsky (Trostsky was not a saint himself). The real reason was because I couldn't spend my life in dark rooms when the sky is like this. I could not believe there would be a revolution here. I blamed the gold, working men with gold in their mouths, but, really, it was the sky. Look at it. It has no history. But is this why you study medicine? To do one fine thing?"

Leah sat cross-legged, her hands folded in the nest of her pleated skirt. She blushed, but although she wished to bow her head, did not. "Do I seem silly?"

"Not at all. But why a doctor? Why not a baker?"

The girl smiled.

"But why not? Have you never smelt bread?" Rosa shut her eyes and her nostrils flared as she smelt imaginary loaves. "You wish to be of use. I was the same. I joined the Party. Of course I was often travelling, on the road, but I did whatever work I could. My husband thought I was mad, but I did dull and menial things for the Party and I felt that being a dancer was of no worth. But a dancer *is* of worth *and* a baker . . . candlestick makers too."

Rosa sat up slowly and rubbed her eyes. "I will tell you why, really, I left the Party. It was because they could not take a dancer seriously. They could not imagine I was a serious person. I was not dowdy enough for them. Do you believe me?"

"Yes, Rosa," said solemn Leah.

"It is a lie," said Rosa, looking out across the harbour where a liner was coming around the point from the Quay, coloured streamers still dangling from its sides. "I am so used to saying it, I believe it." When she turned her gaze was so fierce that Leah averted her eyes and began to fiddle with the loaf of bread. "The bastards expelled me."

Leah blushed.

"Because", Rosa said, "they are puritans and hypocrites, because I had an affair with a married comrade. We used to come on picnics, like this, and tell secrets to each other. But they did not expel him. He was a man. They expelled me. It's quite true. He was very senior too. That is why I can't forgive them." She drank her wine, thirstily, emptying the tumbler and refilling it. "So now, darling, you have my secret. You are shocked?"

"No," said Leah, who was shocked. "Not at all," she said, as if she heard about such things every day. "I was thinking about your son, Joseph, in Moscow."

"What else is there for him to do?" said Rosa hotly, rubbing her eyes. "How could he be anything else but a Marxist? Better a Marxist than some wishy-washy social democrat." And to emphasize the point she threw a prawn head at a scavenging seagull.

"Oh, Rosa!"

"Yes, I know Izzie is your friend, but he is my son." This time it was the wine cork she threw.

"He is very kind," said Leah, "and that is what is important."

Rosa's face then underwent one of those transformations that would always delight Leah – it sloughed off its tired miserable lines and became drum-tight with a splendid smile.

"And that is what's important? Kindness?"

"Yes."

"Yes," said Rosa, shaking out her hair. "Kindness and dancing. Can we agree on that?"

Leah could not say yes but smiled instead.

"I will teach you to dance," said Rosa with a shyness that Leah did not understand. "Then you will understand what I am talking about." But it would be another week before Leah realized how important the dancing lessons might be to Rosa and now she only smiled, relieved that Rosa's mood had passed.

But even then, as they contented themselves with the progress of a tugboat pushing its way back to Pyrmont, a man came up to them and asked them for money. His eyes were downcast and he had cardboard tied to the bottom of his shoes. He was a young man too, no more than thirty. Rosa gave him the money and he went away.

They watched him trudge around the path beside the seawall.

"I am suddenly struck," Rosa said, her smile quite collapsed, "by how evil we are." She looked down at the empty prawn shells, the broken heads, the long thin feelers and something – perhaps it was only the flies crawling on them – made her shudder.

16

Secrets sheltered within secrets, boxes within boxes, and in the heart of this secret world, in the ultimate box, sweet as sandalwood, Leah Goldstein danced, felt her heart pump, her glands secrete, savoured the sweet ache of unused muscles and knew herself – beneath the eye of her stern-faced but contented teacher – to grow beautiful.

In this final box, the stories had no moral. They were dancing stories set in country halls, flapping tents. Here Rosalind danced for miners. There Leonard bent his iron bar and swallowed fire to wild applause, while the man he had become drove his trucks through the Sydney streets unaware that, in his own house, his wife was romancing about their difficult past, turning those country halls into theatres as glittering as the fortune they had never found.

It was months before they were sprung and by then it was too late. The women, both of them, were addicted. So when Lenny found them – having arrived at the house in the middle of the day, his heart set on nothing more complicated than cheese and pickles – there was nothing he could do to stop it. He opened the door of the spare room as Leah Goldstein – moving to the rhythms of Lou Rodana's Orchestra – dropped a coloured scarf to reveal her small leotard-clad breasts.

There was a silence then. The gramophone clicked noisily. Lenny fumbled for a cigarette in his blue overalls, but even while he discarded wet matches, one by one, his eyes took in the scene –the electric radiator glowing in the corner, the wind-up gramophone in the empty fireplace, the girl's shapely legs, the sweat on her upper lip, the old scrapbooks spread across the little table beneath the cobweb-covered windows and – last of all – his wife's pleading eyes as she stood and smiled.

"Show me", he said to his wife, "where you keep dry matches."

"You know where," she said, not wishing to be alone with him.

"Show me," he said.

Rosa laughed, a high scratchy laugh, and followed him out of the room. Leah lifted the arm from the gramophone and wound it up again.

She could hear Lenny's angry voice. She removed the needle from the arm and searched through a tiny tin box looking for a sharper one.

17

Rosa gave him his matches, holding the box at arm's length, and watched him light his cigarette. He looked around for an ashtray and, obedient as any wife in a woman's magazine, she found one amongst the unwashed dishes in the sink, rinsed it beneath the tap and dried it. Ash smeared the tea-towel, and she thought, defensively, so what?

"Why?" he said. He did not sit at the table when she sat down. He leaned against the kitchen door and folded his arms across his chest. She took a dirty casserole off the chair so there would be somewhere he could sit, but he watched her silently and did not move.

"Why?" he repeated.

"Why what?"

"Why? For what use? A dancing doctor?"

Rosa shrugged.

"What would her people say to you, filling her head with rubbish?"

She would have liked to say that it was not rubbish, that it was wrong to call her new happiness rubbish.

"What would her mother and father say? She is meant to be studying. What will you feel if she fails her studies?"

"She wanted to . . ." Rosa began, but she could not meet her husband's eyes. She wished she had the kitchen tidier. She stacked two plates inside the greasy frying pan.

"Is that what you want?" Lenny said. "You want her to fail? You want that on your head?"

Rosa shrugged again.

"You force her to do things. She doesn't know how to say no. It is like the Passover."

"It is *not* like the Passover," Rosa said. "The Passover was not my idea." She was beginning to feel guilty and it was wrong. It was a trick he had. "She wanted," she whispered, worrying that Leah would hear them.

"She wanted, she wanted."

"She *did* want."

"She wanted so much, she ran away. That's how much she wanted."

Of course the Passover had been a mistake, but who was to know it? None of them. Not until it was done. The girl had been so alight, so eager. On the eve they had swept the house together and thrown out all the bread. Leah had been full of questions. Why this? Why that? They had made the charoset together. They had boiled the eggs. Rosa had shown her how the tray was set. They had starched the white tablecloth and set the table.

On Passover she had arrived in a new dress. It was almost a real Passover. Lenny's father and brother were there. The old man was frail and doddery but when he began to read from the book his voice, though high, was strong and clear. She did not like the old man and he did not like her, but out of his corrupt old mouth the words came – so clear and clean that she stopped hating him and was pleased he had come.

It had happened at the very beginning, when the karpas was taken. She had not known the girl well then and had not understood her. She had looked at the girl as she took the karpas and when her face changed she thought it must be the bitterness. But then Leah had stood, suddenly, with an awful scrape of the chair and, just as the old man began ("This is the bread of affliction . . .") she ran from the house. Thank God the old scoundrel was deaf and never heard Leah spitting and coughing as she ran out the front door. But he was not blind. He saw Rosa run after her. And Rosa, as she went down the front steps, heard his voice squawking in outrage like a caged bird.

She had found Leah weeping, hunched over and hugging herself behind the lavatory and she took the shuddering body in her arms and held her.

"What is it, little Leah? What is it?"

Leah wept and wept. "I am a fraud," she said. "I am a fake, a fake, a fake. I cannot be anything."

"You are the sky," Rosa said, trying to find medicine in words. She held the girl's head to her breast. "You are the sky." She meant that big sky, that vast clear cobalt sky without history, clean, full of light, free of sombre clouds.

But she did not explain herself and neither the sky nor her arms could give Leah Goldstein any comfort.

Now, in that kitchen, her husband came to sit next to her in the vacant chair. He put the back of his dirty hand against her cheek, gently. "She is very young," he said, softly, "and you will damage her."

"All right," she said, but she promised nothing.

"You have plenty of other things to amuse you," he said, looking around the kitchen, the open cupboards, the spilt flour, the stacks of yellowing newspapers.

"Yes," she said. She found some cheese and pickles then and saw him to his truck. She admired the load of roofing lead he had bought from the old Turramurra Seminary and promised him meat and pudding for his dinner while Leah Goldstein, who had heard almost every word, held the head of the gramophone ready. And Rosa, returning to the spare room, found her protégée swaying her hips lasciviously to the accompaniment of Lou Rondano's "Boompsy Daisy".

18

In October, Leah Goldstein had to give up her dancing. Her final exams were approaching. She was also working late into the night, Roneoing pamphlets, addressing envelopes and moving from dreary street to dreary street stuffing election material in letter boxes. She felt herself engaged in a fight between good and evil. It was no longer a theory to her. In the final hectic weeks Izzie had been badly beaten by the New Guard, dragged down from the platform outside Colgate Palmolive and kicked and pummelled as he lay on the ground. He had screamed like a child, a high piercing terrible sound, and although he was ashamed of this it made Leah admire him all the more. She developed a passionate hatred of large men, New Guardsmen, policemen, bailiffs with moustaches and returned soldier's badges. When Jack Lang was finally elected and she met him, at last, face to face, she was made uncomfortable by his size, the harshness of his voice, the width of his shoulders: the Socialist Saviour looked like a bailiff.

There were parties, of course, when Lang was finally elected, but the party she chose to remember was the one Rosa and Lenny threw for Rosa's birthday during the first week of her exams.

"My *silly* friends," Rosa had told her with an odd grimace that at once celebrated her theatrical colleagues and denied them totally.

Rosa's silly friends had red mouths and huge hats. They were walking scrapbooks. There were dancers of every type, bit actors, second-rate cabaret performers, and short men with wide lapels who could tell jokes for three hours without repeating themselves. They filled the house, surrounded the caravan, and spilled out into the street. They chucked Izzie under the chin as if he were still a little boy and told each other different stories at the same time. Leah was entranced by them and did not notice that Rosa was bored and dissatisfied with all this vapid talk which reminded her only of the days before her expulsion when her friends had been serious people.

Mervyn Sullivan arrived in a giant black Buick, bringing two beautiful actresses and a huge bottle of champagne with a silver ribbon around its neck, and Rosa, surprising herself by the dazzling quality of her own hypocrisy, pretended to be flattered that he had come.

In the later afternoon they all walked along Bondi Beach and strolled along the sand in colourful defiance of the rude realities of life. This was the day when Mervyn Sullivan, hearing that Leah had learned dancing from Rosa, grandly presented her with his card, a deckled masterpiece like a wedding invitation. "There is always work for talent," he said and made her put the card in her handbag.

Jennifer Valamay sang a rude song about a dicky bird and Leah, emboldened by a single glass of sweet sherry, kissed Izzie on the cheek behind the laundry. It was not an unqualified success, for the skin she had felt such compassion for when it was bruised by the fists of bullies also had an upsetting clamminess; the kiss made her shiver; she hid the shiver in a laugh.

19

When she returned to Malvern Road at Christmas that year, Leah Goldstein had no idea that she was, already, well on the way to being a snake-dancer. She felt, inside that monstrous house, on the way to nowhere. She was bored and lonely. She listened to the magnified sounds of clinking cutlery and, in this atmosphere as thin as her mother's consommé, she found herself yearning for the coarseness of the Kaletskys, for hunks of potato and chunks of sausage, for things not cut but torn, for breadcrumbs on the tablecloth, for shocking flatulence, accusation, discord. Even the way the male Kaletskys moved, their slightness, frailty, their sparrow-fast heads, their darting eyes, the movements of their ironic lips, all this purified in her mind until their skins became buffed and ivory smooth with so much taking out and putting away, and the Kaletskys metamorphosed into exquisite characters, like a family of little Balinese gods and exhibited a variety-show vulgarity that was, at the same time, so finely worked that the images must be wrapped – like Joseph Kaletsky's translation of Engels that Rosa had so proudly shown her – in fine layers of jeweller's tissue paper.

Her mother, it is true, saw something was amiss, but blamed Sydney for making her daughter noisy and opinionated. If she could have known that snakes would be involved she would have, of course, blamed the snake. But the snake is not a Cause but an Effect, not a Serpent but a simple snake, and if we are to be scrupulous in laying blame it is better that you know: it is the chooks that are responsible.

Soon you will find yourself with chooks all around you, shitting, pecking, puddling in their drinking water, but before we get to that insanitary situation, perhaps I should recount my own experience of chooks – and I do not mean the difficulties, with lice, mites, fowl pox, pullorum or bum-drop about which subjects Goon's otherwise taciturn cousin gave me enough information to last a lifetime. Nor do I plan to debate with you the comparative virtues of the Plymouth Rock, the Rhode Island Red, the Silkie, the White Leghorn or the Australorp, although I have always thought the White Leghorn a particularly degenerate example of the species. Nor, madam, will I sign your protest letter about the battery hens. I wish only to recount an incident that occurred in that summer of February 1931 while Leah Goldstein was hiding in her room in Malvern Road pretending to be a socialist.

I was, at that time, still dithering around Central Victoria and giving my son the deceitful impression that Sydney and his mother were 20,000 miles from Melbourne.

Now I know I told you I had given up on the motor trade, but in February 1931, just as I was coming down the steps of the Woodend Post Office, trying to keep my hat on my head and the hot wind-blown dust out of my eyes, I ran into Bert McCulloch, the local Ford dealer.

Now dealer is a tricky word: it suggests something sharp and clever, monied, propertied, something, in short, not at all like Bert who was a blacksmith by birth, a jack of all trades, a clever wheelwright, an ace welder, a plumber of rare ingenuity. He could carry a piece of hot metal between grease-black thumb and forefinger in such a way that – even though the metal had suffered half an hour beneath his welding torch – he was not burnt. His knack, he said, was partly in the protection offered by the grease but also by the feather-lightness of his touch.

Bert told me he had a Prospect out at Morrisons, a woman with silver rings on her fingers, a cert to buy an A Model. He had offended this woman in some way. She would not speak to him. Would I, he asked, take on the job? There was fifty quid in it.

Bert needed the sale as much as I did. Before I had time to think about it his wife was ushering my children out of the northerly wind and into the shelter of the earth-floored shed where Bert did his welding and where she answered the phone and did the books. I would have taken my children with me, but she stole

265

them away, fearful I suppose of any further hindrance to the sale being made – you could see the McCullochs were having hard times too.

Next thing I knew I was sitting behind the wheel of a brand new A Model and Bert was offering me – he held it delicately between thumb and forefinger as if it were a freshly welded intake manifold – a map, hand-drawn on gasket cork, to the property of Miss Adamson of Morrisons.

Bert had a nice face, round and regular with a fringe of snow-white hair, a tanned pate, and a pair of rimless spectacles that gave him, blue singlet or no, a distinguished air. His lower teeth, however, were stained and worn away by the hot torrents of his tea drinking and when he winked and grinned at me, the face took on a cock-eyed malicious quality: a trick of the teeth, but unsettling to a fellow so desperate for a quid and so fearful of failure at the same time.

"This'll test you, Sonny Jim."

"Why would that be?"

"She's a spinst-ah," he leered. "And a crack lick-ah."

Bert had a healthy interest in sexual matters. It had been he who informed me, years before, about what ladies who are affectionate towards each other do in private, and I suppose I must conclude he was correct about Miss Adamson's sexual predilections. But the interesting thing about it is that the place where the lady was supposed to put her tongue, this delicate and private matter, so occupied the minds of all Woodend that it assumed the nature of a cloak that the hot wind of gossip wrapped around the woman so tightly, so effectively that – even while they all sniggered and pointed – it obscured from view that which otherwise would have been glaringly obvious, to wit – Miss Adamson was not the full bag of marbles.

Sex was their obsession, but Miss Adamson's, as I soon found out, was chooks.

I did not realize straight away. I was struck, of course, by her physical appearance which was at once eccentric and aristocratic. I remember, most of all, her hands. These were not in the least aristocratic, but were large and broad and thick-fingered, as tough as farmers'. Her fingers not only showed broad, chipped, broken cuticles but three big ornate silver rings whose classical allusions were lost in convoluted forms and black silver oxide. Her face was strong, heavily jawed, big-nosed, but very handsome. Her hair was a lustrous grey and it was cut simply in a fringe. She wore a faded grey men's work shirt and big serge trousers of a weight unsuitable to the day. She was, I suppose, about fifty.

I liked her immediately.

Of course I liked her. I had seen Bert's wife's eyes, close to panic in the way they looked at me and when she gathered my children about her I realized, suddenly, how pinched and threadbare they were. Of course I liked Miss Adamson. I was going to sell her a car. I would have loved her if I had needed to. My stomach was swollen up with air and all that hot blown summer landscape had taken on a slightly unreal focus so that the edges of the wattle leaves looked sharp enough to slice your fingers off.

She was very civil to me. She was not the type to offer scones – she confronted me at the gate in front of her shiny little cottage – but neither was she the type to send me off without a demo. She reckoned (she ordered) that we might take a spin up to the back boundary where, she knew, the fence was sure to have been broken in a recent flood. She asked me, most politely, if the A Model could ford her river and I, having inspected the crossing, assured her, even more politely, that it could. I had the feeling in the back of my neck that I have always had when a sale will be made – that creamy tingling feeling, sharp and smooth at once, calm and excited, abrasive and soothing. I did not mind the musty smell about her person or the sour mud she introduced into the vehicle. I could not keep my eyes from the tangled wealth of story suggested by those silver rings and broad strong hands.

The river was only a foot high, the rocks small. We sailed across and didn't even get our feet wet.

The trouble was that we spent too much time on her boundary which, by the by, was the most disgraceful fence I have ever seen and it was, like dirty underwear, a contradiction to her front fences, her little green-painted cottage, closed sheds, neat haystacks – here, swept out of sight behind an unusual stand of wattles and box-thorns was a fence (which may, long ago, have been tight and strained with six bright tight strands of wire you could play a tune on) which was now as sad as a half-unravelled sweater on a scarecrow – cobbled together out of bits and pieces with not a single whole piece of wire, I swear it, more than a yard long, and most of them so rusty they broke when you twisted them, and some of them no more than poor thin binding wire, and others pieces of barbed stuff so archaic you found yourself wondering about its history. The posts were no better, most of them rotted off at ground level and the general situation was so bad that it was very easy to spend an hour there, poking around looking for bits of wire to fix it with. My feelings, so far, indicated that the sale was mine. I was already eating café breakfasts, hotel dinners, mixed grills, steamed puddings, ordering a beer for myself and green jelly for the children.

When the fence was fixed as well as possible, we got back into the car. Miss Adamson took in her broad belt a notch and made complimentary remarks. Not a word about Chooks or Tinkers. She even praised the paintwork, insisting that there was great depth and beauty in the black. If there were no upsets the fifty quid was mine.

We returned to the crossing, passing slowly through the high rusty stands of dock weeds and the fleshy beds of dense paspalum. We hit no hidden rock or stump.

What, an hour before, had been a pleasant little creek was now a swollen raging torrent down which broken trees rode pell-mell and beneath the rush of waters could be heard the low rumble of boulders grinding on each other like a gravel-crusher. Anyone who knows the district knows how this can happen – you have a blue-skied day but there are storms and thunder upon the mountain. I did not know this at the time, but Miss Adamson, having lived there for twenty years, must have known. In spite of which, she turned on me.

"You tinker," she said.

I had brought the car to the crossing. I was, already, disorientated. I could not understand why the creek was the way it was. It seemed impossible and I was as confused as a fellow suddenly, without warning, rolled out of a boat trying to understand his new environment.

"Madam?" I said, but I was staring at that monstrous river whose waters were puce and bruised from so much violence.

"You pesky little tinker," she said. "A tinker's trick," she roared. "But I", her eyes were hard, hostile, her mouth suddenly thin and severe, "shall not buy."

I knew she was a crack lick-ah, but it did not occur to me that she was crazy, not even when she blamed me for a flood. It is obvious enough now, now I alert you to the condition, but had you sat there with your head awash with astonishment and worry as to how you would get home to your children, knowing one had a sore throat and temperature and that the other would make himself ill with bawling, not knowing how it was – how, anyway –that a perfectly sedate creek could convert itself like this without benefit of a single cloud, and had you sat here beside me and shared my confusion, then the accusation of being a tinker, if you bothered to take it in, would be merely one more cannon shot in the chaos of battle and you would not think it madder or less reasonable than the river itself.

So, no, I did not doubt her sanity. In fact the opposite is true: she looked at me as if I were some ant, some low form of life, and she looked at me so confidently that, in spite of the fact that her trousers were two sizes too big for her, I believed her. She was musty to smell but her eyes were eyes accustomed to deciding what way the world shall be run. At that moment I abandoned any hope of the sale.

That was my disappointment, a disappointment so great I could have cried. I wanted only to be with my family. I thought of my boy who would soon be bellowing in the foreign dark. I considered fording the river on foot, but even as the thought entered my head I saw a log, as big as a battering ram, surfing down the river as if powered by its own angry engine.

I thought the business finished. But it was, alas, merely starting, for the excitement of the river seemed to have served the function of priming the engine of Miss Adamson's madness and it began (roughly, with coughs, curses, and small explosions) to ignite, and then to turn, and soon the whole mechanism was huffing and chuffing, ready to run all through the night up and down, down and up, along one track whose point of departure and point of arrival were identical: chooks.

I did not notice at the beginning. I did not notice that she was speaking about her chooks in a peculiar way. She was worried about them. That was only natural. She said Maisie had no idea how to look after them. But she was not cross with Maisie, but with me, for luring her across the river.

She pulled a notebook from her pocket and showed me her breeding plan, all little tiny boxes and arrows at angles, but still I did not think her mad, merely unfriendly. She accused me of not understanding the diagrams. She was right. She did not do this in any hysterical way, but as proof, if you like, of my inferiority, that I was a man so stupid I could not understand a chook. My ignorance was a thing I was, I have admitted it before, most sensitive about. I collapsed easily before her attack.

She may have stopped talking, but I don't remember it.

At dusk a woman with a kerosene lamp came down to the crossing and waved it about. Miss Adamson got out of the car and screamed instructions at the raging river. It was quite obvious Maisie could not hear her, but Miss Adamson shouted at the light until, at last, it went away.

It was night before I really started to understand that I was trapped with a mad woman. By then she was stretched out on the back seat, her muddy boots on the upholstery, smoking.

"We have no right," she said, lighting a cigarette (I did not ask her where she was putting the ash and butts). "We have no right to make them so stupid. God did not make them stupid. Men did. All we do here is repair the damage."

"What damage?" I asked, but I was thinking of the damage she was doing to Bert's upholstery.

Then she sat up. The moon was just rising. I could see her very clearly. "Does nothing stay in your head, tinker?"

She then set off up and down her one track. Half the night she huffed and puffed while I drifted in and out of nightmares.

Her opinion, as I gathered it, was that the chook should be discontented. She found their content and their stupidity to be unnatural. She gave me chooks, chapter and verse, history, breeding, the Asian jungle fowl, the works. She had some jungle fowl which, she said – and I am sure she meant nothing vulgar – would put some spunk into her leghorns. They were on a verge of flight, she said, of freedom, anguish, life, love. She shook me awake to make sure I understood.

I had not eaten for three days. I told her this, but it did not affect her. She would not permit me to escape my hunger with sleep.

At dawn we saw a slight middle-aged woman in a black Edwardian dress. She was standing on the other side of the much reduced river. She was compressed by severe stays. She wore high-laced boots and a netted little black hat. She was carrying a bucket and hollering and pointing, but I could not make out what she was on about.

The object of her excitement was obscured by the tall avenue of blackwoods that lined the river, and then, in the grey imperfect light I witnessed what was, I suppose, in the history of noxious weeds and feral beasts, an important moment.

I thought at first they were sulphur-crested cockatoos.

But they were not. They were white leghorns, the most stupid of chooks, rising, white and heavy into the soupy summer air.

Miss Adamson was standing beside me. "There," she said to me, her eyes no longer cold and hard, but wet and shining and full of hurt like a wronged child. "There, tinker," she said. "You see."

There they were all right: ignorance, stupidity, malice, flying free and unfettered. They circled, their overdeveloped wings working at too fast a rate for birds so big. They set off south, the least hesitant one leading, down between the river blackwoods.

These were the progenitors of the wild chooks that caused so much trouble in the Wimmera wheatfields and of the leghorns who were soon to invade Leah Goldstein's story.

20

On her first day back in Sydney Leah went with Izzie to Bondi. The world shone with the light of picnics and Leah was delighted with everything she saw. The ordinariness of those little Bondi streets did not dismay her. She loved their mess, their crass. She liked the paspalum growing in the grass strips, the white clover with its rusty heart, the nettles poking out of chain-mail fences. A man in a cotton singlet was asleep in a kitchen chair on the footpath and around the corner came a nanny-goat, its chain rattling behind it, pursued by a woman in Sunday curlers and her husband's dressing gown.

"You mongrel," said the woman to the clever goat. "Lovely day," she said to Leah and did not even seem to see that Izzie, the source of Leah's happiness, was busy being a chook, not just any chook, but a chook belonging to Lenny and Rosa's new tenants.

Last night, on the platform at Central, he had tried to kiss her and she had found herself, involuntarily, shrinking from him. She had felt a flinch of disappointment exactly equal to the gap between her ivory-smooth idea of Izzie and Izzie himself, this little scarecrow with rag-doll sleeves, bad skin and hair (she wrinkled her nose) that badly needed washing.

But she had forgotten: Izzie was funny. And now, as he thrust out his bantam's chest and drew his hands into his flapping wings, she laughed in delight. God, what a chook he was. He clucked and chortled and scratched amongst the clover. He had feathers and a comb. He clicked along the paving stones on his pointed shoes.

"Teddy's chooks", he whispered, "do not stand on pavement cracks."

"Teddy's chooks", he leaped on to a low brick wall, "riding on the tram to Bondi."

The chook was so well behaved on the tram seat. It tucked its head in and snoozed absently. And this (it was now history) was how the tenants' chooks had travelled to Bondi after their eviction from Newtown, their right to free travel defended by three militant members of the Tramways Union, one of whom – the famous Arthur McKay – insisted on paying full fare for the rooster.

"I cannot wait", Leah said – and felt how pleased Izzie was when she took his arm – "to meet your famous chooks."

She could not have avoided them. The new tenants' chooks had taken possession like a conquering army. The front fence – never a pretty sight – was now ugly with chicken wire. The chooks scratched and pecked at the remains of the front lawn. Their droppings marked the concrete path around the side of the house and – in the ravaged back garden, between house and caravan – she walked into a scene of execution: a headless Rhode Island Red spurted its last spasms of bright red blood beneath the picnic sky and then fell, drunkenly, and lay twitching in the dust.

A man in a woollen round-necked singlet and serge trousers stood watching the bird with an air of puzzled curiosity. He had a big boozer's nose, tender with fragile capillaries, and – as he saw Izzie and tucked his lower lip beneath his upper – a manner that was at once self-effacing and sly. He pushed the dead bird with the head of his axe.

Izzie introduced Leah. Teddy called her "missus". He squatted and poked at the small fire he had lit beneath Lenny's copper cauldron. The bottom of the cauldron was streaked with black and it was full of dark steaming water.

"Hang on," Teddy said. "Got a prezzie for you." He rose and disappeared into the house and they could hear a woman's voice shouting at him in anger.

"Nice bloke," Izzie said.

"Where are Sid and Rosa?"

Izzie nodded his head towards the caravan and, seeing Leah's confusion, explained: "Teddy's got a wife and four kids."

"Oh," said Leah, looking at the dead chook and wondering how it was possible to be evicted in Jack Lang's state.

"Here ya are," Teddy said. He had returned with a chipped

bowl full of hen's eggs. "Nice fresh cackleberries for your mum and dad."

As they walked the few steps to the caravan, Teddy dunked the headless chook into the cauldron and the rank smell of its steaming feathers filled Leah's nostrils.

21

One expected discord amongst the Kaletskys, but nothing had prepared Leah for the dull air of misery she found inside that caravan on whose floor the sand of lost holidays, sand that had once stuck between Izzie's toes or clung to Rosa's brown calves, still lingered, cold, hard-edged, abrasive.

Rosa looked ill. Her face was sallow. Those lovely lines around her eyes and mouth had deepened and set into unhappy patterns, and although she embraced Leah and made a fuss of her, her eyes stayed as dull as the windows of that gloomy space. They crammed in together around a tiny table, oppressed by the weight of uncomfortably placed cupboards.

Leah had returned to Sydney vowing to work hard at her studies, to give up her picnics and her dancing, but she had not been in the caravan five minutes before she found herself resolving to get Rosa out on a picnic.

"So," she said, bright as a nurse, "you have tenants, Rosa."

"I hate them," Rosa hissed. "I want my house back."

Lenny sighed and screwed his eyes shut. "If you want them to go," he said, "all you have to do is tell them." He lit a cigarette, made a face, then put it out.

"Why should I tell them? *He*," Rosa pointed a finger at her son who stared, ostentatiously, at the metal ceiling, "*he* is the one who asked them here."

"You have a short memory, Rosa," Izzie said. "Who offered them the house?"

"How could they live in the caravan? It is hard enough for two people."

Lenny was trying to catch Leah's eye. He was making secret fun of his wife. Leah was embarrassed. She took Rosa's hand and stroked it but Rosa did not seem connected to her hand. "I am a prisoner in this nasty box," she said, but to no one in particular. "I cannot go into my garden, I have to ask them if I

273

might please use the shower. The shower is filthy. The walls in the kitchen are covered with grease. . . ."

"Whose grease?" said Lenny.

"It smells. I hate it."

"Rosa," Lenny said, "you are being selfish," but he put out his hand to her, to touch her shoulder. Rosa shrugged his hand off.

"Of course I am selfish," she yelled, suddenly very angry. "I have always been selfish."

"*You* gave them the house," Izzie said and Leah, who had begun to feel physically ill, found a strong shiver of dislike pass through her.

"What else could I do? You make it impossible for me to do anything else with your stupid charity. You are a wishy-washy. You know you are."

Izzie's face tightened and his pretty mouth became a slit. "Who owned stocks and shares? Some Marxist!"

"I did," Rosa shouted. Leah wanted to block her ears, to run away and hide from this nightmare. "I did."

"You are making Leah embarrassed," Lenny said, but Rosa was staring at her son and something nasty was happening between them.

"Joseph would never have done this to me," she said. "A real communist would do nothing so sentimental."

Izzie stood up, his face quite pallid. "Shut up," he screamed. He looked ugly with hate. "Shut your damn mouth."

Lenny began to rise. Leah put her hands across her ears. The caravan rocked and swayed as Izzie ran from it. They heard his feet on the path and the squeak of the gate.

"Go and find him, Leah," Rosa said wearily. "Go and find him. Tell him you love him."

When she had gone, husband and wife went back to the matter that they had been discussing for two days. They circled round and around it, talking, talking, but in the centre of their talk there was nothing, a hole – the scrap-metal business was bankrupt.

22

Amongst some fleshy plants with leaves like ear-lobes, she found him, high on the cliffs of Tamarama where the wet Cellophane wrappers of Hoadley's confectionery assumed the same wet snotty look as the used contraceptive – that repellent thing – she had found there while walking as a dancer, her head high, her arms swinging, as fluid as a seagull, on a day when Rosa had been happy with the world and that other fleshy plant, the one called pig-face, had lain across a corner of the cliffs like vivid pink shantung flung across a draper's counter.

He was curled inside a weather-worn piece of soft yellow stone a hundred feet above the sucking sea. If he had wrists like a girl, he suffered hurt like a man, privately, ashamed of tears or perhaps, Leah thought, seeing the black ball of pain in the arms of the rock, like an animal withdrawing from the herd. It seemed to her to be a deeply conservative attitude to pain – to withdraw from society as if one would be destroyed for one's weakness or incapacity.

All away to the south the sky was hung with thunder blue and down along the beach at Bondi the sand glowed an odd deep mustard yellow and she wished she had been up on the cliffs on the day of Rosa's birthday party to see the procession along the beach: the mauves, the yellows, blacks and pinks, the wonderful Silly Friends parading noisily and emptily along the sand.

She chose a course towards Izzie that would allow him to witness her approach and thus have time to compose herself. She walked with her head down, one hand on her hat, the other controlling her dress which rose recklessly to show the sky her dancer's legs.

When she arrived at the rock he was sitting up, looking sheepish. She sat down beside him and took his hand, not as a lover might, but as a concerned stranger taking a pulse, and indeed it crossed her mind to wonder if such skin could ever be truly familiar, if it might not always be slightly alien.

"Talking to my mother," Izzie said, not looking at her. "Talking to my mother is not a game you can win. You are in check from the first move."

"Do you know what I think?" Leah said at last.

"What do you think?"

"I think the chooks are making everyone unhappy." She smiled, but she was quite serious. When Izzie had made the chooks they had been snow-white creatures with wise black eyes but now they were malevolent and mad-eyed and their red combs were obscene.

Izzie shrugged his shoulders irritably.

"She has never been any different," he said. "It was always

275

Joseph who could do no wrong. Whatever I did, it didn't matter–
I was wrong. Oh, Goldstein, if only you could meet my slimy big
brother. She loves him. She thinks he's the ant's pants. Have
you seen how she wraps up his dull translations in tissue paper?
Jesus Christ! He's such a fraud."

"Izzie, why didn't you tell me about Rosa?"

"I am telling you, Goldstein," he smiled, "now."

"She's unhappy. She looks sick and miserable. And your
father has a funny look too – disappointed and bitter."

"I forgot."

Leah looked at him incredulously.

"How could you forget?"

"I *forgot*. And there's a southerly buster coming." He pulled
her to her feet and they began to stroll back to Bondi. "You don't
know how busy I am. You don't understand what I do. You
haven't even *asked*."

He gave her an odd sideways look. "I've got more to worry about
than Rosa and Lenny." He pulled his grubby hands out of his
pockets and started striking off points on his dainty little fingers.
"Each day I teach. I get up at five. I do my preparation. I get to
school at eight thirty. I'm busy till four. Then there's work to do
with the local branch. Then," he hesitated, "I've got other stuff."

"I am going to take Rosa on a picnic."

"Leah, it is a secret. I'm working for the UWU."

"Oh," she said. "I see." But in fact she didn't understand at all.

"The Unemployed Workers' Union."

"Good," she said, still not appreciating what this meant, that the
UWU was mostly communist and that Izzie's membership of it was
enough to have him expelled from the Labour Party.

"I train speakers," he said.

"You're a good speaker, Izzie."

As they walked back to Campbell Parade he began to talk about
his dissatisfaction with Lang, that he was nothing but a fraud, and
Leah – who remembered all those nights they had worked to get
Lang elected – suddenly felt weary and sick of all these bright
futures.

Campbell Parade was rich in leather shoes and double-coned
ice-creams dripped frivolously on to the sweaty footpath. Izzie was
still talking, gesticulating, bumping into people.

"Izzie," she said when he, at last, paused for breath.

"Yes-sie," he grinned.

"What Rosa said about Jack Lang was right."

"Yes."

"Well, why don't you tell her so?"

"I will," he said. "I promise." And then he went on telling her how he took his speaker's course at the UWU at Glebe, how a man named Bill Darcy introduced him to the class: "Youse fellows reckons you're not too impressive on the platform. Well, I want youse to cast your eyes on this little fellow I saw some of youse laughing at when he stepped in. Well, youse can start laughing on the other side of your faces because he is the darndest little speaker we got, so better sit there and listen to him while he gives you the drum and if you clean out your ear-holes you might get a bit of sense into your heads."

Leah began laughing.

"You'd be proud of me," he said.

"I am proud of you," she said, suddenly serious. She was pleased that in all this awful world there was someone who was trying to do something decent and she wondered what was wrong with her, that her emotions ran so hot and cold about this man who now, as they withdrew into a bus shelter, shyly took her hand.

It was then that he told her what he had begun by hiding, that he had lost his job. The Lang Machine, with cold vindictiveness, had not only expelled him from the Labour Party but dismissed him from his job at a state school. He had been arrested after a fight with police at evictions in Glebe and it was this, his new criminal record, that was used as the excuse.

"Oh, Izzie. The bastards."

The bus shelter was a bleak place. Drunks had pissed in it. Someone had gouged "Bread not Bullets" into the seat. The letters were jagged. She found herself embracing Izzie. His hair was greasy and unpleasant, and confused, in her mind, with the smell of the stale urine. It was an appropriate perfume for such an evil, loveless world.

Small boys ran past. "Hubba-hubba," they called to the embracing couple. "Hubba-hubba."

Leah did not hear them.

When she looked, at last, at Izzie's face, she was startled to find him grinning.

"I've joined the Party," he said.

She remembered thinking that Rosa, at least, would be pleased.

23

But Rosa was not pleased. She called him names: ultra-leftist, adventurist, names, it seemed, that described his behaviour in fighting policemen.

But then, all squeezing in around that table again, they became quiet as they realized the bleakness of the position.

Leah's mind spun. She considered wiring her father for money, and then, quite properly, dismissed it.

"But what will happen?" she asked.

No one answered her. It wasn't necessary. She knew herself exactly what would happen: they would have to live on hand-outs. There would be government stooges around the house asking questions about chooks and tenants. If they received payment for either they would get no hand-out. Rosa would unleash her tongue on officious felt-hatted spies who would never believe they had no income and, even if they did, life would be a misery, trudging all the way down to Number 7 wharf for a meal ticket, then back up to the other end of the city to collect a gunnysack of food – no vegetables, no fruit, and a lump of meat chopped up just anyhow.

"I think, Lenny," Leah said, "that you will have to rent your house, for money."

Lenny ran his hand through his wiry grey hair. He opened his mouth a fraction and his false teeth – Leah had never noticed them before – gave a small clack.

"Leah, Leah," Rosa said. "Do you really think we would evict them?"

"We would do no such thing," said Lenny quietly. "It would kill us."

"But you must do something." Leah was impatient, not for the first time, with the Kaletskys. They seemed helpless to her, like children, and now they were, it seemed, overcome with some family emotion that excluded her completely.

Rosa put her arm around Izzie and hugged him to her. "You are a good boy, Izzie."

"An ultra-leftist," he reminded her, but their cheeks, mother and son, were still pressed together.

"Better an ultra-leftist than a Menshevik," said Rosa Kaletsky. Leah had forgotten what a Menshevik was and, anyway, did not care. She did not see what application the in-fighting in Russia had to do with a caravan in Bondi where the immediate problems had to be solved, i.e., how to feed the stubborn Kaletskys who were blowing noses and smiling to each other unaware that there, in their midst, was a girl imbued by the dangerous ambition to do One Fine Thing.

24

Whenever Leah thought of Mervyn Sullivan she thought of liquids, water, tears, sweat, the whole of his large handsome face surrounded by an envelope of liquid that, itself invisible, left a fine smear of condensation on his big features and made him appear sentimental or weepy when in fact he was neither.

She had carried his card ever since he had given it to her that afternoon at Bondi.

"You never know," he had said.

"You never know," she repeated to herself on every occasion she had considered throwing it out.

His office she discovered on the fifth floor above an arcade at the dingy end of Elizabeth Street down near Central.

The sign on the door proclaimed MERVYN SULLIVAN THEATRI-CAL AGENT but the scene inside the door showed nothing but disarray. There were open filing cabinets with their insides falling out and, on the floor, yellowed clippings, photographs, letters lying next to indentations in the carpet that betrayed the recent removal of a desk and chair. A woman's dress, brilliant with spangles, hung from the picture rail.

Amongst all this Mervyn Sullivan sat hunched over a metal waste-paper basket, his left hand on his chest, carefully keeping his silk tie from harm whilst he ate a meat pie, the watery contents of which dripped messily and landed noisily amongst the crumpled papers in the bin.

She carried her emu suit in a paper bag.

"Mr Sullivan," she began, "I am Leah Goldstein and you met me at Rosa Kaletsky's birthday party at Bondi. You gave me your card and invited me to call on you."

Mervyn Sullivan did not say anything. In fact, he did not even look up. He had, always, tremendous concentration on anything he took a mind to tackle, and the meat pie did not allow anything else.

279

It was to this concentration on the task at hand that Mervyn Sullivan attributed his now doubtful success.

Leah waited for a reply. If there had been a chair to sit on she would have sat, but as there was none she stood uncertainly at the doorway and waited. She watched Mervyn Sullivan complete his meat pie and carefully wipe his fingers with newspaper cuttings.

Then he stood up and did up his suit coat.

"Mr Sullivan . . ." Leah began again.

"A long way from Romano's," Mervyn Sullivan said. "Lobster thermidor and French champagne, crêpes Suzette and yes sir, no sir. A long way too, girlie, from when I saw you last. Don't you want to be a lawyer any more?"

"Doctor," Leah said. "You see, Izzie lost his job and. . . ."

Mervyn Sullivan held up his hand. "Spare me, please. I listen to these stories all day. Please."

"You said you'd get me work."

"I'm packing in this game," Mervyn Sullivan said, indicating that Leah should sit in the chair next to the waste-paper basket. "I'm finished. I can't make a quid any more."

Leah looked at the shining handsome face and mistook the liquids for signs of emotion. In the middle of her own disappointment she found room to be sorry for him.

"How terrible," she said.

Mervyn Sullivan did not seem to notice her sympathy. "I have girls like you in here every day. Dancers are a dime a dozen, girlie, I promise you. There's nothing. If you don't believe me go and see All-Star, go and talk to Jim Sharman. Ask him about dancers. They all think they're star material. They come in here and then they want to argue with me. Anyway, I'm packing up, I'm going on the road again. Who would have thought it? Fifty years of age, and back on the road. Jesus wept."

"I'll do anything," Leah said. "I learn quickly."

"Dancers are too much trouble," Mervyn said. "Give me a good vocalist, a fat lady and a magician. Why do I want to break my heart with dancers?"

"I brought my costume."

"What difference does a costume make?"

"It's an emu costume," Leah said, and held up the feathers. "Don't you remember Rosa Kaletsky's Emu Dance?"

"So why would feathers make you co-operate? It's your age, girlie. You'll think you know everything. Give you a week and you'll think you're it. You'll be telling me how to run my business, you'll be arguing with me, having headaches, going sick, falling in love with the first decent-looking cocky who comes ogling you in the front seat."

He was standing now, staring at a photograph on the floor. He stooped and picked it up. "Prunier's," he said, handing it to Leah who saw Mervyn Sullivan with a beautiful woman on either side of him. "I was the King," he said. "I got Sheila Bradbury, that's her on the left, a hundred quid a week. She's an alcoholic now. If you want sense from her see her at breakfast while she's still shaking."

"I don't drink."

"But could I trust you?" Mervyn Sullivan said softly, his eyes watering and his upper lip swelling. "You're at the university. You think you've got brains. You think you can dance. You'd argue with me all day long. I'm getting too old to argue, girlie. Mervyn knows what's right. You're a good kid," he said, coming to look at the photograph over her shoulder. He was very close, but she was not frightened. But when she felt his hand on her neck, she knew, with a shock, what was required.

"Would you co-operate?" Mervyn Sullivan said. "That is the question."

They were five floors above the street. A fine rain was falling and obscuring the outlines of the world outside. Leah shivered.

"You see," he said, and took his hand away.

They stood there, staring intently at the photograph of Mervyn Sullivan and two women at Prunier's. There was a vase of flowers, roses, on the table. The black-trousered legs of a waiter hovered by Mervyn's left shoulder. The woman who was now an alcoholic had her hand on Mervyn's right shoulder. Lost in the black and grey world of the photograph, Leah made her decision.

"All right," she said.

"You won't argue," Mervyn Sullivan said, turning her by her shoulders to look at him. Her nose came level with his splendid tie. It was a big tie, and tied into a luxurious fat knot. "It's hard on the road," he said. "The towns are ratty. We sleep in caravans. There is no damn glamour, just hard work," he said smiling. He brushed her breast with the back of his large hand and she thought, again, that he would burst into tears. "The magician is a fairy," he said, taking her hand and placing it against the hard thing in his trousers. "And I can't pay you like a professional. Two quid a week would be tops."

281

"Three quid," Leah said, thinking of Rosa and Lenny.

"Three quid," Mervyn Sullivan agreed, unbuttoning her skirt. "Just for the legs."

As the alcoholic Sheila Bradbury could attest, Mervyn Sullivan was a bully and a bastard but he was a masterful lover and although not totally denying the watery emotion suggested by his face, performed with such lingering brutality that Leah, who five minutes before had been a virgin, found herself in Elizabeth Street, spread out across a desk and making tiny bird-sounds she did not at first recognize as coming from her at all. Mervyn Sullivan had been a tap-dancer. He was brilliant, alone in a spotlight, which itself suggested there might be an audience for the event; and Leah, in the darkness, vibrated like a tram on metal wheels and felt an electric pleasure as she raced over cold wet bitumen.

When it was over, he was matter-of-fact. "OK," he said, "now you can dance."

"You hired me already."

"Christ," he said, "You're arguing already."

"You said three pounds."

"Look, girlie, I don't even know you can dance. Now, please, just for Uncle Mervyn, put on your feathers. And let's hope you do a little better on your feet than on your back."

She danced, without music, with hate in her heart.

"All right," he said. "Meet me down in the arcade on Wednesday morning and bring a photograph so I can get a sign painted."

25

She was nineteen years old; her eyes were clear; she was so young that Rosa could not even bear to contemplate it. She placed her hand next to Leah's, silently, as if the evidence presented there on the oilcloth-covered table should be argument enough: the corruption of one, the innocence of the other.

Leah's brow contained not a line. It was so smooth that Rosa ran the tip of her finger across it, from the bridge of her nose up into the dense curly blue-black hair that never, in any light, revealed the scalp beneath.

Rosa opened her mouth to speak and then shut it. What was

there to say? How could she un-say all those dances, wind back all those scratchy pieces of silly music?

In just this way had she lost Joseph, through the power of her stupid mouth. But you could lose someone to Lenin with a clear conscience. You could not abandon someone to Mervyn Sullivan so easily.

Lenny, crumpled, unshaven, unhappy Lenny, said nothing. She could not meet his eyes. She knew she would see blame there. She felt blame enough.

So they sat, in silence, while the westerly wind buffeted the little caravan and rain dripped slowly through the leaking hatch in the roof.

Rosa would have liked to say some of the things she felt about Leah's decision. For instance: it suggested an enormous arrogance, to undertake this change of career for the benefit of people who had not requested it, people far tougher than she was who had – anyway – survived a lifetime of difficulty without such monstrous charity, this bright-eyed, shining One Fine Thing.

Yet she could not say this with any confidence because Leah stubbornly refused to admit that Lenny and Rosa had anything to do with it. She said nothing, not even half a hint, about sending them money and no one could bring themselves to ask her this most embarrassing question or say that whatever money she made she would need herself, that even if she starved herself on their account, she could not, on a dancer's wages, be a breadwinner.

The turmoil of this meeting will be best understood if you imagine Rosa, now, as the caravan rocks in the wind, begin to speak sternly, harshly even, and all the time stroking Leah's smooth pink-nailed hand, and both women's eyes full of tears.

Rosa and Lenny begged Leah, jointly and separately, to reconsider. They spoke badly of Mervyn Sullivan and painted unattractive pictures of life on the road. But all this flowed off her smooth and untroubled skin which was, like all young skin, thin as paper and thick as cowhide.

Leah, excited beyond belief at this daring swerve in her life, refused to admit that she had done anything earth-shattering. She was insouciant, arguing against the skipping rhythms of her heart.

"Why", she asked Rosa, "is a doctor superior to a dancer?"

Rosa flinched, feeling her own words turned into knives and used against her.

"When the bills come," Lenny said, "then you will see the difference."

"Leah, if this is for us . . ." Rosa began.

"No, Rosa, it is not for you." And indeed she felt that was true, and although she felt a little frightened of what she had done, she also felt an enormous relief. She was too stupid to be a doctor. She could not have borne another year of feeling so inadequate. Everything around her conspired to make her feel stupid, even Izzie whom she admired so much.

"When I was a young girl," Rosa said, "I used to dream that one day my mother would get sick and old and I would look after her. I would tell her, Mamma, I will look after you. She would smile at me. She liked me to say it to her. She repeated it to grown-ups to show what a nice girl I was. Later, when I was older, I did look after her, and I was happy to look after her. But I've thought about it lately, Leah, and I don't think it was a very nice sort of happiness. It was like a revenge: 'Now I have you. Now you will wash your hands when I say. Now you will eat your meal. It will be *this* meal – which I have cooked without consulting you – because I am very busy and you are a lot of trouble.'"

"So," said Lenny. "So what is your story?" He butted out his cigarette and then placed it, not in the ashtray, but on the top of the table, lined up with all the other butts each one of which had been put out at precisely the same moment.

"The story is that all young people dream they will control their parents. They wait, like crows, while they get weaker."

"But you are not my parents, Rosa."

"Then I will not have this on my conscience. We did not ask you to." She looked up and caught Lenny's eyes. He nodded his head slowly. See! he was saying. See!

"Yes?" Rosa said belligerently. "What is it?"

But Lenny would say nothing. He ran his tongue over his chipped teeth and studied her with his calculating man's eyes.

"And it affects nothing," Rosa said to Leah. "Don't you understand? It is so naïve. It is too naïve to bear. The world stays just the same as it was before."

"I wasn't trying to alter the world. Rosa, Rosa, don't cry. The Kaletskys are the ones who alter the world. We Goldsteins are more humble."

"Humble. Listen to her, Lenny. I could smack your face. What will your father think of us?"

284

"Too late to think now," said Lenny.

"I sent him a list", said Leah, whose father still knew nothing of the Kaletskys, "with two columns. In one column I put all the pros and in another I put all the cons."

"You left some out."

"How do you know, Rosa, you haven't seen the list?"

"You have left out all the things you are too young to know, because you have never been a dancer. All you have listened to is my silly stories. I'm sorry I ever told you."

"Rosa, Rosa, don't cry."

"I'm not crying. It is such a waste of life, for nothing. You will lie in bed in some dump, some rat-hole in Benalla and the fleas will feed off you and you will stop yourself going to sleep because when you are asleep you will scratch yourself, and if you scratch your belly or your legs – you tell her, Lenny – then the customers see it. So you go to sleep anyway, you are so tired. You drove a hundred miles. You had a flat tyre. You did a show. You are so tired. You are so tired you stop listening to the drunks in the street calling out your name. You are too tired to be frightened when they break their beer bottles in the gutter and call out filthy things about the body you showed to them. So you go to sleep and you wake up at four in the morning because it is market day and the cattle are bellowing outside and you have scratched yourself all over and you will have to do the show with make-up all over your body and who will pay for the make-up? Lenny, you tell her."

"You do," Lenny said.

"So you wake up and you look at your face and it is getting a line, just here." She put a fingernail, light and sharp as a surgeon's scalpel, against the edge of Leah's mouth. "And you think how much nicer it would be to be a doctor and what a fool you were to ever listen to a bored old woman telling her sentimental stories."

"Oh, Rosa, you won't listen to me. I don't want to be a doctor. I want to be a dancer."

"A dancer, yes. The Tivoli. Her Majesty's. Even Romano's. But not Mervyn Sullivan on the road. He is such a wolf and poor little Izzie in Sydney half mad with jealousy. I thought you would marry him."

"Oh, Rosa."

"Marry him," Rosa said, hugging her fiercely. "Marry him. Stay here with us, Leah."

285

Lenny stretched out his hand across the table. He knocked the ashtray and broke the careful line of calculated butts. He took Leah's hand and held it hard.

"Stay, Leah."

Leah wept. She felt such a rush, such a huge upsurge of both happiness and misery that she was overwhelmed by something close to ecstasy. At that moment, in that rocking caravan, she would feel, she imagined, all the pain and happiness in the world, and she wept, nearly drowning. It was the last time she was so young.

26

The ructions in her own family were predictable but abated after the first flurry of telegrams (TOO UPSET TOO UNWELL TO WRITE LIFE IS A BARREN FIELD LOVE FATHER).

Leah wrote a long and detailed letter in which she introduced the Kaletskys, one by one, and explained her motives for both of her seemingly precipitous actions. With this careful testament to his daughter's seriousness in his hands, Sid Goldstein ceased his melodramatic telegrams and wrote a long letter.

Leah treasured this letter for years, and not merely because the flowery copperplate hand seemed more considered than usual, but for the whole list of good advice it contained, i.e., Read if you can. Keep your mind alert. To describe the towns you visit will be a good exercise and train you in much more than English composition. It will encourage a critical frame of mind – to describe an object is to ask why the object is shaped the way it is. Likewise a horse, a building or a nose. All this will be good for you, whatever you do. I will not insult you by offering money, but if trouble strikes please be assured that your parents are always here and here to help you. I send my kindest regards and best wishes to your husband and hope some time we shall have the pleasure of meeting this young man.

The whole of this letter, by the by, was a masterful piece of deception. Sid Goldstein was depressed, miserable and unhappy but considered, wisely, that venting spleen on his daughter would merely drive her from him. One gets a whiff of the real state of his emotions in the irritable PS: "I cannot see",

286

he wrote in broader, fatter strokes, "how you can possibly have betrayed Wysbraum. Are you thinking of the rooming house he rushed you into?"

27

The eccentrically spelt letters are all, I suppose, gone now – stranded in drawers with perished rubber bands and verdigrised door keys as companions, or have – worse – become the accumulated capital of fastidious great-nieces who marvel at the time you could send a letter for tuppence and regret – having consulted a stamp dealer on the subject – that their great-aunt did not treat the perforations of her stamps with more respect. She was not like Rosa who tore corners off and stood the King on his head, but she did not treat the perforations with the care her crabbed handwriting led one to expect.

The great-nieces would do well to examine the dates on the stamps: the badly torn perforations are from winter in Victoria – their dancing great-aunt had chilblains on her pretty hands.

Following her father's instructions, Leah managed to forget who it was she was writing to. She lost sight of his mournful eyes, his prim mouth, his watery silence, his fear of discord. She wrote things in her letters she would never have dreamed of saying to his face and, as a result, he also wrote things that he would have considered previously unthinkable. He began to use words with a recklessness quite foreign to his speech. I do not mean that he used words incorrectly or inaccurately – he remained, to his death, a pedant – but that he did not stint himself in the quantity of words and this is attested by the increasing value of the stamps on his long manila envelopes and the rare black one- shilling Kookaburra is directly attributable to this new garrulousness.

Sid Goldstein filled page after page with an often disjointed but touchingly vulnerable inquisition into the nature of his life, his business, the depressed economy and, at last, his Jewishness. "It is not enough for you to say that it might be 'useful' or 'comforting' or that you feel a fool not knowing the simplest Yiddish word or are an outsider when you sit at Passover. Technically speaking you are not a Jew anyway because your mother is not a Jew. You do not show concern for the important issue, which is whether there is a god or not, and if there is a god if he is likely to behave as the God of the Jews is reported to. Obviously I have made my decision as best I can." They discussed the secular state. Leah spoke favourably of Marx, Sid unfavourably of communists he had known, saying that they were men who appeared to have left no room in their lives for kindness. Leah replied with a passion. Her father wrote of Russian anti-Semitism revealed in the indignities of life in Minsk. All the while they described for each other's eyes the more ordinary stuff of life: thistles by a roadside, a man playing a saxophone on a crowded bus.

The postmarks of Leah's letters show the progress of Mervyn Sullivan's Chevrolet. They dip down towards Bateman's Bay, halt, lose courage, and the next day they have crossed the mountains and materialized in Yass. Albury must have been successful for there are many letters to and from Albury Post Office, even a rare letter from Izzie in his distinctive loopy hand: vast tails to the "y"s and "g"s that tangle with words two lines beneath, long crosses to the "t"s that fling themselves emphatically beneath the line above, appearing to underline, to add emphasis where none was intended, with the result that to read his short letters is a stuttering process, a series of misunderstandings, halts, clarifications.

But it is not this that makes Izzie's letters so frustrating to read. It is because he never once talks about the things that are on his mind. He forgives his wife for something we will come to in a minute but which he does not dwell on, will not even touch. The words are plain, short, hurried: a man cooking without benefit of a pot holder, and they become more understandable when you realize what he is replying to.

Here, in this note from Shepparton: "I have done it again," she confesses. "I would not be your wife if I could not tell you. I would be a cheat and a liar, not merely unfaithful."

The longer she is away from him, the more her idealization of him continues. She thinks of him as "a good person, absolutely GOOD; it is for this reason that I love you and will never love anyone else. I am proud of you, my darling Izzie. When I see men humping their swags along these dusty roads I know that at least one of us is doing something useful. I love you."

Four times he jumped the rattler, his knuckles bleeding from punching walls. Twice he found her, once in Benalla, as the truck pulled out, and, again, in Shepparton where they spent a night as tearful as their wedding night, taunted by the watery ghost of

Mervyn Sullivan who winked at Izzie lewdly at breakfast and asked him how old he was.

He could not tell her. He was not brave enough to tell her. She put such weight on his goodness and usefulness, that he could not tell her what had happened to him, that he, like his mother before him, had been expelled by the Communist Party of Australia.

28

The committee of the NSW branch of the Communist Party were, with a single exception, decent men and women. They were embarrassed that they could not yet produce evidence to back up their charges, but they had no doubt that the evidence existed. They been advised of its existence by none other than the Comintern.

To understand the effect of this upon them, you must realize that they often imagined that the Comintern had forgotten that the Party ever existed in Australia. Certainly it was not in the habit of displaying an interest in individual comrades. So when they were advised that the Australian I. Kaletsky had indulged in activities against the revolution, they not only believed it, but were sure that the activities must be particularly serious.

It was a misunderstanding and it came to play an important part in Izzie's life, to be, for months, *the* business of his life. And in this he was supported by his mother.

"Fight them," she said. "If you accept it, you will always be sorry. What have you done? What have you said? Don't shake your head. There is always something."

He became like a fellow who has been sold an unsatisfactory Vauxhall who will stand in front of the town hall with his whole sad story written on a blackboard. He attacked, buttonholed, angered and confused any comrade who would listen to him. There was a stage, in August 1931, when the CPA headquarters in Sussex Street had its door locked for weeks on end and it was necessary to knock out a code to gain entrance. This was not as a precaution against fascists or Australian Intelligence but against Izzie Kaletsky who would not give up.

He wrote letters to the *Tribune* which were never published and to the Comintern which were opened by Intelligence and copied by hand before they were sent on their slow way by ship across the world.

Izzie changed that year, like a man who has been tortured and who, walking down the street amidst his fellows, shows no crude scars or telling limp – merely a weariness in his smile which sometimes gave the impression that his lip had curled.

He tried to live off the money Leah sent him. But just the same, when de Groot cut the ribbon on the Sydney Harbour Bridge, Izzie and Lenny were there selling bright balloons.

"Buy a balloon," Leah's husband said, "buy a balloon."

29

Both Leah Goldstein and my son seemed to have interpreted my disappearing as a clever stunt which might be useful. They did not tremble on the edge of an abyss, or question the substantiality of matter. Leah began to sew spangles on my suit and Charles tried, belligerently, to disappear in class before the incredulous eyes of Mr Barry Edwards and twenty-eight children who suddenly erupted into wild hooting and cat-calling when Charles Badgery stood in such a queer way.

Mr Barry Edwards giggled, even while he strapped my son's winter-white legs.

The red weals of pain were still there later as my son continued his obsessive game with his sister, near the camp. He tugged at his odd socks (one bright blue, the other overchecked with brown diamonds) but the socks would not stay up. They fell, and revealed the marks of Mr Edwards's handiwork.

"I need garters," he announced.

"What are garters?"

"Hold your socks up."

My son is stubborn. He has always been stubborn. If the milky poison – that curdling creamy stuff in the whisky bottle that the actress procured in Carlton – could not budge him from his mother's womb, then neither could Barry Edwards's strap change his mind. He decided on garters, firstly to hide his marks from me, to stop me discovering that he had been playing the game he was forbidden; but also because it seemed to him – quite suddenly, but very clearly – that they were the ingredient he lacked. As a grown man he would have the same attitude towards electronic equipment, hi-fi, ham radio, things in black boxes with dainty buttons, glowing dials, esoteric wiring diagrams and languages of their own, as if these products and their associated rituals would somehow bring about the changes he wanted in his life.

It was getting dark and the air was dank like a stone church with a defective damp course. The crows mourned above the darkening waters of Crab Apple Creek and Charles slashed at the tall column of a blackwood wattle with a heavy stick.

He was thinking about garters, about how perfect it would be to have his socks held neatly on his chubby calves. His sister watched him. She wanted to know about garters and how they worked. He stopped to explain it to her, with a solemnity that made the simple gadgets fittingly mysterious. He pulled up his socks again and folded them over an inch from the top.

"When you do that," he said, "it hides the garters."

Sonia knew he was mistaken about the garters, but she could not tell him. Unlike Charles, who saw new opportunities for escape, revenge, triumph and – most of all – making money, Sonia knew that this was not a trick. Her child's fingers had silently questioned my skin, hugged my heavy thigh, or held the fob watch that had disappeared with me, looking inquiringly at its coded face.

"If you disappear," she asked her garter-worshipping brother, "where do you go?"

"Nowhere," Charles said, hitting the tree. "You're just invisible."

Goon Tse Ying's dragon was not a great scaly monster that any fool could see. It was a tiny thing, a thread, a slippery worm. It had entered my daughter without me even glimpsing it. It slunk into her viscera and lodged there.

"You go to heaven", she whispered, "and see Jesus."

"Bullswack."

"*You* can't do it."

"I can. I can. If you help me, please, Sonny."

"No."

"Pur-leeese." Charles put his big arm around his sister; it was a wooden hug carved from Mallee root, the big head grotesquely askew, pleading gracelessly. "You take the stick," he said, putting it across her pleated lap and folding her little hands around it. "And you run at me, and say Ching Chong Chinaman."

"I won't."

291

"And hit me," Charles said, "hard."

"No," she said, and moved away from the stick which dropped to the ground.

"What do you pray?" asked ingratiating Charles.

Sonia said nothing.

"I need garters," Charles said firmly, and with that settled strode on ahead of his sister, leaving her to hurry through the last light towards the little hessian humpy I had made for Leah Goldstein who was now busy sewing spangles on to my best suit coat and arguing with me about the write-up I had got for her in the paper.

"It's all lies, Mr Badgery," she said, threading one more spangle on to her relentless needle. "I have never been to Gay Paree, as you call it. I will not dance with a death adder, not in any circumstances. And it says nothing about you and your act which you were so desperate to impress me with."

I watched the spangles unhappily and saw that I had not, as I believed I had, delivered value to her. It was a first-class write-up in anybody's language.

I tried to explain the nature of publicity to her. She listened to me patiently enough. I explained how I had been written up in papers everywhere and that a good editor expected a little exaggeration – the colours strengthened, so to speak. And it was my understanding of this that had allowed me to get a page-one write-up for her when she had been unable to get any. No one at the paper had ever heard of Mervyn Sullivan but everyone in Bendigo would now know about Leah Leonda, as I had called her.

"Well," she said, holding up the suit coat critically to the kerosene light. "I don't want to have a barney with you, Mr Badgery. You've been very kind. But if I can't do a show honestly I don't want to do a show at all. It's a good show. It's not like some old-fashioned aeroplane that you're ashamed of, no offence. I don't need to tell lies. We did ten shows in Myrniong. We got everybody in town, and some of them twice. And now we've got your act, Mr Badgery, which is really breathtaking. I think you underestimate the effect of your own act."

The aim of the write-up had been to make my so-called act unnecessary, but she was too flinty-faced to tell the truth to. I opened my mouth. I was prepared to begin a truthful sentence and not worry where I ended up, but my son barged through the doorway, demanding garters.

I told him there would be no garters but Leah, sitting on the bed I had made for her (hessian stretched across two wattle poles) had already produced some black elastic from her small cane sewing box.

Charles did not dare look at me. His lower lip went all plump, like a cherub, and he went and sat beside Leah while Sonia came and squatted beside me, hugging my calf and questioning my shoelaces.

30

Charles oiled the snakes as he was instructed and took them, one at a time, so they might attend to matters of toilet. The snake is a neat creature, and most fastidious about where it drops its shit. My son took them to a grassy patch and waited while they extruded their firm dark pellets. From time to time he adjusted his socks and examined the curious red patterns the garters made on his legs.

Sonia washed our dishes in the creek and managed not to break anything. She rubbed the greasy plates with river sand while Leah cleaned her single gramophone record with petrol and soft cloth. She did various exercises and displayed the emu feathers to the sunshine.

And I put on my spangled suit coat and was much admired.

The magpies chortled merrily, their feathers clean, and I was like one of those ageing farmers, Gus Housey comes to mind, who get behind the wheel of a motor car for the first time and know, before they do a thing, that they will crash. They hold the wheel rigidly. They stare ahead defiantly. They release the clutch with the jerk of someone who must get a nasty business done with. They give off the smell of men who are victims of their own excessive pride and now must pay the price. Their eyes seek out fences or trees and you cannot triumph over them in any wrestle for the wheel.

"There is population in this town," Leah told me, "and there is money, and we are not leaving until we have shown them what we can do."

Anticipating disaster, I persuaded my partner to let me negotiate a suitable venue for our première.

31

I have heard people describe Bendigo as a country town. They mention it in the same breath as Shepparton or Ararat. These people have never been to Bendigo and don't know what they're talking about. The Town Hall is the equal of anything in Florence; the Law Courts would not look frumpish in Versailles. And if there are farmers in the streets, dark cafés with three courses for two and sixpence and, in Hayes Street, a Co-op dedicated to Norfield Wire Strainers and Cattle Drench, it does not alter the fact that Bendigo is a town of the Gold Age. If cattle are driven through the streets on the way to the ammoniacal sale-yards it does not make the streets less grand, does not diminish their width by as much as half a chain, and even the bellowing cattle must see, if not understand, the great white fountain near the Kerang turn-off that promised (and promises still, for all I know) a return to days when men would once again build solicitors' offices like wedding cakes and put towers on hotels and art schools alike. One could ignore, as I had chosen to, as the townspeople tried to, the men with cardboard tied to the bottom of their shoes who shuffled through the town with billycans clanking and sugar bags tied across their bent shoulders.

There was no shortage of good venues for a variety act. For instance, there was a great big place near the Town Hall (gone now) that had a great circular upstairs gallery, electrically operated curtains, and a bank of lights which the caretaker, a newsagent and cricket fanatic named Perry Thomassen, was at great pains to show me, but not before he had demonstrated the correct wrist action for a googly and told me that he had been on the wireless, in a sporting quiz, in Melbourne. He was a lanky stooped fellow and too clumsy to be trusted with a cricket bat, let alone the fifty-foot ladder he mounted to demonstrate the spots, dimmer and floods. He got his pigeon toes tangled in the rungs and dropped pennies from his pockets while he recited the names of the men who made Australia the greatest sporting nation in the world. So keen was he to establish his case that he added Dame Nellie Melba and Mo McCaughey to his list, the point being (I think) that both of them had performed in this very hall. He was promising to show me Mo's braces (left behind in a dressing room in amusing circumstances) when I slipped quietly out into the street. I had no intention of making an idiot of myself in such a central location. Instead I booked the little wooden Mechanics' Institute in a laneway behind the back entrance to the Catholic Seminary. I got the place for two bob but had to sign a piece of paper saying I· would not hold a political meeting.

I had to tell lies, of course, to explain this miserable location to Leah, but she was naïve about halls at this stage of her career, never having had to hire one herself.

So there I was, at seven o'clock of a rainy night, shivering before the fly-spotted mirror while spiders kept on at their business on the bare tin roof above my head.

Leah made tea and talked to me softly about stage fright, but it was not stage fright that was the point at all: if the business in hand had been juggling or card tricks, I would have been in my element. I would have enjoyed those spangles and thought them my right for they provided an aura no less dazzling than the one that surrounded me when I walked down Ryrie Street in Geelong with my dreams intact and a Shaftesbury Patented Umbrella in my hand.

32

Charles marched before the gaping entrance, squeaking back and forth on his brand-new boots, clicking on steel toecaps, clacking at the heels, his garters itchy-tight around his wounded calves, his short tweed trousers rubbing at the knee, his jacket buttoned tight below his jutting chin, his hair parted with a knife edge and held flat with shining oil, his button eyes afire with dragon light.

Before him he held a jam tin. He jangled it – prouder than a blackboard monitor – jiggled the eleven separate shillings up and down and was pleased (triumphant) that the audience contained his hateful teacher and giggling strapper, Mr Barry Edwards Esq. who was known to grown-ups, it seemed, as 'A-plus-B'.

So Charles marched before that door waiting for his revenge or, at least, his vindication. His bald-headed father would soon arrange himself in the style that Barry Edwards had mocked, had compared to both standard lamp and ballerina.

The walls and ceiling of the little hall were lined with tongue-and-groove boards that had been, mistakenly, coated with kalsomine. Along each wall some well-intentioned person had placed coloured light globes (blue, yellow, green) at six-foot intervals, just below the empty picture rail.

In this evil light the eleven paying customers, all great supporters of Douglas Credit, all from the one bar of the Shamrock Hotel, hawked and spat and conversed in echoing voices about the banner for the Eaglehawk Bowling Club which, having been left behind five years before, now billowed in the draughts above the proscenium arch.

Sonia stood on a chair in a kitchen, her hand already on the heavy brass switch that would soon plunge the hall into darkness while her father transported himself, she had no doubts, into the arms of Jesus Christ Himself. She took her hand from the switch and pressed it against her arm, nervously assuring herself of her own solidity.

Leah had wrapped herself in a moth-eaten red robe which covered her emu feathers in a lumpy sort of fashion. She shivered. She rubbed her legs. It was not cold. She jumped up and down and declared that she was petrified, that she hated this life, that she would vomit any moment. A huge flake of silver paint detached itself from her shoe and revealed a bright red slash, like a wound.

"Please, Mr Badgery," she said. "Don't let me down." And went on stage, before I had a chance to make an escape. I sat hunched on my chair. I saw the back of her cloak disappear around the corner of the tea urn, and then she was on stage, making a very formal speech. Her voice was a tight-stretched mirror of anxiety as she publicly confessed the lies I had persuaded the newspaper to print. This unexpected piece of entertainment fell, shivering, in spooky silence: there were to be no death adders, no Gay Paree. They shuffled their boots. Charles clicked his money together apprehensively.

"But", the snake-dancer said (Charles' boots creaked), "I am one hell of a dancer."

There was applause.

"And I will dance with venomous snakes. I will dance with two red-bellied black snakes and also a python big enough to choke a grown man. But if this is not enough, you can have your money back now."

Charles held his jam tin very still, but he need not have worried:

no one wanted their money back. Someone wanted a drink. Someone else wanted to see Leah's legs. They were in a good mood and did not complain about the leaking roof.

"But," Leah said, and her voice was suddenly sleek, groomed on the oil of their approbation. "But", she said, "there is more." She was so confident about my act I could not bear to listen to her. I plugged my ears and sucked in my breath. I stood up. Sonia smiled at me. She jumped down from her chair and kissed me on the hand, then jumped again to stand guard beside that dreadful switch which was to put me in the centre of attention.

Leah finished singing my praises. The applause was strong and riveted with whistles. I began my walk towards the stage. On the steps: Leah, pink, glowing. She patted my bald head and I got a laugh as I stumbled (missing floorboard) on to the dusty stage.

And there I stood.

I stood there for a long time without doing anything. Neither did the audience. We regarded each other. I blinked and peered miserably into the gloom.

Charles creaked at the back of the hall and it was for him that I arranged myself in the position for summoning dragons, the foot on knee, the stretched hand, etc. It was, I stress, merely the position, nothing more, as harmless as an unarmed grenade.

"Badgery," roared Barry Edwards in the dark. I peered out at him. "I swear it must be a Badgery."

The hall tittered. Charles's boots creaked in anticipation of a delicious revenge. His dragon stretched itself.

"Ha ha," said A-plus-B, "Two ballerinas, two lampstands. Not one, but two."

"Shut up, A-plus-B," a woman hissed. "We come for his show, not yours."

"Sorry, Kathleen," said brown-voiced Edwards. "A million pardons but I thought you come for the beer."

This was considered funny. They laughed for a while and when they had finished I was still standing there. I shut my eyes.

"God help us, he's gone to sleep."

I opened them.

"He's awake," they shrilled, "he's awake."

There was a rush of feathers and I received a clip across the head and a push in the back. I fell, heavily. A four-letter word escaped but was stamped to death by the hooting, squealing audience.

There was an emu dancing over me. It lifted its net-stockinged legs high. It stamped on my hands and on my legs. I retreated, crawling, but did not escape the final indignity – a simulated peck on my dusty backside.

"Get off," the emu hissed, putting on the gramophone with its beak.

"Get off," the mob echoed joyfully, for no matter what faults the Bendigo Mechanics' Institute may have had, bad accoustics could not be numbered amongst them.

"Oh God," roared A-plus-B, "God save me, this is wonderful."

Charles opened his mouth in pain.

My son gripped his hands together and was given coiled visions of revenge no less luminous than Sonia's angelic hosts who fluttered in her mind's eyes, as disturbed as pigeons who find their coop door boarded shut.

I crawled off the stage and left the show to Leah Goldstein. My daughter came down off her chair and held my hand, but I did not want the shy sympathy of children, not that my son offered any. He would not even look at me. He put his precious jam tin on the kitchen sink and sat on the stairs where he could adore Leah without obstruction.

The Emu Dance was a great success. When the emu chick hatched they applauded the cleverness (Charles also, noisily). When she did the Veil Dance even the woman whistled her (Charles stamped). The tap was a triumph and when she returned for the great finale, the Snake Dance, the hall was as quiet and vibrant as a shiver.

My bleeding hands curled into fists and I could have punched the dancer on her little parrot's nose. I was far too jealous to watch her, and thus missed the moment when it started to go wrong. Perhaps, as I have seen her do, she held a clutch of assorted snakes in her hands and let them drop on to her head. It was called the Shower of Snakes. In any case, she attempted too much for the credulity of the big-voiced woman who asserted, loudly, that the serpents had obviously been defanged, their poison sacs removed and that fraud was being openly committed on stage. This was not, in itself, what stopped the show and Leah did not, as she often did later, make a simple speech about the technical difficulties of either defanging or removing poison sacs. She could explain the operation required with scientific precision and point out the adverse affect on the health and happiness of the snake. What did stop the show was A-plus-B's footnote to the charge of fraud and this was made *sotto voce*, beneath his hand, under his beard. I did not hear the complete sentence, but heard him say "three by two" which is, in case you did not know it, rhyming slang.

The arm of the gramophone dredged a painful channel across "The Blue Danube" and left a repeating click which was to accompany Leah's dancing for many months to come.

Leah, shivering in a harem suit, decked in gauze and goose-pimples, stood with hands on her hips, her head thrust forwards, trembling. She ordered the lights turned on and singled out the man with the large black beard who seemed not the least perturbed by becoming the focus of attention. He folded his hands complacently in his lap and chewed his large moustache.

"I heard you," said Leah Goldstein, "and I heard your name."

"What if you did?" said the big-voiced woman now revealed to be quite tiny, weathered and shrunken like an old iris bulb. She had a fox-stole round her shoulders and a large fur hat jammed over her head. "What diff does it make what he said? The point is, Jew or no Jew, their sacs are gone." She nudged her bearded companion with her sharp elbow. "Jew or no Jew," she said to A-plus-B, "what's the diff?"

There were dragons breeding in that hall: they cloaked their activities in the smell of stale orange peel and leaking gas, and Leah, getting a whiff of it, felt her guts knot hard.

"There is no '*diff*', Kathleen," said the ironic pedagogue, "until she starts to make money under false pretences. Then", he smiled at the shivering dancer, "it means everything. Here we have, in Bendigo, a perfect illustration of the world financial crisis. You, madam", he told Leah Goldstein, "are a cartoon."

"Your name is A-plus-B," said Leah.

"Correct weight," said the woman. "What's his birthday?"

"Shut up, Kath," said an equally weathered man in grey overalls who was sitting at the back of the hall. "You've had a fair innings."

"They call you A-plus-B because you believe in Douglas Credit. It's a fraud," said Leah Goldstein, launching into a five-minute attack on the whole system of Douglas Credit, the history of which she briefly provided, with special emphasis on its derivation from Social Credit from which system it had excluded all radical and humanitarian aspects. Further, she implied,

Douglas Credit was a breeding ground for fascists, Jew-haters, and worse, the central algebraic proof of its feasibility (in which A-plus-B plays a central role) was a trick, a fraud more serious than anything to do with snakes and poison sacs. "You can't even add up," she said, in conclusion.

"Spoken like a Jew," said A-plus-B. "Always adding up", he said, "and subtracting."

"Substracting," hollered fur-hatted Kathleen. "Very good."

"Shut up, Kath," said the man in grey overalls. "You're pissed."

"Subtraction," said A-plus-B, "as in cheating."

"Address yourself to the question," shrieked Leah.

"Shut up, Kath," said the man up the back, and fell off his chair.

"I'm a Jew all right," said Leah. She summoned Charles to her side (the first time he ever walked the boards). She whispered in his bright red ear. He returned with the jam tin of money. Leah took the tin and emptied all eleven shillings into the canvas snake bag. Then she took the two remaining black snakes, who had remained gently entwined around their mistress's warm body during the entire argument, and lowered them with their fellows. "I'm a Jew all right. I don't take money from fascists." She was having trouble speaking and I, who minutes before had wanted to punch her on her lovely nose, felt nothing but admiration for her courage. She, who could be so lithe and sensuous, stood in her harem suit, skinny, trembling, small-breasted, no longer in control of the shape of her normally austere lower lip.

Barry Edwards, previously flustered by a philosophically literate snake-dancer, could now smile confidently. He was blessed with a bully's subtle sensitivity – he was taking his cues from her voice. He was not thinking about the snakes which were now being carried towards him by Charles Badgery who felt then, that night, the shiver of power of a snake-handler. He would feel it all his life, but never so intensely, so exquisitely, as now, as his warty hand goes into the bag, glides sweetly past the sleeping python, in amongst the black-snake coils, smelling like a friend. The grubby little hand finds a shilling and holds it up to A-plus-B.

His garters itch, a pleasant feeling, providing the sweet anticipation of a gentle scratch.

Barry Edwards's hands reach out, greedy for the shilling, are nearly there, the nicotine-stained pincers, when Charles (you little bastard!) drops the shilling back into the sack.

How sweet my little son looked on that night. How angelic was his smile as he looked at his teacher's thoughtful face.

No one else would put their hand into the sack. Charles was enjoying himself, could have prolonged his little pantomime for minutes, hours; but Leah screamed at him to give the man his shilling; which he did. People scraped their chairs across the floor and gathered coats. They swarmed, moved erratically towards the door and back to where Barry Edwards remained stubbornly in his chair.

So Charles began to lay his pretty snakes at Barry Edwards's feet. He held the little black snake and showed its oil-glistening red belly and its smooth little head. He let it crawl around his neck and then he placed it on the floor like a child playing with a moulded-lead toy car. He pointed it carefully towards Edwards's odd scuffed shoes and watched as the aforesaid shoes moved themselves, one after the other, towards the door.

Imagine the Mechanics' Institute as a box of yellow wood with cold sickly light globes like a necklace around its picture rail. Arranged at random, pointing this way and that: some wooden chairs. In their midst: a jut-jawed child in short pants, playing with a red-bellied black snake, cooing to it on the floor.

33

We were magicians that night. We made futures and summoned up pasts. We sent up flares loaded with words that spewed like broken glass across the sky, and I knew the dancer so little I imagined this normal.

It was, my God, like Halley's Comet – for Leah to loosen her tongue and talk for the pleasure of it (lolly-paper talk) fifteen different factors must all coincide and I will list just eight of them.

1 A dancer's walk.
2 Danger overcome.
3 McWilliams Autumn Brown Sherry or equivalent.
4 Her correspondence fully up to date.
5 No uncertainties threatening, i.e., no camp to shift, or new hall to hire.
6 Puddles dry and mud absent.
7 No sickness in camp.
8 Her mood itchy, but not scratchy.

The style of discourse she favoured when these conditions were satisfied was totally unrelated to her normal approach which was as functional as a hacksaw. You could hardly call it flowery but it did leave room for sentimentality and whimsy and was fuelled by both optimism and remorse.

So when she summonsed up Izzie I swear I saw him stand before me on the skirts of shadow round the fire, his big eyes wet with hurt, his pointy toes kicking moodily at a fat fleshy thistle whose obstinate root would not leave the soil.

He was the Good Man.

There were, as yet, no shades of grey in Leah's mental menagerie, and Mervyn Sullivan was summonsed up to be the Evil Man. She could not bring herself to say exactly what she meant, but made herself so clear that I could feel I was lying in bed with him too, looking at his false watery mask while his prick gave odd vibrations to my perfect hatred and I grew breasts to press against his broad hair-matted chest and sharp nails to dig into his buttocks. She had Good and Evil, Strength and Weakness, had them paired and opposed in such a tangle that I grew giddy following her.

I paraded Jack and Molly, and displayed the Parrot Poem. I listened, light-headed, while she demolished Phoebe before my eyes, pulled her to pieces like a cheap celluloid doll, flung her arms into the blackberries and her hair into the fire.

"She made the cage," I was informed. "She was a spoiled brat."

The smoke from the fire was pleasantly intoxicating. I hastened to find a few favourable things to present in favour of my missing wife. I made a few fast lies, jerry-built things with bright colours and badly fitting lids. I talked aeroplanes and motor cars, all the Australian products that had begun so brightly. When I talked about these failures, Leah told me later, they sounded like little swallows that had fallen from their nests and died.

She showed me her father's suit, Wysbraum's red lips and broad bum, the white scalp beneath Rosa's hair, and that splendid canvas, that huge complicated composition of moulded grey forms that Marx made, which she at once admired but could not bring herself to enter.

I was not quite so frank. I was (as Leah said later) "secretive". I made no confessions of electric belts although the battery hung heavily on my leg; nor did I talk of ghosts and snakes.

"I did not like you, Mr Badgery," Leah said, beneath the vast star-powdered sky, "until you did your act."

"I did not like you, Miss Goldstein, until you finished yours."

"God, you were funny, Mr Badgery." She snapped a gum twig happily and threw it on the fire. "You should have seen yourself."

I made a mud map in the dark.

She said: "I thought you were a spiv, excuse me; but when I saw you on the stage I changed my mind."

I asked her why, and for once she was not interested in teasing the greasy hairs of reality apart to find The Truth.

"I dunno," she said. "I did. Excuse me, I can't see your face. Come and sit over here."

I went and sat beside her on the log. She grinned at me in the dark. "I was nearly a doctor," she said.

"Fair dinkum?"

"Dinky-die. Pass the bottle. I'm very partial to this stuff. It's not good for you. Nothing's good for you, nothing nice," getting down to the core of her problem. "How old are you, Mr Badgery?"

"Forty," I lied.

"I'm twenty-four," she lied.

And yes, I know I promised there would be no hanky-panky, but that was a lie as well.

"I'm partial to a number of things," she whispered, on the log, by the camp fire, at Crab Apple Creek.

"I'm a bit partial myself," I said.

"I'm very partial," she said, "but for God's sake, be careful."

34

Dear Izzie, she wrote, I love you and miss you. I have done it, again, and I detest myself. There is no point in my lying about it. I must tell you and you must forgive me if you can. I have also said things about you to strangers which I should not have said and did not mean. You are the only man I ever cared about or respected. You believe what I believe. You stand for what I stand for. You are brave and good and I send you letters that cause you pain.

I dreamed about you two nights ago. You were in an odd black suit with belled cuffs and you were weeping. When I tried to comfort you, you did not know who I was and I woke up crying myself.

Anyway, here is a money order. It is less than it should be because I wasted four shillings on wine. Izzie, one day we will be like ordinary people. We will have a house and a baby with big black eyes and Rosa and Lenny will play with it. I am frightened of everything. Everything seems dark and ignorant. I try to read the Gramsci but am so tired. My mind is rusted and full of rubbish. Please be careful. I am sending you a map of the camp site as usual so if your work calls you this way, you could find me. DO NOT MAKE A SPECIAL TRIP. It is only in case you are doing Party work in the area. Will be in Bendigo some days yet I imagine.

Your loving wife,

Leah

35

The flesh of the morning was pink and tasted of mud like a rainbow trout, and I was the Prince of the Bedroom, the King of Liars. The urge to build was on me already and I looked at the world through imaginary windows and possible doorways. Leah snored in her palace and I hardly saw my children, although I must have dressed them, inspected their shoes, their socks, their nails, parted Charles's hair and retied the ribbons on Sonia's plaits.

I remember nothing of driving them to school. I was under the illusion that it was my day; it was really my son's. On this day, the 23rd September 1931, he added the final card to his hand and climbed a giant eucalypt and carried down a yellow-tailed black cockatoo. Expressed thus, it sounds easy. But this is not your sulphur-crested cockatoo, often caught, usually caged, taught to speak Pet's Lingo. This is the giant cockatoo sometimes called funereal, and if you have ever watched these monsters ripping branches to pieces, seen them screeching at the top of river casuarinas, or seen, at close range, their odd faces (more like a devil's koala than a bird) then you would know, without being told, this is not an easy bird to catch or tame.

He did not choose it. He was driven to it by Barry Edwards's sarcastic comments when the birds were observed above the schoolyard. Badgery was good with animals, he said, and would bring them down a cockatoo.

My son had warts and smelly breath, but he was not a fool. He knew there was no choice but to up the ante in this game with his teacher. Having driven him out with snakes he would shame him with a cockatoo.

The cockatoo, therefore, was a means, not an end, an instrument of revenge, a card in a game, but yet, when Charles was finally eighty feet above the ground, wrapping his useful bandy legs around the rough-barked eucalypt, edging carefully out towards his goal, he had forgotten what it was an instrument for; he began to coo.

He swung in the high branches above the schoolyard where Sonia stood, with all the school – it was now recess – whispering eccentric self-taught prayers to Sweet Jesus Meek and Mine.

The headmaster was yelling at Mr Edwards and Mr Edwards was biting his moustache and trying to get the headmaster to yell at him in private but the headmaster ordered Miss Watkins to ring the fire brigade and then he could not wait, and – he was a young man – tried to climb the tree himself but tore his Fletcher Jones trousers and showed his bottom and Miss Watkins took the girls to practise assembly drill in front of the shelter shed.

The fuss in the playground hardly intruded on Charles's consciousness, for he was blessed with very particular powers of concentration. The commotion below merely warmed him as he moved closer to communion with the dark brown eye with its delicate pink surround. My son had a great store of affection he could not give to people properly; he just didn't have the knack. He could not hug his little sister without awkwardness, but when he confronted this steel-beaked bird his affection issued from him readily, like a net, a finely knotted gauze which the bird felt and stayed still to accept. As he took the bird it emitted a small noise, not the loud raucous noise of a yellow-tailed black cockatoo, but a small grizzle, like a new puppy will give, as it surrendered itself to the webs of Charles's affection.

Charles descended, to applause, down the ladders of the Bendigo Volunteer Fire Brigade and into the anxious care of Barry Edwards who gave him no trouble – quite the opposite – from that day. In class that afternoon he sat with the cockatoo who, having entered an alien universe, was ministered to as a royal guest, was brought gifts of hakea pods and pine cones, was permitted to screech and shit, and was thus given the illusion that it was a god, being waited on by superstitious savages.

36

I was in an excellent mood. I called in at the tip and found good roof guttering awaiting me. On my way back to camp I nicked twenty foot of fencing wire from the bottom string of a squatter's fence. I never bought a nail in my life and I never understood why anyone would bother when there are millions of miles of fencing wire available to do the job. Eight gauge is best. Cut it square one end, angle it at the other, and there's your nail.

I drove back to the camp constructing towers with pretty windows.

I parked the Dodge and noticed Leah was boiling something up in a four-gallon drum. She did not look up to greet me and, imagining she was washing her female particulars, I did not intrude. Instead I busied myself with the guttering and the fencing wire. When Leah spoke she was right behind me. She made me jump.

"One," she said, "I was drunk. Two, it won't happen again. Three, I don't love you."

I covered my confusion by dropping the rest of the guttering on the ground.

"Did you hear me?" she asked.

"I heard you."

"Good," she said, and walked back to the fire where she was – I discovered later – punishing her overcoat by boiling it.

I fiddled with the fencing wire for a bit, making a few nails to start with. I like making things. It is always soothing, and the very simple things are the most soothing of all. The squatter's wire felt as soft as lead between my pliers. I made three-inch nails, each one exactly the same as the one before.

"What are you doing?"

"Making nails."

"This camp is filthy," she said (untrue). "Your truck is filthy. I don't know how you live like this. Come on, move. Move your nails. Help me with the mattress. How long is it since you aired it? How long is it since you washed your children's clothes? Orange peel!"

She emptied the back tray of the Dodge and started scrubbing. I took the guttering over to her hut. I fetched an empty petrol drum to stand on and began to measure for the gutter. In a minute she was behind me with her wet arms folded across her breasts. Her neck seemed longer, stretched, her shoulders more sloping, her eyes larger.

"Excuse me, what are you doing?"

"Fixing up."

"You sleep with me once and you think you own me."

"No." If you had seen her once you would know that she could not be owned. "Just making a place."

306

"This is *not* your place and never can be."

I recognized the tone. This was not lolly-paper talk. It was hacksaw stuff, the annoying tone with which she had entered camp.

"It is public land," I said. "It's a reserve, and if I take out a mining lease I'm entitled to build a hut here, providing I continue to demonstrate that I am actually working my lease."

"There you go, land–house, house–land, you can't help yourself, can you, Mr Badgery? You're true blue. Dinky-di. You think you can put up some shanty and that makes it your place, but you can't, and it never will be. Are you listening to me?"

I did not want to lose my temper. "Leah, what have I done to deserve this?"

"Forget what we did. The matter is obvious. The land is stolen. The whole country is stolen. The whole nation is based on a lie which is that it was not already occupied when the British came here. If it is anybody's place it is the blacks'. Does it *look* like your place? Does it *feel* like your place? Can't you see, even the trees have nothing to do with you."

"This is my country", I said quietly, "even if it's not yours."

"Meaning, excuse me?" She put her hands on her hips.

I scratched a line on the guttering and threw it to the ground. "You're a Jew. You don't have a country."

"Of course we have a country. It was stolen from us."

"Tough. What do you want me to do?"

"I don't want you to do anything. I don't require a hut or nails."

"Leah," I held out my hand.

She brushed the hand away.

"Don't touch me," she said. "Touch me and I leave, right now." And she walked across to the kero drum, her legs perambulating beneath her rigid spine, and began to fish out her boiling coat.

I cannot stand being brushed aside. Most serious tempers begin with being brushed aside, kindness rejected, conciliation spurned. "And if I don't touch you, what then?"

"How would I know?" she said, dropping the coat back into the water. "Don't you have any ideas of your own? Don't you read anything? Don't you think about anything but skin?" She suddenly burst into tears, calling me a bully.

If you expect me to take her in my arms and quiet the tears, to stroke her hair and whisper into her ear, you have mistaken

307

me for someone else. I lost *my* temper. Not slowly, not neatly, but like an overwound clock flying into separate parts, with useful cogs and gears all converted into deadly shrapnel. I will not repeat the rough words I said. The gist of it, however, is essential: I had not invited Leah into my camp or my bed and she had no business attacking me for either.

I turned my back on her and went back to nailing the guttering on the hut, splintering timber, bending nails, full of homicidal strength. I was as mad with fight as a bar-room brawler rolling out into the street; when her apology came it was the last thing I expected.

She did not look like a woman apologizing. Her eyes were strong, and her manner thoughtful. One could not confuse apology with surrender.

It was quite an apology, and not a short one either, although the length was not dictated by a love of words; she had a lot to say. On certain difficult matters, of which skin was perhaps the most important, she did not make herself clear, or I did not pay attention properly. Other things I grasped a little better – of all her conflicts, she admitted, the greatest was between weakness and strength. She saw herself in an alliance of the weak against the strong but (paradoxically, she thought) was much attracted to male physical strength which also (in the form of police, bailiffs, armies and Mervyn Sullivan) most terrified her in life. Her adultery had, therefore, been a more complicated betrayal and she had been wrong, she admitted, to blame me for it.

I am prepared to wager that she never laid out the central nervous system of the dogfish as carefully as she exposed these nervous systems of her own; I was much affected and stepped down from my drum, with my own confession tumbling from me. I admitted I could not read and that the landscape had, indeed, always seemed alien to me, that it made me, in many lights, melancholy and homesick for something else, that I preferred a small window in a house, and so on.

I must describe this to you coldly. I step back from it a little. Excuse me, but our hands are trembling, mine and Leah's, all these naked things of ours nodding to each other, shining wet and sensitive to sunlight.

We consider each other, our eyes so sharply focused that the periphery of our vision is smeared with vaseline.

We retire to bed. If there are curtains, they are drawn.

37

It is not the skin of young women, their firm breasts, buttocks, undimpled backsides, unstretched stomachs, etc., it is their expectations of life that I have lusted after, have drunk like a vampire with a black mouth and pink tongue; I have stolen their passions, enthusiasms, mistakes, misunderstandings, and valued these more than their superior educations.

The steps of the Bendigo Post Office are not a private place on a Friday afternoon. When you hear Leah scream at me you will think – casual bystander – that my new lover is nothing but a screaming shrew, is less attractive than the big-faced yellow-tailed black cockatoo my son has chained, temporarily, to the external rear-vision mirror of the truck, a cockatoo whose tail feathers conveniently echo the colour of the telegram in Leah's hand, a pretty coincidence not noted by the idle clergyman who stops to stare or by the two taut housewives with string bags full of sausages who do not bother to hide their interest in the Jewess, her silver shoes, and the rude-faced boy who is pulling her towards the truck.

There: Leah waving the telegram. She is a splendid creature, her whole soul trembling with love, with fear, feeling itself to be caught between good, evil, weakness, strength, duty, indulgence, crude appetite and fine asceticism.

All around her people worry about sausages or neatsfoot oil.

"You will punch him down," she said. "You think you can control him because you are stronger, but you can't and never will."

The telegram, you must realize, is from Izzie who will shortly arrive in Bendigo armed with information about his wife's infidelity, and I – hurling the cockatoo into the back of the truck above my son's protests – am in love with his wife.

38

The world was wet and smelt of rancid butter and they huddled into the caravan, as miserable as rain-sodden chooks. Denied the company of his comrades, this was the size of Izzie's life. He was, within these confines, like a terminally ill patient whose uncushioned vertebrae show through wasted flesh which is Buddhist yellow, royal purple, mottled with bruises no cushion can protect him from.

He was rubbed raw by his wife's letters; he spent her money; he hated her; also, perhaps, vice versa. And yet he waited for her to send him some impossible letter, some combination of words as particularly structured as laudanum.

However it was not just one letter he required, but two. The stamps of this second letter would not be perforated. They would be cut. Sometimes, courting sleep, he would imagine the scissors would cut these stamps. Now, he thought, at this moment, they are cutting the stamps from the sheets. The Comrade has mittens and red fingers with chilblains. The stamp has no adhesive. She dips a brush into a pot of paste and there, my name. In two months it will be in my hands. Sixty-one days. He willed the letter across oceans, saw it impatiently through dawdling ports where incompetent officials delayed the ship with unnecessary fire drills.

Rosa would give him no comfort. Perhaps she intended sympathy, but it was no help for her to criticize the Party. She would not leave it alone. She dredged through her memory for instances of stupidity, ambition, avarice she had witnessed in communists. She poured vitriol on the Comintern while she waited for a letter from her other son.

Only from his father did he draw some comfort. In these long featureless days, unable to concentrate on a book, not wanting to do anything but sleep until the letters woke him, he felt a real compassion for the man he had so often slighted. Now they made sandwiches together. Izzie held out a slice of bread in each extended palm while his father, patient and uncomplaining, brushed on the melted butter. When these two slices were done, Izzie waited, palms extended, while his father placed the two buttered slices on a sheet of newspaper on the floor, cut two more slices of bread, balancing the stale loaf on his thin knees, placed these two slices on Izzie's hands, and repeated the process again.

It irritated Izzie that his father should accept this inconvenience so meekly; that he did not demand the table where Rosa now sat.

Rosa had the table. She was conducting her interview with Dora, whose theatrical career had been ruined by an unexpectedly ballooning backside and who was now well spoken of as a fortune-teller.

Dora's arms and thighs and face had quickly followed the

310

example of her backside without ever losing the complexion ("real peaches and cream") of which she had always been so proud. She positioned herself carefully on the chair and placed a large cane basket on the table beside her. She sighed and smiled vaguely at Rosa who had not yet guessed the contents of the basket. Rosa returned the smile which offered a diffused sort of goodwill but no real affection: the two women had known each other too long; each had said too many indiscreet things about the other.

There was a movement in the basket. Rosa, a red scarf over her hair, cocked her head. Her interest was diverted by Dora who now displayed a small gaily-coloured purse. It was made from tiny beads and had a striking floral pattern. Rosa murmured her admiration. Dora's smile tightened its focus a little.

The fortune-teller's hands had too many rings on them. They were the same rings she had owned when her hands had been thinner and the flesh had risen around the rings like the bark of a tree that will shortly engulf a piece of old fencing wire. Yet here again Rosa was prevented from critical concentration because the hands were now delving into the pretty purse and producing grains of coloured wheat and scattering them at random across the table. There were many different colours, all as bright as the beads of the bag.

Rosa kept her own hands beneath the table and watched. She felt critical of herself, and foolish, just as a married man catching sight of himself in a brothel mirror may suddenly see himself in a more objective light.

Indeed, looking at the two men, she discovered them both smiling at her.

"If you don't like it," she told her son, "you don't have to stay." She imagined them sneering at her. They were smiling because they had guessed the contents of the basket and were waiting for her reaction.

When, less than a minute later, Rosa saw the chook, she did not shriek. She caught her breath silently and took herself in a notch.

"I am allergic," she said softly to Dora, begging her with her eyes to put the thing back.

"You cannot be allergic to the future," said the insensitive fat woman, clasping the bundle of white feathers so that the inert chook moulded itself to her and became a feathery extension of her bosom.

"It is blind," Dora confided.

"Ah," Izzie said, "so the future is blind?"

311

"No," Dora corrected him, "the future is not blind. We are blind. The chook is blind."

"I cannot believe in a chook," Rosa said, looking for help from her husband. Lenny, perfectly capable of exacting small revenges, was suddenly busy cutting bread.

"If you don't believe," Dora said hurriedly, placing the chook on the table, "it makes no difference." The chook cowered, a soft centreless thing. "It is not like a seance where you have to believe. Are you swimming?"

"No, I am not swimming."

"I am swimming, every morning." The chook stood and started tapping at the tabletop with its beak.

"I am sleeping," Rosa said.

"Ah, now, you see. It has taken a green one. You must write this down."

"You write it, Dora. I am paying you."

"No, no, you write. Quickly, now it is blue."

"I will not," Rosa folded her arms firmly and sank back against the caravan wall. "It is stupid. I am allergic."

"Suit yourself," said Dora sulkily. She produced a slim tortoiseshell pen (Rosa withheld admiration). She wrote down the colours of the grains of wheat as the blind chook ate them. She did not write down the ones that were knocked from the table. "Tell me, why don't you swim? When you first came here, always, you were swimming. Every day, you told me."

"Can it smell colours?" Rosa asked.

"It can smell smells, not colours."

"Colours, though, have smells. I can smell yellow."

"How does yellow smell, darling?"

"It has a yellow smell – what else? Are you writing down the colours? Such a nice pen," she said. "I think it was the green again."

"How is your other business, Dora?" Izzie asked. The bread on his palms now held slices of cheese and grated lettuce.

"Miss Latimer to you," Rosa said.

"It doesn't matter," Dora said. "Mrs Davis," she added. "Not so well," she told the industrious end of the caravan.

"There is more demand for fortunes than enemas?"

"Yes, there is more fortune in the future," she giggled. "That's one of my sayings, one of my slogans. I think success makes one rather American, don't you?" (Izzie scowled.) "Now, darling," she said to her client, "we have ten colours written on our chart so

312

we can put our chookie back in its little house. Bad times", she told Izzie, "are good times for fortune-tellers. Rosa is worried about money. She is worried about her son."

"I am her son."

"The other son, your brother, the clever one, Jacob."

"Clever?" Izzie asked. "Who told you he was clever?"

Rosa blushed. "Such a jealous little boy," she murmured. "Since he was little."

"Clever? Joseph, my brother? Clever?"

"Always this one did things," Rosa whispered. "Steel wool in with his brother's Weetbix. You understand? The same shape. He tried to kill his brother. Now his brother is in Russia," she raised her voice, "who knows what has happened to him, but this one is only worrying about itself. He is safe and sound. His wife sends him money. He does not need to work. So rich. All around him, people worry. He is a king. His father makes sandwiches to sell. See: what is the son doing? He holds out his hands."

"Leave him alone, Rosa," Lenny said. "You know why he is upset."

"He is expelled. From what? From nothing."

"Why do you pick on him? Leave him alone. Talk to your chook. Gossip with it." Then, more quietly, he told his son: "Take a walk. I'll finish these. Maybe you meet the postie."

Rosa went back to her conference with Dora who had now produced a large volume, like a telephone book, that explained the significance of the chook's choice of colours.

"He won't give me my mail," Izzie told his father. "He says it must go into the letterbox. If I stand at the gate and hold out my hand, he won't give it to me. 'How do I know this is your letterbox?' He is a little bureaucrat exercising his power."

"You have much pain," Dora was telling Rosa, "much pain with children."

"Sixteen stitches. *This* one. I was torn."

"Oh shit," said Izzie and walked out. Rosa shrugged. Lenny put the tops on the sandwiches he would try to sell at Circular Quay. Izzie waited under the eaves of the house until he saw the postman drop two envelopes into the small tin letterbox. Neither of them was airmail and he approached them with no expectations.

The first one ("Darling Izzie, I have dun it again") was from Leah, although he did not open it immediately. The second was, in fact, the letter he had waited for so long. Its stamp was

313

perforated, not cut, and it bore a profile of an English monarch, but it was from the comrades in Sussex Street and it invited him to come and resolve certain matters in respect of his membership.

His first feelings were light and joyful, but by the time he had walked six miles in light drizzle he was cold and slightly bitter. He rehearsed a small speech he was to make to the comrades. He amended it, forgot it, and made another one. He looked forward to their apology.

And yet when he was in those little rooms on the fourth floor above Sussex Street it became obvious that there would be no resolution, no discussion, no apology. Instead they asked him to write a pamphlet on Japanese militarism and said, straight-faced, that the Unemployed Workers' Union needed someone to train speakers for the field.

He should have been happy. He wished to be happy. He looked at these two men and the greying woman whom he had respected and wished to emulate and found they could only meet his eyes with difficulty. It was not because there had been a mistake, but because they did not know what the mistake was. They were decent people who were embarrassed to be found acting contrary to their principles. He tried not to despise them.

His suit was soaked through and he began to shiver. The ink of the sentences in Leah's letter began to run, blurring the outlines of the letters and giving them a soft blue woolly character out of keeping with their meaning.

39

We lay in our truck, us Badgerys. The children kicked at me with their feet, and put their elbows in my eye.

"Do you love Izzie?" Sonia asked me.

"I don't know, Sonny. I haven't met him."

"Leah loves Izzie."

"Yes, I know."

"Izzie is Leah's husband," said Charles. "They were married, but not in church. Izzie is a communist. He doesn't believe in God."

"I *know*," Sonia said. "Do you love Izzie, Charlie?"

"No," said Charles. "And I want him to go away."

I lay on my stomach and looked through a chink in the back door. The hessian hut glowed yellow with the light of a kero lamp. Leah, dressed in white, sat up in bed, writing. The whole hut was her veil. Charles farted. Sonia giggled. I was a fool again, in love.

40

Izzie stood there, for some minutes, just inside the door. His wife was writing, jabbing impatiently at the paper; just so must she have constructed the cloudy outlines of his jealous dreams. His eyes were bloodshot with travel; they took in the dirt floor, the small objects on the packing case beside the bed, a tiny black-and-white photograph pinned to the hessian wall. The photograph reassured him. It had been taken during the party for the Silly Friends.

She looked up and smiled. She looked neither young nor old to him, merely very beautiful.

He was as frail as a sparrow. His face was very white, his lips very red. He wore his shiny dark suit with books protruding from the jacket pockets.

"You found us?"

"A good map, Goldstein," and although he grinned he was already irritable because he felt so shy. He shoved at one of the bush-poles that supported the roof. He pushed at it angrily.

Leah stopped herself asking him not to shake the pole. She patted the bed and when he sat – reluctantly she thought – took his hand in hers.

"You smell like a dog," she said, squeezing the hand.

"Sweat. Jumping trains." He was looking into her eyes, trying to find some reassurance. "Where is *he*?"

"In the truck, with his children."

He nodded. Although he had left Sydney in a rage, he had made himself become strong and positive along the way. He had exorcized his jealousy. He had patiently, mile after stolen mile, rebuilt his life, at least in his imagination. But now all this gave way before a flood of emotion, all these good intentions floating like broken packing cases in swollen waters. He was overcome with a desire to hurt.

"Is this where you do it?"

"Izzie, please."

315

He did stop himself, but not before he had sipped the exquisite flavours of his hurt and experienced an intoxicant so potent that it made him slightly faint.

He crushed her against him. It was a rough, demanding embrace, made cold and clammy by his rain-wet jacket, and Leah tried not to resent it.

"Your lips are hard," he accused.

She shrugged. "What would you like them to be?" She too tried to smile, but she was now as irritated as he was, irritated that the man she wrote to so tenderly should embrace in so wet and cold a manner.

She looked up and saw him curl that fondly remembered lip. He showed her his teeth right up to the gum.

"Izzie, what has *happened*?"

"What do you think I *am*?" he hissed. "What do you think I can *take*?"

"I promised . . ."

"I never asked for it."

". . . to tell the truth, to never lie to you, Izzie."

"I won't be your confessor."

"You want me to lie to you?"

"I want you to come home with me." His hand, on hers, was gentle and not demanding. The voice suggested no recriminations, but Leah felt herself shrinking from him. She did not want to go home. This was too shocking for her to admit to herself: she could not bear to be so selfish. So she made excuses and the excuses contradicted each other and made no sense.

The truth, in comparison, was a simple thing. Leah was enjoying her life. She liked travelling and she enjoyed, even more, the life in the letters she wrote to everyone, to her father in particular. You can see the pleasure in their yellowed pages now: the minute details of life, whole streets of towns peopled with bakers, shoppers and passing stockmen. The life in the letters has a pattern and a shape if not a meaning. Here, in the letters, she can come dangerously close to admitting why she remained on the road and what she got from it. But when Izzie told her, perhaps untruthfully, that the dancing was financially unnecessary, she could not admit to him that she did not want to give up the life.

Also, as she lay beside him on the bed in awkward intimacy, separated from his body by a tugging blanket, she was shocked, once again, to feel that shudder at the prospect of his skin. In memory she had blanched it and smoothed it, but there was no

316

denying it here and she was overcome by guilt and confusion by her feelings for she thought it *wrong* to be repelled by his skin. She had liked his skin well enough as a friend. There was no *reason* why she should not like it now, as a wife. And the skin, more than the coarse blanket, continued to keep them apart and bring the conversation to matters that seemed safe. It was then that she learned of the whole ordeal he had gone through with the Party. She did not ask him why he had kept it secret from her, but as she watched him and saw the hard gleam in his eyes as he talked about his vindication she thought, not of the unsympathetic nature of his triumph, but of the extent of his shame during the period of his expulsion and she remembered the way – the day in Tamarama – he had curled up in hurt in the hollow of a rock above the sea.

He held her hand as he talked and began to stroke her arm. She was ashamed to not welcome this intimacy. She distracted him by quizzing him about the mechanics of his vindication. They were, the two of them, alike in many respects and she smiled to listen to his approach to the problem. There had to be a *reason*. There was a reason for everything. The comrades in Sussex Street knew nothing about it, therefore the reason for his dismissal must exist outside of Australia. He had hypothesized another Isadore Kaletsky and begun a search of leftist papers and periodicals from 1911 to the present day. In this he had been helped by old friends of Joseph's, political academics but not Party members. Finally, when he found the article he had known, from theory, must exist, he felt, he said, like an astronomer who posits the presence of a star by mathematics before locating it with his telescope. The article, written in 1923 for a little English Marxist periodical (*New Times*) was most critical of Lenin and very warm towards Comrade Trotsky. The article concerned issues in Australia. He then wrote directly to the Comintern pointing out that he had been only twelve years old at the time and had never been to London. In short, he was not the I. Kaletsky they thought he was.

"But who", Leah asked, "dobbed you in?"

But he would not see the issue as dobbing in, but as a quite correct approach for a party that did not wish to fall into error. Leah, hearing his confident use of "correct" and "incorrect", felt uneasy.

"Who", she asked, "is this I. Kaletsky and what will happen to him?"

"He'll be expelled."

"And if he lives in Russia?"

"The same."

"Put on trial!"

"Goldstein, Goldstein, you've been reading the capitalist press."

"Look at your face. You know it's true."

"*Perhaps* there have been trials of anti-revolutionaries. What else should they do?"

"Izzie, look at me."

"I am looking at you, damn it."

Leah held her husband's hands and looked into his eyes. She nodded her head slowly as she saw that it was true: that it was J. (Joseph) Kaletsky who had written the article, who had lived in London in 1923, who Moscow now knew about, who would be, she assumed, dealt with. She felt such a confusion of pity and revulsion that the two opposing tides made her whole body tremble.

"Poor Izzie," she said. "Poor, poor little Izzie."

From this they proceeded, misunderstanding on misunderstanding, until, finally making clammy love, Leah wept while Izzie asked her why.

When he came outside for a piss, I was so close to him I could have tripped him over.

41

It was an odd, bright, windy sort of morning. The gums tossed above our camp and showed the silver undersides of their leaves like a million dazzling knives. The grasses were mirrors and even the pebbles we kicked aimlessly beneath our boots were peppered full of glittering mica. We sat beneath a contradictory sky (a soft, chalky blue) and pretended everything was normal.

Leah sat on the petrol drum I had used in the installation of her guttering. She leaned her back against the doorpost of her hut. The October 1923 issue of *New Times* flapped its pages in the wind, fluttering like a captive dove or fortune-telling chook. She soothed the pages and held them against her thigh.

She now rested her forefinger on her bottom row of small white teeth and watched us, and only the dark rings around her sunken eyes told anything of the sort of night she had had.

318

As she sat on the petrol drum she was trying to write a letter, not a real letter to a real person, but some imaginary construction, flawless in its logic and clear as ice, a letter where one fact attaches seamlessly to the next, where *just* conclusions are sensibly reached. There was no one to whom she could bear to send this letter to and, in any case, she was so agitated she could not get the disparate elements to stay still:

"If he has betrayed his brother from fear and weakness, should I then abandon (betray) him? Is this not to double the crime? Why should I reject him because he is weak? What is wrong with *me* that I do not like his skin? Is my skin flawless? Have I been a liar to write to him as I have and then to wish to undo my words because of his skin? Is it skin I am rejecting? Is it something else? Am I merely asking the skin to represent something else for me? How long has this skin been a problem? When I met him in Mrs Heller's I thought him fine-looking and witty. If he is my husband and he murders a man (which seems likely) I should stand by him. If his victim is his own brother, what then? I do not ask perfection of him, only the right intention."

The article Joseph Kaletsky had written in 1922 flapped on her lap and she pretended to read it while Isadore Kaletsky stood beneath a gum tree talking to Herbert Badgery who, I assure you, had in no way been prepared for his rival, either in appearance or personality.

At night, as a spy, I had judged him physically my inferior, but now I could not keep my eyes off his face which was so foreign and so fine, girl-like with its long lashes, limpid eyes, dark ringlets, archer's bow lips; not a soft face. Its nose, chin, cheeks all shaped by the handsome curves of good Semitic bone, the curves of scimitars but also those of harps. His skin, I assure you, seemed quite normal.

He shook my hand, a small hand, but hard, and his speech was staccato, enthusiastic, quiet, light. He charmed me, disarmed me; and while Leah – who I would have understood better had she held a judge's black cap in her pretty hands – stared vacantly, her husband inquired about my experience as an aviator, was knowledgeable about the Australian motor industry, and expressed the opinion that it was a bad thing that the Holden Body Works had fallen into the hands of General Motors.

I once heard Melba sing and knew, from the first note, that I was in the presence of extraordinary gifts. Izzie had that quality, without me even knowing quite what that talent was. If you had given it to me, I would have sold cars with it, one a day.

I cannot even pretend to understand all the resonances that were alive on that bright, tossed day. I cannot imagine that Izzie knew what was going on in Leah's mind; but then I also find it difficult to imagine that he was ignorant of her turmoil.

He did an odd thing. Let me tell it.

Charles was sitting on the bonnet of the truck. The cockatoo was tied with dunny chain to the outside rear-vision mirror from which perch it shrieked and wailed and attacked its own reflection. (If you are, from habit, seeing a white cockatoo in your mind, I must beg you to change it for the correct one, three foot long, funereal black, its yellow fan of feathers at present clasped shut beneath its tail.)

Izzie, his hands in his pockets, his suit jacket bulging with books, came to stand in front of Charles who had disliked him the moment he knew the man existed. And just as, years later, Charles would not be able to pass by an aggressive or frightened animal without attempting to befriend it, so, it seems to me, Izzie approached my suspicious hostile son.

Izzie held out his dainty hand towards the cockie which tilted its ferocious head to one side and examined the approaching meal. Izzie began to spill out an immense amount of information about cockatoos including such historical titbits as the fact that its close relation *Calyptorhynchus magnificus* (the red-tailed black cockatoo) was the first Australian parrot to be illustrated. This little sketch was executed not by Joseph Banks, but by his draughtsman, a chap called Parkers or Parkinson, in 1770. The information, however, was not merely historical (that would have lost Charles's attention very quickly) but covered breeding, questions of diet and inclination to travel. My son hoarded away everything he heard. The result, however, was that he felt obliged to give something in return. "It bites," he admitted.

"Yes," said Izzie. "Yes," he added, offering his fingers as if they were egg sandwiches. He was not a fool. He not only knew the bird was female (Charles had not), he knew that its beak must be powerful enough to crush a pine nut or hakea pod. So for what did he offer this sacrifice? For Charles's admiration? For silent Sonia's? Or for Leah, who remained with the white wings of the article for which Joseph Kaletsky was later tried? Did he reduce the value of his courage to that of a gimmick?

Leah watched him calmly. She passed her hand across her eyes a second and yawned. The eucalypts tossed above her head and the casuarinas shed needles with a sigh that meant nothing more than windy weather.

And the cockatoo, at last, took what was offered and Izzie gave an odd, high hoot. Charles slapped the bird across the head. The finger was released. Blood streamed.

We all, I think, looked at Leah. This is why I am sure we understood more than we knew. We looked, all together, towards her and she, hearing the hoot of agony, looked up, saw the blood flowing from the finger, and looked down again.

This is one of the few moments of childhood that Charles can accurately recall (for the rest it is imaginary slights, fictitious hardships) and on this day in Bendigo he too saw the blood flowing down the lacerated finger and I am indebted to him for the recollection of a dirty fingernail atop it all.

It was not to be a simple day for at this very moment, while Leah was returning to her magazine, while the finger was still aloft, before the cockatoo had stretched and spread itself, levitated above the bonnet of the Dodge with its sulphur tail feathers splayed out beneath it, a black Chevrolet, with a wireless aerial running along its roof like the outlined drawing of a knife blade, rolled over the rocks into the camp with its engine cut.

It was the town police from Bendigo.

As a car salesman you have many dealings with police, particularly in regard to registration of vehicles. Up until that day I always got on well with them. At Barret's we gave them a bottle of grog at Christmas, nothing dirty, but enough to get my plates through the system quickly. In short I did not, as Leah now did, begin to shake like a leaf, nor did my face, as Izzie's did, set into a scimitar sneer.

The police were not, however, here to inquire about motor-car registration plates (although they made a note of mine before departing). They were here to advise a communist agitator and his collaborators to move out of town. They did this with a mixture of weariness and primness that I was later to recognize as characteristic. They searched no one, and made no inquiries as to why their major interest had blood streaming down his finger. We were given sixty minutes to pack and it all happened so fast I did not even argue. When they called me "Baldy" I did not raise a fist.

Even when they departed I had no time for *post mortems* because now I found Izzie's wrath was focused on me. He was under the illusion that I had informed the local police. I had somehow, it seemed, done this during the night. I had walked five miles into Bendigo, like Curnow betraying the Kelly gang, to give the warning. What bullshit. I have seen drunks get themselves into this sort of passionate rage, a time for ultimatums, bottles with broken necks, drawn knives and shotguns grabbed from under car seats. But it was only nine in the morning and there was no alcohol to justify it.

The charming man I had enjoyed ten minutes before now became a hateful little sparrow to whom I would happily have fed poisoned wheat. He splashed blood on my clean shirt, and that upset me almost as much as the silly ultimatum he now proclaimed, demanding that Leah choose now, once and for all, between the pair of us.

Leah walked across from the petrol drum to which she had returned for the magazine.

"Come," she said, holding his arm. "I want to talk to you."

"Talk to me here," Izzie said.

"Izzie, please."

"Talk here," he said. "What can't be said?"

"All right," said Leah Goldstein, no longer fair, no longer rational. "All right."

It was then she told him, in front of everyone, she could not bear his skin.

I think of a suit of scar tissue, ripped and broken, beside which agony a lacerated finger is nothing but a young man's prank.

42

"What sustains you, Mr Badgery?" Leah asked me, rattling northwards in a hurriedly packed utility, hounded by small-town police who imagined us revolutionaries. They were waiting for us at Heathcote and Nagambie, Tatura, Kyabram and Shepparton itself. They found us entering town, or buying a pie or a few gallons of petrol. In Nagambie we got our camp set up before they were on to us, Brylcreemed Irishmen with cabbage soup on their breath. They were familiar with our names and our business which was, they informed us, the overthrow of lawful government. We packed our things and moved on, driven across the

322

state like the legendary sparrows the Chinese eliminated by never letting land.

"What sustains you?" she asked, as I turned down one more unlabelled gravel road which promised an escape from the tyrannical coppers of the soft-fruit country.

I attempted an answer. The car crashed hard into deep pot-holes. I was thirsty. Dust went muddy in my throat.

"Nothing", she said, "sustains you, Mr Badgery. You are walking on hot macadam, quickly. All that sustains you is your filthy belt, excuse me, but it is true. You are sustained by a gadget. The gadget does not believe in anything. It does not have an idea. It is just a product. The workers who make it are serving a mindless thing."

"It prevents dizziness."

"Dizziness, you told me, fearfulness. The verdigris on the battery makes your leg green. Have you noticed?"

"What is 'sustain'?" Charles asked, leaning forward like a scabby sultan from the pile of bedding in the back. Leah had charcoaled a small moustache on to his face and it was Leah, now, who answered his question with such patience, at such length that I derived great benefit myself.

"What is wrong with us all", she said when she had satisfied my son's curiosity, "is that we are sustained by gadgets, or desires that are satisfied by gadgets, when someone like my husband," she swallowed, "whatever his faults," a long pause, "is sustained by something more substantial."

"And what sustains you, Mrs Kaletsky?"

"Movement," she said, displaying her white feet. "I admit it. I am really the one dancing on hot macadam, not you: town to town, dancing, writing letters. I cannot stay still anywhere. It is not a country where you can rest. It is a black man's country: sharp stones, rocks, sticks, bull ants, flies. We can only move around it like tourists. The blackfeller can rest but we must keep moving. That is why I can't return with my husband as he wishes," she announced, seeking rest in a simple theory, "because I am selfish, addicted to movement."

She was wrong about herself – what sustained her were the threads from the famous suit which she had woven into something new and personal, something finer than that sour greasy object which she had, if not misunderstood, at least imperfectly comprehended. With the threads of the suit she had woven kindness into a philosophy that was as simply practised as sending money to Rosa, picking up bagmen on the road, teaching me to read, sharing her food and being attentive to someone else's children. What she had made had little in common with Izzie's giant dream, was like one of her proverbial baby swallows beside his giant canvas of smooth grey forms, that complex ants' nest bathed in golden light.

"My husband is sustained by a better world, you see, not by fear or selfishness."

"Yes."

"He has probably killed his brother," she said, as if talking to herself, "and he thinks this is permissible. He thinks this is just. He thinks it is Correct."

"And that is better than being sustained by a belt?"

"Probably," she shivered, and tried to shut the scratched side curtains. "The intention is better. The intention is generous, not fearful."

"But why did he have to dob in his brother?"

"Not dob in."

"Do the Russians have a patent out on communism? Why does he have to explain himself to them?"

"It is a science," she said without conviction. "And the Russians have performed the first successful experiment. You'd have to ask him, Mr Badgery," she said bleakly. "I don't understand either."

"I liked him," I said.

"People do," she said and sat hugging her bare arms, no longer curious about the rabbits leaping from the bracken-covered paddocks we were passing through.

"No one asked *me*," said the voice from the back. "No one asked what sustains *me*."

What sustained my son, it seemed, was his new friendship with the cockatoo and Leah, guilty, weary, gritty-eyed, hugged him awkwardly across the back of the seat, and, with tears running down her cheeks, told him he was a good boy.

"I won't hurt her, will I, Leah?"

"No, Charles. I know you won't."

"I won't let her down."

"No."

"I know what sustains Sonia," Charles whispered, putting his arms around Leah's neck.

I turned to look at the sweet smile on my daughter's sleeping face.

"Disappearing," said duplicitous Charles, attempting to see what reaction this would get. "She tries all the time," whispered the little informer. "She says prayers to Jesus to make her disappear."

I couldn't help smiling. I never had a high opinion of the power of the Christian god: electric crosses, holy pictures, Irish priests at country football matches.

"Jesus doesn't know the trick," I said.

"I told her," Charles said.

"And who should she pray to, Mr Badgery?" said Leah who had never, once, referred to my act since the Bendigo fiasco.

"You don't pray to Jesus, I promise you that."

"But who", she insisted, "do you pray to?"

"Matilda," I grinned.

She frowned.

"Goddess of Fear."

Leah did not laugh. She put her hand on my knee. "Do you become afraid, Mr Badgery?"

"Sometimes,"

"Let's buy alcohol," she said suddenly. "Let's buy alcohol in Violet Town."

43

Alcohol sustained us, it is true, and had it not been for this (and a packet of French letters I was forced to buy in Benalla) we would have made it across the border with petrol in the tank and five bob to spare, free, ready to make an honest quid without the help of the Victorian Police Force.

Alas we ran out of petrol in Wodonga and Charles, to his everlasting pride and eternal shame, sold his yellow-tailed black cockatoo to the man in the pet shop outside whose establishment fortune decreed we should come to rest.

There is nothing to tell about this except to let you see the expression on my son's face when he had bid up the price from ten shillings to one pound. His face seemed to swell, as if ruled by air or fluids; it became quite pink and taut and his eyes brightened with moisture and his mouth quivered at that odd uncertain point – a point I would like to leave it at forever – where, tickled by pride, made loose with relief, it may burst into the broadest smile or, alternatively, fall in on itself, feed on itself, a bitter meal of self-hatred that might sustain a man forever.

44

I would rather fill my history with great men and women, philosophers, scientists, intellectuals, artists, but I confess myself incapable of so vast a lie. I am stuck with Badgery & Goldstein (Theatricals) wandering through the 1930s like flies on the face of a great painting, travelling up and down the curlicues of the frame, complaining that our legs are like lead and the glare from all that gilt is wearying our eyes, arguing about the nature of life and our place in the world while – I now know – Niels Bohr was postulating the presence of the neutrino, while matter itself was being proved insubstantial, while Hitler – that black spider – was weaving his unholy lies.

Lies, dreams, visions – they were everywhere. We brushed them aside as carelessly as spider webs across a garden path. They clung to us, of course, adhered to our clothes and trailed behind us but we were too busy arguing to note their presence.

So while Arthur Dempster discovered Uranium 235 I was learning to be a funny man, mocking the dragon, standing on a dusty stage in Bellingen, NSW, and looking like a fool while an emu pecked my bum.

I had painted a map of Australia on the soft canopy of the Dodge and marked our path in red. "Badgery & Goldstein (Theatricals)" it said. Later I added "& Pet Suppliers" in acknowledgement of Charles's role in our survival.

Charles grew large and strong, but in an awkward way, with powerful bullock driver's thighs atop his bandy legs. He had a long trunk, a huge head with a powerful jaw, a face painful with pimples. He suffered his adolescence, talking to various animals in a breaking voice. When he should have been masturbating or spying on girls in the changing sheds of shire swimming pools, he was caressing some bright parrot or persuading a carpet snake to give up its freedom.

During some bad times in the Northern Rivers, it was fourteen-year-old Charles who kept us alive, selling birds to a charming old American, a fellow named Parson who wore rimless glasses like Teddy Roosevelt. He robbed us, of course, but we didn't know any better. He paid us a shilling for king parrots, sixpence for a galah, and we stayed in Grafton while the jacarandas dropped their lilac carpets across the streets and Charles went out each day with his nets and his climbing boots, a sanctimonious look on his face.

We paid for all this, the rest of us, paid for it in Charlie's moods, his slammed car doors, his stamped foot, his flood of tears.

It was also in Grafton that I bought Sonia a pretty white dress so she could go to Church of England Sunday School. Leah, who dressed drably off stage, disapproved of this. I was never religious myself but I thought it a harmless sort of thing. I would rather have my daughter pray to Jesus and sing Christmas carols than flirt with dragons. Besides, I had nothing against a pretty dress and I liked to dress up my beautiful daughter, to brush her hair and tie her ribbons. I was not approved of and later, in a moment of heat, Leah would scream at me: "All you saw of her were pretty dresses, not who she was. She was just skin to you."

Ah, skin.

We cannot avoid it. Ever since her husband had walked, glass-eyed, mask-faced, from our camp, skin had been an obsession with my puritanical partner who suffered her guilt, that she had rejected her husband for an unworthy reason. She did not even understand her own reasons. She put all the weight on that poor envelope and would not let herself see beyond it.

She wrote to Izzie once a week, but she said nothing to him of skin. I was the one who bore the brunt of her obsession.

45

Sonia was at Sunday School in her pretty dress and Charles had been taken up to Mapleton in the schoolteacher's jinker to remove an alleged taipan from the Post Office toilet. Leah and I –temporarily rich – had retired to bed in our room at Donaldson's Commercial Hotel, Nambour. It was the wet season: mosquitoes hung in clouds outside our net; the air was sweet with the smell of the sugar mill just up the road.

A romantic afternoon had been planned. Bundaberg rum was purchased. And then Izzie and his skin came greasingly into the room, sliding into the bed, and I found my lover looking at me with that calculating grey gaze of hers as if, had she been able to focus her stare finely enough, she would have cut away the bone on my shaven head and laid bare the smelly secrets of my dogfish soul.

"In what respect", she said, at last, "am I like your wife?" She propped herself up on her elbow and displayed her small flaw, the nipple of her left breast which had the habit of popping inwards and which she, when washing, and I when kissing, popped out again, in readiness for the day when she would feed a child. Sometimes we discussed this possibility, this furry-edged future, but not today. The nipple remained inverted.

"I will tell you in what respect," she said, "it is skin. Give me the rum."

"Empty."

"Show me."

I dropped my hands into the skirts of mosquito net and dragged the empty bottle into bed. I held it up against the light. The bottle was empty but she drank from it anyway.

"Young women's skin," she said. "She was twenty-three when you left her."

"She left me."

"So you claim, but who could believe you? You told the newspaper in Grafton you were an ex-serviceman. You believe whatever falls out of your mouth because you don't really believe anything, just Product. You don't care about people, you only care about skin."

"Leah, Leah, I love you."

"Skin," she said. "Skin, you told me – the feel of skin."

"Let me. . . ."

"And when it stretches and sags you'll throw me out, trade me in for a new one."

"Let me tell you a story."

"Don't touch me."

"A story."

"A lie."

"A true story. How I got my electric belt."

"How you got your Product to worship."

"It's about skin. Do you want to hear it or not?"

"Yes," she said, suspecting a trap.

The story was, more or less, as follows. Most of it is lies, but I could think of no other way to tell Leah Goldstein that I loved her and not her skin.

328

46

Molly was practical. She had always been practical, even if she had spent half her life pretending she was not. "You are a commercial asset," Mrs Ester had told her, and Mrs Ester, may she rest in peace, had been right.

She enjoyed driving home in the T Model taxi, enjoyed it far more than the Hispano Suiza, which was a fine car doubtless, but did not have "Boomerang Taxi" written on its door, or a commercial licence plate, or a "Not for Hire" sign displayed on the roof. She was not plying for business, but rather celebrating her occupation and enjoying the smell of lavender that emanated from the small muslin bag hidden beneath the back seat.

As she turned from Flemington Road up to Ballarat Road towards Haymarket she reflected that she was tired. Waiting while a wagon turned into the timber yard on the corner she checked her face in the rear-vision mirror and was pleased to note that the tiredness did not show. She was a handsome woman, a little plump, but handsome none the less. She patted her cloche hat and wondered if she appeared hard. She had dismissed Inky O'Dyer that afternoon, but her face did not suggest she was capable of it and Inky O'Dyer, small, swaggering, chewing a match, had been slow to understand. But she would not have the public being cheated, and Inky had cheated. She felt sorry for him. She felt more sorry for his wife, and had posted her a cheque for twenty pounds. For those who suffered she brimmed with compassion. Towards those who erred she was less than generous and when she thought of the insolent Inky, his cap pushed back on his head, his hands in his deep pockets, her mouth diminished in size a fraction, an event she did not witness in her mirror, for by then the wagon had finally entered the timber yard and she was almost at the corner at the Haymarket yards.

As she came down the track beside the yards (the same track I had met Horace on that afternoon) she saw the steer before she saw Charles. It was a large black animal with a white blaze on its forehead and one ear missing. The beast had been cut proud. It pawed the earth and dribbled, blocking the road, glaring malevolently at the taxi. She thought of Jack, who had become the subject of puzzling and angry dreams. She found herself, asleep, slapping her dead husband's face. She was not the sort of person to inquire as to why she might be so.

The steer annoyed her. She stopped the car and tooted the horn and, when it did not move, got out of the car and approached it with the crank handle. The beast hesitated, retreated, and then, kicking up its heels, dodged round the car and up towards the main road.

It was only then, suddenly frightened by the risk she had taken, that she saw Charles standing in the middle of the track, shoeless, mud-faced and blubbering.

She knew then what had happened. She had heard the whisperings in the house on the Maribyrnong and known something evil was afoot. Her daughter was a stranger to her and the colluding poet (who would not lift the seat when he urinated) could not meet her eyes. She had watched Annette Davidson silently, with a stock-taker's eyes, and measured, in that wide red mouth, the extent of her deviousness.

She swept up Charles from the roadway and while she chattered to him and called him dearie and little man, she was preparing herself. She drove fast on to the property, noted the aircraft gone, and, carrying her bulky bawling grandson in her arms, entered the house.

It was like a place where a murder had been committed. The very breadcrumbs on the oil-cloth table gave witness to it. Flies rose from an unwashed frying pan. Sonia was crying in her cot. Her nappy needed changing. She found me, in tatters, underneath the bed, my head bleeding – a broken window nearby attested to the cause. Nearby she found an axe, its blade chipped and ugly from its battle with the poems.

"Lord save us," she said. "May God strike them," she muttered. "May lightning hit them. Molly's here," she said. "Molly's here."

She did things in an order that had its own logic. First she attended to Charles. She washed a saucepan and heated up some milk. When she had done this she poured it into a large mug and added a very generous portion of her *crème de menthe*. She sat him on her knee and spoke to him soothingly. She took off his shoes and socks and played this little pig went to market and when the *crème de menthe* seemed slow in acting, made him another one. She was, perhaps, too generous, for Charles went to sleep before he had finished his second mug. She put him into bed fully clothed and then changed Sonia.

I heard all this but it did not touch me. I was in my own fever world, composed of whirling aeroplanes, spars, rotary engines, guy ropes, and buildings with splintered towers. Herbert Badgery, who does not cry, whimpered like a child.

As she cleaned out the bedroom she spoke to me, as she removed the bits and pieces Phoebe had left behind (three dresses, a silk scarf, two petticoats, scribbled poems crumpled on the floor, a chamber-pot– unemptied – a vase, lipsticks, the dress she had been married in) she talked to me.

"You were a doormat, poor man. Don't mind, don't worry. God will have mercy on you. Molly is here. Dearie me, look at it." She hurled things from the room as she spoke, bustling around. She tore sheets from the bed, removed prints from the wall. "You'll see," she said. "You'll see. Good riddance. Bad rubbish. Little Miss Uppity, little Miss Spoiled."

She carried the wreckage from the room down to the river, squelching through river mud in high heels, and threw what she had not dropped into the oily waters.

She removed her muddy shoes and stockings outside the door and threw these, as if they too might be tainted, into the ashcan on the doorstep. Then she lit the wood stove and stacked its firebox full. She riddled the grate. She washed the dishes. She did her work with a passion, crashing dishes and saucepans. "They'll die," she said, "you'll see. You're a good man. Too good, too kind. Built her a house", she said, "with his own hands. Fed and clothed, the little riddance, the little uppity."

Thus Molly set upon her cure. First the clean house. "Thought I was silly," she said, mopping the oilskin table. "Looked down at me. Laughed."

She came to me then to attend to my wounds, smelling of disinfectant and Velvet soap. My mind was not right. I blubbered like a baby, howled and hugged her, raged like a warrior, giggled like a girl. She persuaded me into the bed. I sat up and talked like an adult. I told her I had been fired and then, in the middle of this, a great black blind came down over my head and I wanted to bang my head against the wall until it broke.

I ran out to the birdcages and released them. I shooed them out, as if this magic might bring back my wife. I wrung the neck of a parrot that would not leave. Not just wrung its neck, but pulled its head off. Molly got me back to bed and washed the blood and feathers from my hands. She got me undressed. I had no vanity or modesty. She got me into pyjamas and sat by my bed sponging my face with a warm wet towel.

"It's a death," she said. "That's what it is, a death. Grieve. You can howl. I howled when Jack died, howled and howled. She is dead", she said, "and gone. Poor man, you were a doormat. Mud on you, mud from her feet. Miss High-and-Mighty, and left her babies."

I woke up in a dark room and plunged back into the pit. Molly sat in the kitchen. She had the firebox door open. I could see the flames. She came in, dressing gown pink, soft fluffy slippers, her hair brushed out.

She sat on my bed and held me.

I am sure, to this day, that she did not plan what happened. To plan such a thing would have been repugnant to her. Had someone suggested she do such a thing she would have been outraged. Perhaps I did it. I do not know. But somewhere between my search for comfort and her desperate desire to provide it, my head found its way to her breasts. Not young girl's breasts, dear Leah, not firm, pert, but large, and pendulous. Don't wrinkle up your little puritan's face and turn away. Face me. Look at me while I tell you that I, Herbert Badgery, took a breast in my mouth like a child, while the north wind turned to rock the little house of my disgrace. The dark and the wind isolated us from reality, from her god even, from the priest and the dusty confessional, and Molly was the angel of sleep, claimed that right, that role, out loud. "To make him sleep," she told her fierce and vengeful god, and I hope her god heard her. I hope he saw her discard her belt, heard it clunk to the floor, the slippers flop, the gown shed like a whisper; saw her body, the fleshy arms, the red corset marks on her generous stomach, the appendix scar, the blue veins on her thighs, the dimples of her sagging backside. Hope he saw them and found them beautiful.

"In it goes," she said, "poor baby."

"Molly, Molly, what's happening?"

"Shush, shush, slow and easy. Mama's got you, slow and easy."

No, my darling Leah, I will not plead normality and go rifling through my bureau to pull out birth certificates to show she was only six years older than I was. For making it normal would miss the point. We did not think it normal, either of us, it was abnormal, extraordinary, wonderful, embarrassing, and it did not happen just once, but merely raised the curtain on a time of my life when I was not the me I thought I was, and she was not the she she thought she was.

I will tell you, my mother-in-law and I became lovers, but there was never in it anything as casual as the life of lovers, no waking together, no dropping of clothes on floors and piling into bed. There were firm rituals (as set as the Latin incantations by which she reached her god) that must be gone through. There were lines that must be said which soon would assume the form, not of words at all, but odd-shaped keys to doors that were otherwise locked tight.

Our mornings were as proper as you would expect, both waking on our own beds. The demands of life ensured that breakfast would be made, fires lit, Molly's car be started, a formal but friendly goodbye be given while she left for work.

I stayed at home and did not go into a world where I was a fool, a cuckold, a man without a job or a wife. I made myself into a small man and sat in the sun with a blanket over my knees with no more future than that suggested by the peas I slowly shelled for dinner.

When I did finally venture out into the world with a new Dodge truck I was as shaky and nervous as any invalid, not surprised to find myself unwanted by employers. I read no newspapers and so made no connection between my misfortune and that of others.

But this is leaping ahead a little and there is more skin, my darling, to regale you with. And why is your nose so wrinkled while your eyes are so bright?

47

Oh, how pleasant it is for a man to be looked after, and if I have made myself a pitiful thing, a broken spirit, an invalid with no dreams left, I do not take it back but present to you the other side of the grubby coin: that year with Molly in which I did not need to strive, to impress, to make a sale, to do anything other than sit in the sun or by the fire. Here I had the childhood I had never had, was petted, cosseted, indulged, and if there was a dark wound in my soul, if the yellow dusk and the white smoke from the tannery sometimes filled me with melancholy as I waited for my mother-in-law's car headlights bumping over the paddock, flickering like motor-cycle lights on the rough land, then that, I am sure, is the natural order of childhoods: that certain lights produce sadness, that the night be full of threatening shapes, and the sight of ants crawling along a windowsill is enough to induce an inexplicable terror.

My children ran wild, with dirty faces and, often as not, empty bellies.

In the evenings we ate puddings.

And when my brood were safely asleep our little rituals would begin, everything in its place, one thing at a time. Brush your teeth, Herbert, in water so cold it hurts them. Empty your bladder into the stinking mysteries of the dunnycan. Bid your mother-in-law good night and climb into bed.

Sit there, wait, toss a little, turn a little so that she, still sitting by the fire, can inquire:

"Can't you sleep?"

"No, not yet."

"I'll get some warm milk."

The warm milk is produced, yellow with cream, in a thick chipped mug that has travelled all the way from London to Point's Point, to Geelong, to Maribyrnong, to sit beside my bed, clinking on the marble-topped dresser beside my wristwatch with the luminous dial and the sweat-sour leather band.

The milk will not work, but it must be used, as part of our ritual, as the raising of the cup is in the other.

"You must sleep, poor man. I'll sponge your face."

"Ah, thank you."

Yes, step by step, through this door, up this passage, jangling our keys, we proceeded, until the last door open we were permitted, as reward for our best endeavours, to cover each other with plum-soft kisses, while the half-drunk milk wrinkles its yellow face and separates itself into an edible impersonation of ageing skin.

I never blamed the holy pictures for bringing our idyll undone. They looked down on us, I thought, benevolently: Jesus with his heart showing, like an ad in a chemist-shop window; Mary ascending into heaven. I liked to have them there. Had Molly taken them down I would have complained.

No, I blamed the Irishman at Essendon, to whom Molly – worrying about persistent pains in her insides – at last made her full confession. The pain, it turned out, was only wind, for which charcoal tablets proved quite effective. But by then the Irishman had done his work and it had been decided that Molly must not keep me from my wife.

I was plump from puddings and my hands were soft. She

bought me a brand-new Dodge. She took me to Stobbit's in Little Bourke Street and had a suit made for me. She dressed me, weeping, in her own electric belt. She knitted a sweater for Charles and a pair of socks and a balaclava for Sonia. But in the end there was nothing more she could do but make a thermos of strong black tea – it took only fifteen minutes – and present me with two tins of cake with pussy cats painted on them.

She stood in front of the old church hall that I had stolen from the Methodists. She plucked at the tall sedge grass that had invaded the grounds. She wore an unfashionably long cream dress which billowed out in the cold morning wind. She had used too much lipstick on her smile and her skin was dusty with powder, like the wings of a moth damaged from its adventures. She wore a cloth flower, a cream rose, in her gold-dyed hair. She held out a long-gloved arm and waved.

The gearbox in the Dodge was new and stiff. It moved reluctantly into first.

Charles kicked his new boots against the floor.

Molly, her soul now guaranteed safe and sound, retreated clumsily towards the solitude of the house.

I turned and drove straight back. But two days later we made our farewells for good. I headed up the Sydney Road, accompanied by St Christopher towards whose talisman I never felt anything but sentimental affection.

48

My attitude towards religion was not that of a serious man, and I did not think it odd that Sonia would have herself confirmed five times, not, that is, until the Church of England man in Ballarat brought it to my attention. This was in 1934 when Badgery & Goldstein lost the Dodge and my daughter decided on another confirmation.

I had no objection. She already had the dress.

I forget the minister's name, but I vividly remember the boiled lollies he offered me. The rooms of his manse were stacked high with cardboard boxes, large glass jars filled with Eucalyptus Diamonds, Black Babies, Humbugs, Tarzan Jubes, and Traffic Lights. He did not explain himself but I have seen the type before: clergymen with an itch for commerce who must satisfy their natural cravings in odd ways. This fellow was obsessed with buying things in bulk. He had me taste the marmalade he favoured, an orange Seville in a four-gallon drum, enough to last him a lifetime. He was a pleasant enough man with a great pile of fair wavy hair atop a high forehead. He had a hooded brow, bright blue eyes, and a small innocent mouth carried with him from his childhood.

He postponed the discussion of heresy (there was nought else on his mind) to show me the demijohns of water he had imported seventy miles from Melbourne. In the bathroom he demonstrated the comparative softness of Melbourne and Ballarat water by lathering his thin hairy arms and wrists – smeary Ballarat on the left, creamy Melbourne on the right.

We then sat in the front parlour and watched my pretty daughter play too roughly with his son. She did somersaults on the rough green lawn outside the leadlight windows and did not worry that she showed her panties.

Was I aware, he wished to know, of my daughter's frequent confirmations?

You cannot suck a man's humbug and be uncivil to him. I admitted to having seen her in her confirmation dress in another town, in other towns, with the Catholics in Sale, the Methodists in Yass. I had the photographs in my wallet – the pretty girl with the prayer book looking at the camera, sometimes alone, or, at Sale, in front of that redbrick barn of a thing, lined up with all those Irish eyebrows, pale skin, dark hair, squinting at the sun.

Did I believe? The reverend man inquired of me, proffering a second humbug which I declined.

In God?

His mouth wrapped around his humbug. His forehead creased. The big head nodded.

I confessed that I did not.

I did not, however, confuse the issue by admitting the pleasure I got from my daughter's confirmations – to see her there with her mother's green eyes alight with a passion not entirely selfish, that Bible clutched in her gloved hand. I envied her faith like I envied her careless tangle-armed sleep.

The clergyman did not come to the point right away. I realize now that he must have been busy with his humbug, wearing it down to a manageable size so that he might speak unimpeded, but at the time I was confused by his frown of concentration, his inexplicable pauses and frequent swallowing. Finally he got his sweetmeat into a suitable state and he was able to explain the nature of my daughter's heresy which he was now convinced she had inherited from that popish lot in Sale. He showed me the holy picture he had taken from her: the Assumption of the Virgin.

It was a beauty.

The Virgin rose above a great cloud of smoke while down below the adoring crowd raised their heads to what they could not see.

Sonia had assured the clergyman that she herself intended to do likewise and that her father Herbert Badgery (who art in heaven) could do it any time he liked.

"Oh dear."

"Oh dear," agreed the minister and bit his humbug so hard that it shattered in his mouth.

I looked at my daughter. I could not imagine what constellations whirled within her brain, how many angels she fitted on the heads of her pins, let alone how many she wedged under the edge of her broken fingernails.

I promised to attend to the matter as soon as possible but explained that we were newly arrived in Ballarat and busily establishing ourselves.

So if I may leave my daughter to tumble innocently upon the fresh-cut lawn, I must get down to explaining how it was we were in the Golden City at all.

49

By November 1934 I was a different man. I could read without moving my lips. I was an old python with his opaque skin now shed, his blindness gone, once again splendid and supple, seeing the world in all its terrifying colours. I had been drip-fed on Rosa's letters and Leah's monologues. I read the newspapers with the sensitivity of one liar regarding the work of another. An unemployed boilermaker from Williamstown, picked up on the road, was not just a witty fellow with a runny nose and a knowledge of horses, he was a symbol of the injustices that threaded all the way from the railway police who had most recently bashed him to Adolf Hitler and Mussolini.

People were still starving in Australia although the newspapers now denied it. When the Australian car industry at last capitulated and General Motors began manufacturing the press trumpeted the triumph.

I had become an armchair expert, busting for a fight.

I built my huts wherever we stayed, and left them for others to shelter in. This pitiful charity was hardly satisfying to a man like me. And yet I could think of nothing better. I slandered the communists for mindlessness and the Labour Party for racism. And at the same time I envied Izzie whose letters rubbed at me, irritated me, judged me, were sand between the skins of Badgery & Goldstein.

And it was in this mood that I took on the railway police.

I would not have minded the railway police if they were weak or unprincipled men trying to survive. Christ knows I have been both, am both, will always be both. But the railway police did not have the grace to lower their eyes in the face of decency, acquitted themselves like bully boys, enjoying the thwack of their three-foot batons. They evicted human beings from carriages carpeted with sheep shit and thought themselves righteous for doing it.

The battle was not planned in advance and started quite by chance. We were carrying a swag of rosellas down to Melbourne and stopped, somewhere between Maldon and Bendigo, to inquire directions from a group of bagmen who were milling around the railway line. They were trying to get up to Shepparton to pick fruit. Fifty yards up the line I could see the cause of the blockage – there were half a dozen railway police leaning against a siding platform. They leant like men in a bar, sticking out their potato bellies.

There was a communist amongst the bagmen. He had got up a deputation and had conferences, but with no useful result – the johns had sworn to massacre the swaggies if they jumped the rattler. The men were now in disarray, some for fighting, some for staying, some for walking into Maldon to get the dole there.

What I did was not done like a nice man. It was done with spit on my shoe, swagger in my walk, a nasty glint in my eye, a charming smile on my face. As I walked up that railway track to talk to the bully boys I was my father's son. I had a vision of myself that sunny morning as I had not had a vision of myself for years: I could *see* Herbert Badgery again. I was delighted to hear the crunch of railway gravel. I was pleased my shoes were spit-bright, my handsome head newly shaved. I adopted the bearing of a brigadier and swung the silver-topped cane I used in my act as an idiot. I could feel Leah's eyes (wet, bright, big) boring into my broad straight back, but I was not doing this for her admiration. I was doing it for my own.

I tipped my Akubra to the gentlemen in blue who hung around the siding drinking tea from their thermos. They had, of course, observed me speaking with their enemies, but they had also witnessed my walk towards them (need I stress, *again*, the importance of the correct approach to walking?). They were uncertain as to how to take me. Perhaps they brought me an inspector in disguise and they offered me tea and gave up the rest of their soiled lumpy sugar when I demanded it.

I was, by then, an accomplished Thespian; I understood the value of silence on a stage, how it can be used to induce suspense, and then hysteria. I used a long cloak of silence to examine them. The smallest one was the most dangerous. He was none other than John Oliver O'Dowd, the same who was later responsible for Izzie's misfortune at Albury, a bully of a rare and dedicated sort, short, broad-shouldered, small-eyed, a type often mistaken for homosexual by people trying to explain the odd seepings of sentimentality in that otherwise impassive, excessively masculine face.

The others were bully boys to be sure, all leaning towards one another for support, thick-necked, broad-armed followers of orders, and my game made them edgy and uncertain. John Oliver O'Dowd was a good ten years older than his "bhoys" and it was to him that I addressed my remarks. I informed him of the numbers of men who waited on the track and said they only wished lawful work in the orchards, that they would be using carriages intended for animals already slaughtered or still in the fields, that they would be causing no financial loss to state or individual enterprise and that, if John Oliver O'Dowd should turn his official back, then these presently useless men might get on with producing wealth for the benefit of the state.

I spoke to him nicely. I could have sold him a Ford or a cannon. I did not permit him easily to hate me. I stroked the bastard like a trout until my demands made him turn, reluctantly, from me.

"All very decent, Mr Badgery," O'Dowd said at last (carefully, carefully). He pulled a hair from his nose and gazed at it a second. "I dare say. But we are policemen and we have our orders and intend to obey them."

His zombies dragged their heels through gravel, intent on underlining their boss's remarks.

"If you obey your orders, Mr O'Dowd, I will drill these men for half a day and then I shall march up here and we will go through you lot like a hot knife", I smiled, "through a block of lard." I made myself *like* him as I spoke to him. And liking him, of course, was more than half of it, to understand why this miserable O'Dowd with his short arms and thick wrists should be the animal he was, to imagine his miserable cot, his nights beneath hessian bags sewed into quilts, his early frosty mornings, his loveless dusks, his unbending father, his withered disappointed mother. You cannot fake this affection, and O'Dowd knew, in the very moment I threatened him, that I also *liked* him. It weakened him horribly.

"That's as may be," he said, smiling himself.

"As will be."

"Come, Mr Badgery, those buggers is all commos."

"Have you not heard of me?" I inquired, spitting out my tea-leaves daintily at his feet. He shifted a boot sideways just in time.

"Can't say I have."

"You would be familiar with the International Workers of the World?" Oh, what pleasure it was to counterfeit this belief, this membership, to see his small eyes blink at my lovely, shiny lie.

"You're not a Wobbly?"

"I'm a human being, sir, and you won't be permitted to treat these men as animals." I drew myself up taller. I gave a beautiful account of my career with the Wobblies. In a brief circuit I visited Chicago and Perth. "Write it down if you must," I told the fair-haired galoot who was making earnest notes of my confession. "Do a fair draft and I will sign it."

O'Dowd snatched away the notebook before his man made a fool of himself.

"All right?" I asked O'Dowd. He did not answer. "I'm giving you mugs half an hour to make up your mind. If you haven't given us reason to change our minds, we'll come down here and do you."

"Youse was going to do drill," sneered the man who had lost his notebook.

"That was before I looked you in the eye, son."

And then I walked back along the line to report my progress to the men. I swung my cane. The magpie, a lovely bird, gave such a clear happy cry, like an angel gargling in a crystal vase.

50

Of the fifty men gathered at the siding, only three had no inclination for a fight, and one of these was an old fellow known as "Doc" who shouldered his bluey and whistled up his lame fox-terrier before formally wishing them all well. He made a small speech with many classical allusions. The other two made off without a word to anyone, walking slowly up the road past the railway johns who were still lounging against the siding platform. O'Dowd called out to them. They slowed, then stopped. The big stooped one took off his swag and gave it to his mate. Then he walked across and was surrounded by the bullies for a good three minutes. Finally he departed with his mate.

O'Dowd knew the bagmen were solid. I looked at my watch and sipped my tea.

Leah had the commie over to one side by some black forty-four-gallon drums. She listened to him with a bowed head and then, lifting her dark eyes, asked quiet, intent questions. The bagmen, I saw, were starved for the softness of children's skin and the agitation of small squirming bodies and you could see it in the eyes of those who did not even acknowledge Charles and Sonia that they, too, "'ad one just like 'im". The homesickness was palpable.

A big bushman called Clout was at work with a tomahawk making batons. When he had trimmed a bit of ironbark to size, or knocked the worst splinters of a split fence post, he would swing it around his head a few times before crashing it down on the rails. Yet in spite of Clout's displays of violence, it was a very quiet, pleasant, sunny day, only spoiled by the excess of blowflies which gathered on the bushman's sweat-dark back and hung in clouds around the mouths of those inclined to yarning.

At twenty past the hour we heard a train. It was not the one we wanted. It came around the river flat below at enormous speed, getting up chuff for the slow crawl up the hill on whose crest we sat. This spot, fifteen miles from Bendigo, was known to bagmen all through the country as "Walkers' Hill" because you could – from either side of this crest – jump the rattler at a leisurely walking pace.

O'Dowd now stood and began to stroll towards us and Clout, reckoning the hour had come, began to distribute his batons, the ends of which he had lewdly sharpened "for playin' quoits".

O'Dowd came walking carefully, showing great regard for the welfare of his boots at which he stared with great attention. When, at last, he showed his face, I saw what he'd been hiding – a smirk I could not understand.

"All right, Mr Badgery," he said to me. "You've won."

The men cheered. Someone clapped O'Dowd on the back.

"There's a train coming now," O'Dowd shouted. "Youse can all get on it."

"That's the Ballarat train," the communist said, pushing through. "These men want to go to Shepparton. It's going the wrong way."

O'Dowd could not help himself. He split himself with a grin. "Tough," he said. He could already feel the uncertainty amongst the men as they hovered, lifted a bag or put one down, whispered to a mate or cursed or spat. Their acceptance or rejection of the train was showing in their dusty irritated eyes.

"It's this train or no train," O'Dowd said. He was a clever bastard. He knew they didn't want to go to Ballarat, but he gave them a small victory which was enough to make them go soft and lose their fight. He smiled at me just like I had smiled at him. He was *making* them do the exact opposite of what they wanted.

"There's no work in Ballarat," I said.

The smile swallowed itself in the cold slit of his mouth. "There's work", he said, "everywhere, for them that want it."

The train engine was in sight now at the bottom of the hill. The men started to check their swags, to arrange a billy, tighten a strap, hoist a bundle, kick a fire apart. They came around and shook my hand. They lifted Sonia and kissed her cheek and hugged her till she grunted. They ruffled Charles's head and we were all, in spite of our defeat, warm – we had won the most important battle, so we thought.

The train drew beside us and we stood in full sight of the driver and the fireman.

There were sheep wagons, not clean, but empty. The men waited for the protection of closed boxcars, rolling back their doors in good leisurely style. It was then, as they boarded the train, I saw Leah. She was running towards me carrying the snake bag in one hand, pulling bawling Charles towards me with the other.

"Come on," she screamed. "Get on the train."

I laughed.

"Get on," she said. "For God's sake, I beg you."

O'Dowd, I found, right behind my shoulder. "Better get on the train, Mr Badgery," he said.

"Hurry," Leah said. She did not wait but helped my son aboard, and then my daughter. She was climbing on, and I was stumbling along the track, tripping on abandoned sleepers, O'Dowd at my side. By the road I saw O'Dowd's bully boys setting to work on the Dodge. They had, at that stage, only slashed the tyres. The brush hook they used was razor sharp. They drew it round the walls "like a hot knife", O'Dowd said, "through lard."

He started laughing. He could not stop. He was hysterical. Tears rolled down his face and he could not speak for a good minute, by which time he was standing still, we were pulling away, and Charles was bawling about his lost rosellas. The train wheels obliterated his last crow of triumph.

And that was how I lost my only asset, for lose it I did, good and proper. When I finally got back there two weeks later I saw the sort of mess the "bhoys" had made of it. They were not so stupid as to steal it. They simply destroyed it. They had been at the body with an axe. They had used no spanners or wrenches on the engine, just the sledge-hammer.

Everything stank of dead rosellas.

51

There is no doubt about it – I have a salesman's sense of history. I do not mean about the course of it, or the import of it, but rather its scale of time, its pulse, its intervals, its peaks, troughs, crests, waves. I was not born in some Marxist planet out near Saturn where the days last a year and the inevitabilities of history take a century to show. I am from Venus, from Mars, and my days are short and busy and the intervals on my whirling clock are dictated by the time it takes to make a deal, and *that* is the basic unit of my time. And even if I have boasted about how I was a patient man when I sold Fords to cockies, shuffled cards, told a yarn, taught a spinster aunt to drive, I was not talking about anything more than a day or two of my life, and *then* off down the road with the order in my pocket.

I was not some Izzie with a twenty-year clock in his daggy pockets.

It is true that I was the one who took on the infamous John Oliver O'Dowd and organized the bagman against him, but when

343

the battle was lost, I could not, as Leah begged me to (with tears in her big eyes), return to the struggle. For Christ's sake, I had lost my *car*. But in the boxcar that day, Leah was beyond such trivial things as cars or making money. She did not have a stomach, did not need food, drink or even air. All she could think was that we should take on the enemy again.

She was the saint with shining eyes. I was the shark, the lounge lizard. I took the family to the saloon bar at Craig's Hotel and performed the snake trick for money.

Leah submitted, glowering – she drew a line between cheating and entertainment that I never saw as clearly.

The trick was one we had performed many times before when we were desperate. Everybody had a part: it was up to reluctant Leah to release the snake into the bar. It was up to me to find it and identify it as venomous. Then Sonia, drinking her lemon squash, would declare she knew a boy who would catch it. She fetched Charles. Charles then caught the snake for a fee (and, inevitably, much admiration).

The trick did have its dangers. In Rockhampton a drunk policeman splattered our best black snake with the publican's pistol. In Gympie a bank clerk got one with a billiard cue.

We had many assets to replace in Ballarat and we could not content ourselves with one pub, but moved from Battery Hill all the way through the east and up into the smarter pubs around Lydiard Street. We moved fast, keeping ahead of any grapevine, as voracious as an army of ants. The cheeks of the Badgerys were flushed but Leah betrayed her emotions with a nasty rash along her slender neck.

My pocket contained a damp bird's nest of crumpled currency from which drifted the unmistakable odours of Ballarat Bitter. I clicked my cane, tap, tap, a light filigree of sound woven around the military beat of Charles's great clod-hopping boots which he stamped heel first, into the ringing pavements of Sturt Street. Behind him came Sonia, her white socks betraying the lack of garters and behind her was Leah whose bulging black handbag contained a dangerously compressed snake whose welfare was much on her mind. Leah wore what she had escaped in, a light floral dress with an unflattering stain she had collected on a boxcar floor, and a wide-brimmed straw hat whose generous shade did not manage to hide the fury dancing in her big grey eyes and, it must be said, the dancer was limping. I am tempted to suggest that the blisters she habitually collected were caused, not by shoes, but by the same thing that caused the rash to rise from beneath the neat collar of her summer dress.

While Charles dropped back to lean against the wall, the rest of us entered Craig's Hotel in style, through the revolving glass doors, a quick inquiry at the desk and then through to the saloon bar with me no more than three inches behind Leah so that I might hide the stain that marked her backside.

It was that quiet sleepy time in the afternoon when the people who inhabit saloon bars do so quietly, where the work of the barmaid is betrayed by small quiet sounds, and no wolf-pack laughter or hen-party screech offends the ear of the sensitive visitor who may peruse the photographs of famous racehorses at his leisure while the other drinkers whisper quietly to each other, or read their copies of the *Courier Mail*, turning the pages quietly in respect of the hour of day.

The snake, of course, disrupted this calm a little, but Charles was soon found playing in the street and introduced to the ashen barmaid and then the dour licensee. And while those drinkers who remained found themselves huddled together in a suddenly talkative group, the snake (a Children's Python) worked its way across the slippery linoleum towards an extraordinary-looking man in a yellow-checked suit. He had a bald head, a little goatee beard, an ascetic high-boned face, and gold-framed spectacles over sunken thoughtful eyes. While Charles, blushing red as usual, conducted his stubborn negotiation, this other fellow carried on his own silent conversation with himself, resting a gold-ringed finger on his pale lower lip. He rolled his eyes like a fellow trying to multiply 23 by 48 without using a pencil.

It was easy to see the licensee was not an easy man with a quid. It was not that he haggled, but that he did not move. He regarded Charles with sleepy-eyed suspicion. I expressed the view that the snake was venomous, and relied upon the fact that pythons are not native to Ballarat. The snake paused, lifted its head from the linoleum, and flicked its tongue at the smoky air.

"God damn," said the man in the yellow-checked suit. He spoke in the purest American.

The licensee blinked his lizard-lidded eyes; the snake lay flat as a fallen stick. A green pound note was passed, at last, into my son's custody.

"God damn. You're Lee-anne. The snake-dancer. I saw your show." He picked up his hat, stepped over the snake, and took two gliding steps across the floor, his hand extended to my

345

blushing lover who was huddled back against the photographs of racehorses, pretending snake-fear. "Nathan Schick," he said, smiling crookedly but charmingly to reveal a gold-filled mouth, "I saw your act in Nambour, Queensland."

I did not see Charles leave, but a scream from Sturt Street told me he was accompanied by the python.

Nathan Schick seemed quite unaffected. He fussed around the table and forced Leah to sit down. He shoved out his pale hand and gave me that charming, weary, gold-speckled smile.

"Badgery," I said, trying to keep the publican in view.

"I know, I know," said the splendid American, patting a small round stomach which looked like a tiny cushion shoved down his trousers. "You, sir, are a funny man. A very funny man." I could not listen to him. I watched the cardiganed licensee approach. I kept my eye on the door and smiled at Nathan Schick. "Yes, sir, I saw your show. You should see her," he told the dour-faced publican who had come to block my exit. "You should see this young lady work with snakes."

The licensee had the fine red veins and slow poached eyes of his caste. "I just have, Mr Schick."

Nathan Schick blinked and made his mouth into an "O". What a ham he was. I am nine-tenths convinced he betrayed us to the licensee and then rescued us to that we would feel ourselves in his debt.

He gave the licensee a crisp new pound note, ordered a round of drinks, sent Sonia to fetch her brother, and told the barmaid she was lucky to have such talented performers patronizing her bar. Schick could talk a line of bullshit like I never heard before, and in this he had the distinct advantage of being American and therefore never hesitant about expressing an opinion. Australians, in comparison, lack confidence, and it is this, not steel mills or oilwells, that is the difference between the two nations.

Schick also had that peculiar deafness that Americans adopt towards Australians (not dissimilar to the deafness city people adopt when listening to country people). It comes from not understanding the rhythms of their speech and assuming they would not live where they did if they were more resourceful.

So Nathan Schick, while regarding us benevolently, misunderstood our ironies and took them for firmly held beliefs, contradicted them, dropped names around the bar, criticized the act he had recently praised, suggested "improvements" without a beg-your-pardon, asked us to join his troupe which would soon play the Tivoli in Melbourne, then thought better of it and asked us to audition.

This, for people who had lost ten rosellas and a Dodge utility, was very heady stuff. When Nathan ordered straight gin, so did we. The angry blotches left Leah's neck and rearranged themselves into a rosy aura. She toasted me silently across the gin-wet tabletop, and even the line of her Victorian shoulders suggested relief.

Nathan Schick had ideas to take our act to America, or so he claimed. He caught me pulling a funny face at Leah, and hamming up his hurt feelings, produced a little gold-embossed notebook in which he had written: "Lee-anne, snakes". We had left Nambour, he said, before he could talk to us. He was full of ideas. Most of them – he freely admitted it – were lousy.

It was after five o'clock now and the bar started to fill. In pubs all over Ballarat thirsty men had only one hour's heavy drinking before they were expelled into the street at closing time.

"Hell, Lee-anne," shouted Nathan Schick, now hemmed in by a forest of trousered drinkers, "hell, *I know*, I'm not an artist. I'm just making a suggestion. Look, an example only. If you want to play, say, Dallas, Texas, you need a hook. You're Australian. You got to have an Australian hook. Something in your act, not a snake – all snakes look the same. Not your ostrich. Something Australian."

"It's an emu."

"Who cares? This is an American audience. Do you say to them, Ladies and Gentlemen, this is an emu even though you think it's an ostrich? Does Herbie make a comedy routine from this?" He raised his pale eyebrows from behind his gold-rimmed glasses. He considered the idea of my comedy routine, flicking his wide eyes from one face to the next. I wondered how it was that, no matter how I hated Henry Ford, I always loved Americans. "Nah," Nathan smashed the idea flat with his ringed hand. "Nah, you need something Australian in your act."

"A kangaroo," said Charles, and momentarily stopped kicking the table.

"Yes," said Nathan Schick nodding his head at my blushing son. "But no. I took a herd of boxing kangaroos out through the Middle West at the end of the Great War and no one was too interested. They are a vicious animal, Herbie, did you know that? Yes, they are. They ripped each other's guts out – excuse me, Lee-anne – but it's true. You can't have that sort of thing in family entertainment, as I'm sure you know," he said, obviously believing we knew no such thing. "Now you two kids should not be scraping around Ballarat pulling bad tricks in second-rate hotels. Neither should I. If Jack Benny could see me here, he'd say, what the hell is Nathan doing in Bell-A-Rat. My answer is: Jack, I am making a living. His answer to me: Nathan, it is not a living, it is a death. My reply: don't I know it. We are getting too old for all this. What I want is an Aussie act for the States. This is a great country, but it hasn't even started to be exploited. You people don't realize what it is you have to sell."

"Wombats", said Charles, "and koalas."

"There are problems with the wombat," Nathan Schick said. "I was interested in wombats in '29. I went up to your zoo in Sydney and looked at the wombat. The fellow said you could train them but God, Herbie, no offence . . . Lee-Anne . . . but the wombat is not star quality. They would laugh at you in Pittsburgh. You know what I mean, uh? Pittsburgh?"

We didn't.

"They would laugh at you and your wombat. And the koala – sure, it's cute, but they pass wind and they're intoxicated all day. You can't work with those sort of people. The koala is not a commercial property. You need something very original. Maybe you should have some abos in your act. They do a war dance? Tie you up? Herbie rescues you? No, it's not enough. It's the wildlife that I like, and that's where I think you two are on to something."

And what did puritanical Leah think of Nathan Schick? Leah Goldstein, who put Izzie Kaletsky on a pedestal and then worried about the ethics of skin, this same Leah Goldstein sat in her chair with her gin and water, and beamed at him. She loved Nathan Schick's vulgar suit and ringed hands. She liked the garrulous checks, like leftover material from a Silly Friends party. Even as he had walked across the saloon bar, stepping over the snake so carelessly, even as he opened his gold-filled mouth to expose her for fraud, she liked him.

Leah became light-headed more quickly than mere gin could explain.

She laughed, that great wild snort of a laugh that was her trademark, and gave not a damn that heads in that noisy bar turned to look at her. She was talkative, almost (for her) garrulous. She told a story about Rosa, one about a snake; she held my hand and patted me on the head. When we stumbled out into the gin-bright street she liked Nathan enough to kiss him, first on one cheek and then the other. She made his sunken eyes gleam like diamonds and she glowed herself, realizing the importance of her gift.

Nathan had a soft spot for us too. He was to tell us so, continually. He exploited us in his crummy show in Ballarat and had us work at starvation rates, but still he liked us. He was lonely, divorced three times with all his children either in hospital or gaol, but he was an optimist. He quickly became Dear Nathan, Bloody Nathan, Poor Nathan, Nathan-won't-shut-up, Nathan-won't-go-home.

I grew to love the bony-faced bastard and his schemes, and I thought that Leah did too. She worked hard, laughed more often, told her awkward jokes, but the letters from Ballarat show the true condition of her soul: they lack joy. It does not matter that she had a real job in a big city, three shows a day, write-ups in the *Courier Mail*, a new act with a Distinctive Australian Flavour. All this, it seems, was froth.

She wrote to Rosa: "The lesson I have learned is that what you say will happen, *will* happen. I declared myself a dancer when I had no right to. I had no skill, no experience, nothing. And yet, today, here I am writing to you from Ballarat and telling you about our show, and that I have spangles on my tits and a regular Yank to tell me when I am out of time. How pathetic I have been. I am like someone God has given three wishes to and all I have asked for is ice-cream. I have been wasting time trying to get deep satisfaction from something that cannot provide it. Ho-hum!"

In the light of this one could be cynical and say that the telegram telling her of Izzie's accident was a gift from God.

52

Leah felt the jerk of the train physically rip her out of Ballarat. She saw dry-eyed Herbert Badgery standing waving, hiding his emotions in the shadow of his Akubra hat, grey, formal, unsmiling. Beside him Nathan Schick showed his gold teeth in crooked-faced regret. Mr Schick was bare-headed of course, because he had given his Panama hat to Leah ("A lady cannot travel without a hat") and had replaced its band with a burgundy ribbon he "just happened" to have in his pocket. Dear Mr Schick, she reflected. Dear Mr Schick was a good man although, paradoxically, quite dishonest. He had them working for less than a stagehand, had lied to them about his Tivoli show, but had come to the station, given away a fine hat and stood there now with his eyes gleaming with tears in his ascetic bony skull. Sonia held a handkerchief to her mouth. Was she pretending to cry? Leah did not care for Sonia who had been, she thought (and said), spoiled by her prettiness, and her father's loneliness for female company. She was a product of Skin, stroked too much, fondled, indulged and should have had her knuckles rapped and her backside paddled instead of being permitted to display all these parodies of female fine feeling of which her gooey-eyed religion was only one example. She had been permitted to say a prayer in the carriage. Dear God let Leah travel safely to Sydney and may Izzie be better soon. Amen.

Leah moved irritably in her seat and considered the other occupants of the carriage: old ladies of the type you no longer see: thick stockings, hanging drawers, stretched cardigans, ruddy faces, dead fur, powder, flatulence, all for ever in the process of arrangement and rearrangement while they looked for their tickets and called each other Mae or Gert. They smelt of dust and ignorance, like front rooms that need airing.

Leah's cheek was smeared with tea-tree oil, the remainder of Charles's goodbye kiss which she would, in fact, carry with her all her life for she would never be able to smell tea-tree oil without remembering that acned face shining bright beneath the aromatic sheen. He had made her promise she would come back and she had phrased her promise like a clever lawyer. She was ashamed of herself for the promise, and unsure as to the correctness of what she was doing. Regret hovered, waiting to be let in. And yet, as the train tore her free of Ballarat, she was mostly aware of having done something, at last, that was fine, something selfless, something that did not cater for what she imagined to be her mindless hedonism: the pleasures of movement, the tremors of skin, the sensualist's love of description. She did not relish Izzie, and for this reason she was pleased to go to help him but even while she savoured the pleasure of this fine decision she was pulling herself up sharp, criticizing herself for smugness and self-righteousness.

She was surprised to be on that train. Like a child who imagines herself locked in her room and then finds the door not locked at all, she stood uncertainly in the corridor, wondering if she would not, after all, be better to stay in her room with her dolls and her books.

She had not expected to be let go so easily. She had, of course, announced her intention firmly and then, to her surprise, found no one to question her. She had expected Herbert Badgery to fight her fiercely. Herbert Badgery, however, had not known this, nor had he guessed as she had, that once she had offered her services to Izzie it would not be easy to relinquish them. Later, when Herbert understood that his silence was based on a wrong assumption, he much regretted that he had not protested.

Not a simple regret either, it turned and turned, as endless as a corkscrew in his heart.

Leah did not overvalue Schick's easy emotion at the expense of Badgery's silence. She had lain in Herbert's arms often enough to have absorbed him, to have achieved that almost complete understanding of a character by osmosis. They had passed fluids between each other. She knew that this refusal to display emotion was not heartlessness but a dam wall of emotion on whose deep side she had also swum, silently, in a place not suggested by the flashy talk and loud opinions of Herbert the urger.

The train shuddered down through the hills of Ballarat and travelled through the greedily cleared land which produced in her a melancholy unrelated to her own experience in this landscape. (It is true that she had danced in all these towns between the barren hills, first with Mervyn Sullivan and then with Badgery & Goldstein, bleak halls in frost-clear nights, potato farmers clapping (a padding noise) on thick callused hands.) But she saw the landscape with Herbert's eyes. It was his, not hers. She could feel nothing for the place, and only sense the things he had told her: how he had flown there, crash-landed here, sold a car to a spud cockie there, at Bungaree. Even Ballarat had been like that. She had seen it as one might see a triple-exposed photograph: streets in which Grigson drove, Mrs Ester strode and through which the horse dragged Molly's mother's coffin. All of this she saw, but it was nothing to do with her.

Tonight she would see her father in Melbourne and she intended to ask him (took out pencil and paper to make the note) about his own feelings and why he had abandoned the rituals of their race which might have sustained them better in a foreign place. Why then had he denied himself (and her) this comfort?

Neither did she understand the old ladies in the compartment and although she recognized the squashed lamington cakes they produced (wrapped in wrinkled greaseproof paper) and could give them a name, they produced no echoes in her own experience. She listened to their long conversation about the dryness of the country from which seemingly poor material they were able to knit a conversation, or, if not exactly a conversation, a series of calls and answering calls like crows will do just before sunset. The word "dry" repeated itself, joined itself to other words and then fell away into silence to be replaced by the subject of erosion ("rear-rosion") which they clucked their tongues about. On the panel behind their heads the railways had framed photographs of ferny glades and cool green places on the other side of Melbourne where the Goldstein family had once motored in search of walks, single-filed, silent walks where they had all moved and stopped with a single mind, to listen to a bellbird, to hasten to a clearing, to taste the clean spring water.

She felt lonely, no longer joined to anything.

She took out her writing pad – never, ever, did she travel without one – and began the first of many letters in a long and complicated correspondence:

My darling Herbert, it began.

I had never been addressed by her so tenderly.

53

She was surprised that her mother had not come, and startled to see Wysbraum at her father's side, grinning widely and stamping his big feet while Sid Goldstein held out the parcel to his daughter. So intent was he on offering this parcel, so triumphant was he, so inexplicably delighted by the poor state of the thin bare cotton dress his daughter wore, that the embrace was awkward and became a defence of the parcel rather than anything else. Too many things were said at once, questions about bags and journeys, platform tickets (Wysbraum had lost them), concern for Izzie, all orchestrated with a triumphal note regarding the parcel and the dress.

"You see, Wysbraum," said Sid Goldstein, "you see, I told you. I told you she would arrive with nothing, Try it, try," he said to his daughter. "You are as thin as I imagined. Isn't it true, Wysbraum, didn't I tell you?"

Wysbraum nodded and smiled at Leah. He had become fat. His belly bulged against his shirt ungracefully. "Try it," he nodded and she was shocked, again, to see how monstrously ugly poor Wysbraum was and her heart went out to him. He was so ugly that people stopped to look, even the dusty old women from her carriage had paused for an open-mouthed moment to consider the spectacle of Wysbraum as he took the parcel from Sid and, there, right on Platform 1 at Spencer Street, undid the string and held a grey silk dress out towards Leah. He pressed it against her shoulder and made her – she was laughing and embarrassed – look at herself in the Nestlé's chocolate display case in whose mirrored back wall she saw herself reflected. The dress had fashionably wide shoulders and narrow hips.

"The latest thing," said Wysbraum, parroting what Sid had told him. "Your father knows. It is his business to know. Feel it, feel it."

Leah felt it.

"Silk," he said, as if it was somehow her fault.

"Very nice."

"Silk, from silkworms," he said, almost angrily, nodding his big head and making funny blinking signals with his eyes.

It occurred to Leah, quite suddenly, that he was signalling her to kiss her father and when she had tested the validity of this theory and discovered – what a beaming smile she received from Wysbraum – its correctness, she was shocked that he should take such a proprietorial attitude.

"Change," instructed Wysbraum, attempting to bustle through the gates without showing a ticket. The ticket attendant tried to stop him but he bustled through (rudely, Leah thought) with calls of "Come, come, you can change here."

There was a small fuss about Sid's ticket, but it was eventually found, together with Wysbraum's, in Wysbraum's pocket.

"There is a good ladies' here, right in the station," Wysbraum said (stamping away, coming back). "I have a friend from Colac, she comes up here often and she tells me the ones in Flinders Street are bad, disgusting, you would not ask a dog to use them, but for the country people they take trouble and the ladies' toilet here is always clean, no problems with paper and it is mopped out four times a day, so she tells me. The cleaning woman has a sister in Colac, this is how my friend knows. I said to your father that if you wished to change this was the best place because it is better you go into the Savoy dressed in your new dress. You can make the correct entry. Very smart," he said, rubbing the silk in his grubby fingers. "Real silk."

Leah escaped into the ladies' toilet. She sat there longer than necessary, trying to still her irritation. She liked Wysbraum, of course, but she wished to see her mother. She wished to see her sisters. It was three years since she had seen them, and that was the Christmas she was in love with Izzie and had hidden in her room. And now that she was here it was because Izzie had been hurt, badly hurt, in Albury, and it was not correct that the two men should be jostling each other and talking loudly and being like schoolboys on holidays when the occasion of her visit was something so terrible.

She emerged to receive praise, and indeed she knew she looked attractive in the dress and that it suited her well. As she mounted the steps of the Savoy Plaza she walked with a dancer's walk and felt the eyes of the doorman on her. She had no make-up and her eyes were sunken a little but she knew she was a striking figure. She walked as if she were famous. And, although one part of her was guilty and irritated, there was another part that thirsted for something as rich as the Savoy – after years of counting pennies, eating Bungaree trout and lard and golden syrup on stale bread, she was anticipating the white tablecloths, the long menus, the American cocktails with sugar around the rim of the glass. It was a big event not just for her, but for her father who would not normally have eaten in such splendour.

"Anything you want," he whispered in her ear as they walked towards the dining room, "anything, just order. Beef, chicken, whatever you want."

Men in black suits were attentive to them, although she thought she saw the *maître d.* look askance at Wysbraum whose suit wore the marks of less illustrious meals.

They were seated at a table overlooking Spencer Street where, as Wysbraum pointed out, they would be able to view the arrival of Leah's train in three hours' time. He ordered a Corio whisky although Sid urged him to have a Scotch. Sid then also ordered a Corio whisky. Wysbraum urged him to have a Scotch and not to deny himself on Wysbraum's account, that Wysbraum drank Corio whisky because that was what he preferred, not because it was cheaper and that if Sid – the drink waiter shifted weight from one leg to the other – if Sid preferred Scotch then that was what he should order because he did not have his daughter, the famous dancer – the drink waiter sighed – to toast every day. Sid weakened and ordered a Scotch. Leah ordered a Brandy Cruster and Wysbraum, as the waiter was leaving, changed his order to Scotch.

"It is true", Wysbraum said to Leah, "that I prefer Corio whisky because I am used to it. One glass each evening and I sit on my balcony and watch the lights of the city. It is a taste I am used to.

And yet if I drink Corio whisky and your father drinks Scotch then, you see, it will not give him the pleasure it should. All the time he will be worrying about me. He will imagine that the Corio whisky will burn my throat while the Scotch is soothing his, and there will be no pleasure because instead of the smoothness of the Scotch he will taste what he imagines is the roughness of the Corio, not rough at all, but he imagines it is. Now, tell me Leah, you are finished with this fellow?"

"What fellow?" She had been watching Wysbraum and thinking that he was, after all, in love with her father, that he spoke in this embarrassing obsessive way because he loved Sid Goldstein more than anyone on earth and that, she realized, was how he had always spoken. He had spoken in exactly this tone at the dinner table in Malvern Road but then, when she was younger, it had seemed the way things were, and everyone had smiled at Wysbraum, but now it seemed a rudeness, that he should have made love to Sid Goldstein at Edith Goldstein's table.

"What fellow?" she asked, not really thinking about the question, but seeing the abnormality of her family and shuddering mentally to feel herself free of it.

"Badgery, this fellow you have been in business with. You are through with him?"

"Oh no, Wysbraum. No, I very much doubt it."

"But", said Wysbraum, tucking his table napkin into his collar and picking up the menu, "you are returning to your husband, so your father said, who has been in trouble with the police. His photograph was in the paper. A nice-looking boy," he said. "Your father has been very worried for you."

"Wysbraum, Wysbraum," said Sid Goldstein. "Leah, don't listen to him. She writes to me every week, sometimes three times," he told Wysbraum, tugging at the menu to make him listen. "She writes to me. She tells me everything."

"You showed me the letter," said Wysbraum. "Very nice," he told Leah. "Very brainy."

"I showed him one," Sid told Leah apologetically, polishing his glasses with his handkerchief and leaving his big eyelids as soft and vulnerable as a creature without its natural shell. "How is your husband? He will have no use of either leg?"

The Brandy Cruster arrived at this moment. Leah looked at it doubtfully. She shook her head to her father's question while Wysbraum made some fuss about the Scotch. Her father would not ask, she knew, the extent of the injury; it would be something they could write about.

"Where is Mother?"

"At home," he said, again embarrassed. "She sends her love, and Grace and Nadia also. Nadia is doing very well in her secretarial course."

"You told me," Leah said. "Why didn't they come?"

"It is my fault," Wysbraum said. "Tonight is the night, Tuesday; every Tuesday your father and I have a meal in the city."

"So why couldn't Mother come?"

"It is Tuesday," said Wysbraum firmly and Leah saw her father's uncomfortable look, the way he cleaned between the tines of the fork with his napkin, a boarding-house habit he still exhibited when nervous or agitated. It was Wysbraum's night, just as it had been Wysbraum's suit, and it could no more be taken from him than the suit could.

"You have all this," Wysbraum would have said. "Monday, Wednesday, all the days. I, I only have Tuesday."

"So tell me," her father said. "How is Mr Schick and what will happen to Mr Badgery now that he cannot perform with you?"

And she managed, in spite of her irritation, to construct a story for him, not in the form of conversation, but as a letter. Sid waited silently, patiently, his hands in his lap while his daughter answered the question and even Wysbraum tried not to interrupt, although there was the fuss about oysters, and then the discussion about pork, which Wysbraum ordered very ostentatiously, so loudly that the group at the next table, a large flowery lady of sixty and two younger gentlemen in suits, all giggled and began – Leah heard them – to tell a joke involving Jews and pork.

"Ah," said Wysbraum, "I like a good piece of crackling," which sent their neighbours off into fresh peals of laughter.

"In any case," Leah said, "I would like to talk to Mother, on the telephone."

She pushed her Brandy Cruster away from her, as if the thing was now too expensive, too frivolous, something she had merely imagined she wanted, like a spoiled child crying for sample bags at the Easter Show. She rose from her seat awkwardly. "Please," she told the men. "Excuse me a moment." And when she saw her father begin to stand: "Telephone, that's all."

But having descended the grand stairs to the front foyer where she intended to telephone, she found her father, his napkin still clutched anxiously in his hand, right behind her.

"Please," he said. "Please, no."

The foyer was a large open space whose floor was chequered with squares of black and white marble. They stood next to each other, like pieces opposing each other on a chess board, oblivious of the interest of the ageing porter with the Lord Kitchener moustache and the Harris-tweed squatter who sat in tall uncomfortable chairs in the shadow of the grand stairs.

"She does not know," Sid whispered.

"Does not know what?"

"How could I tell her? Imagine the trouble I would have." He tried, unsuccessfully, to hide the table napkin in his trouser pocket. The pocket was too small or the napkin too big; he withdrew it.

"What trouble? How?" demanded imperious Leah beneath Nathan Schick's Panama; she took the napkin from her father and folded it carefully.

"It is *Wysbraum's* night. I told you already. Come over here, we are in the road. Here, Leah. Wysbraum is a poor lonely man. There is nothing else in his life. You cannot take away his Tuesday. He would not permit it."

"Here." She gave him back his napkin, tightly folded. He took it absently.

"Leah, you will see your mother again, soon. We will visit. I promise."

"Why can't he have his night, and Mother be here too, and Nadia?"

Her father could not meet her eyes. He was ashamed but also not ashamed. "Leah, they are all listening."

"Let them listen." She failed to stare down the porter who insolently refused to hide his interest. "You mean," she whispered, "Mother does not know that I am in Melbourne?"

"He is a strange man, Leah. Every year, by himself, stranger and stranger. No one else will bother with him. For everyone else he is too much trouble. About everything he is difficult, and proud, too proud."

"But I always thought you liked him."

"Yes, yes. Like him. A fine man, and very kind. But you must not phone your mother from here. I will give you money and you telephone her from Sydney. Have a good talk, an hour if you like. Here, ten pounds. Talk to her from Sydney with this."

"Here it is cheaper." She was already shocked by the prices on the menu in the dining room. "I will ring from here and say it is Sydney."

"No, no," said Sid Goldstein, truly shocked. "You must not lie to your mother, not ever."

Leah sucked in her breath long enough to stop her telling her father that he was a hypocrite. She contented herself with saying that she did not understand him, a suggestion that made him irritable.

"How can you not, my darling? How can you not understand? We write a hundred letters to each other and you say you do not understand. You have a brain. You have imagination. You think about things. Well, think, please. If you think about Wysbraum you will understand why you should not telephone your mother, why I could not tell her, why he could not have her here. Think, please."

"Father, I don't understand. I really don't."

Now it was his turn to suck in his breath. "You are going to look after your husband who you do not live with. Why?"

"It's obvious," she said angrily.

"Yes, he needs you. You love him, only, in the most general sense."

She tried to demur but now it was she who could not hold his eyes. She tried to remember what confessions she might have inadvertently made.

"In the most general way," he insisted. "In the sense that one loves one's fellows. I am not belittling this love. He is a human being, in trouble, and naturally you must go. I am proud of you that you should go."

"It is not to be proud of," she said defensively.

"And in my case," her father smiled palely, "it is just the same."

"What?"

"Wysbraum," (he was talking so quietly she could hardly hear him), "Wysbraum is the same."

"No." The single word rang like a shot through the troubled corridors of their talk. It was a cry from the dock, from the back of the court, a noise more dreadful than the judgement that had prompted it. She saw a vision of a future she did not want and had not guessed at. Even the snobbish moustached porter lowered his eyes and then turned his back, struck by the pain in the exclamation.

"It is a fine thing about humans," Sid Goldstein said. "It is the best thing." He held her shoulders in both hands. His grey eyes contained a small hard ball of fierce emotion. "I am proud of you."

It was thus that Wysbraum found them and, quite literally, prized them apart. Wysbraum walked up the stairs ahead of Leah, tugging possessively at his friend's sleeve.

As for the dinner, she endured it. She watched Wysbraum with disgust, seeing only a child, a limpet, a parasite living on her father's emotions and she could see nothing fine in the relationship at all. She said little but only her father, casting miserable glances across the table, noticed it.

Later, boarding the train to Sydney, she knew that what she had decided to do was not fine at all. Embracing her father at the door of the second-class carriage she was tempted to go, to pass through the turnstile, to tear up her ticket, to walk out into Spencer Street, a free woman. Instead she wrote a letter. She began it before the train reached North Melbourne. The letter was to Herbert Badgery and in it she expressed her feelings about the joy of the merry-go-round, the whirl of colours, the pleasures of movement. "I have not valued", she wrote, "what I have loved."

54

Spawned by lies, suckled on dreams, infested with dragons, my children could never have been normal, only extraordinary. Had they enjoyed the benefits of books and distinguished visitors they might have grown as famous as they deserved. They had the mark, not just of originality, but also of tenacity and, had they not spent their childhood in one poor school after another and their evenings bookless in the back of a Dodge, you might be reading this history, not to see how it was I failed as an Aviator or their mother as a Poet, but to see how it was that my wards, my child, my ghost's child, came to take their place in history.

But as it was they had no books, no brainy visitors. They made their futures in the same way that people fossicking in a tip must build a life, from the materials that come to hand. They made their philosophies from fencing wire and grew eccentrically, the one obsessed with birds and reptiles, the other with God, the insubstantial nature of life. Of birds and reptiles we will have plenty more to say later on, but on matters to do with God there will not be overmuch. And the difference, I guess now, between Charles and Sonia was that Charles, once he could see no *result* from his efforts to disappear, gave up and concentrated on things that were of more *use*, whilst Sonia would not give up and was like someone who has survived a cyclone and can never quite believe in the solidity of a house or the permanence of a tree. She felt herself walking over ice an inch thick, and splinters all around her. She was eleven years old and did not hide her holy pictures from me. If she wished to dress like the Virgin Mary I had no objection. I was lonely and miserable. I brushed her hair one hundred strokes each night and hugged her too tightly. I spoke to Nathan about the costume and he had his wardrobe mistress make up a blue robe of the type indicated by the Catholics in Sale on their holy picture.

Dear Nathan. He was kind to me. Now I was the one who would not sleep, would not shut up. He played cards with me and listened to me talk about Leah Goldstein until the passing dunnyman announced the coming dawn. He had no use for me in his show, but he hired me as his chauffeur. I drove him here and there on matters of business, and sometimes, on Sundays when there was no show, to pursue his hobby of fishing.

It was on one of these excursions to Clunes, near Ballarat, that the incident I will now relate took place.

Nathan and I sat at the foot of a steep bark-slippery ridge where a small creek wound through a rocky eucalypt forest. The creek was reputed to contain blackfish and Nathan, dressed in plus-fours, his bald head covered with a deerstalker hat, arranged the extraordinary collection of American lures he had inherited from an uncle. Nathan did not know which lure was which or when or how to use them. Yet who could doubt the efficacy of the set-up? There was a splendid cane box with a lid and inside the cane box were those colourful mechanical creatures, an octopus with feathers hanging from its bright pink head, dazzling silver swivels, jewelled bronze blades, soft feathered bodies adorned like peacocks, transparent bubbles, all so beautiful you would never think that their purpose was death.

While the ever optimistic Nathan lit a pipe and fiddled with his gear, I made a camp fire. We were not to fish until night and we would spend the afternoon yarning about this and that, but mostly Leah Goldstein.

Charles and Sonia went up the ridge. I opened a bottle of Ballarat Bertie's famous brew, leaned against a tree and listened to the Buick's hot radiator as it contracted quietly in the cool air. I did not worry about my children. They knew the bush.

Sonia arranged her robe in the manner of the holy picture. She drew it over her head and let her auburn hair show just a fraction beneath this bonnet. She drew the cloak around her shoulders and tugged at her little white dress which would not, no matter how she tried, come down as far as the Virgin's dress had when she hovered in the clouds above the astonished worshippers below.

Charles watched her, impatiently. He had grown out of all that rubbish. He wanted his sister to give him a bunk-up on to a difficult branch of a tree where a pink-nosed possum warranted his attention. He was like an opponent in a football match trying to distract a man kicking a goal. When Sonia clasped her hands in imitation of the holy picture, Charles made vomiting noises. He waved his hands and hooted.

But Sonia arranged herself, exactly.

Charles sighed and squatted with his back against the tree. He picked at a scab. He looked up into the tree's umbrella watching birds flick to and fro. He could identify most of them, even the smallest, by their silhouette. He knew his sister's stubbornness was well equal to his. He waited for the ritual to be over. He yawned, closed his eyes. When he opened them my daughter had gone.

Charles, I can see him, gawped. He called out her name, not loudly, but politely.

"By golly," he said. "By jiminy." He forgot about his pink-nosed possum and sat and waited for his sister's return. He was always patient and he waited with his mind a blank, watching the lengthening shadows and the final loss of colour to the night.

When he came, at last, to the camp, it was already dark.

Clunes, in case you do not know it, is bored full of mine shafts.

55

I remember the case of Mrs Chamberlain who was condemned for murder, almost certainly, because she did not show adequate grief for her lost child. She did not howl and pull out her hair in tufts. She was therefore universally derided as an unnatural mother and a monster.

I can only pray that my jury, unlike hers, possess imagination equal to their task, because I will not shriek and groan before you.

Instead, let me tell you:

It is alleged I hit my son and caused him lasting damage to the ear.

There was a funeral with no coffin.

At the funeral there was a small upset we need not dwell on. As a result of this upset my friend Nathan Schick drove me to Sunbury where he placed me in the care of doctors. Perhaps he imagined grief was medical.

56

The train had not run across Izzie's legs neatly, but torn crudely, splintering bone, crushing flesh; it took the right leg above the knee and the left across the thigh; then, like some Corsican bandit who wishes to leave a sign, cut the top of an index finger with a neat razor slice.

He had not been jumping the rattler, although that lie appeared in the *Albury News*. He had been fleeing from John Oliver O'Dowd who ambushed the boxcar Izzie was riding in (it had pulled into a siding in order to give the new *Spirit of Progress* right of way).

Izzie was out and running when the *Spirit* came hurtling up from the south, its brakes locked, sparks showering from its wheels while the driver, white-faced and bug-eyed, whimpered quietly as he sliced across the fallen man whose pointed toes had tripped on a spike.

The driver's name was Jack Fish, a shy and pessimistic man who had always thought himself a coward. But it was Jack Fish who ran back two hundred yards beside his hissing train, Jack Fish who pushed the bully boys aside, applied tourniquets in the midst of screams and hot, pulsing bright red arterial blood.

Something quite wonderful happened to Jack Fish that night, and it was no less wonderful for occurring in the midst of so much agony. He could not explain it to anyone but as he carried that bleeding mess, running, tripping, his eyes filled with sweat, he felt what religious people call God, and the experience of holding that ragged mess of flesh, that man, in his arms, all that blood, that beating heart, that screaming journey down the last twenty miles to Albury, the sheer terror of it, would give him a comfort about life he had no right to expect. It was not the business of being a hero, being given a medal, or having his picture taken. All of this made him uncomfortable and embarrassed. Nor was it the recollection of his dramatic entrance at Albury where the *Spirit of*

Progress had stopped half-way along the crowded platform and the driver had leapt down with the mutilated body of a mercifully unconscious Izzie Kaletsky. About all this, Jack Fish felt what someone else might feel about waking up in church naked.

This experience did not transform Jack Fish's personality, did not make him soft, gracious, or even very understanding. For this same man was able to write to Izzie in Albury Base Hospital: "I am pleased to have been of assistance to you, even though I hear you are a commie."

This letter was about the only thing that made Izzie laugh during that extended stay in Albury Base where his missing legs not only continued to send him signals that the morphine could not block, but the part that was left became infected and had to be dressed and redressed, painfully.

He fought his despair in Albury. It was more difficult when he came home to Sydney where the house had been emptied of tenants on his behalf. He was installed in the room where Leah had once learned to dance, where his mother and father now planned to look after him. The tenants' greasy walls had been repainted in a blinding "cheerful" yellow. A print of sunflowers hung over the old fireplace which was now fitted with a large electric radiator. Blue curtains with puckered hems hung across the dirty windows. They tried to give the room a new history with curios, framed photographs, but they had never decorated a room in all their travelling lives and it showed in the final effect which was jumbled, discordant, slightly desperate. It was then that it was hard to be brave. He was ashamed that his old parents should be forced to confront the ugly lumpy reality of his slowly healing stumps. He had been their future. Was it arrogant of him to feel that he contained the best of them, that he was a truer embodiment of their virtues than the brother who had disappeared into the steaming cauldron of the revolution? Perhaps, but the brother, anyway, was not discussed, and this painful place which could not be touched intensified his feelings of despair.

His body had let him down. If Leah had seen something unsympathetic in his lemon-peel skin, he had not. He had been proud of his body, of its unapparent strength, its ability to withstand hunger and violence. He had loved his body but at the same time he imagined it could be seen as ugly. He had, when occasion permitted it, looked at his frail blue-white form in the mirror with all the amazed tenderness of a lover. He had always expected to be let down by his mind, to be betrayed by fear or panic, but never, ever, by his body. And although his anxieties about money were an ingredient in his distress, they were nothing compared with what he felt when he saw his parents' cloudy old eyes confront his mutilation.

And yet he must be nursed. He must have dressings changed, be carried to the toilet and he was humiliated, guilty and angry to have wheezing Rosa and rheumatoid Lenny push him on a tubular-steel office chair which they used like a sled to push him to bathroom and toilet.

They had never been a tender family. They had been bright, ironic, combative, and the tenderness they now showed him was another source of pain.

So it was Izzie who insisted on the telegram being sent to Leah and it was Rosa – guilty about the marriage which she believed she had manipulated – who argued against it.

"Leave her, leave her. We can manage. She has her own life, Izzie."

"Let him send it," Lenny said. "She has a right to know. Ask her for nothing," he said to his son, "just tell her, so she knows."

Of course they all, as they conferred around the invalid's bed, arguing about the wording of the telegram, knew what would happen. They assembled the words like people wishing to escape responsibility for their actions.

Izzie did not approve of the anger he felt. He bottled it up tight, this defeatist counterproductive emotion which grew fat as a slug on his self-pity. But in the end it did not matter what he approved or disapproved of, and he was made angry by the tread of the milkman as he ran, soft, padding on his worn sandshoes, past the window. And even on those evenings and weekends when comrades came to sit in the room – sometimes there were ten or twelve people, smoking, drinking, talking – he had to fight to keep the resentment from his voice. There were those who saw it in his dark eyes and these, more sensitive than the rest, would soon find excuses not to come, or would come and then be unable to stay long.

Yet, for the most part, he was admired for his courage, for his persistence, for his lack of self-pity – even while he was learning to fight the pains in his phantom legs, to convert these signals into something bearable, he was writing pamphlets for the CPA and the UWU. He read voraciously.

His true emotions were not able to surface until his wife

arrived, one winter's afternoon, wearing an expensive grey silk dress and a Panama hat with a burgundy band.

She stood in the doorway and he found her, to his surprise – for he had not been thinking kindly of her – very beautiful indeed, a fine austere beauty whose slightly sunken dark-shadowed eyes gave a sorrowful sugarless edge to what prettiness might be in her lips.

Leah, standing in the doorway of the room where she had learned to dance, could not stop her eyes going to that ambiguous area of rumpled blanket.

"No good, Kaletsky," she said throatily.

And there was, for that little while, great tenderness and shyness, a more sombre, subtle version of the emotions they had felt in Mrs Heller's when she had perched pretentiously above her badly dissected dogfish.

Their problem, both of them, was that they believed too much in the scientific and the rational and they thought they could – like Marxists changing the course of rivers – prevent the floods and earthquakes of primitive emotions. They sat beside each other and spoke what they imagined was the truth. But Izzie could not untangle his anger from his love and Leah did not help him when she explained her terms: that she had come to nurse him, to be, as she called it, "of use", but not to be his sexual partner for she would feel that to be duplicitous. She did not mention the subject of skin, but it was not to be forgotten and it was Izzie who would use his sharp knife against them both, while she was changing his bandages on his shameful stumps and trying to ignore the erection he presented her with.

She *was* useful. She found the Kaletskys' finances in an appalling state and borrowed, in the first week, five hundred pounds from her father. Most of this was used to pay back loans that Lenny had arranged. She bought a wheelchair. With the twenty pounds that remained she bought bowls and cake tins and at night she learned to bake the rich Jewish cakes that Lenny would deliver by day. She made sure Izzie was at meetings he would never have gotten to otherwise. She arranged chauffeurs, had him wheeled here, carried there and stood beside him on platforms while he used his formidable talents in the service of a new world. But the price she paid was to become the focus of all his anger and this was less to do with his envy of those who could walk and run, more to do with the fact that she could care for him but not love him.

Rosa and Lenny, in their caravan, could not help but overhear the painful arguments of son and daughter-in-law. They moaned out loud in their separate beds, pulled pillows over their heads, and had stilted conversations whose sole function was to block out the bitter voice of their son.

"Please," Rosa heard, "please go. I would rather crawl like a snail. I would rather sleep on a mat on the bloody floor. I would rather be lonely and shit in my pants. Please go."

And later she would hear the sound of weeping, a nasty choking noise she had first mistaken for vomiting, but it was, she knew, the sound of her son begging Leah Goldstein to stay.

And that is how Leah Goldstein made a little hell for herself and the Kaletskys, like a child who crawls into an old-fashioned refrigerator so easily, shuts the door, and finds there is no corresponding latch inside.

Yet she was saved, as she had been saved before, by her letters, and when she continued her correspondence with me she used some of the art I had taught her and which she had once so vigorously rejected. Now she began to invent a life outside her walls, to send squares of sky to me (cobalt blue and saturated with life) to invent joy, to sustain it, and to write a hundred times about Silly Friends she must first manufacture. She arranged them on the mustard-yellow sand of Tamarama – indigos, crimsons, violet and viridian, people who were never born, walking on a beach she had stolen from 1923.

57

If you had seen me in 1937 you would have thought me finished. I had no suit. My hands trembled. I no longer shaved my skull and the hair that grew across it was white and wispy. Yet I was a young man, only fifty-one. My eyes were good and my muscles strong enough to ride a bicycle from Nambucca to Grafton.

I had been pumping gasoline and repairing bicycles in Nambucca and when I got my annual holidays I made the long journey up to Grafton, not for the pleasure of it, but to see the General Motors dealer, a Mr Lewis. I had filled his tank with petrol often enough and he had invited me to call on him if ever I was in Grafton. I was angling for a job.

Grafton is a prosperous town. There is sugar cane, timber,

rich river flats beside the Clarence River and I was already building mansions in my mind when I noticed the sign: GOON & SONS: PROVIDORES. It was just beside the bridge, as bold as brass, and I must have passed it twenty times before and not noticed it.

I could not believe that Goon would be still alive, but when I called at the providore they told me that the old man was asleep. I should come back in the morning. I left a visiting card and went to find a boarding house. I slept badly, although the weather was not yet hot, and in the morning I was back at the providore before the doors were open. I waited while they hosed down the concrete and hung out their wares by the big sliding doors.

A young girl, Chinese of course, but with a broad Australian accent, took me out the back, along a high catwalk, and up some old splintery stairs to a small room where an ancient Chinaman sat with the Clarence River running sleepily behind his shoulder.

The room was sparse, containing a widower's tiny bed against one wall and a simple wooden desk near the window. On the walls were many framed photographs and advertisements for various Chinese associations; they had thin black frames. The girl ran lightly down the stairs and left me with the old Chinaman who wore an inappropriate three-piece English suit. He was shrunken as a Chinese plum and his white collar, loose around his neck, showed its stud behind a drooping tie. His hands had the transparency of the old but it was I, the young man, whose hands shook.

As I entered he looked up and gave me a fast intelligent glance; he then continued with his writing.

When he spoke at last his voice was not like gravel but as weak and thin as jasmine tea. It was also clear and the English was perfectly enunciated.

"You must excuse me", he said, standing carefully, "while I take a leak."

I stepped back so that I would not block his passage from the room, but he turned his back to me and, having fiddled with his buttons, piddled into a chamber-pot he kept behind the desk. The pot had not been empty when he started and he did not add much to it. I turned to look at the wall. "Charlie" Goon had been president of the Grafton Chinese Commercial and Cultural Association from 1923 to 1926. The sombre group photographs seldom showed more than five members.

"Better out than in," said Goon Tse Ying brightly, fiddling with his fly buttons and seating himself. "I don't suppose you carry barley sugar? No? Just as well."

"You are Goon Tse Ying?"

"Yes, yes. Please sit down. Sit on the trunk. Pull it over, that's right. They tell me we have met before, but I do not know the name. I am eighty-one years old, so I forget many things. Where was it that I had the pleasure?"

"In Melbourne. In 1895."

"Ah, Melbourne, yes, yes." His foot moved the chamber-pot further under the desk.

"Mrs Wong is your cousin."

"Mrs Wong, ah yes."

"You bought this business in 1896."

"Not this one. Another one, further down the river. But I came to Grafton about then. That's right. I couldn't forget that."

"And you translated for a herbalist."

"Poor Mr Chin, yes, I did."

"I am Herbert Badgery. Surely you remember me."

"No, no," he shook his head.

"I was a little boy. You found me at the markets. Remember the Eastern Markets? I was a little boy. You called me 'My Englishman'. I slept at Wong's. I shared a room with old Hing."

His eyes clouded. It looked as if he had stopped trying to remember. He fiddled with his fountain pen and looked down at the book on the table. I kept talking. I described everything I could remember. I told him about the things he had taught me. I showed him my brightly shone shoes. He smiled and nodded. I told him how I had eaten porridge and he had drunk brandy and the smile widened into a grin that made his rice-paper skin crinkle like an old paper bag. I became excited. With every memory I produced a nod. My teeth were aching again but I did not let that stop me. I described his horse. He agreed it was black. He had been fond of that horse, he said, and began to tell me about it, how he had haggled over its purchase. I was too impatient for politeness. I interrupted his triumph to tell him about the morning he had taken me, with this very horse between the shafts, to make a camp. I told him about the place. I described the rocks, the thistles, how he had oiled his hair flat on his head.

He interrupted me for another leak. I listened to his penis dribble while I studied the Chinese–Australian Friends' Assocation. There had been a national conference in Brisbane in 1931.

"Yes," Goon Tse Ying said. He pulled up his trousers as he sat down. "Yes, yes. I remember. I was a young man then, full of life, and with no family. Now I have great-grandchildren and I am writing down everything for them. All my secrets," he smiled. "In this book. I must write them in both Chinese and English. The young ones don't understand Chinese – they're real little Aussies."

"You taught me to disappear."

He smiled, but I know that Chinese smile. It means nothing. I repeated myself.

"No," he said. "Oh no. I'm not a magic man. Disappear? Is that what you mean? No, no, I taught you to clean your shoes."

"To vanish," I insisted.

"Oh no."

"Don't you remember? You said, 'I am teaching you this because I love you, but also because I hate you.' You did not like the English or the Australians."

"My children are Australians."

"You were at Lambing Flat. Your uncle Han", I said, "was run over by a cart. His broken bones poked out through his leg."

"Oh," Goon smiled. "I remember you. Hao Han Bu Chi Yan Tian Kui, we called you: 'Small Bottle, Strong Smell'. You made up stories, all the time. You told me your father was dead and then you made Mae Wong cry when you said your father had beaten you and gone to Adelaide. To Hing you told another story, I forget it. Perhaps you have some barley sugar? Yes, yes, I remember you. Hing said you were a sorcerer. Mrs Wong was frightened of you. You made her frightened with a story about a snake. She could not have you in the house any more and I had to have you go to my cousin who did not want you either. Yes, yes. It all comes back. It's astonishing – you think a memory is all gone, and then there it is, clear as day. Yes, my Little Englishman. Small Bottle, Big Smell. Did you become a sorcerer after all?"

"I disappeared. You taught me. That's why Mrs Wong got ill."

He smiled and shook his head. "And my children tell me that there are no sorcerers in Australia, that we are all too modern for such superstitions."

We were interrupted by the girl who had shown me up. She brought us a pot of tea and two stout chipped mugs. Her grandfather introduced her as Heather. The girl giggled and ran down the stairs.

"No," Goon said. "No, I do not come from Lambing Flat." He

poured the dark tea with a steady hand. "My father had a store in Tasmania at a place called Garibaldi. Before that he looked for gold in Queensland. He was at the Palmer rush. Then he became a pedlar, and when he married he bought the store in Garibaldi from a relation he had never met. The relation was going home to China and my father bought the store because his mother wrote from China and nagged at him until he did. I was born at Garibaldi and I don't know any magic tricks except how to", he demonstrated, "take the top off my thumb which I learned from my Australian grandson."

"The fact remains, I have done it."

He waved me down, like a conductor quietening a noisy brass section. "Yes, yes," he said, and called me by that insulting Chinese name. "Possibly. I don't doubt you."

"Before witnesses."

"Be quiet," said Goon Tse Ying. "You make too much noise."

"So what are your secrets, Mr Goon?" I poked at his book, this splendid volume, black, red, gold, the colours of dragons.

"Shopkeeper's secrets," he said, sliding it out of my reach. He would not hold my eye. He moved his chamber-pot, nervously, with his foot.

"You were a small child," he said, stirring three sugars into his dark tea. "You misunderstood the things I tried to teach you. I was kind to you, but you did not understand. Perhaps your life had been too hard. Perhaps you were one of those fellows who sees tricks everywhere and thinks that nothing is what people say it is. I wanted you to know practical things, so you wouldn't be tempted to be what Hing said you were already. He was superstitious, a poor man from a village, and I did not believe him. I told you, I suppose, that you should not make a dragon. My English was not as good as I thought it was and you misunderstood me. A dragon, Little Bottle, was my mother's name for a frightening story. Also it is a name they give to liars in my mother's village. In Hokein, they say 'to sew dragon seeds' when they mean gossip. My mother also used to call the castor sugar she put on dumplings 'dragon eggs' but I wouldn't have a clue as to why."

He pushed the bowl of sugar towards me. "Quite all right," he said, seeing my hands shaking: "Not castor sugar." And then he roared with laughter.

But my shaking hand had nothing to do with sugar, either fine or coarse. It was a condition I had not been free of since my time in

Sunbury. "I lost my little girl," I said. "I made a dragon and lost my little girl."

Goon looked at me warily. "What do you want?" He edged his chair back an inch or two and looked expectantly towards the door.

I tried to calm myself. I picked up the mug of tea but my hands shook so I slopped it over his desk. Goon moved his book a little further away.

"I can tell you nothing, Mr Badgery." He picked up the book and placed it in his lap. "If what you say is true, you're the sorcerer not me. Poor Hing was right. He hung himself, did you know?"

My hand trembled uncontrollably. I placed it on top of the desk. I gripped the edge to steady myself, but the desk itself began to shudder and the open bottle of ink and the cups of tea set up opposing splashing surfaces of liquid. Goon Tse Ying picked up the bottle of ink and slowly screwed its cap back on.

"If a thing can disappear, it can reappear."

"You are the sorcerer, Small Bottle, not me. I'm a business man."

He had been kind to me as a father is meant to be kind to a son. He had sat me on his bony knee and pulled my toes. He had let me smell brandy and laughed when my nose wrinkled. He had tricked me and found a whole fistful of dirt in my ear. He had taken me promenading, "doing the block" as they called it, holding my hand proudly. He dressed me in a sailor suit. And now, with polished eyes inside his wrinkled, shrunken hairless head, he dared deny me.

I did not drink his tea, nor shake his hand on leaving.

58

I was not well. I went to my boarding house and lay, fully clothed, on the bed and there I thought about the book that the Chinaman had been keen to keep from me. It was not an ordinary exercise book, not a journal or ledger, not the sort of thing you could buy across the counter at any newsagent or stationer's. It was bound in black leather with a bright red spine. On the front cover was a gold panel surrounded by a red border. On the gold panel were three Chinese characters.

The landlady came in without knocking. She asked me to take

371

my shoes off her quilt and asked for money. I took off my shoes. I gave her money. I was thinking about that book. She inquired after my health but I only heard her, in my memory, after she had gone and there was little, anyway, to be said about my health. It was not what it was.

59

The haze of jacarandas in November gives Grafton an insubstantial look and I am no longer even certain that the Grafton I visited in 1937 is the Grafton that lives, so solidly, on the fruits of tree-killing, by the banks of the Clarence.

But certain parts of the town are very clear to me: the bridge over which I walked to and fro, the graceless metal trough which allows few views of the mighty meandering river beneath.

It was there, on that echoing bridge, I decided to steal *The Book of Dragons*. Dusk went; dark came. I wandered the streets, past houses where families were eating. I waited under trees, hovered by corner stores, trod the purple carpet of jacaranda petals. Cicadas trilled. The air had a sweet slightly mouldy smell. I went up to the General Motors dealer but there was nothing to see. The doors of his shed were rolled shut and padlocked. I took my bicycle from the boarding house and went up to the highway to cycle. I was nearly killed by an Arnott's Biscuit truck. I came back, once more, across that dog-legged bridge.

I crept down through the tall grasses on the steep bank of the Clarence and approached the providore from the back. The Goon family were all downstairs, sitting in their kitchen. The daughter was doing her homework. Two sons were crouching over the wireless. Such signs of domesticity cut across my heart and I thought of you, Leah, of your nipple.

There were empty molasses drums at the back. Mosquitoes bred in their rusty lids. I climbed up on one and hoisted myself up to the catwalk that led to the old man's room.

My shoes were well shone and supple of sole; it was not they that squeaked but the filthy Chinaman's floor. I fiddled and fumbled on his desk. The mugs of tea were still there. So was Goon Tse Ying. I could hear him breathing. I knocked the pen – I had observed it earlier, can see it still, black with a thin gold

372

band like a wedding ring – and it rolled and dropped, a little bomb, on to the floor.

He spoke, whispered, reed-thin, my insulting Chinese name.

I had *The Book of Dragons*.

I had great hopes for that book, and he, obviously, the same. He was on me like a spider, a hairless huntsman dropping, flop, off the ceiling, stinking of garlic. When you do battle with a master magician you do not enter the quest lightly. You know what he can do, how easily he can grease from your grasp, oil away, and take his information with him. I held him round the throat with both hands. The book dropped to the floor. You would not think a chap would get loose from a grip like that, my fingers interlocked like a golfer with a club, but he escaped me, hissing. I grabbed for the book and found it. His hand was at it too. There was, as they say, a struggle.

A moment came when I realized Goon Tse Ying was no longer there. I held *The Book of Dragons* in one hand, his bleeding finger in the other.

60

If I had not laughed out loud, I would never have gone to court and never known that musty labyrinth known as Grafton Gaol. When I entered my room in the boarding house I was not expecting laughter. I had walked the passage shoeless, had not stopped on the way for so much as a pee or a flush, had unlocked my door quietly with *The Book of Dragons* tucked inside my Fair Isle jumper.

Inside my room, the door locked, a chair under the knob, I sat down on the bed to study. My hands could not hold it still. I stood and laid the volume on the dresser.

On each left-hand page were Chinese characters. On each right-hand page were words in English.

A white ant hatch erupted in the night and the winged creatures pushed their way through the insect wire and flooded hungrily around the light, abandoning their wings and crawling around the shining white reflecting surfaces of my sweating face.

I approached the book no less desperately:

"It is my secrets of business which I fear you, my sons, have not yet understood. Therefore I write them down for you. Please attend.

"1   In purchasing stock, first of all, consider the demand. Do not stock a large quantity, firstly for fear of moths and secondly for fear of deterioration. If the goods are in demand at profitable prices it becomes an exception. In an exceedingly cheap article there is no harm to buy a large quantity."

The English made no more sense to me than the Chinese characters. I felt myself confronted with a code I could not decipher.

"2   Always serve your customers with courtesy and patience. Show patiently as many samples as you can.

"3   In wrapping up articles for customers make sure there is no mistake blah blah blah.

"4   Where there are too many customers to enable you to attend to them all at the same time, then ask courteously . . ." (the rest obscured by a brown sticky fluid).

"5   When a customer becomes lax with his account blah blah blah.

"6   At closing time lock and guard against fires."

By now I was giggling. Some fool was hammering against the wall. It was my giggling, of course, that brought me undone. I could have cycled back to Nambucca. There was a splendid widow there, the owner of a shell shop and a pair of gooey romantic eyes.

"7   In case of heavy rains. Ha-ha-ha. Loss by flood is unthinkable.

"8   Influence people by virtue, not subdue them by force. 'They who overcome men with smartness of speech for the most part procure themselves hatred.'

"9   Calmness is to be prized. If you succeed in this, prosperity may be expected in a short time.

"10   If a matter does not concern you, do not forcibly interfere. It is an old saying that it is the mouth that causes shame and hostilities. If one does not meddle with anything outside his own sphere he will be free from sorrow throughout his life. So beware of it."

I was roaring with laughter, heedless of whatever fools might stamp on my ceiling and belabour my door. I was later informed my listeners thought I had hurt myself.

"Oh Wing, my son, guide your brothers Lo and Wah, and obey my commands. Do not forget that if one does not alter the way of the father he is considered filial. *The Book of Poetry* said 'For such filial piety without ceasing there will be confirmed blessing on you.' "

When they took that sticky brown book from my hands I had begun to weep, and Sergeant Moth – that famous entrepreneur – picked up the finger and put it in a paper bag.

61

I am not sure how much later it was. I could not even tell you the owner of the house; but I have described it before – it was the house I invented to frighten the draughtsman in Geelong – that hairy-knuckled Englishman – when he would not put my name at the bottom of Bradfield's aircraft plans.

This house was exactly where I had placed it: three doors from the post office. It was a big stone place with leadlight windows, encircled with elms. The lawn, I saw as Sergeant Moth's Ford rolled up the drive, was dotted with daffodils.

Inside, at the head of the table, was a man with one finger missing from his bandaged hand. It was not the Mr Regan I had once described, but Mr Goon Tse Ying whose angry eyes I could not meet.

So it was, at a time when it seemed too late, that I began to have some understanding of the power of lies.

But read on, read on, and do not concern yourself about my years in HM Prison, Rankin Downs: I found my solace where I always would – in the blue pieces of cobalt sky, the mustard-yellow lies sent to me by mail, composed by Leah Goldstein.

Book 3

1

Marjorie Chaffey laid down her broom and squatted on the sun-silvered boards of her front veranda. A mouse ran across her bare foot; when it returned to nibble at her big toe-nail she brushed it aside. She was in her middle forties and when she squatted, she squatted comfortably, with her unusually large feet flat on the sandy floor and her thin arms folded on her knees. She could stay in that position for hours, and would do so, if the mirage would come back again.

The mirage had appeared at the bottom of the driveway. It had occupied the lonely road for four hundred yards on either side of their mailbox. There, shimmering above the hot Mallee sand, she had seen the main street of Horsham. This had occurred two years ago, two days after Boxing Day. She had been able to make out the parcels in the women's string bags. She could see the butcher cutting down a string of sausages and his name (Harris) was written on his glass window. She saw an old farmer with a bent back lead a reluctant fox-terrier on a string lead. She had seen the white-aproned grocer's boy riding on a black bicycle.

This, by itself, did not have the makings of a secret. If this had been all there was, she would have fetched her husband and they would have looked at it together.

But she had seen something else, and this "something else" had filled her with such joy, such a sweet mixture of happiness and loss, that she could tell no one. The "something else" was a young boy, dressed in cricket whites. She had only seen him for a moment. Another boy, the grocer's boy, had leaned his black bicycle against a wall and, when he had entered his employer's premises, the bicycle had fallen noiselessly to the footpath. The farmer had been led away by his fox-terrier. And then the boy in cricket whites passed the butcher's window, did a cartwheel, and was gone.

It was the cartwheel, the slender tanned arms, the careless joy of it, that pierced her heart, for she thought she recognized – although she knew it was impossible – her husband. She knew it

379

was not her husband. She could hear him then, could hear him now, up at the forge. His nose had grown and his eyebrows had skewed like a house whose foundations are sunk in shifting shale. And yet it was her husband and she remembered what he had been like when he was a young boy, swift and pretty as a rabbit. He had played on the wing for Jeparit and he had such a dainty, fast, brave stab kick – it fairly zinged – and she had married him for a young girl's reasons not like they said.

But now she heard a motor cycle approach and her interest shifted towards it. It was not a mirage. It was a real motor cycle, a hard metal object that was causing a soft orange feather of dust to rise into the cobalt sky behind it. Watching the motor cycle she began to forget her boy in cricket whites and, although she had no idea who rode the motor cycle, she willed it to stop.

"Stop," she said, not loudly, but very clearly.

The motor cycle stopped. It was beside the mailbox, four hundred yards from the veranda. It stayed there, its engine beating erratically.

When the rider got off his machine, Marjorie Chaffey felt – it came on her suddenly – irritated. She stood and picked up her broom.

She would have to offer the visitor some water.

2

The motor cycle fired and misfired, hesitated, surged ahead, misfired and spluttered. Charles gritted his teeth and felt the sand between his fillings. His kidneys ached. He had tied a woollen scarf around them, then tightened his money belt around the scarf, but the bruised kidneys still ached and the cause of their pain – roads made from saplings laid side by side, a technique known locally as corduroy – showed no signs of getting any smoother.

There was nothing wrong with the motor cycle, a ten-year-old 1927 H-series AJS. The fault was with the petrol. In all this drought-stricken Mallee it was the one place a traveller could be sure of finding water.

My son was seventeen years old. He had powerful thighs and thick arms hanging low from sloping shoulders. His great carved wooden head was marked with a black eye that was more yellow than black and from this spectacular bed of bruised flesh the eye itself, sand-irritated, bloodshot, as wild as a currawong's, stared out at a landscape in which the tops of fences protruded from windswept sand.

The hearing aid was in his ear but not connected. The ear spluttered and exploded, crackled and fizzed as it always did, whether connected to the hearing aid or not. With this ear he remembered me – the grief-mad father who had struck him one awful evening at Clunes.

The new Mercury sidecar, a heavy attachment better suited to a large motorbike, proclaimed his business: "Snake Boy Badgery" and the crudely painted warning ("Take Care. Snakes in Here.") did not lie.

He saw the mailbox when he was still a mile from it – a pale blue thing sitting on the sand which slowly revealed itself to be what he had known it was anyway – a four-gallon drum on its side with a small veranda soldered on to keep the weather out. A soft sandy track led from the mailbox through a stand of stunted Mallee gums and up a gentle rise to where a house – its corrugated iron walls gleaming silver in the heat – stood on a bare orange patch of earth.

Charles stopped at the mailbox and read the sign. "Chaffey." He was already nervous. He wondered what sort of person Chaffey would be, if he would be suspicious, or sarcastic or rude, if he had sons who would taunt him or daughters who would laugh at his funny looks, if they would refuse him water, deny him a feed, or give him both and then send him out into the dark unfriendly night without wondering if he had a bed to go to.

The gate was not made from wood or iron, was more of a trap than a gate, a strained contraption made from fencing wire and a complicated series of loops and levers that served to tension the wire and slacken it off. He had not come across the system before (not surprisingly – it was the product of Les Chaffey's ingenious mind) and so took some time to get it open and even more time to get it shut.

Marjorie Chaffey saw Charles undo his scarf and belt and place them in his sidecar. When she saw him comb his hair she thought: "Salesman."

It was late in March but still very hot. The wheat had long been taken in but still lay in sacks at railway sidings where it was being eaten by mice. The earth had been ploughed and seeded twice but the expensive seed had never germinated and the paddocks, the subject of mortgages and other substantial documents, were drifting like bad dreams in the wind.

Marjorie Chaffey tried to read the sign on the sidecar as it approached but she had left her distance glasses on the mantelpiece and so could not make it out.

The veranda was only two feet above the sandy soil, but it gave her the advantage over strangers and she remained there as she always did, looking down at the machine (shining black, glittering gold) which fell silent, not sharply or cleanly, but like a noisy meeting slowly brought to order.

The rider did up the buttons on his suit coat. He was, she saw, only a boy.

Charles tried to see her face, but the sun was in his eyes and the woman was in shadow. "G'day missus."

"G'day." The reply was as flat as a shutter on a window.

He squinted up at her. It would be a small exaggeration to say that he sought love in the stranger's shadowed face, but none at all to say that he wished approval and acceptance. He was a stranger moving amongst strangers, finely tuned to acceptance and rejection.

"Hot enough for you?" he asked.

"Hot enough."

He was sweating inside his heavy suit, but he wished to appear a man. He also wanted to say, I'm just a boy. I won't harm you. All I want is a feed and a place to sleep.

The woman on the veranda was as still as a goanna that knows itself watched and even the feathery touch of her broom as it shifted on the floor reminded him of a goanna's forked tongue as it smells the air.

"Boss home?" he asked her. He knew the black eye made him look unusual. He would have liked to explain the black eye to her. He was sure she was a nice woman and kind to her children. He could not explain the black eye. He was ashamed of it.

"What you after?" she asked.

"Oh," he blushed and made an arc in the sand with his boot, "bit of business."

"What sort of business would that be?"

A mouse ran across the veranda and she flicked it half-heartedly with her broom. The mouse ran up the handle of a rusting shovel, along the horizontal corrugations of the wall (Charles saw it, soft as a shadow across the silver) through the window and into the house. She removed the prop from the corrugated-iron shutter so that it dropped closed with a clang.

"Mice bad?" he asked.

"Bad everywhere," she said defensively.

"I come from Jeparit today," Charles said. "They were bad up there. By Jove they were. Eat your buttons."

"Eat your buttons everywhere." Charles did not hear her, nor did he notice the three safety pins on the front of her floral dress. "Eat your toenails in the night," she said.

Charles was fiddling with his hearing aid, a heavy metal box that pulled his suit coat out of shape. It came on with a roar. He grimaced.

"Sorry," he said, putting his head on one side as if he might, from this angle, penetrate the shadow. "I'm a bit hard of hearing."

"Ah," she said, suddenly sorry for him. "You didn't miss nothing. Just talking about the blankety mice."

"Got a cat?"

"Got two," she said, defensive again, "but it does no good."

Charles could smell, already, although he was not yet invited on to the veranda, the sour dank smell of mice. "I got something better than a cat, missus."

"Better talk to my husband if you're selling, but he won't buy nothing. If you've got mousetraps or that sort of thing you're better off to save your legs. He's up at the forge," she said, becoming angry, again, about the glass of water she would have to offer him.

Charles trudged around the back, past the hot silver walls, around the corner of the kitchen house. He had hoped that the man was not at home. He would rather, any day, deal with a woman for there was always a soft spot to be found in the hardest of them.

He was careful not to tread on the dead, sandy vegetable patch. He threaded his way through a rusting garden of ploughshares, tines and scarifiers and made his way, without hope, towards the dark mouth of the bright-walled shed. His hearing aid crackled and he missed the sounds of a man smithing and the cries of white cockatoos, three of them, as they passed overhead on their way to a stand of trees above a dry water-hole; their cries, coinciding with the slow powerful movement of their wings, were like big creaking doors in need of oil. Charles saw the birds but they only depressed him. He had swapped his nets for petrol.

The forge was set up at one end of the large earth-floored shed and he saw the red glowing piece of metal in the gloom before he saw the farmer himself. As he walked towards the shower of sparks he did not take in the unusual nature of the shed – the shelves packed with odd-shaped pieces of metal, the neat hand-written labels. He walked past a drill press and a lathe without wondering why a farmer would have such equipment. What he did notice was the tractor – an old T Model cleverly converted so that the heavy chain transmitted power to large metal wheels.

"Petrol," thought Snake Boy Badgery.

The farmer was one of those quick-eyed finely built men whom farming has made strong and wiry but who, in the end, are not suited to their work because they like the company of people too much. He was pleased to see the stranger standing in his shed. He did not immediately break off what he was doing – shaping a metal wheel cleat to replace the broken one on his tractor – but he finished it only roughly and when he had dunked it, sizzling, into a drum of year-old water, took off his apron and shook hands.

Charles was relieved to see the man's face, and not just because it grinned at him, but because it was, anyway, a friendly face, cocked, crooked, with pale eyebrows at extreme angles and deep wrinkles in the corner of pale blue eyes. This was Les Chaffey, a man with a dictionary on his shelf, a map of the world on his wall, a habit of poking at things with a fork or a screwdriver when they interested him.

Charles liked him immediately. He liked his waistcoat with the silver watch he had won at the rifle club. He liked the three different pens and the propelling pencil he carried in the pocket of his collarless shirt. But mostly he liked the way he cocked his head and listened carefully to what Charles had to say.

"Is that a fact?" he said when Charles, in an untidy rush of words, had told him about the snakes, i.e., that they were not poisonous and that they ate mice. "And that's your line of business, is it?"

Charles said that it was. His price was a gallon of petrol, a meal and a place to sleep. As he named the price he feared it was too high but, when Les Chaffey shook his hand to confirm the deal being done, he was sorry he had asked so little. Charles's eyes betrayed him by suddenly watering. He hid his emotions in the dark pockets of the shed.

As they walked back to the house a wind sprang up and the farmer tried not to think about his drifting paddocks, a hard thing to do when they are stinging you on the back of the neck. He took refuge in fancies about the young visitor's black eye, wondered if it had happened in a farm or a pub and whose daughter had been involved. There was something about the Snake Boy that made him confident a daughter had been involved. He got it wrong. What he was seeing was a need for affection that could have been best satisfied by a big woman with an apron and floury hands. But Les Chaffey saw the oily remains of pimples on his neck and big chin and thought he secreted an odour of sexual need as obvious and all-pervasive as the smell of the mice who covered, in their teeming breeding millions, the land from Jeparit to the South Australian border and this parallel brought him back to the very things he wished to forget – drought and mice, mice and overdrafts.

The shops in Jeparit, even the butcher's, smelt of mice, and in the grocer's you could see where they had eaten the paper around the lids of the Brockoff's biscuit tins and pushed the hinged lids open. At the railway sidings they ate the wheat bags from the bottom until the bags collapsed in on themselves, worthless, empty, a year's work inside the guts of mice. There were mice jokes and those who had children – both of his were at the Gordon Tech in Geelong – made little chariots from matchboxes and raced the diseased creatures in teams of four and six.

It was the mice that had brought Charles so far from Sydney, riding a motorbike he had never intended to buy. He had read about the plague in the Sydney papers, but he had not been prepared for the extent of it, the fearless armies of squeaking creatures, the stink you could never escape, the red sores they spread on the children's arms and faces.

No one had money to buy snakes and he had no talent to persuade them to change their minds. So he found himself broke and lonely in unfriendly towns, swapping the services of his pythons for a meal and a little petrol, knowing that tomorrow the snakes would be as sated as gluttons on Boxing Day and that if he wished to eat at all he would have to perform the Snake Trick. And it was the Snake Trick that had resulted in the black eye – his amateurish deception had been exposed in Dan Murphy's Commercial Hotel in Jeparit.

The Chaffeys' home was hot as an oven and smelt of mice and sweat but Charles was thankful to be invited inside and be formally introduced to Mrs Chaffey.

Mrs Chaffey was small and faded; however her worn pale eyes were still capable of transmitting signals of sharp alarm and warm affection on behalf of the husband called "Dad". She showed both of these emotions in the dark kitchen house as she listened to her husband explain the snake boy's business. She allowed herself to be persuaded to touch one; it was not the pythons that alarmed her, but rather the quantity of enthusiasm they might generate.

Mrs Chaffey recognized enthusiasm as something vital in her husband's life, but she also knew it must be measured most precisely, like one of those potions (so beloved of quacks) that are vital in a small dose, and lethal in a larger one. When she had finished assessing the snakes she gave them back to their owner. Then she offered him a glass of water and cut extra potatoes for the Irish stew.

3

It is difficult to give the flavour of my son's life at this stage, and although he would later romance about it, claim that he had been a scholar of boarding houses and a citizen of the highway, that he had friends from Moe to Minyip, his grown-up eyes would still show the truth to anyone who cared to look at them: he had passed along those roads a total nonentity, had felt himself a no one, worse than a no one: shy, ugly, nervous of grown men, anxious when confronting boys his own age, a blushing fool with café waitresses, an easy target for teasing children.

Yet he also harboured an idea of himself that contradicted all of this: that he was someone special, someone who would one day do great things not just for himself, but for his country. And these contradictions, the triangular tensions between his shyness, arrogance, and hunger for affection, made him a difficult person to get to know, made him belligerent when nervous, a stammerer when confident, weepy when approved of, brash when he would be better off being quiet.

He was hampered further by his deafness which sometimes made him imagine slights where none had been intended.

These things were quite enough to make him a poor salesman, but he suffered a further handicap – he was so eager to tell the truth that he could never simplify. I have seen in him my own dizzy desire to throw all one's being at a friend's feet, to show the tangle, the contradictions, the good and the bad, and say – there I am. I did it myself one evening with Jack McGrath. I have done it on other occasions, but with Charles the truth was an obsession. I don't know where it came from, but it made him a poor salesman. And this is not, as you may have imagined Professor, because a

386

salesman is required to lie. It is because the truth, told thus, is of no interest to the average punter.

And even with someone like Les Chaffey, it seldom brings a benefit.

Chaffey was interested in every word my son had to say. He sat him in his big gloomy dining room before the sun was down and put a big plate of stew in front of him. There was gristle on the meat and fat floating in the gravy, but Charles was so hungry that both his head and his belly ached. He picked up his yellow bone-handled knife and his verdigrised fork without waiting to hear if the Chaffeys said grace or not. Then Mrs Chaffey gave him a napkin so he put his knife and fork down and spread the linen on his lap.

It was then Les Chaffey asked him where the pythons came from.

Now if Charles had been able to forget an isolated pocket in Papua and a reported sighting in the Gulf, he could have answered this question in four words and got a potato into his mouth before the next question arrived. But he was not capable of such deceit and there was, anyway, such interest in the faces of both host and hostess, that he wished to present them with everything, not only about the snakes, but in the way that he himself, in the daily course of his life, had collected the information. So he not only mentioned the isolated pocket in Papua and the sighting in the Gulf which, he had to confess it, he had not read about himself but had been told by a man who he had met in a café in Ararat, a schoolteacher, a Mr Gibson, originally from Moe, who was not a teacher of natural science but of English but who read science as a hobby.

I am abbreviating. For every road Charles took he came to a fork that had to be noted if not explored. He covered many points, including the origin of his suit and the explanation of the oil stain on the cuff, before he revealed that Mr Gibson had told him that the sighting in the Gulf was not the python in question – there had certainly been no scale count – but another python or rather a snake commonly called a python, but in fact not a python at all.

His host and hostess were mopping up their gravy with big lumps of snowy baker-shop bread and Charles was still trying to get the first lump of spud into his mouth but he had not, even though he had abandoned Mr Gibson, been able to complete his answer.

He sat talking, his elbows resting on the checked oilskin table,

387

while his pythons ate their fill, lazily doubling their bodyweight; they oozed their way through holes in the hessian wall-lining and lay plump and lumpy amidst the dry black seaweed insulation Les Chaffey had brought all the way from Geelong. Charles watched a skin form on the top of his stew. He spoke faster and faster. He was grateful for his host's kind attention and, at the same time, although he knew it was wrong of him to feel it, he was angry and resentful that they would not let him eat.

And yet he might have eaten in the end for his answer, although it seemed, as it uncoiled itself, to be never-ending, eventually began to taper and, finally, showed the divided subcaudal scales of the very tip of the tail itself. He should have had time for a quick mouthful before his host's next query, and would have, had he not noticed the aforementioned person leaning forward and staring unashamedly at his black eye. He was, as I have already said, ashamed of the story behind his injury but if he were asked a direct question about it he would have no choice but to tell the truth in all its humiliating detail.

The sun had now gone and kerosene lamps had appeared in the course of Charles's answer. They cast a deep blue shadow and it was the quest for this soft hiding place that made him push his chair back and turn his head in such an awkward way. Once he had his eye tucked safely out of sight, there was nothing the Chaffeys could do to persuade him to eat. He patted his stomach and declared himself satisfied. He could have cried with disappointment.

"Did you", Les Chaffey said, helping himself to his guest's uneaten food, "have a barney?"

Charles stared at his host, transfixed.

"A blue?"

He had a headache, and his neck hurt too.

"A stoush?" Les Chaffey suggested, leaning across his laden plate with knife and fork poised, his eyebrows skew-whiff in anticipation.

Charles shrugged miserably.

And then, as Marjorie Chaffey watched in the soot-curtained lamplight, something occurred that she would remember for a long time but never be able to do justice to in words except to say: "What a lovely smile."

But this is an inadequate description of such a miraculous thing. The smile that Les and Marjorie Chaffey received from their guest was a request not to persist with the question and a generous reward for not doing it. But it was also much more than this and his Messianic grandfather, had he possessed such a gift, would have had all Victoria queuing up to buy his cannon.

That night Les Chaffey would dream of chopping wood, splitting open an ironbark log and discovering a red rose, miraculously untouched, within its hollow core.

4

Les Chaffey was a man who could not see a loose thread in a pullover without pulling at it, or spy a horse without trying to pat it. If he met an Italian he would want to hear the Italian language spoken and then have many common English words translated ("Now then, what would be the Italian word for 'generator'?"). If he ate a stew he wanted to know how it was cooked and what went into it. This behaviour gave him a name as a sticky-beak and a gossip. It made no difference that he had also invented several ploughs and a device for grubbing Mallee country or that people had journeyed all the way from Melbourne to inspect them. This gave him the additional reputation, not totally undeserved, of being dangerous.

He had a gramophone and several Tommy Dorsey records. He sat in the hot dining room or on the veranda with shirt sleeves rolled up, his waistcoat unbuttoned, his white ankles showing above his slippers, his head cocked on one side, listening like a dog to an inexplicable sound. He did not give the impression of a man listening for pleasure, but one wishing to make sense of a complex language.

Les Chaffey had left school on the day he turned fourteen and he had always regretted it. But he had come to believe that if he asked enough people enough things he would end up with an education regardless. He had, therefore, trained himself to ask questions.

So as his wife stacked up the dinner plates, Les smiled at his guest and combed his wavy fair hair, not from vanity, but in the style of a good mechanic who wishes everything in order before a machine is stripped down. He removed the odd hairs from his comb and dropped them fastidiously on to the floor.

A mouse, running for its life, slipped and fell from the rafters, upset the sugar bowl and scampered off the table.

Les Chaffey sat, smiling, in the lamplight.

Charles shifted in his seat. He had the feeling something was about to start and he did not know what it was. They were waiting, it would appear, for Mrs Chaffey to return from the kitchen.

She hurried in, shuffling softly in her slippers, and scraped her chair and folded her hands in her lap.

"What would you make", Les Chaffey began, tucking his comb neatly into his shirt pocket, "in your line of work, in an average week?"

Charles was wondering if they might give him an aspirin or a slice of bread, but he decided to deal with the question first. But when he had answered, it was quickly replaced by another.

What was his experience with the red-bellied black snake? How did it differ from the blue-bellied variety? What was his mother before she was a Badgery? Would they be any relation to the Minyip McGraths? What does your father do? What do you reckon about Mo McCaughey? Who do you vote for? What's your opinion of General Franco?

Charles answered this last question carefully, but when he discovered his host was both a nationalist and a socialist he told him the truth: that he had been on the brink of going to fight against "that mongrel Franco" when he had been waylaid.

Les, of course, was interested. He herded the spilled grains of sugar with the edge of his hand and when he had them into a little pile he swept them into the sugar bowl. Then he placed the sugar bowl on the shelf behind his head.

"Now," he said, "how did it happen?"

Charles was thinking about the Harrises' house at Horsham – they had served him six lamb chops for breakfast and cut a lunch for him to take when he left. They had put sweet gherkins on his cheese sandwiches and he had thrown them away because he did not like gherkins. Now he regretted it. He could, for instance, have taken the gherkins off the sandwiches. He could even have washed the gherkin taste off the cheese. He had been a mug. He would never throw away good food ever again. Even if he could not have got rid of the gherkin taste from the cheese he could, at least, have kept the bottom slice of bread which the gherkin had never touched.

"You were on the boat?" Les Chaffey suggested.

"No, I never saw the boat."

"He had the ticket," suggested Mrs Chaffey. It was the first time she had spoken, but Charles liked the way she leaned towards him as she spoke.

"I had the money for the ticket to get to London."

"Right," said Les. "You had the do-re-mi. You had it in your pocket."

"In my money belt."

"In your money belt, right you are. Then what happened?"

The shutters were all propped wide open and Charles could hear the cry of a solitary owl, *Mo-poke, Mo-poke*. He was about to ask for a slice of bread and then he looked up, the question on his lips, and he saw how keenly Mrs Chaffey was listening. He decided to tell the story first.

5

He had, in the beginning, no intention of going to Spain at all. He had been going to Sydney, to find his mother. As the train swung and swayed in between the dingy backyards of Sydney he felt that his life was about to begin. He imagined his mother would live in a house similar to the ones he saw by the railway line and this did not dismay him at all, quite the contrary. He was expecting warm embraces and hot tears, soft beds, big dinners; the noise of the trains passing his window could only increase his happiness.

He had brought his last two, his best two, rabbit skins to give her. She could make them into a hat or a stole. They were hard on one side and soft on the other and when you bent them, they made a crinkly noise. They were his best-quality skins and he took them out of his bluey on the last leg up from Liverpool. He showed them to the sailor.

"They're for my mum," he said. "I haven't seen her since I was a little nipper."

The sailor advised him to find his mother whatever effort it took. He himself had grown up in an orphanage. He offered to help, but Charles said he already had a friend who was helping him. When the sailor learned the friend was a female he showed Charles a French letter in a paper envelope. It was stamped "air-tested" and he insisted on Charles taking it.

Leah Goldstein was not expecting him. If she had seen him in the street it is doubtful if she would have recognized him, for he had grown large and the dress he now adopted was of his own choosing – a combination of cast-offs from municipal tips and certain flash items for which he had paid too much money. Thus he wore a big checked jacket with bright blue and gold squares

391

which had been refashioned from a man's dressing gown, a pair of heavy hobnailed work boots which, judging from the number of eyelets, might have been thirty years old, and a big white Texan hat bought by mail order from *Smith's Weekly*. He carried a rolled bluey, but not across his shoulders. He had made a leather handle to buckle on to its straps so that he could carry the bluey at his side, like a suitcase. He did not wish to be thought a swagman.

Leah Goldstein would not have recognized him in the street, but she could do it – did do it – before she turned on the porch light and saw him standing there still holding his tram ticket in his hand. The smell of tea-tree oil came to her, blown on the westerly wind, and the austere set of her face was already softening and her lips were forming the shape of his name before she reached the light switch.

For a moment she feared he would, like a new puppy, burst through the flywire. But he contained himself and in a second, with the flimsy screen door still intact, he was crushing her to him and she was laughing out loud. She was pleased to see him, more pleased than she would have imagined, but just the same she had to shush his croaking voice, his joyful shouts, because there was a meeting in progress inside and she – the minute book was in her hand – was secretary. She put her finger to her lips and said he could come in and listen, that they would not (she pulled a face) be too much longer.

In the little room, sitting on the floor, on broken chairs, on the bed, were a number of men and women who would be, or already were, famous as artists and writers. They were meeting to organize an exhibition to raise money to send Australians to fight against General Franco and when Charles entered they smiled at him in a good-natured way and went back to their business. Charles blushed bright red and sat in a corner against the wall.

There was a fierce argument proceeding about whether there could be any such thing as proletarian art. Charles was surprised to see that Leah, whom he remembered most for her strong opinions, took no part in this. Neither did she write down anything that was said. She sat beside and a little behind Izzie's wheelchair and, twice, smiled at Charles. No one seemed to take any notice of Izzie's mutilation and Charles was shocked that he did not take the trouble to throw a rug across those trousered stumps.

Charles felt self-conscious and ill at ease. He understood almost nothing about the room or the situation. He could not see why a man should wear a fur hat or a woman have green stockings. He did not understand the abstract print on the wall or even the language that they spoke. He listened to Izzie Kaletsky pouring scorn on the possibility of proletarian art but he could not understand what he was talking about.

And yet he had trapped rabbits and sold birds. He had been fencing in Western New South Wales. He could trap rosellas with no other bait than a cup of water. The total of his savings was a hundred and five pounds six shillings and twopence. This was more, he thought, than most of these people were worth. They had no right to make him feel so stupid. He sought a way to move the ground to something that would be more favourable to him. He was not so ambitious as to attempt to make the Picasso print disappear or the problems of proletarian art vanish, and yet this is precisely what he succeeded in doing – he opened his swag and took out his snake, a little green and yellow tree snake, startlingly beautiful and very active, which he had bought that afternoon in Campbell Street.

He sat in the corner, casting secret smiles at Leah and soon the meeting was finished because everyone was looking at the snake and no one could concentrate on what anyone else was saying.

It was not long before he was telling them about his work with the fencing contractor and his experience with snakes out west. He was, after all, a Badgery.

When everyone had gone, Leah excused herself (it was time for her to make Lenny's cocoa) and Charles and Izzie were left alone together.

Izzie was irritable, not with Charles, but with his comrades who were so easily distracted from their work, like children in a schoolroom on a summer afternoon. He rocked himself back and forth in his chair, lit a cigarette, and tried to stop the tide of desolation that always overcame him when the meetings were over and he was left alone with his wife. He fidgeted, balanced his ashtray, bit his lip and tried to feel sympathy for his unwanted guest.

"So," he said, "what are your plans for Sydney?"

Charles missed half of the sentence but he understood more from Izzie's face than he would, anyway, have gathered from the words.

"I'm a bit hard of hearing," he said belligerently.

Izzie did not repeat himself. Now he was reinstated as a

teacher his days were long ones. He nodded, wearily. Charles interpreted the weariness as hostility.

"I suppose you think I'm a bit of a mug," he said.

Izzie shook his head. "No," he said, and smiled.

They sat and looked at each other. Charles was soon in a panic. If he was not an idiot he should be able to say something. He did not know what to say or how to say it.

"I remember you," he begged. "We met before. My cockie bit your finger."

Izzie would have preferred to be kind to the fidgeting boy, but Charles chose to remind him of the day he would prefer to forget.

There was another silence.

"I came down to find my mum."

Izzie said something but Charles missed it. He started fiddling with his hearing aid. He banged the metal box on his knee.

"Do you remember me?" he demanded. "I remember you. I was only a young fellow."

"I'm sorry. I'm tired."

"What were you talking about when I came in?"

Izzie explained but Charles gave up understanding almost as soon as he started and when he spoke again it was on another subject entirely.

"I owe Leah a lot."

"Everybody seems to." Izzie just wanted to go to bed and sleep. He did not wish to hear talk about his saintly wife, but he did wish her to come and rescue him. He looked expectantly towards the door.

"I'm going to take her to the theatre."

In fact Charles had been going to take them both to the theatre. He did not even know that he'd changed his mind until the words came out of his mouth and he had excluded Izzie from it. "And to a rest-er-raunt."

"Good for you," said Izzie Kaletsky, now thoroughly impatient with his bumptious guest. He leaned over and started to pick up the typed pages that were spread on the surface of the bed.

"Yes. I'm going to take her to the Chinese acrobats."

"That's nice." Izzie placed the pages in a dun-coloured folder.

"It will be nice. There are twelve boy acrobats, from China. I've got the money."

"You're very fortunate."

394

"I worked for it, every zac and deener. I was going to take her to a pub, but I met a bloke on the train who said a resteraunt would be better."

"Then you should take her to Prunier's."

"What's that?"

"Prunier's. Here, I'll write it down for you," said Izzie Kaletsky with a malice that was no longer new to him. "It's the very best restaurant in Sydney."

"That's what I want."

Charles took the piece of paper Izzie gave him and painstakingly copied the name and address into a small marbled notebook.

But he was to cross out the address the following morning when Leah, declining his invitation, laughed. It was then he knew Izzie had made a fool of him and he never tried to like him again.

6

It was Leah Goldstein who wrote to me to say my missing son was found at last. She described for me his half-grown-up face, his smell, his clothes, his croaking voice, his snake, his bankbooks. On the first morning she cooked him a big breakfast with grilled sausages, steak, kidney, onions, eggs, chops, buttered toast, cups of tea. She served this monstrous meal on a plate with a blue rim. This is what she told me, and I am not saying it wasn't kind of her, or even typical of her, only that you can't rely on it being true – by 1938 my puritanical friend was as addicted to telling lies as another woman, equally unhappy with her life, might be to a sherry bottle.

Yes, yes, I am asking you to believe that Honest Leah had become Lying Leah. I am not saying that it happened overnight. These things don't happen like that. Lies were not on her mind at all. She had sought to do no more than deliver some happiness to me, each day, for every day I lived in gaol. She wrote me letters.

She did not tell me that this enraged her husband. Neither did she describe the weather when it was unpleasant. If she was ill she would not trouble me with it; she would write as if she were well. This, of course, is not quite lying.

She did not begin to tell real lies until Rosa was in hospital suffering that filthy rot that left her all eaten out inside, as light

395

and fragile as a pine log infested with white ant. It was Leah who calmed down Rosa's husband and her son. It was Leah who cared for and nursed her angry friend, washed the sheets and nighties she was so ashamed of, sat with her, watched her sleep until she felt herself to be soaked in the gassy odours of death itself. Later she would think of these months, when she helped her friend die, as one of the most important times in her life.

But she wrote not a word about it to me. Instead she described long walks with Rosa along the clifftops to Tamarama. She did not date these walks, but the impression given was that they had happened an hour or a minute before, that Rosa sat across from her at the kitchen table, drinking fragrant tea. They were beautiful letters, bulging with powerful skies and rimmed with intense yellow light. Every blade of grass seemed sharply painted, every word of conversation exact and true. Perhaps these things had once taken place. Perhaps she invented them. In any case they gave me that electric, unnatural mixture of emotions that every prisoner knows, where even the best things in the world outside come slashed with our own bitterness or jealousy. This confusion of love and hurt is very powerful. I came to crave it even while I dreaded it. It is a more potent drug than simple happiness.

Rosa died and was buried. Leah eliminated her presence from the house, threw away stubs of pencils and old ball gowns, yellowed letters, scraps of lace. No one tried to stop her. Lenny and Izzie mourned like Jews. While they sat on floors, Leah sat at the table and brought Rosa back to life. Now that, God damn it, is no longer mere politeness. She sent me descriptions of Rosa swinging her arms, Rosa burping, Rosa raising her lovely face to the sun. When it gets to this point she is no longer doing it for me alone. She is doing it for herself. And before a year is out she has the whole thing out of control and she has presented imaginary Rosa with imaginary grandchildren, made curtains, planted passionfruit and worried herself about the whooping cough in a world that exists between nine and eleven o'clock in the morning.

There was a time, when I finally learned the truth, that I could have killed her for her deception, to have made me feel so much about what revealed itself as nothing. I will tell you, later, how I got on the train with my bottle and my blade. But when I think about her now I cannot even imagine my own anger. I see only the empty air around her, the coldness of the surfaces, the gloss on the linoleum, the yellow stare of the shining cupboard doors, the brown hard glaze on the cracked bread crock, the rusty drip mark on the empty porcelain sink, and my Leah sitting alone writing these letters to me, manufacturing a happy family.

It was dangerous work and it is hardly surprising that she got herself addicted.

And although she could put up with Lenny's whingeing about his bowels ("I'm all bound up, girlie") and even the cruelties of her husband's tongue, she would permit nothing to prevent her letter-writing and even Izzie had learned to leave her alone when she was occupied with what they both now chose to call "bookkeeping".

Do not imagine that she was lazy in regard to her other duties. Leah, at twenty-five, worked as hard and unrelentingly as any widow who does not wish to think. She rose at five thirty every morning, washed and dressed her husband, made him breakfast, cut his lunch. At six thirty they left the house and she pushed the wheelchair up the steep hill out of Bondi, right up as far as Neil Street where they met Izzie's headmaster, a Mr Wilks of tory views. Together they would pick up the crippled teacher and strap the light wheelchair to the spare tyre. Mr Wilks would not have the chair inside the car (although it was a collapsible American model and would have fitted easily) and complained about scratch marks on the paintwork on the outside.

Leah then walked briskly down to Campbell Parade, sparing no time to admire the pounding surf, bought a newspaper for Lenny, returned to the house, did the washing if it was a Monday, went shopping if it was Tuesday or Friday, and because these were the days of the Popular Front against Fascism and there were demonstrations, meetings, anti-war rallies, seminars and fund-raising exercises like the Artists Against War exhibition she – being only a young wife with no children to care for – was always busy organizing something, arranging a hall for an exhibition, begging paintings from artists, borrowing a tea urn from a union who wanted her to pay a deposit. She did all these things without complaint, but she would not give up the time allocated to "my bookkeeping" for anyone. During these two hours of every day she would not answer a telephone or door or even make a cup of tea. She sat at the kitchen table celebrating imaginary birthdays and picking fruit from unplanted apple trees.

Even when Charles arrived in Sydney to find his mother, even though Leah was delighted to see him, although she may have cooked him a huge breakfast with steaks and chops and kidneys and bacon and sausages and eggs and onions, although she accepted his invitation to see the Chinese boy acrobats, she would not give up her letters to help him find his mother.

Of course she was guilty. She probably cooked him fried bread and liver as well. She apologized more than was necessary. She hovered around him with a teapot. But she would not give up her bookkeeping.

Instead she conscripted Lenny, who was doing nothing better than studying the racing form and worrying about his constipation, to help in the search.

They were a bizarre pair, the neat little Jew with his dark suit and black hat (which he wore like a Riley Street larrikin, tipped forward over his eyes) and the wide-hipped, pear-headed youth who did not know what to do with his big red hands. Thus she was able, when they finally left her alone, to incorporate a truthful portrait of the pair into the letter that began "Dear Herbert"; this reflection of the real world was like a little piece of mirror glass sewn into the fanciful patterns of a Hindu bride's dress.

7

Charles had never talked to a "foreigner" in all his life. He had met Englishmen, of course, and the Yank who taught him how to trap the rabbits, but he had not met a real foreigner. Yet by ten o'clock on his second day in Sydney he was sitting in tea-rooms at Bondi and the tea-rooms were full of foreigners. Lenny bought him a cake and showed him how to eat it with a fork. The fork was tiny and hard to use. Charles pressed his knees together and tried to keep his elbow to his side. When the cake was finished they set out for the Bondi Post Office. It was still early, no more than ten, but there was a dance hall already open and they stopped to peer through its open lattice walls at the couples gliding on the floor. Lenny nudged him and winked. Charles blushed. He would never have the nerve to go into such a place.

"You know how to dance?" Lenny asked him. They were walking past the newsagent's towards the Post Office.

Charles admitted that he didn't.

Lenny then showed him how the foxtrot was done, right in front of the newsagent's. Even though Charles was embarrassed he was also impressed at the light graceful movements of the silver-haired man. He was so dapper and neat. He held his hands out as if embracing a slightly taller woman.

"Foxtrot," Lenny said, and smiled. "You can teach yourself." They then went into the newsagent's and picked up the *Sporting Globe*.

At the Bondi Post Office they telephoned every Badgery listed in the Sydney phone book. It was Charles who supplied the pennies and Lenny who did the talking. They invested pennies in Miss A. B. Badgery and Mr W. A. Badgery, in a Badgery who imported and in another who manufactured rope; but they had no luck. Then, with hands smudged with phone-book ink, their cuffs soiled with post-office grime, they took a tram, a bus, another tram, and went to St Vincent's Hospital, not in search of Phoebe (which is what Charles had imagined as they walked up the steps) but to visit a friend of Lenny's, an old man, also a foreigner who described himself to Charles as "a common tout and racecourse urger".

Charles showed the man his snake and the man gave Lenny some money.

After that they went to a café in Rowe Street and Lenny asked questions about Charles's mother. It was a café for artists and poets and he thought she might be known there.

Lenny went patiently from table to table. He began the same way, exactly, each time. "Excuse me, please, gentlemen, perhaps you can help." Or: "Excuse me, please, sir." Charles put his hands in his pockets and jingled the pennies he had left over from the Post Office. He stared around at the posters on the wall. He tried to appear nonchalant, but he hated it. He wanted to go. He did not know why he was being stared at.

When Lenny arrived at the last table, Charles was already at the door.

"Excuse me, please, sir," said Lenny, "perhaps you can help."

The man was very fat. He had wet red lips and slicked-back hair. He sat sketching in a book no bigger than a matchbox but Charles noted none of this. Neither did he listen to Lenny's speech. He was hot with embarrassment. He was wondering what item of his wardrobe was incorrect, if it was the coat or perhaps the hat.

"Know her?" the artist's voice was high and fluting. "I should say I know her. Casually," he said, "artistically, socially, biblically."

Charles was brought back from the open door to meet the man who knew his mother. The man's hand was soft as a pillow.

"Your mother", he said loudly, "is one of the great characters of

Sydney. One of the great *hostesses*. One of the great free *spirits*. Go," he said, tearing a page from his tiny sketchbook and giving it to Charles. "Here is her address. See her. Talk to her about your wardrobe."

The whole café burst into laughter and Lenny, escorting his young charge out into the hot street, suggested he might like to look at some clothes at Anthony Hordern's.

And that was how Charles presented himself at his mother's doorway looking for all the world (as Mr L., her visitor at the time, remarked) "like the very latest thing in bank clerks".

8

Svelte cats named Swinburne arched their backs above the harbour and rubbed their silver fur against the fluted plaster columns that Annette Davidson had painted chrome yellow and kingfisher blue. The walls were pale peach and the great window uncurtained. On the polished wooden floor were rugs of exotic origin and on a low table (a snazzy thing of glass and chrome) sat a single white bowl with nothing in it but a dying beetle.

Charles, imprisoned in his new suit, pressed his knees together as he perched himself on the tiny chair. His neck burned beneath his collar. His mother had not, as yet, so much as touched his hand. There had been no embrace. No lipstick marked his cheek and every eye was free from tears. She had taken the parcel of rabbit skins but had not even opened it. He tried not to blame her. The fault was with the other visitor, this Mr L. who droned on and on in a voice that Charles, having limited experience of such things, thought must be that of a clergyman, the mistake being made because of its mellifluous nature, its lack of self-consciousness, its easy assurance that its audience would not escape.

Charles balanced his cup and saucer on his knee. He had already finished it but he did not know where to put it and this problem occupied his entire mind. He felt himself observed and wondered what was correct. He was inclined to put the cup and saucer on the glass table and yet it was so ostentatiously bare that he felt it might be wrong to do so and, in any case, the table was glass and would make a loud noise and draw attention to his mistake, if mistake it was. So he continued to hold the saucer on his knee and looked, with what he imagined was polite attention, in the direction of Mr L.

The famous Mr L. sprawled in the settee while remaining, somehow, as neat as a pin. He was boom-voiced, big-nosed, with a sensuous mouth below oddly pinched, slightly disapproving nostrils. His hair was cut fringed like a boy's but was flecked with silver and Charles, attempting to understand the gist of the argument, gathered only that the speaker did not like communists, Jews or proponents of what he called "Bank Clerk Culture". He went on and on about "LCD" and it was twenty years later that an older Charles realized, one insomniac night, that he had been referring to Lowest Common Denominator and that what he was most frightened of was democracy.

But it was to my wife that Charles gave the bulk of his attention, and it was not the polite uncomfortable look he felt obliged to give the self-satisfied Mr L., but something its object felt to be a reprimand. Charles stared, his eyes heavy with love and censure. His mother was, in her mid-thirties, still a young woman. If there was something dark and shadowy around her eyes it suggested no more than the burdens of beauty. Charles's mother was like a gypsy. She was totally beyond imagining. Everthing about her (the painted pillars, the arching cats, the smooth honey colour of her skin) was unlike anything Charles had ever seen. She wore a scarf wrapped around her head and its tail fell, a cascade of tiny roses, over one bare shoulder. Her hands were shapely, the fingers long, flexible and expressive. When she spoke a throaty contralto came from lips which hardly seemed to move and yet enunciated her vowels in a manner that her son could only describe as posh; the manner of speaking suggested great passion and great control.

He waited for a pause in the man's speech, imagining that, when it came, his mother would have a chance to explain that he was Charles Badgery, her son, and that they would, of course, wish time together and then the man might look at him less oddly. She had introduced him, with a jerky motion of her hand, as Charles, then held her bare throat and laughed. It was a jarring, silly outburst. Mr L. had blinked and continued with his speech.

The pause, at last, arrived. His mother stood. She took the saucer and cup from his knees and departed, with a murmur, to the kitchen.

Charles, disappointed, stretched himself inside the confines of his suit. He knew that Mr L. was staring at his brown boots and knew that Lenny had been right and that he should have bought shoes, or, if he were intent on boots, at least black boots. Now he was sorry he had been stubborn about the brown boots, but he had always wanted them, although this would be difficult to explain, just as he knew – looking at the man's pale sleepy supercilious eyes – that he could not explain that the suit was only so ill-fitting because he had been in a hurry to get here, that it was to be returned to Anthony Hordern's tomorrow where the legs would be lengthened, the sleeves let down, the backside made more generous.

"Nice day," he said to Mr L., unable to stand his staring.

"Noice day," said Mr L., and Charles could not believe that he was being mocked.

Meanwhile Phoebe clattered around the kitchen in a tizz, not knowing what it was she should do. Afterwards she would regret (particularly when in her cups) not having sent the famous little satyr away and thus removed the problem of having to socialize with two such different personalities at once. Yet both of them had arrived, almost together, and both without warning; she had found herself trapped between what she had once been and what she would like to be.

One always gave boys biscuits. She looked for biscuits but Annette had been up in the night, prowling the house, and had eaten them all. Her son (she found it hard to credit she had ever had one) and not even a damn biscuit to give him. He had smelt (she wrinkled her nose, looking for sugar lumps) distinctly odd. He was like a yokel in a suit. He was odd, repelling, ugly, with frighteningly demanding eyes that she was tempted to label as insolent but could not, of course, because she was his mother. Also there was this: that he was disconcertingly familiar, like photographs of her father as young man, and she felt towards this image a halting pulse of affection that was no weaker than the undertow of her irritation.

Yet she could not send Mr L. away. She had laboured long to get his attention, had done what she always had – mixed up her literary ambitions and her powers of sexual persuasion. It was, as Annette was never slow to remind her, a bad habit to have fallen into. But to this Phoebe would bitterly reply that their whole life was a bad habit, a habit none of them could break, not even Horace who, although he was presently away, working as a purser on a coastal steamer, would return as soon as he had forgotten how sharply he was cut by frustration and jealousy, or when he was dismissed for epilepsy and put off the ship, whichever was the sooner.

402

There were other bad habits too that Phoebe was not aware of, the worst being the whole system of illusion whereby Horace and Annette propped up Phoebe and made her believe herself a poet. Perhaps Horace, aroused by the sensational subject-matter, could not see the awfulness of the poems; but Annette (sarcastic, bitter, put-upon Annette, the history mistress with the wide beseeching mouth), Annette said nothing, perhaps from fear that Phoebe would, at last, turn on her and reject her totally, unconditionally, for ever. The nearest Annette would ever come to speaking the unutterable was, when most miserable, "We have spoiled you."

Thus, Phoebe: surrounded by her menagerie: Annette, Horace, the cats arching their backs. She had allowed herself to become ridiculous and did not know it. Mr L., who sat in the next room idly and elegantly mocking her son, was not about to publish her poetry in *Isis* although he was doubtless aroused by the potency of some of the sexual imagery which made up for in literalness what it lacked in subtlety. He could not take the poems as anything other than a menu for the pleasure that might await him in the curtained bed referred to with such passion in one infamous unpublished sonnet that the men who drank at La Bohème would never publish no matter how often they passed it, smiling, from hand to hand.

While she looked for biscuits she knew already eaten, Phoebe imagined herself on the brink of publication and she could not ask Mr L. to leave to allow herself to have time with her son and she resolved to ask Charles if he would come back tomorrow. She intended to take him aside, and explain all the complexities. She would cook him a lunch tomorrow, or perhaps Annette might cook something tonight, and she would serve it to him tomorrow.

She returned to make this arrangement at a time when Charles had at last realized the snobbish and malicious nature of his interrogator and, having had his suit insultingly admired for ten minutes, was at the end of his tether. Phoebe, seeing the wildness in his eyes, panicked, and made her request there and then with the result that he stood in an urgent rush of limbs, scraping the chair along the floor, his eyes imploring, clutching for some sign from hers, but ready, belligerently, to reject it. She found herself rushing after him, up the steps and out into the road, where he stood trembling all over like a difficult horse. She quieted him, slowly, but ruined it again by being worried about Mr L. to whom she must return. She leaned towards him to kiss his burning cheek and he – realizing her intention – flinched from her and stamped off down the street where he was to become hopelessly lost, split his trousers, and all but ruin the rest of the suit in a storm that all of Sydney had seen coming.

When Phoebe returned to her flat she found that her guest had drawn a caricature of her son as a wombat which was as marvellously executed as it was cruelly accurate. He inscribed it to her, and signed it. She laughed and thanked him and made a great fuss about how she must have it framed.

But later, after they had disported in the curtained bed, a bitterness welled up in her so strong that she could not maintain her silence. It is to her credit that she told the artist that the wombat was her missing son and resembled her late father. It is also characteristic of her that she should also have the work framed and display it prominently; for although she would have loved to destroy the caricature she could not bear to part with the inscription.

9

He could not admit to anyone that his mother had not hugged him or asked him to come back and live with her. Neither would he lie about it. Yet his actions were lying actions, for he stayed out at dinnertime and generally behaved like a young man with a busy social calendar.

Leah imagined him being entertained by Phoebe while all the while he was mooching along George Street eating a pie from a paper bag or sitting in the stalls at the Lyceum by himself. When she asked him about his evenings she received the same smile the Chaffeys had when they wanted to know about his black eye; she squeezed his hand hard and felt, in the answering squeeze, what she thought was joy. He was miserable.

He went back to Neutral Bay where Phoebe lived, not once, but three times. He walked up the steep street from the ferry and stood across the road from her flat. On one occasion a man entered the building just as he arrived and, imagining that his mother might, once again, have a competing visitor, he departed. At another time, a steamy Sunday afternoon, he entered the flat itself. There was a party in progress and the room was full of very peculiar-looking people. Charles took a piece of cheese and ate it defiantly before he lost his nerve and fled.

For the most part, however, he wandered the streets of the city itself, hot, tired, too shy to do business with the impatient tram conductors. He took his suit back to Anthony Hordern's to be altered and repaired and was roared up by the old salesman for treating it so badly. He spent a lot of time in Campbell Street pricing birds in those dark crowded little pet shops most of which – although he did not know it at the time – had whorehouses out the back. He stared at French sailors at the Quay and bought half a pint of prawns from an itinerant barrow man. And in Bathurst Street, amongst the shops of pawnbrokers, second-hand clothes shops and tyre vulcanizers, he found Desmond Moore's now famous bookshop where he inquired after a book of poetry by Phoebe Badgery.

The bookseller was a slim young man with a blond moustache. He looked at Charles and frowned. He took in the loud checks, the large hat, the hearing aid, the shape of the head, the width of the neck, the bow of the legs, the size of the boots, all the time wondering how such an apparition fitted in with Phoebe Badgery whose charms he much admired.

The bookseller asked where it was he'd heard of such a book.

Charles fiddled with his hearing aid, banged it with his fist, and placed it on the counter. His eyes were as big and soft as a sheepdog's. His hands were large and tightly clenched. His fingernails were broken.

"Where", the bookseller said, unnecessarily loud, "did you hear of this *book*?"

"I was told." Charles's face was aflame. He wished he had never come to Sydney where everyone wished to insult and abuse him.

"By whom?" said the bookseller, enjoying the game of speaking so loudly. He glanced around to collect the tributes of his fellow workers, the rolled eyes, the wry smiles, the hand across the lipsticked laugh. "By whom", he said, ending the word with a real hum, "were you told?"

Charles became angry and stamped his foot. "That's for me to know, and you to find out."

"Now, now." The bookseller extended a pale placating palm. "I meant no offence."

"None taken." His voice was too loud. He could not hear it exactly, but he could feel it was too loud. "Just get me the book."

"There is no book."

"Then I'll go elsewhere." He began to stuff his hearing aid away in his jacket pocket.

"There is no elsewhere. There is no book by Phoebe Badgery. I take it", he said, "that you are a friend of Mrs Badgery's?"

Charles's ear suffered a hurt, a sharp crack, and he misheard.

"Then you're a fool for saying so," he said.

In the street outside, amidst the stink of car tyres, he burst into tears, and when he arrived back in Bondi (having spent ten shillings on a taxi rather than put up with the rudeness of one more tram conductor) Leah was alarmed to see his swollen face. She asked him what the matter was and he burst into tears again.

It was then he told her the whole story and they sat at the kitchen table, drinking tea, both crying together.

It was in the aftermath of this incident that he decided he would go to Spain. There was much in his decision, of course, that was immature and there was a part of him that looked forward to his death in Spain as a suitable punishment for the mother who had not loved him sufficiently. Yet there were other, finer threads to the fabric of his character, motives so simple and obvious that when Izzie and Leah quizzed him about them, he moved them, even Izzie, with the simplicity of his answer.

Charles said: "Because I am for the weak and against the strong, not the strong against the weak, and I've got the money for the fare."

That, at least, is what Leah reports him to have said, and I have always intended to ask if he really did make so fine a speech. I was much affected by it at the time.

Whatever he said, Izzie Kaletsky was the one who wrote down the address of a comrade who would help make the arrangements.

10

George Fipps was not meant to vet Charles. Nor was he meant to accept the fare money from him. All he was meant to do was provide the boy with a letter of introduction to the International Brigade in London. And, indeed, he came to the meeting with the letter neatly folded in the breast pocket of his shirt.

But in the steamy beer-sour shadows of the Sussex Hotel, Charles – who had misunderstood the purpose of the meeting – pushed an envelope towards the comrade who left it where it was, not an inch from his beer glass. The envelope contained one hundred and twenty pounds in purple fivers.

Perhaps George Fipps already sensed what the outcome of the meeting would be and that was why he neither pushed the envelope away nor picked it up. He studied it, as if it were fate itself lying there on the damp towelling, slowly darkening.

George Fipps was thirty-six years old. He was a big, handsome, sleepy-lidded man whose blond hair, after twenty-one years of Brylcreem, had begun to take on a slightly green tinge. In his youth he had been a larrikin and a street-brawler and he was still proud of his strength and his fighter's skills. He rolled his white shirt sleeves as high as they would go.

He had not intended to go to Spain himself. But then he had not realized, until his meeting with my innocent son, how much he hated permitting young comrades to fight when he could have done it better himself. He helped collect the money for their fares –those painfully arrived at zacs and deeners – but he had never let himself know, until he saw that envelope, how much he loathed being one of those old men who send young men off to war.

This was not a thing he could confess to afterwards. All he would say was that Charles had not been suitable. He told Izzie: "He was a keen young fellow, but he didn't have no theory. Jeez, mate, I couldn't let him. I couldn't have the comrades in Spain think we was all so bloody ignorant."

But to Charles he said nothing so cruel. He talked to him gently, talked so softly that he might have been with a woman in bed and Charles had to bring out his hearing machine and put it amongst the spilled beer on the bar. By the third glass he had convinced Charles that the best thing for the international working class would be for Charles to buy George's motorbike and sidecar and for George to go to Spain instead.

You would expect both men to be surprised by the outcome, but in the daylight darkness of the bar, with the soft nasal excitement of the horse races on the wireless, it had seemed – to both of them – sensible. It was only in the street outside that they saw what they had done. George Fipps began to spit and slap his hands together. Charles stood and grinned at his new motorbike – it was black and gold and it gleamed, it dazzled, in the sun.

George quickly taught him how to drive it and then they went over to the Balmain Police where George's brother-in-law issued a driving licence.

Outside in Darling Street the two men grinned at each other and shook hands. George Fipps spat three times into the gutter, winked, and set off towards his boarding house. Charles drove back to Bondi, drunk in charge, singing tunelessly, with a sidecar full of whitewash cans.

It was only when he started to tell the story to Izzie and Leah and he saw the look on Izzie's face that Charles saw his story could be looked at from other angles, i.e., that he had been cheated, that he had let himself be cheated because he was a coward. It was then, his head aching from beer, that he shouted at his host and threatened to punch him. He said he hated Sydney. He said it was full of liars and cheats and snobs. But what made him really angry, what he couldn't admit, was that he suddenly felt the sneer on Izzie's face was deserved. He was relieved he no longer had the money and no longer had to go.

The next day he read about the mouse plague in Victoria.

11

It was seven in the morning, and although it was not cold, although he had wrapped himself in a greatcoat, my boy's teeth were chattering in his head. He sat on the crackling AJS while Leah talked intensely, holding his gloved wrist as if, by doing this, she would retain him.

He had overfilled the machine with oil and it sounded, idling, like someone slapping jelly on a plate. Lenny came and stood on the front doorstep in his pyjamas, his hands, comically, over his ears. When Charles did not see him he went back inside and waited for Leah to fetch him his paper.

But Leah was suddenly too overcome with guilt to notice anything as silly as Lenny. She had neglected the boy. She had been selfish. She had left him alone to be patronized and insulted by city people. He was alone in the world and she, his only friend, had betrayed him.

"Listen to me," Leah said. "Somebody has to give you advice. Don't stay in the country whatever you do. The city is a lot better than you think. When you come back I will have more time. I'll forget my bookkeeping. I'll take a holiday. I promise. When you come back I'll work on an education for you somehow. You can live here with us. You can go to night school. Would you like that? You could have a pet shop, anything, to make a living."

Charles' ears crackled, shrieked and knocked. The AJS slapped and spluttered. Against all odds, like a willow seed lodging in a

408

hair-split rock, the pet shop slipped through the explosions and found a welcome.

"You could have a pet shop, anything, to make a living."

12

Kevin Simmons (and that other chap whose name eludes me) escaped from Long Bay in 1958 and you may remember what celebrities they were, running all over the country with the coppers panting at their tails. It was Simmons who was the smart one, and it was him the coppers hated.

The gaol they put him into was Grafton and you only have to drive through those ugly big gates to get the smell of what sort of place it is. Even before I saw my cell I knew this was no ordinary country lock-up. And although they boast in Grafton (town) that there has been only one execution in their gaol, the Brylcreemed chemists and clerks who tell you this do not mention the sane men who have hanged themselves in their cells.

It is a gaol dedicated to knocking the bejesus out of people, and if you are a tough guy they put you in "trac" and the warders come and visit you in your cell each night until you weep and beg to God to let you die. They are not nice noises to hear coming through your walls at night and, believe me, you hear everything. You hear a button brush against a wall and when poor Simmons hanged himself at last, his biggest problem was doing it so he would not be heard and I have read no sadder thing than the official account of how he used blankets and coir mats so he could take his life in total silence.

When I was an author I was party to a book called *Gaol Bird* which claimed I was a prisoner in Grafton Gaol, but once I had read the tattooed messages on the screws' arms I knew that I must get myself transferred out of there. *Gaol Bird* was a pack of lies – I spent no more than one soft month in Grafton during which time I made myself into a nice old man. I shuffled and tottered and you would not recognize the fellow who came cycling up from Nambucca a week before so cocky about his life that he abandoned a pretty widow with a business of her own.

Oh, you would not believe what a brown nose I was, a smiling snivelling wretch of a thing. I bent my spine and let my dentures clack when I smiled.

I got my transfer. They shipped me up to Rankin Downs near

Coraki. Rankin Downs was brand new at the time, a sort of Promised Land for prisoners according to the Grafton grapevine. There were no locks on the door and you could get an education or work in the bush planting flooded gum.

Rankin Downs was a lovely idea. This was not apparent when you first saw it, but I am sure the intentions behind it were good. I am sure it was not the plan, not originally, to build it on the edge of a paperbark swamp, but perhaps its creator, its champion, had too many enemies in the department. Perhaps he lacked stamina and they wore him down, getting him to accept one compromise and then another. He saw it on a map and it looked perfect. It was only later that he saw they would have to build the camp on a gravel platform on the edge of a swamp, but he was an optimist. He kept going forward. He nearly lost his scheme countless times and in the end he was pleased to accept the long huts from the army. Perhaps he did not appreciate that they were cold in winter and boiling in summer, or perhaps he did, and still thought it a superior situation to a proper gaol. He was right, this weak tender soul in the Department of Corrective Services, but there is many a man who would have thanked him if he might have fought, just a little harder, and got us some wire to keep out the mosquitoes.

Rankin Downs may have been a prisoners' paradise, but it was the lowest rung for the screws who did not care for either the isolated site or the standard of their own accommodation. We were not put in the charge of bashers – they were right at the top in Grafton – but we got the moaners, the whingers, the ones with flatulence and bad breath, the ones their fellows could not stand to watch eating.

I could give you a long list of my complaints about Rankin Downs, that bleak, muddy, dusty, shadeless place – but I will also say this in its favour – you were permitted to look the screws in the eyes and you could sleep at night without listening to beatings. One slept without fear in that place but when Reg Moth was let into my so-called "cell" that night, my balls went tight and my mouth dry. Moth was not a screw. He was the sergeant who had arrested me, a wide square-headed fellow with big ginger eyebrows and thick hairy arms. He had a dented chin, big fleshy ear-lobes and a pair of very pale blue eyes that bulged demandingly from his florid face. He had a voice like a man who smokes forty Craven As a day – hoarse, cracked, given to phlegmy interruptions – but I don't recall him smoking. He parted his hair straight down the middle, across the flat plateau of his big

410

head and although he was neat and polite, there was something contradictory in his eyes as if he were a neat polished chest of drawers full of tangled laddered nylon stockings.

It is not the normal practice for arresting sergeants to pay social calls upon their victims, and even if it were, it would take a keen man to make a journey up from Grafton at night. The last hour to Rankin Downs is along a straight, rutted gravel road cut right through the paperbarks. Having arrived at night I can speak with some authority on the desolate feeling the road produces: the white fire-scarred trunks, the unsettling vision of yabbies moving from one side of the road to the other. In the daytime, they tell me, the squashed yabbies make the bush smell like the Sydney fish markets.

It was the custom at Rankin Downs to receive visitors in the shade under the big tank stands. There was no provision in the "cells" for a visitor. I offered Sergeant Moth my bed. He took it and I squatted on the floor with my back against the cracked asbestos-sheet wall. When my knees got stiff and sore I asked his permission before I sat on the floor.

He talked. I watched his mouth move. I could not understand why he had come and I listened to him talking about Peter Dawson who had sung the "Floral Dance" at the Jacaranda Festival the year before. I had, on the one hand, a thirst for all the details of normal life. I wanted to hear about Dawson, what he had sung, what he had worn, how the trees had looked along the avenues of Grafton. In another way I did not want to hear at all, loathed every word he said, just as I sometimes loathed every word of Goldstein's letters. At the same time I was frightened of being bashed. His manner was not a basher's manner. It was fussy and finicky. This did not calm me, but somehow made the prospect of bashing more certain. I would have liked to stand up and not be so defenceless on the floor, but now I was there I did not like to attract his attention with any sudden movements. I could hear my next-door neighbour, a little apprentice mechanic from Coff's Harbour, crying in his sleep. It was a soft whimpering noise. At first I thought it was a bird. His name was Jacko and he was getting out next week. He wouldn't help me if I was bashed.

Moth brought a bottle from his pocket, an old Vegemite bottle with something – I took it for a little yabby – floating in it.

"I thought", Reg Moth said, giving the bottle a good shake, "that it was a shame to throw it out."

Throw what out?

411

"So I went", he said, "down to Phelan's, the chemist chap in Grafton, and I said, have you got a little formaldehyde and he gave me a drop of it in a Vegemite jar. It's very expensive, formaldehyde. Have you ever purchased it, Badgery? Shockingly expensive. But he gave it to me, out of the goodness of his heart. Gave it to me and I put Charlie Goon's finger in it, and here it is, see. I've kept it for you, a souvenir."

"Thank you," I said. I tried to smile politely and look grateful but I had a gagging feeling in my throat.

"You like it?" It was hard to get the meaning of those bulging eyes, but he looked surprised. I felt hot and dizzy. I was disgusted with myself for having torn off an old man's finger. It floated before my eyes, suspended in a Vegemite bottle with a little torn skirt of skin.

"You like it?" He picked his lower teeth with a big square thumbnail. "It makes me want to vomit."

For a moment I thought he was a basher after all and that he had to make himself angry before he could get his fists to me. I pulled down my shirt sleeves.

"But I can see", he said, examining his thumbnail, "that it'd be a different matter for you. It could even be valuable to you. Now, to someone like me, it's a very unsettling thing to have around the house, and there's also the question of the expense I put into it."

"But this chemist chap. . . ."

"Phelan."

"Phelan. This Mr Phelan gave you the formaldehyde." I did not mean to argue with him. I was trying to point out that I had not put him to a lot of trouble. This is how your mind starts to work after two months in gaol.

"*Gave* me the formaldehyde? Who says so?" He peered around the cell. There was not much to peer at – we had the big black cockroaches that year, not the smaller German ones which, now I think of it, were probably not German at all. He studied the gaps between the floorboards, then the single shelf which was, so early, already crammed with Goldstein's letters. "Who says so?"

"There are no witnesses," I admitted.

"That's right, Badgery." He grinned and winked at me. You couldn't help liking him when he was like that. He didn't look like a copper at all, but a farmer about to set off for the pub. "So who's to know if I paid for the formaldehyde or not? Perhaps I have a receipt, here, on me, from Mr Phelan. He's not exactly what you'd call a Mason.''

"Is that so?"

"It is." He was, suddenly, very solemn.

In the silence that followed I realized that I was not to be bashed. It was only bribery that was required. The night was full of the high-pitched whine of the swamp.

"Here, take it," Moth said, suddenly blown along on the gust of a new mood so that where, a minute before, he had been pensive, as still as a pig on a butcher's hook, he was now all eyes and elbows. He thrust the Vegemite bottle at me. "Here, take it. Take it for a pound. I'll settle for a quid. It's a nasty wormy thing you've done and it's a nasty wormy thing in a bottle, and I don't want it. I hope it gives you nightmares, Badgery. I hope it makes you see things when you're awake."

"Done," I said, giddy with relief.

"Three quid," he said, "and it's yours."

"Done." I did not care about the three quid. All I had in my bank account was the money he had arrested me with: three pounds, two shillings and sixpence.

"Three pounds two and six, and you have a deal."

"Done," I said, and happily signed the withdrawal chit he had brought in with him.

Moth rose and, having fussily arranged his genitals, knocked on the door to be let out. This was habit, but quite unnecessary. The door was unlocked, and there was no one except prisoners to hear him knock on it. All he had to do was open it, walk down two steps, cross the so-called "quadrangle", duck under the big rainwater tanks, cut through the big shade house full of eucalypt seedlings – a nice cool place with a pleasant smell of damp earth and sawdust – and he would be at the front gate which would not, probably not, be locked either. The prisoners were either very young and in for very short sentences or, like me, too old to consider the fifty-mile walk.

Moth stood at my door, waiting. He drummed his fingernails against the plywood.

"I'll tell you, Badgery. I would have given it to you. I would have paid you money to take the nasty thing. Have you ever noticed", he said, "how in a dream nothing ever stays still? Things are always moving, Badgery. Have you noticed?"

I stood up and opened the door for him. I just turned the handle and moved it in an inch so he would feel what I had done, but he no longer seemed interested in leaving.

413

"Always moving. You look at a face and you think you've got a fix on it, but it changes. The mouth opens and becomes a fish or if it's pretty it turns ugly and all the white skin is suddenly scars. You have noticed it, haven't you?"

"Yes," I said.

"That's right," he nodded in satisfaction. "And lovely roses turn into lumps of meat. You cannot grasp it, isn't that right, like mercury between your fingers?"

"Yes," I said.

"That's right," he said. He stared at me with those odd pale eyes that seemed to shift mercurially from belligerence to puzzlement. "I knew you'd know," he said.

He blinked and looked at me for a moment before he realized that the door had been opened. Then, without word, he turned and left me. I watched him pass out of sight under the tank stands. A minute later – he must have been running – I heard his car start and saw the lights sweep across the so-called "cottages" where the screws were obliged to live with their unhappy wives.

I understood a little more about Sergeant Moth when I met his brother and heard he was famous in the Clarence River region for his enterprise in the field of small bribes. He made his money from after-hours drinkers, two-up schools and SP bookies and it was only natural that he would, like a careful housewife, hesitate before throwing out the scraps of an arrest.

I didn't look at the ugly "souvenir" for weeks. I avoided it. I hid it behind Goldstein's envelopes – those perfumed razor blades – and when I saw it again, by accident, it had gone mercifully cloudy. There was a particularly hot February night in 1939, the one in which the yabbies caused so much trouble, after which the liquid in the bottle turned gin-clear. It was then that I noticed what looked like a wart behind the knuckle. But by 1939 I had other things to worry about. I had become a student. I had the privilege of a desk and extra shelves. Never mind I cracked the asbestos sheeting putting up the shelves – I got written up in the *Rankin Downs Express* and when my exam results came out they made an even bigger fuss.

I had the bottle tucked away behind the dictionary that the governor had given to me. Every time I removed the book I could not help noticing that the wart was growing bigger. This worried me as much as if I'd found a growth on my own finger, one that frightened me so much I couldn't confess it to myself, let alone a doctor.

414

I started to take the dictionary down, not for a useful word, but to glance at what I'd hidden behind it. I saw it happened just as Sergeant Moth said it did.

The finger changed. It changed all the time. It changed like a face in a dream.

I will not upset myself by describing the slimy monsters that tried to free themselves from that bottle, but rather tell you about the morning I woke early and found it filled with bright blue creatures that darted in and out of delicate filigree forests, like tropical fish feeding amongst the coral.

Is it hard to understand why an old man with his dentures in his hand would suddenly show his pink gums and grin? There: Herbert Badgery, Apprentice Liar, as delighted as a baby with a bright blue rattle.

13

The AJS had been wheeled into Chaffey's shed where it had been, solicitously, covered with a tarpaulin to keep off the shit of wandering chickens.

It was a hot night and the smell of the mouse plague was heavy in Charles's nostrils as he lay in bed. He could hear the mice gnawing at the walls and scampering across the ceiling and, occasionally, a small squeak to indicate that one of his snakes was still dining.

He was hungry. His stomach was tight and he had a taste like iron filings in his mouth but it was, just the same, lovely to lie in a bed in a room by himself, even if the room was just an open back veranda. The mattress smelt a little unusual, but he was used to other people's smells, strange sheets, hessian blankets, beds shared with bony children, pissing children, pinching children. He could sleep anywhere, on kitchen tables or in hay sheds, it made no difference, and when he was an older man, suffering insomnia, he would look back nostalgically on those lonely nights when he could escape hunger or heartache just by lying down and closing his eyes.

He slept easily, dreaming instantly of his pet shop in which environment the smell of mice (now gnawing at the salty underarms of his carelessly discarded shirt) was nothing more than the aroma of a pet's cornucopia.

So as Charles contemplated a rare golden-shouldered parrot, a being so beautiful that its dreamer's face showed a beatific smile, Les Chaffey quietly slipped the tarpaulin off the H-series AJS and stood there, contemplating it. There was a look on his face that could be mistaken for hostility, the way he narrowed his eyes and pushed his head forward, but it was no more than intense curiosity, and it was easy enough to imagine that it was the sheer force of his gaze that had worn away at his wife's face until it had taken on the look of a pretty fabric that has been laundered too often, the bright blues gone chalky pale and the pinks almost white.

The AJS, Les Chaffey thought, was an interesting machine. He squatted beside it for a moment. Then, like a fellow reaching for his pipe, he pulled a small wooden-handled screwdriver from his back pocket and, in four fast neat movements, removed the single screw from the pilgrim pump. He could see, before he touched that screw, what the pilgrim pump was, i.e., a device for automatically controlling the oil feed to the engine, but that was not enough. He wanted to know how it worked. He fetched a spanner and disconnected the pipes that led to it. He removed the little knurled nut on the pump itself and was surprised by the spring-loaded cams. He had not expected spring-loading and the spring escaped him, flying beyond the circle of lamplight. He collected what remained (a worm and roller, two cams, the knurled nut) and held them in the dry cup of his hand. He thought about the spring a moment but decided to wait for daylight.

Having fiddled with the worm and roller, having learned the rate was controlled by the magneto sprocket, the mystery was more or less explained and, glancing over the bike again, he was struck by the small clearance between rear tyre and mudguard. How, he wondered, would a fellow change a tyre on a machine like this? Indeed, at first sight, it looked impossible.

He was busy removing the chain guard when his wife came in and stood behind him, eccentric only in her nakedness.

"Come on, Dad, leave it alone."

"Nah, Marjorie, just looking." He looked up and gave her a creased smile and tapped her bare ankle with the screwdriver. "You go to bed."

"What is it?" She squatted, and her body, had anyone been interested to look at it, was what you might expect of a forty-five-year-old woman accustomed to hard physical work. She was slight, like her husband, and her biceps showed a similar

416

wiriness. They both had suntans that stopped just above the elbow.

"A pilgrim pump," said Les, opening his hand to show her the parts. "A wonderful thing. But what I'm worried about is this rear wheel. Could I trouble you to hold the lamp, Marjorie?"

She held the lamp for him while he placed the chain guard gently on the floor. He unclipped the chain and folded it neatly. He put the chain clip in his shirt pocket.

"I'm going to hold up the back of the bike," he said. "Now if you could just wiggle this back wheel around, we'll see what's what."

She sat on the dusty floor behind the cycle, heedless of the dirt on her naked backside and, while her husband took the weight off the back tyre, she wiggled it as asked.

"Did you ask his permission, Leslie Chaffey?"

"For God's sake, Marjorie, don't nag."

"I weren't nagging."

The back wheel suddenly found its way free, just where it had appeared impossible, slipped neatly out beside the guard, and, taking Mrs Chaffey by surprise, rolled gently away from her to fall down in the shadows.

Les Chaffey waited until his wife was clear, then lowered the rear of the bike. "I'll have it back together by morning."

"You forget."

"What do I forget? Hold this a sec."

He handed her the chain while he fetched, from a high shelf in the unlit upper half of the shed, a stack of old newspapers. He spread these out, slowly, like a man laying out a hand of patience.

"You forget," she said, holding the oily chain in her two outstretched palms. "You forget."

He was now at the clutch, or rather at the place where the clutch cable attached itself to a small lever on the gearbox casing. She came and squatted beside him and, when he held out the lamp to her, she placed the oily chain on the newspaper and took it from him. "You forget," she repeated. "The threshing machine."

"For God's sake," he grunted, "that was twenty years ago. You didn't even know me."

"I heard about it just the same. You forget what you're like." Just the same, she held the lamp high, and helped him to find the small metal ball when it popped off the end of the gearbox spindle.

"The thing I can't understand", said Les Chaffey, digging out

417

the parts of the pilgrim pump from his pocket and rolling them around his open palm, "is how they got the bank manager to lend them the money. How could you explain it to a bank manager?"

"Oh, pity's sake, don't go on about it."

"It was a good plough, Marjorie. Everybody said so."

"They did," she said. She stood up. "I'm filthy and we've got two hundred gallons of water." When he didn't answer she shrugged and walked back to the house, hanging her head and kicking out her legs like a fourteen-year-old girl. She washed quietly, with three cups of water, and left the dirty water at the back door for her husband to use later.

She lay on her bed and was asleep almost immediately. She opened her eyes – it seemed like a minute later – to see her husband standing there with a piece of glistening metal in his oil-black hands.

"Marjorie, come and look at this."

"I want to sleep."

"Marjorie, this is a beautiful thing."

"Oh, for Pete's sake." She sat up. She was cold. It was the cold that made her look at the clock. "Dad, it's five in the morning."

"I know, I know, look how it's *turned*."

"Oh God," she realized what it was. "God, it's the crankshaft." If he had stood before her with a pulsing red heart in his hands she could hardly have appeared more horrified.

14

Charles would never have any understanding of machinery. It eluded him. His mind, confronted by something as simple as a tyre valve, would suddenly go blank and refuse to function sensibly. This was not such a disadvantage later in life when he could afford to pay a mechanic to do the work for him, but it made things difficult when he was young and poor, and never more so than on the occasion that Les Chaffey went to work on the AJS.

Charles woke early and went to sit in the dining room. He waited for ten or fifteen minutes. His stomach was drum-tight and very noisy. He stood up and walked around, examining the map on the wall, the dictionary on the shelf, the trophies from the rifle club. He was not so interested in these things but hoped that the sound of his boots on the floorboards might attract attention – he imagined his host and hostess sound asleep. He coughed once or twice, then he went out to the kitchen house where he found the stove cold. He opened the bread crock and discovered the end of a loaf of bread. He ate it in a nervous rush, chewing it so little, swallowing the crust in such a big lump, that he thought he had cut his oesophagus. He opened the sugar tin and ate a cupped handful, leaning over the sink so he would not put sticky signs on the floor. He brushed the spilt sugar down the plug hole and stepped outside. He did up all three buttons of his suit and walked (lifting his boots high as though his path were sticky mud) across to the shed where he hoped he might find Les Chaffey blacksmithing.

It was gloomy in the shed but he saw, with some relief, that his host and hostess were both there. But even when his eyes adjusted to the light he did not understand what they were doing. He certainly did not recognize his AJS which was spread, in little pieces, across the freshly newspapered floor while Chaffey and his pyjamaed wife argued with each other about the gearbox.

He did notice the amputated sidecar, but his brain, eager to find the most pleasant explanation, suggested to him that Les Chaffey must have a sidecar of his own. There was nothing to connect the oily parts spread across the Melbourne *Argus* with the motor cycle he had parked so carefully the night before.

"Ah," said Les Chaffey. He looked up at Charles with weary red-rimmed eyes. "The man himself. Did you sleep well?"

Mrs Chaffey, in oil-smeared striped pyjamas, smiled apologetically.

"You weren't in a hurry to be off?" Chaffey asked him. "You could spare us another day I take it?"

"Yes, Mr Chaffey," said Charles, who had noticed tell-tale sugar on the front of his suit. He brushed off the granules and thought himself bold for doing so. "Thank you," he said, and stepped closer to see what it was Chaffey was fiddling with.

"How's this work?" Chaffey asked. "When I took it out I assumed that the primary shaft must mesh like this but the knurls on second gear go in an anti-clockwise direction, so I must have been mistook." He looked up at Charles. "Am I right or am I wrong?"

"I dunno."

"It's your cycle, son, and you should know."

Charles's ears started to buzz. His eyes swept the shed as if tracing the flight of bats. Mrs Chaffey made sympathetic clucking noises but he did not hear them. He looked at the oily puzzle in Chaffey's hands. "This is *my* bike?"

419

"It's not *mine*," said Les Chaffey who did not realize the distress he was causing. He was not inclined to offer an apology or even an explanation. In fact, he seemed to be chastising the owner for his lack of knowledge and it was with something close to disgust that he put the gears to one side and started fiddling with the engine mountings, but a rubber grommet was missing and he had to abandon even this for the moment.

"You'll never drive it properly," he said, putting on a pair of horn-rimmed spectacles which gave him a severe owl-like appearance, "you'll never drive it properly if you don't know what makes it tick."

Charles then asked how long the reassembly might take.

Mrs Chaffey smiled at him, shaking her head, but her meaning was not clear.

As for the mechanic himself, he would not be drawn. He knew, like any experienced tradesman working in such circumstances, that it is a mistake to make a promise you cannot keep. In a job like this one all sorts of unexpected problems can crop up. A broken ring may be discovered where none was guessed at, and then there is the delay in waiting for the new part, going to the parcels office at the Jeparit railway station once a week, irate thirteen-word telegrams to the distributor in Melbourne, and so on. Besides this, there are the problems of rogue dogs, or packs of them, who can sneak into the workshop in the heat of the afternoon and carry away a con-rod to bury or play with. Or, even more likely, the English manufacturers, typically ignorant of life in the colonies, unaware of the technical effects of mice plagues, might have made some part from a milk by-product – an insulator perhaps – and this is then lost to the mice and can only be replaced by the previously described rigmarole involving railway stations and thirteen-word telegrams – a costly and time-consuming business. So when Les Chaffey, in due course, made his answer about the length of time required, he answered sensibly.

"No longer", he said, "than it takes, I promise you."

If this had happened in the city, Charles would have seen plots and thievery all around him, but he was eight miles from Jeparit and so he blinked and tried to understand why his host, a kind and decent man, would pull his AJS to pieces in a draughty shed, gritty with abrasive Mallee sand and redolent of Mallee mice.

"One thing's certain," Chaffey said, folding his glasses, rubbing his eyes, smearing black oil across his weary eyelids, "there'll be no more done without a drop of sleep. I've been up all night on this." He dropped his glasses into their case and snapped the lid shut. "Do you have anything planned for the day?"

"I was heading up to Horsham."

"Ah well, Horsham will still be there tomorrow. It won't run away." He put his arm solicitously around Charles's round shoulder. He only did it for a moment, because, being shorter, it was not comfortable. "Come on, Chas. We'll have some bread and jam and then I'll get my forty winks."

There was no bread so they had jam in the tea. While his host snored across the corridor Charles sat at the big table with Mrs Chaffey while she apologized for her husband.

"There's nothing here", she said sadly, "to challenge his mind. I see him some days on the tractor and I know he's gone off into a daze. It's very dangerous to ride a tractor not thinking. That's how I lost my brother – sitting there, not thinking, and next thing you know it's rolled on top of him. Wife and five children. I'm sorry about your motor cycle, son, but I've got to be honest and say I'm pleased you came. It's woke him up. It really has. Did you see his eyes? Well, you wouldn't know the difference but he's been going to sleep after tea and sleeping half the afternoons as well. There's nothing for his mind. The mice ate all his books. They ate all his plough drawings too, but he didn't even seem to mind. He took the bits that were left and threw them in the fire. Well, he doesn't know how to put your cycle back together, but he will, I promise you. He'll teach himself. When he made the plough he read up all about engineering and he made these little gadgets for telling about stress. I don't claim to understand it all, but there was a professor up here from Melbourne who looked at them and he said to me, 'Mrs Chaffey, it's a marvel.' Mind you, his mother told me he was a genius. She never forgave me for laughing at her. I wish she was still alive so I could apologize to her face. Sometimes I dream she's alive, and I'm so happy because I know I can say I'm sorry. But really, it's all for the best. She'd hate to see him now. He hasn't been the same since the banks pulled out of the plough and he lost his patent. There's an American crowd, I hear, who are making it now. It makes me so cross, I could spit."

The tea and jam had done nothing but accentuate Charles's hunger. He was eager that the talking finish so he could go outside and raid the chook house for eggs. He knew that anything he said would extend the conversation, but he could not help himself – he felt sorry for Mrs Chaffey and being a young man he imagined that words might help her.

"Still," he said, "you've got the farm."

She did not quite laugh, but she expelled some air. "He only bought the farm because it was so bad, to demonstrate the ploughs. Wally Jenkins," she explained, nodding down towards the road where an old Chev made the leading edge of a feather of soft dust. She watched Wally Jenkins's progress for a moment. "To demonstrate the ploughs," she said. "We've got a rocky paddock and a paddock full of stumps and we've got a bog which will be boggy if it ever rains again, and he was so happy when he found it. Just like a little boy. We were boarding with the Ryans in Jeparit at the same time and he came home and said, 'Marjorie, I've found the perfect bit of land.' Oh dear," she said, smoothing her dull hair back over her head.

Charles made a sympathetic noise.

Mrs Chaffey placed her oil-smeared hands palm downwards on the table and Charles – the urge came on him suddenly – wanted to pat them.

"I must say I'm pleased you came," she said. "I must say you are like an angel to me." And she touched *his* hand. Perhaps it was the hunger, but his head started humming and he felt a not unpleasant sensation on his neck, just where the hair was cut short and prickly. She did not pat his hand, as he had considered patting hers, but grabbed it, and squeezed it hard until it hurt.

"If you had wings on your back", she said, her forehead creased with frown marks, "and a halo round your head I couldn't be happier."

And then she stood, made a jumble of cups and saucers, and left the room, accompanying the soft brush of her feet with the light clink of crockery.

It was such a gloomy room. It faced the west and the mornings were spent in deep lifeless shadow. Charles sat alone with his back to his host's rifle-shooting trophies, staring down at the bright yellow ribbon of empty road. It was so still that Mr Jenkins's cloud of dust still hung like a chalky smudge across the sand-washed landscape. His head still felt odd – probably, as I said, only hunger. He looked down and found the oily mark Mrs Chaffey's hand had left on the back of his, and in the face of all the forces to the contrary, the gloomy light, his empty belly, the melancholy snoring of his host, the lost snakes, the various stinks of mice, sweat, must, seaweed, the dismembered motor cycle, the flies fucking on the jam spots on the table, this oil smudge of affection was enough to make him happy.

When he heard Mrs Chaffey splitting firewood he went out to help her.

15

The next morning was as fine and clear and windless as the one before. Wally Jenkins drove past and made his chalk plume of dust. They ate porridge with golden syrup, fresh soda bread with plum jam and cocoa made from new cow's milk. Charles saw a little lump of snake's shit and kicked it under the table.

There was no talking during the eating although Les Chaffey took out his wooden-handled pocket knife and, very carefully, cut the weather map from his two-day-old copy of the *Argus*. He placed this on the table where his bread and butter plate should have been; then he put on his spectacles so he could study while he ate.

When breakfast was finished and the table cleared, Mrs Chaffey ripped a big rag from an old floral dress and gave it to her husband. Charles heard the rip but did not think about it. He was still seated in his chair, his head back, his eyes patiently combing the cobwebby rafters, looking for his snakes.

Chaffey had to ask his guest to move. Mrs Chaffey invited him (wordlessly) to stand beside her and watch Mr Chaffey wipe down the oilskin. Mr Chaffey did not do this like a husband performing a chore, nor did Mrs Chaffey watch him as if he were.

Mrs Chaffey smiled at Charles. Mr Chaffey spat on the rag and worked on the hardened gravy spots. He rubbed like a demon. He polished the oilcloth as if it were made of first-quality cedar. He felt the surface with the flat of his hand and was not easily satisfied.

When he was done with spitting and rubbing, he tucked the rag in his back pocket from whence it hung like a bedraggled bantam's tail. Unconscious of the comic effect, he took down his dictionary from the shelf, opened it at the beginning, and removed his collection of yellowed newspaper weather maps. He then spread these on the table like a hand of patience.

"Come here, Chas. I'll show you something."

Mrs Chaffey nodded encouragingly, although she herself remained leaning against the open window.

Charles went and stood beside his host but because he was

423

confused as to what was happening he did not listen properly to the first part of the explanation and thus found himself saying "yes, yes" when he was, in reality, totally bamboozled.

Les Chaffey was explaining the weather to him. He was doing it in terms of a game of snooker. There was rain coming. It was there, sure as chooks have chickens. It was not on the map yet, but it would be. There was a high, there, which would be snookered. It would wish to move across, but would be blocked. Then this low would come in and drop, plop, into the pocket in the Great Australian Bight. This itself would not bring rain, but it left the field wide open, any mug could see it, for this one, here. Les called it the "Salient Low".

When he had finished his explanation, Les put away his maps. Charles did not understand the implications of what he had heard until later when he went out to the shed and found Chaffey furiously welding the cleat on to his tractor. Mrs Chaffey had an oilcan and was going over the spring-loaded tines of the "Chaffey Patented No. 4 Plough".

No one said to him, "Excuse us, but your motor cycle will have to wait."

Rather, Chaffey said: "Here, pull this," when he could not get the tractor linkage to line up with the plough.

Often, during the next two weeks, Charles came to the brink of asking about when his motor cycle might be ready, but he could see the time was not right, that Chaffey was too tired, or too busy, and so he waited, working the tractor himself for the last three hours of every day. Using the ingenious Chaffey plough, they did the rocky paddock and the one full of stumps. The tractor leapt and thumped and reared and left Charles's kidneys in as painful a state as when he arrived. At night he dreamed of furrows and his sleep was tense with the problems of keeping them straight on rocky ground.

Finally the clouds began to arrive, jumbled and panicked like bellowing beasts in a sale-yard, and Les Chaffey drove before the coming storm, seeding at last. He drove recklessly along the steeper banks in high gear, looking behind him at the bunching clouds, ahead of him for any hole or stump that might send him rolling. He had seeded the Long Adams and the Boggy Third and was on the last run of the Stumpy Thin when the rain came in great fat drops which brought out the perfumes in the soil. He finished the run in a flood of lovely aromas (minty dust, musky clay), drove out the gate, parked the tractor by the back door, put a rusty jam tin over the exhaust stack to keep out the damp, and went into the house where his wife and guest, woken from their naps by the din of rain on the roof, were celebrating with a pot of tea.

"Now," Les Chaffey said, "now young fellow-me-lad, we can get stuck into that AJS of yours."

The next morning there was water for baths and for washing clothes. Mrs Chaffey laboured over the copper, stirring the clothes with a big pale stick, while the rain continued to fall. It was good rain, gentle and persistent, and Les's unlaced boots, as they returned to the house from the shed, were caked with gritty red mud. He took off his boots and left them on the back porch. He came into the kitchen where his prisoner was watching flies fucking on the table.

"There's nothing to it," he announced, filling the kettle recklessly with water. "Half a day's work, and I've got it beat."

Charles was so elated he came and shook his host's hand. The mice were busy dying of their own plague. His snakes had all escaped. There was nothing to keep him in the Mallee any more, and he had resolved to return to Sydney to open a pet shop. He did not know that Les Chaffey was afflicted by a disease common in clever men: he was impatient with detail and when he had finally worked out the gearbox and seen how quickly the rest of the machine could be put together, that the problem was licked, the cat skun, etc., he no longer had any incentive to complete the job, with the result that the motor cycle would be left to lie beneath a tarpaulin like a body in a morgue and only bereaved Charles would bother to lift it, although he no longer hoped that a miracle had been performed while he slept.

Every night Les Chaffey would promise to fix the motor cycle tomorrow, but when tomorrow came he would rise late, dawdle over breakfast, perhaps go into Jeparit to the rifle club, come home after lunch, and fall asleep while his wife shook her head or clicked her tongue.

"Tell him stories about your family," she implored the prisoner, while they sat over empty cups of tea, weeded the vegetable garden, stirred the copper or pegged clothes on the line.

"I tried, missus. You heard me. He's not interested." Charles, in spite of his good nature, was becoming irritated with Mrs Chaffey. He thought she should say something to her husband. Instead she put the onus on him.

"Tell him something mechanical," she said.

Charles tried to relate the story of his father's aeroplanes but being unable to answer such simple questions as the type of engine that powered them, he soon lost his host's attention and (unfairly, he thought) his hostess's respect.

All Charles's stories were like matches struck in a draught, and when he had exhausted his box and Les Chaffey's enthusiasms remained unkindled, he despaired of ever seeing his motor cycle in one piece again.

He told Marjorie Chaffey that he didn't mind, but this was false generosity intended to regain her affection. The truth was that he was so angry he could have burnt the shed down.

Easter came and went. The weather turned clear and cold. The wheat showed green above the yellow paddocks and whatever Les Chaffey should have been doing, he didn't do it. He snored, or listened to his Tommy Dorsey record, or brooded over an old Melbourne telephone directory.

And Mrs Chaffey began to act as if even this was Charles's fault. It was cold on the back veranda, but she pretended she had no extra blankets to give him. She no longer offered to wash his shirt. She spoke to him less often, and less kindly. In the afternoons she withdrew to the front veranda, darning socks or shelling peas in the winter sunlight, or squatting on her haunches to watch for something that never came. In the evenings she knitted mittens and scarves for her children in Geelong. When slugs got into the vegetable garden she spoke as if it was his fault. There was never any pudding at night. And when Charles offered his only money –a florin and two pennies – towards his keep, his wan hostess enraged him by accepting it – she dropped the coins into the pocket of her grubby pinafore where they stayed (he heard them) for weeks.

When he lay in bed at night he wore his socks and his shirt and he spread his suit across the top of the blanket. He learned to sleep on his back, very still, so that he would not crush his suit and have to borrow the iron again.

He could hear the Chaffeys talking on the other side of the wall, and he did not need to poke his hearing aid through the convenient hole in the hessian lining to understand that it was he who was the subject of their conversation.

"Fix his bike."

Silence.

"Leslie Chaffey. . . ."

"I heard you."

Silence, then the movement of springs.

"Why won't you fix it for him?"

Charles lay still and breathless.

"He should be able to fix it himself."

"He can't."

"He should learn."

"He's a dunce," said Marjorie Chaffey, no longer whispering. "He can't learn."

"For God's sake, Marjorie, it's *simple*."

Another silence and then, without any warning, without so much as a spring squeak, came a bellow of pain so loud that Charles could not believe it came from his friendly-faced host.

"WHY IS LIFE LIKE THIS?"

"Shush, it's all right, shush, Leslie, shush. It's all right."

"WHY?"

"I'm here."

Les Chaffey wept. His wife cooed. A mopoke cried in the scrub to the north. Charles removed his hearing aid and locked himself in, alone with the noises of his blood.

16

It occurred to Charles that he had fallen amongst mad people and he would be wise to escape. Still, he did not rush at it, and when he did make a move it was in exactly the opposite direction to what you'd expect, not down the drive and past the mailbox, but up the back and into the scrub. He poked around amongst the tussocked grasses and stunted trees. He found a couple of mallee fowl who opened their mound each morning to let the autumn sun warm their eggs, but he did not study them. The mallee fowl is too depressing and lifeless a bird to have any commercial value and my boy's mind was occupied with the idea of the pet shop in Sydney.

Had he already decided it would be the Best Pet Shop in the World? Probably. It would not matter that he had seen no more of the world's pet shops than those cramped cages in Campbell Street. He suffered from the Badgery conceit and was not concerned by what competition he would have to face. He knew only what he needed to know, which was that the Splendid Wrens he could see around him were worth five bob in Sydney. There were Golden Whistlers at half a crown. And, best of all (he could see the ticket-writing already): Blue Bonnets, 1 guinea.

Charles was feeling belligerent towards the Chaffeys and, having lost his motor cycle, did not feel inclined to ask permission to use their binding twine for nets or fencing wire for net frames. He made his nets (badly) from two sprung halves, like big netted oyster shells. He took the garden spade and did not own up when it was missed. He dug holes in the red sandy soil in the scrub, and in these holes, amidst the amputated wattle roots, he placed stolen pudding bowls of water – the only bait necessary for the job.

He was soon, on paper anyway, a rich man.

And yet I must not make my son's motives appear solely mercenary and you must see how gently he handles the birds when he traps them, and how those big clumsy hands suddenly reveal themselves as instruments of affection. He worries excessively about their diet, their comfort, the size of their improvised chicken-wire cages, separates the meek from the aggressive, finds company for the gregarious. And when he at last succeeds in trapping a one-guinea blue bonnet he can sit happily for hours marvelling at the beauty of its feathers, the rich blue around its parrot's beak, the yellow of its lower breast in which lovely sea you find a soft-edged island of rich blood red.

He did not feel the need to explain his growing menagerie to anyone. Marjorie Chaffey saw him using their seed wheat to feed galahs and, as was her habit when angry, said nothing. Her mood was not helped by her husband who, having passed the birds every day for a week as he walked to the dunny and back, finally noticed them, became excited and started feeding them himself.

It was then that Marjorie Chaffey began to dig the hole. Perhaps it was for compost. Perhaps it was for something else. She didn't care. She was so angry she made it four feet deep while her thick-skinned husband squandered his intelligence and enthusiasm devising a more efficient bird-catching net. She heard his excited voice coming from the shed. She flung down the mattock and took up the crowbar. He came and showed her what he'd done. She dropped the crowbar and picked up the spade and he waited patiently for her to finish removing the loose dirt.

Then he explained the bird net, pointing out the simplicity of the spring which he had made from an old inner tube, and the trigger release which was as sensitive as a mousetrap. He did not notice that she had been crying and when she made no comment about his invention it did not seem to dampen his enthusiasm for it.

That night she cooked him curried lamb, a meal he hated. He ate the lot without commenting, talking to the silly boy about a pet shop.

"Fix up his bike", she said, "so he can go."

Charles heard her, but he was so frightened of her he could not look her in the eye.

"Fix it," she said, pulling her knitting out of a brown-paper bag.

But Les Chaffey did not seem to hear, or perhaps he did hear and decided that there was no point in addressing the question until the present matter was settled. He was making some clever shipping cages. Using no more than galvanized iron and solder he was constructing a feed dispenser and a tiny water cistern that would not spill no matter how roughly the cage was handled by the railways.

He also spent a lot of time (now he was privy to Charles's ambitions) giving advice. Half of the advice was about banks and the other half about wives. Marjorie Chaffey's knitting needles clicked as fast as a telegraph key.

About banks he said: "You are doing the right thing, Chas, to have a pet shop. By that I mean – you are handling a product that already exists. My big mistake in life was to make a product that had not previously existed. You see, these fellows at the bank are only there for two reasons. The first is that they've got no imagination. The second is that the bank is a secure job. So they've got no guts and they've got no imagination. They lack every bloody thing you need to make a quid. So what you need, when you approach them, is something they can understand without thinking. You won't have to make them imagine a pet shop, because they'll have already seen one. You won't have to give them drawings of cockatoos or prove to them that a cockatoo can actually fly and talk and that, if it could, people would want to pay money for the privilege of owning one. The cockatoo already exists. This puts you in the same league as importing or manufacturing under licence. They'll lend you money whether your suit is pressed or not."

About wives, he said: "Now you reckon you're too young to go into marriage, and I grant you that there is not a lot of talent in Jeparit to change your mind, but you should not consider opening a business without a wife. You think you can do it, and then you realize there are books to be done, bills to be sent out, and women are particularly good at this sort of work."

"Fix his bike."

429

"If you've got a telephone," said Les, blinking at his wife, combing his hair, holding the comb up against the light so he could remove the hairs properly. "If you've got a telephone," (he put the comb back in his pocket) "if you've got a telephone. . . ."

"I'd need a telephone."

"You would. They're a great aid to any business. If you have a telephone, you need someone to answer it."

"I like a woman's voice. . . ." said Charles, as Mrs Chaffey rose, quite suddenly, and walked out of the room, across the passage, and into the bedroom where she threw herself on to the bed so heavily Charles could feel her misery through the soles of his boots.

"But not only that." Les got up, went to the door, peered across the corridor, shut the door, and sat down again. "Say you're called away, someone's got to answer it. You can't, because you're not there. Now you can employ someone, of course, but then the money is going out of the family, and you won't get the same intelligence, or diligence either." He paused. "A guinea for a bloody parrot," he said, and whistled. "It's a bloody marvel."

"Mr Chaffey, please, I'd appreciate it if you'd put my bike back together."

"You're a funny fellow," said Les Chaffey who could not understand how anyone who was such a no-hoper with machinery could display such a talent when it came to a more difficult thing like birds. He would, of course, be lost without a sensible wife and in this respect the motor cycle would prove to be an important asset. Girls liked fellows with motorbikes. He began to think about the various local girls who might look kindly on his lodger, but could not, immediately, think of any. They were either too pretty (and therefore too up themselves) or too clever or too stupid. He completely forgot about the young schoolteacher who boarded with Chook Carrol out at Red Hill and might never have thought of her had he not had his attention drawn to her by chance.

17

Charles only went into Jeparit that day because he was frightened to be left alone with Mrs Chaffey. He did not like Jeparit very much. It was a small town where everyone stared at a strange face, and he had only gone into the general store to escape the ordeal of the main street. He was poking around amongst the rolls of pig wire, trying to fill in time until Les Chaffey came to fetch him, totally unaware that Robert Menzies (that famous kisser of royal hands) had escaped from the same shop – he had been born there – and was now on his way to being Prime Minister of Australia.

Les Chaffey, meanwhile, was standing in the street outside and wondering if it might be worth his while to teach his guest to dance. It was then that he saw the bank manager walking at an unusually brisk pace. The bank manager had wrapped up a revolver in a handkerchief but the handkerchief was not large enough to hide the weapon from Les Chaffey who introduced himself to the man's attention and demanded to know what he was up to.

The bank manager had only walked fifty yards from his office but he was already puffing and he was in such a state of excitement that it took all of Les's skills to extract the story from him.

He had been contacted by the police, who had no pistols themselves, to ask him to go up to the school where Miss Emma Underhill was bailed up in the schoolyard with a large goanna on her head. The goanna was a big fellow and, being cornered by teasing children, had run up Miss Underhill (as goannas will) thinking her a tree, and now Miss Underhill was bleeding and hysterical and the goanna must be dealt with.

"And what," asked Les Chaffey, reaching for a comb which he had left at home, "what were you going to do with a firearm in a schoolyard?"

The bank manager thought that the pupils should be sent home.

"You would evacuate the school? On account of a goanna?"

The bank manager knew that Les Chaffey was a sticky-beak and a trouble-maker, but he was also nervous of the firearm. "Do you have a better idea?"

Les Chaffey did have a better idea. He ran into the general store and pulled Charles out, holding him by the collar and leading him (still holding the collar) along the main street, past the giggling draper's, in front of Dan Murphy's Commercial Hotel, and up the sandy path into the schoolyard where a high-pitched scream (the goanna had just shifted position) attracted him to Miss Underhill who stood, isolated and lonely, on a bitumen square in front of the shelter shed whilst four teachers and thirty-six pupils stood in an arc and stared at her.

431

"There," said Les Chaffey to his panting puzzled friend. "Isn't she lovely?"

18

Years later when she was being eccentric, had shed her corset and let her arse spread unhindered by anything but her perpetual dressing gown, Emma showed her youngest son a tiny foetus – it was no more than an inch long – which she claimed was his half-brother and which – she tried to make him look in the old Vegemite jar that contained it – was half goanna and half human.

Hissao was disgusted with his mother (who wouldn't be?) and not least because she allowed her upper denture plate to drop at the moment of this disclosure. He did not look, or looked only briefly at the "thing" floating in cloudy liquid.

He shuddered, he who accepted his mother's peculiarities more easily than any of us.

Hissao was well informed about the genitalia of goannas. He had known, from a very early age, that the male has not one penis, but two. These are pale spiny things no more than two centimetres long, and normally kept retracted in little sheaths under the rear legs. It is hardly surprising, therefore, that Hissao stumbled on the mechanical reality of such a coupling, but he should have known better than to approach the problem in this way. There is no doubt that some unlikely things have happened within the wombs of the women of the family but there is no question that they have been able to affect the shape of their offspring as easily as children idly fooling with some Plasticine. Why, if not because of this, is Hissao himself not only named Hissao, but also snub-nosed and almond-eyed? Why? Because the Japanese were bombing Darwin and Emma was not a stupid woman.

The goanna foetus in the bottle was to cause us all a great upset and no one was to be more upset than Charles for whom it was to prove quite fatal.

When he stood beside Les Chaffey in the schoolyard in Jeparit he could not see what the silent girl would become and – untroubled by wild visions – he was able to admire her composure and her sturdy limbs. His hearing aid crackled and hissed. He looked at her sternly. She had pronounced hips, a barrel chest and a broad backside, but it was not simply her shape that he found agreeable; it was her stillness in the midst of all the hysteria that surrounded her. She had screamed, of course, from pain. But now the reptile (a Gould's Monitor) was still again, the girl's pleasant moon face was composed; only her brown eyes displayed any agitation. When she heard that Charles intended to remove the goanna, she smiled at him, lifting her top lip to reveal pretty pink gums and small neat teeth.

The goanna had its leathery chin resting just above her fringe. It tested the air nervously with its forked tongue. Its front claws gripped her broad shoulders, its baggy muscled body moulded itself to her cotton-clad back and its hind claws gripped the soft mound of her generous backside. Its tail, striped yellow like all its body, did not quite touch the ground.

Charles then transformed himself from an acned, red-faced, awkward youth into an expert. The schoolchildren who had whispered and giggled about his funny face and bandy legs saw the change and fell into a silence.

"Get a chaff bag," he told the bank manager, with such terseness that the man did as he was told. Charles turned off his hearing aid and walked out into the no man's land that separated the assembled pupils from the frozen girl.

Emma, seeing him stand before her, observed the hearing aid, a small brown bakelite knob protruding from his fleshy ear, and it made her trust him. He seemed older and more experienced. She felt his personality to be round and smooth and free from nasty spikes. She smiled, a smaller, shyer smile than last time, and this raised, from the ranks of the children in front of her, the same magical incantation that had greeted Leah Goldstein and Izzie Kaletsky when they embraced in a Bondi bus shelter.

"Hubba hubba," the children shouted.

The bag arrived. When this fact had, at last, been drawn to Charles's attention, he walked slowly towards the goanna. His neck was tingling. He felt a warm hum at the base of his skull. The goanna blew out its neck. Charles made a noise deep in his throat. The goanna hissed and then, before anyone had time to gasp, Charles had it off and into the bag, causing no more additional damage than a ripped patch of dress which revealed a blood-spotted petticoat underneath.

"Thank you," she said, and waited for Charles to fiddle with his hearing aid with one hand while he held the agitated chaff bag with the other.

"Charles Badgery," he said, blushing now that the expert performance was ended and he found himself, a shy boy, faced with a girl he liked the look of.

"Don't hurt it," she said.

She placed her hand on his wrist, a pressure so light Charles could barely feel it and, at the same time, could feel nothing else. "It wasn't the goanna's fault." Her voice was as light as her touch. "It was them," she nodded at the pupils who were still, for the moment, quiet. "The little beggars were cheeking it. Promise me you won't hurt it."

"You have my word," he said, quite scarlet, but now they were being crowded and, like aviators just landed, were taken away by the mob, Emma by her pupils, Charles by Les Chaffey and the bank manager.

19

Never in Les Chaffey's life had a plan worked out so neatly and it took him by surprise. He had developed plans more rational, more reasonable, prettier plans, more optimistic plans but these – carefully detailed to the last screw – had been stillborn while this careless doodle, this idea that Charles must fall in love with the schoolteacher, now came to pass exactly as he'd envisaged.

"Well, I'll be damned, I'll be euchred, I'll be a Dutchman." He grinned and rubbed his leprechaun mouth and gazed at his raw red friend who would only confess that Miss Underhill seemed "like a nice sort of girl".

The motor cycle, it was obvious, was an essential aid to courting and Les, having belted his truck up the drive in a cloud of dust, did not stop for tea or a chat with his wife, but pulled his overalls on over his good Fletcher Jones trousers and set to work immediately. It was not in his nature to work so quickly, but he could see that an hour lost would be a dangerous hour, so he put his head down and did not stop until the AJS was back together. It was because of this, or because of Charles impatiently circling him, getting in his light, kicking over his tools, that the quality of the job was less than it might otherwise have been and the machine would ever after be troubled by faults that originated in those two excited days.

As it turned out such haste was unnecessary and no motor cycle was required to woo Miss Emma Underhill who, tired of her landlady's son who was building an outhouse specially to please the young miss, walked the six miles across from Red Hill to inquire, she said, about the well-being of the goanna. The Underhill women were all great walkers and Emma did not come traipsing along the sandy road in high heels and white lawn dress. She put on her white short socks and her strong brown brogues. She wore a heavy tweed pleated skirt that did not show the dirt, and a black twin-set, a colour that suited her complexion. She did carry an umbrella, but she used it energetically, like a walking stick, and she put her shoulders back and held up her head and walked with a good stride, strong and determined, but not without grace or sensuality either. Whilst walking, Emma Underhill showed a part of her character she kept hidden the rest of the time and for an hour and a half she did not lower her eyes once.

She handled the complications of the Chaffeys' gate without hesitation and she walked, more sedately, up the long drive, aware that a woman was squatting on the front veranda watching her. She put up her umbrella and realized, for the first time, that she was being bold. She would be talked about.

She introduced herself to Mrs Chaffey and said she had come about the goanna.

She was directed around the house to the back where she found Charles and the goanna, both together, inside a stout stockade on the edge of the scrub. The monitor was already well on its way to being tame.

She did not go into the cage at once, but stayed with her hands clutching the chicken wire while Charles showed her how the monitor would let its back be stroked and its head rubbed. He was very shy and this made him stern. He said he had begun by using a long piece of cane, and when the animal was used to being rubbed with this, he had used his hands. He said he was lucky, that another monitor, identical in age and appearance, might have stayed wild forever, but this particular one was different. It was quite safe for her to come into the stockade. He gave her his word she would not be harmed and this last commitment he made very solemnly indeed.

Emma entered, clutching her handbag to her chest. She had already decided to get married. She squatted beside the prone reptile, even though it made her wounds hurt. She had had a single stitch on her bottom and a tetanus shot as well. She touched the hard scaly back with the tip of her finger.

"Hello, Mr Monster," she said. Charles loved her voice. It was so soft and blurred, like pastels. It made his neck tingle just to listen to her. It gave him the same delicious feeling he had as he hovered on the brink of sleep and this feeling – until now – had been the single most pleasant feeling in his life. It was the voice that coloured everything he now thought about her. It was shy and tentative and musical. Sometimes he did not manage to hear the words she said, but he did not let on about his deafness.

Emma had withdrawn her hand and stayed squatting in the dust. "You're its friend," she said. "It likes you more than me."

"It can't tell you from me, I reckon." Charles drew a doodle in the dust with a broken stick. "All it knows is that we are the sort of animals that bring it food."

Both of the Chaffeys were now hovering around the chook pen, pretending to be mending a laying box. It was Mrs Chaffey who observed, tartly, that if they swapped the goanna for a bag of cement it would have made no difference. And, to be fair, the goanna, being well fed and contented, was not unlike a bag of cement. It lay flat on its belly in its heavy timber and wire stockade while Charles Badgery and Emma Underhill squatted on either side of it and rubbed and patted, patted and rubbed, their cheeks flushed.

This part of the story is still popular around Jeparit. They say the goanna lost so much skin from all this patting that it soon began to bleed.

20

It is not true, of course, that business about the goanna bleeding – no one in Jeparit ever said such a thing. Not even the town that produced the Warden of the Cinque Ports could stretch to such a grotesque idea. It was I, Herbert Badgery, who said it. I was struck with a passion to make my son look a ninny. I did not plan to. I love him. I have always loved him. My greatest wish is to show you my brave and optimistic boy struggling against the handicap of his conception and upbringing towards success. And then, just as I am almost achieving it, I think of the way he walks, lifting his feet high and stamping them down. He walks like a yokel, a moron. I want to grab him by the ear and drag him to a quiet corner where I can teach him to walk properly. I love him, yes, of course I do, but I wish to mock him, not only him but his ladylove, not only her, but the landscape they inhabit, not merely the landscape in general, but the paddocks of Chaffey's farm in particular. I would like to take them, each one by name, and convert the dreary melancholy of the place into a very superior and spiteful kind of beauty, to caress the damn paddocks until they too begin to bleed.

Look at them, the three of them: boy, girl, goanna. They are all desert creatures, accustomed to eking out what they can from poor circumstances. In the goanna's case it does not irritate me. I expect it to behave like an opportunist, to eat twice its body weight when the food is available, because there may be nothing else available for a month. But when my son takes the affection Emma Underhill offers him, he does it in exactly the same spirit – as if no one, ever, will be affectionate to him again. He would fall in love with anyone, a butcher's cat that rubbed itself against his legs. And once he had done it he would be loyal for life. Of course I am angry. I am not an unreasonable man. I don't wish to deny him affection and love. I would not mind if he was likely to go flying off on a waltzing binge and get himself engaged to a waitress first and a telephonist second.

Can't dance? Of course he can't dance. Fa. He does not need to dance. He could not have seduced her better (made her head go numb, gormless, silly, her eyes go wider), not if he had spun her in her peach organdie ball gown round the Jeparit Mechanics' Institute.

They stroked the goanna until their hands were sticky with its juices. Then they borrowed a little dinghy and went rowing up on Lake Hindmarsh. He told her the names of the waterbirds. He kissed her. He wrote to his mother for permission to marry. And when May came they packed up all the birds and made a new cage for the Gould's Monitor and shipped them all down to Bacchus Marsh where Emma's family lived. They left the AJS temporarily in the care of Les Chaffey.

Bacchus Marsh is another town entirely, quite different from Jeparit. No Robert Menzies has been invented there. No, this is the town of Frank Hardy and Captain Moonlight. But my apologies to the Shire President, for I am not suggesting it is a town peopled solely with Communist Writers and Bushranger Priests, and I tip my hat to you Sir, Madam, to the Claringbolds, Careys, Dugdales, Lidgetts, Jenszes, Joungebloeds, Alkemades, Dellioses, and those of you who know Bacchus Marsh should skip the next ten pages for they concern only Henry Underhill and his family, and far less about these matters than you yourself will know already. There is only a mention of the plane trees in Grant Street, a nod in the direction of agricultural matters, and a description of the Underhills' house, i.e., the Underhills occupied a long low single-storey brick cottage on the corner of Gell and Davis Streets – where the panel-beater's shop is now. As you came down Davis Street you could look down into the backyard where Henry Underhill kept his dogs, those snarling chained bitzers that threw themselves so frantically against their chains that they appeared, at times, possessed of a desire to hang themselves.

It was in this house that Charles and Emma came to stay before the marriage which took place in that little weatherboard church with the high galvanized-iron steeple. I was not at the wedding, being still retained at Rankin Downs, but I can see the steeple in my mind's eye, a slender shining dunce's cap protruding from an electric green field of the sugar cane for which Bacchus Marsh is so famous.

The bell inside that steeple is deep and sonorous and many people will tell you that this special quality is attributable to the fundamental resonance of the galvanized iron and not to the bell. Others say that it is the intrinsic quality of the bell that Captain Bacchus brought with him from Burma in 1846. This is a good example of the stupid arguments that seem to arise wherever churches are built and Emma's father, besides being a pound officer, was a passionate participant in all of them. He not only held strong views about bells but (to take only one instance) on the crucial matter of whether an altar was really an altar or a communion table. Disagreement on this subject was enough to make the vein on his forehead take on the appearance of a small blue worm.

In short, he was a fool.

Henry Underhill was a man who felt he had been called upon to rule, and he was not put off by the fact that no one else seemed to have noticed. Instead he patiently collected, one by one, those small positions of authority left vacant by others' indolence. When no one could see the point in drilling the militia, it was Henry Underhill who had his wife iron his uniform and blanco his webbing, who tucked a baton under his arm, and barked at the young men until the street lights came on and even he had to admit it was time to go home. He was secretary of the Progress Association and seconded the resolution to have public benches placed in the main street. He was the head chap in the vestry. And, last of all, he was the pound officer, even though he did cut a funny figure on a horse.

Now, as only the last of these positions paid a wage, and that not a very good one, he was not a rich man. And although responsible for the Progress Association's bookkeeping, he was a nervous fellow with money. When he heard that the first of his three daughters wished to marry he did not, as his wife did, worry about the quality of the unseen boy. His first emotion was relief, that *that* problem was out of the way. Then he became – it took only an instant – nervous. There was a wedding to pay for. Worse than that, the Education Department of Victoria, having paid for his daughter's expensive training, were expecting her to fulfil her obligations to them. He had signed a bond guaranteeing that she would teach for five years. But now she was going into the pet business. The Education Department therefore required their money back. Five hundred pounds. This figure put him in a panic proper. He did not know what to do about it. If he had calmed down a moment and reread his agreement with the Department he would have seen that he could pay off the bond in instalments. If he had been the sort of man to share his worries with his wife, she would have been sure to have pointed it out to him, and even done it nicely, so that he would not feel stupid. But he had a stern sense of a husband's responsibilities and it would never have occurred to him that he might show such a frightening document to a woman.

So he did not reread the agreement calmly. He did not discuss it with his wife. Instead he decided, even before he met Charles, that he would extract the sum from him.

Now all that, in its mingy way, is logical enough. It is not difficult to persuade yourself that it might even be fair, and a simpler man would have set to work extracting the money. But Emma's father was not a simple man, being burdened not only with officiousness, meanness and nerves, but also with a sense of honour. He was therefore duty bound to make something clear to Charles before he began to lever away the five hundred quid.

What this "thing" was has never been made clear. And while you will find plenty of people in Bacchus Marsh prepared to smirk and roll their eyes about it, they don't seem to know very much about the particulars. Whatever the "thing" was took place when Emma was thrown from her family home into the

439

teachers' college. One would gather that the strength of her reaction against being thrown out from under the parental roof gave rise to fears about her sanity.

Henry Underhill had a full month to consider how he would communicate this to Charles Badgery. The matter so concerned him that he thought of nothing else but how to express it diplomatically. And yet when he saw Charles Badgery help his daughter down from the train, his heart lightened. He saw the way he held her hand, how he fussed about her coat. The boy was infatuated. He smiled. The job would not be so difficult at all.

Charles, for his part, was eager to like Emma's father. He was also preparing himself to confess that his own father was in gaol. He had spent more time worrying about his confession than Henry Underhill had with his. Further, he had seen a photograph of his future father-in-law, and the photograph had frightened him. In the photograph Henry Underhill wore jodhpurs and carried a riding whip. He stood ramrod straight and his countenance was severe and military.

When he saw the smile his future father-in-law showed beneath his moustache, Charles, also, felt relieved. Henry Underhill was not only nicer, but far shorter than the photograph had showed. He was no more than five foot two. He was also energetic and brisk. He was a fellow who liked to get things done. He was also touchingly shy and awkward when he embraced his daughter.

"Right," said Henry Underhill, retreating from the embrace and slapping a rolled newspaper against his thigh. "We need a trolley for your cages. Clancy Shea has a good one in the parcels office. You and me, young fellah, can get the trolley. Emma, mind the birds."

Charles liked this. He didn't think it bossy at all. They walked off down the platform as the train pulled out of the station and laboured up towards Parwan. Soon you could hear the starlings again.

"It's a beaut day," said Charles, by way of approaching the question of Rankin Downs.

"I'm sure you'll be very happy."

"Oh yes," said Charles, who had not expected to be liked. "You bet."

Henry Underhill smiled, and stopped walking. Charles stopped, and smiled too. He was sorry to be so much taller.

"Do you know horses, Chas?"

"I reckon I know enough." Charles kicked a large lump of quartz gravel across the black bitumen platform. He sensed a birds-and-bees talk coming. He was wrong.

"Our Emmie", smiled Henry Underhill, showing perfect white teeth beneath that handsome brush of hair, "is what they call flighty."

Now "flighty" only had two meanings to Charles – either (a) Flirty or (b) Crazy – and Henry Underhill had the disturbing experience of watching the young man change before his eyes. He had, until this moment, stood round-shouldered as he tried to minimize his height. He had stood with his hands politely behind his back and his head in a permanent deferential bow. But now he grew a full six inches and if Underhill did not see his big fists curl he must have witnessed the other symptoms.

"She ain't," said Charles.

"No, no, not like that." Henry Underhill saw how badly he was understood. To him the word "flighty" had suggested something nervous, tentative, even beautiful. It had suggested prancing, spirit, fine breeding and the acceptable nervousness that often accompanies it.

"You may be her Dad, Mr Underhill, but my Emma is not flighty."

In any normal circumstances Henry Underhill would have started to lose his temper here. He could not stand to be contradicted by an underling. He would have had one of his outbursts, gone red in the face and threatened the stock whip.

In any normal circumstances Charles, also, would have begun to shout.

But they were both, although very red in the face, smiling amiably at each other, although they stood so still that the starlings, unaware that they were human, scavenged spilt grain from the platform at their feet.

"Nervous, I meant," said Henry Underhill. "Nervous like. Lacking in confidence."

"I see," said Charles, furious that his beloved had been compared to a horse. It was this that stuck in his mind, this big-haunched image which would stay with him and offend him all his life.

"I'm her Dad. I know my girl."

Charles now noticed the way Henry Underhill's bushy eyebrows pressed down so heavily upon his eyes. It made him look mad. "I'm sure you do, Mr Underhill." He was tired and

441

dirty from the journey, but he could have picked the pound officer up and knocked him down. He had the Badgery temperament and he imagined all sort of things, pushing him off the platform, smacking him across the cheek, cuffing him across the back of the head. "I'm sure you do," he said.

"She's flighty." Henry Underhill frightened the starlings with a single slap of his rolled newspaper and, relieved to have at last done the right thing, he led the walk towards the trolley. "Like a horse."

It took a little while to get the birds and the goanna down to the wagon. When they had, at last, tied everything down firmly, Henry Underhill dropped his first hint about the five hundred quid.

This offended Charles as much as the description of his daughter. He despised the sleazy way Underhill sidled up to the matter, just as they were taking up the tension on the last knot, came breathing up beside him as if he were selling a dirty postcard.

When he was at last sitting on the bench seat beside his fiancée, he silently resolved to pay the whole bond himself, but not to tell Underhill a thing about it. So as they set off at a trot beside the park, Charles began to plan his moves as carefully as if Underhill was an animal who must be trapped. He was already involved in the technique of it, how he must secretly contact the Education Department, arrange a box number at the post office for mail. And no one looking at him, or talking to him, would ever guess that this sort of cunning could coexist with such clumsy, awkward honesty.

They came up to the High School, turned right, and crossed the Werribee River bridge. Seeing Charles so silent, Emma, her big hands folded contentedly on her lap, told her father about the Best Pet Shop in the World.

"Now, Emmie, don't talk fibs," her father said, looking across to Charles and giving him a wink.

"It's no fib, Mr Underhill." Charles took Emma's gloved hand and squeezed it.

"Pish."

Charles did not understand the term and so was silent.

"Posh and pish," said Henry Underhill, belting the horse's rump with the reins. "Have you seen the world?"

Charles did not answer. He concentrated on the arch of plane trees above the road; the trees were losing the last of their leaves and the air was sweet and smoky with the fires of tidy householders.

He squeezed Emma's hand again and although he hurt her she did not complain. She could feel her father's happiness, and she was limp and tired with relief. She had worried that there would be trouble, but now she could see there would be none.

Henry Underhill was indeed happy. His daughter would be married and this piece of insolence would be persuaded to pay part of the bond. "Best in the world," he said, "you're just a boy."

"Yes," said Charles, thinking that he would have to tolerate this odious hairy-nostrilled chap for another thirty days. He was pleased he had left the AJS at Jeparit. He would go back and fetch it.

"Best pet shop in the world!"

Emma smiled. She was so used to her father's teasing she found nothing offensive in it. She had made herself believe, so long ago, that he did not mean to be nasty, that now she could not see just how infuriated he was made by the Best Pet Shop in the World.

21

Winter came very early that year. It was not even June and there was snow lying on the ground for three days at Ballan. It was on the wireless and the Melbourne papers took photographs and put them on the front page. One Sunday afternoon they saw cars with yellow headlights and snowmen on their roofs. The cars crawled in procession down Stanford Hill, along the main street of the dusk-grey town, in the direction of Melbourne. Neither of them had seen snow before, but not having the AJS they could not go.

The day after the snowmen drove through the town, there were falls in Bacchus Marsh itself, but although you could catch the flakes in your outstretched hands they melted there, just as quickly as they did when they hit the ground. Emma went to Halbut's to buy Charles a pair of long johns. Marjorie Halbut, who had sat behind her in sixth grade, served her. At first she was condescending, but when she learned that Emma was to be married her manner changed. "My," she said when Emma made her bring out the biggest pair, "he must be a footballer."

Marjorie's father said she could sign for it, but Emma said that they were going to live in Sydney so there was no need for an account.

The long johns were a little too big, but Charles did not think to complain. The little white loops showed on his braces and he was very touched by the present.

They went for long walks together, up towards the Lederderg Gorge, or down through Durham's Orchards, or out along Grant Street to the park at Maddingley. They kicked through the deep dead leaves on the footpaths and talked. Really it was Charles who talked. Emma was surprised, and pleased, that he had so many ideas – although it was not the ideas that struck her but the kindness she recognized behind them all, even if he did, sometimes, express himself badly.

"You should go into politics," she said once, walking back from Saturday's mud-caked football match.

"Nah," he said. "Not me." And he was quiet then. They walked hand in hand past fields of cabbages, split-rail fences, then the big new houses with their stucco walls and arched porches. They walked for half a mile with the rest of the rustling crowd who kicked at the leaves or walked hunched, hands deep in pockets, hiding their faces from the fine drizzle that was now falling.

"You know what I like best?" he said.

By then they were standing in Main Street in front of Hallowell's milk bar. His eyes were suddenly full of emotion and Emma, quite consciously, treasured the moment, just as she might "treasure" a wild flower picked on a honeymoon. Her father, she thought, had once been like this. All men, she thought, are once like this, and then life begins. So she remembered the little shining brown tiles outside Hallowell's and the drawn holland blind in the window and the family walking past with woollen beanies in the yellow and black Bacchus Marsh colours, and how he held both her hands and she thought he was going to kiss her there and then in the Main Street with the victorious Dustin family (Darley supporters) tooting their horn as they made a left-hand turn at the Court House Hotel and headed back home to their market gardens at Darley.

"What do you like best?"

"Sitting in the kitchen," he said.

He never explained it. She could see the pressure of his emotions pressing against the back of his eyes, and she did not like to ask him what it was he meant.

He could talk at length about the injustices of the world. He knew he was poorly informed and badly educated, and he would

444

never pretend to know more than he did, and this gave to his feelings the extra strength of his natural honesty. But he could, at least, in his own way, talk about poverty, hardship, unfairness, even the subject of being Australian – these were emotional subjects, but not nearly so loaded as what it meant for him to sit in the Underhills' kitchen – the steam, flour-dusted hands, women's laughter, hairbrushing, the short hiss of a damp finger on a hot black iron, aprons with pockets full of wooden pegs, shining peeled potatoes, spitting fat, hot jam on steamed puddings in the middle of the day – these were things too precious to be spoken of.

Only Henry Underhill could spoil the kitchen; introducing his harsh opinions, his barked orders, his acrid tobacco odours, and it was only then, after work, or during weekends, that Charles felt such a desire to take walks, or to visit the dunny down the back.

The wind whipped down into the town from the cold stone churches on the Pentland Hills and when you left the kitchen to go to the dunny the dogs threw themselves, yellow-eyed and broken-toothed, against their chains. It was cold out there and a draught as thin as a knife blade blew through the trapdoor at the back of the can and froze your bum and shrivelled your balls. You wiped yourself in the gloom with old government forms, all torn neatly and hung on a nail. The paper was cold and hard and the hair-trigger dogs barked every time you ripped off a sheet; a well-informed stranger, walking along the street, could look down across the top of the link chain fence and see the closed dunny door and the dogs straining towards it and imagine, exactly, what it was you were doing.

Charles did not like Underhill's dunny, but when Henry Underhill was home he stayed there for long periods, luxuriating in the remembered kitchen.

Among the things he pondered, with his trousers pulled around his goose-pimpled thighs, was why his father-in-law had singled out Emma to say that she was like a horse. For Emma's mother and her two sisters were just like her. They were broad and strong with comfortable backsides and nicely shaped big-calved legs. They all wore skirts with lots of fine pleats and twin-sets which they washed carefully – each of them following an identical procedure – rolling them dry with several bathroom towels before leaving them to lie flat on a little table near the kitchen stove and thus contributing a sweet clean odour of soap and wool to all the other feminine perfumes that Charles found so comforting and kindly. And as for being flighty – there were no signs of flightiness at all. If anything they seemed the opposite – they had soft placid brown eyes, round untroubled faces, black fringes, and small even white teeth. They all had the endearing habit of murmuring as if they were reluctant to commit themselves to an exact opinion, and Charles did not feel critical of this – how could he? – this soft wash of sound.

Charles liked these women as much as he detested the man. It did not occur to him that one might be the product of the other, that their way of talking might be the consequence of Henry Underhill's intolerance for opinions other than his own. The mistake is understandable because they did not carry themselves like meek women – they walked confidently with their heads up and their shoulders back – and yet when little Henry Underhill came into the kitchen, there was nothing they would not do for him and the whole mood of the place was ruined. They polished his brass and blancoed his military webbing, not reluctantly, but eagerly. If he complained about his tea, they brewed a new pot, and looked happy to do it. They laundered his whites for boundary umpiring. They stood in Lederderg Street at night without overcoats, their arms folded beneath their breasts, watching while he drilled the surly militia up and down. They, alone in all Bacchus Marsh, could not see what a fool he looked.

Charles did not confess his true feelings about his future father-in-law. When Henry Underhill was in residence Charles took the lowliest seat, near the doorway, and drank the dark black tea the man of the house required. While Emma cleaned her father's boots, filled his cup, or warmed his newspaper, Charles watched silently. When she laughed at some joke against the Best Pet Shop in the World, Charles smiled.

He was having his own quiet revenge and he was conducting the whole affair with a nicety that would surprise those who thought him clumsy. It was not in his nature but (if you take my meaning) well within his ability, and he tortured Henry Underhill without the victim realizing that it was intentional. He did it very simply. He refused to discuss the bond. Hints on the subject he ignored. Even the most direct questions seemed to produce a malfunction in his hearing aid. So while the two appeared to be great friends, there was really a war in progress. Underhill insulted Charles's business ambitions. Charles refused to discuss the bond while, at the same time, he conducted his secret negotiations with the Education Department from a post office box in the main street. And this was the real reason he went back to Jeparit – because Henry Underhill discovered he had been sneaking down to the post office, cutting through the sale-yards and the side lane in the Lifeguard Milk Factory. Charles did not have the nerve to lie to a direct question and that was why he and Emma returned to Chaffey's. Their excuse was the AJS but the real reason was to avoid questions about the bond which Charles had by then, formally, committed himself to paying off, at the rate of five pounds five shillings and sixpence a week for three years.

They arrived back in the middle of the wedding arrangements and found Henry Underhill ill with nerves. He had swollen lumps on his legs like water-filled pigeon's eggs and, less dramatically, a measle-like rash across his chest. Charles was thus not only permitted, but instructed, to remain away from him.

On the wedding day itself Henry Underhill coated himself with calamine lotion before dressing in his best suit. He had striped trousers and a long black coat. It did not occur to Charles that his refusal to discuss the bond had produced Henry Underhill's illness and he did not mention it until after the wedding itself, when they were lined up for photographs outside the church.

The photographer was Jack Coe, of course, and he was darting around in his usual style, making sure everyone was in their place. He moved the itchy Underhill a fraction closer to Charles Badgery.

"I paid the bond," Charles said.

An odd smile surfaced from beneath Henry Underhill's moustache, a vulnerable nervous thing fearful of being squashed if it came out into the sunlight.

"You what?" he said.

"Now," said Jack Coe, "Mr Underhill, could you please. . . ."

"I took the responsibility", said Charles, "to pay the bond."

"Ha ha," said Henry Underhill, looking at the camera. "Ha ha."

"That's right," said Jack Coe, hidden under his black hood. "Mr Badgery, please, a smile."

"You'll never make a business man, lad," said Henry Underhill, scratching himself in the secret of his pocket.

"I am a business man."

Emma murmured in her young husband's ear.

"I would have paid *half*," said Emma's father.

"Right, now, steady," said Jack Coe.

"I would have paid *half!*" yelled Henry Underhill. "You'll never make a business man. You'll never make a business man's *bootlace*."

It was the best photograph taken. Both Henry and Charles had spoiled the others but now they beamed at Jack Coe's camera and Underhill's face was so creased you could not notice the swellings. No one looking at the photographs since that day has ever doubted the quality of their happiness.

22

It is obvious to anyone – Emma Underhill was Henry Underhill's daughter. This was not, it seems, so obvious to Charles. When he paid his five hundred quid and took possession of the daughter, he imagined himself to have liquidated the father and erased his influence. So if the Marching Martinet had once fathered Emma Badgery, now he was forced to magically un-father her, to withdraw his penis and blow it like a nose in his checked handkerchief, to fold the handkerchief like a table napkin and slip it through a silver ring, to leave his seed where it would do no harm, on the kitchen table. Emma had emerged, *de novo*, untainted. Charles had paid his five hundred quid and Emma, therefore – I trust you follow – had never made her father's tea, blancoed his webbing, held out her hand for the sharp burn of his strap or her lips towards his frosty affections.

Once they were safely in Sydney Charles never mentioned his father-in-law again and the only message he ever sent him was each year at Christmas when he added his signature (C. Badgery) to the card his wife sent. And because his memory, like any river, changed its course, cut a corner here, exaggerated another there, soon all he could remember was that Henry Underhill had said Emma had a backside like a horse. It certainly did not occur to him that he had been warned about her mental stability.

If it had not been for the war (whose slow birth he had watched so keenly and also so wilfully ignored) I doubt that the question would have arisen. In almost every respect Charles and Emma were well suited to each other.

Leah, who came to visit their little shop, saw (typically) what was good about the place – that it had a murmuring, nurturing quality. It was a place of succour and tenderness. Leah was delighted with the variety of life, the rabbits, big and fat, the lorikeets as richly coloured as oriental rugs, the dull white-eyed python waiting patiently to lose its skin, the not-for-sale Gould's Monitor, the little seas of kissing jewels which were aquariums, the smell of straw, apples, grain, and the volatile odours of faeces which were, mixed together, pleasant and repugnant all at once.

Amongst these charges the newlyweds were like a pair of giant children, forever kneeling or bending, pacifying, supplicating their easily upset charges. They both had big hands and big feet and young faces and Emma's speech, although shy and indistinct, did not feel timid but rather sensuous and sleepy. She seemed to speak with the drowsiness of a happy lover.

It is true that Charles talked a great deal but he did not do it to exclude his wife and looked, continually, to her for agreement, so that the whole business enterprise was flavoured with their great tenderness together. And although Leah was interested in the problems facing the best pet shop in the world, what really pleased her was the couple's affection.

She was impressed too that they wished to do everything properly from the beginning, had made appointments to speak to people at the zoo, made notes and constructed cages that were really too big for the little shop. It was a mistake, perhaps. But they were happy not to have a prison like those overcrowded holes in Campbell Street. The big cages did create problems because they had to bunk one species in with another. The pretty blue bonnets had showed themselves to be pugnacious in the extreme. Feathers had flown. Blood had run.

And Emma had been wonderful, Charles said. The girl blushed and lowered her eyes. Leah could imagine those strong-wristed hands offering succour to wounded rosellas or rescuing a terrified guinea-pig from the well-meaning attentions of a buck rabbit.

She could not think of anyone who would suit Charles better. She seemed earthy, practical, loving and unpretentious. They both prepared the pets' meals together, working side by side at the kitchen table, carving dark hunks of horsemeat, breaking eggs, crumbling Madeira cake. They already had their own moth trap and would soon start breeding flies for their pupae. They did not seem to notice that their flat had a funny smell, but even this smell, unpleasant at first, soon came to be associated, in Leah's mind, with happiness.

It was 1938. Hitler was in Austria. Bukharin and Rykov were already on trial in Moscow. Bondi Beach was not yet strung with barbed wire, but the cafés were already filling with Jews from Europe. Leah Goldstein stood on platforms beside her husband while he spoke against fighting the Nazis.

She would appear, standing erect in that severe grey suit of hers, her flinty face unsmiling, like the popular image of a severe communist, but it was from this time that her letters began to fill with the sweet fecund odours of the little pet shop where she would go, more and more often, to drink tea with Emma, to watch her belly swell, to breathe deep of air rich with straw, rape-seed, molasses and fur.

She was as happy there as in a letter. She did not speak. The two women sat behind the counter. Emma knitted.

23

Phoebe came to borrow a pound and was shocked by Emma's kissing. It was not Emma who started it. It was Phoebe who was a great one for kissing everything that crossed her path. It was not the act of kissing that was shocking. It was the quality of the kiss itself. You could feel in those kisses the juices of Emma's contentment and Phoebe – who had thought her daughter-in-law's big straight toes quite disgusting – was much disturbed. It was embarrassing, like walking into the middle of someone else's love-making, and Phoebe, who had come to flaunt her newest young man as well as get a pound, left the shop feeling old and out of temper.

She was not alone in being affected by those kisses. Leah wrote me a page about them. Emma was a plant grown in an austere climate suddenly transplanted into a fertile tropical latitude. She stretched herself luxuriously and felt her toes uncurl in the warm red soil. She was all abloom with kisses.

The extraordinary thing is she had not even loved Charles when she'd decided to marry him. She had thought only that he was a decent manly man and she had been comforted not only by his hearing aid but by his funny looks. He was like that dog-leg bridge the shire had built out over Parwan – stumpy and awkward but no one ever questioned its reliability. When he promised to honour and obey, you could rely on him. Anyone could see he was not a flash Harry or a lounge lizard or a drunkard. He would look after her.

She had expected so little, and now she was almost drunk from the richness of her life. It is true that she did not like Sydney, but then she had never liked Melbourne. Cities were too noisy and confusing to suit her. She was a homebody anyway. She was happiest amongst the pets, or upstairs in the little flat which she was modestly redecorating with what money they had left after the Education Department took its tithe. She stripped the peeling wallpaper, killed the earwigs, and ladled on new kalsomine.

Instinctively she reproduced elements of her mother's house. She bought a ha'penny brass hook on which to hang the hot water bottle, just behind the stove, in which place it had been awkward and inconvenient in Bacchus Marsh, and it was just as awkward and inconvenient in George Street, Sydney. She begged a calendar from the butcher's and hung it behind the door so that one had, as in Bacchus Marsh, to shut the door in order to know what day it was. And she found a framed picture of the King of England in Bathurst Street. It was very dusty and its frame was chipped but it was only tuppence and she brought it home and hung it (with difficulty – the picture rail was precarious) above the kitchen table. And she had just completed this last improvement when Charles, suckled on hatred of all things royal and British, walked in the door (his mind more occupied with the Snake Exhibition in his shop window) and stood, gawping, at the King of England.

It would never have occurred to Charles that the King of England had no more importance to Emma than a brass hook or a butcher's calendar. The colour rose from beneath his collar and washed upwards like spilt ink on blotting paper. And it is no good trying to decide whether his reaction owes more to Herbert Badgery or Leah Goldstein or his own reading on the subject in *Smith's Weekly* and the *Bulletin*, but react he did, as instantly and instinctively as if he'd been punched in the nose; he struck straight back and his wife, big-bellied, weary-legged, did not recognize the monster who took possession of the man she loved. She felt a fear grip her guts and the baby kicked back against it, panicking inside her. She saw the tendons on his neck go tight as fencing wire one notch before it snaps. He put his wide-brimmed hat down – too slowly – on the table and leaned across – his arms seemed horribly strong and far too long (he could reach the picture rail without the aid of either chair or ladder) and pulled at the bearded King of England who, refusing to abandon his position, finally brought the whole picture rail springing after him. The rail bounced on the table, knocked Emma's teacup, broke its handle, and while the handleless cup rolled smoothly across the table on its way to destruction, Charles carried the picture of the King to the kitchen sink, opened the window behind it, and dropped it into the moss-covered concrete lane below.

Charles had the family temper: the fast flare-up, the instant die-away, nothing left but ashes, contrition, embarrassment. So when he turned and saw her crumpling face, the monster left him. Now he knelt beside his shaking wife and tried to explain. He kissed her eyes. He was sorry. He nuzzled her neck. She was his little lamb. She was a precious, a pet, a possum, a mouse.

But she, it turned out, was as ready to deny the King of England as he was to criticize his own childish temper. She no longer cared that the monarch had been an important man in her father's house. She despised him. Would never say his name again. She felt safer than ever in her husband's arms and her extraordinary kisses, those tropical blooms, were dark and heavy with fear-born adrenalin, cups of it, enough to make them both quite drunk.

24

Father Moran told me he had seen a fairy on a mushroom. It was a very small little gentleman, with tiny boots and laces. He was very specific. He could describe those little boots, brown with metal eyelets like his own, and laces that – although necessarily fine – were made from real hide – you could see by the fall of the bow. It had a pair of short trousers, a tailored jacket, a brown tam-o'-shanter. Father Moran had been only a boy when he saw it but he could now recall the most minute details. It had been at the end of the day. He had been with his brother Reginald and his father and they had gone out on the road by the Clarence looking for mushrooms. It was hot and steamy and the light was all hazy and golden and he had bent with his knife, an old bone-handled one gone yellow from being dropped in boiling water, and was about to cut the mushroom when he saw the fairy sitting on it.

While he was telling me this I was looking at those round shining pop eyes of his and I had the oddest feeling that I had known him before. Yet he had a very distinctive manner and you would not easily forget him. He was a square-headed fellow with curly grey hair and a florid face. He was a size too, with broad shoulders and a chest bursting out of his priestly black. But it was his eyes, big and bulging, and filled with all sorts of demanding emotions, his eyes that put me on edge.

He was in the habit of staying for hours. I couldn't ask him to leave. For God's sake, I was in gaol. I had all sorts come to look at me. Doctors from America detoured via Sydney to meet me and then talked about me as if I was not there. Rankin Downs was like that. They told you how lucky you were to be in such a place and then they wrote your name on index cards, folders, assembled pieces of blue paper you might occasionally glimpse peeking from a stained manila folder on the Boss's desk. Your door could open at any time, for any reason. They did not need a key to do it. Anyone could walk in. Someone from Poland? Why not? I had a man from Poland. He was there to look at my gums, but when he was left alone with me he measured my head with callipers.

So Father Moran was no more trouble than the rest. I did not mind him poking around in my bookshelves, but he worried me. It was not that he saw a fairy. I did not mind that he had seen a fairy. What upset me was the way his grey eyes bulged when he told me. He gave me a smile, neat and white as a wooden doll. By itself the smile was nothing. A display of teeth. But marry it up with the eyes in that big square head and you have what I would call a spectre.

He moved from the bed and sat on top of my kerosene heater. The heater was not lit. It was September, already warm, although sometimes I used it when the rains came, to keep the mildew out of my papers. You never saw such rain as we had at Rankin Downs and the youngsters working out in the bush would come back covered in grey slimy mud, snivelling and homesick under their blankets of wet earth.

"I never told a man in twenty years," said Father Moran. "And perhaps I am using the wrong term in calling it a fairy. I never studied these things. It might have been an elf or something. But I'll tell you this, Badgery, whatever he was, he was. And I suppose you're thinking that it was something else, a sparrow, or a doll, and that I was just a little fellow and easily confused. But I know what I saw because I saw its face. It was so cross. You never saw such anger on a human's face. You never saw such a filthy scowl as the one it gave me. It was the sort of expression you would expect a bull ant to have, if it had a proper face to give expressions with. Do you follow me?"

He went on and on. I was not only alarmed by the emotion, I was also concerned for my heater. You do not accumulate these things easily, even in Rankin Downs. I had some Feltex on the floor, six bookshelves, a chair, a desk. I did not get this stuff by violence or bribery or dobbing-in my fellow prisoners. I got them by using frailty and decency. This is a very potent combination. It does things to screws who you would otherwise describe as heartless and before they can help themselves they are running to fetch you a square of carpet from their own house and smiling at you like a mother when you have it. I got this sort of treatment at some cost, for making yourself into a frail man is a dangerous thing and much of it is not reversible. I lost an inch in height during my ten years in Rankin Downs and I have had trouble with my sciatica ever since. My skin never recovered its tone. But excuse me, because the damn heater is crumbling beneath the priest and it is not cowardice that stops me telling him, but his story which is reaching a delicate stage and has become frail and flowery and as easily bruised as a baby's arm. *Attendez-vous!*

"I went and got my brother. I begged him to come and look. But he wouldn't come. He laughed at me, Badgery, and he would not come. You can imagine it, can't you? Me knowing this little gent is over there, no more than a cricket pitch away, and my brother refusing to come and look. That was like him. It was so like him. He enjoyed what it did to me."

"Perhaps your father. . . ?"

"My father beat me," the priest said. "For lying."

It was getting late. I could hear the slow diesel thump of the Fergie tractor bringing the trailerful of boys back from work. The kitchen was pumping out its rancid steam and the mechanics were already showered and thumping their tennis ball (bom, bom, bom) against the wall of my hut and Father Moran was demanding something with his eyes. I felt what a dog must feel, a dog who wants to sleep and is interrupted by a master who wants something the dog can't understand. I did all a dog can do. I showed him my eyes. They were a fine colour. I also asked him how fairies might fit in with Catholicism. I thought this might be the trouble. But if it was he wasn't ready to admit it.

It was only the kerosene heater crumpling beneath his sixteen stone that finally brought him to his senses. He broke the mantle and burst the fuel tank and when he picked the whole thing up in his big hands, kero dripping on to his boots, he looked dazed like a man after a traffic accident.

"Oh, Badgery," he said. "I'm sorry. I'm a clumsy fool. I beg your pardon."

There was nothing I could say. My face said what I felt. You are a lucky man to own a kero heater.

"I'll replace it," he said desperately. "The sisters at the convent have some the same."

"Don't worry, Father." I stood with a grunt. I made my kidneys hurt and the pain showed like a shadow on my face. I grimaced and shuffled towards him. "I'll get another."

He looked at me: frail decent Badgery shuffling to pick up the wounded heater. My aim was to make his heart near burst, but this – as I found out later – was not the case at all. But if Moran did not think me frail and decent, he was quite alone in all the gaol.

You would not dream of the numbers of young men in gaol who dream only of being decent men. You won't observe them in such numbers in any other place. I was first amongst them. I was their leader, their example. There was no kindness I would not stoop to perform.

It was my frailty that gave me power. It ruined my body, but I was respected by young ruffians known to have put hot smoothing irons on young girls' faces. They came with offers to protect me.

Was it admirable? Did I claim that it was? Of course it was not admirable. I took it up, originally, to stop myself being bullied by my fellow prisoners. If I had been younger, stronger, richer, if I could have defended myself with a fist or a knife or a bribe, then I would have done so. But I had none of these things. I had only decency and frailty to rely on.

But there was another aspect to it. I was preparing myself to take my place at the Kaletskys' on Sunday afternoons. To this end I was acquiring an education. I wished to be a decent man in a grey suit. I wished to be quiet and polite. I did not want to be an ignorant fool full of noises and bombast, I wished to acquire ideas and opinions, to sit next to Rosa at the big table and talk about philosophy and politics. I wished to accept scones and tea, and walk amongst the orange groves with Leah's children, return through the French windows to play chess with her husband. I was preparing myself for a gracious old age, with friends.

"We shall be", Leah wrote, "your *de facto* family."

To this end I was busy learning to be an intellectual. I was in correspondence with the University of Sydney and you may judge, of course, that my motives were the wrong ones for the proper study of any subject, let alone History. It is true that I was often impatient, that I was in too much of a hurry to find some little snippet, some picturesque fact that would serve to impress the Kaletskys with my erudition. I persisted just the same. And all Rankin Downs was proud of me. Juvenile sadists who might otherwise have tried to rip my balls off came to stand in my cell just to watch me studying. The Anglican Bishop of Grafton, reading about me in a local paper, had books sent to me and I am much indebted to him for providing most of the dreary Australian history books that were available pre-war.

But it was to the Catholic side, to Father Moran in particular, that I owed my real thanks, for it was he who gave me, on his very first visit to my freshly painted yellow room, M. V. Anderson's famous work which opens with that luminous paragraph which I will quote without abbreviation: "Our forefathers were all great liars. They lied about the lands they selected and the cattle they owned. They lied about their backgrounds and the parentage of their wives. However it is their first lie that is the most impressive for being so monumental, i.e., that the continent, at the time of first settlement, was said to be occupied but not cultivated and by that simple device they were able to give the legal owners short shrift and, when they objected, to use the musket or poison flour, and to do so with a clear conscience. It is in the context of this great foundation stone that we must begin our study of Australian history."

Reading these words I always imagined the man who wrote them. M. V. Anderson was a thin stooped fellow with a big nose and a high-pitched voice, a tea drinker, a gossip with dandruff on his shoulders and nicotine on his long fingers. M. V. Anderson enjoyed himself. There was nothing to excite him as much as a lie. I imagine the glint in his eye and the pendulous lower lip as it begins to blow up and expand with blood as he tells his reader that Bourke and Wills were not involved in simple exploration but were spies for the colony of Victoria, sent to steal a piece of Western Queensland that had, by error, been omitted from the proper survey.

It was M. V. Anderson who showed me that a liar might be a patriot and although, at the time, I thought this a lesson learned too late, it was not so. So if I say some unkind things about Father Moran they must be weighed against the positive aspect, i.e., that it was he and no one else who drove two hours along rutted gravel roads to introduce M. V. Anderson into my life. The book, of course, had another name on its flyleaf. Stephen Wall, it said, 6B. When I pointed this out to Moran, and suggested that Master Wall must miss his book, he merely said that M. V. Anderson was unsuitable for boys.

Moran did not always annoy me. Often I was pleased to see him. He could be amusing. He had a rare ability to tell a football match from beginning to end and he would sometimes arrive late on Saturday night with beer on his breath and his cheeks flushed with excitement. In fact, I realize now, he did not really give me trouble until the football season was over. It was then he started going through my bookshelves. The screws occasionally did the same. Every now and then there would be whistles and searches and they would find homemade knives or dirty pictures. Moran did not search like a screw. He did it like a man browsing in a bookshop, but he was at the same thing, pulling out books, looking behind them, flipping through the pages, peeking into Leah's letters. I waited for him to get on with his trade and start talking about God, but he was reluctant to do it. I tried to bring the subject up once or twice, but it made him hostile.

"What would a fellow like you want to talk about God for?"

He was right, of course, but I was surprised by the venom when he said it. It puzzled me even more as to why he came to see me and I might have been kept in suspense a lot longer if I had not blundered into the matter by mistake. I mentioned – in connection with what I now forget – Sergeant Reg Moth.

Moran was standing there with one of Leah's letters hidden inside an Oxford Dictionary, pretending to look up some word or other while all the time he was prying into my private life. But when I mentioned Moth, his mouth opened and his brow furrowed.

"You didn't call him *that*?"

"Call him what?"

"Moth."

"I might have called him Sergeant. Sergeant, or Moth, or Sergeant Moth." I shrugged.

He was such a big man and it was a very small room so his moods always seemed too bulky for the space. They pushed at me, bumped at me, seemed as if they would swamp or suffocate me.

"He cannot stand the name," he said, shutting the dictionary with the letter still in it. "It drives him mad. You would have hurt him if you called him Moth."

"His own name."

He put the dictionary back in the shelf and – an annoying habit of his – lined up the spine exactly with the edge of the shelf. "His nickname," he corrected me. "Aren't you going to ask me why?"

"Why?"

And suddenly all his big solemn red-faced officiousness was gone and he was grinning at me like a schoolboy. "The Moth

– because if there's a light on, he'll turn up." He giggled. "I shouldn't laugh. It's my own brother after all."

Of course he was the loony's brother. Of course he was. He had that same square head and bulging eyes. "Well, well. . . ." I said.

"Come on, Badgery," he smiled. "Don't pretend you didn't know." He started to lower himself on to my damaged heater, changed his mind and went to the bunk. His smile pulled at his face as tightly as his buttoned-up suit pulled at his big footballer's body. "I saw the way you looked when I told you about the little fellow on the mushroom. You knew what I was alluding to. You understand my intention."

"Father, I swear, I understood nothing."

"But what could you swear by – that is the thing. Perhaps you might tell me later, but I saw at the time that you understood my point, that my brother would not look at devilry, that he did not think such things were even possible. You appreciated the irony."

"Now you call it devilry."

"Of course it is devilry, man. Or would be, if I had not made it up. Do you think God makes tiny men to sit on mushrooms? Of course it is devilry, and you know it too."

I felt disappointed. I had liked that little man on the mushroom more than I knew. I asked him why he made it up.

"To trap you," he said, clapping his big hands together, and giving me that white picket-fence grin. "I know you've got that thing in a bottle somewhere. I thought if I told you that story, you'd bring it out. But, like my brother says, you are cunning as a rat."

I was an old man, decent and frail. I put the cap on my pen. I smiled. I showed him my lovely violet eyes. "Come, Father, we're both grown men."

He withstood the powerful blast of affection I sent his way. "Are we?" he said. "Are we? Are we now, *men*? Reginald came to me up at St Joseph's. I was taking a class. He came to the door. He said to me, 'Michael, I have seen the devil.' You know his voice, loud and rough. 'I've seen the devil,' he said. I thought he was drunk. God forgive me, I was angry because he interrupted my class. I saw the tears in his eyes and I denied him. I never got on with him, Badgery. He was never a happy man. He would not let God into his heart. Always the Moth. It wasn't the bribes he was after when he pestered the illegal drinkers. It was the company. They knew that, of course. That's why they gave him his name.

But now he can look back on those times, when he was sneaking round Flanagan's backyard, arresting people and letting them off for a quid, he can look back on them as happy times. Father Doyle has heard his confession, but he has no peace, other than what he can get out of a whisky bottle. There have been policemen up from Sydney to witness his behaviour."

I didn't know which brother was the maddest. There is no doubt, however, that the priest was the biggest, by a good two stone. "Father," I asked him, "do you really think I'm the devil?"

"Perhaps you're just a witch."

I took the bottle out of my pocket where I'd had it all along. I held it out towards him. He would not look at it. He peered away from it, into the corner, as if he was looking for cockroaches. "Is that it?" His voice was quite excitable.

"It is."

He took it from me, but still he did not look at it. I remember the enormous heat I felt radiating from his hand. I got out of his way. He went to the desk, I to the bed. He took out a little black book from his suit pocket and read some Latin out of it. I didn't understand the words of course, but he was a fearsome reader. I suppose he was exorcizing the devil or some other trick of his trade. When he finished he put the book away. He stayed where he was. And then he knelt. I thought he was praying, but no. "Badgery," he said, "come here."

I went. He was looking at the bottle, moving his big square head around, peering from one angle then another. There was a strong odour of camphor, but that came from his suit. He looked up at me and smiled, a lovely smile, not that straight picket fence of a thing he'd shown me up to now.

"What a lovely thing," he said. "What a lovely thing."

Indeed it was.

"Would you deny to me that these are angels?"

I could not.

"Angels, whizzing around in a bottle."

"Take it," I said. "Have it. Keep it. Please, for Chrissakes."

It was the blasphemy that changed him. He jerked like a fellow who has given himself a shock off his own car battery. He dropped the bottle as if it were a spanner. He was going to shake hands with me – he usually did when he was leaving – but something made him change his mind. He shivered. The silly ninny thought I was the devil. I know I cannot prove it, but I am

459

sure it's what he thought. In any case he did not visit me again and, when the football season came again, I missed him.

I was saddened to hear that he had died on the Kokoda Trail. I thought of that big strong body lying broken in the mud and I wished I had been with him, not a useless old man in a gaol, anxious that my families would be killed and taken from me. I dreamed, often, that Charles had been broken on some battlefield. I dreamed about his pets, unattended. They ate their last corn, expecting more. They had no idea that anything was wrong.

25

When people recall the character of that infamous goanna it is always devious and bitter, given to counterfeit affection, slow sidlings followed by razor-sharp attacks, but it was not always so and (as Emma would later point out) this change coincided with the loss of its front left leg on September 11th, 1939, and was the direct responsibility of Charles Badgery and a result of his inconsistency about the King of England. On the one hand he considered England and the English the scourge of all humanity; he knew them as hypocrites, snobs, snivellers, and past masters of the economic swifty; but on the other hand who was it (she asked) who, on that clear September Monday when the newspaper declared Australia would stand side by side with England in the war, who was it who went to enlist in the company of that well-known urger and bulldust merchant, Harry the rabbitoh?

They stood in a long winding queue at Victoria Barracks. It was ten in the morning. The rabbitoh was drunk. He botted cigarettes from the younger men and told them stories about "Good Ol' Jack Monash". Charles was nervous and solemn. He carried the two gang-gang cockatoos in a ferret box. The ferret box was on loan, but he had purchased the gang-gangs from the rabbitoh in a lane behind the Ship's Inn at Circular Quay.

While Emma knew all about the purchase of the gang-gangs, she knew nothing about the dreadful queue at Victoria Barracks, the very smell of which would have been enough to frighten her, for the group of men shuffling their shoes, rustling their newspapers, plunging their hands into their pockets, feeling their balls, tilting their hats, had the distinct odour (as pungent as sweat) of war. Even had she smelt the smell, had she known about the queue, Emma would have been confident, complacent even, that her husband would never stand in such a thing – she knew, she thought, where he stood *vis-à-vis* the King of England.

There were problems, that morning, more pressing than war. It was unseasonably hot and the arcade was packed with schoolchildren who had been brought in to see Charles's latest merchandising idea: the Cockatoo Exhibition. ("Every cockatoo known to science", the *Sydney Morning Herald* said, "will be presented this week by a George Street business man, Mr Charles Badgery.") The arcade became hot and airless. The teachers pushed and prodded at their charges and shouted at them to quell the noise. O'Dowd the jeweller sent his handsome nephew across to complain that the schoolchildren were keeping away customers, which he did, but not before he had complimented Emma on the beauty of their window display: the palm cockatoo with its katzenjammer haircut and bright red cheek, the pink cockatoo whose raised crest was a sunrise of red and yellow, whose plump chest showed a pretty blush that descended as far as its leather-gloved claws. There were red-tailed cockatoos, casuarina cockatoos, a little corella and a galah. Only the gang-gangs were missing, but their food tray contained the long blackened seed pods of wattles and some hawthorn berries for which exotic food gang-gangs have a great weakness. Emma had hung a carefully printed sign on its front door: "On its way". There was some confusion about this sign (some imagining that it meant that the bird had departed) but not nearly so much confusion as the other sign ("It's a boy. 9 lbs.") that Charles had stuck in the window when Henry had been born; this gave a misleading impression about the sex and weight of the long-billed corella now gorging itself on Wimmera wheat.

It was a noisy and confusing day. Emma tried to feed the baby behind a plywood screen but was interrupted by children wanting to know how much the cockatoos cost. She had stained the front of her dress and was embarrassed. The proprietor of the sandwich shop, a woman with a growth on her hand the size of an apple, came to tell her about the war and all the men rushing off to enlist. Emma murmured vaguely, nodding her head, patting Henry regularly on the back, feeling the damp spreading from his napkin on to her dress. She was not worrying that her husband would leave her to fight a war. It was bad enough that he was away for two hours. She was in a panic about technical questions.

A murmur did not suffice. Perspiration formed on her lip and she observed, helplessly, an old lady poking her soft pink fingers into cages where they had no place. The bed was not made. The kitchen was littered with millet and cake crumbs. The whole flat stank of bad apples and overripe horsemeat and, although they said you couldn't get pregnant when you were breast-feeding, she knew she was.

Through all this confusion the goanna wandered and was, as usual, quite at home. He could be trusted to stay within the confines of the shop and he was learning, Emma thought, not to frighten the birds who died easily from what the vet called "trauma". It seemed never to have occurred to the goanna that he was a prisoner, rather that he had blundered into some cornucopia and his manner, although hardly charming, was amiable enough. He pressed himself against the bubbling aquariums and blinked a slow, meaningless, reptile's blink.

But on the day that war broke out all this was to change. First the woman from the sandwich shop returned to say that Mr Badgery was enlisting. He had been seen, she said, at Victoria Barracks.

Emma dissented, struggling with a napkin pin on the shop counter, watching two boys poking at the goanna's pale underbelly.

"No," she told the boys, but lacked confidence.

"With two galahs", the woman from the sandwich shop said, "in a cage, in a queue."

Only when the galahs were described in detail did Emma realize that the story was correct.

The front of her dress was stained with milk and damp with pee, but she did not pause to change, nor, when she issued her instructions, did she murmur. She put the baby firmly on her hip. "Look after the shop," she said to the woman from the sandwich shop. "I'll be back in half a mo."

"It's the lunch hour. My Sylvie's by herself."

"I'll tell her where you are," said Emma Badgery and pushed herself through a panic of children's legs into the confusion of George Street where the war was declaring itself, flapping on the wings of newspapers.

It was then that the goanna who had, perhaps, been prodded one time too many, decided to make its move. Under the illusion that it was a free agent it dragged its leathery belly along the cool tiles of the arcade, passed safely through a forest of thin legs and

462

got itself as far as the fruit shop, right on George Street itself. The fruiterer, a young fox-faced man, took fright and slammed down the mesh grille with which he locked his shop at night.

The goanna was alarmed and climbed to safety. He got to the top of the grille and stayed there, thus preventing the fruiterer from opening his door again. The fruiterer could afford to wait a minute or two, but he was not prepared to see good business pass him by. He therefore began poking at the goanna with a broom handle. His wife managed to sell two bananas through the grille, but had her situation exploited by the customer who walked away without giving money in exchange.

The escaped prisoner was dashed to the floor with a broom stick and set upon by a passing fox-terrier.

The monitor reared up and stood on its back legs. Its throat inflated and it hissed like a dragon. The fox-terrier was small and fat. It had its teeth into the monitor's front leg and hung there, its back legs quite off the ground. No one passing seemed to notice. The monitor was six foot tall and it brought up its back legs and raked the fox-terrier's belly. The foxie yelped, dropped, walked a few yards, and collapsed, its green-grey intestines spilling out while it died, twitching, in the George Street gutter. It was Sylvie from the sandwich shop who put the rubbish bin down over the goanna. The greengrocer then helped her turn it and put the lid on. He swept its amputated leg out into George Street.

The Gould's Monitor was never quite the same again and all because, as Emma pointed out, Charles Badgery had gone off to enlist on behalf of the King of England.

26

Emma never did like those old toast-rack trams. She did not understand which was the green line and which the red. She was confused by the hieroglyphics they displayed on their front. She did not like the way they threatened to throw you out the door on bends. She had organized her life so that she avoided them completely.

But on this day she had no choice. She and the baby travelled by tram to Victoria Barracks. The army had set up a tent at the front gates and the men all queued to have their particulars taken down. She smelled the smell all right. She did not like it, but she would not be beaten by it. She pushed her way to where the odour was strongest, inside the tent itself, and demanded to see her husband. The men smiled at her. She saw the smiles, distant detached things like little red purses full of teeth. It was some time before she could be made to understand that if her husband was not in the queue and not in the tent then he had already been "done".

She turned to face the terrors of the trams again. She was dizzy. She went to a milk bar at the tram stop and asked for a glass of water. It was unthinkable that he would leave her. He had promised, in a church. She did not wait for the water. There was no time. She was dizzy like the other time, but worse. She was his possum, his mouse, his cherub, his delight. She rode down Oxford Street in a daze and when she found herself close enough to home – she recognized Hyde Park – she got out of the tram and began to walk. It was not her strong legs or country-woman's walk that drew comments from passers-by. It was the unfocused look in her big round eyes. The pin (never properly clipped) dropped from the napkin in Liverpool Street, and the napkin itself flopped to the footpath on the corner of Pitt Street. There was something in her manner that prevented it being returned to her.

She pushed through the schoolchildren outside the shop and, finding her place behind the desk already taken by the lady with the growth, crawled quietly into the big cage that rightfully belonged to the goanna. The goanna, however, was in a rubbish bin behind the counter and so Emma was able to stay where she was, curled up, quite still, while conferences took place around her. The jeweller's nephew tried to speak to her but she did not seem to hear. It was decided best to leave it to her husband and so they put up the closed sign and shut the door.

Charles did not get home until six at night. He had been rejected from the tent because of his hearing and told, loudly, that there was no point in his name being written down. The rabbitoh persuaded him to go out to Bankstown where there was a fellow with his backyard full of golden-shouldered parrots. So when he arrived home he had the gang-gangs and a pair of golden-shouldered parrots as well. He did not realize anything was wrong.

He busied himself making the gang-gangs at home, whistling to himself all the while. He assumed Emma to be upstairs with the baby and took the pair of parrots up to show her. When he found the flat empty he came downstairs again and only when

464

his son, asleep on his wife's breast, gurgled, did Charles see the situation.

He squatted before the cage.

"Emma," he said.

She murmured.

"Emma, what are you doing?"

Emma was not so dizzy any more. She drank some water from a bowl. He could not go and leave her without water. When it got cold in the night, she moved enough to let him push a blanket in around her.

27

Charles did not know what to do. He did not dare telephone a doctor in case they took her from him and locked her away in an asylum. He was still only eighteen and had no experience of such things. He was very close to panic and because he was so frightened himself he adopted a very firm approach that gave no indication of his true feelings.

He prepared a meal and set a place for her. He told her the meal was there, but he did not bring it down to her.

That night he slept on his own side of the bed with his hearing aid connected and turned up loud. In the morning he found Emma's side of the bed still empty, disturbed only by his dream-churned limbs. He had a headache. He rose wearily, tucked his hearing aid into his pyjama pocket, slipped his big feet into felt slippers (once the very symbol of his perfect happiness) and padded into the kitchen. He sat on a bin of millet and stared for a long time at the meal he had left out for her. The heavy mantel clock struck seven. He stood. He examined the meal closely and found two tiny scratch marks where a mouse had sampled the congealed white fat on the plate. Towards the centre of the table were two small droppings.

A cacophony of cockatoos vibrated the diaphragm of his ear. He could make out, in the midst of this din, the peculiar calls of the gang-gangs, cries they would normally have made in flight, but he was too depressed and frightened to take pleasure from anything so simple and everything that might have delighted him on a normal day now caused him pain, even – in the bathroom – the sight of Emma's worn-out toothbrush produced an agony that could not have been greater had she actually died.

He washed his hands fastidiously and returned to the chops. He fetched a sharp knife and began, slowly, to cut them into cubes of a size that might be acceptable to a puppy. Then, with one chop still to go, he changed his mind, laid down his knife, tied up his dressing gown, licked his larded fingers, and went downstairs.

Emma already had the baby at her breast. She looked up at him and murmured. There was nothing mad about her face, nor the slightest sign of any hostility. But when she made goldfish motions with her lips there was a look in her eyes that did not go with kissing.

"Emma," Charles said, squatting beside her. "Emma, I'm going to make you a really good breakfast."

Emma made goldfish kisses.

"But you've got to cut this out. Stop it. Stop it, Emmie. You've got to come upstairs and eat like a human."

No matter what words he said, his voice betrayed him and Emma saw that she did not *have* to do anything. She showed him her gums and her teeth but her eyes remained alien, connected to rooms full of curtained thoughts.

"Please, Emmie."

She frowned and shifted her bulk within the tight confines of the cage. At this stage she still wanted to get out. She was hungry. She wanted to eat bacon and eggs and chops and then have kisses. She wanted everything to be normal, as it had been before, and she did not guess that she was already clearing a path for her emotions to travel along, that the path would soon be a highway, cambered, sealed, with concrete guttering along its edges. She wrenched the baby gently and shifted him to her other breast and felt his lips begin their pleasant rhythmic contractions.

"All right," said Charles, standing so suddenly that the guinea-pigs next door suffered a nearly fatal terror. "All right," he said, stamping his foot, causing the ceiling of the fishes' world to see-saw, sickeningly, upsetting the sea perch which now began to bite the rufous redfish, tearing its pretty tail which flowed behind like a bloodied bride's dress.

"All right," he said, "if that's what you want."

He started to clean out the finches' cage, then, with tears streaming down his face, slammed the door shut.

He inspected his cockatoos and found the Major Mitchell already biting its feathers so severely that its glory was almost gone. The moth-eaten bird only reflected his emotions.

"All right," he said. "All right."

466

Emma saw his face as it came back to her cage. It was red and terrible. The eyes were bloodshot and the forehead creased. He squatted in front of the cage and groaned and Emma felt a pulse of pure pleasure. It did not last long. There was fear as well, fear mixed up with it, but the feeling was lovely. Those great red hands clenched and unclenched as if they would circle her white neck and throttle her and those brimming wet eyes were worshipping her, begging her. Henry Underhill's daughter had never experienced such a thing. She felt trembling weakness and steely power, was tiny and huge, was a wren within an all-protecting hand that might, at any moment, crush her.

Charles did not know what he had just done. His temper left him on the stairs. He went to the kitchen and fussed over the second chop, cutting it even more finely than the first. He placed the meat in a cereal bowl together with some mashed-up vegetables. He brought the offering downstairs and placed it in front of his wife's cage.

When she saw the bowl, Emma knew that she was stronger than the men in the tent. Her big straight toes curled and stretched. She murmured her thanks, but did not eat, letting him guess that she would prefer a drink first. He fetched milk and poured it into another bowl. This she drank, not like an animal, but like a two-handed primate.

"Fork," she said and Charles was so pleased to hear a clear word from her that he pounded up the stairs and down again. Emma felt the heavy footsteps. They set up reverberations which lasted much longer than the simple journey upstairs. She felt the eggshell edges of a pure white ping-pong ball that would not stop bouncing.

She became languorous and heavy-lidded. She accepted soap and water. She had no objection to fresh napkins and pins, but she had no inclination to abandon such a pleasant place.

"Emma," Charles said. "Emma, it's going to be a big day." His calf muscles were weary and so he kneeled beside her. "Come on, fair's fair. We have a shop to open."

Charles did not, at that moment, give a damn about the shop. He wished only for everything to be as it had been before. He was not saying what he really felt, and this did not matter, because Emma was not listening to the words themselves, only the emotions behind them.

"I can't open the shop and stay here with you, Honeybunch. Honeybunch, are you listening? I can't do business with my wife in a cage. Why don't I help you upstairs? Do you want a cage? I'll carry it upstairs for you. Would you like that?"

He knelt before her in his dressing gown. It was a rich diet for anyone brought up in Henry Underhill's house.

28

There were already people at the door who wished to be admitted. Charles was in his dressing gown and he had not shaved. The customers rattled the door handle and poked their fingers through the brass letterflap and although he did not wish them to come into his shop he was like a man who is incapable of leaving a telephone ringing – he opened the door.

In order to distract them from his wife he told them many facts about cockatoos, e.g. that the pink cockatoo is just another name for the Major Mitchell, that its scientific name is *Catcua leadbetteri*, that it is less popular as a pet than you might expect because it cannot learn English or (ha ha) Spanish either.

He succeeded in getting rid of customers almost as soon as they arrived. Only the jeweller's nephew would not be easily put off. He went straight to the cage and was surprised to find Emma where he had last seen her.

The young man made Charles feel both uncouth and guilty. He could think of nothing to say in his own defence.

The fox-faced fruiterer came next. He also handed Charles a sealed envelope with a signed petition inside it. Charles was, by then, so distracted that he did not even realize that the fruiterer was angry with him, and when the man left he locked the door behind him and hung up the "CLOSED" sign. He sat behind the counter. Emma blew him goldfish kisses. He was frightened.

29

Leah slept on an old couch in the wide passage that led from the front door to the living room. She was careful not to be seen there by visitors but anyone passing down that echoing passage could hardly miss the evidence that the couch was occupied. There were folded rugs and pillows stacked neatly. Beneath the bed there were glasses of water (usually two, sometimes three), an ashtray, a writing pad, a pen, a Westclox alarm clock with a cracked glass and a loud tick.

It would be misleading to say that she slept here, because she slept so little. She napped, on and off, with the light always on. If those comrades who thought themselves her friends could have seen her they would doubtless have been shocked – all this insomnia and secret note-making. Sometimes she was shocked herself. She was a light living on its own reserves, a snake devouring its own tail. She could not see where the nourishment came for her feverish imagination. She had never thought herself inventive or clever. Yet now she had a nicotine-stained callus on her writer's finger and spent her night making orange groves and children, views from windows and waving fields of talk.

Sometimes she thought it was useless and wasteful but she knew, at the same time, that it was not useless and wasteful to knit, say, a sweater to send to someone one loved. She looked at her face in her compact, peering at three a.m. for signs of selfishness. Sometimes she found them, sometimes not. Her view of her face is not worth a pinch of shit. Let me tell you it is not a selfish face. Even her comrades could tell you that much. But who would expect to see selfishness anyway? You might, more reasonably, expect to see a young woman already marked by years of waste and disappointment, to see a face corroded by her husband's acid jibes. Yet there is no trace of bitterness or disappointment and those flinty features of hers, which should have become gaunter and beakier, have done quite the opposite. The eyes, which were once so steely and unforgiving, now show something gentler. Also she has developed a way of lifting her chin and raising her eyes, an expectant look, as if someone has just knocked on the door and she is looking up to see who it might be.

She, who had made more silly decisions than anyone has a right to, now showed both curiosity and optimism.

She endured her insomnia quite calmly, not fretting after sleep. She sat up in the sexless heavy flannel pyjamas she wore in those days. Occasionally she might read, sometimes she might write, but more often she would simply sit with her hands folded on her lap. The clock ticked. Lenny coughed and spat in his room. Leah thought.

On the night of September 12th, 1939, she thought, of course, about the war. She was shocked to recognize that there was a part of her that welcomed it and, while once she would have put this part away and not examined it, now she chose to touch it. It was as if the war would blow away the house she sat in, shatter it, throw clothing and dishes and newspapers out across the smoky street. The destruction was vicious and beautiful. She day-dreamed, walking out along the street and down into laneways. She saw bodies, about five of them, piled on top of each other beside a metal garbage bin and saw, as she peered, her father's body; shining green intestines protruding from his white starched shirt.

"No," she said, out loud. Her fingers clenched. She shut her eyes, and opened them. It was three forty-six.

This was eight minutes after Charles Badgery had woken to find his wife standing beside his bed. She was holding a very sick goanna with a roughly amputated leg. The goanna was so sick it did not try to escape. It dug its claws (five-fingered and child-like) into the pink eiderdown on the bed.

"Oh, Emmie, Emmie. Emmie, what have you done to it?"

Emma had come because she thought the animal was dying. She had not come to be accused. It was his fault. He was the one who had abandoned them. She filled her lungs with air and left the room. Her blood was coursing with chemicals she had learned to make herself. She was like a plant producing flowers, seeds, berries, suckers, buds, everything, all at once. She shut the cage door behind her.

Charles was now very scared. He examined the wound and saw the leg had not been cut off, but torn. He carried the creature into the kitchen and chloroformed it and then, having removed another inch of the stump, dressed the clean wound with sulphur. He then bandaged the goanna and put it in the ferret cage. He hid the ferret cage under the bed. He would have phoned Leah then but he imagined her in bed, beside her husband, sleeping. He waited as long as the dawn before he dialled her number.

He tried to tell Leah that his wife was mad but every time he approached the dreadful word he broke down and cried. He could not say it. He did say, however, that she was in a cage and was attacking the pets.

"Oh God," said Leah. "No."

This exclamation served to frighten Charles even more and so she quickly became brisk. She was standing in the kitchen, already shedding her pyjamas. "All right," she said, "you come here and look after Izzie. I'll come to the shop."

"He hates me."

"He hates me too," she said simply, folding up the pyjamas on the kitchen table. "That's beside the point."

"Leah, she's gone mad."

She could hear him crying at the other end of the phone. It was a terrible noise. She closed her eyes. "Listen," she said. "Listen to me, Charlie. I'm leaving now. You meet me in Taylor Square with the key for the shop. I'll be there in thirty minutes." She could hear him crying still. "Hang up," she said, and waited until he had.

Yet when she let herself into the pet shop she did not feel as capable as her voice suggested. She moved slowly, warily, unsure of what to expect. In all the rich variety of smell the shop contained, she now detected the unmistakable odour of human shit and, by going to the place where the smell was strongest, she found Emma and the baby in the cage next to the rabbits. She saw a wild-haired dirt-smeared woman lying amongst the damp straw on the floor of the cage. The baby's face was covered in yellow snot and its eyes seemed gummed together. Leah held out her hand and had it taken. Emma murmured affectionately but her nails were sharp and painful. Leah looked at her eyes and wondered if she was drunk.

"All right, Emma." She disengaged the sharp nails slowly, so as not to give offence. "We're going to get you clean because I can't talk to you when you're dirty like this. So I'll take you upstairs and get you washed and I promise you I'll bring you back here. Is that agreeable?"

It seemed to be. Leah escorted mother and child up to the concrete-floored bathroom where she found both of them equally dependent. She did not talk except to say which way she wanted the woman to turn, simple practical requests, e.g. lift your arm, your leg, turn your head, now we wash your botty, etc. She was not used to handling women's bodies and although she tried to do what she had to do without looking, she was fascinated by the difference between herself and Emma who had such large nipples on her shiny swollen breasts and white stretch marks on her young stomach and hips, like white rivers on the map of a foreign country. Leah tried not to stare, but Emma was as lacking in modesty as her little boy and closed her eyes happily to let the shampoo be rinsed from her hair by saucepan after saucepan of steaming water.

When Leah had them both washed and had combed their hair,

dried between their toes and the cheeks of their bottoms and powdered them with talc, she took them downstairs, the one in a clean napkin, the other in her husband's dressing gown. She changed the straw in the cage and, before returning them to it, introduced the pink eiderdown as a mattress – the baby had several scratches from that rough straw.

She then squatted on the floor beside the cage and, amidst the piercing din of birds, the low hum of aquariums, and the baby's gentle gurgling, tried to talk to Emma quietly.

She understood, she thought, what it was that Emma was up to, and she said so.

This single comment produced such a look of hope in her friend's eyes that she immediately set out to explain, in detail, what it was she understood.

"I know," she said, wondering if she should towel Emma's hair dry. "He loves them so much, and then he cages them. He has always loved them, ever since he was little."

Emma frowned. Leah did not notice.

"He picked up my snakes. I'll never forget it. He was just a little boy and he had no fear at all. Then we have all this." She waved a hand around the shop where lorikeets and wrens hopped and fluttered, fidgeted and fussed, forever in nervous motion. "It's tragic. He loves them all so much and then he cages them. He turns them into a product and you can look at it, if you want to, as a perversion. Izzie agrees with you. But you won't make the point by climbing into a cage. You'd be better off to discuss it with him because, I can tell you, he's missed your meaning."

"He's not the only one," said Emma, but the unusual clarity of this statement was lost amidst an outburst from the cockatoos.

"What?"

Emma murmured irritably.

"Am I barking up the wrong tree?"

Emma murmured assent.

"Is it because you are ashamed of being kept?" asked Leah, but in spite of the reasonable tone of her voice she was becoming irritated by Emma's manner.

Emma murmured again.

"For God's sake, don't make me play idiot guessing games. What is it? Tell me."

Emma blinked, and told her: Charles had enlisted in the army.

"Oh shit," said Leah. Her legs were weary from such uncomfortable squatting. She stood up. "What in the hell is the

472

matter with you? I live with a Jew who claims he cannot distinguish between Adolf Hitler and Neville Chamberlain. But your husband is a decent man and you are lucky to have him. He feels things. He has a heart. He tries his best. I thought you were good and kind, Emma. I watched you with animals and with your baby. But you're as stupid as the rest of us."

And then she was crying – fat hot tears rolled down her cheeks. "I hate the world." The words surprised her as much as the tears did, like huge white tails on tiny blackheads. "I wish I were dead. Look at what we've done. Look at all his cages. Look at you. We are all perverted. Everything good in us gets perverted. I wanted to be good and kind and I made myself a slave instead. I lie awake at night planning how I am going to leave him, but I can't. When he touches me he makes my skin creep. He has lost his legs and he thinks that's a licence for selfishness and spite. When he speaks in public everyone admires him. A woman in Newtown told me he was a saint."

Leah sat on the floor again, crossing her legs, and not worrying about the filthy straw that prickled her legs and laddered her stockings. "Oh, Emma," she said wearily. "I'm so sick of it. I wish I was with Charlie's father, dancing and arguing and drinking sweet wine."

Emma looked at Leah Goldstein – the flinty face now contorted in misery like a crumpled newspaper unfolding in a fire, the slumped shoulders, the clenched fists, the slender crossed legs leading to a pair of bright red high-heeled shoes that had seemed so gay when they had first clicked through the early-morning gloom.

Emma murmured. She moved to one side of her cage. She was large and the cage was small but she managed to make some room. She patted the eiderdown and held out her hand.

Leah gave a self-mocking little laugh, but she joined Emma in the cage and let herself be embraced and comforted by her murmuring friend who dried her eyes with the rough sleeve of the dressing gown and stroked her hair and neck until she was, in the midst of all those pet-shop noises, sound asleep.

30

When Leah woke up she was so refreshed as to be almost light-hearted. Cramped by wire, prickled by straw, she was as elated and optimistic about human beings as she had been despairing an

473

hour before. She forgot her stern judgement of Emma's selfishness and remembered only her kindness, the quality that she most closely approximated to goodness, her thirst for which would always lead her to idealize and oversimplify the characters of those who displayed it.

She kissed the sleeping woman on the forehead, and re-arranged the baby's blue bunny rug around its chubby legs. She felt heady, almost silly. She crawled out of the cage and dusted the straw from her severe black suit.

She looked up to see Charles standing behind the counter. The shop was closed.

Leah hoisted her skirt a fraction and did a small dance for him, smiling broadly and tapping (dangerously) on her bright red shoes.

Charles was too worried to smile. He had returned to the shop and found two women in a cage that had previously held one.

"Treasure her," Leah said, panting a little. "She loves you. She worships you. You are a lucky man to have a wife who will be so mad on your behalf."

She sat herself, athletically, on the counter, spilling roneoed notes about the feeding requirements of various cockatoos and these yellow sheets now sliced through the air and floated so much longer than expected that Leah giggled to see it, as if the yellow sheets were a circus arranged on her behalf.

"She thinks you have enlisted. Is that right?"

Charles, stooping to pick up his precious yellow notes, straightened. "They didn't want to know me, Leah."

"Don't be so solemn, Charlie. Everything will be all right."

"They rejected me. But Emma doesn't even know I went."

"Oh, she does, Charlie Barley, Gloomy Moony. She thinks you were accepted."

"Oh."

"That's right. 'Oh!' Why wouldn't they have you? Of course, your hearing. I'll write to your father about this. I'll do it this morning. He'll enjoy it."

"He hates me."

"When you say Izzie hates you, Charlie Barley, you may have a point, although personally I think that hate is far too strong a word. But when you say your father hates you, you are very, very wrong."

"He didn't even write when Henry got born."

"And you didn't write to him either."

"He hates me."

"Wait, Charlie Barley, and you'll see."

"He blames me for what happened to Sonia." He assembled the yellow sheets and brought them back to the counter where he fiddled with them, taking too much trouble to make them all line up square in the stack he had made. He looked up at Leah defiantly. His eyes were puffy. He went back to the stack of paper. "Sometimes I dream I skun her. Skun the skin off her. . . ."

"Don't."

"And she smiles at me. She don't know what's happening to her."

"Shush," Leah said, brushing hair from his suit shoulder and doing up his coat buttons. "Only happy talk now. There's a terrible war starting and all sorts of rotten things everywhere, but go and look after your wife who loves you. Tell her you are not in the army. Do you have any money? Here, I'll lend you a pound. Go and buy – no, I'll go and buy some sparkling hock – don't argue, and you can put candles on the table tonight and you can celebrate that you won't be making her a widow after all. I'll be back in a moment. And then I must do my baking and cook something suitable for that person whom your wife", she giggled, "insists on calling 'Hisy-door', the little rat – not her, him – do you know that he has the cunning to be having an affair with a colleague at the school? His nasty headmaster, the one who gives him the lift to work, came and told me all about it. He seems most disturbed by the horrid idea of a man with no legs having sex with a woman with two. That was at the heart of it. He just wished it stopped and he thought telling me would stop it, but I don't live in the real world any more. I write to your father and tell him how happy I am. I tell him such fibs, Charlie Farlie, can you believe that?"

"I s'pose so," said Charles, who was disturbed by the turn of the conversation. He locked the till and then unlocked it. He did not like Leah using the word "sex" and he liked even less the personal nature of her confession. Worst of all he did not like to hear that she told lies.

"Do you disapprove?" Leah leaned over the counter but he shrugged and pulled the handle on the till so the drawer flew open with a little "ding".

Charles shrugged. "I dunno," he said.

Leah held out her hand and he shut the till. "Don't disapprove of me, Charlie." She looked intently into his eyes. "If I told him the truth I would drown. What are you thinking?"

He could not hold that gaze. It embarrassed him. "What you taught us," he said.

"Don't disapprove of me, Charlie. I will tell him the truth later, not now. When he gets out, I'll tell him the truth. There is plenty of time. But for the moment I will be unprincipled. Did you notice my red shoes?"

He hadn't. He came round from behind the counter to inspect them.

"I feel I have invented them." She giggled and covered her mouth with her hand. "I'll get the hock. You give her the good news after I've left. I think I'd weep if I was here."

Charles listened to the red shoes tapping across the grimy floor of the arcade. He was disturbed by her confessions. He disapproved of Izzie's infidelity. He was disgusted that she should tell lies. But he was also excited by the pressure of her hand and the appeal of her grey eyes when she begged him not to judge her.

31

It was thus lodged in Charles's brain that his wife had entered a cage to punish him for something he had done, and he saw how, from her point of view, he had been insensitive and thoughtless. He did not think her mad at all, but only saw the degree to which he had made her so unhappy.

He could not apologize enough. Whenever the shop was empty they kissed, great blood-swollen kisses, tender and easily bruised. Emma huddled into her husband's strong arms and bent her broad shoulders. She shrunk herself against his chest, all the time awash with the most delicious emotions.

She did not know she had become addicted, not even at four o'clock when they could stand the ache no more, locked up the shop, pulled down the blind and made love to each other on the dirty floor and with every stroke he slid inside her, hard and big as a bull, he was, at the same time, nothing but a baby, sucking at her breast. He smeared and bubbled her with her own warm milk, spread it across her smooth white chest and in the pink maze of her little ear whence he poured – even whilst he began to bang her, push her, thump her, rearing back with bulging eyes – his milk-white apologies, his child's requests for love.

They did not know what was happening to them. They had a

celebration dinner and got tipsy on Goldstein's hock. They went to bed early and were asleep, immediately, in each other's arms.

So far, you see, nothing so remarkable. And yet some time that night Emma Badgery rose from her bed, and without waking herself enough to ask herself what she was doing, crept groggily down the stairs and evicted the Gould's Monitor from its cage. And there she was to stay, on and off, not every day, not every night, but more often than not, as long as she lived.

She never felt compelled to find reasons for it. It was guilty Charles who would always torture himself with reasons. As for Emma, she never once talked about the pleasure she felt, our little queen, to be there safe and warm with her husband dancing his love dance around her, big and strong, as dangerous as a bear, begging, threatening, pleading.

The shy little plant from Bacchus Marsh was soon raging, bright red and dazzling pink like wild lantana, across the entire landscape of her husband's life.

32

Hissao was too young to remember it but everyone else (i.e., Henry and George Badgery, the famous dullards) can tell you the story of how their father acted on the night of Nathan Schick's first visit to the Pitt Street premises. It was in the season of westerly winds which would explain why the children would be wide awake when their father came stumbling in drunk at that hour of the morning. They were not used to him being drunk and did not know it was him. They lay very still in the cage, pressed tight against the smooth skin and silk-clad breasts of their snoring mother.

Emma had been eating bacon sandwiches again. They had all been eating bacon sandwiches. The monster stood on the plate and when it broke it sounded like a rifle shot.

Of course they were frightened. They were frightened even before the creature began to crash up the stairs. The westerly was howling and threatening to drag the roof, screeching, up into the night. Clouds scudded across the top of the big skylight which always illuminated their dreams and nightmares. Through this frame they saw warty faces illuminated by thunderstorms. They watched for enemy bombers and, having freed themselves from the tight clamp of their mothers's sleeping embrace, saw torn newspapers pass across the sky like migrating birds.

Henry saw his father trailing a hose, but he did not recognize either the father or the hose. The teapot was kicked against the wall and the air was wet with alcohol and tannin. Henry shook his mother, shook and shook her, but she slept on. George was crying. The creature was cursing and fumbling with the kitchen tap.

Charles was drunk on black-market Scotch. It took him an age to get the hose connected. He flooded the kitchen and drenched his Dedman suit. Then he turned on the lights and tried to blast his family from the cage. They would not budge. The children clung to their mother. The mother clung bleakly to the bars and, afterwards, lay shivering on a sodden mattress on the floor.

When Charles – bawling and remorseful – tried to dry them, Emma bit his finger.

The wind was still blowing when he woke at five a.m. He lit two kerosene radiators and placed them near his family. He went to the lavatory and tried to vomit. He bathed his finger and put mercurochrome on it. He believed he had deserved to be bitten. He thought himself loathsome.

The idea that his wife was in the cage because he had done something wrong was now fixed very firmly in his head and could no more be dislodged than she be moved from the cage itself. The trouble was not the cage – the trouble was that she would not tell him what he had done. He asked her. He even suggested. But all Emma would do was murmur. And although he would begin calmly enough, smiling, nodding, rubbing her back, bringing her a white-fleshed peach on a plate, or a bacon sandwich or a pair of silk stockings wrapped in holly-speckled paper, although he would whisper sweet things in her small ear or make porridge with illegal butter melting on it, he would, in the end, lose his temper with all the non-specific murmuring. Then he would behave like an animal and say nasty things.

Later, when he remembered the things he had said and done, he would easily understand why she might wish to punish him.

Leah Goldstein, their one real friend, did nothing to help. Partly this was because Charles never lost his temper in her presence, and so she never witnessed anything as spectacular as the hosing-down. However, she was well aware that Emma, her friend, lived in a cage. Oh, she was often out of it, it is true, shopping, showering, visiting the cinema, but it was where she liked to spend her time, where she would entertain her friend, read her romances, and sleep with her children, like a silky sow contented with its litter.

And Goldstein saw all this and would not criticize. She pretended it was all quite normal. Not once did she say to Emma that it was not a useful way to behave, was not good for the children or even herself. Instead she stubbornly stuck to her first impression which was that Emma was kind and affectionate and the thing she found remarkable about the cage was how attractive Emma made it seem. This was not merely because Charles had bought her tributes of satin sheets or that the blankets she slept in were of mohair so soft that you had to – it was quite impossible to resist – stroke it against your cheek, or that her doting husband always seemed to be able to find her fruit out of season and butter when they had no butter coupons left. Goldstein was not untouched by this luxury, although she would not let herself admit it, but what impressed her most was the way she was with her children – she whacked them across the head when they misbehaved and nuzzled them when they were good, and Leah, who so much wanted children of her own that she invented them in letters, was in no mood to criticize the woman she called "A Perfect Mother".

There were things that you would expect to make Goldstein uneasy – the youngest boy's Asiatic face, for instance – but she does not seem to have noticed it. You would expect her, also, to have had stern words about Emma's penchant for silk stockings and leg-of-mutton sleeves, both of which were banned for the duration, and yet she did not. Even when she herself was getting blisters and a bad back in the Land Army she never saw Emma in an unfavourable light. When she had leave she would come up from Narrabri on the train and she and Emma would go to the matinée together. Sometimes they just sat and knitted and, on a rainy afternoon, with the sky falling gently on the glass above their heads, it was hard to imagine a nicer place to be.

If Leah had once, only once, said that Emma was crazy it might have helped. It was left instead to Nathan Schick who delivered the opinion while they sat drinking in the gutter in William Street. But while his diagnosis was accurate, his advice was not good and led only to the incident with the hose.

Nathan liked Charles, but he did not understand his situation. For instance, when he saw that a wife in a cage had done nothing to deter the boy's ambition to have the best pet shop in the world, he admired him for it, and saw it as an example of that characteristic he admired most, i.e., GOING DOWN THE GODDAMN MIDDLE. This was about as big a misunderstanding of the situation as it was possible to have.

Charles did not have his magnificent new shop in spite of Emma. He had it because of Emma. If he had not been so bluffed and bamboozled by his wife he would have been, deaf or not, in the army.

Nathan Schick admired Charles for keeping out of uniform. Charles, on the other hand, was embarrassed to be a young man in plain clothes. He imagined himself a coward. He was the proprietor of a non-essential industry. He camouflaged himself in an old grey boiler suit. He gave an elderly impression. He walked close to the cages and kept his head down. He hired women who would have been better used as telegraphists or machinists or Land Army labourers and he paid them money so they would sell pets for him. He was ashamed of the very thing that gave him so much pleasure.

When Nathan Schick came looking to buy that inappropriate mascot for General MacArthur, he did not have to go poking around in the dark end of Doyle's Arcade. The pet shop had moved twice and it was no longer a mere pet shop. The sign said it was an emporium. It was too. Charles was renting (and would soon buy) the old Stratford Arcade in Pitt Street. No matter how inconspicuous he might wish to be, he was still a Badgery. He had grand visions. So even though he saw that an emporium like this must draw attention to his non-essential status, he could not resist those four wooden-railed galleries stretching upwards towards that lovely skylight, a delicate thing of lacy iron and clear glass. Each gallery was a good twelve foot wide, enough to build deep cages and still have room for customers. Here you could accommodate a cockatoo in the proper manner. You could have a wallaby run. Possibly, one day, you could install a platypus. On the Pitt Street end of the gallery there were proper rooms. In one he could breed flies. In another he could place incubators in preparation for the day when the war was over and there was kerosene enough to run them. On the top floor they could have a flat and they would be able, on summer evenings, to bring deckchairs out on to the top gallery and stare down into the canyon and watch parrots flying to and fro in fifty-foot-long cages.

Once my son, in a perfect echo of Henry Underhill, bellowed at me that I was not a business man's bootlace. He loved to style himself a practical man. It was bullshit. He was an enthusiast, a fan. He did not even calculate the money he would need to fix the arcade which had been disused since the depression. He signed the lease without getting a quote for building cages or aquariums. He did not even think about the extra cost of feed if he was going to stock the place in accordance with his dream which was, I must tell you, an expression of the purest patriotism – pure Australiana – definitely no bunny rabbits or pussy cats no matter how tearfully his little boys begged him.

There was no one to tell him that Sydney was not big enough to support such poetry. Any real business man would have told him that the best pet shop in the world would be a failure.

The Americans, however, saved his arse. They arrived just when he needed them and although everyone remembers them for nylons and candy bars, they also paid big money for rosellas and lorikeets, blue bonnets and golden whistlers, all varieties of cockatoos, king parrots and western parrots, finches, warblers, even a pair of dancing brolgas courtesy of Harry the rabbitoh. The GIs handed their money across the counter like children sent shopping by their mothers. You took what you wanted and you handed the rest back to them. Charles did not cheat them, but he did put his prices up until he reached the delicate point where they no longer said they were low.

Gang-gangs cost a fiver. Australians came to stare at the mug Yanks wasting their money. They put Charles in a temper. He thought them ignorant and ill-educated and would have liked to give them a piece of his mind. But being a non-essential coward in a boiler suit he could only bump into them belligerently as they stood in front of the pretty white cages.

Normally he tried to keep away from customers. He was happier in the fetid room where he bred his fly pupae, or away on the lakes around Kempsey collecting stock. Petrol was rationed but he had an old Essex with a gas producer and he went hunting in this.

So when Nathan Schick did arrive he was lucky to find the boss home. Charles had a termite nest in a hessian bag. He had his head down and there was something in the walk, the suggestion of a limp, that gave the impression of someone old and smelly although he was only twenty-four.

"Charlie Badgery," said the Yank, blocking his access to the stairs.

Charles may or may not have heard him; he tried to push past.

"Charlie." The Major had a bony hand on the round fleshy shoulder. "Don't say you don't recognize me."

Maybe he did, maybe he didn't.

The Yank removed his cap and revealed a bald head. Nathan was now ten years older, but there was no denying the crooked regretful gold-toothed smile.

"How nice to see you, Mr Schick."

Charles did not feel nice at all. He felt ill. This face before him was the face of his nightmares. His sister was skun and this was a face licked by camp fire. There were American baubles on the end of a fishing line, hooks, razors, blades, balloons, feathers, knives. Soon his ear would go dull and fill with blood.

"God damn, Charlie. I read about your shop last year and I wondered. . . ."

Charles lowered his bag. "That was a different shop."

"And I've been wondering if this is the same boy I knew."

Charles could not help himself – he smiled. He liked Americans. He liked the careful round way they spoke and the way they never hesitated to give an opinion. He liked the smart lines of the Major's jacket and the floppy officer's cap. Most of all he liked the sense of cleanliness that emanated from Nathan Schick. The real Nathan Schick had little to do with the grotesque figure in his recurring dream.

It was lunchtime, and the shop was busy with browsers. Charles wanted to get out of the stair entrance but Nathan, oblivious to the pushing people, wanted to talk. "Remember the corellas," he said, releasing Charles's shoulder and holding his upper arm instead. "The corellas you got for the show in Ballarat. And the first one shit on Shirlene Maguire."

"Don't talk about Sonia," Charles said.

Nathan blinked.

"I know you weren't going to, but . . . don't. . . ."

There was a soft part to Nathan Schick. It was as mushy as marshmallow, all sweet and sentimental. And when Charles said that to him it was almost enough to bring him undone. Charles backed off the entrance to the stairs, dragging his termite sack with him. Nathan followed him and began to pat him, comfortingly, on his shoulder but when he saw the look on the boy's face, he stopped.

"Hell's bells," he laughed, a silly false laugh. He tapped out a battered Lucky Strike and lit it. "I'm not here to talk about the past, Charlie Badgery. It's business. The U. S. of A. requires your services."

It is difficult to convey the impact of this simple slogan on Charles Badgery. He was like a man struck by love for whom all the world – a minute ago so clear, delineated by crisp lines and sharp colours – now runs at the edges until it is nothing more than a blurred velvet frame for the object of its affections. It did not matter that the saleswoman with the bruise on her throat wished a confirmation of the price of a children's python or that, having smiled and excused herself to the Yank, she shouted in the direction of his hearing aid. Not two feet away an old man was stuffing breadcrumbs through the bars of a mynah bird's cage, although there were signs forbidding it. And even when Henry's slipper fell four levels and landed – dead on target – at his father's feet, Charles did not react, and his children, leaning over the rail, got no fun.

"What services?" Charles put down his bag of termites.

"Professional services, what else?"

"How?"

"General MacArthur", said Nathan Schick, "has asked me to buy him a mascot."

And that is how Charlie Badgery came to provide MacArthur with his celebrated cockatoo. It was he who taught the bird to say, "Hello, Digger." He put the cage on the preparation bench and sat on a cage in front of it for five hours every night. Every time the bird said "Hello, Digger" he gave it Vegemite on toast.

The important thing about this episode was not the cockatoo's brief blaze of glory in the newsreels and newspapers, nor was it the letter MacArthur wrote to Charles declaring his emporium the best pet shop in the world. No, the important thing – our whole future hinged on it – was that he renewed his acquaintance with Nathan Schick.

33

Nathan Schick was a juggler. He had so many schemes going on in his head at once that he rarely got any of them going. I don't think this disappointed him. The soft burr of sadness in his ascetic face was not produced by this, but rather, the contrary: it was the schemes that took the edge off his sadness. I do not believe that his business was to make money. It was to make schemes, and in this you must class him a runaway success. It did not matter that there were five schemes smashed and bleeding at his feet, he had another one arcing through the air and it was this his eyes concentrated on.

With Nathan, nothing was what it seemed. The show in Ballarat, for instance, was not a dry run for the Tivoli in Melbourne, although that is what he told Badgery & Goldstein. He set up the show in Ballarat to attract a certain Gloria Beaudare. There were sixteen complicated moves to checkmate, and I forget how it was meant to work, except it didn't.

Likewise with MacArthur's cockatoo. MacArthur was almost incidental to the scheme. He had not wanted a mascot. It was Schick who convinced him that he needed one, and the last thing on Schick's mind was how the "Hello, Digger" would be received by the Australian public. He did not have time to worry about details. The bird had to say something. Nathan knew enough about Australia to know that people would take offence at a cockatoo calling a Yankee "Digger", but he was in a hurry and couldn't think of anything better. MacArthur liked it. Nathan did not care. It was not important to the scheme, because he also knew that once the cockatoo had been in the newsreels and in the papers it would be worth a lot of money. He did not bother to analyse why this should be so, that the public would pay good money to own a party to a presumption. What he knew was that one cockatoo looked exactly like another, and that he could produce fifty MacArthur's cockatoos, or even a hundred, and sell each one as the original. It was a good scheme, as smooth and flawless as an egg.

He was not ready to discuss the scheme with Charles. When he sauntered into the shop, he had been ready, but in his memory he had confused the character of the father with that of the son. He had not been prepared for Charles's earnestness, and he was now embarrassed by his enthusiasm for the Allied cause.

Charles did not want money. He told Nathan it would be an honour to be involved in any scheme at all – he did not even ask what the scheme might be.

Nathan smiled, a regretful smile, the smile of a man who remembers honour and knows what it feels like. He folded his soft hands behind his back and moved along the galleries behind Charles, gliding on thin-soled American shoes, as light as a dancer. He observed the silent incubators and dry-retched in the fly-breeding room. On the fourth gallery he met the three-legged goanna and Charles's unconventional family. He did not inquire as to why Charles's wife should have a small Japanese child at her breast. He watched the pets' meals being prepared in the family kitchen. He then went out to the gallery again and stood and watched his countrymen in the canyon below. It was then that the second scheme came to him. This scheme was so much bigger than the first that it immediately claimed all of his attention. When he had thought it through a little he went and found Charles and persuaded him that they should go down to King's Cross and discuss business. He smiled at Emma, but she unnerved him, and he went to wait on the wide creaking stairs while Charles changed from his grey overalls into his Dedman suit.

They went to several clubs. They ate steak and chips and oysters. They drank Scotch. Charles had few of the social graces and he was only at ease when he could discuss birds, marsupials or mammals. Nathan was not bored at all. He was delighted to listen while Charles shouted about necrobacillosis in wallabies, neoplasia in a palm cockatoo. Nathan asked questions, nodding and frowning and showing sympathy. Charles confessed his plan for a whole factory staffed by budgerigars. He revealed his plan for a goldfish sleep-inducer. Nathan advised him to see a patent attorney.

In a taxi on the way to Double Bay Charles confessed his delight to be doing something for the war. Nathan shifted uncomfortably. In a room above a fruit shop they played poker with two giant negroes who mesmerized Charles out of five pounds. Then they walked three miles to Darlinghurst amidst streets of wind-blown garbage cans. Here, at last, they were in harmony, both becoming lyrical about the uniqueness and beauty of Australian birds and animals.

They knocked on some doors, which turned out to be wrong.

They were already drunk, but Nathan stopped a Yankee captain in Crown Street and bought the rest of his Scotch from him. They went down to William Street and sat in the gutter to drink it. The westerly wrapped newspapers around their ankles.

There is something about a westerly. When you're inside a house, there is no nastier wind. It pulls and tugs at you. It howls and shudders. But when you're in an open space it is a different matter entirely and it affected both of the men. Charles was struck by a desire to remove his clothes and let the wind wash around him; he was almost drunk enough to do it.

"So," Nathan said. He detached a sheet of newspaper from his ankle, and held it up fastidiously between thumb and forefinger before releasing it.

"So," he said. The newspaper sailed through the air and wrapped itself eagerly around a lamppost. "So what are we going to do?"

"We're going to get drunk."

"We've done that." Nathan handed over the whisky all the same. He noticed, as he did so, that the street was totally empty, all of William Street from King's Cross to Hyde Park. Something went tight in his chest and he put his hand to his face and held it. But then two taxis appeared beside the New Zealand Hotel and came up the hill towards them.

When the taxis passed, Nathan tried to light a cigarette but the wind was too strong. "What", he put his Lucky Strike back in its crumpled packet, "are we going to do when your customers have gone home?"

This was the Intro to the Scheme. It confused Charles. He could not see how the "we" had got itself messed into "your customers". He pulled the cork out of the bottle and raised it to his lips.

"The war can't last forever," Nathan said. "Then all your rich Yanks will go home. My question to you, Charlie, is have you thought about this?"

Of course he'd thought about it. It had kept him awake at night, wandering around his galleries, sitting in pyjamas on those wide lonely stairs, staring into the aquariums in search of sleep.

"I want the war to end tomorrow," he said. "I would give my right arm."

"Yes, yes, I know." Nathan did know. He was not without sympathy. He merely wished to get to the scheme. "But what will you do?"

Suddenly Charles was lurching to his feet and roaring into the face of the westerly.

"How in the fuck do I know?" His eyes were watering, but possibly it was only the wind. "How . . . in . . . the fuck . . . do . . . I . . . know?" Some girls in a taxi drove past and waved at him, and he waved at them. His mood suddenly changed. He stood smiling after their tail-lights before returning to sit, more or less neatly, beside Nathan. "I'm shikkered. I've never been so shikkered before. Do you know how I know? Because," he started giggling, "because I don't normally fucking swear. Nathan, I don't know what I'm going to do."

It was then that Nathan said all that stuff about Emma needing treatment. It was unnecessary. He regretted having said it immediately.

"What do you mean, treatment?"

"Believe me, Charlie, it costs. I know. My first wife is the same."

"There's nothing wrong with Emma."

"Charlie. . . ."

"There's nothing wrong with her. I love her. . . ."

"Charlie. . . ."

"Do you love your wife? Course you don't. You said you didn't. I feel sorry for you, Mr Schick, but I love my wife and my boys."

Nathan took the bottle and felt the golden liquid dull the pain in his cigarette-sore throat. It was a long drink, as long as drowning, and when he had finished, and fumbled with the cork, and got it, at last, firmly into the throat of the bottle, he looked up and saw that his partner had gone.

Then he saw him, lurching at an angle across William Street.

"Shit," said Nathan Schick.

The big pear-shaped figure paused in the middle of the street. It turned and shouted ("I love her") and before the cry had been swallowed by the wind the figure turned and stumbled on its crumbled way. It tripped on the kerb on the other side of the street, kept its balance with vaudevillian precision, and disappeared into the darkness of the Forbes Street steps.

Nathan moved lightly across William Street. He regretted having said anything about his wife. He could never guess that his comment, so vigorously denied, would lead to a hosing down within the hour. Nathan took special care at the kerb. He crossed the footpath as dainty as a shadow and started to ascend the unlit steps.

"How the fuck do I know?" said a voice from the sixth step.

Nathan threaded his way past a nest of knees and elbows and sat on the step above him. He felt the cold in the old stone steps and resisted the strong desire he felt to talk about love and loneliness.

"I'm sorry," he said.

"How in the fuck do I know?"

"Charlie, listen."

"I listen."

"Do you want to go back to selling puppy dogs in a one-room dump?"

"I never sold a puppy dog in my life."

"All right, Mr Clever Dick." He gave the boy the Scotch and watched him drink it. There was a lighted window in a house above their heads and he could see the flow of the whisky as it ran down the boy's big chin and dripped, in a dotted line of liquid light, on to his shirt and tie. "All right, Mr Wise Guy, you tell me. How are we going to make a quid when the Yanks go home?"

Charles saw the answer, right there, in the piss-sour gloom of the Forbes Street steps. The whisky stung a cut on his hand and he saw it – this patch of dazzling clarity in the middle of the murk.

"Export," he said.

Nathan leaned forward and tried to hug him. He poked a finger in his eye before he got an arm around his head and squeezed his ears. "That's my scheme," he said.

"Me here, you there."

"That's right."

"Hands across the fucking ocean."

It is true that the discussion on the Forbes Street steps led to the hosing down and thus contributed to the loss of the affection of his two eldest boys, but it also led to the formation of a company with Nathan Schick, to the printing of letterheads with a Los Angeles address, and to one (only) cockatoo that could say, "Hello, Digger."

By 1949 Charles Badgery could afford to buy his wife a pearl necklace the price of which – he told me so himself – was one thousand guineas.

34

In 1949 I was sixty-three years old. I was now perfectly equipped to live in a world that did not exist, the world of Goldstein's letters. Had you seen me you would have been amazed that a place like Rankin Downs could produce such a specimen. I was educated, frail and decent. My voice was soft. I had a pretty stoop. My handshake was as smooth and as animated as a kid glove. I had the complexion of a eunuch and a Degree of Arts from the University of Sydney. You wish to discuss the Trade Union Movement in the 1890s? I'm your man. I can do it as if we are walking across streets of autumn leaves and there is warm cocoa waiting in the study. An interesting theory about the Shearers' Strike? Please be my guest. The role of lies in popular perceptions of the Australian political fabric? You have my speciality.

I was a marvel. Of course I was. I did not even mind that the Rankin Downs' Parole Board thought the credit was theirs. They could never imagine the work, the endless boring work, it takes to achieve this sort of transformation. I modelled myself on M. V. Anderson. I got his way of hunching his narrow little shoulders together and sinking his chin into his chest and bringing his long

488

nicotine-stained fingers together and looking up, a little coyly, at his questioner, pursing the lips and raising the eyebrows, etc., etc. Oh, I was a cute little popsy. You would have loved me.

I told the Parole Board I was off to write a book; I was lying. What I really had in mind was no more complicated than drawing my pension, getting visiting rights to the Kaletskys, and effecting a reconciliation with my son. This last was a difficult matter. I wrote to him once, a short note I admit it, to say I was sorry for belting him across the ear. He never wrote back, and although Goldstein explained that it was due to excess of emotion – too many thoughts and feelings for his stubby HB pencil to control – I was angry just the same.

But damn it, I had a weakness for grand buildings and I liked the sound of his shop. It was not merely a building with a tower. It *was* a tower. Goldstein, of course, had not informed me about the situation on the fourth floor. I did not know I had a grandson named Hissao or that his mother lived in a cage. I did not even know that the whole edifice depended on the Americans' enthusiasm for Australian birds and reptiles. I will tell you the truth – it would not have put me off my plan to get myself put up there.

Various women have threatened me with the prospect of a lonely old age. They have said it in the desire to frighten me and they have said it again when they've seen how it has worked on me.

So I admit it – I spent my ten years in Rankin Downs with one real aim, i.e., that I would end up with a place in this rotten lonely world. I invested an entire decade so that I would not end my life hiding amongst dead cabbages in the Eastern Markets. It was monomania, I admit it, but not overly ambitious. I did not seek wealth or even fame, merely a fire to sit in front of, a friend to trust, some company for the summer afternoons which are the loneliest time in a city of beaches.

I did not escape, although it would have been easy enough. It was not the type of dangerous thing M. V. Anderson would attempt. Neither, being a tea drinker, would he have an interest in a still, or kicking a football end to end inside the wire-walled enclosure. There was no adequate company there for M. V. Anderson. He was happier inside his books, resting his monstrous lower lip against the tip of his index finger. He was a person made for a sole purpose, to fit a very particular niche in life. He was no good for selling a car or anything practical, just this one purpose that I spent my ten years perfecting.

It was an eccentric jerky clock that marked those years, like one of the faulty mechanisms that drag their heavy hands upwards and then, whoosh, drop them down. Slow, yes, very slow – ten years were an eternity. But fast too – it took hardly a second.

And then, on the very eve of my release, I received a letter from Leah Goldstein. I suppose the letter was written as something joyful, i.e., that she, now, had done her time too, that she was free, available, without children, without Rosa, was unencumbered by french windows or orange trees.

Lucky man, you say, to be so old and frail and yet, at the same time, to inspire such devotion. Bullshit, Professor. You think I squander ten years of my life on a fancy. Ten years, and there she is slaughtering children, diminishing a husband, burying a friend, rolling up a carpet, pulling down the wallpaper I had arranged myself to harmonize with. Lucky man. To become an asthmatic tea drinker, for nothing.

Suddenly I could not even remember what she looked like. I could remember nothing but how she came into my camp so long ago, criticizing me, eating my food without being asked. She took an extra piece of Bungaree trout. Four slices, she ate, and did not even beg your pardon. Four slices. I was shaking all over. I could not keep my hand still. It was not nerves, not one of those weak-tea emotions I had been refining through sixteen filters. No, this was rage of a type M. V. Anderson could not even imagine, the poor sissy. I could feel bubbles coursing through my blood and the skin around my finger joints stretched tight. I was Herbert Badgery and I was a nasty bastard, no doubt about it, and I traded my wireless – I had been taking it as a present – for a blade.

You would expect me to remember my exit from Rankin Downs, to remember that long jarring journey over wet-season gravel. I cannot remember a thing. I have been planning to tell you a story about those yabbies (they were as big as beer bottles) but there is no time now, and I cannot remember whether we saw any on the road out or not, or even who the "we" might be.

I remember the train when it came into the siding and the shock and disappointment when I saw how filthy it was. The seats inside were green. I was expecting brown, but they turned out green. They were sticky with jam and spilt ice-creams. I had the knife strapped on my leg with an old tie. I had the Vegemite bottle in my pocket – you shoud have felt it – hot enough to burn you – I had it wrapped up in handkerchiefs. It was full of dragons but I did not look at it. I sat on the edge of an unpleasant seat and waited. Oh Christ that train was slow. It creaked and whined and shunted itself back and forth before it began to creak dismally towards Grafton. No one could tell me how long it would take to reach Sydney.

I walked up and down the train for a while then. Do not mistake this for a celebration of freedom. I was not admiring the lovely scenery or the pretty faces of the passengers. I was battling with spasms of anger that came on me when I thought how skilfully she had lied to me EVERY DAY FOR TEN YEARS and I knew why she had never had the courage to visit because *she could not look me in the eyes*.

In one of the carriages I came across two fellows playing knuckles, young fellows with old eyes.

I invited myself to join the game. I still spoke droll and wheezy like Anderson but God I was fast. My frailty seemed to fall away like dandruff. I smashed my fist down on one knuckle and then the next until they were sore and blue and they asked to be let off.

It calmed me for a moment.

The bigger one told me he had travelled round Queensland playing knuckles, with his mate as a tout. He said the Spags there would bet on anything. He showed me his roll and reckoned he couldn't spend it as fast as he made it. I told him I was just out of the slammer and he gave me twenty quid. That was a lot of money in 1949 – a doctor's salary for a week – and I wrote down his mother's address so I could return the money to him but I lost it and never did.

Did I tell you I was on my way to kill Goldstein? I did not form the words, but there was only one conclusion to my journey. For ten years I had suffered the exquisite pain of her letters, the mixture of jealousy and happiness, all those razor cuts, for nothing. I had bound my feet. I had cut off my balls.

I had made myself into an intellectual, for nothing.

The train journey took twelve hours. It arrived at Central. I got a taxi to Bondi. New-model cars were all around me. That is what I noticed most. They gave me the feeling of riding through a dream. The weather was warm, overcast, threatening thunder. I had the money to pay for my ride, but I jumped out at the lights at the esplanade just to spite the bastard. The driver was up and after me. Jesus, I ran. I left asthmatic M. V. Anderson at the first corner. I was over a fence and across a rusty-roofed chook-shed, on to another chook-shed, down into a lane, up the stairs of a block of flats with steel-framed windows. My back hurt, my leg hurt but I didn't care. Everything I did was on the premise that I was an old man who would soon die and I will tell you I savoured the rasp of my breath, like a rat-tail file in my oesophagus. I was Herbert Badgery, alive.

I waited in the block of flats for a while and then I went off to find the Kaletskys' number. I have no recollection of the house itself. All I remember is the crumbling concrete path, the tall rank weeds, and the leadlight in the peeling front door. I broke the leadlight with my shoe and let myself in. There were stacks of newspapers around the walls.

The house sucked. It was a sour, dank, rotten place. You could smell it was unhappy and no little children had run along that wide corridor for a long long time.

In the front room, I found an old man sitting by the fire although, outside, as I mentioned, it was a summer day with big bruised anvil-headed clouds, the sky full of cold holes and giddy updraughts. I came into the centre of the room, holding my blade. It was a villainous thing, the best the youngsters at Rankin Downs could produce, made from car-number-plate metal and strong enough to saw its way into a rib cage.

This faded old fart with silver hair looked at me. He was sitting on an upholstered cushion of that type that is called, I believe, a pouffe. He leaned over and picked up the poker.

He put the poker between his teeth. I watched him. He looked at me and bent the poker into a U.

Then he spat out the blood and broken teeth into his lap.

35

I robbed Lennie Kaletsky of five quid, just to throw him off the scent. Then I wandered down to Bondi Post Office and applied for the pension. I gave my address c/o Southern Cross Hotel.

I was nervous of approaching my son, not because I thought Goldstein would be in his care, but because I now suspected the pet shop itself might be a lie, that no such glorious thing existed, or that if it did it would reveal itself to be a grimy little hole with widdling guinea-pigs in sour straw.

I paid cash money for my second taxi. I checked into the Southern Cross Hotel. First I tried to sleep, but after I had lain on my lumpy mattress for an hour I got up and went to the barber's for a shave. Then I began to approach the pet shop. I pretended to myself I was not doing it. I window-shopped up Pitt Street, looking out of the corner of my eye, scuttling sideways like a crab.

I saw the word BADGERY first, high on the pediment of the building. I felt ill, as if the thing might evaporate. My back pained me and my teeth set up a throb, my body protesting about whether it was to be frail or no, and would I please make up my mind.

I cross Pitt Street, threading my way between the queues of trams, not furtively, not like a murderer, not quite like a gentleman. I am non-committal in my movements.

I approach the shop, looking down at the footpath. Outside there is a crowd of fellows, all arguing about some motor car. I excuse myself and they make room for me so I can stare up at the building.

Of course it thrills me: BADGERY, as bold as brass, in Pitt Street. Badgery Pet Emporium. It is better than she described. This window is thirty feet long and is set out with a design of pretty flowers. I make out the map of Australia. There are some words, but I am more taken by the little rock-wallabies which hop to and fro across this pretty scene and one of them, in particular, eating an apple, holding it daintily between its two front paws.

The men go on with their argument about the car and I get out of their way. I cannot know that the wallaby will die of influenza in Beverly Hills and I am, of course, proud of my boy. I begin to remember things more fondly than I am used to – the day he brought the yellow-tailed cockatoo down from the tree at Bendigo School, how Izzie had his finger bitten, and how Charles sold the bird when we ran out of petrol in Albury.

I enter the shop. Do I suddenly look like a Narrabri cocky on his first day in Sydney? Well, why not. Look at those galleries, those beautiful birds behind shining white wire, the glistening snakes coiled beneath spotless glass, that huge skylight, just as Goldstein described it to me, and now, as I watch, two white-overalled men work with buckets and water, cleaning off the week's supply of pigeon shit against a background of delicate stratocumulus.

The galleries are crowded. Ascending the stairs it is necessary to be polite, to allow two nuns to come down, to wait for three clattering boys with high voices and heavy boots.

I lean, at last, over the rail of the first gallery and look down. The cashier sits at a high desk in the middle of the floor, but he is deep in a book. I watch for some time. The cashier continues to turn the pages indolently, and yet the shop is obviously prosperous. The shop attendants are everywhere. They wear red-peaked caps and dicky little yellow jackets. They squat beside a cage here, gesture like a fisherman there, close eyes to dredge up information from the cellars of their memories. These are not salesmen. They are enthusiasts.

I am too delighted to dwell on anything in particular. I wander from exhibit to exhibit. I find the famous regent bower-bird which is trained to dig sapphires. It takes its blue stones from a pile of sawdust and places them, one by one, on an apothecary's scales. In the next cage I put two bob in a slot and see two apricot-coloured budgies tap an illuminated button. They get some seed. I get a drink coaster printed with the legend "Best Pet Shop in the World".

I slip this into my pocket. I walk up the last flight of stairs to the door marked "Private". And there, for a moment, with the door not properly locked, I hesitate. For this is the part I most care to see, to meet the affectionate wife I have read so much about, to play with my grandchildren, to be offered scones and the comfy chair. I am a coward in the face of that door. I thrust my hands in my pocket to make them still, and I am still vacillating when two youths come tearing out the door, their faces bright with embarrassment, and go thumping down the stairs past me. On the floor below they suddenly burst into ugly laughter.

I funk it, and turn, not knowing the woman I have come to damage is not five feet from me, quietly knitting. I do not meet Mr Lo, puffing from his exertions, nor Emma Badgery, the real cause of the upset boys I have just witnessed, who is adjusting her dress and retiring to a corner, a well-fed spider retiring to the centre of its web.

36

Emma knew it was wrong. She knew she would go to hell for the things that she did. It was not right to love your husband more than your children, or to spend your afternoons in a cage or to tease him so much that he banged his head against the floor like a defeated wrestler in a Pitt Street newsreel. She was steeped in wrong, soaked in it – it was probably wrong, it felt wrong, to eat mangoes the way she did, to suck the wide flat fibrous stone and have juice running down your arms, to have it well up in sticky pools between your fingers, and who, in her father's house, would have even imagined a fruit like a mango? It would have made him angry, her dearest daddy; he would have hit her bare legs with a razor strop. What a giddy temper he would have had at the suggestion of such a fabulous and filthy fruit.

And it was wrong, she did not need to be reminded, to make those two boys go running giggling down the stairs. She had heard them come through the "Private" door. She had seen them long before they had seen her, the minute they put their spotty noses inside and sniffed the musty odours of her home. Their upper lips were smudged with adolescent hair. She had watched them lift the mist nets and heard them croaking to each other. She had been in her slip and bra and she did nothing to make herself more decent. Leah was nearby, but was busy working and did not notice. Mr Lo was asleep. Emma pretended the boys were not there and she had opened her compact and dusted a little more blusher on her cheek. She heard them see her – the sucked-in breath, the whispered conference – and from the corner of her eye, as she checked her smooth reflection in her mirror, she waited to see what they would do.

But they were only boys, and easily frightened. When she turned to look at them, they fled, hooting and hollering down the stairs.

Once she had looked up and seen a policeman. He had watched her, smiling at her quietly, from the other side of the bars. Then she had become all milky and languid and had drawn on her lipstick, pouting her lips proudly towards that little mirror she owned then, and had let the clean biting line of neat teeth show underneath that firm silk-hard flesh that glistened like the innards of a freshly cut heart, bright, almost iridescent, slippery, muscled, secret.

He was not the only one of her uninvited visitors who gave her that sweet calm smile of recognition, merely the first. He had sat and smiled at her, she knew, because he knew she was like him and he like her. This kindred feeling was so soothing that her whole soul became as cool and limpid as tank water.

But to listen to most of the people who saw her, those all-but-burglars, you would think that her presence in a cage had affected some vital thing in their innards. She could not, ever, predict what it was they were going to do when they saw her, but the reactions were nearly always violent or loud or crude or angry – and she knew it was sinful to sit safely inside her cage and enjoy it, but she did anyway.

She preened herself. She had become vain and was not even ashamed of it. Once she had been a young girl and worn short socks and sensible skirts, but now she arranged her powder and her lipsticks and her rouges, mascaras, eye-liners, her emollients, astringents, foundation creams, moisturizing creams, her egg creams, her enamels, her nail-polish removers, emery boards, nail files and other aids to femininity.

And although her cage was directly opposite you as you walked on to the fourth level – so that you had only to come to the rail in front of you and look across – there was such a tangle of objects, such a confusion of lines or rope, netting, electrical cable, string, so many shapes you could not immediately understand, so many fascinating perspectives of the emporium below and the sky above, that you did not immediately notice the woman in the cage, or the child that was so often with her. In fact you were more likely to notice the lattice structure – it was very pretty and was often lit from within – that was next door to her. This was a cube measuring about ten feet in every way and you would not immediately describe it as a cage at all. It was far too pretty. It was a place for ferns and creepers and there were, indeed, some terracotta pots whose dried dead vegetation suggested that it was intended to have plants growing over it. Charles had given this to Emma in 1944, for Christmas. She had thanked him of course, and given him warm kisses, but she had not been so simple as to be tricked into living in it. And this, as it turned out, was just as well, because when Leah Goldstein arrived to live, one tear-stained afternoon, there was immediately a suitable place to put her.

There was another cage on the left as you entered from the stairway, and this one was often noticed first, and it was certainly a far more splendid structure than that rusty tin-floored affair that Emma had crawled into to remind her husband of his obligations. This latest cage was also a present from Charles. It was strong enough to hold a polar bear, but its ironwork was beautiful. There were pink venetian blinds, a little day bed, and a fluffy rug on the floor. Originally, too, there had been bottles of Coty and Max Factor on a glass shelf, but Emma could not be induced to move.

Neither, of course, would she live in the flat itself – and this is more easily understandable because it was a small and dark and poorly ventilated area on the Pitt Street end of the fourth gallery. Charles slept there. Emma often cooked there. But the family's real home was in and around the cage where its most determined member lived, out on the gallery floor itself. This fourth gallery was more like a storehouse, a warehouse, a garden shed with spiders and old yellowing newspapers, which were dry and unpleasant to touch. It provided a marked contrast to the hygienic emporium below where the shining white-enamelled cages were so regularly wiped clean that, first thing in the morning when the staff arrived, there was a distinct change of air, as if the wind had changed its quarter and was now blowing off the sea, and then the emporium was all awash with bleaches and antiseptics, and although that might be all very comforting for some, Emma preferred the chaos of that big rectangular doughnut of private territory, the fourth gallery, where she lived amidst old mist nets, broken-down refrigerators, children's toys, mouldering laundry, lost sandwiches and those abandoned tricycles which had once raced round and round, but could no longer – Charles had stacked other cages, plainer, smaller, rusty birdcages, in such a manner that they blocked the children's favourite racetrack.

It was a madhouse, so he said.

When he was angry he said that they were all demented, himself included, and that their children would grow up to be insane, capable of theft and suicide. He called her a slattern and a slut and madwoman and then she would go cold as ice and she could do that trick with her eyes so they went blind and hard as steel ball-bearings and it frightened him and he thought she would never love him again. Then he would come to her in the night, begging as if she were a queen in satin and silk, a queen in a cage, and then she would spurn him.

Oh, what a game they had, what a sweet lovely perversion it was. You could feel the rage. You could feel the whole building, the actual building, shimmering with it until it was a violin filled with parrots, fluttering, panicked in their cages, and the fish in terror, swimming round and round in their bubbling tanks and some timid possum, illegally trapped, in the boss's office, lying mute with fear while its heart, no more than half an inch across, drove itself into a red and dangerous frenzy.

It was wrong, of course it was. She did not need to be told. She thought up the most disgusting things, God strike her. She took his big bull's pizzle in her mouth and made him weep and moan and once she dreamed she had decorated it with lipstick and rouge and smoothed depilatory cream on his hairy sac. She read the women's magazines but it seemed that they would not address themselves to what a woman's life might really be.

And dear Jesus, how he had tried to get her out of that cage. He thought he wanted her to be like "normal" people, but he did not really. Who would want to be normal after this? They would die of boredom, and besides, she had grown to love the cage when it was quiet and calm, and she would lie in there on the long sweet sunny afternoons and listen to the goanna drag its handbag belly across the dark wooden boards and lie beneath its ultraviolet light and when the late afternoon began to turn to early evening it would come right to her door, like a cat at feeding time, and she would open the box the staff brought to her and feed it "pinkies", those baby rats they bought for the reptiles.

Hissao would help her sometimes. Henry and George were not at home with pinkies or goannas. They would hide themselves away at the far end amongst the wire netting and make themselves tunnels and cages and hide in case – they never told her but she knew – in case a schoolfriend came and saw them. But Hissao was never ashamed. He was different from the beginning. They both liked it in the cage. Leah Goldstein said it was not good for Hissao to see his mother in the cage all the time. She did not say it sternly, but gently, as a womanly friend, while she brushed her hair. So Emma tried, she really did, to play outside with him for a certain portion of the day, but he also liked the cage.

It was the inner sanctum in which they were both, mother and son, loved and cared for, protected from the world, and they felt themselves to be circled by so many loving defences, walls, moats and drawbridges that it was a shock, sometimes, to look up and see the skylight was thin, so brittle, so fragile a barrier between their comfort and the cold of a storm.

So when uninvited guests found her and became angry with her for being in a cage, Emma truly believed that they were jealous.

Indeed, in just eight hours' time from my hesitation on the stairway, she was to offer me, as a mark of special favour, a cage of my own. This, I am pleased to say, was already taken by Mr Lo, and I must, in all politeness, ask you to bear with me, juddering, shell-shocked in the doorway, give me time to take a breather while I tell you a little about Mr Lo and how he found himself in such an odd accommodation.

37

One day, and not too many days before my own arrival – more than a month but less than a year – Leah Goldstein returned from shopping, her string bag heavy with potatoes with which she planned to make a lovely cake, and found a gentleman sitting in the cage with the pink venetian blinds. He was twenty-two years old, a professional man, and was very nicely turned out in a grey double-breasted suit. He had a golden heart-shaped face and dark, sunken, unhappy eyes. He was Mr Henry Lo, marine architect, illegal immigrant.

Leah turned left as she came, puffing slightly, through the door, and there he was. Mr Lo smiled. Leah smiled. Mr Lo held out his business card. Leah placed the heavy string bag on the floor, very carefully and slowly in case a potato should tumble out and roll with the natural fall of the floor, and drop four storeys by which time it would be a lethal weapon falling at 200 miles per hour and capable of breaking the cranium and lodging itself, pulped and soggy behind the eyes – Charles had told her this, even shown her the mathematics of the fall, kindly provided by a staff member – and so, even though Leah was interested to read the new arrival's card, she was particularly careful with the potatoes, washed King Edwards from Dorrigo, picked early from loose red soil, and so round and easily rolled.

When she had the potatoes as stable as was likely, she placed her feet on either side of them, smiled apologetically at the young man in the cage, and read the card carefully.

Emma was wearing her pearls and her New Look suit. She was out of the cage and playing dutifully with her youngest son over on the southern gallery, racing a heavy lead motor car up and down and fighting for possession of it without taking the slightest trouble to protect her expensive nylons.

Leah offered Mr Lo his card back, but he insisted – he held up his soft pale palm to indicate his meaning – that she keep it. Leah and Mr Lo then bobbed at each other and Leah picked up her dangerous potatoes and squeezed her way past the rusty birdcages and made her way round to Emma's side. She squatted, not only because she was tired, but because she wished to speak to her friend in confidence.

"Who's that?" asked Leah Goldstein.

"That's Mr Lo." Emma gave Hissao the car and found herself a wooden truck to crash into it with. "There," she told the pretty rouge-cheeked boy, "now you're dead."

"Not dead," Hissao said. He started running around the gallery but stopped when he saw the adults were more interested in whispering than chasing.

"Why is he there?" Leah Goldstein hissed and Hissao came back to listen. He snuggled in against his mother, picking at the soft cotton of her dress, rubbing it against his cheek and smudging it, although no one realized.

"He wants to stay," Emma said. "He wants a job, so I gave him one."

"Gave him what?"

"I gave him a job," said Emma and, although she did not smile, there was something happening with her face, as subtle as her perfume.

"Emma!"

Emma pouted but she was not unhappy. She was almost never unhappy. Soon Leah would be going away, as soon as Charles's daddy came to get her, and she would miss her, miss the custard and rich soups, the games of canasta, the long companionable silences, but she would not be unhappy.

"Dear Leah," she said. She was about to fetch some perfume to dab on her friend's wrists when she heard her husband's great big feet – she saw them in her mind's eye, those punched brown brogues, size eleven, on the worn stair treads – they were coming this way. She could hear Charles and cranky Van Kraligan shouting at each other about the budgie factory. Van Kraligan's voice came up over the gallery – he was working below – but Charles was already up the stairs to the fourth level.

"Balt," Van Kraligan said. "I am not a bloody Balt. Balt is from Baltic. I am not Baltic. Fix it," he yelled, "fix it your bloody self, mate."

Charles strode through the door. He had shed his wartime camouflage and emerged with tailor's stitching on his gaberdine lapels. His suits were pressed each day by the American Pressers in Angel Place. He came through the stairs like a wealthy man, turned right rather than left, and thus missed the melancholy but hopeful Mr Lo standing at attention inside the cage Charles had commissioned from Spikey Dawson.

Charles walked – twenty-eight years old and still lifting his feet too high – round to the west side, as far as the door to the kitchen,

500

and then he leaned over the railing so he could shout at Van Kraligan on the gallery below. Don't worry what he said – it was all to do with his ignorance about geography – but rather that Mr Lo heard the tone of voice and did not need to look for a gold watch to know that this hairy giant was definitely the boss.

He therefore readied himself, exposing his cuffs the correct amount and placing a white handkerchief in his breast pocket. When Charles had finished with Van Kraligan, Mr Lo gave a cough, very small, and very polite, which Charles did not hear – he noticed, instead, Emma and Leah staring in the direction of the cage.

When Mr Lo saw that he had the boss's attention, he proceeded to show him what he could do.

38

He did not mind if she was mad – he would look after her, just as he had looked after Leah when she arrived, with one thin summer dress crammed in her handbag; just as he gave money to his mother and provided for his children. He got great pleasure from providing. It was a miracle that he could do it. He, Charles Badgery (who did not know what order the letters of the alphabet went in, who was ugly, awkward, shy, deaf, bandy), could provide.

When he threatened to call in doctors, which he often did, it was not because of her madness or lack of it. It was because of the thought that she mocked him. It was the look in her eye, secretive, malevolent, wrapped in thin clear plastic.

And it was this look that he saw, or feared he saw, on the day she put the Asiatic in the cage.

Charles leaned across the rail and watched Mr Lo thoughtfully, as though he were nothing more than a newly arrived cockatoo whose responses he was attempting to judge, to see if he would adapt to his cage readily or would end up noisy and a nuisance to his fellows.

Mr Lo bowed to Charles, bowed as he had not bowed except to Grandfather. Then he spoke a high-flown poem, badly remembered, which his accomplished sister had often recited before visitors. (The poem was in Mandarin. Charles Badgery did not notice the mistakes.) Finally he turned five somersaults and would have done a sixth except that he was out of practice and feared a disgrace.

"Please," said Mr Lo, suppressing his greedy lungs.

Charles was considering the thing that he never considered, the thing that he could not even admit that he thought about, but which had lacerated him since that day in 1943 when he emerged from the damp little church in George Street and discovered – it was his outraged mother who brought it to his attention – that his son was not named Michael, as he had thought, but Hissao. Now, six years later, he compared, point by point, his son with the man in the cage. He saw, quickly, that the visitor bore no resemblance to his son. His eyes were round, not almond-shaped at all, and they were sunken into shadows.

Seeing the proprietor's thoughtful face, Mr Lo realized that his tenure was in question. He began to sing a small sad song he had learned from his grandmother. Charles, hearing the sadness in the song, was at once moved and disgusted. He walked around the gallery rail but he would not look at the human being performing like a monkey in a cage.

He had ordered that the door of this particular cage be made big, like a normal door to a normal room, so when he decided to enter, he entered easily enough. Still, he found it difficult to battle the nimble Mr Lo who clambered up to the barred roof and hung on.

"Please," said Charles, "I cannot have you here."

While this all took place on the north side, Leah, on the south side, extracted Mr Lo's real story from Emma and – while Charles stayed inside the cage and Mr Lo hung on to the ceiling with aching arms – Leah came to the bars to explain the situation to the proprietor. Mr Lo, she said, wished to remain in Australia. The Australian government, having regard for the colour of Mr Lo's skin and the shape of his eyes, did not wish him to stay. They had given him the same iniquitous dictation test that they had given Egon Kirsch, although they had done it in Dutch not Gaelic, and they did not wish him to stay. They were wrong. Mr Lo was right.

This opinion had a confusing effect on Charles. First he had an excessive respect for the law which he must – there is no other explanation – have picked up from the Rawleigh's man who, having failed to abort him, had nursed him instead.

Second, he had immense respect for Leah Goldstein's firm opinions.

Everyone, he knew, was watching him. Leah was saying that

Mr Lo shoud be harboured. His wife was edging around the rail towards him. There was a man from the Customs Department – a government officer – waiting in his office downstairs, "making inquiries" about certain activities and although he had nothing to hide he was fearful about it and was now made doubly fearful by this illegal activity being conducted above the government official's head. He did not want trouble. He began to sweat. He could feel his deodorized armpits were sweating.

"Perhaps", said Mr Lo, who felt himself unable to hang on much longer, "you think I want money. No money," Mr Lo said, even though he was frightened at what he had got himself involved with. He was beyond thinking. If only he could have a night's sleep without worrying about arrest.

"No," Charles said.

Mr Lo dropped wearily to the floor and examined the painful impressions the bars had made on his hands. He had soft hands. He was proud of them, but now his hands would become rough and calloused, his long nail torn, and it was just as the fortune-teller had said – "Bad fortune, much hardship, great wealth follows."

It was cramped in the cage. Mr Lo was fond of garlic. Charles was not and so – although he did not wish to – he retreated from the cage and stood, with Leah, Emma and Hissao, looking in.

Mr Lo, although weary, managed a somersault.

"Let him stay," Emma said. It was a murmur, of course, but her husband knew what it meant. He turned and looked at his wife's eyes and thought, "Do you love me?"

For answer she released the strand of pearls that she had been clutching, and touched his sleeve, a habit she had, which, for all its restraint – no skin touched, little pressure applied – signified her most tender moods.

"It's not decent," Charles said, and his tone was exactly the same one he used when he found her stroking the goanna in such a way – no one else could do it – that its pale hemipenes emerged pale and spiky from their sheaths. He said it as if he was waiting, passively, to be contradicted, to be told it was perfectly decent.

"There's no privacy," he begged. "What if he raped you?"

"You lock me in," said Mr Lo. "Please." He shut the door and made a passable imitation of a padlock with his soft and slender hands.

Charles would have loved to snap a heavy lock just in the place where Mr Lo suggested. He also found the idea of locking a human being in a cage disgusting. And so he stood there, staring at the marine architect's hands, caught between his humanist ideals and his sexual jealousy.

In the end it was the gentle pressure on his sleeve that won the day, and Mr Lo was not only permitted to stay, but he stayed with no padlock.

You will understand how fine the balance was when you see Charles, late that night, earlier on other nights, come sneaking out of his flat, sliding his stockinged feet along the polished floorboards in case he should knock over Henry's Meccano or stab himself on Nick's donkey engine, holding his breath, the torch in his dressing-gown pocket. He gets himself right up against Mr Lo's cage before he turns on the torch. Mr Lo lies on his back, fully clothed, his dark eyes wide open.

Mr Lo, as it turned out, was nothing but a gentleman. Every evening he lowered the pink venetian blinds so the ladies could undress in privacy and he would inquire of them, with a small cough, before raising them each morning.

When Charles at last calmed down, he engaged Henry Lo to draw the plans for the new loading dock at the Ultimo warehouse. This activity did not stop Mr Lo trying to make himself agreeable to the customers who continued to wander on to the fourth-floor gallery.

By the time I met him he could execute a perfect triple somersault.

39

Later, when my grandson was an international traveller, he experienced similar feelings to those I felt on the wide stairs of the pet shop. I had the sense of stepping into a vision, of every edge being sharp, of every colour intense, of viewing the whole through glass as carefully cleaned as the great skylight in the ceiling and, had I sat on the roof and gazed down into this world, like a Barrier Reef tourist in a glass-bottomed boat, I could not have felt more entranced or more alien.

I could not separate my son's industry from Goldstein's lies. I could not tell where one stopped and the other started and I dithered, my knife against my leg, my hat in my hand. All right, all right, I was intent on getting put up and I should have discarded my knife there and then and twice I tried, stooping down on a landing between galleries, pretending to retie my shoelace, only to be interrupted by loud-booted boys or gawky teenagers with comic books in their back pockets. So I left my knife where it was, although it felt too tight, and I wandered down to the ground floor, sorry I had not taken more trouble to write to my son.

On the ground floor I tried to peer up into the fourth gallery, to see if I could get some indication of the standard of accommodation, but the galleries were so deep and the canyon so narrow that it was impossible to see a thing. I should have written to him. I often wrote him letters in my head, eloquent loving letters, but when I sat down to write them my hands went cold and dry and I could not bring myself to form the words required. Now I would have to go away – it was the sensible plan – sneak down to Wollongong and start the correspondence from there, wait a year if necessary until the boy invited me up to stay. But even while I developed this careful plan, my hands began to shake. I went out into the street to calm down. I turned my attention on the little pink-nosed wallaby in the window. It was then I realized that the Badgery Pet Emporium had entered into what is known in the car game as a "joint promotion", that the whole of the window was an advertisement for the new Holden car, that the map of fake flowers the wallabies stood on bore the legend: "Australia's Own Car".

This was bullshit. The car was about as Australian as General MacArthur, although it was not MacArthur but General Motors who had taken the government to the cleaners. It was a simple deal. GM permitted the Australian government to provide all the capital. In return the Australian government permitted GM to expatriate all the profits.

Twelve years before this piece of deception would have got me particularly excited, but now I saw it from M. V. Anderson's point of view, and noted it, not as something new, but one more element in an old pattern of self-deception. This is the great thing about being an intellectual. It is very calming. I felt no anger. Not a touch. I hoped Charles had been well paid and I was not at all offended when, via the medium of the tannoy above my head, Lou Topano and his Band of Renown gave forth with "Holding You in My Holden".

I had tied my knife too tight. It was most uncomfortable. I stopped to pull it looser but it would not come. It was then I found myself in the midst of men still arguing about a car. The tail of the tie was showing at the bottom of the trouser cuff. One of the arguing men was my son, Charles Badgery.

His suit was silk, shot with threads of silk, but it did not hide his extraordinary build. Neither did the wide-brimmed Yankee hat cast a shadow deep enough to soften the crude features of his head: that huge thick neck, that jutting jaw, the mouth that could be mistaken for cruel.

I stared at him a moment, proud of him, irritated by his loud voice, but also embarrassed by my own suit which was fifteen years old and hung in great folds around me. I had lost weight in Rankin Downs. My shirt was too big and its collar sat loosely around my crêpey neck. In short, I looked a no-hoper.

The car they were arguing about belonged to C. Badgery Esq. It was a Holden, one of the first. It was smooth, everywhere rounded, like a condensed Chevrolet, and the curved body panels shone seductively in the bright grey light of Pitt Street. It was like something from a letter. It glowed like a pearl and I too walked around it and felt my hand, almost against my will, go out to stroke it.

The arguers were cynics and romantics, some of them both, pretending to be rational men. Yet they were so bewitched by the thing they never once addressed themselves to the real issue but rather to such incidentals as the fact that the car was built with no chassis, that a bag of superphosphate in the back was necessary to make it handle properly. Some said it was ugly, some beautiful, and others said it was "tinny" and would crumple if you tapped it. But no one questioned that it was Australia's Own Car and nothing made a dent in Charles's excitement. He plunged his hands deep into his pockets, jiggled his keys, rocked back on his heels, looked up and down the busy street, waved to a passing friend and declared it a great day for Australia.

I should have got on the bus to Wollongong as I had planned. I was in much too confused a state to meet my son. I was a man descending on to a busy railway platform in a strange city with a battered old suitcase tied with string. I was jolted by impatient travellers, bumped by porters while I worried about whether my ticket was in my wallet or my fob pocket when it was in neither.

I held out my hand to him before I knew I'd done it. At first he thought me a stranger congratulating him. He shook the hand while he looked over his shoulder and shouted to someone else.

"Charles," I said. "It's Daddy." I did not know the weakness of the string that kept my emotional baggage together because there, in Pitt Street, the fucking thing broke, and everything I owned came spilling out of me, tangled pyjama pants, dirty socks, love letters, toilet rolls and old silk stockings. I hugged my boy and bawled into his deaf ear. I am not a big one for hugging men, I swear it. I never did it before that day. But I embraced my boy Charles Badgery in Pitt Street, Sydney, and frightened the bejesus out of him until he realized who I was.

It was a warm day, but I was shivering. I started to apologize for the knob in his ear. Don't smirk – I meant it – you should have seen it, the great ugly lump of bakelite sticking out of his ear-hole. He was too young a man to have to tolerate it.

Charles wasn't interested in apologies. He was pleased to see me.

"Have you seen the shop?" He led me towards it by the elbow. The doors were big and solid. Nothing quivered or evaporated. If Goldstein had invented it she had done a damn good job for it looked as solid as the real McCoy. "Crikey, this is wonderful. I always imagine you coming to look at it. I always wonder what you'd think. And here you are, I can't believe it."

He took me around the shop and introduced me to his staff, each one, by name, explaining the sapphire miner, loading me up with drink coasters. He was not ashamed of my ill-fitting suit or the tear marks on my cheeks. He took me into a large cage, all full of logs and ferns and running water and at the back he showed me a female lyrebird he had incubated himself. She was building a nest, he said, and was ready to mate. He was happy, because this meant he had cared for it well, but he was sad because there was no male to give her.

You could feel such a well of tenderness in the boy that I was affected by it too. A bower-bird came and perched by my shoulder and, for a moment or two, I could almost feel myself to be a nice man.

On the third gallery, we ran into a fellow, a seed importer from the Haymarket who wanted to go for a spin in the Holden. So we all clattered down those wide wooden stairs – light-coloured and worn in the centre of the treads, black on the edges – making as much noise as schoolkids let out early on a summer's afternoon, bathers in their hands, towels around their necks. Twenty-four hours before I had been in H M Prison, Rankin Downs.

At the front desk Charles remembered his family and despatched a wizened little fellow to bring "them" downstairs. I never imagined Goldstein was up there. I was trying to get rid of my knife, but Charles wanted me to get in his car. The birdseed importer came along. I got in the middle, and the importer got the window seat. And now, thank God, I could undo my tie. My companion took too much of an interest in my activities, so I merely loosened it off. I had no intentions about that knife one way or the other. I was preparing my plan to get myself put up.

It was too important a matter to leave vulnerable to the chancy winds of human emotions.

40

Mr Lo confessed to no one how he longed to walk the streets of Sydney as a free man and he felt this need most strongly on days like this one – grey, hot steaming February days whose humidity and colour reminded him of Penang, of Sundays when you could stroll out by the sea wall with Old Mother, his sisters, his worldly brother-in-law, Old Mother flicking her fan – he could still hear the noise it made, like a clock – and he, Mr Lo, would always buy them those little glutinous rice cakes wrapped in banana leaf although he was a poor student and had less than all the others.

He would die and never see Penang again, unless it was as a ghost, alone on the sea wall looking for the cake-sellers who were home in bed.

But Mr Lo did not dwell on this. He tried to be optimistic. He dreamed, not of Penang, but of the more attainable streets in Sydney. Just the same, when the invitation was made for him to ride in Charles's new car, he declined, with thanks.

"I will hold the fort," he said, pleased with his colloquialism. "Please."

They did not try to persuade him any more. He watched Leah put on her big white hat and struggle into her shoes. He saw Emma make some last adjustment to her face, while little Hissao, his good friend, whom he entertained with ghost stories and Old Mother's songs, picked up his favourite Dinky toy and stuffed it into his bulging pockets.

Mr Lo smiled and showed them great happiness, but when the door was shut behind them and he had carefully locked it, he sighed, and his eyes lost their fraudulent gloss in an instant, like cheap baubles from the thieves' market which tarnish in their wrapping on the way home.

Once, only once, had he ventured out into the street. But he had only gone a block before he was overcome with his vulnerability, his illegal status, the thought that there was nothing to protect him from questioning, officials, exportation, a gaol sentence in Penang and, finally, conscription to fight the communists in the jungle.

So he returned, and stayed, and did not try to go out again, sad to be locked away from the world and fearful lest he be forced into it.

Mr Lo was an intelligent young man. His teachers had all remarked on his understanding and his diligence. Things did not need to be explained to him twice. Yet he could not, in his present situation, ever understand how he was permitted to stay or what function he had in the workings of Mr Badgery's establishment. He had asked and been answered, but he had not understood and he behaved as he had when, as a child, when his father was still alive, he had gone fishing. He was too young to understand fishing, but he followed the example of his father and uncles. When they jiggled their lines, he did likewise. When they changed bait, so did he. But he did not understand. So it was in Mr Badgery's emporium: he did his somersaults and spoke in languages, but he could be overcome, mid-somersault, with a panic that there was no meaning to his antics. He no longer imagined that he was to be sold. That misconception had not lasted a week, and he had been relieved to realize it, and yet he also dreamed of the day when a beautiful young lady would come through the door – it did not even matter if she was not beautiful, or even if she was no longer young – and she would see him: neat, clever, nimble and she would fall helplessly in love with him. She would not even notice Mrs Badgery and if she did would not be so impolite as to laugh or point. She would stand shyly and lower her eyes, and he would speak to her. On the first visit she would not answer, but she would return, and sooner or later she would speak. She would want to marry him, but he would have to ask her, of course. And then they would walk the streets of Sydney together. He would buy her rice cakes, bright red ones wrapped in green leaf.

Mr Lo began to straighten chairs. He unlocked the little nest of wooden legs that Hissao had made into a "Ghosts' Cage" and lined the chairs neatly along the rail of the gallery. When he had done this he took out his handkerchief and dusted the seats. Then he sat down. He thought optimistic thoughts.

I have never been a great one for returning to my past and thus experiencing that giddy gap between past and present where, in a second, you trip and teeter and, with arms flailing, fingernails scraping against egg-smooth walls, you fall through twenty years.

Yet on that day in Sydney, that muggy steaming day, I breathed the odour of my little boy's manly sweat and plunged and soared in the turbulent air of time.

I met the mad woman. I looked into Hissao's eyes and saw my lost daughter, for whatever Emma had made of him, there was no mistaking that similarity, that sweet nature, that pretty face.

Charles, I assume, introduced me once again to Leah, but there was such a commotion in my mind that I did not hear. I did not recognize her and so wondered at the particular attention this handsome woman bestowed on me.

The birdseed importer had a fat bum and took up too much of the front seat. It was hard to turn. I was blocking Charles's view in the rear-vision mirror. We roared up George Street and headed towards the bridge. Charles was shouting various facts about the car and its performance, accelerating, braking, and showing off. He drove no better than Jack McGrath.

"Mother is in Sydney," he shouted.

"Who?"

"Phoebe, your wife. My mother is in Sydney."

"Oh," I said. I did not wish to hear about wives. I was taken by the handsome woman in the back seat. I wanted to turn so I could see her wedding finger, but the birdseed importer was trying to question me about my business and Charles wanted a coin for the bridge toll. I got my hand into my pocket, gave him the two bob, and saw it safely into the tollkeeper's hand, and then, as we lurched savagely on to that ugly steel structure all Australia is so proud of, I managed to squirm free of the importer's attention and turn in my seat to look at the woman.

I groan out loud to remember what I did. I tipped my hat, although there was little room to do it, "Herbert Badgery," I said, "I don't believe we've been introduced."

For answer I received a whack across the face.

Leah Goldstein had a lovely face. All the angles had become rounded, like a river rock that is so smooth that all you wish to do is place it in your hand, and once it is there it gives you a comfort and a happiness you could not begin to explain, that such a smooth sun-warm rock should fit your cupped palm so perfectly.

We sat on the Argyle steps beneath a Morton Bay fig which is still there today, and I unstrapped the tie and gave her the knife. God, it was an ugly thing – there was no elegance to the weapons made in Rankin Downs. I never did say what it was I planned to do with that blade, but I always assumed she understood. Perhaps she never did, but merely saw it as a symbol of my criminality, something that could be discarded as easily as the dank gaol smell which – she told me later – permeated my clothes and my skin. In any case we dropped the knife into Darling Harbour that afternoon and I wept, for the fourth time that day, and Goldstein wept with me, but perhaps she did not understand. I thought about this often, later. I wondered if I should not make it more clear. When we were lovers again I would be stricken by visions that would make me groan. I would touch her chest or feel her lovely ribcage or lie with my head against her breast listening to her beating heart (it had an odd skip to it, that heart) and think of that steel blade with its grubby rag-and-string glued handle.

I did not ask why she had told me lies so long. All I cared about was the future. I undid my shirt on the Argyle steps. I told you I was a vain man, but I had less to be vain about than I once had. The quacks had been through my back, mining for a kidney stone they never found, but what damage they had done was nothing to what I had done myself in my quest for frailty. I showed her the crêpe-skin around my neck, and the place where my biceps had once been tight before I so cleverly dissolved them in the acid of my lying mind.

I swear to God I will never understand Goldstein's criteria about skin, for she found nothing wrong with mine. She touched it and looked at me with her velvety cat's eyes. She did not flinch. She smiled. So did an old lady who was standing on the wrought-iron balcony above those narrow steps. She was hanging out her washing between her canary and the wall and she stopped, with wooden pegs in her mouth, and smiled.

Once the skin was settled, we moved on. My back hurt like hell, but I did not confess it. There were pains shooting up my legs and my teeth set up an ache as vague and persistent as people talking in the next room. I drew myself up and tried to tell myself I was a young man. I drew up my forearms a fraction and imagined myself on the sand at Bondi Beach. But you do not slough off a shuffle so quickly, and I soon had to admit that I would be an old fellow for a little while and that I could not match the dancer's walk beside me.

At sixty-five years of age, women do not see you. You are invisible. Until, that is, you walk down George Street with a young woman with a dancer's walk and then you go from invisible (flip-flop) to neon-signed and you are, take my word for it, a celebrity, a ballet master, a painter, a famous anarchist, a free-thinker, a revolutionary, an inventor of note, a criminal of power and influence, but look at me, I am only Herbert Badgery and once I was shy about my legs and now all I want is to lie down on my bed and take an Aspro and hope my toothache will go away.

I should have quietly withdrawn myself, gone back alone to my hotel, read an uncensored newspaper and gone to bed early. Charles, however, was busy arranging my life for me.

43

In all her fifty years Phoebe had never once worked for money. She was not ashamed of this. On the contrary. She had, after all, given her life to art and as for money, it always turned up somehow. Visitors to her little flat would look around at the pretty walls, the small works by famous artists, the rugs on the floor, the view of the harbour out the window and – feeling themselves steeped in nasty compromises, pot-boilers, jobs with newspapers, unpleasant sinecures with the Education Department – not only envied her but admired her.

Her poetry, of course, was little known, but by the end of the war she had begun the little magazine that historians now talk about so seriously – *Malley's Urn*, a private joke amongst the literati at the time and if you don't get the joke, don't worry – it was never very funny.

There were those who imagined her to have inherited wealth, but if Phoebe even smelt a whiff of this misunderstanding, she set it straight – her mother had left five coal mines to the Catholic Church. Imagine!

So where had the money come from? First from Horace until his ship had sunk, torpedoed in the English Channel. Also from Annette Davidson until, at an age when you might think her past it, she had run away to Perth – in the middle of a school term – with her own PE instructress. She had arranged a telegram to Phoebe which announced her death but everybody – even Phoebe – knew the two women had a "horrid little milk bar" in Nedlands.

So it was left to Charles to be a patron of the arts and he was not at all displeased by this. You could buy (if you wished – few did) *Malley's Urn* in the pet emporium – there was always a stack on the cashier's desk and Charles had a complete set of that quarterly green magazine in his musty bedroom which he read on his insomniacal nights.

Now all of this seemed firm and settled until the day that I arrived in Sydney and Charles decided that his mother should have the flat in the pet emporium. Charles was so excited by this idea that he did not even wait for the reunion dinner he was planning for that night. He got his mother on the telephone and came straight to the point.

"And leave my flat? My lovely flat?"

"Mother, it's very expensive."

"And take up with *him*?"

"Come and meet him," Charles begged.

"Oh, don't worry, I'll come and meet him. But I will not leave my flat. I refuse, I absolutely refuse, Charles. I value my independence."

It was then Charles lost his temper and said some unkind things about her "independence". He succeeded in frightening his mother terribly.

44

Amongst her friends, Phoebe was not thought to be unkind. Quite the opposite. But as she walked into the private room at the Hyde Park Hotel on that evening in February 1949, she was armed for battle. She was angry with her son who now strode across the vulgar carpet to welcome her, but she kissed him on his rough sunburnt cheek as if nothing was the matter. She nodded to Leah whom she had never liked, and smiled at

Emma, trying to convey fondness while, at the same time, keeping sufficient distance to discourage those soft-centred kisses.

Everyone was standing except for Emma who had seated herself at table. She wore, Phoebe noted, the same ostentatious pearls she had worn on Christmas Day. She had also, through design or carelessness – it was not quite clear which – neglected to wear a corset and her round little stomach rose from below the belt of her long silk dress and disappeared into the floral valley of her thighs.

Phoebe accepted the kisses of her grandchildren. No one would have guessed that she was repelled by all this sticky-mouthed humanity. She was bright. She laughed as she always did when nervous, and put her hand to her throat. She let her eyes go to that place in the room where her opponent sat.

"Herbert Badgery, I presume," she said in a whisky-cured contralto. She laughed again. The feathers cascaded from her little hat.

I stood and walked towards her.

She held out her hand, briskly, with her handbag tucked beneath her arm. I shook her hand and found it damp.

"Well," she said, and laughed again.

I could feel everyone watching us, marooned there in the middle of that room, the long cloth-covered table by our side. I felt dead-eyed Henry sit with a thump on one of the chairs. I had gone for a rum with Goldstein. She said it was good for toothache, but I could see it had been a mistake. I had already called Hissao "Sonia".

"You've got old," said Phoebe.

I refrained from saying that she, also, had got old. Her carefully applied powder did nothing to hide the fine lines which were not those caused by laughing and smiling but were, rather, a fine network, like rivers on the map of her upper lip. Yet she had become the thing she had imagined and there was not, in either her bearing or her accent, very much left that would connect her to Jack and Molly.

A waiter came with sherry on a tray. I could have done with another rum, but I kept my hands jammed in the sticky pockets of my derelict suit, producing, doubtless, an effect that Phoebe would think was "common". She took a sherry. The boys said they wanted lemonade and I was pleased to feel that I was no longer the centre of attention. Henry was pinching Nicky and making him cry. Hissao wanted a pee and I could see Charles making toilet inquiries of the waiter. Emma started murmuring over Leah whose face she had so carefully made up, producing a doll-like beauty which, while foreign to her character and everything I liked about it, none the less made my wrinkled dick stretch and unwrinkle as if it were lying, not in the dark discomfort of my underpants, but in the gentle warmth of tomorrow morning's sunshine.

The windows were open on to Elizabeth Street and the hot night was suddenly filled with the frenzy of exhaust pipes, slipped clutches, the distinctive slap of engines wrecked by wartime gas producers. I liked the smell of car exhausts and I sniffed in the stinking air as Goldstein would have sniffed in jasmine.

"I mean no malice," Phoebe said.

A strange expression. I looked to match it against an expression on her face, but she had her face bent from me, looking for something in her handbag – a white envelope, smooth, unbent, unmarked by powder.

When she looked up I thought she was frightened of me. She handed me the envelope. In my confusion I imagined it was money, compensation for that aeroplane she had stolen from me. I thanked her, and tucked the envelope into my pocket. It felt thick and comforting. Perhaps there would be sufficient to pay my son some rent.

"You see," she said, "I know you are a bigamist." She finished her sherry and looked around for a waiter. There was no waiter. She put the glass down on the table. "You were already married when you married me. You were married", she said, "to Marjorie Thatcher Wilson in Castlemaine on October 15th, 1917, and you were never divorced."

I said nothing.

"I have all the papers." She was quite gay. In the next room a dance combo began to play. There was a saxophone, I recall, and a piano player with an American accent. The waiter came and filled her glass. "It won't matter if you tear it up, because I have the real thing. It's a little folio tied up with a ribbon and it cost me forty pounds. But the point is, dear Herbert, that I will not give up my flat."

I had no idea what she was talking about, although I remembered Marjorie Wilson very well. She was a nice woman, and I was sorry I left her but the problem was not her but the screeching mother she would bow and scrape to all day long. I was silent. I was thinking about Marjorie and how we had to do it in the laundry while we took it in turns to keep the squeaky wringer moving.

My silence seemed to make Phoebe gayer.

"If you force me, I'll have you charged with bigamy and then, I believe, I'm entitled to sue you for all sorts of things."

She laughed again, and I was reminded of her mother in the days when she thought something was wrong with her brain, when, caught in Geelong, with no faith in her normal manner, she had crooked her finger and adopted a plummy accent and revealed her terrors in continual laughter.

I was feeling quite anaesthetized. I had another sherry to help it along. My teeth stopped hurting and I promised Phoebe that I would cause her no trouble. I congratulated myself on having moved beyond a young man's rages.

I winked at my flirty lipsticked Goldstein as I sat down at the table. She touched my calf and smiled softly. I felt myself master of the situation. I said as little as possible but smiled politely at everyone. I asked them questions about themselves, an old salesman's habit guaranteed to make your prospect think you both sympathetic and intelligent. I did not imagine there was a risk of an argument about Australia's Own Car. I did not think I cared about the subject. I imagined I had no passions left except those involving shelter and the comforts of skin. I would do nothing to jeopardize either. I was going to have a place, with Goldstein, inside that wonderful building of my son's. I was going to wake each morning and gaze up at the skylight and know, straightaway, what sort of day it was.

Charles sat himself between Leah and his porcelain-faced wife. When the oyster shells were removed, he stretched and yawned and put his long arms along the back of Leah's chair, a gesture perhaps accidental, but I did not take to it.

"So, Father," he said.

Phoebe, on my right, whispered that he only shouted because he was deaf.

"Tell me, Father," he removed his arm from Leah's chair, and leaned forward intently. "You haven't given your opinion of the Holden."

I was not insensitive to his feelings about the car. I had questioned him about it at length. I would have thought this enough to do the job, but he was not such a simple fellow as he looked.

"It went well," I said. "I couldn't pass an opinion without driving it."

"You can pass an opinion on one fact: it's an Australian car. I thought of you the day I read about it. I thought, Father has lived to see his dream come true. An Australian Car. Did he ever tell you, Mother," he turned to Phoebe who was now looking very bored and was taking exception to Charles's great pleasure in saying "Mother" and "Father" at the one table, "did he ever tell you how he walked away from the T Model on the saltflats at Geelong? When we were kids we used to ask him to tell us that story. He must have told it to us a hundred times. He. . . ."

"There are no saltflats in Geelong," Phoebe said. "He was lying."

"The saltflats are at Balliang East," I said.

Phoebe shuddered. "A dreadful place."

"Very close to where I met you."

"That's what I meant."

Goldstein was the only one to laugh. It was also Goldstein who, on the subject of Australia's Own Car, made the point about the extraordinary deal General Motors had done with the Australian government. She talked about this in detail while Phoebe sighed loudly and shifted in her chair.

The roast beef arrived and for a moment it seemed as if the conversation would pass on to something less difficult, but Charles had no intention of letting it go.

"Yes," he said, polishing his fork with his table napkin. "There is money here to do things. There's no doubt about it."

"Yes, dear," said Leah. "It's our money, but the Yanks do get all the profit. They won't risk their money because we have – or they think we have – a socialist government."

"Who can blame them?" said my feathered wife. Her voice was not quite firm and bobbled uncertainly on its perch.

"Excuse me," Comrade Goldstein put her fork back on her plate and sat up straight in her chair. "Excuse me, but I do."

Phoebe ignored Leah. (Perhaps this made me angry, but I didn't think so at the time.) "I can't bear the way they speak," she said. "I just can't stand their vowels."

"I like it better than the Poms," said Charles. "It's not stuck up. Now, you've met Nathan. . . ."

"No, no," his mother tapped the table with her dessert spoon. "I don't mean the Americans. I mean the Labour Party. They've all got pegs on their noses."

"It's the Australian way of speaking."

"It's pig ignorant", said Phoebe, "and if I were an American I wouldn't trust them either. They talk like pickpockets."

"Say again," said Charles. He placed his hearing aid on the table, propping it up against the blue packet of de Witt's Antacid Powder which he brought with him wherever he ate.

"They're thieves, pickpockets." Phoebe looked at her son's contrivance with disgust. "Put it in your pocket, Charles. Show some manners."

"He can't hear you if he does," Leah said, but Charles put his machine away, looking a little hurt. Phoebe smiled at Leah. She was too polite to call her a pinko.

Emma, in the meantime, had Hissao on her lap and was feeding him although he was now five and quite old enough to have his own chair and feed himself. Emma did not contribute to the argument although she smiled at me from time to time and occasionally I heard the barely audible sound of her murmurs. She popped mashed-up messes of food into her son's pretty mouth while his dark watchful eyes roamed over us. Once, in the middle of an argument, he smiled at me and for a moment I heard nothing that was said and smiled at him like a man in love. So late in my foolish life I was to acquire a real family after all.

"So, Father, what do you say about the Holden, eh?"

I shrugged. I am not a shrugger by nature but I wished to avoid saying anything hurtful.

"Come on. Come on." He put his ape arm behind Leah's chair and beamed at me.

When I had done my years of study in Rankin Downs this was not the context in which I had planned to unleash my learning. I had imagined dispassionate discourse, conversation as restrained as teacups quietly kissing their saucers. But still I answered my son in a considered way, avoiding anything that could be considered personal.

"I would say", I told him, "that we Australians are a timid people who have no faith in ourselves."

It was then that the trouble started. It was not with my comment, which was quiet and civilized. It was my son's reply. He roared with laughter as unmusical as the chair he scraped beneath him. I felt my temper begin to rise. I tried to bottle it. I had my heart intent on entering his household and I would not – not this time, please God – go hurling snakes around the room, ranting with a young man's passion, destroying the very thing I wanted.

"You don't believe me?" I asked him quietly. I fancy you could describe my smile as wry but my eyes, I felt them, were small and showed themselves as an intense violet blue.

Charles laughed again.

I did not lose my temper. I spoke sweetly, so softly that he had to produce his machine again and listen with a strained expression. "Then why. . . ." I said.

"Speak up."

"Then why", I waited for him to get the thing adjusted, "are we so easy to fool? Why do we let them call it 'Australia's Own Car'?"

He did not obey the rules. He did not know them, the bloody ignoramus.

"Because it is." He thumped his fist on the table and made the plates jump. Emma's eyes slanted and she hunched her shoulders. Leah stared at the tablecloth. Phoebe examined the little watch she had pinned to her breast and the two bigger boys, the apprentice dullards, put on their deadman's eyes and looked to the front.

"No," I said. I was still quite calm. "It's a lie. And the shame is, it's not our lie; it's their lie."

"Your father", Leah said, "uses the word 'lie' in a slightly eccentric way," and she touched my leg again, beneath the table, recalling the tender conversation we had conducted over our Bundaberg rum.

"There are several meanings to the word 'lie'," said Phoebe, speaking as a professional in matters to do with language, "but only one to the word 'liar'."

"A lie", I said, "is something that isn't true at the moment you say it."

I saw Goldstein's smile – it spread to her eyes and suffused her skin as pervasive as a blush.

"E.g.?" my son demanded.

I had lived with my Vegemite jar so long that I did not find its contents disgusting. Often it was frightening but mostly it reminded me of the trivial nature of my imagination – for I had no doubt that it was this that controlled its contents. I could do no better than some warts, a fish, and – for a week or two – a tiny fox-terrier (it was only half an inch long) that finally changed into something like a cauliflower. Even mad Moran had made angels.

"E.g.?" my son demanded.

When I placed the bottle on the table, I was pointing out our lack of courage and imagination. It was all so clear to me that I felt no need to explain it further.

"E.g.," I said.

But all they saw was a finger floating in a bottle.

Emma grabbed for it, but it was Charles who won possession. He looked at me with disgust but I was too far along the line of my argument to go back and explain it to the slower ones.

"What is this *thing*?"

"Almost anything you're brave enough to make it into."

"I don't understand you," Charles roared.

"I don't understand you either, mug." (I was blowing it. Tough shit. Rough tit. Too bad.) "How can you turn your shop into a wing-ding for a Yankee card trick? Australia's Own Car! It's bullshit, boy. You've been done like a dinner."

"I haven't *been* done, Father. I *have* done. I've done more than you ever did. You lied and cheated and passed dud cheques. You never fed us. We never had clothes. We were cold and hungry when you looked after us. Now look at you. Look at you all. Jeez, you get up my nose. I'm sorry, Leah, but it's true. I feed you all. I put food in your mouth, and yours, and yours, and yours, and yours. It's my worry, my responsibility, and no one here lifts a finger to help me." His voice went up an octave. "You come along here with your socialism or your poetry or your sarcasm or this, this *thing*, but none of you actually do anything. In real life, someone has to talk to the bank manager. It's me. I'm the one. I'm a business man. All those years, Father, you talked as if you were a business man, but I can see now you weren't a business man's bootlace. You moaned and groaned about the Pommies and the Yanks but you never did anything. And now you've got the nerve to criticize my car. Well it's Our Car. There's not another one like it in all the world. Is there one in Russia? Ha. In America? No, it's ours and we made it."

Everyone was silent, but Charles was at that point – I know it well – where the climax of a rage is not quite reached and something, some definite thing, must be done to cap it off. The flag must be driven into the snow.

"But," he said, thrusting his hand into his jacket pocket and pulling out a crumpled quid note, "but, seeing you are all so independent, here's a quid from me towards the food and grog. I'm sure you can all pay for yourselves. Put that thing *down*," he said to Emma, but his wife was entranced by the Vegemite jar and did not even look up when her husband left the room and stamped down the stairs into the night.

Henry and George sat rigid. Emma and Hissao were already busy with my bottle.

"Well," Phoebe said brightly. "I must be off, too." She kissed me briskly on the cheek and she had been borne out into the night on black feathers before anyone had a chance to ask her for a penny towards the meal.

I must have looked miserable because Goldstein kicked my ankle and smiled at me.

"Don't worry," she said. "He'll be back in a minute."

It happened just as she predicted. He was away no longer than it takes to walk around the block, up Castlereagh, into Liverpool, and back. He came into the room holding his hat in his hand with his shoulders rounded, his long arms pressed against his sides. I did not want him to apologize. I thought him entitled to say what he said, even if I did think he had been tricked by the Yanks. I tried to stop him, but he insisted. He did not do it briefly. He went on and on and I had to listen. He was in the habit of it: apologizing for things he was not to blame for. I could not look at him, only at the tablecloth.

"I hope you will stay," he said.

"Oh yes," I said.

"Not just tonight."

"Thank you."

"But always."

It went on, we will leave it there. Let me say only that there were soon more tears – even Goldstein joined in – and soon I was walking through the warm bright streets of Sydney with my dancer on one arm and my gentle son upon the other. We proceeded towards my tower and you will understand that at a time like this a Chinaman's dead finger might easily escape my notice.

45

You, my dear sticky-beak, already know the conditions of life on the fourth gallery, but for me it was a revelation.

My son had made his workplace like a cathedral and I had expected him, therefore, to live in a palace, not a prison. It was easy to see why the most normal person would not wish to sleep in the so-called flat where my boy (presuming me well past such a grubby thing as copulation) made up a bunk for me, throwing on children's bunny rugs and heavy eiderdowns although the night was warm and the air stifling. The flat had no windows, merely small opaque skylights which – I could see the rusty trails – leaked every time it rained. No wonder his children preferred the company of their mother. There was a ripe odour of horse meat and ageing apples, both of them pervasive smells that get themselves soaked into every surface so that a fellow trying to block his nose from them will find his blankets are as contaminated as the air itself.

How could you compare this with the prospect from the fourth gallery where you could gaze upwards and find the sky full of bruised thunderclouds or blinding blue, on whose varnished rail you could lean, like a first-class passenger on an ocean liner and watch the customers perform their antics on the ground floor below? Here you could have the most beautiful birds on earth to amuse you, and at night you could find your way into the green watery depths of sleep via the cool tanks of dreaming reef fish.

And yet, for all this possibility, the style of life on the fourth gallery had none of the poetry I had imagined when, just that morning, I had stood below and craned my neck to catch a glimpse of it. And yes, I admit it, I was disappointed at first and I did not like the way they permitted the overweight goanna to drag its peeling belly across the floor so that one had to be reminded – constantly – not to trip over the nasty thing. Emma tried to persuade me to pat it, but I merely touched it.

They had made a slum of it.

It is true that Mr Lo kept his cage tidy. And Goldstein, likewise, living in the rejected lattice, kept everything neat and spartan. She had a chair and a little desk. There was a newspaper photograph of me hanging on the wall in a neat black frame. But the rest of the place was – you know already – like a toolshed, a warehouse, a junk room, a repository for broken toys, empty saucepans, dispossessed chairs, unhung curtains, rope, nails, women's magazines and leftovers laid out for the goanna and then not found suitable by the recipient who spent its mornings next to Emma's cage, basking under an ultraviolet light.

When I saw the fourth gallery my face, I am told by a dancer, went very odd. She said my skin went taut and then rather grey and after that it took on a white waxy sheen. Doubtless she tells the truth, but this pessimism, this shock, while quite natural, would not have lasted for a moment. It did not take me a minute to see what was to be done, what I was to do, and I was not angry or irritated, but delighted, that I had been given an occupation, that I could deliver value to my family so easily and quickly. I did not disapprove, as Leah thought I did, of the tangle of humanity. It was the tangle of objects that I loathed. It was the objects that seemed to rule.

To reach the bedroom one had to pass through the kitchen where meals were prepared for both pets and humans. There was no decent lighting. The feed bins were smeared with broken egg. Fortunately the wall that separated it from the gallery did not appear to be structural. I would need a sledge-hammer to begin the opening out. There were a number of tools I would need at the same time, and a quantity of rough-sawn hardwood.

So even while my son was busy making sure I did not share a bed with Leah Goldstein, I was turning my mind to his fourth gallery. I thanked him for his bed quite graciously and accepted a loan of a toothbrush for my dentures. I was then taken to say goodnight to everyone, and I shook the older boys by the hand and accepted a kiss from their younger brother. When I said goodnight to Goldstein I gave her a wink and a grin and kissed her on her nose. Neither of us argued with our sentence.

They put me in my hole and turned off the light. Was I resentful? No, I was not. I threw off my blankets and pulled a damp sheet over my ears and nose and waited for sleep.

My aches began to set themselves up like instruments in an orchestra. First the low grumbling oboe of my back, then the violin sciatica in my leg. Teeth and kidneys arranged themselves and I greeted my afflictions by name.

I was used to a coir mat in Rankin Downs. Its substitute was too small and soft. I dragged it off the bed and set it up on the floor, but the apple smell seemed worse down there, and anyway I could not stop my brain from spinning. Too much had happened in one day, to have passed from prison to freedom, from murder to love, and now, as I lay on the floor in this airless room, to the problems of architecture.

It did not come to me immediately. I was down there wrestling with it for an hour or two before I saw it. This was no job for hessian or tin or chicken wire. It should be thin and elegant, with glass and steel and walls full of swimming fish. There wasn't a pencil in the room. I turned out the drawers but they held only socks and school reports. I put on my tired and sticky shirt and went out to the kitchen to find a pencil. I could see through the kitchen window that the gallery lights were out and I was reluctant to draw attention to myself. I flashed the kitchen light on and off but could see no pencil. I stood on something nasty but it was perhaps only a grape – although if you were guided by your nose you would think it a fish's kidney or an eyeball. I could feel millet and other seeds beneath my bare feet.

I slipped out the door to the gallery. It was very quiet, but also full of the currents of breathing air. Emma was lying on her back and was the loudest, but I could hear them all, the soft whisper of children's breath included. I went to the rail and looked up at the skylight. There was no moon and the stars were bright. I could make out the giddy powder of the Milky Way and I stood there, craning my neck, trying to make out the Southern Cross. I could not find it, of course (what Australian ever can?) but that is not the point at all and you will appreciate that a skylight full of stars is not a thing that a prisoner, even one from Rankin Downs, is used to. I began to incorporate a telescope in my plans. I would need to drop a concrete pier through four storeys, but it could be done elegantly, I knew it could, and you can imagine what it would be like to lie in bed with skin touching skin and the two of you looking, sighing, staring at the rings of Saturn.

My thoughts then, although occupied in the most sentimental way with copulation, were really more concerned with architecture, the placing of the concrete pier in such a way that I did not destroy the open space I loved so much.

I was, as they say, a million miles away, when Leah Goldstein put her lips one inch away from my ear.

"I'm a bit partial," she said.

We will forget the fright she gave me, the wild alarm of skipping rhythms she triggered in my heart so that, for a moment, it careered around like a car on a wet corner, and remember rather, that we kissed, most gently, and retired to the privacy of my room.

But here, I must confess it, I was as nervous as a boy. I had not been sorry to put off the moment I also wanted so much, and when Charles locked me away I did not complain because it suited me. Ten years in a prison does not engender confidence in these delicate matters which one, at the same time, has spent so many hours dwelling on, so in the end one has enough material to make a palace from the leftovers. I had not, as Goldstein imagined, come seeking her out. Had I known she was waiting for me I would have stayed alone on my mattress on the floor.

A prisoner's memory turns love-making into something at once sweet and coarse, as saccharine as a pin-up, as rough as his hands on his cock, all worried whether his semen will splash on to his clothes or go into the bucket and I had forgotten the tiny intimacies of that ache I had named a fuck, the small pinching fingers on my nipples and belly, the ripe musky honey beneath the sweet bush of shampooed hair, the way a face in the dark (in the light too) changes its meaning and how words you thought yourself too old to say, sentiments you imagined dead and drowned, bubble up from the muddy floor and burst in such explosions of light, of perfume, floral yeasts and uric acid, and my Leah's eyes were huge and shining (nebulae, supernovae) and as she arched her back and locked her legs around mine so we were held hard, tight in a rack, Herbert Badgery was caught by surprise to find himself awash with gratitude, a prisoner in a rocking-horse of sighs.

46

Herbert Badgery lay in Leah Goldstein's arms. She smelt the musty odours of Rankin Downs seeping from his skin, like old rags kept in a cleaner's bucket for too long a time. He was already asleep.

Down in Pitt Street a drunk was pouring forth an endless mantra of echoing abuse against the empty summer streets.

Herbert Badgery began to snore, quietly. She was sorry she had not told him what she meant, had not said it properly. She had belittled herself. It was a stupid habit. She had made light of her ability to earn ten quid a week, as if it had been bought lightly or maintained easily. She had told him that the stories were hack work, which was true, and that they were women's stories, which was true in that they were written for the demands of the editors of women's magazines. But she had not told him that this constant production was like walking, each day, through a field of thigh-high mud. The fiction editors were arrogant and stupid enough to think themselves superior to their readers. You could only supply them with what they wished by thinking badly of human beings.

And yet she had taught herself to do this work because it was work that could be done anywhere, in a café in Sydney or sitting by a roadside at Goondiwindi. It would provide enough, with

Herbert's pension, to live free of Charles's charity – they would not need to be family pets like Mr Lo.

She dreamed of landscapes cut with raw red roads, hills sliced by deep crimson cuttings, yellow ochre rocks striated with the long straight stabs of jack-hammers. Her mind, perversely perhaps, found peace in pictures of wide khaki seas around small treeless towns with the paling fences so new you could smell the tree sap in them. In these landscapes, by these roads, she found a shrill, ragged, unaesthetic optimism. It was ignorant and guiltless, and she had not yet told him but it was what she craved.

She could tell him tomorrow, but tonight she could now tell herself something else – she could allow herself to feel the hate she had for the pet emporium. And, indeed, lying in the unventilated dark, on a mattress on the floor, with the grease of cosmetics still on her face, she allowed a ripple of hatred, an electric jolt to pass down her body.

"I hate this place," she said. She said it out loud just to make herself hear what she thought, so that she could no longer pretend to herself that she thought otherwise.

"Signed," she whispered, "signed, L. Goldstein."

Herbert rolled on to his back and she dragged her arm out from under him. She loved him, but she would rather go and sleep in her own bed by herself. It was a habit, probably a selfish one. It was this last thought that made her stay and, also, her wish not to hurt him. She put the sheet over him and sat, hunched, on the edge of the mattress.

She hated it. She wanted to leave so much that tomorrow would not be too soon. She would not waste another moment of her life, that river filled with jetsam which had once – it looked so sad and pitiful now – been so important to her.

No longer would she be understanding Leah. She liked and cared for Charles but her feelings for Emma and her children were false emotions and she tasted their taste in the cosmetics on her face. She had cooked their bland meals for them, wiped their noses, mended their socks, done all the simple things they all appeared to be incapable of doing. She had accepted the mindless ordinariness of their lives because she did not wish to live alone, perhaps, or because she could never explain to Charles why she might want to leave his custody.

But she was not a young girl any more. She was thirty-seven years old and had a crease beneath her bottom and a little roll of fat on her middle. She was thirty-seven and had, for the most part, wasted her life as if she hated it.

She started to make pictures in her closed eyes, a habit she had developed on her insomniac nights in Bondi. She could make perfect pictures: twisted white eucalypts at a corner of a white road near Cooma, bristling khaki banksias in the foot-burning sand at Coolum, Gymea lilies in the scrub around Dural, like burning weapons on long shafts placed defiantly to warn intruders. She saw the cliffs and waters of the Hawkesbury lying in the water like the scaly back of a partly-submerged reptilian hand.

"Cdwerther," said Herbert Badgery.

She turned her head. He also was sitting upright.

"What?" she asked.

"C-wder. Ah, strewth, I can't even say it." Then, laughing, he lay down again, still asleep.

Leah Goldstein started giggling.

Tonight, when he lost his temper with his naïve son, she had been so pleased. She had been pleased, anyway, to see again her blue-eyed scoundrel and confidence man, but she was pleased, particularly, to see that he still could care about a thing like that, care enough to lose his temper.

At last, she thought, I've done something right.

"You're so much nicer," she told the sleeping man. "You're not hard and scratchy any more. Can you hear me?"

"Mm," said Herbert Badgery, and started snoring.

"I love you," said Leah Goldstein.

She peered at him closely in the dark. His eyes were shut. He was breathing through his partly open mouth. "You *are* asleep, aren't you?"

"I hate this place," said Leah Goldstein.

47

You may recall me mentioning a certain widow in Nambucca. I said she had a shell shop and it was her I left behind when I cycled up to Grafton looking for a job with the General Motors dealer.

In truth it was a milk bar, but I always liked the idea of a shell shop. I had a picture in my mind of glass cases with those twisted shapes, soft and pink on the inside, all set out neatly on beds of tissue paper. I had no objection to cleaning the glass myself. I knew all the bus drivers on that route and many of them said they would have stopped there if there had been shells but we never got around to it.

I came into that shop in 1937. I had been working for an oyster farmer down at Port, and that was pleasant work most of the year, but I was not getting ahead. I did not have a scheme in mind, but I bought a second-hand Malvern Star bicycle and thought I'd ride it up to Queensland. There was a small buckle in the back wheel, but in every other respect it was a good machine. I left Port at sun-up and I was in Nambucca for lunch and that was where I found Shirl's Milk Bar (although it was not called that at the time) and I parked the bike and went in for a pie.

You know the sort of place. It stands back from its own little patch of yellow gravel. It has a peppercorn tree or a big old gum tree in front of it. There is a wooden veranda with its floors a few feet up from the ground. The boards are a bit rotten. When you walk into the shop there is a torn fly-screen and a little bell rings down the back. You look at the curtain hung across the passage and you expect to meet a big-bellied woman with breathing troubles, or a bent one with a dangerous mole in the middle of her forehead. You look at the lollies behind the streaky glass – tarzan jubes, traffic lights, licorice allsorts, musk sticks in three colours, freddo frogs, jelly babies, eucalyptus diamonds, and just the way they sit there in their cardboard boxes tells you to expect goitre, canker, wall-eye, gout, crutches.

So when I heard Shirl coming – click, click, click, click – it was not the right walk for a shop like this. I knew what she looked like the minute I heard her – short, broad, verging on muscly, with brown skin and a nice set of lines around very lively eyes. She emerged from behind her curtain with her make-up properly done, the seams of her stockings straight, and her hair fresh from the domed oven at Mrs M. Donnelly, the Nambucca hairdresser. She could not have been more than fifty.

I put off the pie a moment and bought a threepenny glass of lemonade, to give me time to consider the matter.

I asked her if the shop was hers. I was surprised to hear her say yes, because it was a shop for dying in, and she did not look like the dying sort. Then she told me about her dead husband and I understood.

When I finished the lemonade, I ordered a strawberry spider. I told her she didn't belong there. I came straight out with it and

528

although she did not look up – she had her arm deep into the ice-cream tub, scratching around to get enough into the scoop to make my spider – I could tell she was pleased to hear me say it.

"No," she said. "I deserve a ruddy big palace, and silk sheets and a little black boy to do the housework and rub my back." She dropped the scoop of ice-cream into the glass, ladled on the strawberry and splashed in the lemonade. The spider frothed up pink inside the glass and spilled down the sides. She had bright red nail polish on and her nails looked pretty holding that frothing pink glass.

"You do," I said.

If I'd been stuck with the shop I would have opened the place out a bit, like one of those Queensland fruit stalls, or even like a Sydney milk bar where all you have at the front is a sliding door, and once it is open you are truly open. You smell the ocean and the dust. You'd be alive, not half dead.

The truth does no harm on occasions. I told her what was on my mind. I gave her a bit of a sketch. I used a piece of wrapping paper which she was kind enough to tear off a loaf of bread.

She leaned across the counter. She had that smell of a woman fresh from the hairdresser. "That's all very good," she said, "but you're forgetting the westerly."

"Your shop faces east."

"That's so," she said, but she did not lean back, or start wiping down the counter. She ran her finger over the plan, as if it were a road map. "So you're a handyman, are you?"

She looked up and we considered each other a moment.

"I was looking for a place to board," I said. "Give me a room and my keep and I'll do the job for you. It'd be a pleasure. You could have oranges in racks right down the wall. . . ."

I could see the choice of oranges, or perhaps the numbers I suggested, puzzled her.

"And sea shells," I said, "in glass cases, for the tourists. The main thing though is the light. It's that mongrel wall that makes the shop so miserable."

"What about materials?"

"Don't worry. I'll supply them."

"You'd have to have a permit from the council."

"You like to dance?" I asked her.

"Don't mind."

"There's a dance down at Port tonight."

"Oh yes."

"You want to go?"

She pursed her lips and looked at me. "How would we get there?"

"I got a bike."

She laughed. I laughed too. Any mug could see we were not discussing bicycles.

"You're going to double-dink me," she said. I always liked women with lines around their eyes. "Put me in my ball gown on your bar."

"I'll double-dink you," I said. "It'd be a pleasure."

"You think you're capable?"

"More than."

I was too, and by three o'clock we'd made a mess of her clean sheets and I was lying on my back with her hair in my nose, thinking how much nicer the room would be if we could lift the roof like the hatch on a ferret box.

Shirl was a good woman. She had a great appetite for life and would have a go at anything. We went rabbit shooting, fishing at night, swimming, dancing. We won a silver cup for mixed doubles at Taree. She liked to play the piano and sing.

She wasn't much of a cook but neither was I. We ate meat pies and baked beans and fried eggs. She used to fart in her sleep.

I got a job at Bobby Nelson's garage, working the pumps when he was away driving the school bus. This gave me enough cash to buy materials and I soon had the front of the shop pulled out and I put a big steel RSJ right across the front of it. Then I built the sliding doors myself, modelling them on the ones at Nelson's garage. This was more expensive than I thought, but Shirl made up the difference. I felt happy ripping open that bloody coffin of a shop. I rigged up a clever canvas canopy to go out the front for the summer mornings, and we started to buy in fruits and vegetables and I would stack these out there.

I put signs up and down the highway. "SHIRL THE GIRL FOR FRUIT & VEG", "SHIRL THE GIRL FOR ICE COLD DRINKS", "SHIRL THE GIRL FOR A CUPPA TEA".

Naturally it wasn't long before she wanted to marry me. I was not averse to the idea at all, although there were a couple of previous arrangements I would have to sort out, and I think I went as far as to write off for my old wedding certificates. I was under the impression, I think, that they might have lost the old ones, but this was not so.

But the impediment to marriage was nothing technical. It was a dog.

If the dog had been there on my first day, I would not have spent my money buying lemonades and spiders. I would have doffed my hat and off up the road. But little Rooney (that's right, and yes, named after Mickey) was in the care of the vet at the time, suffering from mange, being shaved and painted with some violet-coloured tincture.

Now I have never liked corgies. So you can imagine how I felt, a week after having got myself a woman, a house, a scheme, to see her cuddling a purple one to her bosom.

I was prepared to be friends with Rooney but Rooney did not feel the same way about me. He would growl and bare his teeth if I went near him. He would lie across doorways and snarl as I stepped over him. He did not bite me once, but he managed to take the edge off my happiness. He would lie in a corner and watch me. He had mad eyes, and when we made love he would lie under the dresser growling.

We were so well suited, Shirl and I. We had arguments about nothing else but Rooney, and the worst ones were about the chocolate logs she gave the little rat. It was disgusting to watch.

"Dogs don't eat chocolate."

"Rooney does. Don't you, Rooney?"

"It'll rot his teeth."

"It's a reward."

"What for?"

"It encourages him to eat his dinner."

"You don't need to encourage a dog to eat. He'll eat anything. Look at him."

"Rooney needs to be encouraged."

"How does he know? Jesus, Shirley, how does he *know* why you're giving him chocolate?"

"He knows, don't you, darling?"

Rooney turned and looked at me. He tried to stare me down, and I would have won if I had not had more important things to do.

I made inquiries. I learned that corgies lived to ten or twelve. There was only eight years to go, and I should have been patient and waited him out, but I was a young man with a young man's ignorance about time, so I tried to hurry it up. I did not actually do anything, but I discussed it with Bobby Nelson. I gave him to understand that I would not mind if someone put Rooney in a sugar bag and dropped him in the estuary. This was a very stupid thing to do, because it got back to Shirl who came flying at me with red nails and bared teeth.

"I was only joking, Shirl. I was just joking with him."

"Get out."

I had been there exactly six months. I got my bicycle clips off the mantelpiece and put them on. I hadn't had breakfast so I took a cold pie. I got on the Malvern Star and I expected her to say to me to come back, but she didn't. She stood there in the shade of the canvas awning. It was a lovely place, cool and breezy and you could smell water and dust in it. She stood there with her arms folded and Rooney sitting at her feet. I don't remember what expression she had on her face, but I remember the dog's eyes. I never expected to find eyes like that in a human being, but that is another story and we will come to it in a moment.

48

There is nothing like a bit of opening out to get people to declare their position. You'll find that this does not happen until the bricks are actually falling and you have your handkerchief wrapped around your nose to keep the mortar dust out of your lungs and, with your twelve-pound hammer making that lovely soft noise as it gets in amongst the bricks, you will find people all around you, each one expressing a point of view about what you are doing, some saying it is dangerous, some illegal, others beautiful, and there is always someone else who will be concerned about the temporary and trivial inconveniences, e.g. the problems of mortar dust which they insist is poisonous to certain fishes.

And you can say that I should have left well enough alone, that I should have been grateful to have a roof over my head and not be some poor wretch shuffling along the passage of a Darlinghurst boarding house. Of course I was grateful, but what do you want me to do? Put up a cordon, take out an injunction, call the National Trust to make sure no one changed so much as a window and that the smell of old socks, bad apples, stale horse meat, minced liver, that this rich brew would be embalmed forever just the way it was? Would you have me sit on my arse and die – in the midst of my new happiness – of boredom?

Of course not.

You would have me go ahead, but cautiously. You would advise me to be democratic, to consult those who lived here before I arrived. This, you would imagine, would prevent the onset of blind enthusiasm and monomania.

I imagined so myself. I did consult. But there are many difficulties with consultation. The first of these is that it relies on people having an eye for what you are talking about. They can say yes but not understand. It also presupposes that they have some idea of why they are living the way they are. So you can hold all the discussions you like and the truth is that it will make no difference – you will only get your final yes or no when the bricks are falling.

The second difficulty is with those who will not tell you the truth. Goldstein was in this category. She told me yes, when she meant no. She went into her little latticed box and how was I to know she was dropping fat tears on to her writing paper while I, she told me later, marched around the fourth gallery like a little sergeant major, ignoring Mr Lo, flattering Emma, going down into the shop to find my son and frightening the customers with my enthusiasm.

Young Hissao, of course, thought the whole thing great fun. He marched up and downstairs with me (whoops-a-daisy) hand in hand. But young Henry and George were not my sort of people. I had looked forward to their friendship but they stood at a distance with their arms pressed against their sides and stared at me with an expression that – had you not known the innocent nature of my work – you could have mistaken for terror. You could already see that their great passion in life would be normality and they would seek out the tiled roof, the small window, the locked door, the clipped hedge, the wife who never farted, lacy pillows on the marital bed. They were frightened by my opening out. They did not see the beauty of the process – how the great four-storey space was filled with dust like an old cathedral and motes of light came slicing into the canyon, as if Jesus Christ himself was standing above the skylight and you might as well know it – it was the skylight I was really interested in, not the kitchen wall. I am not saying that the kitchen wall was not best removed. It was vital. It was, if you like, the Overture. The point is this – that the best approach to opening out is to begin cautiously – you do not, not

533

ever, leap straight to the main performance. A patient man would be wise to begin with a small window and enlarge it a fraction at a time. A less patient man does best to content himself with a wall. This will give the occupants some confidence. They will appreciate that they have previously lived their lives inside a coffin and now they may begin to stretch and breathe. When you have them at this stage you can safely begin to discuss the roof. A roof is a much more emotional matter than a wall, and in Nambucca, for instance, I was just starting to hint at it when Rooney finally won his battle and I was handed my bicycle clips.

So I told no one, not even Goldstein, that I had a plan for the skylight. What I had in mind was to rip off the roof completely and set up a system which would open and shut like an eyelid above us. This sort of idea tends to strike the uneducated as impractical, possibly dangerous, so for the time being I kept it to myself and pottered around with my sledge-hammer.

The wall did not appear to be structural. I went down to Nock & Kirby's and bought a wrecking bar and took out the window without much effort. I took the door off its hinges and took out the frame. It was pleasant to do things with my hands after all those years of M. V. Anderson-type activity. I took another stroll down to Nock & Kirby's and bought a new hacksaw. Then I came back and took out the old kitchen sink and closed off the water pipes. It was a warm day, so I did not rush at it. I strolled at my grandson's pace. I carried my hat in my hand and my various pieces of shopping under my arm. I nodded to the staff and smiled at those members of my new family whose eyes I could catch. When it was time to get stuck into the wall I took off my jacket and folded it and put it inside Goldstein's apartment. It was dim in there. I did not notice any redness around the eyes. I warned her of impending dust and she looked up and, I thought, smiled. I did not know she was an author. If she had told me, it must have slipped my mind.

It was eleven a.m. precisely when I began my attack. I did not rush at it like a young fool. I opened out from the existing window. The bricks were old and handmade, soft and pink and very crumbly. I took them out slowly, working at it so there was a natural stepped arch left in the wall. By noon I had a space twelve foot wide and I had just decided to leave it at that for the day, to see how it settled, when Goldstein crept up and shouted in my ear.

"Fool," she said. "You impossible fool."

534

49

Leah had become like the old-maid aunt in a Victorian story, forever puffing up the stairs and down, first awake, last asleep, a repository of patience and kindness, taken for granted, never arousing curiosity except of the most perfunctory sort about her ambitions and her hopes because she showed the world so little sign that she had any.

But she was, of course, beneath her river-smooth exterior, full of the tumbling currents of ambitions that she had been rash enough, gambler enough, to postpone ten years.

She felt, that morning while I consulted about the wall, like a runner who has paced herself to a certain distance and when the distance is extended, cannot run another step. She was exhausted.

I asked her about the wall.

"Oh yes," she said. "What a lovely idea."

She went into her latticed room. She had a mattress there, along one wall, and a desk along the other. It was cramped, but she was used to it. She sat at the desk and arranged her papers as she would on any other morning. She took out yesterday's work and placed it at her left elbow. The tears began to drop and she rubbed them with her finger, as if they were errors to be erased.

Outside she could hear Mr Lo arguing. She did not need to look. It was an amusing performance on the first occasion, but after that the spectacle quickly palled. Mr Lo amused himself, each morning, by playing imaginary baseball. He did not even have a bat. He would walk to the eastern end of the gallery, the opposite end to Herbert Badgery's wall, and position himself above his imaginary plate. It was just as well he did not have a real bat for he would have hit a ladder on the back swing. He never swung quickly, always slowly, and it was hard to ascertain which was a strike and which a ball. It was obviously hard for the umpire too. Mr Lo was always arguing with him and for a quiet man, a polite man, these arguments had a frightening ferocity. Mr Lo bellowed. He stamped and shrieked. Leah did not know what he was saying, but at these moments she felt closest to him.

Mr Lo was like everything in this place. It was easy to understand why he did it. In one way it was perfectly sane and normal, but sometimes you could look at it with that other eye, and it was terrifying to realize this was what your life had become.

Emma was sitting on a big overstuffed armchair in front of her cage – she looked like any overweight woman in a seaside camping ground. Her skin had loosened, her face now showed a tendency to jowliness. She sat, leaning forward on her open thighs, talking on the telephone. She liked to talk on the telephone. Her sister had sent her a Bacchus Marsh phone directory and it was her great pleasure to look through it and telephone people who were often most surprised to hear from her.

Goldstein lit a cigarette and watched. She could hear me talking to Hissao but she blocked that out of her mind – that blowfly noise – and watched Emma who, having finished her first phone conversation of the day, was fossicking in a large cardboard box she always kept near her chair. She took from it a single iridescent pink hair curler and rolled her straight black hair deftly into it. She clipped in a pin and patted it. There was a finickiness, a silly vanity in her actions. That was, at any rate, one way to see it. But the other way was to see her as a great courtesan.

Emma looked up and smiled, presumably at her father-in-law. She then hid her face and retreated, dragging the cardboard box after her, into her cage. She shut the door behind and sat herself on a little stool with a bright blue lambswool cover. She was just a heavily built countrywoman with a pink slip. She had meaty shoulders and fleshy upper arms. Her stomach bulged against the satin of the slip. She leaned forward, pressing her face towards the glass of a small round shaving mirror which was tied – with blue electrical flex – to the wall.

"Yes," thought Leah Goldstein, "she is a great courtesan. She is not the most beautiful woman in the world. She is not overendowed with intelligence. Yet her ambitions are quite extraordinary – nothing less than to be adored and worshipped. She is a great artist. Her husband can think of nothing else but having her love him. If she was beautiful everyone would understand. She could lie around in baths of ass's milk and her behaviour would be perfectly normal. They would applaud her and write poetry about her. They would think it quite permissible for her to be her husband's pet."

But it was not permissible for her, Leah Goldstein, to live her life so uselessly. It was not permissible to be in this undignified position, to be kept by a keeper of pets. She loved Charles, but it was not permissible for her to stay here. And here was this idiot,

536

this fool, making a home for himself, jumping from one prison to another.

It was unbearable.

She sat and tried to write. She prided herself on her professionalism, that she could write her thousand words of pap whether she was well or ill. But all she felt was an enormous anger welling up in her, that she had wasted ten years of her life on a misunderstanding.

She stood up. She had not been intending to say anything. But when she emerged Herbert Badgery turned and smiled. His blue eyes looked false, like a doll's eyes.

"You fool," she said. "You moron. You want to be a pet."

"This is my old age."

"How disgusting then. What an old age. You want to lie on your back and have your stomach rubbed."

"Shut up."

"Pet," she said.

"Why not? I've earned it."

"What about life?" she cried. She was bawling now. Her face contorted. Tears coming down, splashing her sandalled feet. "What about *life*? I thought you were full of it. I used to tell people you had more life in your little finger" – she held it up, indicating a pink tip with a sharp slice of her other hand's index finger – "than most people, more moral people, better people, had in their whole bodies. Now look at you."

There was nothing to say.

She kicked at a brick. I suppose it hurt her, for her foot was covered with nothing more than a small blue slipper.

"Five years we were together, Mr Badgery, and I have drawn on that time ever since. It has sustained me. Not just you – don't look so smug – the life. The life was a life. When I visit my father his house is depressing, full of death and dying, and I read the letters. You could build a country from the towns and streets that I described, even a good country, a happy one. I was alive."

"So you want to be a dancer again."

"Don't be a smart alec," she said, but she was not shouting any more and there was sadness in her voice. She rubbed the foot with which she had kicked the brick.

"Well, what do you want?"

Her shoulders slumped, not much, perhaps no more than a quarter of an inch, but it was a definite movement and Mr Lo must have observed it too because he stopped staring at us and went

back to his game of imaginary baseball and my daughter-in-law –
standing powder-puff in hand at her doorway – winked at me.

And even I, with sweat in my eyes, could see that Goldstein did
not know. She had what she always had, I thought – a yearning,
and that was fine, but I would not be blamed for it. It was the same
misunderstanding that had plagued me all my life. All I ever
wanted was a fire and slippers. But the women never saw, or if
they did, they looked the other way.

"We are going to *die*," said Goldstein, moving closer, speaking
softly.

"So?"

"So you are out of one prison, and making another one."

"And what would you suggest?"

She was close to me now, so close I could smell the Ipana
toothpaste on her breath. "I'd rather have leeches on my legs. I'd
rather be damp and freezing in the fog in Dorrigo."

"You'd rather have nails through your hands," I said.

"Shut up," she yelled. I thought she was going to strike me, or
spit, but she turned to walk away.

Emma, Hissao, and Mr Lo were all staring at her from their
separate corners.

"Pets," she shouted. "Fools."

She turned back towards me and brushed past on her way to
the stairs.

As she ran down the stairs there was a small sound, a dzzzzt, a
fine fast jagged noise like electricity passing from one surface to
another.

A fine crack appeared in the southern wall and then the 'dzzzzt'
shot across the ceiling. I ignored it. I knocked out some more
bricks to give it something worth cracking over.

50

There is always someone who will get in a panic about a crack.
Next morning the Chinaman revealed himself to be the person
who would take that part. He dragged me out of the nasty
bathroom (all blue laminate and aluminium edging) to show me
what I already knew. You will understand, I trust, that I was
irritable about a number of things and when Mr Lo drew my
attention to the crack, I misunderstood his character. He spoke to
me about Rowe Street Joyce but I did not inquire about who she

was. A crack is a threatening thing to a layman, but to someone like me it is an architectural instruction, more precise in its message than any draftsman's pencil.

I thanked Mr Lo and went back to the bathroom and washed the soap off my face.

As I walked out to find my son, Mr Lo was already playing baseball and Emma was putting new curlers in her hair. I could see a light shining inside Goldstein's latticed apartment, but I did not enter. I went downstairs to find my son in his office. I did not tell him about the crack, only that I would need cash for more materials. He took it well. He showed me a regent bower-bird he had hatched from an egg. I watched him feed it with an eye-dropper and he was as tender with it as he was when he combed the wet hair of his sullen boys.

Charles did not become alarmed till later, when the fellows from Jordan Brothers' had their block and tackle fixed to the steel roof-trusses. He emerged from his office with an egg sandwich in his hand just as that big RSJ slowly lifted from his shop floor. An RSJ, in case you are not familiar with the term, is a steel beam, a rolled-steel joist, and in this case it was fifteen feet long, one foot deep and four inches wide. It weighed a ton.

I can understand why Charles might wish to get the customers out of the shop. But it was quite unnecessary for him to evict the staff as well. If he had not lined them up in Pitt Street in their uniforms, the newspaper would never have been alerted and the whole operation could have been done quickly and safely.

I am not saying it is his fault. I am saying it was unfortunate. The photographers wanted a pic of Charles riding the beam and so the whole thing, which was nearly in place, had to be lowered down to the ground for him to stand on. Then they wanted a photograph with me on it beside him. Then Charles wanted to tell them about the best pet shop in the world and the point is that it all took time.

When the reporters and photographers had gone, the RSJ rose again. They had it at the third gallery, and it was moving sweetly towards the fourth. The foreman was already applying pressure on the rope that was to bring it rolling sideways and his offsiders were standing ready when an entire section of skylight crazed and fell like drops of water in sunlight, like a diamond necklace dropped by a careless thief. This fleeting moment – this fleeting chandelier – was followed (or so it seemed to me – that the noise came after) by a sharp hard crack like a bullwhip.

The fellows from Jordan Brothers' worked like aces. They got the RSJ over to one side and into place. They had the stress off the truss in a minute and so you would think no serious damage was done.

I had no time to worry about the subjective reactions of the other tenants. There was too much to do. We got the RSJ bolted into place and I saw, just as we finished, that we were going to need some more steel for the sides, just to stiffen the whole thing. There were arguments about money. I suppose I was not tactful. In the heat of the moment I may have forgotten that it had been my idea in the first place. I may have referred to it, in conversation with my son, as "this scheme of yours".

Jordan Brothers' went off for the extra steel, and I leaned back against Mr Lo's quarters looking up at the skylight. Thunderclouds were tumbling in from the south pushing up great columns into the dizzy air. I would need to rent a tarpaulin and I had no money of my own.

I smelt the Chinaman behind me: soap and ironing.

"Rowe Street Joyce," he said, emerging from his cage, as neat as a *maître d*.

"Beg yours?" My hands were blistered from the sledge-hammer and my white shirt was rusty from the RSJ. I looked at Mr Lo and wondered if he could lend me a quid.

"Rowe Street Joyce," he said. "RSJ."

"Ah, you mean Rolled Steel Joist."

"Of course," he said, a little curtly, I thought. He gave me his card. I did not notice the rain begin. I was listening to Mr Lo. He had come to Sydney, he said, for only one thing, to become a top man in building Hi-Li. He saw that Hi-Li would come to Sydney before it came to Penang, so his plan had been to get experience with Hi-Li here and then go home when they started Hi-Li there.

I felt the rain. My head was running with sweat and the rain was pleasant, but I should have been out getting a tarpaulin. I got the architect to accompany me downstairs and I took some money from the till. I gave him enough to buy a T-square and kept enough for the rent of the tarp. Then, because I could not wait to brief him, I walked with him up to Sayer's. I did not want him worrying about the skylight, but he could get to work on the accommodation. I had a lovely plan for making rooms with walls of fish tanks and venetian blinds in front. It would have worked. We could have had light, movement, the sky, privacy, the works. I did not realize that he did not understand, that all he wanted to do was build Hi-Li, that I was bamboozling him with fishes.

But I made a bigger mistake, i.e., I imagined my client in the matter of the reconstruction was my son. Quite incorrect. But as I walked back through the storm with Mr Lo I did not know this. I used the phone at the town hall to order a tarpaulin from Jordan Brothers'. I entered the emporium already calculating the weight of water the fish tanks would add to the fourth gallery.

When Goldstein grinned at me I knew something was up. She stood at the rail. She smoked a cigarette and had a glass of beer in her hand. I did not realize what had changed her until I saw, not ten yards from her, Rooney's eyes. They were, of course, in Emma Badgery's face.

She showed me her teeth. I lifted a lip. No more was necessary between us.

51

While all other directions afforded great security, that eggshell roof, even when intact, sometimes made Emma giddy with anxiety. When she heard the bullwhip crack and saw the sky fall in, she felt a terror so great that it was necessary for her to crawl – she could not stand – down the stairs to find her husband.

Her arrival was heralded by the staff, and Charles, already in a panic about his building, ran up the stairs to meet her.

I knew none of this. I did not understand Emma's requirements in terms of shelter, sustenance and protection. I did not know about the meeting on the stairs. She had defeated me, but I was not yet aware of it.

I sat, that night, on the rubble in the middle of the kitchen trying to work out a way to get the broken bricks down to the ground floor. The tarpaulin flapped like a spinnaker above the skylight and although the wind came through the missing section it was not unpleasant to me – no more than sea air and spray – and I never thought it would be to anyone else. I sat there on the pile of bricks with a leashed lightglobe circling above my head, an echo, if you like, of the old goanna who lay beneath its similarly moving ultraviolet light elsewhere in the gallery.

My view of the gallery, and the goanna's swinging light – a necessary medication to prevent the onset of rickets – was nicely framed by the stepped edges of the high brick arch and, within that, the hard black lines of the RSJs. On the right-hand side I could see, through the lattice, Goldstein at work at her desk. She had a moon-warm light beside her and, as I watched, I saw her stop writing and run her hands through her tangled blue-black hair. I was still under the impression that she was writing a letter, and that, of course, is the trouble with schemes, that they begin as a celebration of happiness and end up leaving you blind to the people on whom your happiness depends.

I could not see Emma, but I knew she had locked herself up in her cage and would not talk to her husband. I had seen him pacing up and down around the bars and pleading with her. She had the children in there with her and I could make them out, could see Henry's dark unhappy eyes as he stared out into the gallery. He would not wave when I waved to him.

Mr Lo was at his drawing-board.

I sat on my pile of bricks and tried to work out a simple lift. I picked up a brick and started to scratch a plan on to it with a nail. It was then I noticed the thumb print in the corner. This is common enough with bricks of this age, produced by convicts down at Brickfields, but I had never been so struck with it before.

I was looking at this, considering a man's thumb print baked into a clay brick, when Charles came up the stairs he had exited so furiously an hour before and, rather than going grovelling to his wife, he came to me.

I was pleased to see him. I made room for him on my pile of broken bricks.

"You see this brick," I said. "You see the thumb print. You know how that got there? Some poor bugger working at Brickfields a hundred-and-fifty years ago did that. He turned the brick out of the mould and, as he did it, he had to give the wet clay a little shove with his thumbs, see. This one, and this one. They've all got it. So there you are. All around you, in your walls, you've got the thumb prints of convicts. How do you reckon that affects you?"

We, both of us, looked around. It was a big building. It was a lot of thumb prints to consider.

"Father," he said, "do you know how much money you've spent today?"

I was very tired, but I did my best to be polite. I explained that once you start a job there is no going back. Then, to get us

542

back on a peaceful plane, I started to talk to him about bricks. I told him how some of them have special marks, the shape of clubs or spades for instance, pressed into them.

"For God's sake," he shouted in my ear, "at least have the grace to say you're sorry."

"I'm not," and, by Christ, I wasn't. I looked out from where I sat. Anyone could see I'd improved it out of sight.

"Not sorry?"

"Charlie, look what I've done."

"It's a mess."

"I'll clean it up. All I need is. . . ." I was going to tell him about the cables, but he wouldn't let me.

"There's no water."

"I'll connect it."

"Don't touch it." He moved himself off the rubble and stood over me. I stood up too. "I'll get a tradesman."

"Why pay a tradesman?"

"You're retired, Father. You're on the pension."

"I've got to do something."

"Go to the beach."

"I'm too old for the beach. No one wants to look at an old man on the beach. I'll trap birds for you."

"I already employ people to trap for me."

"Then let me finish this." My voice went a little strange. I didn't realize I felt so emotional about it.

He came and put two hands on my shoulder. "Father. . . ."

Then I saw her. She was out of her cage. She was standing in the corridor between Leah's lattice and the gallery rail. She had my Vegemite jar in her hand, but if there was a time for getting it back, it was past.

"Father . . . it's the money."

Emma was smiling at me, but the smile was not friendly.

"Have the grace to admit the truth."

"What truth?"

But we never got into it, because Emma came past me and embraced her husband. There, right in front of me, she hugged and kissed him. She gobbled his nose and licked his ear. I had to go away. I could not stand it. It was not the kissing and cooing. It was the bloody words.

"Oh, Emmie," I heard my son say – a big man, fifteen stones – "Oh, Emmie, Emmie, I'm sorry."

52

Rosellas fucked, fertilized their eggs, laid them, hatched their young and did all the hard work feeding them. Fish, marsupials, and snakes all reproduced themselves for our benefit. We were, it seemed, sitting on a gold mine. There was no shortage of anything. My son bought me shirts and suits. Anything I wanted I could sign for at Hordern's or Grace Brothers'. A Parker pen? Yes, sir. Crocodile-skin shoes? Please be seated. A blue dress for the little girl? Fifth floor, sir.

At home there was a special room for me, to compensate, I suppose, for my disappointment. When I say special, I mean it was the same room they put me into in the beginning, but they let me put a window in the wall so that I could look out into Pitt Street. I chose a modern window, steel-framed, and when they put the neon sign out on the front of the building – only a month later – Charles made them design it around my window although Claude Neon, the manufacturers, wanted him to brick it up.

They were so nice to me. They bought me a bed with a drawer under it for my underpants and socks. They built in a cupboard, and then they left me alone. They all had lives of their own, worries, occupations, hobbies, whatever. The bed they bought me was only two foot wide. There was no question of me sharing with Goldstein, not if it was ten foot wide.

Yes, I blamed her for having my scheme stopped. Yes, I was wrong. Yes, I knew at the time. Yes, I was a cranky, bad-tempered old man. All that much would be clear to you anyway. Goldstein, to top it all, had problems of her own and very shortly afterwards she moved out to be an independent woman on her ten pounds a week. As to whether she got leeches on her legs or frostbite on her hands, I have no idea.

I, for my part, sat on my chair. It was a brand-new one (Danish Deluxe was the brand) and I could look out at the signs in the sky. They put up a big blue one a block or two away. ALCOA AUSTRALIA it said. It did not go on or off but it was both beautiful and enigmatic hanging there in the sky, not bothering to explain how it could be both Alcoa and Australia at the same time. It was the first of many. I pretended to myself that they amused me, these visions as fantastic as flying saucers.

When I was bored I would go to Randwick and lose my pension

to the bookies and then I would come back and stand in the street and look up at my window. Not so much my window, but rather the neon sign that surrounded it. Everyone said it was the best neon sign in Sydney. People came from interstate to look at it. It had a flight of king parrots whizzing in a circle round my window, red, green, red, green, you could see their wings flap and their genuine parrot flight pattern, up down, wings out, wings flat. All around the edges were little lights representing golden wattle and the wattle blossoms fell in the electric breeze. It was a beautiful thing – a hundred per cent pure Australiana – and you would never guess that the emporium it advertised was owned thirty-three per cent by Gulf & Western and twenty-five per cent by Schick & Co.

Once I persuaded Charles to stand in my window while I went downstairs to look at him, framed by it. He would only do it once. He was busy with government departments who kept banning the export of his birds. I would have asked his wife to stand there but we were not on speaking terms. So it was Hissao whom I persuaded to stand there instead. I would have him stand on my Danish Deluxe. He would jump up and down on it – I didn't mind that – and I would make that interminable journey down the stairs – I always forgot what floor I was on – and go and stand and look at him.

I was using him, of course, but not in any way that was harmful to him. I was looking at him, but imagining myself as a passer-by and looking up to see ME in there. The question is: how would you take me, sitting there in my chair, neon lit, surrounded by these swirling signs? Am I a prisoner in the midst of a sign or am I a spider at its centre?

Hissao and I had a natural affinity. We had lots more to do than pose in windows and I suppose Charles was pleased to see his father get on with at least one member of his family. The truth was that we both had time on our hands.

So while Mr Lo played his imaginary baseball and Emma occupied herself with her courtesan arts, my grandson and I explored the city of Sydney. We ate waffles at the Quay and raspberry lemonade at the Astor in Bondi. We walked miles at a time and he did not complain when his sturdy little legs were tired. He did not grumble or want drinks when there was nothing but sea water available. We visited Phoebe for dry biscuits and mouldy cheese. We went, hand in hand, round the winding paths of Taronga Park Zoo, through the deep drifts of sand at Cronulla.

We criss-crossed the harbour in ferries and knew the tricks of all the wharfs; the treacherous current, for instance, at Long Nose Point where the water from the Parramatta rushed at the turn of the tide like water roaring out a plughole. We travelled up river past Drummoyne inside the wheelhouse of the *Karingal*. We crossed the heads to Manly in the *South Steyne*, riding the big August swell while tourists vomited their pies into the grey-slicked harbour. We took the creaking *Lady Woodward* to Cockatoo Island and were given a special tour of the dockyard. We saw the innards of a submarine, and afterwards, at smoke-oh, I entertained the men with my story of the bagman's battle with John Oliver O'Dowd. At the time I was fascinated by my grandson's appearance – it seemed to change with the light, or the company. In any case none of the men at Cockatoo Island expressed anti-Japanese feelings towards him.

No one at home seemed very interested in our excursions or what we did. We tried to tell them, but they had other things to think about. They had done nothing to fix up the mess I had made with my opening out and they would not let me do anything to remedy it. The RSJ still bridged the ragged arch. The sink was reconnected but there were still piles of bricks on the floor. In the middle of this mess Charles now cooked the family meals. They did not have time to hear that Hissao was a genius.

You see, I had discovered he could draw. I do not mean like you imagine, not with little red houses and bright yellow suns and a doggie and a chookie in the corner. No, I mean draw, in perspective. He was a prodigy, but no one in the mad house had noticed.

He was only six years old but he did a drawing of me standing in the window. Then I had him do a drawing of the gallery with all the opening out completed. Anyone could tell he had talent.

I knew I did not have a lot of time. I knew they would take him away from me. Some days I did not shave, I was so keen to get him out of the building and on to the streets. He was only six years old, but he understood everything I showed him and when he talked and discussed what we had seen he did not mumble or lose his way in a sentence or forget what it was he was trying to say. I showed him how to look at Sydney and also how to change his walk etc., etc. Goldstein heard all this and paid me a visit to change my mind. She said it was not necessary for the education of an architect, but she knew nothing. An architect must have the ability to convince people that his schemes are worth it. The better he is the more he needs charm, enthusiasm, variable walks, accents, all the salesman's tools of trade.

I showed him, most important of all, the sort of city it was – full of trickery and deception. If you push against it too hard you will find yourself leaning against empty air. It is never, for all its brick and concrete, quite substantial and I would not be surprised to wake one morning and find the whole thing gone, with only the grinning façade of Luna Park rising from the blue shimmer of eucalyptus bush.

I began his education in April, on the day I marched him up the five hundred and eighty steps inside the South Pylon of the Bridge. We were both knocked up when we reached the top, but we were not doing it for pleasure. I was showing him that the pylon was a trick, that while it appeared to hold up the bridge it did no such thing.

Then I took him down to Martin Place to show him the granite facing on the Bank of New Zealand. I was keen for him to see that the granite was only a face, a veneer, and that behind this make-up was a plain brick building, but when I dug around with my pocket knife I discovered that the granite was not granite at all but terracotta tiles, clever forgery by the Wunderlich Brothers who made their "granite" from soft dirt they quarried at Rose Hill.

Hissao could smile and laugh. He did not appear bookish or dull, but he was the equal of the subject. I bought him a blue book with unlined pages and I had him do drawings, of buildings that lied about their height, their age, and most particularly their location. There was not one that did not pretend itself huddled in some European capital with weak sun in summer and ice in winter.

The family looked at his drawings and were pleased, so they said, although I could see they were uneasy. But it was not the drawings that gave them their reason to take him away, but another matter.

You see, the little fellow was the spitting image of Sonia in certain lights, and you can say it was mad, but I bought him a little blue dress and a pinny and I had him put them on. There was no danger in it. I got him to do it in the privacy of my room. Then I got him to stand up on the chair and I went down to the street to have a look.

I arrived on the footpath. I turned, pretending the sign had just caught my eye. I looked up, and there she was. What a pretty little girl my Sonia was. She tugged at the long sleeves of her dress and then waved her hand. I was still standing there five minutes later when Charles and Phoebe Badgery appeared beside my little girl. Then they all looked down at me but it is Charles whose figure now comes most strongly to mind – I will not easily forget the beckoning finger he put my way.

53

I was not myself. I was not as calm as I would have wished. I knew they were within their rights, but I thought it unnecessary for them to take him away from me so soon. I know they meant to do their best for the boy, but I had not hurt him. I showed them the book of drawings, but Charles was grim and pale and he said Hissao was going to a boarding school in Melbourne.

Boarding school. He was so young. It was painful to think of him in his little cap and uniform, by himself, six hundred miles from home.

I went to Charles's office and begged him to reconsider. He was not nasty to me. He was very gentle. But he would not change his mind.

There was nothing left for me but to teach myself to be an author. It was the only scheme available.

54

Dear Mr Badgery, she wrote, her head on one side, her pencil crooked between her finger, her handwriting so tiny and exact you would never believe she had once danced so fluidly.

Dear Mr Badgery, she wrote in a room in Pitt Street while I lay in bed two miles away with half my brain collapsed and nurses whispering around my peripheries.

Dear Mr Badgery, (so sarcastic)

Dear Mr Badgery, my name is Leah Goldstein. I am forty years old and, as you have already noted, my arse has begun to drop. Sometimes I exaggerate. Sometimes I like to imagine people are better than they are. Oftentimes I prefer to overlook some little fault and make them appear more beautiful than they really are. But I am not a liar, and these notebooks of yours are – excuse me – unpardonable.

I do not mind that you have stolen so much of what I have

written. Is that what you were doing crawling around on the floor pretending to kill cockroaches or kissing my feet when I already told you they were dirty? A hundred things come to me, things that amused me at the time, touched me – and now I see they were only excuses to thieve things from me. And even then you have not done me the honour of thieving things whole but have taken a bit here, a bit there, snipped, altered, and so on. You have stolen like a barbarian, slashing a bunch of grapes from the middle of a canvas.

If only you had said what you wanted, I would have helped you, gladly.

And why have you been so unfair to us, to yourself most of all? Why this desire to make yourself appear such a bad man? Do you think it is sexy? One would never know from your writing that you were a man worth knowing, a man worth waiting for. If you had not been do you not imagine I would have found another? They were there, don't make me list them, decent men too, and I was not in any case the Victorian Aunt you so smugly pass me off as. You do not, of course, mention where I went in '49 when I moved out. All you can bring yourself to say is that I was set on being an independent woman with my ten quid a week. You wonder, sarcastically, if I got my leeches and frostbite while what you worry about is that I took a young man's penis into me and you have the discomfort of knowing that young man and having met him and having his gentle brown eyes and strong features taunt you. So your casual superior tone does not match those great dramas you and I suffered in the name of "love".

It is not polite of me to write these words in your own book. But vandalism begets vandalism and, anyway, I am drunk. I am angry and it makes no difference that you are lying in hospital with tubes in your arms and down your throat or that I only found your little hoard of notebooks looking for your lost pyjamas.

Why do you pose as the great criminal, the cynic? Why do you always make me seem such a dull goody-two-shoes? Why do you not say how we laughed and danced together and lay in each other's arms on warm beaches and smelt jasmine and honeysuckle and admired fish with silver scales? You were a kind man, or I imagined you were, and you would cry like a woman for someone else's pain.

You seem to delight in making yourself seem stupid and I suppose that is your business if you want to. But why do you give no credit to anyone else? You know very well how it was you were transferred from Grafton to Rankin Downs and it was not because "I knew I had to get out of there" but because Izzie worked very hard on someone at the Department of Corrective Services and that there was a large bribe involved which your son paid. Wasn't this worth remembering?

Likewise with Mr Lo – you are content to have him with his imaginary baseball and his somersaults. This is all true, but why do you leave out the part your son played fighting the Immigration Department through to the High Court? You know how expensive it was, and also how proud he was to do it, and how proud you were of him as well.

But instead you choose to dwell on things like the American ownership of the firm and our dependence on it. It's all true. But it is not the whole truth, and I admit that I spoke in a derogatory way about that dependence, that I said we were pets, but when I came back in '51 we did some good work together.

You say you had to teach yourself to be an author, which you know is a lie. But I will not dwell on that. Would you have written about the books we wrote together – *Gaol Bird*, particularly? Probably not, but it is just as well because you would have made them sound like smart stunts and deliberately forgotten that each one of those books had a purpose, that we tried to do some good things and were not embarrassed about it either.

Oh, Mr Badgery, what an old heartbreak you are. You have left out everything worth loving about the emporium. You left out the pianola. And when you leave out the pianola you leave out the very possibility of joy, and suddenly there is a dreadful place, gloomy, oppressive, without music. But don't you remember the singalongs we had that went to four in the morning with Charles rocking back and forth at the pedals and Nathan Schick in his seersucker singing those songs from *The Student Prince*? You used to love it. "Come boys, let's all be gay, boys, education should be scientific play, boys." But where the pianola sat you describe some sheets of plywood leaning against a wall, so you left it out on purpose, just as you leave out Henry and George, and this is really, I am sure, because Henry bit your finger.

You have treated us all badly, as if we were your creatures. I forgive you for not mentioning my lover, but not for omitting my membership of the Labour Party and the success of the books.

I have always been optimistic about you. I have always thought that you would finally respond to love and kindness and that, in the end, you would feel safe enough, loved enough, to have no need for bombast and exaggeration. But tonight – writing down these lines in the full knowledge that you may well recover and actually read these lines – tonight, I don't care if you die.

55

It was a cool morning in September 1961 and the fishermen on the sea wall at Deloitte Avenue, having been lured from their beds by clear skies and bright sun on their whiskered faces, now found themselves replacing their soggy baits with numb fingers. A breeze had sprung up from the south-east; you could hardly call it a wind, but it was thin and penetrating none the less and the fishermen drew their coats around themselves and clenched their soggy cigarettes between their lips while they waited for the tide to turn.

There was, however, no weather in Charles's office, nor any sign of it, unless you count the creaks and groans of the old building as it weathered the sea of commerce, as ancient floorboards adjusted to the shifting weight of the staff or anticipated the arrival and departure of customers. Because it was still early you could hear the squeaking wheel of the old pram they used to carry the trays of food to the pets. There was the distant whine of the floor polisher. Somewhere a shop assistant with a high nasal voice was relating a joke from the *Perry Como Show* but, because of the eccentricities of the building itself, it was impossible to tell where he stood. The cash register, having rung once (to have its change checked) and rung a second time (as its drawer was shut) was now silent.

There were no windows in Charles's office, although there was a frosted-glass panel in the door which bore the legend, "Knock and Enter". Charles sat behind a large cedar desk, the surface of which was obscured by a great many papers, some flat, others crumpled. He wore a single-breasted navy linen suit and a striped navy tie. If you saw him in a photograph, Leah thought, you would see the image of a powerful business man and you would think him cruel and efficient, a cold ally of Gulf & Western, a smuggler of threatened species, a briber of customs officers. You would see the pouches beneath his eyes and you would not understand them; you might not even think about them but they would guide you, just the same, to the conclusion that he was debauched; it would not occur to you that the bags were caused by weeping.

His hands were still shaking as he tried to get a Viscount Kingsize from Leah's pack. His fingers were too big and – because it was a

551

new pack and the cigarettes were still tight and his nails were clipped short – he had difficulty. She wanted to take the pack from him and do it for him, but he was upset enough anyway, so she waited.

"There are times", he said, when he had at last lit the cigarette, "when I could kill her."

Nothing changes, she thought. We have the same battles over and over. He forgets how many times he has said this to me. She wondered if passion, like pain, was something that could not be truly remembered, that one could only remember that one had felt the pain but one could not remember the pain itself.

"Kill her, really kill her."

Perhaps he did remember. Perhaps he was trying to tell her that this time was really different, just as he had tried, on all those other occasions, to stress how different they were.

"Murder her." He held up his two hands. The right one held a smoking cigarette. "I can imagine how her neck would feel between my hands."

He was not capable of killing anything, Leah thought, and it would do no good to tell him that he would soon smother his anger in the warm roundness of Emma's belly.

"I keep her, I feed her, I do anything she wants. She wants to send her sister a koala bear, I do it for her. I could go to gaol for it, but I do it. But now I ask her to do something for me, what does she do?"

He sucked on the cigarette and exhaled it, Leah thought, just like a little boy blowing out a candle.

Leah Goldstein was nearly fifty years old, and although she had put some weight on her backside she normally presented the world with a thin, dry, nicotine-stained cynicism. She flicked open the Viscount pack and when she lit her cigarette she revealed her liar's lump, the callus where her HB pencil fitted against her finger.

They sat there then, the pair of them, in silence, smoking. A yellow shadow came towards the frosted door, hesitated, then turned away. Has he really forgotten, Leah thought, is he capable of forgetting the number of times she has stoked him to exactly this point?

And then, because she was Leah Goldstein, she looked for parallels in her own life, and found them in the number of times she had left the comforts of the pet shop and returned to them again, the number of times she had immersed herself in Labour politics and then become bored and impatient and given them up for the pleasures of beer on Bondi Beach where, beneath that fool's blue sky she had sought the company of flash characters, racecourse touts, used-car salesmen, and each time, through each cycle, she had been like Charles, like a person waking from dreaming and forgetting that she had been through all these things so many times before.

And here she was, back living in the pet shop, amongst the fatally flawed Badgerys, and here was the nicest of them feeding off his own rage.

"How many times", she asked him, although she had intended not to, "do you think you have had rows like this one? A thousand? Two thousand?"

Charles put out his cigarette, not neatly, but so the paper was torn and its warm tube of tobacco was exposed, lying ruptured amongst the dry ash. "This is different."

"Oh yeah?" You could see in the smile, in the softness of the voice, that the dry cynical tone was a pose and had no more connection to the real Leah Goldstein than her black turtle-neck sweater or her brown desert boots.

How many times had she hated Herbert Badgery and then forgiven him? And why was each time so new, her feelings so fresh as if they had never been unwrapped before?

"Look," he said.

"I'm looking."

"Look, if *Time* magazine wanted to write *you* up for one of your crummy books. . . ."

"Thank *you*."

"You say they're crummy."

"Only about some of them. Some of them are very good."

But he was too obsessed to detour and discuss her work and even if he had not been, he had no feeling for the subject and would never see what their author now saw – that the real subject of Goldstein's work was not the people, but the landscape and its roads, red, yellow, white, ochre, mustard, dun, madeira, maize, the raw optimistic tracks that cut the arteries of an ancient culture before a new one had been born.

"If *Time* magazine were coming to interview you," Charles said, "you wouldn't want them to see the circus on the top floor. How would you explain it to them?"

"I'd say, this is my wife and this is Mr Lo who won't go home. Please excuse the mess."

He laughed then, at last, but soon he was serious again.

"All I wanted was for her to make an effort. For one day."

"Simmer down, chum. Have you got an ashtray or are you going to hog it all to yourself? Nothing catastrophic has happened. You've been like this before and it'll pass. Every time she rubs the stupid goanna's belly. . . ."

"It's not its belly she rubs."

"Every time she does it you want to kill her. That's why she does it. You even know that's why she does it. And you can stop enjoying your temper, it's a nasty habit."

"I can really imagine killing her."

"I bet you can," she said, watching him prolong his feelings, like a man getting the last drag out of his cigarette before he burnt the filter and made himself ill on the taste of burning synthetic.

"I can feel my hands wanting to go round her neck like you want to put your arms to hold someone and. . . ." He stopped suddenly, blushing. He hid his confusion by picking up a pile of papers, vets' reports for the month of August. "Pneumonia and trauma," he read out, as if this was something to do with it. "Trauma, Air Sacculitis, Too Decomposed, Trauma." He read belligerently, as if these were Emma's fault.

"We can imagine all sorts of things, sausage," Leah said gently. "That's why we're not living in the trees any more."

Charles flicked through the pages, and then placed them roughly in a manila envelope from a drawer. He wrote something on an envelope.

"One day I'll do it." He placed the envelope in a wire basket. "I'm sure that's how murders happen."

There was something rather prim and self-conscious about this. Leah did not believe it and she did not like it. She put out her cigarette and lit another one. The phone on the desk gave a small "ding" as the switchboard operator began work.

"Will you please ask Emma to tidy up?"

"Work is already in progress," said Leah Goldstein, grinning widely. "Your father is supervising."

"Supervising. How can he supervise? He can't even wipe his bottom properly."

"He's supervising."

"She can't stand him. She won't do a thing he says."

"She's co-operating. She listens to him very carefully."

"I can never hear a word he says."

"Charlie, are you listening? We are making you look ultra-respectable for tomorrow."

"Why didn't you tell me before?"

"I wanted you to appreciate how clever I am."

They laughed then. They enjoyed each other's company. They always had. And I will not, in demonstrating this, discuss the first night that Leah Goldstein lived in the emporium, when she had taken up residence in the flat itself, was made a bed, had a proper room, etc. All I know is what anyone else knows which is that someone drank a bottle of whisky that night and on the following night Leah took up residence out on the gallery next to Emma.

Charles picked up the telephone and ordered tea. He pushed back his chair and put his feet up on the desk. Leah smiled to see that he had white tennis socks showing between his navy suit and black shoes.

"I'll tell you what I'm worried about."

"Your socks, I hope."

He sighted along his legs, frowned. "Maybe they're doing a story on bird smuggling. They might think that's what I'm up to."

"Are you?"

"Ha ha, Leah. Very funny."

The girl brought the tea in and they watched her pour it. She was thin and fair with almost no eyebrows. She could not have been more than sixteen. Leah was shocked to see that she was nervous of bringing tea into the "boss's office" and also to see that Charles hardly noticed it, that she did not even exist for him.

When she had gone, Charles said, "Nathan wants me to. He won't say it on the phone or put it in writing, but that's what he wants."

"Wants what?"

"He calls it expediting, but he means smuggling. I think the bloody government wants me to as well. Every week they ban the export of something and they wonder why the economy is in a mess."

"What's the girl's name?"

"What girl?" he looked up, blinking irritably. He still had his legs on the desk but he leaned forward, put sugar in her tea, stirred it for her and pushed her cup and saucer as far as he could.

"The fair girl."

Charles understood. He looked towards the door, staring, it seemed, at the diffused images of suspended neon lights, and then he shrugged. "Maybe it would be better not to do it. I don't

555

have to be interviewed. They can't make me." And then, seeing the expression on Leah's face – "Glenda. Her name is Glenda."

Leah drank her tea silently. Her view about the interview was complicated, even contradictory. She was as suspicious of it as Charles was, although for different reasons. She knew that Gulf & Western and Schick wished to buy out their Australian partner and she suspected this was, somehow, part of the ploy. She was wrong, but the mistake is understandable. It was a time when the Americans were making their first big push into Australian industry.

Her second thought was that it was rather pathetic to need to be well thought of by *Time* magazine, to tidy your life, to sanitize it enough to be acceptable to Henry Luce.

But when she had finished her tea and placed the cup carefully in its saucer she knew that she would say neither of these things to him, that it would not only be cruel but also fruitless. And it was to compensate for her secret unkindness in thinking such thoughts that she let her other feelings, her simple love for Charlie Badgery, dominate.

"Maybe", she said, "it would help if Hissao was here. He could talk to them first and if there was going to be trouble, you wouldn't need to talk to them at all." She did not really trust Hissao, but she judged him perfect for this job.

"Do you think he would?"

"For God's sake, you're his father. He'd love to." And when she saw him hesitating, measuring, again, how much he was loved by his family, "Come on, Charlie Barley, do you want the Yanks to write you up or not?"

It was a speech that she was to remember afterwards with much regret.

56

Hissao remembers the day well. Really they were two days – September 11th and 12th, 1961 – but in his mind they are only one day. He remembers them as days full of unlikely events, days that coincided with the real beginning of life as an adult, days of great beauty, but also of grief. Actually one must include a third day, although, placed in order, it is not the third day, but the first of three. On this day, September 10th, a Monday that had predicted the full-blown arrival of spring, he had smoked marijuana for the first time, lost his heterosexual virginity in the back of a '52 Humber, and listened to a record – forever to be associated with these events – of Miles Davis and John Coltrane playing "Round Midnight".

The next day, the eleventh, was quite cold, cold enough for him to huddle into his leather jacket as he sat in his corner seat at Gino's, a small Italian coffee bar which was tucked away in a little lane on the edge of Chinatown. He was hardly in hiding – the place was a common meeting place for a certain set of students from the university – but it was a most unlikely place to meet any of his family.

Hissao liked Gino's. You could buy a minestrone and a bread roll for two and sixpence. There was a printed menu that showed a cartoon of a beatnik type walking up the walls above the heads of jiving couples; he left footprints on the ceiling and these footprints were repeated, in real life, up the walls and across the ceiling of Gino's although no one had ever been known to dance there.

Hissao had been there, at the same table, the evening before, and had bought the willowy clarinettist a Bacci which, she insisted, was Italian for kiss. So he was not hiding. He was merely sitting there, playing with the sugar bowl, writing her name with salt on the table, dreaming through the clouds of espresso steam. He had finished his coffee, had scraped out the rim of remaining froth with his teaspoon, and he sat there wondering what he would do next.

Hissao was eighteen years old. He was unnaturally short for a Badgery, a little over five foot tall, but he was also nicely proportioned. When he removed his shirt, men were either surprised or thrilled (depending on their sexual predilections). He had a gymnast's body and it was obviously the product of some serious work; yet it was made charming, almost comic, by the biscuit-barrel chest which had come to him, via his mother, from Henry Underhill.

The chest excluded (or even included) he had somehow slipped through the genetic minefields his progenitors had laid for him. Not only were his legs straight but he avoided the lonely excesses of masculinity represented by his bull-necked, jut-jawed Easter Island father. He had curling black hair, smooth olive skin, and red cherubic lips which suggested, strongly at some times, weakly at others, an oriental parent who did not exist.

This, the question of Hissao's name and his face, was not a

thing that was, any longer, discussed in the family. It had been discussed on only one day, the day of Hissao's christening in October 1943, when Charles had emerged into the bright light of George Street and discovered – it was brought to his attention by his angry mother – that his son was not called Michael at all but had – his mother was so cross she was spitting as she spoke – an enemy name. You could not, to be precise about it, really call this ruckus a discussion, so we can say then that the matter had never, ever, been discussed within the family. Outside the family, of course, was another matter and, as a boy at school, he had been granted no immunity.

By 1961, however, the only signs left of his childhood battles were the gymnast's chest, the unexpected biceps, the pronounced pectorals, and the tendency to slur his name on occasions so that it came out "Sau" which was often mistaken for "Sal" or "Saul".

For the most part he did not act like a damaged young man and his laugh, that great indicator of personality, gave the clue. When he laughed (which was often) he produced a singularly awkward noise, a great tottering tower of a laugh with chains hanging off it and odd cubicles protruding from its shaking upper storeys; not quite normal, but not damaged either, and endearing for being so awkward and, once you had got over the shock, infectious. It was a laugh to stop an old man being cynical, to make him smile, toothlessly perhaps, but smile to see that the product of a fearful imagination could turn out to be so likeable a young man.

The laugh made everyone in Gino's look up, not at Leah Goldstein, whose unexpected entrance had precipitated it, but at Hissao.

"I want to talk to you, laddie," said Leah and made him laugh even more and thump his foot as well. He was laughing at the joy of coincidence, the magic of chance, that Leah, who had never walked up this cabbage-dank, milky-drained laneway before should not only do it now, but choose to open Gino's unwelcoming door, just at the time she wished to speak with him.

Consider though, as they scrape their plastic chairs around and order espressos, that here are two people who can watch a Chinaman's finger change into a leech without suffering any great alarm. The woman once saw a man disappear before her eyes. The young man has a face that no one can satisfactorily explain. Yet they do not greet each other like beings who might, between them, change the shape of cities, of past, of future. They do not, as they might, embrace as the children of magicians, as magicians themselves who could, if they decided to, fill the night sky with brand new neon. No, they behave like servants. They giggle like idiots because of a . . . COINCIDENCE.

They drank strong black Italian coffee and ate great fat Italian doughnuts with that little blob of jam always lying unpredictably just at the place where you cannot, even if you wish, save it to last.

Hissao, perhaps influenced by his surroundings, looked rosy-cheeked and Tuscan. Goldstein wore a silver medallion with her black roll-necked sweater. She wore a white leather coat, not because of the weather, which she had been unaware of as she dressed, but because of a shyness about her widening bum which no one who knew her would have guessed at.

"But why can't he ask me himself?" Hissao asked when Leah had made Charles's request. He was pleased, just the same, to be asked. His father had never before thought of him in so adult a way.

"You know he's shy."

"I'm his son."

"Then you should understand him. He's frightened you'd say no."

"But why me?"

"Oh, you Badgerys." Leah was smiling, but the irritation she expressed was real enough. "Why do you always angle for compliments? You *know* why."

Hissao coloured, but he also grinned.

"It's because I'm personable." And Leah marvelled that it did not sound in the least conceited. It was conceited, of course. It was a classic Badgery conceit. (Perhaps not a conceit, in that it was true, but it was unpleasantly complacent.) She realized, looking at this young man whose ructious christening she had attended, that she did not know him at all, only in the way an aunt might know a nephew. He was so pretty and so sure of himself that she gave him no credit for any ambitions other than selfish ones, and even while she admitted that she was prejudiced against him, she believed her prejudice well founded.

"Whoever this man is from *Time*," Hissao said, still smiling at her, "I'll get on with him. That's why you're asking me."

"That's about it, I suppose."

"I won't lose my temper, no matter what he says."

Leah nodded.

"This is very important to him," Hissao said, spilling sugar from the shaker into a neat pile on the table. "It is probably the most important thing in his life. It is like an exam for him, what do you think?"

Leah shrugged. She lacked the young's enthusiasm for simple explanations. She was irritated by the growing pile of sugar on the table, by Hissao's very red lips, by the dark long-lashed eyes he held her eyes with.

Don't you try and con me, you little smarty pants, she thought.

"I wish he would ask me himself, just the same."

"Oh, he will," Goldstein said, standing suddenly, and she left the little coffee lounge without even shaking hands.

That afternoon his father visited him in his rented room and, as one man speaking to another, asked his help. Hissao was very moved. He shook hands with the grating firmness that men use to express their gentler emotions.

That night he went to find the clarinettist but she had returned to Melbourne and he found himself, at half-past ten at night, in bed with her friend, a very plump young lady who liked to drink rum with clove cordial in it.

Eighteen is an age that gives a false impression of life, as if every day will bring with it similar surprises. The next day was only to confirm this. Hissao still had half a reefer, a gift from the departed clarinettist. He smoked it looking at himself in the mirror of his wardrobe. The room itself was very small and gave no indication of being the room of an architecture student. There was no hint, no sketch or notebook, no paperback or snapshot, to suggest the importance of the work he would later undertake: the building that might yet – who knows – change the history of his country. Neither would you guess, from the evidence presented by either the room or its occupant, at the fierce nationalism that fuelled him. This was not a boy who would be waylaid by Henry Ford or be seduced by the beauties of cockatoos or the soft hands of Nathan Schick. He had an education. There was money behind him. He did not need to rush out and make a quid and he had an ambition that he had nurtured within him as long as he could remember.

The room will reveal no secrets to you, but I will tell you, anyway, what was in it. It had a window on to a laneway, a very narrow bed beneath the window, a dressing table opposite, and a large walnut wardrobe with a mirror, this last on the wall between bed and dressing table. There was a mirror on the dresser too, but it was the mirror on the door of the walnut wardrobe he looked

560

into as he smoked the reefer. His inquiry was not narcissistic but scientific – he wished to see what the drug did to his perceptions now that he had the opportunity to concentrate on something more neutral than the smooth texture and unexpected perfumes of a woman's skin. He was disappointed to find that nothing altered very much.

"We", he told the mirror, "are going to fix this bastard right up."

He was referring, of course, to the gentleman employed by Henry Luce and you will note, at once, the slightly unpleasant and combative tone of the salesman but there is also so much glee contained in it, an anticipation of the joys of a difficult battle, that even a person of fine scruples, sensitive to the vulgarity of the salesman type (such as yourself, Professor) need not be offended but rather challenged by the contradiction contained herein, ie. that this crass aggression can co-exist with an ability to draw very fine moral distinctions and to see, very objectively, the damage his father's business was doing to the fauna of the country he loved and that, further – like real estate for instance – it was one of those great Australian enterprises that generate wealth while making nothing new.

When Hissao set out to charm the fellow from *Time* he did it because he loved his naïve father and wanted to protect him from hurt. But he did not approve of the pet shop and although he imagined his father as an innocent he thought him a very dangerous innocent. He did not extend the same generosity towards his two elder brothers who were embarrassed by the pet shop for other reasons but who took money, when their father offered it, to help buy suburban houses.

So the boy was acting in bad faith? Perhaps. But he was also an optimist. He knew that the signs in the sky of this city were made only from gas and glass. He knew gas and glass could be broken, the gas set free, the glass bent into other shapes and that even the city itself was something imagined by men and women, and if it could be imagined into one form, it could be imagined into another.

He arrived by taxi outside the emporium at eight thirty to find the footpath had already been swept and hosed. This was a warm morning and the water on the footpath was evaporating. It felt humid, luxurious, grubby, tropical. The window was full of little firetails and the background had been painted with the dun-khaki that is the firetail's dominant colour so that as the little birds flew to and fro their bodies disappeared and only their ember-red tails showed, like flying sparks. This was Van Kraligan's work, not his father's. Hissao checked his reflection in the window. He had worn a conservative suit to make his father feel confident and relaxed, but the bow tie was a secret code addressed only to himself and to those few who might read it – he had stolen it, of course, from Corbusier.

The door was unlocked for the staff. Hissao, however, did not enter immediately but crossed Pitt Street and stood amongst the crowds waiting for the Woolworth's sale. He looked across at Badgery's Pet Emporium, at the neon-signed parrots circling his grandfather's brightly lit window.

His grandfather, Hissao thought, was dying. So he was surprised to see him there, sitting bolt upright in his chair, like the captain on the bridge. He was dressed in a grey linen suit and a panama hat. The elastic of his tie was limp and showing at the edges of the knot, but his eyes were that splendid violet colour they would always show at the beginning of the day. Hissao, without knowing why, shivered.

"Oh, Master," he said, and giggled.

When he entered the emporium the cannabis played its gentle tricks on him and exaggerated the rust on the white-painted cages and the odour of mildew on the stairwell. He suddenly felt very sad.

He went into his father's office – it was tucked in neatly underneath the stairs – and stood staring at the framed photographs that had so impressed him as a boy. But Ava Gardner was already mouldy and Lee Marvin had been damaged by a leaking aquarium on the floor above and even his good wishes, sincerely meant too, had dissolved into a smudged watermark.

The sounds of the morning were all around him: the whining floor polisher, the creaking wheels of the old food pram, the groaning noises of the building itself which seemed to wheeze and fart like an old labrador, old, moth-eaten, too stubborn to die. He sat at his father's desk and began to tidy it for him (and you can look at this fastidiousness of his as one of the few obvious reactions against his upbringing). There were consignment notes from carriers, letters from collectors, trade magazines from all over the world, the vets' reports that his father had read out, so belligerently, to Leah Goldstein. These vets' reports, being roneoed copies and therefore on hydroscopic paper, were damp.

It was the first occasion in his life when he had felt the sadness of time. He was overcome with it there, in his father's office, with the damp paper between his fingers. He felt it in everything. He felt it in the rust and mildew, even in the box housing for the neon tubes above his head which he had once, in his innocence, thought so modern.

He knew why the building was so damp. Its damp courses were defective and it was built on top of the tank stream. He tried to cheer himself by imagining opening up the basement, going down to reveal the historic stream itself, having it run through transparent pipes, but he knew now what the tank stream must look like – a drain, a sewer, no different from other drains and sewers.

His father, coincidentally, had become concerned about rust, and Hissao found him with a pot of white paint trying, when it was already far too late, to hide the evidence from *Time* magazine. He had already put white paint on his good suit before Hissao managed to persuade him to give the touching-up job to Van Kraligan who, for once, did not complain or argue. Hissao watched the stern-faced Dutchman as he took the can of paint and saw that his eyes were all aglitter with excitement. Everyone was waiting for the Yanks.

Hissao then wandered up the stairs to say hello to his mother and was astonished to find all the evidence of normal family life removed. This only exacerbated his sadness. Downstairs his past was rusting, but up here it had been obliterated. It felt cold and sterile. They had removed nets and ladders, the stacks of unread newspapers, the steel drums, the piles of bricks, the abandoned children's toys, balls of wool, lengths of dress material. They had put pot plants in Goldstein's apartment and set her desk outside and put Mr Lo at it so that he was pretending to be a clerk. They had polished the floors and painted his mother's cage. He could see that they had begun to brick up the arch above the RSJ, but had obviously panicked at the lack of time left, and painted over the unfinished job. The goanna had been removed, presumably not without protest from Emma, and placed in a large cage on the ground floor. It had been fed "pinkies" and was now as sleepy and inert as a sunbather.

Hissao shook hands with Mr Lo who was, as usual, so pleased to see him that he felt embarrassed. If he allowed himself to, he would become very cross with Mr Lo who was now free to stay in Australia but who would not leave the building he had lived in so long.

He found his mother in the kitchen sitting on a high stool with her handbag in front of her. He could see that she was bright and excited about the visit too. She had put on a big feathery hat and gloves and lipstick.

He hugged and kissed her. He was pleased – he always was – to see her. She was overweight, she wore old-fashioned clothes, she had no interest in the world outside and only the most perfunctory grasp of his university studies, but she was his mother. They loved each other uncritically. She admired his bow tie and smoothed his hair and then patted the stool beside her for him to sit on.

It was then that Emma produced the old Vegemite jar.

Hissao looked at the bottle with the polite attention another son might bestow on his mother's favourite maidenhair fern, or on a pear tree, new ducklings, a cabbage bed or white-stalked celery growing up through cardboard tubes. The ritual with the bottle was so familiar that he did not even think about it. For the most part the contents of the bottle had been as formless and unpleasant as the sort of stuff you will pull out of a blocked grease trap, but occasionally there were leeches and once a fine creature, as thin as black cotton, which swam with the graceful movements of a snake.

But on this occasion his mother showed him a foetus, half goanna and half human. And I know I said, when I mentioned the subject before, that Hissao did not look, that the liquid was murky, that he could not be sure. BUT OF COURSE HE LOOKED. He was not only polite, he was naturally curious and if someone says that they have your brother in a bottle, of course you have a squint at it. It had fingers (they were perfectly formed) and a face in which you could make out features which had that mixture of soft-mouthed vulnerability and blandness that is the hallmark of the unborn. Where you might expect toes there were long claws, thin, elegant, shining black like ebony; there was also a tail which was long, striped, with very obvious glistening scales.

Hissao, quite suddenly, did not know where he was. His head span. He stood up, and was dizzy, so sat down again. His mother, momentarily, took on the appearance of a total stranger. He leaned across to the kitchen tap, turned it on, and collected water in his cupped hands but when he drank he could taste only the whale-fat flavour of his mother's lipstick. Just the same, he did not realize that he had seen a dragon, only that he was ill and frightened.

"Jesus." He felt ill. "Oh, Emmie, Emmie." He shook his head.

A conversation then took place and I must translate for you, for Emma would rarely speak clearly and although I must write down her question (i.e., "Is my boy cross?") had you been there you would have heard nothing but her murmur, or, if you were lucky, the last word like "doss".

"Just a bit of fun," said Emma to the young boy with the Corbusier bow tie. She took the bottle back and put it amongst the muddle in her handbag. "Is my boy cross?"

Hissao shook his head. He had a heavy feeling around his forehead as if there was a steel band clamped around his head.

"He's your half-brother, after all."

"Emma," Hissao was working hard to gather back his sense of the world. In this he was not helped by the unnaturally tidy appearance of his childhood home. "Emma, you are wicked."

She patted his cheek with a gloved hand and the feeling of kid leather where he had expected skin was also disturbing. He shivered, just as he had shivered, not ten minutes before, standing in Pitt Street.

"Don't you show that to anyone today."

Emma pouted.

"Promise me you won't show it to the journalist."

"All right," she said.

She kept her promise to the very letter, i.e., she did not show that bottle to Charles until the journalist had departed. Until that moment she did nothing but play the humble wife. She was asked two questions and she answered them both with lowered eyes and a gentle murmur. She pulled her fox fur around her shoulders and clutched her bag in front of her. Only the journalist and his photographer thought her peculiar.

Hissao did his work perfectly. When the question of smuggling was raised it was easy for him to answer honestly. He was passionate on his father's behalf. He spoke very quietly, with a sort of hiss in his voice. He attacked the "criminals" who were involved in this activity. He was enthusiastic about the Best Pet Shop in the World. He spoke at length about the necessary protection of Australian fauna. Thus he shuffled true conviction and cynicism, dealt a hand, guessed an answer, did his little act so slickly that when the journalist saw the photographs he was not only surprised to discover that he had been Japanese but that he was also diminutive.

57

Charles's opinions about himself had always been a tangled ball of string and while he thought himself stupid, clumsy and ugly, he also thought of himself as a Good Man. He was generous to his staff, he never cheated on his taxes, he supported any charity that asked him, voted for the political party which would tax him most heavily and distribute his money fairly. He was scrupulous in his business affairs, always meeting the requirements of the Health Department, the Customs Department, the rights (real and imagined) of his customers.

And although he guessed that the journalist from *Time* might talk about smuggling, he was not really prepared for the effect it might have on him. He could not bear to be accused of it.

Later he could not even remember the journalist's face or the sound of his voice. All he could remember was the accusation (what he imagined to be an accusation). Christ Almighty. So they had found suitcases full of dead rosellas at San Francisco airport. Why come to him?

Hissao began to answer. Charles was in such a fury he did not appreciate the great skill with which he was being defended. He plunged his hands so hard into his pocket that he burst the fabric it was made from and his car keys fell down his leg and on to the floor. The journalist's parries were turned aside, but Charles did not notice the turning aside, only the parries themselves, these razor-sharp slashes, stabs and lunges and the proprietor was pricked and cut – there was no shield could save him.

So the McMahons' parrot was extinct? Why come to him? He was Charles Badgery. He had ordered people off the premises for suggesting lesser things, backed them down the stairs and locked them out in the street, for intimating, say, that he used special lights to brighten the colours of a parrot's feathers. These incidents were all family history, funny to recall, but nothing had ever happened like this before and it would never be funny.

The interview was conducted as they moved around the cages. Charles hardly listened. He simply grasped the existence of thirty million Americans who would think him a bad man. They were on the stairs when the man began asking about Herr Bloom in Munich.

Now Charles knew nothing about Herr Bloom, except that he

paid his bills and sent, each year, a Christmas card showing a bird from his famous collection. He had never talked to him, not even on the telephone, and knew nothing of his affairs. But now, hearing a certain tone in the journalist's voice, he was keen to defend his customer. He began to do so.

Hissao, on edge, skating very prettily on ice as thin as a cigarette paper, hissed at him: "Shut up."

His own son!

He began to feel enemies line up all around him. His son treated him like he was nothing but a piece of dog shit. His wife, his wife at least, had smiled gently and squeezed his hand while they took the photograph. When she spoke to the journalist she said that her husband had always been a good provider. The journalist had not understood her, but that was not the point.

Charles had no idea the interview had been a triumph. He shook hands with the journalist and did not realize he had been admired, that the journalist felt himself to be soiled and compromised in comparison.

He heard his son take the journalist down the stairs. He remained in the fourth gallery, shattered.

Even Emma had understood that the interview had been a success. She would not, otherwise, have been so reckless as to choose this moment to display the foetus in the bottle and claim to be the creature's mother.

Charles tried to snatch it from her, but he got the mixing bowl instead. His neck went red and blotchy. He started to say something, but the words got tangled and tripped over themselves and he ran unathletically, heavily, his arms flailing, across the gallery and down the stairs, three at a time, falling on the second landing, rising, bleeding, bawling to Van Kraligan to get a hessian bag.

58

She knew her babies were wrong. They were thoughts that could not be born. And, besides, they would never stay still, and you could not be sure that you had seen what you had seen. It was like looking at clouds drifting across the skylight – one minute you had a knobbly white-faced man all covered in warts and urticaria, and next it was a Spanish galleon in full sail across the top of the yellow Sydney sky.

But this one was different – it stayed the same. It moved, and breathed. You could see the heaving of its tiny ribcage and the clutching movement, just like a real baby, of its elegant, beautiful black claws.

You could see, anyone could see, it was related to the goanna, and she did not show it to her Charlie Barley to tease him, or taunt him, but she did not mind, either, that this had been the result.

She did not quite know what to do with the creature she had made but she was relieved, at last, to have the thing still, and not be so frightened by it.

She took a silk scarf from her handbag and spread it carefully on the kitchen bench. Then she took the magic foetus and placed its bottle in the centre of the scarf. She drew the corners together and knotted them. Next she swept up the shards of the mixing bowl her husband had broken. She swept up in the style of a tradesman cleaning up after a job, that is to say that although she made sure all the splintered pottery was in the dustpan where it would not hurt anyone's bare feet, she did not empty the dustpan itself but left it sitting on top of the feed bin for someone whose responsibility it really was.

She could still hear her husband's angry voice and the voice opened gates to well-used sandy pathways in her brain. She became sleepy-lidded and puffy-lipped. She put her blue patent handbag in the crook of one bare plump arm and picked up the knotted scarf and held it in the other hand. And then she began to walk around the gallery. It was now highly polished and very slippery so she kicked off her shoes and, having let them lie where they fell, walked on. It was still too slippery so she stopped, put down bag and bottle, unclipped her nylons from her suspenders, rolled them down, took them off, picked up what she had put down, and walked on, bare foot.

Emma promenaded. In spite of her corsets which were very expensive, French in origin, black in colour, and her fussily fitted brassière, which, together, pushed her form, as near as it would go, to a fashionable shape, Emma Badgery, whilst promenading, exhibited a barrelling type of sexuality – she walked with a roll of the hip, a long strong slouch, her head high, and, because she walked without self-knowledge or self-criticism, there was something rather dirty about the way she did it. She walked, round and round, unaware that she was, in the eyes of Mr Lo – whose desk she knocked, deliberately it seemed, twice – just a barbarian. She was expecting her husband to reappear and when he didn't she dropped herself, quite suddenly, into her chair which was not where it should be (outside her cage) but next to the stairwell so that she had the unexpected bonus of feeling the excitements on the stair itself, pleasant vibrations that went right through her bones and guided her thoughts, in fits and starts, towards those other vibrations she had experienced as a young dull bride-to-be in a Mercury sidecar when she and the young man had roared down from Jeparit to Bacchus Marsh and all her feelings had been like a foreign country to her and the whole of her young body had felt itself moving to the beat of the engine and she had been safe and cocooned inside with all her old textbooks full of useless knowledge jammed uncomfortably around her feet.

They had come down the first time in the train, because Charles would not let his precious birds travel alone and then, a week later, they had gone back to Jeparit to get the AJS. They had gone together and had been ridiculed by her father for not thinking to put the motor cycle on the train in the first place. What fun he had got from his ridicule, what joy from his temper at the waste of money involved. Her daddy had stamped his polished boots, a quick tattoo, one two, one two, as he criticized them as "spendthrift fools".

And she would never forget coming down the long snake road through the bare cold Pentland Hills towards the Marsh, to be wrapped up so cosily while even the finest winter drizzle felt like a drill of needles against the skin of her young girl's face.

Charles was shouting on the stairs. They were both so lucky. Perhaps the children had suffered because of it, but neither of them had fallen into the businesslike habits of father and mother. She was lucky. It was a pig in a poke and who could have foreseen the poke in the pig? Who was to tell her, who could have predicted, that a man so strong-armed and bristle-faced would suddenly reveal himself to have lips like a baby's when the lights were out? All that kissing and sucking under the sheets.

He had fetched her, from the very first morning, breakfast in bed.

"Brekky," she murmured now, sitting alone in the chair. "Emma wants her brekky." Her Mum and Dad would never have believed that shy Emma would have the nerve to ask for such a thing and yet, precisely because she was not used to it, there was a pleasure in the request itself that was quite extraordinary. It made her nipples go hard, as if she had taken off all her clothes and was standing, brazen, in the middle of a paddock, or up to her knees in

569

swamp water. There was no one to stop her. No one could laugh or pull her hair.

She was lucky and she never forgot how lucky she was and she put him ahead of the children, the two eldest in particular, and they did not like her any more and kissed her only on her cheek with two lips that felt as hard and cold as abalone, all muscle – she would rather they did not kiss her at all – or kept their lips inside hard clamlike shells where they belonged. It was wrong to not love them, to love the youngest more than the eldest, the husband more than even the youngest and sometimes she did care, and she cried that she had made them unhappy, but not often and not for long, because in the end it was what she wanted.

She was lucky to have the business, not only that, to own the walls and roof that contained the business. But she did not like to talk about the business itself, and although she understood – she understood perfectly, exactly – that he might wish to talk to her about it, she did not wish to hear the problems about the business. It was something she would rather not know. It was not a woman's place anyway. And even if it was, it wasn't her place. It was like being in a sidecar and sticking your head out to look at the wheels turning; it could make you fret when you saw how thin the spokes were or that three of them were rusted and five bent, and you should not know, either, about the patches on the tube, or the lack of tread on the tyre. When Charles wished to discuss business with Henry Underhill's daughter she would not permit it.

She sat in her chair and felt that delicious sense of anticipation her teasing always produced in her. It was woman's art. He would not go roaming the streets tom-catting like Mr Schick.

Tonight, or tomorrow night, or even the night after, he would come to her to apologize for the broken bowl. That's why she had left the broken pieces out on the dustpan, so he would not have a chance to forget them. That's why she had left it out. So he would see it when his temper had gone and he could come to her to say sorry. She would judge then what to do, to accept, and hold him in her arms, or to put it off a while longer, to spurn him, to push him to the next giddy level of pleasure.

"Brekky," she murmured, sitting in her chair, "Little Emma wants her brekky."

The journalist, meantime, was walking along George Street carrying a mental picture of her husband – a bubbling baggy-suited enthusiast. He had felt his spine tingle when he saw the man handle the bower-bird. He now found himself wishing, in a way that he imagined he had long ago abandoned, that he might do something decent and sensible with his life. He wished that his days were involved with straw, feathers, simple affections, and he resolved, walking into the Marble Bar, to make Charles the good guy in his story on the fauna-smuggling racket. By the time he had made this decision, Charles had changed into a maniac. He was grappling with an old scarred goanna and pushing it belligerently into a hessian bag. He would not say what it was that he intended although the staff were nervous, knowing this was Mrs Badgery's special pet. They wished no trouble from "her upstairs".

Hissao watched this ruckus without pleasure. He waited to excuse himself, to go back to the university and continue his real life. He was suddenly tired of the pet shop itself, its odd echoes, ghostly floorboards, smells and, most particularly, the caged creatures which should not be caged at all. Having defended his father so skilfully he now felt disgusted, not only with himself, but with the activities he had shielded from attack.

Yet it was Hissao who held the heavy bag of struggling goanna while his father went to get his car keys. They then walked together, father and son, out into Pitt Street where the car, a new-model Holden, was parked outside Woolworths. He waited for his father to unlock the boot. Then he dumped the heavy bag inside, stepped back on to the footpath and, as he did so, his eye was caught by the whizzing parrots. The light inside his grandfather's room was very strong, a vivid blue-white neon so that when the old man sat there, as he did now, as he had before, he seemed as strongly lit as the famous sign that moved around him.

The colour of the eyes could not, surely not, have been discernible from the street, but Hissao was sure it was. He felt, later, that the eyes had bullied him, had made him hold out his hands for the key when he had been meaning to shake hands, to say goodbye.

"I'll drive," Hissao said, and his father dropped the keys into the outstretched hand.

59

Do not think I have no feelings. A stroke may remove one side of your body but it does not cut one's passions in half. No, no, everything is doubled. Twice the pain. Twice the grief. And just because a thing must be done do not imagine that one necessarily relishes it.

No, it is no fun to watch your little boy drive out of your life and my heart, that day, was drilled with icy needles that have never melted. I feel them still, this moment, when I breathe. I cough hard, but all I get is some white dribble to run down the deep unshaven gullies on either side of my mouth which is, no more, I promise, the Phoenician's bow that so beguiled Miss Phoebe McGrath in 1919.

I sat in my chair and watched the hessianed goanna dropped into the boot. I knew, that day, that God is a glutton for grief, love, regret, sadness, joy too, everything, remorse, guilt – it is all steak and eggs to him and he will promise anything to get them. But what am I saying? There is no God. There is only me, Herbert Badgery, enthroned high above Pitt Street while angels or parrots trill attendance.

Hissao put the car into first gear, that insouciant click and clack, made a hand signal (it was the years before indicators became legal) and pulled out into the traffic of Pitt Street as if he was doing nothing more than driving to the corner shop for a *Sporting Globe*. No one saw, no one but me. Goldstein was on her way to have lunch with Doodles Casey, her florid-faced publisher. He was my publisher too, but he thought my brain gone to porridge. Once he visited me in hospital where he wiped my nose; I have never forgiven him, the charlatan.

But Casey is a man of no importance, born for deletion; it is Charles and Hissao we are here to spy on as they cross Darling Harbour on the old Pyrmont Bridge.

They were quiet as they entered the dead-fish stench that hangs beneath the old incinerator at Pyrmont. They said not a word until they reached the hotel that is now known as Wattsies but was, in those days, the plain White Bay Hotel.

"How do I seem to you?" Charles asked.

"How do you mean?"

"How do I *seem*?"

It was an impossible question, and it was expressed in an unusual voice, light, with a reedy vibrato. Hissao put the car into gear when the lights went green.

"Have you seen my bottom?" Charles asked.

"What?"

"Have you", Charles sat sideways in his seat to look at his embarrassed son, "seen my bottom, my bum?"

Hissao smiled but it was not the charming smile of the urbane young man who had discussed the pet business with *Time* magazine. His eyes showed his embarrassment and his smile hurt his face. "Not for a while," he said.

"Was it wrinkled?"

"Oh, Dad! Please."

"Was it?"

"Yes, I suppose so."

"Yes," said Charles, with some bitterness, and then faced the front. They drove on in a silence that Hissao found almost unbearable. They crossed that bridge – I forget its name – the ugly steel box that lay, on that day, across joyless wind-whipped water the colour of a battleship.

"You shouldn't have told me to shut up."

"I'm sorry."

"I bought you your own car. I pay for your university fees, I give you money to live on. I don't ask for much from you. (Keep going up Victoria Road.) I never thought I'd ever hear you tell me to shut up."

Hissao had to change lanes to stay in Victoria Road. He tried to explain, at the same time, why it was necessary to stop his father's comments on Herr Bloom but Charles was not really listening. "Anyway," Hissao said, "he liked you."

"He thought I was a crook."

"No, really. He didn't."

"Thought I was a crook. Maybe I am a crook. Do you think I'm a crook?"

"No."

"Well, he thought I was a crook. All he saw was this big building. He thought I was a moneybags but do you know what I see when I look at that building, all those people employed, all those families fed, all those beautiful pets being shipped away all over the world? Do you know what I think?"

Hissao knew the answer. He had heard it before.

"I think it's a bloody miracle."

They kept driving along Victoria Road while Charles told the story of the business, right from the day when Emma's father had said she had a bum like a horse. He went through his first meeting with a bank manager, the guarantee by Lenny Kaletsky. He could remember every bird he had brought down from Jeparit, and the price of every animal, fish, bird and reptile he had ever sold. He would recall a year in his memory because it was the year that an important specimen had died or another incubated.

At Silverwater Road he had Hissao turn left and they proceeded down through that industrial wasteland across the polluted river and on towards the Parramatta Road.

"There never was a day", Charles said, "when I did not want to be the best at what I did. Do you believe me?"

"Yes, Dad, I do."

"When I was a little nipper no one paid attention to Australian birds and animals. It's all changed now. Me and Nathan, we did that."

"That's terrific," Hissao said and his father looked at him in a way that made him ashamed of the ineptitude of his response.

"I never meant anyone any harm," his father said.

It was a grey overcast day and a low blanket of cloud sat over the industrial puddle-dotted wastes of Silverwater.

"Nowadays you can travel all over the world and find Badgery's birds in all the big collections, Hamburg, Frankfurt, Tokyo."

Hissao, of course, knew all this. He had heard it many times before. His father never tired of repeating the names of cities he had never been to.

"Holland," said Charles, crossing his calf across his heavy thigh. "France, Tokyo."

"You said Tokyo."

"Yes," said Charles. "Turn right."

They drove out to Parramatta in heavy silence. When they arrived at Church Street Charles had him turn right again and it occurred to Hissao that his father was not thinking about where they were going.

"You're intelligent," Charles said as they passed the last of the Parramatta shops. "You can spell, you can write, you've got an education. Do you think there's a God?"

"No, I guess not."

"No," said Charles. "I suppose there isn't."

"Will I go back into Victoria Road?"

"Yes. We'll go to the tip at Ryde."

As they crossed the start of Silverwater Road, Charles said: "Would you say I was a success?"

"Yes."

"And your mother?" His voice was actually shaking. Hissao saw that his cheeks were wet. He did not know what to do. "Would you say she was a success too?"

574

He tried to hold his father's hand but it was clenched into a fist and did not respond to holding.

"Drive," Charles said. "Is she?"

"Yes, in her way."

Later Hissao was to regret his wooden awkwardness, his stiff inadequate answers to all these questions and yet they were not really questions at all, but echoes made by Charles's ricocheting thoughts.

Hissao found the tip and drove, at last, through the low scrub. They bounced over a bush track and arrived at a large bulldozed clearing the perimeters of which were piled with garbage. Magpies and crows rose and settled. Small black flies entered the car through the open windows and then clustered on the inside of the windscreen trying to get out again. The place stank.

Hissao was under the impression that his father was going to release his mother's pet. There would be trouble, he knew, but he did not judge or interfere. He knew that goannas were natural scavengers and imagined his father had chosen the tip because – in all the city – it was the best source of food for it.

Yet when Charles lifted the animal from the boot he also picked up a rifle. He dumped the bag on the ground and clipped a ten-round magazine of .22 bullets into the rifle. Then he untied the string of the bag and emptied the goanna on to the dusty clay ground.

The goanna was nearly twenty-four years old now and rarely moved if it was not necessary. It would lie with its head resting in its food tray and when Emma placed its food there it would eat without altering position. Now it seemed oblivious to any danger, although its tongue flicked in and out as it tasted the new air.

Hissao was frightened.

"You bitch," he heard his father say. "You fucking evil rotten bitch."

Two bullets struck the reptile in fast succession. The noise was empty and metallic. It looked as if he had missed, although the range was only twenty-four inches. Then Hissao saw the blood oozing from eye, and mouth. There were more light, sharp shots. Red marks appeared on the big head, no more serious than sores on the flaking scaly skin. The reptile did not rise up on its rear legs, inflate its throat, slash out with its claws. It tried to get under the car. Charles fired three more times, from the hip, with the tip of the muzzle three inches from the victim.

Hissao turned away. He looked over towards the city. He tried not to hear the things his father said about his mother. He could see the Sydney Harbour Bridge and the AWA tower and he did not see his father do it. He heard a grunt.

It takes only a second, this sort of thing. I have gone through the motions myself – it takes only a second to reverse the rifle and put it in your mouth. It had nothing to do with his financial affairs or his loss of control to his American partners. It was a mistake, most likely because the day was overcast, because the grey sky sucked all the joy from the land, because there were puddles at Silverwater, because the goanna did not die cleanly, because it suffered its wounds in silence, because it could not scream, because there was rust and enteritis and because he misunderstood what he had seen in a bottle.

He left us in charge of Emma, his sole heir, sole proprietor of the Best Pet Shop in the World.

60

Leah Goldstein had worn her suit expecting to be taken somewhere smart, but Doodles Casey had taken her for a counter lunch instead. At first she had been miffed and had drunk quickly and angrily. Then she had seen the funny side of it and drunk quickly and gaily. They had rough red wine and her lips now showed a cracked black mark around their perimeter.

The taxi driver, of course, had not been close enough to see the thin black outline to her lips. He had seen a respectable woman in a suit in Macleay Street and he had picked her up.

Only when she got into the car did he smell the grog. She directed him to an address in Pitt Street.

He drove quickly but also – having had to scrub out the back seat once this week – went very gently on the corners and did nothing to jolt his passenger or make her giddy.

He turned up the radio so that he would not have to talk and thus protected himself from the risk of drunken acrimony.

The news came on 2UE as they were heading up William Street. The first item was about a man who had shot a goanna and then shot himself. The announcer, you could hear it, was smiling while he read the item about the "Bizarre Double Suicide". When the item finished he played "See you later, Alligator".

The taxi driver, in spite of his resolve not to speak to his passenger, made a comment. He looked in the rear-vision mirror and saw his passenger's face collapsed in grief.

Oh shit, he thought, as the volume of the grief rose higher. Drunk women were the worst. He turned up the radio even louder, but he could still hear her howling. He drove quickly, a lot more quickly than he had planned. He dropped her outside Woolworths and she gave him a pound, pushed it into his hand and wanted no change. He saw her in the rear-vision mirror as he drove away. She was standing rigid, staring up at the building across the road.

Leah Goldstein looked up. There was Herbert Badgery, sitting in his chair, listing slightly towards the collapsed side of his brain, surrounded by the waltzing neon rosellas.

"You bastard," she said.

Passers-by made a diversion so they need not brush her. They left plenty of room.

I watched her from where I sat. I saw her cross Pitt Street at an angle. She looked neither to right nor left. When she arrived at the stair inside the emporium, I felt her. I felt the footsteps all the way to the top floor and then around the gallery rail, and through the kitchen.

The door opened.

"Kill *me*," she shouted. "Kill *me*."

She was very drunk and I was exceedingly weak. It was almost impossible for me to move, but I persuaded her to lie down on my little bed and I gave her my basin for when she was sick.

She never remembered what she had said that day, but it unnerved me just the same, as if all my carefully constructed world was unravelling in my hands.

Old men do not need sleep. I sat up all that night beside her. I watched the signs. I held everything in place by the sheer force of my will.

61

Inside that little plastic chapel the widow wailed and wept. Thank God she did. At least it was an honest noise. It was ugly, yes, and full of suffocating gulps and shrieks as big as ripping sails, but I would rather listen to it than the regurgitated pap that poured out of the smiling officiant.

"Chas", I quote his very words, "is sitting with God."

I don't know what brand of Christianity he belonged to (the dickhead) but he had modelled his style of speaking on an American tape recording. He had stood at home, miming the words into his mirror, had folded his talcum-smooth hands the way the manual told him to, had done it again and again until there was only the slightest trace of his Australian accent left and the natural nasal flavour was cloaked in a rich sugary sauce.

It was, he told us so, a happy day for us all.

There was an Acrilan carpet in mottled browns and bright aquamarine chairs to sit on.

When he had said his words they played a Wurlitzer organ and slid the coffin out on rollers just as, in the cool stores in Bacchus Marsh, they slid the cases of apples through the shed. You would never guess that that shiny box contained a man, my boy, a skin-wrapped parcel of fucked-up dreams.

We went out into the sunlight, on to the gravel. Henry's and George's wives made bookends for the widow. Goldstein tried to busy herself with taxis.

All those old people getting confused about which taxi they should be in – stooped thin Sid Goldstein with his paper-dry hands. Wheezy old Henry Underhill trying to order the ranks. Phoebe walking with exaggerated care across the sun-bright quartz worried, as always, that she would fall and break a hip. She had more black plumes than a funeral horse and she approached my wheelchair all netted in black, a pale bony hand extending.

The wheelchair had a curious effect on people. They came and stared at me as if I was a fish at the market.

"How is he?"

I said: "Not long for this old planet now."

They couldn't understand a word I said, and it didn't matter, because I was only lying to cheer them up. Death was their hobby, their dream, their fear, the only subject worth consideration.

Afterwards we went back for drinks at the emporium and George and Henry puffed and grunted carrying me up four flights of stairs.

You would not glorify the affair by calling it a wake. They were all too old and depressing and I went to my room and left them to mutter about how ill I looked, I could hear them sighing and farting and rattling their cups in their saucers, but I had serious matters to attend to – I had my Vegemite jar back.

The thing that killed my boy was not half goanna and half human at all. Neither was it one of the shifting miasmas that had so frightened Sergeant Moth. It was a dragon, a solid being, two inches tall. When it saw me the evil fucker puffed up its throat and showed its red insides to me. Oh, Christ, it was a nasty piece of work. It reared up on its hind legs and scratched at the glass with its long black claws while its whole body pulsed with rage, changing from a deep black green to a bloated pearlescent grey.

I did not start to battle with it immediately. In fact I made myself ignore it. I began by working on the rusty lid with a little piece of wire wool. This may sound simple enough, but when your left arm does not work it is a difficult enough task to occupy all your attention. When the lid was shining clean I used meths and rag on the glass while I listened to Emma's keening through my door.

If the death had not also revealed the financial frailty of the structure on which the family relied, it may well have served to draw us all closer together.

Those jumbled pieces of paper on Charles's desk contained enough information to indicate that the business was not only making a loss, but that the situation was not acceptable to either of the other two shareholders. This was no longer, as everyone thought it was, Schick Inc. and Gulf & Western. Gulf & Western had sold their holding to a Chicago company called Jayoyo Pty Ltd whose function no one knew. The majority shareholders, it would seem – they had not said so in writing – were willing, eager even, to continue their support of the business providing the lucrative banned species could be "facilitated" out of the country. Charles had blithely ignored all such requests.

The state of the books suggested only two possibilities: either the family complied with the majority shareholders or they sold out to them.

Everybody had a different point of view. I heard them squabbling through my door and I know that it is an important part of any funeral, that the squabbling and thieving takes people's minds off their grief. That was the day Henry's wife stole a pair of rare apricot-coloured budgies which she claimed Charles had promised her. George took the mist nets. Even Henry Underhill (whose heart was bad) tried to get away with the ladder, although he had to abandon it on the first landing, where it stayed, propped against the wall, for five years.

Emma would not take any notice of them. It was a week before any one could get her to pay any attention to the question of the future. I took no direct part in this. No one, by the way, asked me to. In any case, I was busy with the Vegemite jar. I crooned to it. I sang it songs as well as I could. In the end it behaved no differently from any nervous horse which, although it may snort and rear and flare its nostrils, can be quietened in the end.

But although I took no part in the discussion I saw, from my window, big bow-legged Henry stride across the street with his pretty wife in trail. I saw all the supplicants – George, Phoebe, Van Kraligan – they all came, all of them. Some carried briefcases, others rolls of paper, others no more than a belligerent face.

Goldstein came and told me of their propositions. I kept my bottle under my rug while she fed me porridge. She talked about how stupid they were, that they could not and would not accept the situation, that the days of the pet shop were over – there was nothing left to argue over. She did not need my answers but I gave her some gurgles anyway. The building would have to be sold, the debts paid off, the company liquidated. You should have seen her eyes – all afire with her enthusiasm. She fed me fiercely, happily, shoving in porridge before I had finished swallowing the last lot. There would be just enough money, she said, to buy Emma a little house and give her a pension.

The rest of us, she said, would have to make our own arrangements.

But Goldstein's agitated happiness was premature because when the widow understood the situation, she became very quiet. She was, at the moment Goldstein finally made it clear to her, sitting behind her late husband's cedar desk, with her thumb under the edge, and her fingers flattened on the top.

"This is my home," she told Leah Goldstein.

"Emma, look at this." Goldstein pushed a bookkeeper's journal towards her, but Emma would no longer look at figures written on paper. "It is not your home at all. It belongs to the Yanks."

Emma murmured and ran her fingertip along Goldstein's arms.

"Emma, you've got to face reality. You are not calling the tune. They are."

Emma smiled. It was the first time she had smiled since Charles had died.

"My boy will look after me," she said, meaning Hissao, although she did not name him.

"Emma, he can't."

"Oh yes he can," said Emma. "You watch him, girlie."

The last person to call Goldstein "girlie" had been Mervyn Sullivan. She did not take to it at all.

62

Leah Goldstein no longer saw the building as a construction of bricks, mortar and other inert matter. It had fibrous matted roots that pushed down into the tank stream. It sweated and groaned and sighed in the wind.

Its whole function was entrapment and its inhabitants could happily while away afternoons and years without any bigger scheme, listening to the races on the radio, reaching out for another oyster, worrying only that the beer glasses were free of detergent and kept, cold and frosted, in the fridge. They discussed the quality of the harbour prawns, got drunk, and crunched the prawns' heads, imagining themselves free and happy while all the time they were servants of the building. It made them behave in disgusting ways.

Leah looked at the cold hard look in Emma's glittering eyes. It was not grief. It was something else and Leah recognized the feeling as one she had known herself.

As she followed Emma out of the office Leah vowed, in a properly formed, silent sentence, that she would stand, one day soon, in Pitt Street and watch the emporium fall to the earth as sweetly as a dress slipping off a coat-hanger, dropping softly, lying formless, broken in the dust.

To this end she took Hissao to a beer garden in Redfern. She did not choose Redfern for any particular reason. It happened to be a hotel that she knew from Labour Party meetings and it was close to the university. Later in the day it would turn into a snake pit and, as it reached its broken-glassed climax at six p.m., it would be a place where crims paid off coppers and, occasionally, shot their competitors. But at this time, eleven in the morning, it was sunny and fresh and the wall-eyed barman had hosed down the bright gravel and driven, with the force of the water, yesterday's cigarette butts and dead matches out of sight. He had picked up the sodden paper napkins and the bare chop bones and Mich Crozier's was ready for another day.

The term "garden", of course, gives a misleading picture of Crozier's – it was a mostly shadeless area of crushed quartz like the Parramatta used-car yard Mich had owned in the 1950s and, in the middle of this blindingly white sea was a redbrick island labelled LADIES and GENTS. If you did not mind the smell you could enjoy the shade the toilet block provided or, if you did mind, which Leah did, you could choose one of the tables next to the lattice that Mich or Rosalie had nailed to the paling fence and screwed to the brick wall of the printing works next door. They had planted jasmine too, but people kept pissing on it and it died.

The tables were slatted, with each slat painted a different fairground colour and, as it was almost impossible to make the tables steady, beer spilt easily and then dripped through the slats.

Hissao sat there with beer-wet knees in his corduroy trousers, looking across at Leah Goldstein, wondering why she had asked to meet him. She wore a pleasantly faded blue-checked shirt, the simplicity of which was contradicted, or at least underlined, by a thin gold chain she wore around her remarkably smooth neck. Her hair was untidy, flecked with grey, and she had pushed it back from her handsome face as if she were impatient with it and had more important things to consider. She lit a cigarette in a very businesslike way, inhaled, exhaled, and lined up her packet of matches with her cigarettes.

"Cheers," she said, and raised her glass as if she were in the habit of drinking beer at eleven in the morning every day.

"Cheers," said Hissao. He was a little frightened of her and also very curious. He had known her all his life and yet knew nothing about her. He guessed, but had never been told, that she had been his grandfather's lover. She had been married to the notorious Izzie Kaletsky. She had been a dancer in the Great Depression. She had had an interesting life and he hoped that, in the hothouse emotions generated by his father's suicide, they would, at last, be able to speak to each other. He felt they would have much in common.

Leah, for her part, was suddenly nervous of Hissao. She had not been expecting nervousness, but she was keyed up about her objective and she suddenly felt that tightness in the throat, the slight tremolo in her voice that she experienced when called to speak in public. She knew nothing about Corbusier and thus missed the significance of the bow tie. She thought he looked unpleasantly slick, like a real-estate salesman.

Hissao began to talk to cover the uneasiness of silence. Nothing in his manner or the timbre of his voice suggested anything but social ease. He felt shy and awkward.

He made some observations about the nature of beer gardens and wondered, out loud, about the habit of painting the slatted tables in different colours. Perhaps, he said (suddenly hit with the idea that she had brought him here to tell him that his father had not been his father at all) perhaps the colours of the tables were really a reference to seaside umbrellas and deckchairs, a signal about leisure and working-class holidays by the sea.

Leah heard only urbane drivel of the type, she imagined, people spoke at cocktail parties. It made her less confident of success, but she waited for him to finish, smiled when he had and, having provided enough punctuation with a deep draught of cold bitter beer, told him what she had come to tell him. Her voice was too tight. She had the sense of talking into a deep well, of shouting against air. She ignored her quavering voice, and pushed on, outlining the risks for him, both legal and moral, of doing what his mother seemed to want, i.e., running the emporium as their American masters wished.

Hissao had no intention of being a lackey. He was not worried about these so-called risks. He was worried that Leah Goldstein seemed serious and unhappy.

"Ah," he said, raising his eyebrows comically, poking gentle fun at the seriousness. He tilted back on the chair and then dropped forward. "Ah so," he said, making himself look as Japanese as anything in Kurosawa, "Ah, so . . . deska?"

Leah misunderstood the performance. She was suspicious of the smiling face and all this animation at a time when he should, given what he had witnessed, be filled with grief. He was spoiled and young and corrupt and she saw, in his white collar and smarmy tie, the salesman's desire to please.

"So I am directed to be a smuggler, eh?" Hissao smiled into his beer. It was easy to forget he was only eighteen years old. "That's the plan. The business is viable after all?" He was being funny, so he imagined.

Leah had never been good with irony. She lit a second cigarette and frowned.

"We'll all be rich," Hissao said gaily. "We could have sports cars and lovers." He was joking of course, but he dropped the word "lovers" into the stream of his talk as deliberately as a fisherman letting a mud-eye float past a watching trout. He wanted Goldstein to talk about lovers, her lovers, his mother's lovers. He wanted confessions, secrets, all the lovely laundry of the past.

It was, however, the wrong approach for Goldstein. She thought him frivolous and silly. She gave him a stern lecture on the American takeovers of Australian industry – a subject she had been researching for the Labour Party – and talked about the political ramifications of it, both in terms of ever-increasing dependence on

American investment and the paybacks a client state must make, like fighting wars in Korea and other places.

It was all unnecessary. Hissao knew almost as much about the subject as she did. He was soon bored and boredom – because he was not a meek young man – soon gave way to irritation.

"I see," he said, now parodying the very quality Leah had misread in him. He filled his beer glass from the jug. "But it doesn't matter, so long as the Resch's is still cold."

She took the bait and that made him really cross. He clicked his tongue loudly. It was an unexpected enough (and sufficiently loud) noise to make Goldstein stop.

"Do you really think", Hissao said, his cheeks burning, "that I don't know all that stuff?"

Goldstein opened her mouth combatively and then shut it cautiously. She tilted her head appraisingly. At last she said: "I don't know you."

"No," he said. "You don't."

They were both embarrassed then. Leah poured more beer for both of them and Hissao began to talk again, deliberately trying, with words and enthusiasm, to bleed the poisonous temper out of his system.

"Leah," he said, "even if I had no principles at all, I wouldn't do what she wants."

"She's your mother."

"Yes, yes, she's my mother, but I wouldn't do it. Out of pure self-interest I wouldn't do it. Out of egotism, I wouldn't. Out of pride, arrogance, ambition."

He listed motivations that, because they were a little unsavoury, he judged she would believe more readily than fine ones.

"You see," he said, smiling, but not calmly. "I'm going to be a great architect."

He took one of Goldstein's cigarettes and lit it with not-quite-steady hands.

Then he was a young man, all afire with enthusiasm and ambition. And Goldstein, who knew herself to be living amongst the rusted wrecks of lives, felt very old and grey and cynical and she envied the smooth skin of his cheeks and the clarity of his eyes and she felt herself giving way to his will as he talked about greatness, *his* greatness, as if it were a thing so certain that he could touch it. He said it made the skin on his fingers go taut – he showed her where – and the quick beneath his nails tingle. And Leah was entranced and repelled by him at the same time. She felt – as she had done when she saw the bow tie – that he was decadent, that his smile was overripe, his skin too smooth, his teeth too white; but there was also something else about him that contradicted this, something untarnished and tough, as precise and unblunted as a surgical blade fresh from its paper wrapping. She had seen this, this tough thing, when he had clicked his tongue.

And yet, through prejudice no doubt, she began to distance herself from him. She leaned back in her chair and dropped her cigarette into the gravel. She listened carefully to what he said – as if the words were a typewritten transcript with no passion or any inflexion. It seemed to her that all he believed in was his ambition. She was wrong, of course, but she was also stubborn in her opinions, and clung to first impressions long past the time when a reasonable person would give them up. And now she remembered a time – she had thought a great deal about this time recently – when everyone she knew seemed occupied with the problems of belief and principle. They had gone about it inelegantly, stumblingly, stupidly often, but at least it had mattered to them and even Herbert Badgery, a blue-eyed illywhacker, had so wished himself to be a man of principle that he had imitated a Wobbly and fought the railway police.

But architecture, she thought, was no better than bird-smuggling. She was not insensitive to architecture. (Quite the opposite, as we have seen already.) The new buildings of Sydney cowed her and seemed, in their intentions, no better than the old ones she wished destroyed. They seemed merciless and uncaring, like machines of war. They rose in disciplined ranks and cast shadows in the streets while the night sky was all abloom with their alien flowers. And this, because it was the only architecture that seemed to matter, was the only architecture she could see. She therefore interrupted Hissao to demand that he confront the path he was choosing, that he admit the companies he worked for (she assumed companies and he did not contradict her assumption) would almost certainly have values that were against the interests not only of fish and birds, but also of marsupials and mammals, human beings included.

By then they were drunk, although neither of them realized it. Their combativeness was not without joy and when Leah dragged him out the side gate (she intended to show him the city skyline, but there were plane trees in the street which blocked the view) she took him by his hand and laughed when he resisted. When the skyline would not reveal itself, no matter how they jumped, they went into the bar and bought another jug of beer. Then they went back into the bright garden which was now, at lunchtime, redolent with burning meat and alive with the small blue flashes of burning chop fat as Mich Crozier's customers cooked themselves their famous five-bob barbecues.

Neither Hissao nor Leah ate. He was telling her that there was not yet an Australian architecture, only a colonial one with verandas tacked on. She said the only suitable architecture should be based on the tent. He agreed with her. She was surprised. She then talked resentfully – Hissao thought – of Mr Lo who was happy to stay where he was and be fed and did not need to worry about what it meant to be Chinese and that she, for her part, was sick to death of trying to decide what it meant to be Australian. She then began to contradict herself, to say there could never be an Australian architecture and he was a fool for trying because there was no such thing as Australia or if there was it was like an improperly fixed photograph that was already fading.

When Hissao objected she told him he was immoral and politically naïve.

Hissao then told her that he had smoked a reefer and had sex with a sailor on the night his father died. He tried to talk about the jumble of emotions he felt about this death and which she too, presumably, felt; he looked for some good thing in the aftermath of the nightmare.

Goldstein was shocked and revolted, but also astonished, that in spite of all the things about the boy that offended her (the sailor most of all, but also the drug-taking, the lack of belief, the lonely egotism of ambition) that they could at least agree on this question of the Badgery Pet Emporium, that it was a business that could no longer be innocently pursued.

She had the numbers. The pet shop had been done in. Stumbling through the glare of Abercrombie Street towards the city, they stopped to formally shake hands on their agreement.

So when she arrived back at the pet shop with a bad headache and blistered feet, she did not pay very much attention to the mumbling grunting conversation being conducted by Emma and Herbert Badgery. She saw the widow had regained possession of her Vegemite bottle. Its lid was now rustfree and, had she cared to look inside, she would have seen it contained filigree, like coral, and that bright blue fish were flitting in and out of it.

The matter of Hissao's future had been decided in her absence.

63

Blame? You wish to discuss blame?

But look – I am growing tits. You may worry about that before you worry about blame. So bring on the dancing girls, bring on your young men with callipers, your snotty-nosed physiologists. Let them poke and calibrate if you think it will tell you anything.

Take my photograph any way you like. I told you already, I don't care about the legs. You wish to know why the breast on the left is different from the one on the right, why their skin, in all my withered chest, is there so taut, so smooth and marble white that you get a bulge in your pants examining me? No? You are more interested in blame?

You wish to know who was to blame for the death of the last-recorded gold-shouldered parrot.

Very well.

The last-recorded golden-shouldered parrot was destined to take its species into extinction, to breathe its last breath in the honey-sweet embrace of a beautiful woman.

Its golden shoulder (or, more precisely, wing) was the least remarkable feature of this creature which now, as the crime commences, is being gently sedated by my grandson Hissao who has been good enough to put his personal ambitions to one side for the welfare of his family.

The beak is now carefully – fastidiously even – tied together with fine white thread and its precious jewel-like wings are likewise being battened down for travelling. This bird is very valuable – the proceeds of its sale will feed us, clothe us, pay our overheads for three months, publish *Malley's Urn*, contribute several thousand dollars to the Vietnam Moratorium Committee, and keep my grandson in the George V for six weeks if he wishes it. So naturally he handles it with great respect. Even when he sews it inside a small pocket where it will lie, head downwards, for the next thirty hours on its journey to Rome there is a gentleness in his movements, a sadness even, a sensitivity unimaginable in a man who felt himself called to be a smuggler. Hissao is not one of those greedy fellows whose suitcases, full of dead birds, incorrectly drugged and badly packed, are occasionally intercepted by customs officers.

This bird is as beautiful as a Persian carpet and it will travel in no suitcase, but nestle inside Hissao's baggy trousers, just beside his penis.

The snakes have already settled inside the lining of his jacket. There are two children's pythons, one in each sleeve. The young man has a natural affinity with snakes and they will, he knows, find the warmth of his body agreeable. No sedation is required.

Hissao now holds out his arm for the coat which Leah Goldstein, having first inspected him critically, hands to him silently. It is ten years since they met in Mich Crozier's and their relationship is cool and formal, and yet neither of their passions is any less and Goldstein, in particular, seems eaten away by her feelings so she has become very thin and gaunt and her eyes have dropped into the shade of their sockets so she gives the appearance of a stern and rather malevolent bird.

Hissao thinks her a hypocrite to accept money from an enterprise she so obviously disapproves of.

Goldstein thinks of him very much as she thought of him that day, except she no longer puts any store on his ambition. And yet it is still there and it has grown, like the roots of a tree constrained too long in a pot, so it is hard and matted and dry, the old wood and the fine hair all compressed into one hard dark knot.

They both stand to admire the effect in the mirror which is now the dominant feature of this room where Charles once incubated the eggs of lyrebirds and bower-birds, an occupation that now, contrasted with its present use, seems blameless. The incubators have long ago ceased to tumble and they stand, silent, heavy like very old-fashioned refrigerators with cumbersome hinges and big corroded brand names. Apart from the incubators there is now a mirror, a small workbench and a refrigerator.

But do not, yet, be in too much hurry with your blame, but rather look at Hissao's reflection in the mirror and you will feel, whether you approve or not, a fondness for the young man in the expensive baggy clothes and you would guess, correctly, that this life, a life he did not choose, is not entirely repulsive to him. There is a new tendency to fleshiness in the face and his body has become, whilst not fat, not even plump, well padded. He has a good nose for good wine, speaks ten languages, three of them like a native, has educated tastes and cultured friends in many countries. He has dined with grouchy old Frank Lloyd Wright at Taelsin West and can tell, in the master's voice, the story of how the architect thundered "strike the forms" when the nervous builder hesitated on the Kauffman job.

He does not think himself either unhappy or bitter and when he bids his mother and grandfather goodbye there is no enmity between them. As he walks down the dusty empty stairwell he does not know how much he hates those of us who remain in those rundown galleries, living in the rusting slum that was once the best pet shop in the world.

He is alive, high on the risks of his profession, and his nostrils flare like an Arab stallion tricked up for show, the inside of those flaring nostrils rubbed with uncut cocaine and ginger powder rubbed on its arse to make it lift its tail so high.

But the hate is there, not so different to the hate that Leah Goldstein wakes with each morning, although in this case it is buried deeply, coiled in him like a stainless-steel spring. It is not obvious in any way, certainly not now, if you watch him walk – the last passenger on QF4 to Rome. You see only an urbane young man with a first-class tag on his brief case. You may notice his oddly scuffed shoes, as carefully chosen as his trousers, but you would not guess that he was holding his breath. This breath-holding is not caused by anxiety – there is no risk yet – he is trying not to smell the smell of airports in which he discerns fear, anxiety, impatience, drunkenness, fatigue, false feelings, a whole Hogarth of smells which he is, fastidious fellow, trying to lock away from the receptors of his brain. It is the breath-holding that makes his appearance slightly rigid and although this is not comical in itself it is made so by the hostess who accompanies him, circling her missing passenger like a Queensland heeler driving home a recalcitrant bullock.

Three hundred and eighty passengers awaited Hissao who had the good grace to act out some mild embarrassment as he took his first-class seat. He folded his large overcoat with exaggerated care and stubbornly refused to give it up to the uncertainties of the overhead locker. He placed it carefully beneath the seat.

The craft was now half an hour late, but when Hissao smiled at the steward, the man could no longer find it in himself to be angry.

The seat next to my grandson was occupied by a large handsome woman. She looked Italian or Spanish. She had olive skin, sloe eyes, a square jaw, and Hissao guessed her age, correctly, at thirty-four. No sooner had he clipped his seat belt together than he settled down to admire her. He did not rush into it like a glutton or a boor, but like a man carefully unfolding a napkin and watching wine being poured into a large glass.

He admired her hands (brown skin and such pink nails like seashells) which seemed to him perfectly proportioned, undeco-rated by nail polish or rings, but soft and supple. He watched them trace unselfconscious paths as they touched each other, her cheek, her forehead. He enjoyed their suppleness, the easy way the fingers could bend back from the pale pink of the palm which was crossed with the clear deep lines of an unhesitant life.

Hissao relaxed into the seat and, as the craft lifted off the tarmac at Mascot Airport, touched the parrot for luck and smiled with satisfaction at the perfection of life.

This business about Hissao and women is difficult. His continual love affairs may be interpreted as a continual need to prove himself as a man in spite of his height. It is a tempting hypothesis. Henry, having read about the Don Juan complex in *Reader's Digest*, suggested to Hissao that his promiscuous behaviour was the result of low-quality orgasms, but Hissao smiled at his brother with such compassion that it was Henry who lost his temper and had to leave the room.

Hissao was one of those rare men who genuinely love women and who, dreaming in bars and coffee shops, amidst the steam of espresso machines, can imagine amorous delights in all the various forms the female body assumes. When he saw his fellow passenger (square-jawed, sloe-eyed) he was not reacting to her money (which he could only guess at) or her fame (which he was ignorant of) but rather his small Nipponese nose twitched to some subtle aroma, the smell of spices in doorways, musky broad-leaved grasses, the heady aroma of a foreign country with its strange alphabets which promise the obliteration of one's personal past and the limitless possibilities of the erotic future.

The 747 landed in Melbourne to take on more passengers, but none of them came to first class. When it took off again, an hour later, Hissao had still not spoken to his companion. They took off into the face of a large black storm. Hissao gave himself up to the power of the engines. He offered himself to them. He felt no fear, only pleasure, in the even greater power of the storm as it pushed the plane relentlessly, breathlessly, upwards before throwing it fiercely into the cold holes in its boiling middle. In Melbourne, as so often happens in summer, it dropped from 35 °C to 18 °C in ten minutes and sweating men in shirt sleeves in Flinders Street prepared to make it the subject of headlines – it was autumn after all.

They reared and lunged above the monotony of Melbourne's west, out across the melancholy wheat plains around Diggers' Rest where Hissao's grandfather had once sold T Model Fords to farmers who could not sign their own name. He passed over Bendigo where Badgery & Goldstein had first performed. They were still in the storm half an hour later above Jeparit where Sir Robert Menzies had been born and where Hissao's father met his mother in the mouse plague of 1937.

They passed the borders of the family history, but Australia stretched on for two thousand miles more and it would be another five hours before they left its coast. An International Vice-President of Uniroyal, returning from firing the Australian Managing Director, vomited his farewell drinks into a paper bag and somewhere else Hissao could hear a woman crying helplessly.

The woman beside him did not move anxiously in her seat or let out cries of fear or even sit like someone waiting for something unpleasant to pass. She was going home after her mother's funeral and her thoughts were full of death and her own mortality and a fine chill of loneliness pierced her.

She had many friends, was much loved by them, and certainly had no shortage of lovers, but both her parents were dead and she had the sensation, now, of being in the front line with none of the conventional weapons of family or children or even country to defend herself against the realities of death and nothingness. Yet she was a strong woman, and an optimist at that; she was not in the least frightened by life, so that when, above Jeparit, Hissao began to talk to her, she gave him the whole of her intelligent attention and warmed her chilled thoughts in conversation.

The most puzzling thing in the entire encounter occurred at a certain stage very late in the conversation, when she discovered she had been talking to a man. She had the feeling of a dream where things and people transmogrify, characters dissolve from one to the other like tricks in a film, monsters in a bottle. She had the sense, the very distinct sense, of her companion's female gender; she had been pleased to find it, had relaxed into it, had been even more delighted to find it coupled with an elegant wit and a sense of both joy and irony. The forces of life, she thought to herself, are flying high tonight.

Later she tried to remember if she had taken pills or perhaps drunk excessively, but there had been only one glass (of champagne) and certainly no pills and yet, in the soft whistling dark above the Arafura Sea she found herself deep in conversation with a man, as in a dream, and her nipples contracted and her vision tunnelled and the sense of what had happened and was happening was disturbed, disorientating, and intensely erotic at the same time. What she saw as through a smeared glass darkly was a Renaissance face, a Bacchus that belonged to red wine, grapes, apples with the bloom of Tuscany on them, a vision saved from decadence by a firmness, a cleanness of will that showed in the intense blue eyes.

591

As she leaned across the last six inches of reserve to kiss him she felt his maleness to be overlaid with a soft blue shadow, the memory of the woman she had begun to talk to.

They were in the back seat of first class. The movie was running. Hissao removed the seat divider. She held his face a moment. Hissao smiled, thinking of the lines of her life held firmly against him, the beginning of her heart line touching the beginning of his smile.

Naturally she misunderstood the smile.

"It's all right," she whispered, "I'm just trying to imagine who you are."

His intentions were not bad. It may be tempting to find in those rosy Tuscan apples the worm of self-absorption, to see in his Bacchus lips the centre of his moral universe. He has, after all, declared himself amoral. He likes to think of himself as a pirate, a brigand, a citizen of risk. But let me tell you, he has the morals of a schoolteacher. Forget the Bacchus lips. He is as careful as a clerk. Even when he removed the seat divider he was beginning to stand, to place the parrot safely amongst his folded coat.

His mistake was to expect caution on the part of his companion. After all, they were not alone. The stewards were sitting upstairs and could return at any moment. The other four first-class passengers were absorbed with *The Railway Children* but that could prove to be indigestible at any moment.

But his companion, Rosa Carlobene, was not known for timidity and tonight, above the Arafura Sea, she was seeking the warm juices of life, defying the tapeworms of habit and order, luxuriating in the complexity of her sexual feelings, flying high on the side of the angels against death and despair.

Thus it was poor Rosa who, in one strong sinuous thrust, ground her pelvis into the head of the golden-shouldered parrot.

Hissao felt the skull squash and wetness spread. He leapt to his feet. He did not care for caution, discretion, customs spies, or Rosa Carlobene. He unzipped his fly, hoping against hope.

And Rosa, who had misunderstood the bump that was the parrot, now misunderstood the blood on Hissao's trembling hands.

"What is it?"

She clutched at his sleeve. He sat down again, but he was fiddling around his fly. "It's nothing," he said.

"Did I hurt you?"

"It's nothing, nothing, I promise. Don't worry." But the words did not match his tone which was cold and angry.

"I have hurt you?"

Hissao did not weep easily, but he wept there, in that aeroplane with the last of the golden-shouldered parrots dead inside his trousers.

Carla felt as if she was having a bad reaction to a drug. She patted at his lap with a handkerchief and was horrified to find it streaked with death.

"It's no good," he said. "It's dead." And he pushed her hand away.

Remembering the incident in later years each of them would physically groan out loud and shut their eyes (each one in their different country, in a different life, carrying the sharp blade of feeling that was unblunted by time or touching), yet the degree of their suffering was different and Rosa's pain, in comparison, was no more important than a stubbed toe or a *faux pas*. Much more was involved for Hissao – it had been his ambition to be recognized as the man who had saved the golden-shouldered parrot.

It was because of this incident, with his guilt, with his contempt for himself, that his hate unleashed itself, a steel spring unsprung, a Japanese paper flower opening up to show its livid heart in a glass of water.

He had loved his country more than he had pretended, and had tried to make something fine out of something rotten. He felt the feelings he had once described to Leah Goldstein as greatness but it was not greatness – it was the same feeling Charles described when he said he would strangle his wife.

64

A bird was a bird to Rosa Carlobene and although she knew her new lover was unhappy about its death she had little inkling of what it really meant to him. He was a smuggler. He had lost money. But he had come through customs without difficulty and, doubtless, he would smuggle again.

She woke in the night to see him climbing on to a chair in the bathroom. At first, half enmeshed by sleep, she thought he was doing himself harm, and then she saw, in the sickly green light of the UPIM sign that illuminated the room, that he was doing chin-ups. She smiled and went back to sleep.

Hissao did his exercises to make the tension go away. He did chin-ups until he could do no more. This of course, did not take place at the Rome Hilton where he was booked. There is nothing to grip on above the doors in the Rome Hilton. They stayed, instead, in a small pensione on the fifth floor of a building in the Piazza Nationale. It was a clean enough place, but noisy. Beefy-armed female singers performed for the aperitif sippers in the square below.

The exercises soothed him for a moment, and then the tension came back. He showered, but the hot water could not unclench the knotted muscles of his strong neck. Then he dressed and went down to the piazza which was now almost empty. Some men hung around the edge of the fountain and, at the last bar, they were stacking away the plastic chairs for the night.

Hissao walked down the streets towards the railway station where young toughs lit matches which illuminated their shirts: brilliant aquamarine, lolly pink, explosions of colour caught in a machismo flare of phosphor.

Hissao walked past, neither frightened by the toughs nor aroused, as he might normally have been, by the erotic possibilities of a new city.

All his skin was tight at the palms and there was nothing he could do to ease it.

Somewhere in a small gritty-pathed park, beside a shuttered kiosk, under warm swaying trees, he said, in English: "I'm going to fix you bastards right up."

And when he said that he felt something click, like a vertebra shifting or a glass skylight cracking under strain. He felt a thing "go" and it made itself known as sharply as a rifle shot and it was there (smelling the sweet scent of some flowering tree whose name he did not know, hearing a nearby Fiat flatten its battery as it tried to start, become weaker and soon give no sound other than the almost mute click of the starter motor and the soft monosyllabic curse of the driver) it was then, while these other things circled his dull tight centre, like flies around something dead, that he felt the hate he had kept himself from knowing. The pain in his skin and in his joints did not go away but intensified, took up another notch, and he was possessed of an acute sensitivity to everything, even the pressure of his silk shirt where it brushed, lightly, against his hairless chest, and he was not sure that what he felt was pain or pleasure, whether he was happy or unhappy to see, at last, the family he had worked so dangerously to support for what they were – an ugly menagerie as evil as anything you might ever see, fleetingly, before your eyes in a bottle.

Then he had the idea.

He had had it before, this idea, and then forgotten it. It was one of those ideas that we find and forget, dig and bury, over and over again, and each time we forget that we have had the idea before. We unearth and bury them like sleepwalkers, frightened of the consequences and only the mud under our nails in the morning reminds us that we have let ourselves fool around with something dangerous.

"I'm going to fix you bastards right up."

He walked back to the pensione in a different style entirely, skipping impatiently at the corners. He was polite to the sleepy concierge. He went into his room and sat by the window for a long time. Rosa Carlobene tossed in her sleep. Hissao opened the window, and heard, from five storeys below, the lonely click of a whore's heels in the empty colonnade. His emotions were those of an assassin. He was small, as small as a grain of sand and also, at exactly the same time, very very large. He was pink and visceral, grey and metallic. He was nothing. He was everything.

He blamed us.

He blamed his foreign face. He blamed his mother for the fear or the opportunism that had changed his natural form. He blamed Leah Goldstein who had wished to see nothing worthwhile in him. He blamed her, particularly, for not understanding that you could enjoy the hotels, the wine, the travel, and at the same time care immensely about the little hearts that beat against your thigh.

Miss Self-righteous, Miss Grim. She would not listen to his plans for this parrot and could not see that Snr Totoro had been sincere, that he wished a breeding pair of golden-shouldered parrots and – he was a clever man, with a proven record – he would have returned parrots to Australia and they could, between them, have begun to build up a flock.

But Goldstein would not listen. No one would listen, and now the cretins would blame him for destroying the species he had set out to save.

He was all afire with blame.

He sat by the window and waited for the dawn, fidgeting in his chair. When the sky began to lighten – a cold hard yellow conquering a bluish grey – he took out his Mont Blanc pen and wrote a very sad and sentimental note for Rosa Carlobene. He placed this on her bedside table and then he took down his coat from its hanger, turned it inside out and lay it across the chair by the window. From his trouser pocket he took a small pearl-handled pocket knife which he now used to slit the lining of the coat. He retrieved the first children's python, very gently, stroked its head and then, in a quick flick, broke its neck.

He made a little noise, like a loud gulp for air.

Then he repeated the process.

He stood, for a moment, very still with a dead snake in his hand. Then he went to the window and threw the two of them out. When he walked out of the room he left his suitcase behind.

He smiled at the concierge and talked to her about the weather. He apologized for waking her in the night. When Rosa came looking for him later the concierge described him – your husband, a real Florentine, she said; such a gentleman.

But by then Hissao was on board the aeroplane to Tokyo where he met Mr Tacheuchi and Mr Mori, both customers. They travelled up to Tokyo, one from Yokohama, one from Mishima, and Hissao entertained them, first in the Ginza and later that grotesque palace of five hundred hostesses, the Mikado.

Did they sense in Hissao the cold fury, the lovelessness of the perfect warrior? Did they realize, that even while he laughed and insisted they take another Scotch, he was not thinking about them but the revenge he planned against his family?

Ah, he was his grandfather's grandson and unkindness was his strongest card. Mr Tacheuchi, a lecherous drunk, was able to put him in touch with the right people at Mitsubishi.

There is no duller man on earth than a Mitsubishi Sarariman. Once you understand how conservative they are, you can easily imagine what distress, what physical pain, not to mention panic, they would feel to do business with a curly-headed, Bacchus-lipped, baggy-suited Australian with scuffed shoes.

Hissao therefore transformed himself. He became dullness personified. He had his hair neatly barbered. He bought the correct English suits and a wristwatch that would declare his rank more clearly than the business cards he had no time to print. In the corridors of Mitsubishi he was all but invisible. It was his destiny. He felt it. He took pleasure from his new politeness, the excessive courtesies, the slow progress, circular, but sometimes spiral, towards consensus.

He still knew himself to be an architect but there, in the endless meetings in Tokyo, the lunches in carefully graded restaurants, the ever-ascending levels of expense and status, he knew that he was born for this, that he was a great salesman, the best the family had yet produced.

He returned on a JAL flight to Sydney with a commitment of one million dollars (US), all of which was to be invested in the best pet shop in the world.

There was a recession on. He was written up in the papers.

65

He ripped the guts out of the old building as if he were a goanna feeding on a turkey. He attacked it viciously, took its entrails first, and left it clean inside, a great empty cavern of slippery ribs.

I lost my window, of course. I was shunted and shifted from ground floor to basement. I did not care. They fed me and wiped my bum. What more can a man want when his grandson is all afire with a scheme? He was my flesh and blood, my creature, my monster. I loved him, loved his barrelled chest, his red-rimmed eyes, the strong broad hands that unrolled the plans amidst the mortar and sawdust. He was opening out the pet shop, living out the destiny I had mapped for him when I took him to the South Pylon of the Bridge. He did not remember, of course, and that is as it should be and I could drink his hate as happily as his love because here, in the city of illusions, he was building a masterpiece.

No one, not even Emma, dared stand in his way. Such was the force of his vision that they all gave way before it and even Goldstein, increasingly gaunt and dark-eyed, Goldstein who would not speak to him, teetered on the brink of admiration for she saw he was pursuing an idea without compromise, that he really did have greatness within his grasp, but that was before she saw what he was up to.

The architects of Sydney all came, sooner or later, for a sticky-beak. They knew that Hissao Badgery, that gourmand, dilettante, deviant, was not capable of such work. They decided he was a front, a shadow for a Japanese architect, and they argued only about which Master it was.

The cretins. There was nothing Japanese in it except the money. He built like a jazz musician. He restated and reworked the melody of the old emporium. The creaking galleries were gone now, but you saw them still, in your imagination. He built like a liar, like a spider – steel ladders and walkways, catwalks, cages in mid-air, in racks on walls, tumbling like waterfalls, in a gallery spanning empty spaces like a stainless Bridge of Sighs.

When Goldstein, at last, saw what he was up to, she tried to stab him in the chest with a knife but she was now an old lady in paisley with weak wrists and arthritic hands and he easily knocked the blade away and then, for good measure, spat right in her face, a great glob of clouded spittle which landed on her ruined cheek and predicted, in its course, the bed along which her hopeless tears would shortly run.

What drove him to this rage was not the knife, but the lack of imagination she displayed, that she could not see what he was doing, what passions ruled him, what love his hate was based in.

66

I have no great pains, no searing agonies to make me scream and weep, but I have nausea, giddiness, the discomforts of incontinence, the itch of psoriasis, and I lie here, with my skin scaling, peeling like a withered prawn.

Naturally they come to see me, not just the men with callipers and bottles, but the ordinary visitors. They journey up the aluminium walkways, they brave their vertigo, they grasp the rail, they tremble to see what a human being can become.

I wish I were well enough to enjoy it properly. I used to enjoy it. I remember the first day he had the boys from Bondi Surf Lifesaving Club bring me up here. They carried me with two poles and a canvas sling.

It seems like for fucking ever ago. It happened in the week Goldstein went to gaol for throwing firecrackers at police horses. They brought me up here. I showed them my write-ups on the wall, framed, behind glass. The morons laughed at me, right in my face, and said I was a museum piece, that I should be stuffed, etc., and then they went downstairs to take up their own positions in the great exhibit, clowning on the sand on the ground floor. They were smug, those lads, about their pay and conditions, but they've been fired now – they got too old. They're probably on the dole, or in the park, getting pissed on metho, remembering the great days when they had work in the Best Pet Shop in the World.

You would think it too hot up here, under the skylight, but Hissao has worked everything out well. The roof disappears completely. He has it opening and closing like an eyelid, and the rosellas, when they are released, fly up towards the open sky. I can see them if I lie on my right side, but it makes me feel dizzy and ill and I try to turn away if I can. Some days I can turn by myself, but on others I need assistance. The rosellas reach the point just opposite me where the sonic curtain operates. When they hit it they falter, lose height, and then, because they now feel as ill as I do, they go back to their perches below. When they feel better they try again. When they die, Hissao gets a new lot.

Of course it is the Best Pet Shop in the World. Who could possibly compete with it? It is not just our owners, the Mitsubishi Company, who say so. Everyone comes. Name a country and I will have met someone who travelled from it just to see us.

And you can say it is simply hate that has made Hissao put so many of his fellow countrymen and women on display. Yet he has not only fed them and paid them well, he has chosen them, the types, with great affection. There is a spirit in this place. It is this that excites the visitors. The shearers, for instance, exhibit that dry, laconic anti-authoritarian wit that is the very basis of the Australian sense of humour. They are proud people, these lifesavers, inventors, manufacturers, bushmen, aboriginals. They do not act like caged people. The very success of the exhibit is in their ability to move and talk naturally within the confines of space. They go about their business, their sand paintings, their circumcision ceremonies, their strikes, settlements, discussions about national anthems, arguments about "Waltzing Matilda" and "Advance Australian Fair". In Phoebe's area the artists and writers all gather for their discussions. Who has not been thrilled to listen to them? Of course there are disagreements, fights, but no one objects. The only bitterness comes from outside these walls, from the jeering crowd of slogan writers on the street who cannot, anyway, afford the entrance money.

Goldstein is not happy. She wishes to leave, but what would she do if Hissao released her? Who would employ her, feed her? Hissao keeps her locked in her cage. The sign on her door says "Melbourne Jew". She spends a lot of time explaining that she is not a Jew, that the sign is a lie, that the exhibition is based on lies; but visitors prefer to believe the printed information. This information, after all, is written and signed by independent experts. The chart on my door says I am a hundred and thirty-nine years old. It also says I was born in 1886, but there are no complaints. The customers are happy.

I have not seen Mr Lo for years, but I suppose he is there, and Emma I see sometimes when she walks out with her boy, proudly inspecting the display on a Sunday afternoon.

But mostly, in the daytime, I see the paying visitors, and at night I see Hissao. Late at night he walks around the clever cages he has made for us, and blames us. And it is I, Herbert Badgery, he blames most of all. He comes after midnight and sits beside my bed drinking brandy. There are all sorts of noises in the night, and I don't mean the keening of an aboriginal woman or the grumbling of a mason, but rather the noises in the street outside where the enemies of the emporium have set up their camp. I have never seen them, but anyone can hear the sirens, the shouting, sometimes the drumming of police-horse hooves.

Our conferences, mine and Hissao's, are not remarkable for their wit or elegance. He pours himself a cognac and insults me, sometimes in Japanese, sometimes in English. His face has coarsened and is showing the effects of all this alcohol. He has become red-nosed, a little pudgy.

"Why don't you die, you old cunt?"

That is the standard of the debate, but there are plenty of times when I would happily oblige him, on nights when my once-handsome face is streaked with white lines. My arteries are as clogged as old drainpipes. They make me feel bad. You would not believe you could feel so bad and still not die, but I cannot die. I will not die, because this is my scheme. I must stay alive to see it out.

"Die, arsehole," says Hissao Badgery.

The poor little fellow. Is he frightened of the enemies who shout his name in the street? Can he feel their passions? Their rage? Is that what it is, my little snookums? He must feel dreadful – he was such a nice boy – everybody liked him – he has not been prepared to be the object of such intelligent and necessary hatred.

For, you see, the emporium is working, sucking rage and hatred towards itself. Such vilifications. Such tempers in the street. Last week we had CS gas drifting through the skylight. The parrots had to be replaced but I drew deep on the gas as if it were honeysuckle. My old optimism is returning.

Did I hear crashing glass, the sound of the first wave breaking as it enters the ground floor? It is this which Hissao fears, this which I wait for, which keeps me alive through all these endless days. But it is not time, not yet.

I take the boy – he is light as a feather – and put him to my breast. His red Bacchus lips pout like a baby. Ah, there. His little lips suck and the contractions are a deep and steady, rhythmic thrum.

It would be of no benefit for him to know that he is, himself, a lie, that he is no more substantial than this splendid four-storey mirage, teetering above Pitt Street, no more concrete than all those alien flowers, those neon signs, those twisted coloured forms in gas and glass that their inventors, dull men, think will last forever.

No, he cannot know.

I close my eyes and do the only thing I can do. I am, at last, the creature I have so long wished to become – a kind man. With my swollen blue-veined breast I give my offspring succour – the milk of dragons from my witch's tit.

It will give him strength for the interesting times ahead.

Also by Peter Carey

The Unusual Life of Tristan Smith

The Unusual Life of Tristan Smith is a dense, funny, moving novel set in the nations of Voorstand and Efica.

Severely afflicted, doomed never to be taller than three foot six, Tristan Smith faces death and danger from the first moment of his energetic and ambitious life.

This is an unprecedented work of the imagination, a modern work as packed with incident and character as a Victorian novel, an allegory that is most remarkable for the thread of love and loyalty that runs through its richly imagined tapestry.

"Peter Carey has an approach to the novel destined to make him one of the most widely read and admired writers working in English."

Times Literary Supplement

ISBN 0 7022 2626 2

Collected Stories

For the first time, Peter Carey's dazzling fables and fantasies from *The Fat Man in History* and *War Crimes* are collected in one volume, together with three ingenious stories not previously published in book form.

"Peter Carey is one of the great story-tellers of our time."

London Evening Standard

"Reading his stories [is] ... like being shot by a firing squad of angels."

Jill Neville, *Sydney Morning Herald*

"Peter Carey writes an intelligent, sizzling, and rapid narrative. He will also do allegories, fables, and astonishing tricks ... I recommend his work to you with great enthusiasm."

Frank Moorhouse

"His imagination is soaring, his style beautifully disciplined, his eye for the truth unblinking."

Geoffrey Dutton, *Bulletin*

"Carey's worlds are quite real. He evokes them with a sense of detail and economy that never labours for effect — it is controlled, witty and chilling."

David Marr

ISBN 0 7022 2712 9

The Fat Man in History

A landmark in contemporary Australian literature, *The Fat Man in History* has brought widespread acclaim to Peter Carey for his brilliant and ingenious fiction. These twelve stories introduce visionary landscapes of intense clarity, where the rules of the game are bizarre, and yet chillingly familiar.

"Peter Carey is a surrealist, a maker of fables, myths, allegories, dreams, nightmares, fantasies."

Douglas Stewart, *Sydney Morning Herald*

"One of the outstanding writers to have emerged during this period."

Peter Lewis, *Times Literary Supplement*

"Carey is that rarity, a highly imaginative writer, verging sometimes on science fiction but writing with verbal economy and a tight narrative grip."

New Statesman

"The most genuinely original of our story tellers — a fabulist and, in some corners of his imagination, a surrealist of disturbing power."

Australian Book Review

ISBN 0 7022 0900 7

War Crimes

The stories in this prize-winning collection are all about power — about those who wield it, those who want it, and those who recall only its dazzling exhilaration and degradation.

"These are true stories, which combine density with clarity, yet in their suggestive power they have the weight of novels."

Bruce Clunies Ross

"His imagination is soaring, his style beautifully disciplined, his eye for the truth unblinking."

Geoffrey Dutton, *Bulletin*

"Peter Carey is one of the great story-tellers of our time, the kind who make you take the telephone off the hook, forget the television and ignore the doorbell."

Miranda Seymour, London *Evening Standard*

"Carey's worlds are quite real. He evokes them with a sense of detail and economy that never labours for effect — it is controlled, witty and chilling."

David Marr

ISBN 0 7022 1649 6

Bliss

Winner:
Miles Franklin Award
NBC Banjo Award
NSW Premier's Award

"Harry Joy was to die three times, but it was his first death which was to have the greatest effect on him, and it is this first death which we shall now witness."

So begins this masterpiece of illusion which marked Peter Carey's brilliant debut as a novelist. The dilemma of Harry Joy is both funny and terrifying, for Harry wakes up in Hell, tortured by those he loves, and by the dreams and nightmares he once created for profit.

"Carey is one of the great story-tellers of our time, the kind who make you take the telephone off the hook, forget the television and ignore the doorbell."

Miranda Seymour, *Evening Standard*

"*Bliss* is outrageous perfection ... madcap, adventurous, engaging, compelling, shocking, moving, funny, sad and inventive."

San Francisco Bay Reporter

"Peter Carey's first novel is a marvel to read ... it's one 'hell' of a good book."

Margaret Smith, *Weekend Australian*

ISBN 0 7022 2759 5

Oscar & Lucinda

Winner:
Booker Prize
Miles Franklin Award
NBC Banjo Award
Adelaide Festival Award
Foundation for Australian Literary Studies Award

"Wonderful is the only word adequate to the imagination that begot, and the assurance that controls, this richly comic novel."

Don Anderson, *Sydney Morning Herald*

"*Oscar and Lucinda* is a novel of extraordinary richness, complexity and strength ... it fills me with wild, savage envy, and no novelist could say fairer than that."

Angela Carter, *Guardian*

"We have a great novelist living on the planet with us, and his name is Peter Carey."

Los Angeles Times

"Oscar and Lucinda are two of the most perfectly realised characters in modern fiction. An immensely skilful and absorbing juxtaposition of a gently comic, obliquely ironic, and deeply compassionate vision of human existence."

David Williamson

ISBN 0 7022 2760 9

The Tax Inspector

The audit of Catchprice Motors looks like the least challenging assignment of the Tax Inspector's life, but she finds the Catchprice family have dangerous dreams the Tax Office were not previously aware of.

The Tax Inspector is a dark and brilliant achievement that is illuminated with a rare humour and compassion. Set in 1990s Sydney, it is a work of astonishing originality by a master of the contemporary novel.

"Peter Carey won the Booker Prize in 1988 with *Oscar and Lucinda*. His new novel is shorter, braver, more painful, and even better ... If you only have time to read one new novel, make it *The Tax Inspector*."

Victoria Glendinning, *The Times*

"His work has a wild, chance-taking quality, an eye for the grotesque, that puts him in harmony with the spirit of his age."

Bruce Cook, *Chicago Tribune*

"A brilliant, powerful and dangerous writer. Dangerous because to read his book involves a loss of innocence."

Sue Gough, *Courier-Mail*

"The novel's greater rewards are its wit and density, its sympathy and wacky inventiveness."

Francine Prose, *New York Times* Book Review

"*The Tax Inspector* is peopled by the sensuous, wilful characters we've come to expect from Peter Carey."

Phil Holcroft, *Sunday Sun*

ISBN 0 7022 2761 7

Dancing on Hot Macadam

Peter Carey's Fiction

Anthony J. Hassall

"The writer has a responsibility to tell the truth, not to shy away from the world as it is; and at the same time the writer has a responsibility to celebrate the potential of the human spirit."

Peter Carey

Peter Carey is one of the world's most gifted and exciting fiction writers. This first comprehensive study of his work follows Carey's career from the nightmare-haunted stories of *The Fat Man in History* and *War Crimes* to the madcap satire of *Bliss*, from *Illywhacker*'s picaresque landscapes to *Oscar and Lucinda*'s glittering achievement, and the powerfully confronting vision of *The Tax Inspector*.

Dancing on Hot Macadam explores Carey's preoccupation with imprisonment and metamorphosis, and the desire of his characters to escape from bewildering roles, relationships and societies. Alert to recent critical debates, this study provides a lucid account of the fiction, its international literary context, and its intriguing critical reception in Australia, America and Britain.

"*Dancing on Hot Macadam* is another volume in the excellent Studies in Australian Literature series, and the second contribution to the list by Anthony J. Hassall. It is a sound and persuasive critique that gets much better as it goes along."

Times Literary Supplement

"The book contains a lot of ideas ... and will be the base from which to draw the map of Carey's fiction as it develops further."

Julian Croft, *Weekend Australian*

ISBN 0 7022 2763 3